Song of the River

Other Books by Sue Harrison

MOTHER EARTH FATHER SKY
MY SISTER THE MOON
BROTHER WIND

SONG
OF THE
RIVER

Sue Harrison

AVON BOOKS

AVON BOOKS
A division of
The Hearst Corporation
1350 Avenue of the Americas
New York, New York 10019

Copyright © 1997 by Sue Harrison
Interior design by Kellan Peck
ISBN: 0-380-97370-7

For the Aleut People
in gratitude and respect

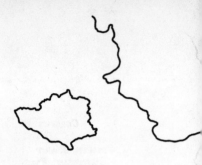

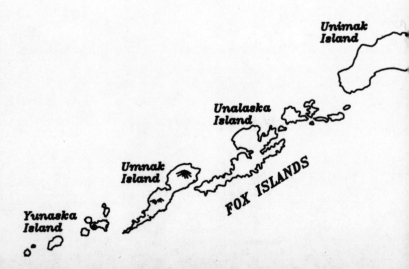

Bering Sea

Unimak Island

Unalaska Island

Umnak Island

Yunaska Island

FOX ISLANDS

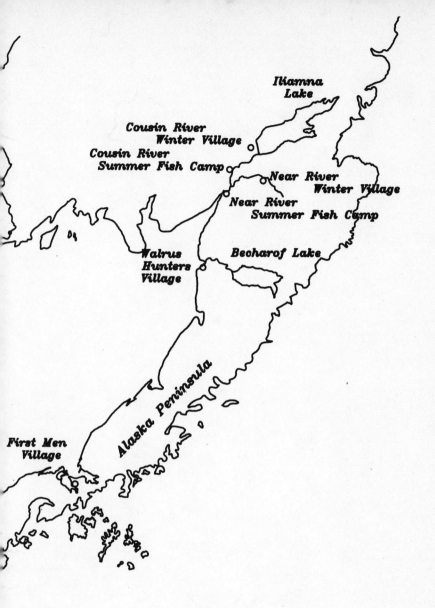

Ikiamna
Lake

Cousin River
Winter Village

Cousin River
Summer Fish Camp

Near River
Winter Village

Near River
Summer Fish Camp

Walrus
Hunters
Village

Becharof Lake

First Men
Village

Alaska Peninsula

Pacific Ocean

Miles

0   25   50   75   100

Song of the River
I

Author's Notes
473

Glossary of Native American Words
476

Pharmacognosia
479

Acknowledgments
482

Song of the River

Prologue

Late Fall, 6480 B.C.
West of the Grandfather Lake
(present-day Iliamna Lake, Alaska)

THE COUSIN RIVER PEOPLE'S WINTER VILLAGE

The pain had been terrible, but that was not what K'os remembered. She remembered her helplessness.

She had fought—scratched, kicked, bit the lobe off one man's ear, gouged another's eye.

She knew their names: Gull Wing, Fox Barking and Sleeps Long. They had come from the Near River Village to trade. Fox Barking had the narrow eyes of a man who lied, and Sleeps Long moved slowly, like someone accustomed to laziness, but Gull Wing carried himself like a hunter. K'os had watched him that evening in her mother's lodge, had smiled if he looked her way.

The next morning she had followed them to the Grandfather Lake, had hidden behind the Grandfather Lake. That rock was a good luck place for women. Those who were pregnant went there to sit, hoping that magic would pass through the rock into the children who waited in their wombs. They spoke their hopes out loud: for a son who was a hunter, for a daughter who would look after her parents when they were old, for an easy birth.

The animals knew the goodness of that place. Caribou, lynx, bear came to drink. Muskrats made their lodges along the banks of the outlet rivers that flowed to the North Sea. In summers there were birds—mergansers, grebes, loons. In winter, the lake was a fine place to catch blackfish, those small soft fish, good eaten raw, full of oil. Just a few would fill a winter belly longing for fat.

It was a difficult walk from their village to the Grandfather Lake, through swamp and muskeg, over tussocks of old grass that stood knee-high above the ground. Hard to walk between, those tussocks were, and treacherous to the ankles of anyone who decided to walk across the tops. Women who went to the Grandfather Lake worked hard to get there. The good luck was worth their effort.

But today it had not been a place of good luck for K'os.

Now, sick and bloody from the struggle, she skirted her village instead of walking through it. Lodge entrances faced east toward the morning sun. She approached her mother's lodge from the back, from the refuse heaps. She pulled the hood of her ground squirrel parka up over her head, drew her face inside the wolverine fur ruff.

She pushed aside the doorflap, crawled through the entrance tunnel. The lodge was large: three tall men could sleep head to toe across the floor, and still a woman had room to walk between them and the lodge wall. River rocks, worn smooth by water, had been brought to the winter village long ago, perhaps by her grandfather or his father, enough to circle the walls of the floor pit that had been dug several handlengths into the ground. Lodge poles, tied in a wide dome above the floor, were covered by two layers of caribou skin to keep the wind from stealing the warmth of the wood fire.

The caribou hide walls were well-sewn, the floor padded with caribou skins, the bedding made of soft warm furs—wolf and lynx and fox.

Her mother, Mink, sighed her relief when she saw K'os, but only said, "You have been gone too long."

K'os had expected more of a scolding than that. Her mother's smiling mouth hid a sharp tongue.

"I told you I was going to the Grandfather Lake," K'os answered. Her words sounded strange to her, as though they came from another woman's mouth. She raised a hand to her face. Her lips felt the same, her nose, her eyes. She stayed where she was, careful to keep her eyes averted from her father's weapons. Blood was blood. Though her flow was not a regular moon flow, it might carry enough power to curse her father's spears and knives, gaffs and hooks.

"Where are the roots?"

K'os inhaled—a quick, gasping breath. She had told her mother that she was going to the Grandfather Lake to gather spruce roots. The black spruce that grew in the dark wet muck on the west side of the lake had long, rope-like roots, strong yet easy to split. She had taken one of her mother's favorite baskets to carry them. She must have left the basket there, after the men found her.

"I don't have them," K'os answered.

"You don't have them? Where are they?"

K'os heard the hard edge in her mother's voice, and she almost told her what had happened. Why keep such a problem to herself? Let her mother and father share her pain. But her mother's tongue was not only sharp, it was busy. Soon every woman in the village would know. Not only the women but the men. Then who would want K'os as wife?

"I started my bleeding," K'os said. "Just when the basket was almost full. I did not know what to do with the roots. I was afraid too much of my moon blood power was in them, so I left them. I know where the basket is. I hid it. If you say the roots are good, I will go back for them. If not, I will leave them."

Her mother began to complain, but her father said, "It was wise, what she did. Leave her alone. What if you used those roots to sew a sael, and later some hunter ate from it? She can go back for the basket when she is done with moon blood."

He frowned at K'os, then jutted his chin toward her face. "You need water. There is blood on your cheek."

Again K'os lifted her hand, touched her face.

She was a beautiful woman, so everyone said, and she had found it was good to be beautiful. There was power in it. You could lie your way out of trouble. You could ask for things, and they would be given to you.

Her beauty was something she often pondered. What was it? A spacing of the eyes? A straight nose; lips, not too small or too large? Shining hair. Was there something else, something that had to do with luck? Surely today she lost whatever luck she had.

She looked at her mother. "I fell," she said.

"The tussocks," said her mother and shook her head. "I told you not to go."

"You were right," K'os told her.

Mink tilted her head toward the side of the lodge where stacks of bundled pelts and skins awaited sewing. "There is enough to keep you busy," she said. "And I will tell my sister to bring your little cousin Gguzaakk to the tikiyaasde. There is room for both of you there. You can watch her while we work."

K'os did not like Gguzaakk. The child had only two summers; she was whiny and climbed into everything. But K'os nodded. Yes, while she was in the menstruation hut, she would care for Gguzaakk. And this time Gguzaakk's mother would have no complaints.

Mink brought her a birchbark cilt'ogho of water. K'os reached for it. There was blood, dried and caked, on the palm of her hand. Mink, looking hard into her daughter's face, did not notice.

"Your jaw and eye, too," she said to K'os, and pressed her hand against her own face. "Bruises."

K'os sat down. She covered her mouth to stifle a groan. Any movement hurt. The pain had slowed her pace during her journey back to the village, and she had been afraid she would not get to her mother's lodge before darkness came. Then what chance would she have—alone and with her luck gone?

The men had hit her hard enough to knock her spirit out of her body, so she did not know everything they had done to her. As she walked that long path back from the Grandfather Lake, it felt as though her belly had nothing to hold it in, so she was sure they had torn something inside. When she urinated, she urinated blood.

She dipped her hand into the sael. They had been foolish, those three men, to lie there, all of them, in the grasses around the Grandfather Rock while she was still alive. They must have thought she was dead, or at least that she would not awaken for a long time.

She had lain there and listened to them, to their boasts, first about what they had done to her, then about other women they had used. They were going to take her again, they decided, then they would leave, return to the Near River Village, to their wives and children.

They had pushed K'os's parka up, baring her belly and breasts, but had not bothered to take it off. Instead they had pulled the hood forward over her face and stuffed a portion of the ruff into her mouth, pressed the fur into her throat until it took all her effort just to breathe. They had found the woman's knife sheathed at her waist, but not the blade hidden on her left forearm, strapped under her parka sleeve.

That knife was a gift from one of her older brothers. He had given it to her before he left to go live with his wife's family at the Four Rivers Village—a man's knife to protect her, because all her brothers lived in other villages with their wives.

K'os had gripped the sleeve knife with both hands and rolled off the rock, the blade out-thrust between her breasts, her fists grasping the haft and pressed tightly to her chest. Gull Wing had been lying next to the rock. She landed on him, drove the knife into his heart before he could react. She pulled it out and thrust it into one of his eyes, then into his neck. His gurgling cries brought the other men to their feet, and K'os took the knife from Gull Wing's throat, held the blade out toward them.

"Which one do I kill next?" she asked, as she sat astride Gull Wing, the man shuddering in death throes beneath her. She dipped her finger in Gull Wing's blood, sucked her finger clean.

She expected them to attack. They turned and ran.

She struggled to her feet, groaning as her belly churned and fell. Then she also ran, away from the lake, away from the rock, away from the dead Gull Wing.

Falling and running, falling and running, she did not stop until blood flowed like a river from between her legs. Then she hid in a clump of willow and stuffed her vagina full of moss and leaves, packing them in to stop the blood.

She stayed there, like an animal, wounded. At first she had been afraid they would find her, afraid she would die, but later she feared she would not die, ruined as she was.

Finally she had decided to continue toward the village, but when she stood, her feet would not move that way. Instead, they turned toward the Grandfather Lake. Instead, they walked her back to Gull Wing's body.

There she cut out Gull Wing's heart and gave it as a gift to the Grandfather Rock.

Four Days Later

THE NEAR RIVER PEOPLE'S WINTER VILLAGE

The child was Day Woman's fourth. The labor should not have been so long, so troublesome. The old woman Ligige' worried about what this might mean. Had Day Woman broken taboos? In all ways she seemed to be a respectful person, yet in the past two years all luck had left her. Her firstborn son drowned while fishing with his father; another child, a daughter, was born dead.

Before those deaths, the old woman Yellow Feather said she heard a raven call at night, and, of course, such a thing meant death. But Yellow Feather was neither aunt nor grandmother to anyone in Day Woman's family, so why, when Yellow Feather heard the call, did death come to Day Woman's children?

Some elders said the problem was Gull Wing, Day Woman's husband. Ligige''s own husband would not hunt or fish with the man. Everyone knew he was careless with animals. He did not cut the joints of wolves he killed, and he laughed when any man placed the gift of a bone in a dead fox's mouth. But if the gift was not given, how would the fox know he was respected? Why would he return the next year to give himself again to The People?

Everyone believed something would happen, and it did. Three days before, two of the village hunters—Fox Barking and Sleeps Long—had returned from a visit to the Cousin River People's Village. Gull Wing, Fox Barking's brother, Day Woman's husband, had also traveled with them. He had been killed by a bear near the lake called Grandfather. The bear had dragged away his body, and they had been unable to find it, so had nothing—not even bones—to bring back to the village.

No one was surprised. A man like Gull Wing earned his problems.

The night she began her mourning, Day Woman's child decided to come into the world, and now, three days later, it was still trying— three days, when her other children had come so easily that Day Woman had laughed at the pain.

Ligige' settled herself into her own thoughts, resting on her haunches, her arms clasped tightly around her knees. She wished she could take some of Day Woman's pain. She slipped one gnarled hand down to her own belly. It was as soft and shriveled as it had been in all the years since the birth of her last child. That child had died, as had all her children, but she had Day Woman, a good niece, always bringing food, things to delight an old woman's tongue, things that were taboo for the young, like the delicate meat of the red-necked grebe, that clumsy bird whose flesh might slow the feet of child or hunter. But why worry over such a thing for an old woman? Old women always had slow feet.

As Ligige' remembered the pain of losing her own children, she decided that if this baby died Day Woman might choose to follow it. Counting this little one, Day Woman would have three dead children and a dead husband. Wouldn't she rather be with them than with Sok, the one son who still lived? Of course it was hard to say. Sok was a large and healthy boy. Fast in running, strong in throwing. The village men said he would be a good hunter, a gifted warrior.

Maybe Day Woman would decide to live a while and watch this boy grow up, then when he was a man, caught in his own life, she would go on to the dead ones. After all, those who are alive can always decide to become spirit. The dead have no more choices left to them.

Ligige''s head nodded, and she turned herself toward dreams, her eyes moving to see those visions that squeezed under the smooth inside skin of her lids. She sighed, almost smiled. Then Day Woman cried out, a scream that woke Ligige' and made her skin rise in bumps from her neck to her wrists. Perhaps there was more than a child trying to find its way out. Perhaps Gull Wing's disrespect had cursed Day Woman's womb.

Ligige' pushed herself to her feet and turned toward the door, ready to run if something horrible came from the bulging pink flesh between Day Woman's legs.

Day Woman screamed again. Ligige' saw the glistening black hair of a baby's head. She breathed one long breath. At least the thing was a child. If it was deformed, it would not be the first such baby she had delivered.

Day Woman squatted, legs spread, supporting herself with a babiche rope hung from the birthing lodge poles. Her face twisted. She pushed, groaning with the effort, and Ligige' knelt between her niece's knees, cupped her hands around the vulva as it stretched wide to allow the baby passage into the world.

The child's head came, then the shoulders. Ligige' caught it, eased it to the nest of moss Day Woman had spread under herself.

"Ah! You are blessed!" Ligige' cried. The child was a boy, his small penis jutting out from his body in announcement. His voice rang in a strong cry.

Day Woman laughed, drew in a quick breath as the afterbirth passed, then laughed again. "Another son," she crowed.

Ligige' handed the baby to his mother. Day Woman put him to her breast, and though most newborns did not seem much interested in eating during the first day of their lives, this child opened his mouth wide over his mother's nipple and sucked. Day Woman grimaced at the sudden letdown of her milk, then again laughed her delight.

Ligige' wrapped the afterbirth in birchbark and tied off the birth cord, then sliced it with her obsidian knife. She took the afterbirth outside, walking carefully with the birchbark packet lifted high so no hunters would cross her path and risk losing their power. After she had buried it, she returned to the lodge.

Day Woman was asleep. The child rested on her chest, birth blood dark on his skin. Ligige' gently picked up the boy and carried him to the bark basket where she had placed ground squirrel skins softened by her own rubbing. She pulled a caribou bladder of water from the lodge poles and, removing the carved antler plug, squeezed a little water into a piece of scraped caribou hide she had softened with fat. She wiped the blood from the baby's face, used a fingernail to flick mucus from his tiny nostrils, then rubbed his chest and belly until they were shiny and pink. She rinsed the hide and smoothed it over his legs down to one foot and the other, then she stopped.

Her belly ached in dismay. The last three toes on both feet were webbed together, and the boy's left foot was bent so the sole pointed in. She flexed the foot down, forcing it until the baby began to cry. She had seen such a deformity once before. The parents had decided to allow that child to die. With a foot twisted so, how would he keep up with The People when they followed the caribou or traveled from the winter village to their summer fish camp? And what of other mothers, those women carrying babies in their bellies? Just by seeing this one, they might pass his deformity to the children in their wombs. Could such a child be allowed to live? How would he ever find a wife? How would Day Woman find a husband when her time of mourning had passed? Would a man want a woman whose son might curse his own unborn children?

Ligige' looked over at Day Woman. She slept in quiet happiness. It would be better if Ligige' put the child out now, but Ligige' was not the mother. The decision was not hers. She wrapped the baby in several ground squirrel skins and laid him on the packed mud of the lodge floor far from his mother's arms. It would be best if Day Woman did not get used to holding him, and best for the child if he did not carry memories of his mother with him to the spirit world. Perhaps, then, he would not call her to leave the living.

Ligige' walked through the sleeping village to her brother's lodge. He was a respected elder and, more important, Day Woman's father. From the time he had been a young man, he had dreamed visions. He would know what to do.

The voice was soft, a sound that seemed like an owl's call. It told Tsaani to prepare for death. He shuddered in his knowledge that owls speak only in certainty, and he wondered if the bird meant his death or the death of someone else in the village. His own death would not be a terrible loss—after all, he was an old man. He had enjoyed many nights of stars, many days of sun. But most likely the owl's call was meant for his daughter Day Woman.

How many women survived a birth labor of three days? Her loss would not be as terrible as losing a hunter, yet she was a young woman, still capable of bearing children, and she was strong. Unusual among The People, she had no fear of water. She was the one who waded deep into the river to repair the fish traps, and once she had saved a child nearly swept away in the fast current of high spring floods.

It was said that their family carried the blood of the Sea Hunters, those men who lived out on the islands of the North Sea. But who could know for sure?

The call came again, and this time, Tsaani realized it was not an owl's voice that beckoned him from his sleep, but that of his sister Ligige'. Tsaani pushed himself from the mound of pelts that was his bed and wrapped a woven hare fur robe around his bare shoulders. It fell in soft white folds to brush against the tops of his feet.

"I am awake, Sister," he said. "Come."

Ligige' came in, and by the dim glow of the hearth coals, Tsaani could see the pinched, worried look on her face.

"My daughter?" Tsaani asked, careful not to mention her name. If she was dead, he did not want to call her spirit into his lodge. Why remind death that he was an old man?

"Day Woman is well. It is the child."

"Dead?"

"Alive, strong, and a boy."

It was good news, but he knew his sister had come in sorrow. "What then?" he asked.

"The child is crippled."

"How?"

"One foot is bent. He might learn to walk. He will never run."

"Nothing can be done?"

Ligige' lifted her hands. "A baby's bones are soft. If the foot was bent and held in place, it might help, but it might not."

"He could draw bad luck to his mother, or worse, his brother. Even the whole village."

"Yes."

"If he is allowed to die, his mother might decide to follow." Tsaani spoke softly, almost to himself. "She is young. It would be a bad thing to lose her."

Ligige' raised her brows in agreement.

"What does the mother say?"

"Nothing. She does not know. She sleeps."

"Has she fed him yet?"

"Yes."

Tsaani hissed, and Ligige' chided herself for her carelessness. She should have noticed the deformity at birth. Milk was as strong as sinew rope, binding mother to child.

Tsaani turned his face toward the top of the lodge. Behind him the hearth smoke rose, as though carrying his prayers. "Bring the child to me," he finally said, "but try not to awaken the mother."

As his sister left, Tsaani turned to watch the smoke in the darkness, then he went to his medicine bag, a river otter skin, the tail, legs and head still attached, the belly full of dried plants, each with its own gift. He found a pack secured with one knot. Cloudberry leaves, dried and crumbled to a fine dust. He untied the knot and carefully shook a small portion of the powder into his cupped hand.

Tsaani scattered the powder into the coals, then spoke slowly, laying his words one by one on the smoke as it rose. He asked for wisdom, for strength, not only for himself but for Day Woman and Ligige'.

By the time his prayers were finished, Ligige' was again scratching on the caribou hide doorflap. He went to her, but made her stay outside. Why chance a curse being carried into his own lodge?

He unwrapped the child. Under the light of full moon, he could see the boy was strong, his head and face well-formed, his shoulders wide. Carefully, Tsaani slipped his hands down the child's legs. The bones were straight, but as in all babies the soles tipped inward. He pulled gently on the right foot, flattened it against his palm. He pushed, and the baby, with surprising strength, pushed back. Then Tsaani placed his hand against the bottom of the left foot. Although the foot flexed slightly, it remained tipped on edge.

Tsaani took a long breath and let it out in a sigh. "This child's foot is bent like a bear's paw flipping fish from water," he told Ligige'. "His mother must have watched a bear catching salmon." Why did women never learn to honor those animals that demand honor? "Did you notice that his toes are webbed?" he asked his sister.

Ligige' nodded. "That is not a curse," she said.

"Yes, but the foot..." Tsaani shook his head. When he spoke again, it was with the quivering voice of an old man. "I will take him to the Grandfather Rock. When Day Woman wakes in the morning, the child will already be gone."

Day Woman called out to Ligige'. Her breasts ached, she said. They were full of milk. Where was the child?

For a time, Ligige' pretended she did not hear. She was sewing a birchbark container. It was as long as her arm, wrist to shoulder, and as big around as a man's thigh. She had pinched the container together at the bottom and whipped it shut with split spruce root. Now she was sewing up the side, punching holes in the overlapped bark with a birdbone awl and securing the seam with long stitches that crisscrossed each other all the way up. It would be a useful thing to hang on her back when she went to the woods to gather plants.

"I need my son," Day Woman said, and using the birthing rope that still hung over her, she pulled herself to her feet. She shuffled to the child's birchbark bed with its nest of ground squirrel furs, then stifled a cry.

"Do not call for him," Ligige' said quietly. "The spirits took him. It was necessary." She explained about the baby's foot.

Day Woman gathered the ground squirrel furs to her breast and sank to the dirt floor.

"I have spoken to your father," said Ligige'. "He offers prayers. The child's spirit is safe. I have promised to stay with you during these days when hunters cannot risk their skills to the powers you hold."

"I may choose to follow my son," Day Woman said.

Ligige' snorted. "You are young. There will be other babies." But she lowered her eyes as she spoke so Day Woman would not see the pity there.

Day Woman moaned and asked, "How will that be? I have no husband."

"Your husband's brother, Fox Barking, says he will take you."

"He has agreed?"

"Your father went to him last night. He has agreed."

For a long time Day Woman was silent, and Ligige' saw that her face was the face of a person deciding. Finally Day Woman lifted the strains of her mourning song. She wrapped her arms over her swollen breasts and lay forward to press her face against the packed dirt floor. Ligige' set aside her birchbark container and fumbled through the fish-skin basket she carried with her when she went to birthing lodges. She took out a comb carved from birch wood and began to pull it gently through Day Woman's hair. As she combed, she, too, sang, mumbling the words of the song The People used to guide new babies to the spirit world.

THE GRANDFATHER LAKE

The lichen on the rock pricked the child's bare skin, and he arched his back. Though the days were drawing toward winter, the sun was bright, hot. The baby squeezed his eyes tight and flailed out with his arms, but there was no closeness of body or wrap, and he startled, reacting as though he fell. Suddenly, a soft robe was thrown over him, blocking out the light and folding the heat down into his face. The blanket settled against his mouth, and he stopped crying. He moved his head and lips, searching for his mother's breast. He caught a bit of the robe and sucked, but there was no milk. In his hunger, the child clamped his gums together against the skin, then sucked hard, drawing a bit of loose fur down his throat. He choked, turning his head to fight for breath. His face darkened; his lips turned blue.

Finally he coughed and dislodged the fur from his throat to his mouth. He pushed it out with his tongue, then gulped in air and began to cry.

The old man walked away; the cries followed him. He lifted his hands to his ears and prayed for protection from the child's spirit.

It was afternoon when K'os reached the Grandfather Lake. She had not wanted to come, but her mother had made her. She hoped she could find the basket quickly.

She searched first at the water's edge. Perhaps during the struggle, the basket had fallen there.

She found phalarope feathers, bear tracks, nothing more. For a moment she squatted on her haunches and allowed herself to rest. She had bled for four days, then stopped, but her belly still ached. She looked out over the lake. The water was still; only the ripples of fish jumping moved the surface.

She kept her back to the hill where the Grandfather Rock lived. Even from this far, she could feel the rock pull her, and it seemed she could hear her own cries, could feel the pain of the men's hands at her wrists and ankles, between her legs.

It will not always be this way, she promised herself. Already she could think of Gull Wing and rejoice. She would kill the others, too. Some way, though she was a woman, she would kill them. If she was strong enough to do that, she was strong enough to face the Grandfather Rock—and Gull Wing's body, rotting beside it.

She turned and walked up the hill, but still kept her eyes away from the rock, instead scanning the ground as she walked, looking for the basket. It was a salmonskin basket, made of six fish skins split at the belly, flayed out and sewn, tail down, to form a narrow base. Each skin was scraped so thin you could see light through it. Her mother had cut off the fish heads, and the curves of the gill slits at the top edge of the basket were like a line of waves, one following the other.

K'os settled her mouth into a frown and lifted her head to see the rock. Grasses hid most of it, and somewhere nearby lay what was left of Gull Wing's body. Memories pressed in, squeezed against her flesh until there was room for nothing but her anger and her pain.

She cried out to the Grandfather Rock. "Give me a long life. Let my hatred grow as strong and dark as a spruce tree. Let it last through all my years."

She repeated the words until they became a song, and she sang until her throat was raw. She crested the hill, then stopped.

There was a woven hare fur robe, pure white, draped over the rock. Who would leave such a beautiful blanket? At the first rain, it would begin to rot. She walked slowly, carefully, watching for Gull Wing's bones. But there was nothing, no bones, no flesh. Of course, a bear might have dragged him away. Or wolves. She thought she could see a swath through the grasses, a flattening, but she was not sure. A hunter would know, a man used to tracking animals.

Perhaps Gull Wing's friends had come back for him, or moved him to the rock and placed the blanket over his body.

She wanted to lift that blanket, to see how the man had rotted, to laugh at the skin and muscles pulling away from the bones, the eyes torn out by ravens, the flesh eaten by foxes. But a part of her hesitated. Who could be sure what was under the blanket? Who could tell what curse might await her?

Better to find her mother's basket and leave.

She walked down the north slope of the hill, then turned toward the black, wet soil where the spruce were thick and tall. She kept her eyes on the ground and finally saw the basket, lying on its side. Her mother would be angry if it was damaged. She picked it up. It was whole; but now she must fill it with spruce roots.

She stooped, ignoring the spikes of pain that cut in from her lower back, and began to thrust her digging stick into the ground. When she felt the stick catch, she pushed it in sideways and lifted until she brought a root to the surface. Using the stick and her hands, she pulled until she had two armlengths of root above ground, then she cut it off and followed it away from the tree, coiling as she walked, pulling, until the root was thin enough to snap. She moved to another tree, took another root, then a third root. She worked until the coils filled the basket.

She knew she should leave an offering for the trees. Her mother had insisted she bring dried caribou leaves with her, but she left the leaves in the pouch tied at her waist. The trees had watched the men come, had seen them take her to the Grandfather Rock, but had done nothing to help her. Why should she leave anything for them?

She started back toward the village, but then decided to return to the Grandfather Rock. She *would* look under the blanket, and sing songs of praise to the animals that had eaten Gull Wing's flesh. Half-way up the hill, she smelled the reek of rotting meat. The smell did not come from the rock. She turned off the path and found the heap of bones, the bits of flesh, that had been Gull Wing.

She stood and laughed, called out to him, lifted her parka, told him to take her body if he thought it was so fine, then still laughing, she continued up toward the Grandfather Rock. If Gull Wing was not under the blanket, she would be foolish to leave it. Why not add it to the blankets she had already set aside for the day she would become wife and have a lodge of her own?

She set the fishskin basket on the ground beside the rock, and for a moment studied the blanket. It was woven from winter hare furs, each pure white, and it lay in a mound, as though it covered something. She lifted one corner. There was a noise, like a bird chirping. She dropped the blanket, backed away.

It is nothing but a bird, she told herself in disgust. You can kill it with your digging stick and take it home for the boiling bag. She lifted the stick, ready to strike, then threw back the robe.

On the rock lay a baby.

K'os closed her eyes quickly, afraid to see some great deformity in the child. Why else were children left?

The baby began to cry. K'os wanted to see it, to know what was wrong with it. She opened her eyes only a crack and looked out through the fringe of her lashes.

The child was whole and plump, a boy, his body long and perfect. K'os squatted beside the rock. Where had he come from? No one she knew had had a baby for at least two moons, and this child was only a day or two old. The scab-like stump of the birth cord still protruded from his belly. Perhaps he was from the Near River People, or one of the bands of Caribou People who traveled, following the herds. She reached down slowly and touched his cheek. He turned his head toward her fingers.

She remembered Gguzaakk when she was small doing the same, looking for her mother's milk-filled breast. Too bad K'os's aunt was not there. She could feed him.

The baby's lips were cracked and dry-looking. He needed milk. K'os dropped her stick, spat into the palm of her hand, and rubbed the spittle on his lips. He tried to suck her fingers, but she pulled them away.

She shook her head. It was too bad someone else had not found him. There were many women who would welcome a son. She did not. Would not. She pressed her hand against her belly. Tomorrow she would go to Old Sister and tell her she had done something foolish. She had slept with one of her mother's sister's sons and did not want her father to know. Did Old Sister have something K'os could take? Surely there were medicines . . . She looked at the baby. He was shivering. His arms and legs jerked in spasms. Yes, too bad.

She closed her eyes and remembered Gull Wing's heart, lying in the center of that rock, exactly where the baby lay now.

Suddenly K'os was very still. She had left the heart as a gift. What if the Grandfather Rock had given her a gift in exchange? There was no sign of that heart, yet here was this child. She bent over him, studied his face. There was something about him that reminded her of Gull Wing. The eyes, the brows? No, that was foolish. Look at the child's long fingers. Gull Wing's had been short, thick. The baby's toes, also, were long and . . . again, K'os stopped. They were webbed; each of the last three toes was joined to the next.

Then she knew.

He was an animal-gift child. Like in the stories. Were not the greatest hunters, the most renowned shamans among her people those who were animal-gift, somehow grown from a clot of blood or a bit of flesh?

This child was one of them. The Grandfather Rock had shaped a child, perhaps from Gull Wing's blood, but more likely from animal blood. Now the rock offered the child to her as a gift, to give her power. To bring back her luck.

She picked up her mother's root basket, then lifted the baby. She wrapped him in the hare fur blanket and spat into his mouth. She had no milk in her breasts, but she could keep him alive until they got to the village, then her mother could find a woman to nurse him.

K'os felt her power grow with each step. She could not keep her laughter in her throat. It spilled out of her mouth and danced ahead of them as she carried the animal-gift baby to the village.

PART ONE

Look! What do I see? Bones cut their feet.

I spoke this riddle to The People before I left my village. I said these words and told them many stories. I spoke long into the night, and The People heard what I said, but I have little hope that they understood.

The bones are those of First Salmon, Caribou Walking, Mother Bear, and all animals who return to give themselves year after year so The People might live. The feet belong to people who no longer show the respect those animals deserve.

The elders whispered among themselves, and I heard their words.

"See what disrespect has cost us," they said. "See what happens when people no longer follow ancient ways. The salmon leave our streams. The young men thirst for war."

So now I, Chakliux, must turn my thoughts to battle, not a battle of knives and spears, but a battle of the spirit. I go to fight for peace. Why else was I trained as storyteller? Why else was I given to The People as animal-gift?

Chapter One

THE NEAR RIVER VILLAGE

Chakliux's thoughts were like the bitter taste of willow bark tea, and he shook his head, suddenly impatient with his self-pity. At least she was beautiful. He could console himself with that. If he did not look into her eyes and see the emptiness there. If he did not let himself hear her foolish giggle, her petty complaints.

What was more important? His happiness or the safety of the people in this village and his own?

He had seen the storm coming, watched when it was only a shifting of stars, a wisp of cloud, but with each incident—the robbing of a snare trap, the refusal of a bride price—the thunderheads built until now it would take only one small thing to set the hunters at each others' throats.

How better to bind the villages than through marriage? What stronger marriage than one between a son set apart as Dzuuggi and the daughter of the Near River shaman?

The older hunters in his village had envied him. He had smiled at their jokes, at the longing in their voices when they spoke of her, this beautiful Near River woman. But Chakliux did not want her. How could she compare to his Gguzaakk?

Gguzaakk had carried her soul in her eyes. Even now, he felt her spirit hovering near him. He was not afraid of her, that she might try to call him into the world of the dead, to follow her and their tiny son. Gguzaakk understood what he had to do, and he could feel her sorrow.

He reminded himself that Snow-in-her-hair was young. Gguzaakk had had more than four handfuls of summers when she died. Wisdom comes with age. Snow-in-her-hair would grow in wisdom as the years passed.

Chakliux watched her as she spoke to her mother, as she laughed and flashed her eyes at the young warriors who made one excuse or another to be near her. She wore a hooded parka of white weasel fur, each slender skin sewn so its black-tipped tail hung free. The parka was something to draw away the breath, and Chakliux comforted himself with the hope that Snow-in-her-hair had sewn it herself. He smiled as he remembered how clumsy Gguzaakk had been with awl and needle. But what had it mattered? Gguzaakk understood things of the spirit. She could look into a person's eyes and know what should be said.

But, Chakliux told himself, it would be good to have a wife who could sew. How better can a woman honor animals than by creating beauty from their furs and hides?

Chakliux also wore a special parka. It was made of sea otter skins—bought in trade from the Walrus Hunters—to remind the Near River People of his powers. His mother had made it. She was a woman gifted with a needle and with quickness of fingers. He wore caribou skin leggings but nothing on his feet. He had known the people would want to see his webbed toes, his foot turned on edge, that sign of his otter blood. Who could doubt he was otter when they saw that foot always ready to paddle?

If it had not been winter, he would have showed them that he could swim.

Even now, he longed for the quiet cold of the depths, the clear silver light shining down into the water. He wanted to teach others to swim, but they would not try, and each year, children, who might have saved themselves if they knew how, were taken by the river. Even Gguzaakk had been afraid to swim . . .

Ah, he could not allow himself to think too much about Gguzaakk. Soon he would have another wife. He must be a good husband to her.

He turned his thoughts to the lodge, to the caribou hides that were stretched over the lodge poles, to the thick mats on the floor. It was a good winter lodge. It would be a comfortable place to stay, and Snow-in-her-hair's father seemed to be a wise man. It would not be difficult to live with this family.

Snow-in-her-hair stood to receive another gift: a willow basket made of roots, split and woven. Inside was a flicker skin. The spotted feathers of that bird—a bird a man might see only once or twice during a whole lifetime—would bring them luck in their marriage.

He thanked the one who had given it—an old woman he had heard called Ligige'. Her back was humped and bent so he could not look into her face, but he saw the respect others in the lodge gave the woman, the place made for her on the honored side of the fire.

She mumbled something when he thanked her, then began to turn away. Suddenly she stopped. She stared at his feet, and he felt the heat of her eyes, as though in looking she had kindled a fire. With effort, she straightened, looked into his face, gasped. She said nothing, only averted her gaze, covered her mouth with one hand. But as she walked away, Chakliux felt Gguzaakk's spirit move like a fitful wind, blowing from all directions.

Sok watched Snow-in-her-hair, let his eyes caress her long graceful arms, the small mounds of her breasts under her parka. Tonight she would become wife of the Cousin River hunter, the man whose feet belonged to otter. Did he appreciate her beauty? Sok had watched the man carefully, saw no great joy in his eyes when he looked at Snow-in-her-hair. Maybe he was more otter than man. Maybe he wanted a woman like Happy Mouth, who looked like an otter.

The first time Sok remembered seeing Snow-in-her-hair she had been a child playing in the dirt outside her mother's lodge. Even then he had recognized her beauty and had stooped to join her play, until one of his hunting partners saw him and laughed, mocking.

He could have waited ten years, saved a bride price that even a shaman would not refuse, but his loins had burned with need. Even when he hunted, he could think of nothing but women. The animals sensed his disrespect and refused to give themselves to his spears. Finally, even his stepfather noticed and told him to take a wife. Sok had taken Red Leaf, a good woman. She had given him two fine, strong sons, but each time he saw Snow-in-her-hair he wished he had waited.

He had considered asking for her as second wife, but a man of The People rarely had a second wife unless his first was barren or sickly, and Red Leaf was neither. His only hope was to become chief hunter or a celebrated warrior. Warriors and chief hunters often had two or even three wives. But now there was this otter man. The stink of the Cousin River Village was still on him. Snow-in-her-hair deserved better.

"Do not let her see him," Ligige' told her brother. "At least until after this night, until they have sealed with their bodies what has been said in words, and her father has accepted the man's gifts."

"Is that wise?" her brother asked. "Truth cannot be changed."

"This marriage gives hope for peace. You know our young hunters seek any excuse to fight against the Cousin River Village. They foul their own traplines to give reason."

Tsaani nodded. His sister was right. And it would not be the first time there had been fighting between this village of The People and the Cousin River Village. With only a two- or three-day walk between winter villages and less between summer fish camps, the people saw each other too often, thought of too many reasons to hold anger against one another, especially since the salmon runs had been poor in the past few years.

But only the few who were oldest in this village—his sister Ligige', Blue-head Duck and he, himself—could remember the last fighting. Words were not strong enough to explain the horror: young men killed, days of mourning, and hard winters with too few hunters in both villages to keep the very old and the very young alive.

To prevent more killing, he and Ligige' must keep this secret, especially from Day Woman.

Tsaani had heard the Cousin River People boast of their animal-gift son, but for some reason he had thought him to be a child yet. Even Near River People had come back to tell stories of his ability to swim. A person who could swim? How could anyone bear the cold waters of The People's rivers? But Tsaani reminded himself that his own daughter had no fear of water, and it was said that their family carried Sea Hunter blood. Those island people claimed to be brothers of the sea otter. Perhaps the man's talents were no more than that—a remembrance of grandfathers long dead.

If so, then Ligige' was right. The young man who had come to marry their shaman's daughter was no animal-gift, but only Day Woman's child, found before he died on the Grandfather Rock.

THE COUSIN RIVER VILLAGE
K'os stretched her arms above her head and curled her toes. She lay on her sleeping mats and watched as Bear Finder adjusted his breech-

cloth and retied his leggings. She was an old woman, they said. She laughed. Bear Finder looked at her, tilted his head.

"You are happy?" he asked.

"I am happy," she said.

Old, yes. Old, but as smooth-skinned and flat-bellied as a girl. Seven handfuls of summers and still like a girl. Her hair was black, without a strand of white, and her face was smooth, her teeth strong. Only her hands betrayed the years, but men did not look at her hands. She had other things they would rather see.

Bear Finder crouched in the entrance tunnel and cautiously moved the doorflap aside.

K'os snorted her disgust. "If you are afraid of my husband, you should not come here at all," she told him.

He crept back from the tunnel, pulled on his parka. She could see the burn of red on his cheeks, but he said nothing. He would return. They always did. And what could Ground Beater do? Throw her out? Kill them? He was an old man. She could tell him anything, and he would believe her. Especially now that her son, Chakliux, was gone. Why worry?

Chakliux. She wondered how he was doing in the Near River Village. She smiled. Had they figured out who he was? Probably not. The Near River People were not known for their quick minds. She was glad he was gone, but she missed him. He was so very wise. He could keep her laughing—or thinking. His riddles! Whose were better?

But he also frightened her. He knew what she was, had probably known since he was a child. But then she knew his secrets also, things he did not even know about himself. Things no one in this village knew.

Gguzaakk had claimed his heart, but she had been no match for K'os. What wife could replace a mother? Especially a wife who had so unfortunately died in childbirth.

Ah well, Chakliux was at the Near River Village now. The shaman's daughter was said to be beautiful. He would soon forget his round, plain Gguzaakk.

Chakliux's powers were great, but they were like the powers of the owl. You did not want to see Chakliux's eyes turned toward you. He did not carry good luck with him. No one was safe. Not even his mother. Not even his wife.

K'os threw back her head and laughed. Let the Near River Village live with Chakliux's luck.

THE NEAR RIVER VILLAGE

The years had weakened Tsaani's legs. He still hunted, but everything he did, he did slowly. Now, as he walked to his daughter's lodge, he planted each foot carefully on the packed snow paths. Mud bled through the ice in the center of the path, and the wet earth smell of it filled Tsaani's nostrils. In that great battle between the sun and night, winter was being defeated once again.

He came to the lodge near the center of the village where his daughter lived. It was a small lodge; the caribou hide cover needed to be replaced, but since she was second wife, Tsaani had little hope that would happen.

Perhaps he would get a few caribou during this year's hunts. His own wife did not need the hides. Her lodge was new. He would not have his daughter live in shame because she was second wife and because her husband would rather sleep than hunt.

He scratched at the doorflap, but no one came. Finally, he crawled in through the entrance tunnel—something he would not have done except in his own daughter's lodge. The lodge was empty.

Fox Barking, Day Woman's husband, was a man whose thoughts were always turned toward himself. He had no doubt taken both wives to see the Cousin River Dzuuggi, thinking the Dzuuggi would assume he was someone important. If a man was too lazy to hunt, what good were wives? When you let your wife live in a lodge that stinks of mildew, who could think you were important?

Tsaani's knees and ankles ached, but he made himself walk more quickly. The shaman's lodge was on the far side of the village. Tsaani's caribou hide moccasins seemed to slip more than necessary, but finally he came to the lodge, to the crowd that had gathered around it.

When the people saw him, they parted to allow him inside.

The lodge was warm, too warm, with too many people, each adding to the heat with words and laughter. Tsaani stayed at the edge of the group, though several urged him toward the comfortable fur mats and willow backrests reserved for the elders, but he remained where he was, watching, listening.

His eyes fell first on the Cousin River Dzuuggi, and in that moment of seeing, he wondered why Ligige' had asked him to come. There was nothing he could do. The young man stood with feet bare, the otter foot and webbed toes uncovered for anyone to see. But even if the man's feet had been covered, how could he hide his high forehead, his wide cheekbones, his well-formed eyes? This was Gull Wing's son. The young man laughed, and it was Gull Wing's laughter. Were they blind? Were they deaf?

He looked at the faces in the lodge. There was no one from the Cousin River Village. Had the man come alone? Perhaps, like Tsaani and Ligige', he realized that too many young hunters longed to become warriors, and so decided to risk only his own life.

Tsaani watched the man for a time, listened as he spoke to the people. Perhaps he looked like his father, but he had wisdom far beyond any Gull Wing ever possessed. It must be the wisdom, Tsaani decided, that closed everyone's eyes to who he was.

Slowly, Tsaani studied each face, the men and women of his village, old and young, wise and foolish. They listened as the Dzuuggi spoke of the ties between the two villages, as he told stories of the battles and the hunts, the grandfathers and warriors who bound them together into one people.

Then Tsaani's eyes found his daughter, and he saw that she knew. There was pain in her face, sorrow etched in long lines down her cheeks. She opened her mouth, and Tsaani was afraid she would speak, would say something to break the spell the Dzuuggi was weaving, but though her mouth moved, no sound escaped.

Tsaani began to work his way through the people, toward his daughter, to warn her, to explain that she could not claim this man as son, that she must make a sacrifice, as she had when this son was born, to protect their village.

More people crowded into the lodge, pressed against Tsaani, so that it seemed as though he were in a dream, each step taking him nowhere, but finally he was only three women from her, then two. He reached out to clasp her shoulder, but before he could touch her, the cry came, a long, loud keening.

As though the cry were a wall, Tsaani felt himself being pushed away. Day Woman flung herself at the young man's feet, clasped his ankles and called out, "My son, oh my son, you have come back to me."

"You think I want a husband who was thrown away?" said Snow-in-her-hair. "You think I want children who are cursed? My children may already be cursed, just because I looked at you. Just because I sat beside you!"

"No one in the Cousin River Village has been cursed because of me," Chakliux said softly.

"That is because they do not know who you are!"

"Nothing has changed. I am the same person I have always been," said Chakliux, but even as he spoke, doubt pricked his heart.

Gguzaakk had died in childbirth. Had he cursed her? He shook his head. No. He knew why she had died. It was one reason he was here. How could he bear to stay in his own village with that knowledge tearing him apart?

Then he felt the comfort of Gguzaakk's spirit close to him, and he reminded himself that even his son had been born whole and perfect. No deformities, no marks that told of curses.

Wolf-and-Raven and his wife, Blue Flower, sat without speaking. They watched their daughter as though she were a dancer, performing. Finally, when Snow-in-her-hair was exhausted, she dropped down to cry, lying with her face in her mother's lap.

After a moment, Wolf-and-Raven cleared his throat. Chakliux waited for the man to speak, and as he waited, he gathered words for his reply. He must convince Wolf-and-Raven that neither he nor old He Talks, the shaman of Chakliux's village, had intended to harm Snow-in-her-hair or any person in the Near River Village. They only wanted everyone to live together in peace.

"There are those who say the Cousin River People sent you to curse us," Wolf-and-Raven finally said. He was a man of long face and loose skin, and his lips were too large for his words, smearing them together so Chakliux had to listen carefully to understand what he said. "I do not believe this."

Chakliux raised his eyebrows to show that he agreed with the man.

"I saw your surprise when Day Woman claimed you. I think you came to bring peace. That is something we need. I do not remember the last time of fighting between our villages, but there are those who do. If what they say is true, I do not want the same thing to happen again.

"I also knew your father, your true father. You have his face, though it seems you do not have his spirit. And Day Woman is not one to lie. Nor Ligige'." He stopped to point with his chin at Chakliux's feet. "She said your toes are like those of a baby she delivered long ago—Day Woman's son. That child was taken to the Grandfather Rock. Even your Cousin River mother has said you were found on the Grandfather Rock."

Yes, Chakliux thought. Found by his mother. He knew the story well. How could he not, being Dzuuggi?

"But we need peace," Wolf-and-Raven said. "I have spoken to your grandfather, Tsaani. He agrees with me. Snow-in-her-hair will not be your wife. I cannot force her. I do not know the ways of your village, but here a woman is not given as wife against her will."

"It is the same in my village," Chakliux said quietly.

"We ask you to stay. To hunt with us and fish with us, to spend this year with us, so our people will see that you are not a curse. The young hunters need to understand that if they choose to fight, they will kill good people—men just like themselves.

"For now, you will live with your brother. Your mother's husband does not want you in her lodge until he knows you are not cursed. Your brother, though, is a strong hunter. He and his wife say you are welcome in her lodge."

"His name is?"

"Sok. You have seen him. His wife makes the pattern of the sun from pieced skins on his parkas and boots."

Yes, Chakliux thought. He knew the man. He was strong-looking, not tall but big. His voice was loud and he laughed often. He seemed to be a man who sought attention, who enjoyed the envy of others. It was strange to think of him as brother.

"For my daughter's sake," Wolf-and-Raven said, "I wish you were animal-gift. For myself, I do not care. Animal-gift or not, we need you to stay in the village, to bind our people together in friendship. Too many will die if we become enemies."

The man's words washed through Chakliux like clear water. If there were men in the Near River Village who hoped for peace, then there was a chance.

"I will stay," Chakliux said.

He lowered his head so Wolf-and-Raven could not see doubt darken his eyes. He had a brother he did not know, a mother who seemed aware of nothing beyond her own needs. Why had she claimed him now, when she had once left him to die under cold and wind and the teeth of animals? Why take away his honor as animal-gift?

But should she say nothing? He was not animal-gift. He was only a child thrown away, a curse.

Then Gguzaakk's voice came to him, spoke in his heart, reminded him why he was in the Near River Village. He must discover how to turn people from hatred to understanding. It did not matter if he was animal-gift. It did not matter if his foot was a sign that he carried otter blood. If he could not bring peace, then many people in this village and his own would die.

Chapter Two

THE FIRST MEN VILLAGE, TRADERS' BAY
(PRESENT-DAY HERENDEEN BAY, THE ALASKA PENINSULA)

Aqamdax looked out over the ice-covered inlet, north toward the sea, then east toward the land of the River People. Perhaps next summer her mother would come back. It had been four years since she left with the trader, but she had promised Aqamdax she would return, and each summer Aqamdax waited and watched.

The wind cut hard from the west, forcing Aqamdax to step forward and brace herself against it. There was no one else on the beach so she called out her words, placed them on the wind, and prayed the message would find its way to her mother.

"You left me in He Sings's ulax," Aqamdax said, lifting her words like a song. "His throwing board is strong. His seal harpoon is cunning, and there is food enough for everyone. His wives still hate me, but I do what I can to help them.

"For two summers now my blood has followed the moon. Soon I will be wife. Come back and share my joy."

She would have said more, but from the edges of her eyes she saw that He Sings's second wife had come to the beach. The woman walked toward her, bent with the wind, her mouth opening and closing like a fish's mouth. She was dragging her youngest daughter by the hand. The child was howling, but the wind pulled away the noise, so Aqamdax knew of her protests only by seeing her face.

When Fish Taker drew near, she set her hands at the center of the girl's back and pushed the child toward Aqamdax.

"I told you this morning, you must take care of her. How will I finish my husband's parka if this one is forever crawling into my lap?"

"She was asleep," Aqamdax told the woman.

"She woke up."

Fish Taker turned back toward the sod-roofed ulas, leaving the girl with Aqamdax. The child was not yet to the age of remembering, but she could talk and walk. Aqamdax knelt down beside her, turning so the girl was in the lee of Aqamdax's body, shielded from the worst of the wind.

"Little Bird, why do you cry?"

"I want eat," she said. She raised a mittened hand to wipe at the mucus running from her nose, then hiccoughed out a sob.

"Here, I have something." Aqamdax pulled a strip of dried fish from the sleeve of her birdskin sax.

Aqamdax ate well in the chief hunter's ulax, but had not forgotten the summer after her father's death, before He Sings had agreed to feed her and her mother. Now she always carried dried meat or fish, even hid some in her sleeping place.

Little Bird reached for the fish, but Aqamdax chewed off a chunk, warmed it for a moment in her mouth, then handed it to the child.

"We should go back to the village," Aqamdax told her. "It is too cold on the beach."

Aqamdax hoisted her to one hip, then walked up the slope of the beach, over the path worn into the snow. She carried Little Bird to Give Spear's lodge. Give Spear was an elder, and never worried if someone chose to sit in the leeward shelter of his ulax. Besides, he was one of the few hunters in the village who had never come to Aqamdax's bed. Even if Give Spear's wife saw Aqamdax sitting outside his ulax, there should be no trouble.

Aqamdax squatted on her haunches and pulled Little Bird close to her. They sat, leaning against one another, and ate. Little Bird chatted in half-formed baby words that Aqamdax could not understand, but the girl did not seem to mind if Aqamdax did not answer her.

Aqamdax let her thoughts go back to the night before. She had not been surprised to hear someone scratch at the curtain of her sleeping place. Many hunters came to her in the night, though only a few had courage to enter He Sings's ulax when the man was home from one of his many hunting trips.

Salmon, Aqamdax had thought. He visited her often. But when she pulled back the curtain, Day Breaker, He Sings's oldest son, was there. Her breath caught so suddenly in her throat that she had not been able to say anything to him, only to open her arms, welcome him into the warmth of her fur seal sleeping robes.

He had taken her quickly, thrusting hard into her body, and she had been glad to feel the power of his need, but that was not what she remembered as she sat with Little Bird.

She remembered what he told her when he left her sleeping place: "Give me a son," he had whispered, "then I will take you as my wife."

THE NEAR RIVER VILLAGE

That day, their hunt had been to stand and look, to watch out over open hills, away from thickets of willow and alder that crowded the riverbanks.

"You will see steam rise, as if from water boiling," Tsaani told Chakliux. "On a day of fog or snow you will not see it, but on a still, cold morning like this, it will be there, coming from the ground, and you will know a bear is waiting, warm in his den."

This kind of hunting needed different songs, different prayers than what Chakliux knew, but during the moon that he had lived with his brother, Sok, Chakliux had learned much. His grandfather had even given him two of his bear hunting songs, a gift as precious as anything Chakliux ever hoped to receive.

But for all their looking, they saw nothing, and finally decided to return to the village. The men quarreled, snapping at one another like unfed dogs, all with eyes averted from Chakliux, ashamed that he had seen their defeat, yet angry also, muttering under their tongues that he had broken their luck.

A good way to bring peace, Chakliux thought bitterly. A good way to turn young hunters from dreams of battle. Then suddenly, Tsaani stopped. Chakliux looked at Tsaani, and Tsaani pointed with his chin toward his dog Black Nose.

Her paws pranced a nervous rhythm against the ground, and she whined high in her throat. Tsaani knelt beside her, and Chakliux saw her tremble.

Tsaani was old, but still he hunted, mostly because of his dogs, Black Nose and Long Tail and the newest one that he had never really given a name, except Dog—as good a name as any, Chakliux thought. All three animals now stood stiff-legged, the fur on their necks bristling.

To Chakliux, it seemed the two males were always at each other's throats, trying to steal food from one another or competing to mount Black Nose, but when Tsaani took them hunting, they worked together, as though each dog knew the other's thoughts. Tsaani told him they had taken down black bears larger than a man.

Tsaani motioned to the hunters behind him, moved his head in a jerk toward a mound of snow-covered earth that bulged from a hill to their left. The men crept up on bent legs, moving their feet in quietness. Long Tail began to dig into the frozen earth near the edge of the mound, flinging chunks of snow and dirt back between his legs as he dug.

A low growl rolled into Black Nose's throat. Tsaani laid his hand against the top of her head and tightened his fingers over the dome of her skull. He had trained her to remain quiet on hunts until the men moved in to kill, but she was pregnant with a litter and more difficult to control.

Sok, a short-bladed knife in his hand, reached forward to slash the air just ahead of the dog's nose. She dropped back to her haunches. In anger Tsaani clasped Sok's wrist. What dog, trained to fear, reacted with courage when courage was needed? Sok's dogs, if Tsaani had allowed them on this hunt, would now be cowering behind the men rather than digging quietly into the den.

Sok glared at Tsaani, his eyes flashing. Chakliux stepped up from the group of men, stood behind the dog and placed both hands against her back. Black Nose again rose to her feet, her muzzle thrust forward, her ears flat against her head.

Chakliux looked at Tsaani, motioned toward the den, then shook his head. Tsaani understood what he meant. There was something wrong. Black Nose did not growl without reason. It was strange, Tsaani thought, how well he hunted with this grandson, even though he had known him only a moon.

Tsaani signed for the hunters to circle the den. Suddenly Black Nose jumped, and a roar more like bear than dog came from her throat. Chakliux lunged to clasp the scruff of her neck but missed, falling forward before he could catch himself.

Suddenly the side of the hill erupted. A bear burst through the earth so that both Long Tail and Dog were flung back toward the hunters.

At first the men did not react. Even Tsaani, in all his years of hunting, had never seen an animal come from the earth in such a way.

Power is working, Tsaani thought. For a moment, he wondered if they should leave the bear. Was there some sacredness here that men had no right to destroy? Perhaps one of his hunters had broken a taboo or treated something with disrespect.

Tsaani's thoughts slowed his hands, but Black Nose leapt toward the bear. Tsaani held his breath. The bear would rip open her belly as she jumped. But her quickness seemed to take the animal by surprise. She sank her teeth into his throat and hung by her jaws, a long swath of white against the bear's black fur.

The bear shook his head, flinging dirt and mud from his face, then swiped at Black Nose, ripping his claws into her back. Blood stained her fur, and Tsaani moaned. Despite her wounds, the dog did not release her grip, and soon Long Tail and Dog also attacked, lunging in to bite the bear's back legs.

The bear rolled his head and swatted at the dogs. He swung toward the circle of men and dropped to all fours, Black Nose still clinging to his neck. The bear turned on Chakliux, who was on hands and knees where he had fallen, his spear and throwing stick on the ground beside him.

Chakliux grabbed the spear and scrambled to his feet, favoring his weak leg, his clubbed foot. Sok moved to stand beside his brother, both facing the bear. Sok gripped his spearthrower and pulled back his arm. He threw, and the spear pierced the bear's right shoulder, a deep wound.

The bear slapped at the spear, then gripped it in his teeth and broke the shaft, but the spearhead and bone foreshaft were still embedded in the shoulder.

Black Nose loosed her grip on the bear's neck and scooted out from between his legs. The bear lunged at her as she ran, but caught nothing more than a tuft of fur. She circled to join Long Tail and Dog in attacking the bear's hindquarters.

Tsaani threw his spear, then the other hunters also threw. The bear reared up one last time on his hind legs, the spears bristling from his head and sides, then he fell forward to lie still.

The hunters cried out when the bear fell, but when Tsaani went to the animal, they were silent. He gave a command to his dogs, and they backed away.

The hunters would butcher and skin the bear where it lay. How could a hunter expect to take more bears if he dragged one over the ground to the village as though it were nothing more than a woman's pack being moved to fish camp?

For a time the men stood in silence, the quietness like a prayer of thanksgiving, but finally Tsaani raised his voice, first in a hunter's singing chant, then in the ancient blessing: "We honor you who have honored us with your life."

He stepped forward, took from his sleeve a sacred jade knife and carefully slit the bear's eyes. If by some oversight, one of the hunters broke a taboo as he butchered the carcass, it was better the bear did not see. Using his long-bladed hunting knife, Tsaani cut off the bear's paws to hold its spirit within, then motioned for the other hunters to join him.

When the butchering was done, they would eat the head meat and the tender, fat flesh around the first few ribs. The rest they would share with their families, but they would leave the hide here at the den, so no woman would be tempted to touch it and in that way destroy her husband's hunting luck.

Tsaani groaned in pleasure. What was better than a full belly and a good wife? He leaned against the backrest Blueberry had woven from split willow. It creaked as he settled his shoulder blades into its mesh. He closed his eyes and let himself remember the hunt. It had been a good day.

Tsaani was an old man—so old he had lost track of the summers he had seen, fourteen handfuls at least. Since Stars-in-her-mouth had died during the winter, he was the oldest person in the village. His sister Ligige' had three or four summers less than he did, though sometimes, when she was in a sour mood, she claimed to be the oldest.

He heard the doorflap open, then his wife's soft steps. He was particularly glad he was not a woman. A woman could not eat the bear's head or rib meat, could not even call the bear by name. The animal was too sacred. At least there had been fat enough for each family to have a share, and the old women could eat the bitaala', the long fatness that rests between a bear's stomach and liver. That would quiet any old woman's complaints.

They were a problem, those old women. He remembered a time when they had kept their mouths shut except to tell stories or give advice, but the old women now! Of course, they were led by Ligige', whose mouth had been noisy since she came from their mother's womb.

Tsaani opened his eyes to look at Blueberry. He had taken her soon after her first moon blood time, less than a year ago. She had not yet swelled with child, but Tsaani was in her blankets often, hoping to give himself a son in his old age. It was his only true sorrow, that his sons and all but one daughter had died in childhood.

Blueberry smiled and raised her eyebrows at him. "Someone thought you were asleep," she said, speaking with the politeness of wife for husband, the young for the old. "Sok is outside. He asks for you."

"Tell him to come inside," Tsaani said. It would be a good way to end this day, a time to discuss the bear hunt, fixing it in his mind with words.

Blueberry crouched to call out through the entrance tunnel. The People were still in their winter camp, in the stout winter lodges. Each was a circle dug into the earth, four, five handlengths deep, roofed with double layers of caribou hide sewn together in lapped seams, then greased to keep out water. The roof had an opening in the center, its flaps propped with sticks that could be moved to keep out rain or direct the hearth smoke.

Tsaani allowed his eyes to linger on the curve of Blueberry's back where it narrowed into her hips. He had been alone many years after his last wife's death, relying on Ligige' to take care of him. It was good to have his own wife again, to know joy in his sleeping robes. It was also good to be away from Ligige''s sharp tongue. There had been times when Tsaani thought it might be easier to do the women's work himself rather than live with his sister.

Sok stepped into the lodge, his eyes respectfully averted from Blueberry and lowered in the presence of his grandfather, but Tsaani saw the smile that twitched at the corner of Sok's face, and he felt the same smile in his own mouth. What man among the hunters today would not smile? A bear during the Moon of Empty Bellies. It was a favorable sign, especially after a third summer without many salmon.

Sok sat across from Tsaani, the hearth coals warming the space between them. Blueberry picked up her birchbark sael and left the lodge. She would probably go to the cooking hearths at the center of the village to bring back something in case he or Sok was still hungry. Though he did not think he could eat more, he would try so Blueberry would know he appreciated her efforts.

In politeness Sok did not speak, waiting, Tsaani knew, for him to begin the conversation. The warmth of the hearth fire and the fullness of his belly made Tsaani's eyes turn toward sleep, but finally he asked, "Your belly is full?"

Sok replied with raised eyebrows and laughter.

"You should be ready for more," Tsaani told him, and motioned toward his wife's empty place on the women's side of the lodge.

When Blueberry returned, she offered her sael first to Tsaani, who saw with gladness that she did not bring more meat, but had gone to

their raised storage cache and brought back cakes of dried berries and
hardened caribou fat. He took a cake and held it up so Sok could see.
Sok grunted his appreciation and took two. Blueberry's cheeks dimpled, and she looked back over one shoulder at Tsaani, like a child
seeking a father's approval.

Tsaani nodded his head at her. Blueberry was a useful woman. She
had been well-named.

Blue-head Duck had told Tsaani that a trader had come to their
village that day. The river ice was strong—would be strong for at least
another moon—so the man had come on foot, over the frozen rivers
of late winter. He might have some small thing that would make a
woman happy, especially if Tsaani offered him a bear claw.

"Black Nose?" Sok asked as he bit into the berry cake.

"The wounds are not deep," Tsaani replied. "Do you have any
goose grass?"

"Yes," Sok said. "My wife dried some last summer. It is not as
good as fresh, but . . ." He lifted his hands and looked at the lodge
walls as if he could see through the caribou skins to the snow outside.
"I will bring you some, tonight if you like."

"No," Tsaani answered. "Bring it tomorrow." He paused and ate
his berry cake, waved away Blueberry when she offered him more
from the basket. Sok leaned forward and took another.

"Black Nose is a good dog," Tsaani said, "but she has never done
such a thing before."

"Many hunters now hope to get one of her pups. It is good she
was not killed."

"This was not her day to die. The great black one, he gave himself
to us. When a man and his dogs are respectful, a bear knows this."

Sok shifted as though he were uncomfortable with Tsaani's words.
Twice he opened his mouth as if to speak, then closed it again. Had
Sok done something to break this good luck that had come to The
People? Tsaani wondered. Sok was a hard man, harsh in his training
of dogs and in the way he treated others, but he acted only as he had
been taught. Who would expect anything different from someone
raised by Fox Barking?

"Another dog has died," Sok finally said.

"Another? Yours?"

"Mine. The young male, black with white blaze." Sok trailed a
hand down the center of his face.

Tsaani shook his head. The best of Sok's young dogs. Two of Sok's
were dead, male and female, both from the same litter. And three other
dogs in the village had also died in the past moon. One was old,

though strong, but the others were like Sok's dogs, young, and with no sign of illness.

"There is some curse," Sok said.

"This is a village of careful people," Tsaani answered. "Every man respects life; every woman observes taboos. What curse could we have? What have we done? Do you know who might have caused this?"

For a long time Sok said nothing, then he spoke quietly, so quietly that Tsaani saw Blueberry, sewing as she sat near the lodge entrance, turn her head to hear him more clearly. "There are few changes in our village. Only Stars-in-her-mouth has died, and she was not a woman to love dogs. So I do not think it is the lack of her prayers. It seems to be something that happened this past moon. During that time, we have lost five healthy dogs and have had several pups in two different litters born dead. Maybe we should not have allowed the healthy pups of those litters to live. Maybe we should have killed them all."

"How many pups are left from both litters?"

"Five."

"Who has them?"

"One was given to me and one to my mother's husband. Another to Sleeps Long. Two went to Blue-head Duck."

"Go to these men," Tsaani said. "Tell them they can each have one of Black Nose's pups if they will kill these other dogs. You also will have one of Black Nose's pups."

Sok nodded.

"We have had these problems for this past moon, you say?" Tsaani asked.

Sok looked long into Tsaani's eyes. "Yes," he said. He stayed for a time, speaking with Tsaani about the hunt. Finally he stood and turned to the entrance tunnel. He paused to raise the last of a berry cake toward Blueberry. "Good," he told her.

She dipped her head in acknowledgment as he left, then came over and stood beside Tsaani. Tsaani slipped his arm around her waist. Without speaking they went to Blueberry's sleeping robes. She slipped off the loose caribouskin dress she wore in the lodge and stood before her husband in nothing but leggings laced to the center of her thighs. Tsaani dropped his woven hare fur robe and guided her hands to his breechcloth. She knelt to untie the thong, and Tsaani slipped his fingers through the smooth dark river of her hair.

A moon, he thought. When did Chakliux come to us? A man like Chakliux—a man raised as Dzuuggi—if he carried a curse, could destroy a whole village. But then, today they had taken a bear. Surely that was a sign of good luck.

Yes, Tsaani thought. We would not have taken the bear if we carried a curse.

The happiness of the hunt returned to him, and so he pushed away all thoughts except those which celebrated the joy of his wife's small and cunning hands.

Sok walked through the village. It was dark, and the caribouskin cover over each winter lodge glowed yellow, lit from within by hearth fires.

He had not told his grandfather the one thing that pressed most urgently in his mind—his desire for the woman Snow-in-her-hair—but at least old Tsaani would begin to think about the problem of having Chakliux in this village. It had been such a foolishness, finding this brother. Sok had not even known he had a brother. Why would he? No one spoke of the dead. Why risk calling their spirits? Why remind the ones who loved them of their loss?

Sok had hoped by allowing Chakliux a place in his wife's lodge that he would gain Wolf-and-Raven's favor, but the man seemed to treat him no differently than he ever had. At least he had not forced Snow-in-her-hair to become Chakliux's wife. And after Chakliux, Sok should seem like a good choice.

Many hunters would not even look at her now. They worried about the bad luck she had gathered by refusing Chakliux. Well, Sok would still take her, though Chakliux would have to find another lodge to live in. But why worry? He could always return to the Cousin River People.

Chakliux had spoken to him several times about the anger building between the young men of both villages, but Sok could not worry about such foolishness. It had always been that way, as long as he could remember. A fight between two hunters, a few angry words, what was that? And if there was a true attack, one village against another . . . Sok could not keep the smile inside his mouth. When did a man have a better chance to prove his worth? Snow-in-her-hair would be proud to have a husband who was also warrior.

If Chakliux was so worried about the villages fighting, then he should go back to the Cousin River People and warn them. He should tell them that this village was the home of strong hunters. If the Cousin Rivers began a fight, they would not win.

Sok walked with his head bent, his eyes seeing only his thoughts, and so he nearly ran into the woman Daes. Both gasped out their surprise, and the woman mumbled an apology.

Sok nodded, then, curious to know what she was doing outside at night, her three-year-old son slung on one hip, he slipped into the shadows near a lodge and watched. She walked quickly toward the brush at the edge of the village where the women relieved themselves.

Why take the child with her on such a cold night? Sok wondered. He should be asleep. Perhaps Daes's sister-wife Brown Water did not allow the child to urinate in the lodge. Most mothers saved their children's urine in wooden troughs. Old urine was good for many things: washing grease from hair and fur, setting dye colors on scraped hides. Daes was third wife of an old man, and everyone knew his first wife, Brown Water, was a woman given to anger and foolish demands. But perhaps, if Brown Water demanded such a thing, she had reason.

Daes had come from those men who live on the sea islands far to the west. The boy, being Sea Hunter, might have some power in his urine that Brown Water did not want in her lodge.

Storytellers spoke of times when the Sea Hunters and The People traded often, even exchanging wives and children, but there were also stories of fighting and hatred. Why trust men who were sometimes trade partners, sometimes enemies? It was best to leave them alone. Men like that were not quite people themselves.

This Daes had been lucky to find herself a husband at all. She had been brought by a trader, her belly full of child. Sok had never understood why the trader had left her. The child was his, even the old women said so, but maybe the trader did not want a Sea Hunter wife, being only part human as she was.

He had come back once or twice since the boy was born. Now the man was here again. Sok smiled. Maybe Daes was more human than he thought. Perhaps she was sneaking from Brown Water's lodge to be with the trader. Why not? She was a beautiful woman. He would not be surprised if the trader welcomed her into his sleeping robes.

Sok thought for a moment of Snow-in-her-hair, and his desire for her was like a fire in his loins. He was a respected hunter, and until Chakliux came, his dogs had been the healthiest in the village. Even old Tsaani asked his advice when he needed medicine for his animals.

Sok's power, his hunting skills, should be enough to satisfy Snow-in-her-hair, especially if Tsaani gave Sok his bear hunting songs and passed his luck to him. That day would come soon. Sok was Tsaani's only true grandson—who could count Chakliux?

Then Snow-in-her-hair might be willing to be his second wife. Sok would give her as much honor as a first wife. He would even give her caribou skins so she could have her own lodge. What woman would want more?

Tsaani slept the dreamless, heavy-armed sleep that came each time he spent himself on his young wife. When Blueberry prodded him, Tsaani, thinking she wanted more, awoke with laughter in his mouth, but then he heard what she was saying and saw that she scrambled to get into her clothes. Someone was scratching at their doorflap.

Blueberry blew into the hearth coals, adding sticks to feed the flames, then let in the one who waited. It was the shaman, Wolf-and-Raven. Tsaani, his woven robe thrown quickly around his shoulders, told Blueberry to go to her mother's lodge, to stay the night and return in the morning to prepare food.

"Wait," Tsaani called, and did not look at Wolf-and-Raven's face. The man would not be pleased to have Tsaani waste time speaking to his wife, but Tsaani did not care. He did not want Blueberry's father to think she had displeased him and been returned to her parents. He found a small ptarmigan foot amulet, handed it to Blueberry. "For your father," he said. "To thank him for his daughter, who is such a good wife."

Blueberry ducked her head, but her smile pushed her cheeks into full, round balls. She left, and Tsaani turned to Wolf-and-Raven, gesturing for the man to take Tsaani's cushioned seat at the back of the lodge. Wolf-and-Raven sat down. For a long time he did not speak, and Tsaani knew he was gathering power into himself. Whatever the man had to say was important, and probably not something Tsaani would be happy to hear.

Finally Wolf-and-Raven said, "I have come about the dogs."

"Your dogs are well?" Tsaani asked. He had given Wolf-and-Raven a fine, large-boned bitch. She would whelp soon.

"My dogs are healthy. But I hear there are other dogs in the village—many—that are dying. It is said they have been cursed. You are supposed to be the one with power when it comes to dogs. The People cannot survive a hard winter without their dogs. How will we hunt? Who will carry our supplies when we follow the caribou? What will we eat in a starving winter if we lose our dogs?"

"You do not have to tell me the importance of dogs. I am usually the one who reminds you to hold them in respect."

Wolf-and-Raven straightened his shoulders and filled his chest with air, but Tsaani saw the man was more wind than muscle, holding his breath to increase his stature like a dog ruffling his neck fur before a fight.

"When Chakliux came to our village," Wolf-and-Raven said, "he came not knowing who he was, but he spoke for peace between our peoples. I decided he should stay with us and work for peace. Now I think he may have brought a curse. If our dogs die, we will be weak. The Cousin River men will take us easily."

"Tell him to go back, then," Tsaani said. "If he has caused this, then make him leave. What is so difficult about that?"

"Some of The People still believe he is animal-gift. They saw him swim at the Cousin River Fish Camp. Some say he himself is an otter."

Tsaani shrugged. "You are shaman. You should know who is right."

Wolf-and-Raven's face darkened. Tsaani had known the man for many years. He was not one to make decisions. But if he wanted the honor of being shaman, then he must also take the responsibility.

"If you do not yet know what is right, then why are you here?" Tsaani asked. "Go home to your wife's lodge. Make prayers. Do what you need to do. You are shaman. You know this. You do not need me to tell you."

Wolf-and-Raven looked at Tsaani; in anger he met Tsaani's eyes.

"Or are you a child?" Tsaani asked softly.

Wolf-and-Raven jumped to his feet. "Watch your tongue, old man," he said, his words short and sharp like the yips of a fox. "I know more of spirits and chants than you do. We already see that your prayers are not strong enough to protect our dogs. Be grateful I am here to fight this curse."

Wolf-and-Raven walked to the entrance and threw back the door-flap. Looking over his shoulder, he said, "Keep Sok away from my daughter. He visited my wife's lodge tonight. Snow-in-her-hair deserves better than to be second wife to your grandson."

Tsaani stood and went to the door. He tied the flap back into place against any wind that might arise during the night, then went wearily to his bed. He lay down and rolled himself into his bedding furs.

"Sok," he whispered into the night. "Why do you always make everything so difficult for yourself? You have a good wife. If you think you need another, choose some widow, someone who will be grateful for your protection yet young enough to make sons."

But as sleep closed his eyelids, Tsaani saw Snow-in-her-hair, the graceful sway of her hips as she walked, her full, round breasts. Tsaani felt his loins tighten. "Ah, Sok," he mumbled. "Ah, Sok. . . ."

Chapter Three

"So someone has decided an old man should not be allowed to sleep?" Tsaani called out, but he got up from his bed and untied the doorflap. "Ah," he said when he saw Fox Barking. "You, too, are out in the night?"

Fox Barking came inside, but Tsaani did not offer him his padded seat at the back of the lodge; he did not even stir the hearth coals. Tsaani turned toward his bed and sat down in the furs. "How is my daughter?" he asked.

"She is good."

"Sok was here, then another man came, now you. Why are *you* here?"

"To speak to you about your daughter's son."

"Sok or Chakliux?"

"Her true son, Sok."

"According to my sister, Chakliux is as much Day Woman's son as Sok."

Fox Barking squatted on his haunches and pushed back the hood of his parka. The parka was beautifully made, narrowing to a long point front and back, with black-tipped weasel tails hanging from the shoulders and wolverine fur sewn around the hood. Fox Barking did not deserve such a parka, Tsaani thought. Most of all, he did not deserve Day Woman. People said that Fox Barking had been brave to marry her, but Tsaani did not agree. Fox Barking was a lazy man and a poor hunter. He took Day Woman not because of his courage, but because she worked hard and was good to look at.

Fox Barking was a thin man with hands too large for his arms. It seemed to Tsaani that they had grown that way to clasp and hold all the things Fox Barking wanted but did not need. He held those hands out now, palms up, and asked, "Sok was here?"

"Yes."

"Why did he come?"

Tsaani turned his head against Fox Barking's rudeness. Even a child knew better than to inquire about a man's conversations.

When Tsaani did not answer, Fox Barking said, "Do you know about the dogs?"

"I know," Tsaani said.

"Do you know about the daughter of Wolf-and-Raven?"

"I know she will make some man a fine wife," Tsaani answered.

"Sok wants her," Fox Barking said, "but her father will not allow her to be second wife."

"Do you think Sok will throw away Red Leaf?"

"No," said Fox Barking. "A man might throw away his wife, but two sons and a good lodge? No."

"Sok does not need another wife," Tsaani said. "He wants too much. He will break his back carrying all the things he wants. When I die, he will own my dogs. I have already given him many of my hunting songs. If he uses those songs wisely, he will be a powerful man. Perhaps then he will be worthy of two wives."

Fox Barking rubbed his hands together and leaned down to hold them near the hearth coals.

"It is dark. You should be in your wife's lodge," Tsaani said, but Fox Barking made no move to leave. "I am an old man," said Tsaani. "Stay if you like, but I must sleep."

He rolled himself in his bedding furs and turned his back on Fox Barking.

The trader's lodge was merely a summer tent. The caribouskin covering was secured by a circle of rocks, then banked for warmth with spruce boughs and snow. A small fire burned fitfully at the center. Its warmth was swallowed up before it reached the lodge walls, but Daes was not cold. She pressed herself against Cen's body. She knew his lovemaking would be quick, but it was better than what she endured from the old man, who was slow and sometimes wept when he could not become hard enough to enter her. It did not matter, she told him, and that was true. He was a good man. He had offered her a home when she had nothing but the curse of a child in her womb.

No, it did not matter, not with her old husband, nor with this trader. She had died more than four years ago, when her First Men husband had drowned. Daes raised her head from the furs of the trader's bed to be sure her son, Ghaden, was still lying in the nest of mats on the other side of the hearth fire. He was awake, his eyes open, but he was quiet, bundled warmly in woven hare fur robes. Daes thought she could hear him hum some quiet River People song. He was a good child, but she did not love him as much as she loved her daughter, Aqamdax. How could she? Ghaden was Cen's son.

Cen pulled her down beside him. "The boy is fine," he told her, then looked over at the child as though making sure what he said was true. "He will be a good trader, someday, but before then I will make you my wife. When your old husband dies, I will claim you," he said, "and someday I will take you back to visit your people."

"Yes," Daes whispered. "Yes." Of course she would be his wife. She would be anyone's wife if it meant she could get back to the First Men and to Aqamdax. Once she returned to her own village, she would never leave it. Until then she would be whatever Cen wanted her to be.

For a time, Fox Barking spoke of Sok's greediness, his selfishness, but then the man suddenly seemed to change his mind. He praised Sok's hunting skills, his dogs and his two young sons. He said Tsaani should pass on his wisdom and his place even before his death; he should give Sok all his bear hunting songs. Who could say, perhaps if Sok was chief bear hunter, then Wolf-and-Raven would beg him to take his daughter.

Though Tsaani lay with his back turned, at first he grunted a few answers. What else could you do with a man who did not understand rudeness? Finally Tsaani was silent, even though Fox Barking began to speak about the village dogs and the curse that had been brought to them all by Chakliux. When Fox Barking still did not stop talking, Tsaani drew his breath in through his nose and made snoring noises. Then he heard Fox Barking get up and leave, but not before he rummaged through Blueberry's food bags.

At least the man did not leave hungry, Tsaani thought, and tucked his laughter into his cheek as he drifted into dreams.

When their lovemaking was finished, Cen wiped himself on the furs of his sleeping place, adjusted his breechcloth and slipped on his leggings and parka. He watched Daes as she dressed, his eyes dark, soft. She could not look at him. Once, she had believed he could fill the emptiness of her first husband's loss. She had been foolish, but her pain had been so great she would have done almost anything to escape it. She had given herself to Cen, breaking the taboos of her mourning. In punishment, she had conceived.

She had known she could not stay with her people, so she had left the village. How else could she protect her daughter from spirits angered by what she had done?

Too late, she had discovered the hardships of a trader's life. How could she stay with him, chance the storms, travel the rivers and tundra, all the while caring for a child? She had asked him to take her to a village where she could deliver their baby, had pleaded that he find her a husband, a hunter, who would care for her.

In sorrow, he did so, and left her, but came back each year, sometimes twice a year. She had told him it was best for their son. Finally this summer, Ghaden was strong enough to make the journey to the First Men Village. This year, Daes would not let Cen leave without her. She laid her hands against his back, stroked his wolf fur parka.

"Yes," she whispered. "I will be glad to become your wife. Then we will return to my village. I will see my daughter again. You can build a lodge there, and when you are not trading, you will have a warm place to stay, and a wife waiting for you."

He turned and looked into her eyes. "Tell your husband he must die soon," Cen said.

"He will not live through another winter," Daes told him, and felt a sudden sadness, knowing her words were true. "But I will go when you say. If you want me to come now, I will come."

Cen narrowed his eyes, tipped his head and stared at the caribou hide walls. "From here," he said, "I go upriver to the Rock Hill Village and beyond. By the time the ice breaks, I will be back. Be ready to go with me then."

"Go away," Tsaani called, and in his need for sleep did not regret his rudeness. "I have had enough people in this lodge. Go away, and do not come back until morning."

Tsaani turned his head toward the doorflap, but the lodge was so dark he could not see. Even the hearth fire, where the edges of old coals should glow red, was dark.

You did not bank the coals, old man, he told himself. But he was sure he remembered doing it—pushing ash over the embers to slow their burning through the night—right after Wolf-and-Raven left. Maybe you dreamed it, he thought.

Blueberry would have to borrow fire from her mother's lodge in the morning. Ah, well, it would do little harm, since her mother would know it was Tsaani and not Blueberry who let the fire go out.

He looked one last time toward the hearth, then saw an edge of light, and another, then darkness blocked the light again. Tsaani's heart thudded, moving from the slow pace of sleep to the quickness of fear. There was some spirit in the lodge, something between him and the hearth.

The bear, Tsaani thought. The bear. Had Tsaani showed disrespect? Had he forgotten some song of praise? Had he eaten meat without gratefulness? No. He had done all things in honor. He had cut off paws and head; he had sliced the bear skin in strips so it would be used by animals and birds for food and bedding, and not wasted. All this was done in respect, following the ways of Tsaani's grandfathers and their grandfathers.

Then he saw that the bear had the head of a person. It had hands and feet, and the dark fur was only a parka.

Tsaani's heart slowed in relief, and he sagged back against his bedding furs, but then anger came to him and he said, "Why are you here? Why do you come to an old man in the middle of the night? You may not need sleep, but I do!"

The one who stood over him did not speak, and when in the black shadows Tsaani finally saw the knife, it was too late.

Daes crouched outside the entrance tunnel of Brown Water's lodge. It was the middle of the night. She should not be outside in clothes she wore only on best occasions. Brown Water hated her. She was always telling their husband he should throw her away.

I should have asked for my own lodge, Daes thought. Happy Mouth and her little daughter, Yaa, would have come with me. Let Brown Water do all the work to keep her own lodge.

But it was not an easy thing for a woman to build a lodge when her husband no longer hunted. Where would she get the caribou skins, especially when Brown Water claimed anything of worth that came to their husband? Besides, why do the extra work? In a moon, maybe two, she would leave the River People's village and return to the First Men.

Daes bent her head to listen. She could hear her husband's snores, but there was no noise coming from the women's side of the lodge, and Brown Water usually snored louder than anyone. Brown Water was waiting for her to return. She would accuse Daes of being with Cen. What defense could Daes offer? The best thing to do was wait for Brown Water to fall asleep, then crawl into their husband's sleeping robes. Daes would claim she had come back early—that Brown Water had been asleep—and if she awoke later to wait for Daes, she was foolish, because Daes had been in their husband's bed most of the night.

But if Daes was going to wait for Brown Water's snores, she needed to set Ghaden down. He was heavy, and her arm was numb from his weight. She looked at her son, but in the darkness could not see his eyes. She ran her fingertips lightly against his lids. He blinked. She pressed a finger to his lips and whispered for him to be quiet, then said that she needed him to stand, just for a little while.

As she bent to set him down, she saw something move in the darkness. Someone was walking past the lodge. A spirit. What else could it be? Even the River People knew spirits moved between lodges during the night.

She squirmed back into the entrance tunnel, but Ghaden slipped from her grasp and ran out into the night—into the path of whatever spirit was walking. Daes almost decided to stay hidden, to hope that the spirit, seeing an innocent child, would pass without harming him, but then she felt the aching loss of Aqamdax and realized it would be the same for her if she lost her son. She crawled from the lodge tunnel and stood up.

The stars were close, as they always were on nights the spirits walked. In their light she saw Ghaden, then drew in her breath as she realized he had clasped the spirit around the legs.

"The boy is mine," she said in a small voice, and fought to keep her words from trembling. Daes reached toward Ghaden, and it seemed that the motion of her arms pulled her body, as though she did not walk but floated over the packed ice path. She grabbed her son and picked him up. She kept her eyes turned down, away from the spirit's face. In the starlight she saw the spirit's furred boots, caribou hoof rattlers tied at the ankles.

Then Ghaden placed something long and hard against her chest. It was a knife, and she pulled it from his hands. It smelled of blood.

"Ghaden," she said, "where . . ." She lifted her head and saw that the one standing before her was no spirit.

"You killed something?" Daes asked. "You need help?" But as she asked she wondered, Who hunts at night? Only animals. So perhaps this is an owl or wolf, and my eyes deceive me into believing it is someone from this village.

"If you need help," Daes said quickly, "I and my sister-wife Happy Mouth will come."

The hunter reached out and took the knife from her hand. Daes gave it easily, as though it were nothing more than a feather lying across her palm. She turned toward Brown Water's lodge, but though her feet had floated easily when she walked away from it, now she seemed to sink with each step.

First her feet went through the ice, then into the soil. The earth was cold and pressed hard against her flesh as it drew her in. It pulled the heat from her body like marrow sucked from a bone.

Then she felt the knife. There was no pain, only the force of the blade plunging. It pushed her farther and farther into the ground until only her eyes and the top of her head remained above the earth. Then she saw that Ghaden, too, was being sucked in, his feet already buried, his legs pale in the starlight so that he seemed like a birch tree growing. But then the knife came for him. He crumpled to the ground, and the blood that welled from his wound ran into Daes's eyes, until she could see nothing more.

Chapter Four

Chakliux's breath was a cloud in the cold air. The dark spruce that grew around the village were rimed with frost, but the early morning sky was clear. By midday, the sun would turn the ice paths into mud.

More than once Chakliux had fallen into the black muck of those paths, but though his clubbed foot affected his balance, he limped only when he was tired or when he ran. This morning, he carried a large sael, the birchbark container full of dried fish for his grandfather's dogs.

Chakliux enjoyed visiting Tsaani. With only a few comments or a simple story, the old man could send Chakliux's mind on a journey that lasted the whole day.

As he walked past Day Woman's lodge, Chakliux lowered his head and hoped he would not see her. She carried her heart in her eyes, and he could not look at her without feeling himself drawn back into being her child, the baby she had left to die. Each day that he spent in this village seemed to pull away more of his power. He wished he could return to his own people and learn to be himself again, but he needed to stay at the Near River Village. Both Tsaani and Wolf-and-

Raven had begun to trust him, to know that he worked for peace.

The raucous calls of camp jays came to him, breaking the silence of late winter. For a moment he lifted his eyes toward the birds, and so did not see the bundle of fur until he tripped over it. He dropped the sael but caught himself with his fingertips. As he stood, he realized the fur was not some blanket carelessly left outside a lodge, but a young woman. He recognized her—Daes of the Sea Hunters—and knew also that she was dead, her eyes open and staring, her cheeks white with frost. She lay on her stomach with her head turned back, as though trying to look over her shoulder at whatever had caused her death.

A curse, Chakliux thought, and closed his eyes in the sudden knowledge that the Near River People would blame him as they blamed him for the dogs. Even his brother, Sok, though Sok treated Chakliux with respect, could not hide his growing worry as dog after dog died.

Chakliux knelt beside the woman, then saw the blood on her back, the wounds. This was no curse. Since when did curses use knives?

So what should he do? Call the shaman? Tell Sok? Each village had it own ways. What did the Near River People do?

Tell the husband, Chakliux thought. The men here had louder voices than in his own village. They expected to know things first and to make most decisions.

Chakliux stood and, in doing so, heard a quiet moan. First he thought it was from Daes, perhaps from her spirit, but when he crouched down, he saw that her little son lay under her. He could not remember the boy's name. The groan came again, and though Chakliux did not want to touch the dead woman for fear of cursing his hunting skills, he pushed her body aside and drew out the child.

In dying the mother must have pulled him under her, Chakliux thought, and in that way kept him from freezing. But the boy was cold, his skin white, his eyelashes and brows frosted. The child cried out, and Chakliux saw the knife in the boy's back, the handle dark with blood.

No, not a curse, Chakliux thought. Something worse.

The girl Yaa was the first in the lodge to hear Ghaden's cry. The sound came from outside. Why was her brother out there? Yaa wondered, her thoughts still mixed with her dreams. She looked over at her mother, but Happy Mouth was asleep, and Brown Water, even if she was awake, would never bother herself over Ghaden. Ghaden's mother, Daes, was not in her bed. She must be outside with him, Yaa thought, but she wrapped herself in one of her sleeping robes and got up.

She bent to stir the hearth coals, then heard the cry again. It sounded as though Ghaden was hurt. She went to her mother, shook her awake. She opened her mouth to explain, but another call came—a man's voice, asking for help.

Happy Mouth nearly knocked her daughter over scrambling from her bed, and though she motioned for Yaa to stay back, Yaa followed her out the entrance tunnel.

"Ghaden!" Yaa cried when she saw the boy in Chakliux's arms. She grabbed her mother's hand. "Mother, he is hurt," she said, and pulled her toward Chakliux, but Yaa stopped when she saw Daes, white and frozen on the ground. Yaa had seen dead people before. She recognized the stiffness and pallor of death. Her stomach rose to her throat and she began retching, dry heaves that seemed to turn her belly inside out.

"Get Brown Water," her mother said to her, hissing the words. "Do not wake your father."

Yaa cupped her hands over her mouth and, sucking in through her fingers, filled her lungs with air until her belly stopped heaving, then she scooted inside. Both Brown Water and her father were awake.

"Mother," Yaa addressed Brown Water in politeness, "your sister-wife needs you."

Brown Water wrapped herself in a robe and said, "You were foolish. I told you to stay inside."

At first Yaa thought Brown Water was speaking to her, but then she realized the woman had tilted her head and was looking around the lodge as though she spoke to someone up by the smoke hole.

"You think we did not know you were going to the trader?" Brown Water said.

Yaa looked up toward the top of the lodge. Had Brown Water seen Daes's spirit floating somewhere up there?

"What has happened?" asked Yaa's father, Summer Face, his voice raspy with age and sleep.

Yaa went over to his bed, a place she was not supposed to be, but this was different. No one had to tell her that Daes was his favorite wife, and of all his children, even those grown and living in other lodges, Ghaden was also his favorite, but that did not bother Yaa. She was her mother's favorite. Ghaden's mother, Daes, though she fed Ghaden and sewed his clothing, did not want to hold him or spend time singing to him or telling stories. It was good their father loved him best.

Yaa knelt beside the old man. He raised himself up on one elbow and looked toward the door. "What has happened?" he asked again. "Where is everyone?"

"They are outside," Yaa said, "but I am here with you. I will not leave you. Do not worry."

Summer Face squinted and peered around the lodge. The bedding where Happy Mouth and Brown Water had slept was crumpled, but Daes's sleeping furs had not been unrolled. "Daes, my wife," the old man whispered, and he raised his voice to ask, "Where is Daes, daughter?"

"Outside with my mother," Yaa answered and held her breath. Her heart pounded in her chest as loud as a drum. "Would you like water or food?" she asked, speaking over its loudness. "I can get you something."

"Yes," her father said, and relaxed back into his sleeping furs. "Water. Daes will bring me food later."

Yaa left her father and stood on her toes to reach for one of the caribou bladder water bags hanging from the lodge poles. She hoped her father's eyes were dim enough that he could not see her hands shake. She carried the water to him and waited as he raised himself to drink from the carved wooden mouthpiece. When he had finished, he lay back and closed his eyes.

Yaa wondered what she should do next. It was strange, she thought, how in some ways her father reminded her of Ghaden—not so much Ghaden now, but Ghaden as a baby, the care he required and how often he slept. Thoughts of Ghaden brought a sting to her eyes, and she turned away. Her father did not need to see her cry, but how could she hold in her tears? Her brother was hurt, and Daes was dead.

There had been blood, so much blood . . . and Ghaden had looked so little and white. The Cousin River man had him. Some of the other children said the Cousin River man was cursed. Perhaps he had killed Daes and hurt Ghaden. But no, probably not. Why would he call for help if he had been the one to hurt them?

She pressed her eyes with her fingertips and tried to push the tears back under her lids. How would Ghaden feel when he found out his mother was dead? He might decide to die himself.

Yaa remembered the times she had taken the best pieces of meat before Ghaden, with his slower baby hands, could reach them. She remembered yelling at him when she was playing with her cousins. She had not always been the best sister, but she would be. From now on, she would be. . . .

*   *   *

Brown Water tried to take the boy away from Chakliux, but he tightened his arms and turned his upper body. "I will carry him to the shaman," he said.

Brown Water bumped against Chakliux's weak leg, using the bulk of her body to threaten his balance.

"If you make me fall, the boy's wound may start to bleed again," he said in a quiet voice, though he wanted to yell at the woman for her stupidity.

"Take out the knife," she hissed at him. "Take out the knife."

"The knife may be holding in the blood. I will take him to the shaman. Is he a healer? Or is there someone else?"

The question seemed to calm Brown Water, and she backed away, considering. "Wolf-and-Raven knows prayers," she said. "Yes, take the boy to his lodge, but I will get old Ligige'. She is a healer with plant medicines. She might know something Wolf-and-Raven does not."

"Good," Chakliux said, and turned toward the shaman's lodge, taking slow steps on the icy path. He saw Brown Water kneel again beside Daes and then with harsh gestures say something to her sister-wife. Happy Mouth went into the lodge. Chakliux supposed she had been given the task of telling the old man about the death.

Daes had been killed. The thought brought fear. During the short time Chakliux had been in this village, he had paid little attention to the woman, had never known her to cause any trouble. But like him, she was from another place. Perhaps there was one who thought she, too, was cursed. Or perhaps . . . No, he could not let himself think that anyone from his own village would do such a thing. Not to Daes. Not to Ghaden.

For a moment Chakliux took his eyes from the path to glance at the haft of the knife protruding from the boy's shoulder. The haft was antler, crudely cut and wrapped with long strands of dark hair. He suddenly realized the knife was much like the ones he and several other hunters had bought in trade the day before. If it was one of the trader's knives, the blade was not long—but long enough to kill.

The boy suddenly groaned and flexed his injured shoulder. His eyes flickered open for a moment, and Chakliux leaned down over him, at the same time trying to maintain his pace without falling.

"Be still," he murmured to the child. "Be still. Be quiet now. Try to sleep."

The boy took a long breath and a seep of blood brightened the wound. Then his voice suddenly rose in a piercing wail. The sound brought people from their lodges, women with stirring sticks in their hands, men still wrapped in bedding furs.

Most only stared, but one man yelled, "You, from the Cousin Village. What is the matter?"

"The boy is hurt. I take him to Wolf-and-Raven," Chakliux answered.

"Whose child?" a woman called, but Chakliux ducked his head and curled himself over the boy, breaking into a limping run.

Ghaden continued to wail, and Chakliux, speaking in a firm voice, said, "You are a man. Do not cry. Be still."

The boy's wail stopped so quickly that for a moment Chakliux was afraid he had died. He looked down. The boy's spirit still peered from his eyes, in fear, in pain.

"Be still. It will hurt less if you do not move," Chakliux said, though he knew his hobbling run jarred the injury. The boy opened his mouth and his breath came in gasps, but he did not cry.

Then the old woman Ligige' was at his side, motioning for people to stay away as she asked, "He is still alive?"

"Yes," Chakliux answered. Pointing with his chin toward the shoulder, he said, "A knife wound."

"Two more lodges," said Ligige', as though she heard Chakliux's thoughts, understood that he needed to know how much farther to carry the boy. "Do you recognize the knife?" she asked.

"It was bought from the trader," Chakliux answered. "It could be anyone's."

. "You think the trader . . ." the woman began, but then they were at Wolf-and-Raven's lodge. Without scratching at the doorflap, with no clearing of her throat or polite calling, Ligige' crawled into the entrance tunnel and gestured for Chakliux to follow.

Wolf-and-Raven was still in his bed, his wife handing him a wooden bowl of food. Bear meat, Chakliux thought, recognizing the rich smell, the melted pools of fat in the broth. Even in the midst of his worry for the child, his stomach growled, reminding him he had not eaten that morning.

"What are you doing?" Wolf-and-Raven asked, his voice loud with irritation.

"Be quiet and help us, little cousin," Ligige' said, addressing the shaman, not in respect but as child to child. Chakliux waited for the man's explosion of anger, but then saw the softening in his eyes. So then they were cousins, Chakliux thought, son and daughter of brothers, according to the kinship term Ligige' had used.

"The child has been injured. A knife wound," Ligige' said. She bent and whispered something in Wolf-and-Raven's ear, something, no doubt, she did not want the boy to hear, probably that his mother was dead.

Wolf-and-Raven's wife quickly arranged a pile of hare fur blankets into a bed, and Chakliux laid the boy belly down on the pelts. The old woman knelt beside the child, but Wolf-and-Raven turned to Chakliux.

"You saw this happen?" he asked.

"Fool!" Ligige' said. The harsh word startled the boy, and he again lifted his voice into a wail, but Ligige' ignored him and continued to speak loudly. "Most of the blood around the wound is old, dark. This happened last night. The child has lost much blood and he is cold. Call away the spirits of pain while I take out the knife and warm him."

Though Chakliux expected Wolf-and-Raven to react in anger, he did not. The shaman went to the back of the lodge and there uncovered several caribou hide pouches, each decorated with the skin of a protector animal—flickers and least weasels. From one he took several folded packets, each filled with a different-colored powder. He mixed the powders with fat into paints to color his face and arms. From another pouch he took rattles and leaves, feathers and shells. Chakliux began to worry that some things were too sacred for him to see. To protect himself and Wolf-and-Raven, he turned his eyes away and watched Ligige'.

She had wrapped the child in warm fur blankets and was now mixing powdered leaves and roots into a cilt'ogho of water. She poured some of the water on a scraped ground squirrel skin, then with a quick movement pulled the knife from the boy's shoulder and pressed the folded skin over the wound. The boy made a tiny mewing sound.

"Hold this," Ligige' barked at Chakliux, and Chakliux knelt beside the boy to hold the ground squirrel skin in place. "Press hard," she said.

Ligige' dipped her fingers into the cilt'ogho and dribbled some of the liquid into the boy's mouth. "It will ease the pain," she told him.

She poured a bit more of the liquid around the wound, using another softened skin to wipe away old blood. Finally she motioned for Chakliux to move his hand. She continued to clean the wound, then prepared another folded skin and tied it into place with long strips of babiche.

Wolf-and-Raven finished his preparations and began a chant, shuffling his feet with the rhythm of his song. Chakliux understood some of what he said, but other words seemed garbled, as though they were not quite The People's language. Soon Wolf-and-Raven's forehead was shining with perspiration. The shaman was almost an old man, already with the pouched belly and thin arms of one who mostly sat, but his feet did not stop, and his song remained loud, clear. If his prayers could keep away those spirits that brought pain, the ones that made wounds fester and fill with pus, then perhaps the child would live—if his mother did not call him to follow her into death.

If that happened, Chakliux doubted that any shaman could do much good. What child would not go with his mother if she asked?

"If you want to stay, you are welcome," Ligige' whispered to Chakliux, "but if you want to go . . ."

Chakliux nodded his understanding. "My grandfather waits for me," he said. "I should go." He watched for a moment as the old woman smoothed back the boy's hair with her gnarled hands and covered him with another blanket.

The child had been a bundle of ice in Chakliux's arms. It would take a long time for the cold to leave him. Perhaps it never would, lying as he had beneath the dead body of his mother. Who could say what that would do to a child? But as he watched Ligige' work, Chakliux felt his hope grow. Her hands were quick and without hesitation as she made poultices and teas.

Chakliux left. Outside, the morning was bright. He walked back toward Brown Water's lodge. He should tell them that the boy was still alive and the knife out, the bleeding stopped. A crowd of people stood at the lodge entrance, but they parted when they saw Chakliux, pulling back as though he carried the spirit of death with him. He looked down, saw the blood that stained his parka from mid-chest to the wolf fur ruff that ended just above his knees. Then Brown Water was at the entrance, her voice firm as she said to Chakliux, "My husband wants to speak to you."

Chakliux stooped to follow Brown Water through the entrance tunnel. Inside, the lodge was large and neat. A caribou hide boiling bag of soup hung near a central hearth fire. The child he had seen earlier when he found the boy—a girl of six or seven summers—was wrapped at the waist with a woven hare fur blanket and sat with an old man, her small hands patting his fur-wrapped shoulders.

She was the old man's daughter; she had the same strong bones beneath the half-moon eyes. The same swirl of hair lifted itself in a peak at the center of a high forehead.

She swallowed, and he saw the dimple at one corner of her lips, like the dimple that had given her mother the name Happy Mouth. It was a face made for someone who laughed often and saw the good things of the earth, and Chakliux was glad the old man had such a daughter.

"The boy is alive," Chakliux said, though the women had not asked, and the old man did not seem to understand what had happened.

"The knife?" asked Brown Water, then glanced to her side.

Chakliux followed her eyes and saw that the dead one lay there. The frost and blood had been washed from her face. Long strands of babiche were knotted around the woman's wrists and elbows, and other strands lay beside her.

"The knife was one the trader brought," Chakliux said.

"I told her she should not go to him," said Brown Water. Then with widened eyes she looked at her husband, but his gaze wandered as though he had not heard her.

"There is no way to know if the trader . . ." Chakliux began, but Brown Water moved her head toward the old man, and Chakliux finished with, "Many men traded for things yesterday." He pulled up his parka sleeve so the women could see the knife sheathed on his forearm. It was similar to the one now lying in Wolf-and-Raven's lodge. "I traded for this."

"You found her as you were going to . . ."

"My grandfather's. I feed his dogs every morning."

"Yes. I have seen you. There is nothing else you know?"

"Nothing else," Chakliux said, then looked over at the dead one. He pointed with his chin toward the strips of babiche. "Do what you can to keep her spirit here."

Both Brown Water and Happy Mouth raised eyebrows in agreement, then Happy Mouth knelt beside the dead woman, picked up a strand of babiche and tied it at her shoulder joint. Once each joint was tied, the spirit lost power. Then perhaps the child would not be called to follow his mother into death.

Chakliux left the lodge. The sael of fish lay near the lodge wall. He picked it up. He wondered if the noise and the mourning cries had awakened Tsaani.

Probably not, he thought. It was early yet, and old men sleep hard.

Chapter Five

Cen was asleep when they came.

They did not enter through the door of his lodge, but through the caribou hide walls, ripping the skins with knives and spearheads. Before he could untangle himself from his sleeping robes, the men were upon him, pinning his arms, hitting him, kicking him. Then the women came, tearing at his eyes with their fingernails, leaving long weals in his cheeks and across his bare chest.

He kicked the women away as the men held him, then screamed out to ask why they were attacking him. He was a respected trader. For many years he had come to this village. Had he ever cheated anyone? Had he ever abused their hospitality?

His last question seemed to renew their anger, and one of the women shouted at him, "What about my sister-wife? What about her little son? You kill them, then say you show respect?"

He knew the woman, her loud voice, her harsh ways. She was Brown Water. Her words pierced his eardrums like birdbone needles. What had she said about killing? Did she mean Daes? Ghaden?

"Who is dead?" he shouted out, but his question brought more screaming, more anger. Several men hit him—hard, heavy blows to his face and belly, so that he curled his body to protect himself. His thoughts swirled as though he lived a dream. He raised his head for a moment to look back at his bed, almost expecting to see himself lying there asleep, dreaming the pain.

Chakliux had watched the Near River hunters and a number of women, Brown Water leading them, leave the village. He knew they were going to the trader's camp. Several men motioned for him to join them, but he shook his head. Because Daes was killed by a trader's knife, they thought the trader did it? What man would be so foolish as to leave such a clear sign?

Chakliux had watched the trader, had seen how skillfully he bargained, how well he judged men. If he had murdered someone, he would not leave his knife behind. Chakliux wanted no part of whatever they planned to do to the man.

"You heard what happened?"

Chakliux turned at the sound of his brother's voice.

"I found her," Chakliux answered.

"You?"

"Yes."

"She was dead when you found her?"

"Yes, and the boy nearly dead."

"Do you think he will live?"

"Ligige' stopped the bleeding, and the shaman prays. Perhaps he will live, perhaps not."

"They think the trader did it?"

"One of the trader's knives was still in the boy's shoulder."

Sok snorted. "Cen is not stupid," he said. "If he killed someone, he would not leave his knife."

"You think they will kill him?" Chakliux asked.

Sok lifted his hands, fingers spread. "Who can say?" he answered. "They will probably bring him back to the village before they decide what to do."

"Should we wait for them?" Chakliux asked. "A man should not be killed for what he did not do. If we talk to them . . ."

"I will wait for them. You should not," Sok answered, then said, "You know what some people say about the dogs."

Chakliux nodded. "Yes." How many had died since he came to the village? Seven, eight? They blamed him. The Near River dogs had been strong and healthy until he came.

"If they blame you for dogs, they might blame you for other things as well," Sok said. "I will wait for them, try to talk to them."

Chakliux turned toward their grandfather's lodge, took several steps along the path before his brother called out to stop him.

"Where are you going?"

"To feed our grandfather's dogs."

"You have not yet fed the dogs?"

"No."

Sok clicked his tongue as though Chakliux were a child to be scolded. "I will do it," Sok said. "Go. Leave the village for the day. Do whatever it is you like to do, but leave the village."

Chakliux could see the irritation in his brother's eyes. Feeding dogs was usually a boy's job. Chakliux did it because he liked being with Tsaani. How else could he show his gratitude for the man's patience, his willingness to accept Chakliux without sympathy or fear of his difference?

Chakliux walked back toward Red Leaf's lodge. His brother was right. He should leave the village, stay away until night. Red Leaf would not be sad to see him go, even just for a day. He was one more to feed, another man to sew for. She was a good wife to Sok and a good mother to Sok's sons, but she did not try to hide her resentment of Chakliux.

Red Leaf was a large woman, as tall as Chakliux and wide of hip and shoulder—a woman who would give a man large, strong sons. Her face was as square as her body, skin dark and smooth. When Sok came into the lodge, Red Leaf's eyes never left him. Her hands, usually capable and strong, fluttered when he spoke, and when she brushed the snow from his parka, her fingers lingered against the fur.

Any acknowledgment of Chakliux came with the downward curl of her lips, the narrowing of her eyes, but this time she smiled and gave him a bowl of meat and broth, then circled to brush snow from his parka.

"You were the one who found her," she said from behind his back. "Do you think spirits killed her?"

Chakliux tipped the bowl to his mouth and drank. He wiped his lips with his hand and said, "Spirits do not use knives."

"You did not see anyone? Someone who might have killed her?" Chakliux squatted on his haunches beside the hearth fire. Red Leaf knelt beside him and whispered, "Night Walking says Brown Water herself might have done it."

"I saw no one," Chakliux answered. "She had been dead a long time when I found her."

Red Leaf's lips tightened.

Chakliux set the bowl on the scraped caribou hides that covered the floor. "I will hunt today," he said, but did not look at the woman. What was wrong with her? This was not a celebration. Daes was dead; her child was badly hurt, perhaps dying. Worst of all, someone had done the killing.

In his own village, Chakliux had been taught the stories of his people, stories to pass down so certain things would not be forgotten. In several of those stories, people had killed others, but that had been long ago, when animals and men could talk to one another. This killing was now.

Chakliux took his weapons and hunter's bag. He pulled his parka hood snug around his face and left the lodge. When he reached the edge of the village, he heard the sudden noise of raised voices, the mourning cries of women. Their songs were like ice against his teeth. The child has died, he thought, and felt his anger rise against the one who had done such a thing.

He peered between the lodges. A crowd had gathered on the far side of the village. They had captured the trader. Chakliux walked quickly toward the river. Sok was right. He did not need to be here. When he got back to the village that night, if he heard any whispers of anger toward him, he would return to his own people. What hope did he have to bring peace to this village if they thought he would kill a woman and a child?

Once he was back at the Cousin River Village, he would listen carefully, watch carefully, and if he discovered the killings were something planned there, he would see that life was given in exchange for life.

When Happy Mouth came for Ligige', she first asked about Ghaden.

"Not dead," Ligige' replied. She had cleaned the wound often, singing when she removed the poultice so spirits would not enter the boy's body through the knife hole.

Ghaden whimpered and Ligige' held up the boy's hands to show Happy Mouth that his fingertips were pink with only a few small patches of frostbite. She smoothed back the dark hair from his forehead. The skin on his face was also healthy, and only two narrow lines of dried blood marked his lips, split from the cold. Daes had been a good mother. Even in death she had fought to keep her son warm through the long night.

"His feet?" Happy Mouth asked.

Ligige' peeled back the blankets. Ghaden's feet, too, were pink, no white blotches or blackening of toes.

"They say you should come now," Happy Mouth said. Her lips

worked in a strange way, as though she fought to keep from crying.

Yes, Ligige' thought. The boy was worth a woman's tears. Now that Daes was dead, Happy Mouth would most likely raise Ghaden as her own.

"I can stay here," Ligige' said. "I have no one in my lodge to feed. My brother has his own wife now."

"Ligige' . . ." Happy Mouth said softly.

Ligige' looked up into the woman's face and realized the pain there was not for Ghaden but for her. Ligige''s heart squeezed itself small as though trying to hide within her chest. "Who?" she asked.

"Your brother," Happy Mouth said. Again her lips worked to hold in tears. "He is dead."

Ligige' bent to adjust the blankets around Ghaden, then she lifted her head, took a long breath. "He was an old man," she said, though in her thoughts he had never been old.

Happy Mouth shook her head. "Dead by the same knife," she said, her voice a whisper.

At first Ligige' did not understand the words. Surely her brother had been called by one of those spirits that brings death to elders— one that stops the heart or slows the breathing, steals speech or reason. But a knife? The same knife that killed Daes?

"Someone killed . . ." Her voice cracked on the words. "Why?"

Happy Mouth did not answer. She helped Ligige' to her feet, guided her from the lodge. Ligige' barely heard Happy Mouth call her daughter, Yaa, scarcely understood her as she told Yaa to stay with Ghaden, to come for her or Brown Water if the boy awoke or if he turned suddenly hot or cold.

Ligige' lifted her eyes into the brightness of the morning. Her brother's spirit was there, watching, she was sure. She saw his face, gentle with a smile, teasing her, laughing with her, sharing stories.

"I am oldest," she whispered, and looked up so her brother would hear.

Cen stared into the faces of the men who held him. One of his eyes was swollen shut, and his head seemed to pound with each beat of his heart. He was sure they had broken his nose, several of his ribs, and perhaps his left wrist.

During the years he had been a trader, he had often faced death. Once his iqyax was destroyed in the surf. Another time he had fallen into a sinkhole while walking overland between villages. He had often been caught in winter storms.

He had managed to drift ashore in the wreckage of his iqyax, though the cold of the waves nearly killed him. In the sinkhole, he had spoken to the grasses around him, asked them to lend him their strength, and so clawed out by pulling and clinging. He had lived through the storms in snow caves he carved with his own hands. But this was different. With winds and water a trader had a chance if he stayed respectful. With men . . .

They dragged him to the center of the village. There they stood him up, naked in the cold wind except for his breechcloth. The hunters and the women shouted at him, threw rocks, hit him with sticks.

The image of Daes came into his mind. She stood before him in her new parka, the one he had brought her from the Walrus Hunters. She opened her mouth. Instead of words, blood flowed, and so he knew she was dead. The knowledge was ice in his heart, and suddenly he did not care if the River People killed him. He and Daes would be together. Away from this village, away from these people. But if Ghaden were alive, could Cen allow himself the joy of Daes? Who would protect their son? Who would care whether or not he grew up to be a good and strong man?

Cen gathered his strength, held himself as straight as he was able. "Tell me," he called out. "Tell me. Is my son still alive?" His question was met with anger, with men lifting fists and spear shafts against him until he had to curl himself down into a ball, his face tucked between his knees, his arms crossed over the back of his neck.

Finally one of the men pulled him to his feet. The man was large, his head broad and scarred, the left side of his face puckered as though he had once been burned from forehead to mouth. "You ask about the boy," he said. "Why?"

"I did not kill him," Cen answered through lips cut by broken teeth. "Why would I kill my own son? Would any of you kill your sons? Then why think I would? Do I look like one of those Not-People who live at the edge of the Far Mountains?" He paused to take a breath, and the pain was like a spear piercing his chest. He spat out blood and hoped it was only from the cuts in his mouth. "I did not kill my son," he said.

The shouting dimmed and the men circled him. Cen felt their eyes on his face. Encouraged by their attention, he said, "Most of you know that when I brought the Sea Hunter woman here, she carried my son in her belly. But how can a trader have a wife? I could not hunt for her, could not train a son to hunt. So I brought them here to this good village. Each year I came back, to trade with you, and to see my son. Someday I hope he will come with me, also be a trader."

A tall thin man called out at this, assured the trader he would not live to see his son grown.

"He is alive then," Cen said, and a woman, hidden from his view by the men around him, hissed at the one who had spoken.

"He is alive," Cen repeated.

"He is," the scarred man finally said. A young man pushed his way to Cen's side. Cen had seen him before. Yes. He called himself Sok, and had traded yesterday for several things.

"The boy is alive," said Sok, "but his mother's spirit calls him, as does the spirit of my grandfather, who was also killed."

The trader stared at the man. Was he saying someone else had died? Three had been attacked?

"Dead by a knife we saw in your hands yesterday."

"You have the knife?" Cen asked.

"Yes."

"Many of you traded for knives yesterday," Cen said. "Do you think if I had some reason to kill the woman and my son and an old man I do not know, I would be fool enough to use my own knife? To leave it?"

There was silence broken only by the moaning of several women, by the mumbling of the men. A wave of pain washed over Cen but he fought it down. "Bring the knife here," he said. "Let me see it. I might remember who bought it in trade." He looked at the men surrounding him. Was there fear in any of the faces?

"Bring the knife," Sok said. "I need revenge on the one who killed my grandfather."

Chakliux walked the river. It was still frozen, some of the ice swept bare, some covered with snow hardened by wind. In one moon, perhaps two, the ice would weaken, and a rush of water, ice and earth from far upriver would roar down to the sea. Even now, Chakliux could see scars from previous breakups, places where whole trees had been uprooted and large portions of the bank swept away.

If he had not seen it happen before, it would be difficult to imagine. The river under ice and snow seemed so quiet, as though it would never be anything but a white path for Chakliux's feet.

Chakliux missed his own village, his own people. He missed telling stories, but at least this village had a river. For as long as he remembered, Chakliux had loved the water. As a child at fish camp, he was told many times to stay away from the river, but still he played and paddled in the shallows. Eventually, he had learned to swim, even though the cold of the water made his bones ache.

He was an otter, the shaman finally decided. Who could deny that? Who could not see his otter feet? Had he not been an animal-gift baby, sprung somehow from a clot of animal blood? Besides, everyone knew people did not swim.

After that, K'os did not try to keep him from the water. His skills were useful in building and repairing the village fish traps, in recovering lost hooks and handlines. He had a place in his village and was honored for his difference.

He was not otter enough to swim in the sea, but once or twice he had seen traders using boats built by the Sea Hunters. Iqyan, they were called, those boats, as sleek as an otter and sheathed with sea lion skins or split walrus hide. How different they were from the clumsy rafts and poles The People used to ferry themselves across the river in summer.

Those Sea Hunters, a trader had once told him, considered themselves brother to the sea otter. Once one of their hunters had come to the fish camp to trade. He was shorter and darker-skinned than The People, with long arms and wide, strong shoulders. Chakliux had seen him roll the iqyax and come up from the river, water dripping over his wide smiling mouth. He wore a birdskin parka, so that some of the women said he was not man but seabird and fought among themselves to decide who would invite him to her bed in hopes of bearing a magic seabird child.

Chakliux and the men had been more interested in the skin coat he wore over the birdskin parka. It was made, the Sea Hunter said, from seal intestines, each intestine split and flattened, then scraped so thin you could see light through it. The strips were sewn together so the seams did not leak water. When the man rolled his iqyax, the intestine parka protected him so the sea could not seep through his clothing and stop his heart with its cold.

Someday, Chakliux had decided, he would have his own iqyax. He did not want to be a trader. It was not a comfortable thing to meet new people when you were different, when you saw questions and worry in the eyes of all who looked at you. He was happy being a hunter. If he learned to hunt from an iqyax, his family would not have to live on fish only, on caribou or even bear. They would also have the fat and oil of sea mammals—seals and sea lions; and walruses, for he would take his iqyax downriver to the North Sea and hunt.

Yes, he was a hunter. He found joy when an animal chose to give itself so The People could live, but it was difficult to keep up with the other hunters, to carry his share, to hold his balance on trails over muskeg and through river brush. His legs were made for water, not land.

Once, according to the old storytellers of his village, the Sea Hunters had even hunted whales. As Dzuuggi he was entrusted with secrets—stories seldom told around winter fires, but which must be
remembered, at least by a few. These stories said there was an island,
almost at the far edge of the world, where men still hunted whales.
The Sea Hunter told them those whale hunters had died long ago
when a mountain in anger destroyed them for some reason no one
could remember.

Since meeting the Sea Hunter, Chakliux had dreamed of trading for
an iqyax of his own, perhaps even learning to build one. Now, looking at
the river, he thought for the first time of seeking those ancient whale
hunter people himself. Were they still there, on that far island? Would it
take a lifetime of summers to find the edge of the world?

The Near River People considered him cursed. The woman who
gave him birth had told him he had been set out to die. Perhaps even
now, in his own village, the people had heard the story and would no
longer want him as Dzuuggi, the one who remembered their past. If
that were true, then why stay? He could not bring peace if no one in
either village respected him.

Chakliux shielded his eyes from the brightness of the midday sun.
The snow was melting. He had trade goods—the bride price of furs
and hides rejected by Wolf-and-Raven—perhaps enough to trade for
an iqyax. Then what would stop him from finding those whale hunters, brothers of the otter?

The pain was almost too much to ignore, but Cen fought it. "I told
you," he said again, "go get the knife."

The large man left the group, and when he returned he carried the
knife, still crusted with blood. Cen pressed his lips together in a tight
line and tried not to show his disappointment. There were several
knives he remembered well—distinctive for the length of a blade, the
shape or color of a handle. But this knife was one from a Caribou
hunter he had met on the trail last summer. His knives were all alike,
with variations so small a man could scarcely tell one from another.
Cen had traded nearly two handfuls of those Caribou knives to the
people of this village.

He motioned for the man to hold the knife closer, and studied it
carefully. There must have been a struggle. Some of the hair that
wrapped the handle was torn. It hung like a black fringe from the
carved antler haft. Cen's thoughts tangled into one another. For a moment he could not remember anything anyone had given him for his
knives. Furs? Yes, he was sure of it. Probably fishskin baskets.

"You see," Cen said, pointing with his chin at the knife, "the handle is loose. The hunter who traded me these knives was from the Caribou People. He glues the handle to the stone blade with spruce pitch."

"What does that matter to us?" the younger man asked.

No, the glue would not matter to them, but the words would slow the people down, make them think. When men took time to think, they were less apt to act in anger. Cen's words also seemed to calm his own thoughts, and he suddenly remembered what he needed to know.

"You bought such a knife," he said, looking into Sok's face, seeing in Sok's eyes the slight widening of surprise. Cen turned to another man. "And you," he said. He pointed to several others, even tilted his head toward one of the men who held him. "You also," he said.

"Yes," said the man holding him, and released his grip on Cen's shoulder. The hunter pushed up his sleeve to show a knife in a sheath strapped above his wrist. "I still have it."

"Mine, also, I have," said another man, and another. Sok, still standing before the trader, held up a knife. Other knives went up, more knives than Cen had traded to these men, many more knives. At another place, another time, he would have laughed.

But why not show a knife? Better to claim having one than to be accused of killing.

The large man, still holding the murder knife, turned to look at the hunters, at their blades lifted to the sky. In that moment, with one arm free and people no longer watching him, Cen moved quickly to grab the weapon from the large man's hand. He roared, but Cen turned the knife toward him, then toward the other man who still held him. That one, a village elder, let him go.

But there were too many of them, and too many weapons. Cen could never get away. Besides, how far could he run with ribs broken, eyes nearly swollen shut? The men were wary. Why be the first to close in on the trader? Why be the one to feel his blade? If he had killed once, he would not hesitate to kill again.

"One of you traded for this knife," Cen said. He continued to hold the blade out, and he circled slowly as he spoke. The men were quiet, but all watched, waited, their own knives in their hands. "One of you killed the woman, and this man's grandfather." Cen lifted his chin toward Sok. "One of you tried to kill my son. For that, I will kill you, whoever you are. If I do not find you during my life, I will find you after I am dead, when I am spirit and can move without being seen.

"I tell each of you this. I did not kill anyone. I did not hurt my son."

Cen steadied his feet against the earth. What good were words if dizziness claimed him?

Suddenly an image came to him, something he had long ago tried to put out of his mind—a mourning ceremony he had seen far to the north, among people he could not now even give a name. A woman had lost her husband, a father his son. They had cut themselves with knives to show their sorrow. That in itself was not so unusual, but the woman had also cut off a finger, the man a strip of flesh from the calf of his leg.

Blood for blood, Cen thought, and called out, "I lift my own voice in mourning." He looked at Sok. "I mourn the man you called grandfather," Cen said. "I mourn the woman who was mother and wife among you."

He waited, but no one moved toward him; no one spoke.

"I did not kill them," he said again. "And I did not injure my son. I lift my voice to spirits who might call my son to their world. I offer blood for blood. Mine for his."

Cen clenched his jaw. They wanted blood, like dogs panting for the lungs of newly killed caribou. He could see it in their eyes. Did these men hope it would ease their pain? Or did they need to show their own strength? Did they believe that if they controlled the power to kill it could not be used against them?

"Blood for blood," Cen said again. He thrust the thin chert blade into his leg and peeled away a long curl of skin. The pain was more than he had imagined. Darkness closed in around his eyes. He clenched his teeth and waited until his mind cleared, then lifting the flap of skin, he cut it away from his leg and threw it on the ground. "To show my sorrow," he said.

He bent over and picked up a fist-sized rock from the edge of the closest hearth fire. Sok moved toward him, but Cen held up his knife. "A trade with the spirits," he explained.

He slipped the rock into his left hand then pressed it against his chest. He gripped the knife and with all his strength cut down across his smallest finger, just above the middle joint. The blade bit through his flesh, a high, screaming pain, then into his bone. Cen felt the deep ache as the knife penetrated and crushed. He did not stop until the blade reached stone.

The severed finger fell to the ground, and Cen dropped the rock. "A trade with the spirits," he said again. With the dripping blade, he pointed at the finger. "For my son's life."

Sok caught him as he fell.

Chapter
Six

THE FIRST MEN VILLAGE

Salmon leaned forward and ran his fingers over Aqamdax's face. He smelled of fish, but his touch was warm, and she felt the slow tightening of her belly. He moved his hand down to cup her left breast.

"It has been a long time for me," he said, his words a whisper.

Aqamdax looked away from him. He had come to her in the middle of the day, interrupted her basket weaving, and when he saw she was alone in the ulax, began talking in sweet and cunning words. His first wife was in her fifth month of pregnancy with their third child. His other wife, a woman who had the same number of summers as Aqamdax, had just given him a daughter. For the sake of his hunting, Salmon should discipline himself to wait.

But why worry about Salmon's hunting or think about his wives? Only two days ago Aqamdax had thought she would soon be wife. She had believed Day Breaker's whispered promises, but this morning, as she sat with He Sings and his four wives, Day Breaker came to them, announced he would marry Smiles Much, a woman whose mother and father lived in the village, a woman with four strong brothers. Later, when Day Breaker and He Sings had gone to visit the father of Smiles Much, Aqamdax had heard Grass Eyes and Fish Taker whispering. They giggled behind their hands, saying that Smiles Much already carried Day Breaker's child in her belly, that she had missed three moons of bleeding.

Then Aqamdax knew Day Breaker's promises had been lies, told to give him access to her bed.

So why should she hesitate to enjoy Salmon, even in the middle of the day? The village women already despised her, spat after her as she walked by. Aqamdax did not care. They only envied her beauty. They saw the desire in their husbands' eyes when she passed. They knew their sons sought her out when the light was long in summer evenings.

Salmon thrust aside his breechcloth and lay over Aqamdax, pushing her back on the woven grass mats which covered the ulax floor. His fingers fumbled at the strings that secured her grass aprons, long woven panels, one hanging from her waist in front, the other hanging over her buttocks, the only clothing First Men women wore inside the ulax.

Salmon's fingers were large and clumsy, and he had not yet succeeded in untying the aprons when Aqamdax heard a screech and knew it was Grass Eyes.

Aqamdax chided herself for her foolishness in not taking Salmon with her into her sleeping place. Though Grass Eyes would have known what they were doing, at least she would have seen nothing, and Aqamdax could have denied the woman's accusations.

Salmon scrambled to his feet, grabbed his parka and ran. He paused long enough to allow Grass Eyes to jump off the notched log propped on a slant from the ulax floor to the square entrance hole in the roof. Then he climbed the log and was outside before Grass Eyes's screams could become words.

Aqamdax would not even look at her. Instead, she straightened her aprons and pushed her long hair back over her ears. Then she curled one corner of her lips into the smile she knew Grass Eyes hated.

Grass Eyes picked up the basket Aqamdax had been making. It was a large, open-weave basket, made for gathering. She threw it at Aqamdax.

"You are worthless," she cried. "All the women of this village are ashamed when they see you. You are worse than your mother. Don't you know the men laugh at you? How can you be that stupid? Get out of my sight. I curse the day your mother left you!"

Aqamdax picked up the basket. "Look at this basket," she said, speaking to Grass Eyes in a quiet voice. "It is better than anything you can make, yet you tell me I am worthless. No one in this village weaves as well as I do. I weave until my eyes burn and my fingers bleed. You trade my baskets and keep the trade goods, then tell me I am worthless. Have you forgotten that Fish Taker is so lazy she does not scrape the edges of hides, but instead leaves them rough and stiff? What about Spotted Leaf? Her fingers are so slow, it would take her a year to make one sax, even using cormorant skins. And I do not have to tell you that Turn Around is only a child. What can she do except please your husband in his bed? Perhaps you are the one who is worthless. Why else would He Sings need three other wives? You must not know how to please him." Aqamdax smiled. "I will be glad to teach you."

Grass Eyes hooked her fingers into claws and ran at Aqamdax. Aqamdax grabbed her birdskin sax from the floor where she had laid it and escaped up the climbing log. She slid down the side of the ulax, ignoring the burn of ice and frozen grass on her bare legs, then ran toward the beach.

The ground was cold under her bare feet. She had been foolish not to take her seal flipper boots. She did not like the feel of them. They were hard against her bones, always trying to shape her feet into the narrow daintiness favored by Spotted Leaf, the chief's third wife—but they were better than walking barefoot in snow. Aqamdax pulled on her sax. It was long, fashioned in the traditional manner of the First Men, hanging loose well past her knees. She crouched beside a hummock of beach grass, her back to the wind, and tucked the sax around her legs and under her feet.

She hated living in the chief's ulax, but what choice had she been given? Without father or grandparents living, and her mother no longer in the village, she had to stay where the elders decided.

Aqamdax tried to think back to the night her mother had left, but with each year that passed, the memory dimmed, and now it seemed almost like a dream.

Daes had come into the sleeping place she and Aqamdax shared. She came whispering her love, then told Aqamdax she was leaving the village, that she was going to the River People. Aqamdax, crying, had begged to go with her, but her mother said the trader would not take both of them. She promised to return, to bring gifts. So Aqamdax had stayed in the sleeping place and only later realized that she did not know which trader her mother meant, or to which River village they were traveling.

During the first year, even in winter, Aqamdax had gone to the beach each day, had waited and watched. She asked every trader who came to the village if he had heard anything about her mother. None had.

She had heard the village women's gossip. They said her mother had run away to be with that trader, but Aqamdax knew the true reason her mother had left.

A moon before, Aqamdax's father had drowned while hunting. After his death, anger took root inside Aqamdax's chest, and she lashed out at everyone, even her mother, until Daes had left with the first man who showed any interest in her.

Aqamdax's throat tightened, but she did not allow herself to cry. Tears would not return her father to life or bring her mother back from the River People. Tears would not even help her live through another day with the chief hunter's wives.

They hated her, those four women. Each was so sure she was the most important woman in the village: Grass Eyes, because she was the chief's first wife; Fish Taker, because she had borne the most children; Spotted Leaf, for her beauty; and Turn Around, because she was the chief's favorite.

The first two years Aqamdax lived in He Sings's ulax, she had hoped he would claim her as daughter. She would have been assured of a husband. Who would hesitate to take the chief hunter's daughter as wife? But when anything went wrong, she was blamed. The sister-wives raised their eyebrows and clacked their tongues, whispered behind their hands and watched her from slitted eyes.

Finally, when Aqamdax realized she had no hope of ever pleasing them, she spent her nights thinking of ways to make them angry. Why not have the fun of mischief when she was blamed for every problem anyway?

How did Spotted Leaf's necklace get into the bottom of Fish Taker's sewing basket? Why did Turn Around eat the berries Grass Eyes was saving for their husband? And the beautiful parka Grass Eyes made, how did it happen to fall apart the first time the chief wore it?

Each year Aqamdax assured herself some hunter would ask for her as wife—perhaps one of the old men, perhaps someone very young—then she would be able to leave the chief hunter's ulax. All the girls she had grown up with, her childhood playmates, were wives. Most of them had babies, but no man claimed Aqamdax.

Then Day Breaker had begun sneaking into her sleeping place at night. . . .

Aqamdax lifted her eyes to look out over the bay. Jagged chunks of ice layered the beach, and a wind blew from the west, ruffling the feathers of Aqamdax's sax. She lifted her shoulders so the high collar rim covered her ears. She needed a parka, an otter fur parka with a hood like the Walrus Hunters wore, but where would she get the pelts to make such a thing?

She could ask the men who slept with her, but they might get angry and stop coming. Then how could she bear the loneliness? Her only hope was to get pregnant, claim the child belonged to the hunter most able to accept her as wife. Yet, in spite of all the men she had pleasured, she had never missed a moon blood time.

She lay her hand against her belly. Old Qung sometimes told stories of women who, in punishment for a taboo broken, were denied children. Perhaps Aqamdax should treat the chief's wives with more respect.

She sighed. It would not be easy; each of them had such a contrary spirit, but if she started with a gift they might believe she intended to change. She looked out over the beach. There was little chance to find something with the bay still frozen. Even the village hunters were home with their wives.

Of course, there was always driftwood, if she was willing to work hard enough to get it. A large chunk of wood, as long as her arm, as thick as a hunter's thigh, had been frozen into the shore ice since the second winter storm. After the storm, several women had worked at getting it loose but had finally given up. Aqamdax could take it back to Grass Eyes. Perhaps the woman would accept it as an offering for peace and forget that she had found Salmon and Aqamdax together.

Aqamdax went back to the ulax and got her seal flipper boots. Grass Eyes's two young daughters were sitting beside their mother, each whining as Grass Eyes tried to teach them to weave baskets.

"I will soon be back to help you," Aqamdax said.

The woman looked at her but said nothing.

Aqamdax pulled on her boots and went back outside. She climbed over the beach ice until she got to the driftwood. About half of the wood was frozen in the ice, but Aqamdax thought she might be able to get it out. She walked up the beach to a scattering of fist-sized round stones, worn smooth over the years by water and wind. She kicked one free and carried it back to the driftwood. She lifted the rock in both hands and brought it down hard against the ice that held the wood.

Again and again, she smashed rock against ice, until her hands ached and her fingers bled. Finally, by leaning her full weight against it, she was able to move the driftwood, less than a finger's width, but still, it moved. She tucked her hands into her sleeves to warm her fingers. They were numb, and, as feeling returned, they hurt enough to force tears from her eyes. She wiped her face on her sleeve and threw herself against the wood until it was loose enough to pull free.

She picked it up, heaved it to one shoulder and worked her way back over the shore ice, past the frozen clumps of grass that marked the line of high tide, up toward the village.

There were three tens of ulas in the village, each warm and strong enough to stand against the assault of the fierce winds that blew in from the sea. Most housed large families: hunters and wives, children, sometimes grandparents, aunts, uncles. The ulas were dug into the earth, roofed with driftwood or whale jaw rafters, then covered with grass mats, thatching and layers of sod.

Inside, one or two large lamps—boulders with tops chipped out to hold oil, or smaller stone lamps, each ringed with moss wicks and filled with seal oil—were kept burning. Their heat was enough to warm the ulax, even in winter.

The chief hunter's ulax was larger than most. It had seven sleeping places, each large enough for two or three people, each padded with sea otter furs and fox pelts, then curtained off from the main room with woven grass panels. Food caches, storage for seal skins of oil and sea lion bellies of dried seal meat, dried fish, whelks and chiton, were also dug into the walls. Caribou bellies and bladders, fitted with carved ivory plugs and bulging with water, hung from the ulax rafters.

The village was a good place to live. Hunters were almost always successful; the children were well-fed and healthy. Even in winter there was enough to eat. Those hunters who were not killed by sudden storms or angry sea animals, those women who lived through child-birth, could look forward to many years as elders, respected, cared for, fed.

Traders came often to the beach. The First Men hunters always had meat, oil. Who made better baskets, finer birdskin parkas than the women of this First Men village?

The wind pushed against Aqamdax as she walked. She turned a shoulder into it, tucked her head down, so she did not see the old woman until she almost ran into her. Suddenly the dark cormorant feathers of the woman's sax were before her, and Aqamdax stopped so quickly that the driftwood slipped from her shoulder, striking her ankle before hitting the ground.

Angry words came to Aqamdax's mouth, but she held them in. The old woman was Qung, the village storyteller, respected by every-one.

Of those who spoke against Aqamdax, the oldest women were often the worst, but in the years since Aqamdax had first welcomed men to her bed, she had never heard Qung lift one word against her.

The thought brought a sudden surge of gratitude. She bent down and leaned forward to look into the old woman's eyes, for the stiffening disease had truly cursed her, bending her until the hump of her back was as high as her head.

"I am sorry, Aunt," said Aqamdax, addressing the old woman in politeness.

"Ah, my eyes are not good, child," Qung answered. She turned her head sideways and up, squinting as she peered into Aqamdax's face. "Aqamdax, is it?" she asked. "Daes's daughter?"

"Yes, Aunt."

Qung patted Aqamdax's hand. "Poor child."

Her words surprised Aqamdax. It was Qung, old and bent, walking with slow steps, who should be pitied.

"You dropped something," Qung said.

"Driftwood," Aqamdax told her. Then, anxious to show Qung that she could easily give things away and should not be pitied, Aqamdax said, "I do not need it. Would you like to have it?"

She waited as the old woman bent even closer to the ground, extended a gnarled hand to stroke the wood. The North Sea had taken its bark, leaving it smooth to the touch but rough to the eye. It was dense-grained, frozen, but not water-rotted.

Trees grew near the First Men's village, mostly stunted willow and wind-sculpted black spruce, but if the storytellers were right, the First Men came from islands with no trees, where any wood they needed for iqyan or ulax rafters had to be scoured from beaches, a gift of the sea. Even yet, it was easier to bring wood from the beaches than to travel inland and cut the living trees.

"You think He Sings does not need it?" Qung asked.

"No."

"Then I would be grateful for it," she said.

She smiled at Aqamdax, and Aqamdax saw that her teeth were worn almost to the gumline. An old one, this woman. No wonder she knew so many stories.

Aqamdax picked up the wood, carried it to Qung's ulax. It was the smallest ulax in the village, a new one, made for the old woman by her daughters, so when Qung told stories the village people could go there, sit and listen, spend long days, long evenings, without interrupting the lives of Qung's children. She lived alone there, though her daughters visited often.

Aqamdax herself sometimes went to the ulax to listen. She thought it would be wonderful to have her own ulax, a place with no wives to scold her, but she had no husband or sisters to help her build such a thing, and how could a woman alone do it? She might be able to dig a place for it in the hills above the beach, gather rock to strengthen walls, but she was not strong enough to raise the rafters.

Even if she were, the village elders would not allow her, a young woman, to have her own ulax.

Aqamdax carried the wood to the roof, then went back to help Qung up. Qung invited her to come inside, promised food and a story.

Aqamdax went gladly. How could Grass Eyes be angry when Aqamdax told her she had spent the day with Qung, that she had given the old woman a gift of driftwood?

The ulax was warm. Moss lamp wicks sent up thin streams of white smoke, and the walls were smooth and dry, well-covered with woven mats. Yes, it would be a good place to live.

Qung brought out food and water, then, taking a piece of dried fish, settled herself on her haunches beside Aqamdax and began telling stories. She started with tales of the ancient grandfather Shuganan, then told of a woman and her brother who became sea otters.

The stories were good. Aqamdax lost herself in them, found herself wishing she had the strength of those ancient people—the man with one hand; the woman who saved her sons from the trickster Raven.

Aqamdax stayed as long as she dared, until the light faded into night, then she crept back through the village to the chief hunter's ulax, to his screaming wives and their noisy children.

She returned to angry words, to accusations by Grass Eyes and her small daughters, the sullen silence of the sister-wives.

"You spend all day away from work that must be done," Grass Eyes said. "You leave the seal skins that should be softened, the baskets that must be woven, the food to be prepared. Yet you bring us back nothing from the beach."

Usually, Aqamdax would have screamed back, would have reminded Grass Eyes who did the most work in the ulax, asked her what anyone brought back from the beach during winter. But this time Aqamdax only smiled.

That night Aqamdax did not allow herself to sleep. Instead, she waited until everyone had left the main ulax room, even Fish Taker, who often waited up in the night to catch some hunter who might come to visit Aqamdax. When everyone was asleep, Aqamdax pushed aside a corner of her curtain, lifted her voice into a high, singing wail and watched, waiting for the wives to come from their sleeping places.

Fish Taker was the first one out, then Spotted Leaf. When Grass Eyes appeared, Aqamdax also came from her sleeping place, her arms lifted to the rafters, her eyes closed. She told the Shuganan story, speaking in a voice soft and singing.

The wives began to argue, each suggesting that one of the others woke her, but Aqamdax ignored them, continued her story, found joy in their confusion. She broke off suddenly, stopped in the middle of a word, opened her eyes and looked around the ulax as though she were surprised.

The wives were huddled together, each clasping the others; the lamp left burning for the night threw their shadows, long and dark, against the wall. Aqamdax glanced toward Turn Around's sleeping place. She and He Sings had the curtain pushed aside. Both peered out at her.

"Oh!" Aqamdax exclaimed. "I am here. Where is Qung?"

"Qung?" the chief hunter asked. "How should we know?"

"I thought she was here with me, teaching me. I thought I was a storyteller."

Turn Around began to laugh, but Grass Eyes straightened and nodded, then went back to her sleeping place. Spotted Leaf and Fish Taker did the same.

Later that night, Grass Eyes, Fish Taker and Spotted Leaf all had the same dream. In the morning, after Turn Around thought about it for a while, she remembered she had also dreamed.

Four sister-wives given the same dream on the same night. Who could deny the sacredness of that? Surely, Aqamdax should go to Qung. She must live in Qung's ulax and learn the ancient stories of the First Men.

They sent their husband out into a day of storm winds and snow to tell Qung.

Chapter
Seven

THE NEAR RIVER VILLAGE

The evening hearth fires glowed golden through the lodge walls, and the sky was the deep blue that comes just at sunset. Chakliux had caught two hares in his snare traps. He carried them into Red Leaf's lodge and laid them just inside the door. Red Leaf would skin them and add the meat and bones to the simmering stew in the boiling bag.

The lodge was empty. It was not unusual for Sok to be somewhere else, but where were Red Leaf and her sons, Carries Much and Cries-loud?

Chakliux stripped off his parka, boots and leggings. He shook the snow from the fur before it melted in the warmth of the lodge, then slipped into a soft caribou hide shirt. Most of the men in the Near River Village wore such shirts when they were in their lodges. The hunters of Chakliux's village did not, preferring their inner parkas on the coldest days, otherwise wearing only their breechcloths. Chakliux was still not comfortable in the shirt, but Red Leaf had been kind enough to make it for him, so he wore it.

A thin cry, a mourning cry, pierced the lodge walls. The boy, Chakliux thought, and sighed. He could still feel the weight of the child in his arms as he carried him to the shaman's lodge. At least he would be mourned. Old Summer Face had claimed him as son, so the boy had a father, sisters, aunts and uncles. For Daes, only the necessary preparations would be made. She had no one except an old husband who would soon join her in death. Next year, when her bones were taken from the raised death platforms, when they were bundled and buried, who would even remember her?

Chakliux got his bowl and, using a dipper made from a caribou scapula, filled it with warm stew. A noise in the entrance tunnel made him turn his head. Sok came in, stood for a moment without speaking.

"The boy?" Chakliux asked. "I hear the mourning cries."

But as Sok moved into the light given off by the hearth fire, Chakliux saw that the man had cut his hair in rough hanks over his ears and that his face was marked with ashes.

"Who?" Chakliux asked. The word scraped his throat like a blade.

"Our grandfather," Sok said softly.

"Our grandfather?" Chakliux repeated, the words a question, as though his doubt would change what Sok had said.

"With the same knife."

The sound of Sok's voice rushed in against Chakliux's ears and the light and smells of the lodge suddenly roared in his head. A weight settled into his chest so that his breathing came hard, like that of a man who has run too far, too long.

"Why?" Chakliux finally asked. "Who would want him dead? Who would want to kill the woman and the boy?"

"The boy is still alive," Sok said, but at first Chakliux heard without understanding, and then with a dullness that allowed him no gladness, no relief.

Chakliux handed Sok his bowl of food. "Eat it," he said. "I cannot."

Sok took the bowl.

"Does anyone know who did it?" Chakliux asked.

"Some say the trader, others say someone from another village." He did not mention the Cousin River Village, but Chakliux saw the accusation in his eyes.

"The Cousin River Village?" Chakliux asked.

Sok lowered his head over the bowl of food and answered with his mouth full. "Some say so."

"Why would someone from the Cousin River Village kill our grandfather, or the woman? What would they have to gain?"

"Honor," Sok replied, and looked up at Chakliux, met his eyes. "Honor as a warrior."

"To start the fighting, you mean," Chakliux said.

"Yes."

"Then why not leave some sign, an amulet or knife, to show who did it?"

Sok shrugged. "The young men say there was something left, but that you hid it."

"Fools!" Chakliux said. "I found nothing but the boy. What about the one who found our grandfather? Was it Blueberry? Did she say there was anything left to proclaim who did it?"

"It was not Blueberry," Sok said.

His eyes darkened, and Chakliux said softly, "You found him because you took the fish for the dogs."

"I found him," said Sok.

"Was there anything that would say who killed him?"

He shook his head. "Nothing," he said. "Nothing."

"The elders and hunters know this?"

"They know, but they say I hid something." He paused. "To protect you, little brother."

How could the men of this village be such fools? Chakliux wondered. Now, because of him, Sok's place of honor, the respect given him by the elders and other hunters, was threatened.

"I am sorry, brother," he said to Sok. "I will do what I can to show them . . ."

"What can you do?" Sok asked, the words harsh, edged with anger. "What if you *had* found something? Would you tell us? You say you have come to bring peace. If a few men from your village killed people here—only an old man and a woman—are their deaths worth losing hunters? Is it worth the loss of children and elders in a starving winter because there are not enough hunters left to bring meat?"

Sok's words sliced into Chakliux's heart. If it had been Cousin River hunters, would he have protected them? Perhaps, if it would save lives. . . . But if they killed once, would they not kill again?

"The trader," Chakliux finally said. "What did they do with him?"

"They let him go."

"They think he did not do it?"

"Most think he would not kill his own son. Daes perhaps. She was a woman of too much complaining. At least Brown Water says so, and Red Leaf, also. But even for that, why would a man who was trader—and did not have to live with her—kill her? Why not just leave her? There are other women in other villages."

Sok continued to speak, but Chakliux could not keep his mind on his brother's words. Instead, he thought of his grandfather, the laughter they had shared, the jokes and riddles. Why would anyone want to kill Tsaani? He was an old man, strong in wisdom, generous in his gifts, yet still able to feed The People with his hunting.

Was it possible that Chakliux had brought a curse to his grandfather? What if Snow-in-her-hair was right? What if his bent foot was not sign of his kinship with otters but of bad luck?

"He had a good life, a long life, with much happiness," Sok said, and the words drew Chakliux from his thoughts. "Two good wives," Sok continued, "one who grew old with him, and another who gave him back his youth. Strong sons, they say, though they died young, and our mother—his daughter—a good woman. Two grandsons. He was glad to have you," Sok said. "He told me often."

Chakliux rubbed his forehead with the heel of his hand. "Do you think it was someone in this village? Do you think there is a man here who would do such a thing?"

For a long time Sok said nothing. Finally he replied, "All day I have asked myself that. All day, others have asked the same question. My answer is this: No. I do not think there is any man in this village who would do such a thing."

"Do you think the trader did it?"

Sok lifted his hands, spread his fingers. "Who can say? No one saw what happened."

"The boy saw," Chakliux said.

Sok tipped his head, seemed to think for a moment. "Perhaps, but he is young."

Chakliux nodded. "Does anyone say it was me?" he asked.

"No, little brother," Sok said. "But if I hear something, I will tell you."

"We should go to our mother."

"Yes." Sok sighed. "Red Leaf is there, and my sons. Our mother is not an easy woman to comfort. She has had too much sorrow in her life."

Chakliux pulled on his leggings, boots and parka, then followed his brother from the lodge. He remembered the last time he saw his grandfather. Since he had come to the Near River Village, Chakliux had been teaching the old man riddles—a tradition in his own village, but not here.

"Look! What do I see?" Chakliux had said to Tsaani. "It grows brown where once it was white."

Tsaani had laughed, then said, "A child's riddle, that one. When summer is near, the ptarmigan's feathers turn from white to brown."

It had been the first riddle the old man had answered without Chakliux's hints and explanations, and Chakliux had felt a strange pride, as though his grandfather were the child and he the teacher.

Snow had begun to fall, large flakes that stuck to the muddy path. They caught on Chakliux's lashes and melted on his eyelids.

A riddle for you, Grandfather, Chakliux thought as he followed Sok to their mother's lodge. Look! What do I see? It bleeds but no man sees the wound. Then speaking aloud, Chakliux gave the answer: "Your grandson's heart."

Yaa watched Brown Water as she greeted another woman, accepted a basket trap of fresh blackfish and a sael of dried blueberries. Yaa's mouth longed for the blueberries, but she saw how quickly Brown Water hid the sael and knew she did not want Yaa to see them. She turned her head, pretended she did not know what Brown Water had done. It went easier with her, she had found, when she acted as stupid as Brown Water thought she was.

But Yaa would tell her mother, and they would both have a few precious berries, though only a taste so Brown Water would not notice they were gone. Yaa's mother would also give some to her husband—a good share—for how could Brown Water complain about that?

Yaa looked over to where her father lay. He seemed to be asleep, but she thought he was not. His eyes were closed, but only so he did not have to see the lodge empty of his wife and favorite son.

At least, Yaa thought, Ghaden might return. When she last watched over him, he had seemed no better, but also no worse. Even Ligige', her cheeks painted black with ashes in mourning for her brother, had seemed relieved when she felt Ghaden's forehead and looked at the wound in his shoulder.

"Why are you surprised?" Yaa had wanted to ask, "I am old enough to care for my brother." But she had known better than to be so rude, and so had kept her eyes lowered in respect as the shaman and Ligige' spoke together about the boy.

Yaa went over to her father, sat down beside him and stroked her hands across his head. He liked that, she knew, having his hair combed, his scalp rubbed. Daes had done it for him all the time. His eyelids fluttered open for a moment, and he looked at Yaa. She thought he tried to smile, but it seemed as though his mouth was too tired even to do that much. He closed his eyes and Yaa used the fingers of both hands to comb through his long white hair. He sighed, and she did not know if it was a sigh of worry, sorrow or contentment, but she saw his lips move again toward a smile, and some of the weight over her heart seemed to lift.

He is too old for these problems, Yaa thought. His bones are too weak. If his heart ached as much as Yaa's, what would keep his ribs from breaking? Under the edge of his blanket they looked as thin as sticks.

"Yaa!" Brown Water shouted, startling Yaa so much that she caught her fingers in her father's hair, jerked his head. His eyes opened in surprise. "You are a useless one," Brown Water said. "Look around you. I need firewood. Go get some and set it inside the door. You know with the snow melting each day, the wood must be left inside to dry."

Yaa knew there was enough wood—dry wood—but it was useless to say so. She glanced down at her father, saw his lips mouth the word "Go."

She smoothed her father's hair one more time, then stood. She had only seven summers, so in the lodge wore nothing but a short apron, something to wipe her hands on and to wrap back between her legs when she sat on prickly-haired caribou hide. Brown Water used full-haired hides on the floor, though the hair shed, getting into their food and bedding.

Yaa had decided that when she had her own lodge she would scrape all the hides, even though it was more work. Her husband would not have caribou hair in every bite of his food.

"You are lazy," Brown Water said. "Better that knife should have taken you than your brother. At least he might be a hunter someday."

Yaa was used to Brown Water's insults, especially when her own mother was not in the lodge, but these words seemed to coil into sharpness and twist themselves down Yaa's throat. She blinked back quick tears, keeping her head turned so Brown Water would not see. Then she felt her father's hard dry fingers against her cheek.

"Good daughter," he said.

Yaa patted his hand and was surprised to see that tears seeped from beneath his eyelids. Then she understood. Her father had taken her tears, had rubbed them from her cheeks and put them into his own eyes so she could meet Brown Water's insults without the embarrassment of crying.

Yaa raised her head. She looked at Brown Water with eyes dry as stones. Still staring at the woman, she pulled on her parka and leggings, her furred boots. Brown Water tried to turn her head, but Yaa used the power of her eyes to pull the woman toward her. Finally, Brown Water began to screech. She threw a ladle at Yaa, but Yaa was too quick. She scooted into the entrance tunnel, then left the lodge.

She did not like to go out when it was dark, but tonight she was glad to get away from Brown Water. She tiptoed over the place where Daes had died. The body was inside the lodge, but it seemed more likely her spirit was here, where she was killed.

Yaa stood for a time looking down at the dark spot near the lodge entrance where Ghaden and Daes had lain, melting the snow with their own blood.

She almost spoke out loud. She almost asked Daes to allow Ghaden to stay with them in this village, but she was afraid of the woman's spirit, of her anger at being dead.

So Yaa said nothing, but instead hurried to the path that led to the center of the village. She would bring Brown Water firewood later, dig it out of the snow that covered the branches she and her mother and Daes had piled around the lodge when winter was new.

Now she would go to the cooking fires. She was no longer a baby, no longer someone the old grandmothers would click a tongue over and give a choice bit of tender meat. More likely they would raise a ladle, threaten her with stories of those tailed ones, the Cet'aeni, who carried children off with them into their homes in the trees. But she was very good at getting food, and today the grandmothers might give her something, especially since her little brother was so sick. Perhaps her chest would not ache so badly if her belly was full.

"My father," Chakliux's mother cried. "Who would kill my father?"

The first time she asked the question, Chakliux had tried to give an answer, some comfort, but now, after he had heard the same words come from her lips five handfuls of times, he merely sat, his eyes staring at nothing, his spirit roaming beyond the caribou hide walls.

In his mind, he gathered his possessions, furs and skins, even the few things he had left in his own village. He gave everything to the Walrus Hunters for an iqyax. How much, he wondered, did Walrus Hunters want for an iqyax? More, surely, than a man would give for a wife.

He did not know how long he had sat when he began to feel the heat of eyes on him. He looked first at Sok, saw that his brother stared at him, a scowl on his face, his eyes narrowed. Sok flexed his fingers, tightened them into fists.

"I need to kill whoever did this," Sok said, his words falling between them like sharp rocks.

"When you know who did it, I will help you," Chakliux replied, and looked down to see that his own hands were also clenched.

"He was a good man, a good grandfather," Fox Barking said, the first words he had spoken to either of his stepsons since they came into the lodge. He moved his lips to point toward their mother. "He was a good father to her," he said.

Sok pressed his fist into the palm of his hand, cracked each of his knuckles, popping them loudly. There was a scratching at the door and several women came in. They carried a boiling bag. Red Leaf stood up and helped them hang it from the lodge poles. They looked for a moment at Day Woman, then left, offering no words of hope, none of comfort.

Red Leaf found three bowls, filled them. She gave the first to Fox Barking, then one to Sok, one to Chakliux. Chakliux shook his head, but his stepfather said, "Eat. Both of you. There is something I must say. Something your grandfather told me the evening before he was killed."

He waited while they ate, leaving his own bowl untouched, watching them as if he were an old woman waiting to refill their bowls. Chakliux finished first. He set his bowl on the floor. Fox Barking glanced at Sok, then turned so he was facing Chakliux.

"Your grandfather asked me to tell you this," Fox Barking said. He licked his lips as though to pull the words he needed into his mouth. "He was the one who decided to . . ." He stopped, tipped his head back and rolled it, shoulder to shoulder, then he looked at Chakliux again and said, "You know, when you were born, it was not your mother who left you. Old Ligige', she came to your grandfather, asked him what to do."

Chakliux was surprised by Fox Barking's words. But of course he should have known. With his grandfather dead, a stepfather or maternal uncle would be the one who made the decision about his life. There had been no uncle. His chest suddenly felt strange, as though the bones inside grated against one another, as though they were pressing and grinding.

"Your grandfather said he made the wrong decision. That is why you were found by the Cousin River girl. That is why they decided to keep you as a son, raise you as Dzuuggi. He told me that someday he would do something to make your life better."

Chakliux looked over at Sok. His brother's cheeks were full of food, but he did not chew.

"He gave me what I needed," Chakliux said quietly. "In the short time I have been in this village, I have learned much. All because of my grandfather's wisdom and my brother's hunting skills."

Fox Barking held his hands palms up, as though to show he had no argument with Chakliux. Then, looking at Sok, he said, "Sok, you are to have your grandfather's weapons. His spears and spearheads, his spearthrower, his fishnets, hooks and throwing stick, whatever his wife does not lay beside him on his burial platform. All that is yours. The lodge, the food in the cache, the baskets and bowls, the bedding and furs, all belong to his wife."

Of course, Chakliux thought. It was strange Fox Barking would even mention such things. Everyone knew the wife owned the lodge, all cooking things, bedding, baskets. It was the same in his own village, but perhaps Fox Barking did not know the customs of Chakliux's village, and gave an explanation so Chakliux would understand.

"You, my wife's youngest son," Fox Barking said to Chakliux, "you are to have what you need to claim a place in this village. Your grandfather wants his wife, Blueberry, to go to you."

The words were like something hard and cold slicing into Chakliux's chest. Blueberry was to be his wife? She was a good woman, had been a fine wife to Tsaani, but she was young. She should be free to choose any man in the village. She would not want Chakliux.

"She has said she would be my wife?" Chakliux asked.

"She agreed." Fox Barking cleared his throat, then said, "This is not the greatest honor Tsaani gave you." Chakliux saw Sok swallow his mouthful of food, set down his bowl and lean forward.

"You are to have his dogs. He thinks you will be a great hunter. He thinks you will keep the bears coming to this village."

Sok made a noise in his throat as though he were choking. When he could speak, he said, "Our grandfather gave Chakliux the dogs?"

"Yes," Fox Barking answered, but his hands moved in a quick nervous dance.

Chakliux looked from his brother to his stepfather. The two men stared at each other, eyes locked.

If Sok wants the dogs, Chakliux thought, he can have them. Blueberry, too. A wife, dogs? I do not need them. If I am not welcome here, I will return to my own village and see what the men there believe. If they think I am cursed, then I will leave The People and go to the Sea Hunters. How can I do that with a wife and dogs?

He looked at Sok. His brother's face was dark with anger, his mouth twisted in hurt. "All these years I have been the one to care for his dogs. All these years, he has trained me."

"They are yours," Chakliux said to Sok. "The dogs are yours. I do not want them. Nor do I want a wife." He looked at his stepfather. The man's mouth was open as though he wanted to swallow up Chakliux's words. "Find someone else for Blueberry. Tell her she is free.

Sok, you are a good hunter. You can support a second wife. Blueberry already has her own lodge. You will probably not even need a bride price to claim her."

Sok and Fox Barking looked at Chakliux as though he were a small and foolish child. "You cannot give away what your grandfather has given you in death," Fox Barking said.

"Some say you are cursed," Sok added, his voice rough as stone. "If you refuse Blueberry and the dogs, you will be. You cannot shame our grandfather in such a way."

But as Sok spoke, he slashed the air with his hands as though to push Chakliux away, out of their mother's lodge.

"Blueberry must mourn one moon," Fox Barking said. "Then, you will go to her. If she displeases you, you may throw her away. If you displease her, she may throw you away, but you cannot refuse her. Nor refuse the dogs."

"The pups," Chakliux said, looking at Sok and Fox Barking. "I may give away the pups?"

"All of them are already promised," Sok said. "One goes to Sleeps Long, another to Fox Barking, two to Blue-head Duck and one to me."

"You will have that one and any others. From any litter," Chakliux promised. "I do not want our grandfather's position as chief hunter. You must be chief hunter. You have his weapons."

"You have his dogs," Sok said, and spread his hands as though to ask a question. "We will see which of us the spirits choose."

"It may not be either of you," Fox Barking said softly, but he laughed when Sok and Chakliux looked at him. "Who can say what the spirits will do? What more can we ask than that the village have meat? With your grandfather dead we must first think of our bellies."

Yaa ran when she came to Ligige"'s lodge. It was best not to get too close. The old man's spirit might be lurking, trying to find someone to accompany him to the world of the dead. It was evening, that time of day when spirits grow careless, drawn by the rich smells coming from smoke holes and hearths.

When she was past, she looked back over her shoulder to be sure there was no spirit following. Suddenly she was pushed, hard. She caught herself with her hands, but felt the ache of her fall in her wrists.

"Stupid!" someone yelled. "Where are your eyes?"

Yaa did not have to look up. She knew the voice. It was River Ice Dancer, a boy a little older than she was and twice her size. He leaned down to where she sat on the ground. Yaa said nothing. She had not been watching, but neither had he. If he had, he could have avoided her. She was small; she did not take up the whole path.

"So where are you going?"

Yaa did not answer. She stood up, brushed the wet snow from her rump.

River Ice Dancer was mean. He would get other children to do dangerous things with threats and dares, then, when someone got hurt, River Ice Dancer would go to the old women and tattle.

River Ice Dancer could not run fast or throw far. He was not accurate with his spear, and he had no gift for catching fish, but he knew how to use fear. That of all things, he did best.

"You will not talk to me?" River Ice Dancer asked.

Yaa tried to step around him, but he moved to block her path. "You think you can get away?"

"Leave me alone," Yaa said. "My mother asked me to bring her something."

"What?"

"Something we need for mourning."

She pushed past him, but he caught her sleeve, pulled her back.

"Do not touch me," Yaa said. "I might have some curse."

River Ice Dancer laughed.

"It does not matter to me if you catch my curse," Yaa said.

River Ice Dancer let go, but he leaned his face close to hers and said, "I think you are right. You do have a curse. You must have after Da . . . you know, that dead one, died in such a way."

Yaa smiled. "You almost said her name. You almost cursed yourself."

River Ice Dancer shoved her hard with both hands, but Yaa was ready for him and braced herself so she did not fall.

"Were you in the lodge when she died?" River Ice Dancer asked.

"She died outside," Yaa said.

"Did you hear anything?" He did not give her time to answer, but instead lowered his voice to a whisper. "I think your mother did it. She's the ugly wife. She's the one who killed her."

His words clogged Yaa's throat until she began to choke. Her mother was a good and gentle woman. She would never hurt anyone. In anger Yaa looked into River Ice Dancer's eyes, in anger she drew back her fist.

River Ice Dancer raised his top lip into a sneer, then spit full into her face. Yaa hit him as hard as she could. The blow landed in the center of his nose.

River Ice Dancer screamed, and it seemed as though his cry released a flow of blood. It poured from his nostrils down over his mouth and chin.

"My mother is good!" Yaa yelled at him.

She turned and ran, and did not look back until she got to the cooking hearths. Her heart beat so hard she could feel it in her eardrums, and her fist ached, but the joy of what she had done flowed through her.

She found a place for herself in the group of children waiting for food. Five hearth fires were arranged in a large circle at the center of the village. Beside each one, large caribouskin cooking bags hung on tripods, and the butts of heavy green-wood roasting sticks were driven into the ground. Hares and ptarmigans, dripping with fat, were skewered on each stick.

Several of the grandmothers gave the youngest children bits of meat, but the older children were ignored. The women were too busy cooking for the families in mourning.

Yaa thought of the meat the women had already brought to Brown Water's lodge, but knew she would get little of it.

Suddenly a dark shape hurled at the children. Yaa's first thought was of River Ice Dancer, then of spirits, but as the children around her began to scream, she realized it was only a dog. He was dragging his tie rope as he ran toward the cooking hearths. The women, armed with ladles, started after him, each trying to keep him away from her own lodge, from her husband's dogs.

The dog flung himself at a large male tied nearby. The two animals twisted and yelped, each going for the other's throat in a tangle of white and dark fur.

Most of the children followed the women, hooting calls and cheers, but Yaa stayed behind. For a moment there was no one at the hearths. She darted forward and grabbed a roasting stick with a fat hare skewered on it.

The stick was hot, but Yaa held on tightly and ran. She sped through the shadows of the village, holding the hare as close to her body as she could, switching the stick from hand to hand until it cooled.

She did not slow until she came to the black spruce that marked a narrow animal path, hidden under the tree's drooping branches. She scuttled under the spruce and, waddling in a crouch, finally came to the den she had found several years before. She picked up the stick she always left at the entrance and poked it inside. The den was empty.

The entrance was so narrow she had to slide in on her belly, but once inside she could sit up, squatting cross-legged, her hair brushing the arch of rock and tree roots at the top of the den.

She took a long breath, then sank her teeth into the hot meat. She swallowed, her stomach too empty to wait for chewing. She felt the meat slide down, settle in comfortable warmth just below her ribs.

"I wish Ghaden was here with me," she said, just in case Daes was listening. "There is enough for both of us. We could have a feast."

Thinking of Ghaden made her throat tighten so she could not swallow. She turned her thoughts to River Ice Dancer, to the satisfying crunch her fist had made against his nose. She laughed, then her throat opened and she was able to eat.

Chapter Eight

Cen pushed his way into the thick brush that grew on the riverbank, then crouched down until his heart slowed. There was no sense in hiding. The soft snow made his tracks easy to follow, but when he rested, he felt safer away from the river. He inhaled the clean smell of the willow around him. The yellow bark was changing to the gray-green of spring, and leaf buds had begun to swell, though the snow had not yet melted back from each thumb-sized bole.

Gripped by the need for sleep, he closed his eyes, but after a moment he jerked himself awake. He needed to get as far from the village as he could. He tightened his right hand on a short stabbing knife. What remained of a throwing spear was slung over his shoulder. If they tried to take him, he would kill at least one of them.

After the River People let him go, Cen had cleaned his wounds, but he knew he still smelled of blood. Wolves are more dangerous than the River People, he told himself. What pack would hesitate to attack something wounded? He had hung amulets around his neck, the amulet his uncle had given him at his birth, and others he had bought in trade from villages as far away as the Great River. Perhaps they would be enough to deter animals.

He wished he had an amulet from the First Men, Daes's people. They had power, those Sea Hunters.

The River People had kept him one whole day, making him wait at the center of the village until the elders decided he could go. Fools! He would never kill Daes or his own son. It was hard enough to leave the village without knowing whether the boy would live or die. But why risk that the elders would change their minds or that some other person would be found dead? Whoever had killed Daes and the old man was one of their own.

During the day he was captive, Cen had been given nothing to eat. Without food, the cold had sunk deep into his bones, but during any distraction, he had moved gradually closer to the hearth fires. There was no chance he could steal food, but the warmth eased his pain, and he was able to inhale the steam that rose from the cooking bags. Shamans said the spirits themselves lived on the smoke from burning fat. If the spirits could, perhaps men could also.

When they finally untied him, small boys and their dogs chased him from the village. Before he had reached the edge of the trees, he had fallen twice, had felt the lashes of the boys' sticks across his arms and legs, had been bitten once on the hand, again on the ankle, but finally they had turned away, allowed him to go the short distance to his lodge. There he found his packs had been scattered, most of his trade goods and weapons taken, and the shaft of his one remaining spear broken. They had left him a handful of dried meat that he stuffed into his mouth even before using his fire bow to relight the hearth.

His warmest blankets and robes had been taken, but they had not touched his sacred bundles or flicker skins. His best parkas were gone, the heavy one of wolf skin and the lighter ground squirrel parka. The hood of the ground squirrel parka had been pieced from tiny patches of fur taken from ground squirrel heads, each head fur only the length of a little finger.

Whoever had taken his parkas had left him an old parka of wolverine fur. It was weak with mildew, would fall apart on his body if he did not move carefully, but it was warm.

He had melted snow in a bag on a tripod and drunk the icy water. Then he went to the back of the lodge, lifted an old moldy mat he had purposely put in that place. He had thawed the ground there with fire, staying awake his first night in the lodge to keep the coals burning until the ground was soft enough for him to dig into it. He had made a hole, buried a bag of meat and berry cakes, a small supply of obsidian in a grass basket.

Cen went back to the fire, hunkered over it, allowed himself two berry cakes. The stump of his severed finger throbbed, and each breath tore into his chest like a knife. His left wrist was swollen almost to the width of his hand. He packed snow around it, and over his face, hoping to bring down the swelling that nearly closed his eyes. Pain muddled his thoughts, but he forced himself to decide what he must do next.

Most of his trade goods had been taken, but because of his injuries, there was still too much for him to carry.

He was strong, able to pull heavy loads on a sled made from his lodge poles. He had carved wooden braces that allowed him to lash the lodge poles together into a sled, and had faced several of the poles with strips of ivory to make runners. Now he could not pull a sled. It was difficult enough to walk. He had to leave everything, even the lodge, taking only food and his amulets.

Cen had gathered what he would take and wrapped it in one of the mats they had left him. He secured the bundle with several of his lodge pole bindings, then he had curled around his fire and let himself sleep. Why not? If they came for him, what could he do?

He had awakened when his fire burned low. He put a coal in a hollowed knot of wood, slung it around his neck, then strapped the pack on his back. It was still night when he left the lodge, though he could see the first edge of dawn above the trees.

He had taken short breaks, ate, once even slept, then forced himself to continue.

Now again he heaved himself to his feet and pushed through the brush to the bank of the river. He walked until in his exhaustion he could no longer think, until his feet were like things that did not belong to him and he could not feel the ache of the bones in his wrist. Then suddenly he was on his knees and could not remember how he had fallen.

He forced himself to stand and turned his mind toward Daes. She had been a good woman—too good to die in the Near River Village, where she had no one to mourn her.

Anger gave him strength. His steps were again firm against the snow. He would have his revenge, and in that way Daes would be mourned. She did have a daughter. Daes had spoken of her often. Cen thought he remembered her. She had been a girl of ten, twelve summers then. By now she was a woman and probably had children of her own.

He should go and tell her that her mother was dead. Cen fixed the image of the daughter in his mind. She had looked much like Daes. Yes, he must go to the First Men, must tell them about Daes, about Ghaden. Perhaps some of the hunters would be willing to help him avenge his woman's death.

The day after the burial ceremony, Chakliux went to Blueberry. Without Tsaani, the lodge seemed empty, cold.

Blueberry did not look at him. With her head lowered, she motioned toward the back of the fire, toward the place where Tsaani always sat, but Chakliux did not want to assume an honor that was not his. Blueberry brought him a bowl of warm meat, the broth dimpled with melted fat and flavored with sour dock leaves. Chakliux raised the bowl to his lips, pushed meat into his mouth with his fingers.

"Good," he said. "Very good."

She looked at him then, and he saw that her eyes were swollen and red, that she had cut her hair so it stuck out in uneven tufts around her ears.

Chakliux's chest ached with the young woman's pain. "I share your sorrow," he told her.

Blueberry scowled. "Why?" she asked. "Your grandfather's death has given you a wife. You think I do not hear the women's laughter? You think I am proud to be given what Snow-in-her-hair did not want?"

Chakliux could not answer. During the short time he had lived in the Near River Village, he had often visited this lodge. Blueberry had seemed to be a quiet woman, not one to throw insults.

It is her sorrow, he told himself, and said, "I do not pretend to be what your husband was, but I have always been a hunter. I will bring food to the lodge. You and your children will have enough to eat."

"Those children," said Blueberry, "will they be otters or people?"

Chakliux, suddenly angry, said, "No one will force you to be my wife."

"You think I will displease my husband, dishonor him by refusing to do what he asks?"

"How does it honor your dead husband when you treat his grandson with scorn?"

She narrowed her eyes and opened her mouth to speak, but at that moment, there was a scratching at the doorflap. "Come!" Blueberry called, anger still loud in her voice.

Sok came in. For a moment he crouched at the end of the entrance tunnel, watching them both. Blueberry turned her back on the men and went to the woman's side of the lodge.

Sok curled his lips, and as though she were not there, he said to Chakliux, "It is cold in here. What happened to the woman who owns this lodge? Can she not keep a hearth fire going?" He picked up several pieces of wood, fed the fire into a blaze, then motioned for Chakliux to sit beside him.

Chakliux sat on his haunches. "Let her mourn," he said in a quiet voice.

"She does not want to be wife again?" Sok asked.

"Not to me."

"Young women are often foolish," Sok said, but he spoke loudly, turning his head to direct his words toward Blueberry's back.

"There is food," said Chakliux, and nodded toward the boiling bag.

Sok picked up a bowl and filled it, then squatted beside his brother. For a short time, he ate, then he said, "It does not seem right without our grandfather."

Suddenly Blueberry turned, her face dark, her teeth clenched. Rudely, she raised her arm to point at Chakliux; rudely she spoke, using his name in boldness. "Chakliux, there is something you should know. Your grandfather was the one who chose to leave you. He was the one who took you from your mother and left you to die. Do you know that?"

"I know," Chakliux said softly.

She stood, mouth open, then grabbed a woven hare fur blanket and wrapped it around herself. "He did not think you should live," she said. "He wanted you dead. So why would he tell me I must be your wife?"

She flung the last words over her shoulder as she left the lodge.

Sok reached out, laid a hand on Chakliux's shoulder.

"I cannot be her husband," Chakliux said.

"You would dishonor our grandfather by refusing her?" Sok asked. "Leave her alone. Do not come to this lodge except to bring meat. In time, she will realize our grandfather was right."

Chakliux pressed his lips together. Now, more than ever, he wanted to return to his own village, his own people. Should he stay where he was not wanted, tied to a place by dogs and a woman who hated him?

"There is something else to think about," Sok said, and his words were slow, sad, so that Chakliux sucked in his breath as he waited for what Sok had to say. "More dogs have died."

"Whose?" Chakliux asked.

"Blue-head Duck's."

Chakliux rubbed one hand across his face.

"The elders are meeting now to decide what needs to be done. They have asked me to come to them at midday. To hear what they have to say."

"Tell them I will leave this village," Chakliux said. "I have had enough. I will be glad to go back to my own people." He did not look at Sok, did not want to see if there was hurt in his brother's eyes.

Sok stood in the midst of the elders. Each was respected in some way, for some skill, some wisdom.

Dog Trainer spoke. He had more dogs than any other man in the village. Of the elders, now that Tsaani was dead, Dog Trainer was recognized as the one who knew most about dogs.

"We have had many dogs die, many who were not sick or old or injured. Puppies are born dead or too weak to live. We had no problems like this until your brother came among us. We were told by the Cousin River shaman that Chakliux was a man of animal powers, a gift from animals. But we in this village remember your mother giving birth, remember her sorrow when she had to give up a son because he would not be able to walk or run.

"We think he must leave our village. We think he might be the cause of our bad luck with dogs. People also say that someone from his village, some hunter wanting to stir our young men to attack, killed your grandfather and the Sea Hunter woman."

"My brother is aware of everything you have just said," Sok answered. "He does not want to make problems here. He came to work for understanding, so his village and ours could continue to live together in peace."

"Some of us think your brother must leave our village," said the elder who called himself Blue-head Duck. Blue-head Duck had many children, all living. He looked at Dog Trainer, though he spoke to Sok. "But some of us think he has power. A child left to die, who does not die, has some favor of the spirits. A child who should not be able to walk, but as a man can walk, has somehow overcome his curse."

"But the dogs die," Dog Trainer said. "You think this village will survive if our dogs die? What if we have a starving winter, what will we eat? How will we move to fish camp? You want our women to carry everything?"

"You know I want our dogs to live," Blue-head Duck said patiently. "But why throw away power?"

"My brother is different from the rest of us," Sok said. His words were careful, slow. "He has powers we do not understand. Is that a reason to blame him for what has happened? Instead we should consider how he can help us. You know we have often tried to get the Cousin River People to trade us one of their dogs—those golden-eyed dogs their grandfathers bought in trade from the caribou followers who live far to the north. What if Chakliux can get one of those dogs for us? Perhaps that would be enough to break this curse."

For a long time no one spoke. Finally Dog Trainer said, "Tell your brother to come to me. I will ask him to visit the Cousin River Village and to make good trades."

Fox Barking raised his eyes from the hearth fire. "It sounds like foolishness, this plan," he said, snorting out the words. "What will Chakliux trade? He has nothing but his grandfather's dogs and his grandfather's wife."

"My granddaughter will not go," another of the elders, father of Blueberry's mother, said.

"Then Chakliux will go alone," Dog Trainer said, "and we will all give him trade goods, so each of us will have a share in the luck."

It was a good idea, Chakliux thought. If he was successful, he would return in one moon, and he would bring dogs from his village for the Near River men. The dogs raised in his village were larger and stronger than those raised here, yet not so given to fighting. Those few marked with golden eyes were known to have special powers, but the hunters of his village did not part easily with them.

A man could get almost anything for a litter of golden-eyed dogs. Anything but a Sea Hunter iqyax, Chakliux thought. Traders said the Sea Hunters did not have dogs. Why should they? They were not like Caribou People, following the herds as they moved spring and fall; they were not like this Near River Village, using dogs to hunt bear. They did not starve in winter and use their dogs for meat. Who starved when there were whales to hunt?

The Near River elders told him they would be satisfied with one golden-eyed dog. Male or female, old or young, as long as it was not too old to mate. Now as Chakliux stood in Sok's lodge, he sorted through the trade goods they had given him, all packed in fishskin baskets, their seams strengthened with welts of caribou hide and decorated with the green head feathers of the male merganser. Some baskets were filled with pelts from beavers trapped in early winter when their fur was thick and shining; others held berry cakes, dried meat or smoked fish.

Blue-head Duck had sent three fine wolfskin parkas edged with wolverine fur; Sok had given caribouskin leggings, shell beads and a handful of narrow chert blades a man could insert in a sharpened length of bone or ivory to make a spearhead that would draw much blood, kill quickly. Others had brought willow bark fishnets and woven hare fur blankets, jade knife blades, caribou antler snow goggles, scrapers, women's knives, bone and ivory fish lures, even a fire bow. Enough to buy several dogs, Chakliux was sure.

Sok had lent him his sled. It was strong and sturdy with frame and runners carved from birch, the body woven of split willow roots. The runners were sheathed with walrus ivory Sok had bought in trade. On the coldest days, when the snow was like sand, or in warmer times, when it was sticky, a man could urinate on the runners. When the urine froze it made a thin layer of ice that moved easily over any kind of snow.

Chakliux tied everything he had been given on the sled, then he added the extra boots, parka and throwing spears he would need for traveling. He also tied on a bundle of his own trade goods. Perhaps he could bring back a dog for himself.

K'os's cousin, Cloud Finder, had several golden-eyed dogs. He might be willing to trade, and that would be one way Chakliux could get an iqyax, at least from the Walrus Hunters. Their iqyan, it was said, were not as good as those made by the Sea Hunters, but unlike the Sea Hunters, the Walrus men kept dogs.

"You are ready?" Sok asked as he came into the lodge.

"Yes. I plan to leave in the morning."

"Red Leaf is at the cooking hearth. She and many of the old women have prepared a feast. Everyone will eat together. Come, there will be drums and dances. What you are doing gives us reason to celebrate."

Chakliux followed Sok to the cooking hearths. He would stay for a little while, then he would go see Day Woman before he left. And also Blueberry. Neither visit would be easy.

An old woman offered Chakliux a bowl of food, but most of the people stood at a distance, watching him from the edges of their eyes. Chakliux took the bowl, then went to find Sok.

He was at the center of a group of men, telling hunting stories. He paused when he saw Chakliux, motioned for Chakliux to join him, then began to boast of his brother's skills.

In politeness, Chakliux listened, but found he could not look at those around him as Sok spoke. He was not used to having others speak about his hunting. It was good to be known as a hunter, though.

He was gifted with his spear, had practiced hard as a boy, thinking a strong arm would make up for his weak leg.

Finally Sok finished. The men looked at Chakliux, and he realized he was expected to tell a story about Sok.

He had hunted several times with his brother, and Sok had done well, acted bravely, though he was harsh with his dogs. Chakliux could speak about these hunts, but in telling such a story, there were many ways a man could be trapped in disrespect. Each village had its own way of praising.

Better to speak truthfully, Chakliux thought, than risk cursing his own brother.

"Someone," Chakliux said carefully, "knows his brother is an honored hunter." He looked at Sok and smiled.

Sok returned his smile, and several of the men called out boisterous praises.

Chakliux continued: "Someday someone will honor him with stories that will stay on men's tongues for a winter of nights, but when a man does not yet know all the ways of a village, it is too easy to curse when praising."

Chakliux looked at the men, met their eyes, saw their eyebrows raised to agree with him.

"In the Cousin River Village," Chakliux said, "there is a tradition started by storytellers. Riddles. I tell you what I see, and each man must search within his own thoughts to know what I speak about. Even grandfathers teach grandsons with riddles. So listen, and try to decide what I speak about."

Chakliux looked at the circle of men. More had come, gathering two and three deep with Chakliux and Sok at the center. Most had bowls of meat, most wore parkas, but some were wrapped in fur blankets, as though they meant only to get their food, then return to the warmth of their lodges. Chakliux looked into each face, not to show disrespect but so they knew he felt himself equal with them, hunter to hunter.

"Look! What do I see?" he said, beginning in the traditional way of his village. "It runs far, singing, and Sok's is the first to fill its mouth with meat."

Chakliux waited. In his own village, where men knew how to unwind a riddle, the answer would have come quickly. What hunter has not heard the voice of his spear as it leaves the spearthrower?

Several men began to grumble, voices low and almost angry, so that Chakliux asked himself whether in avoiding one curse he had walked into another.

"Now," he began, speaking over the discomfort of the Near River hunters, "there is a secret to every riddle. I will tell you this one, and you will be among the few men who know."

Then in the same way that Chakliux had heard grandfathers talk their grandchildren through a riddle, he explained his puzzle to the Near River men. "All hunters know the voice of their spear as it leaves their hands," Chakliux began.

Several men laughed, the boisterous laughter of sudden understanding.

"And what eats first?" Blue-head Duck asked. "Even before the hunter."

"His spear!" several men cried out.

"So the answer is Sok's spear," Dowitcher said.

One by one the hunters began to laugh, a laughter that told their hearts were lifted by new understanding. Then Chakliux slipped from among them, whispering to Sok that he would go and visit their mother and also Blueberry.

"Take food," Sok told him, so Chakliux went to one of the older women, the one who seemed to tell the others what to do. He asked her for food, something to take to his mother, something else to give to Blueberry. The woman filled two small caribouskin bags with meat and broth, then dropped a hot rock from the hearths into each. The stones sizzled and popped as they sank into the meat.

Chakliux held the bags before him as he walked. When he came to his mother's lodge, he scratched and called out, then crouched to slip through the entrance tunnel.

His mother was sitting in darkness, the hearth fire only coals, the soot of previous fires black on her face. She turned her head to watch as he hung the caribou bags from a lodge pole. He scooped out a bowl of meat and handed it to her.

"Eat," he said. "Even in mourning a person should eat."

His mother took the bowl but did not raise it to her lips.

"It is not mourning that keeps food from my mouth," she said. "It is fear." She looked up at him. "For you."

He squatted on his heels beside her, dipped two fingers into her bowl and took out a piece of meat. He pressed it between her lips. Slowly she began to chew.

"You know I go only to the Cousin River Village," he said. "Nothing will happen to me there."

A tear dripped from her left eye, fell to her cheek. "What if they have found out that you are . . ." She stopped speaking, wiped her cheek against her shoulder, then said, "You told me that they think you are animal-gift. What will happen if they find out . . ."

"If they do not already know, I will tell them," Chakliux said. "I am the same person. I still know the stories of The People; I still know how to swim; I still carry the mark of the otter. If what I tell them makes them angry, then I will come back here. If I am not wanted here, I will find another village. There are many villages. More than a man could visit during his life."

Chakliux pressed another piece of meat between her lips. "You think it will make me stronger to know my mother is in her lodge, starving herself? You think it will make my journey easier?"

She seemed older than when Chakliux had first come to the village. New strands of white dimmed her hair. But even though her face was lined, her hair graying, her beauty was strong, the bones standing taut beneath her skin.

"This is something we do in the Cousin River Village," Chakliux told her, and he pulled several hairs from his head, rolled them together in his hands, then twisted them into a knot. He pressed the knot into his mother's palm. "Put this into your amulet. Keep it there. It will draw me back."

She clasped the hair in both hands.

Chakliux stood. "I must go now to Blueberry," he said, and did not miss the quick look of concern that crossed his mother's face.

Yes, what mother would not worry, Chakliux thought, when in little more than a moon, two women tell your son they do not want him as husband.

After his wife Gguzaakk had died, Chakliux seemed to feel nothing—not even the need for a woman. But as the moons passed, the pain subsided into a dull ache, something he could live with. Once again he ate and enjoyed his food; he hunted and celebrated each kill; finally, he again felt the need for a woman.

Both Blueberry and Snow-in-her-hair were good to look at. He could not deny his desire for them, but still, that desire was not as strong as it had been when he was younger. Now, he could wait. He would not marry only to have a woman for his bed.

Blueberry's lodge was well-lit, and when Chakliux scratched she called out in a glad voice. When she saw him, she seemed surprised.

Her face was clean, and she wore good clothes, nothing torn or soiled for mourning.

So then, Chakliux thought as he hung the bag of meat from a lodge pole, she was expecting someone. "The women sent food," Chakliux said, and nodded toward the pouch.

"You want some?" she asked.

Chakliux looked at her for a moment. "Someone else is coming?" he asked.

"No," she said.

"You no longer mourn your husband?" He raised his eyes to her clean face, her brushed and braided hair.

Blueberry covered her cheeks with her hands, then slid her fingers to her braids. She bit at her lips and said, "A dream came to me last night. It was from your grandfather. He told me he did not want his wife dirty. He said he wanted her to be beautiful so everyone would know he had a good woman."

Chakliux listened, saw the too-quick movements of her hands, the many times her tongue came out to lick her lips.

"I am hungry," Chakliux said, and squatted on his haunches as she filled a bowl. The broth slopped over onto his fingers when she handed it to him.

Chakliux said nothing. He wiped his hands on his leggings, fixed a smile on his face. He ate, finished the bowl and handed it back to be refilled.

"You have heard I go to the Cousin River Village?" he asked.

She filled his bowl and gave it to him.

"Yes," she said. A sly gladness came into her eyes.

Chakliux tipped his bowl to drink the broth. He stood and walked to a pile of furs stacked on one side of the lodge. He took several from the pile, arranged them into a bed near the back of the lodge. "It is custom among my people before a journey to sleep in the bed to which you hope to return."

"It . . . it is not a custom here," Blueberry stammered out.

But Chakliux lay down on the furs, wrapped one over himself and closed his eyes. It was not long until he heard a scratching at the doorflap. He opened his eyes, saw Blueberry hurry toward the entrance tunnel, but he rolled quickly from the furs and was there first.

The man Root Digger stood outside, his mouth open in surprise. Chakliux remembered him from the bear hunt.

"Blueberry waits for you," Chakliux said to the man, but Root Digger backed away, mumbling. He slipped in the snow and finally scrambled down the slippery path on feet and fingertips.

Chakliux crawled into the lodge. Blueberry stood with her back to him.

"Do you think I am a fool?" Chakliux asked her. "I saw what you planned as soon as I came into your lodge."

Blueberry said nothing.

"So," said Chakliux, "I will not sleep here tonight. I do not think I want to return to this lodge or to your bed. Do you think Sok will be interested to hear what has happened? You know he searches for the one who killed your husband. Ask Root Digger if he has lost a knife."

He left the lodge, skirted the village so he did not need to walk through the crowd near the cooking hearths. Already the drums were beating; the sky was darkening. If he was to leave in early morning, it would be better for him to sleep rather than dance.

He went to Red Leaf's lodge. It was empty. He unrolled his bedding, lay down in the furs. He tried to relax into sleep, but thoughts crowded away his dreams.

Had Blueberry truly been a good wife to his grandfather, or had she been sneaking Root Digger into her lodge whenever the old man was somewhere else?

If she had been, Chakliux hoped Tsaani had not known. He sighed. He would worry about her later, after he returned. At least he had reason to throw her away. At least there was one less thing to tie him to this village. The woman was not worth thinking about.

The journey to his own village was more important. He looked forward to seeing his father, Ground Beater, and he needed to speak to his mother K'os. In the morning, before he left, he would go to Bluehead Duck. Perhaps the man had some wisdom that would help Chakliux deal with his mother. He needed to know if she was the one behind the murders here at the Near River Village. He did not think that she herself had actually killed Tsaani or Daes. If she wanted it done, it was more likely she had enticed some young man to do it for her. But who could say?

After all, she had killed Gguzaakk.

Chapter
Nine

Yaa lifted her head and stared hard at the smoke hole. Perhaps the sky was lightening, at least a little. She had lain awake all night, drifting in and out of strange half thoughts that were not quite dreams.

She had tried all the things she usually did when she could not sleep: counting, naming her friends, remembering games and telling herself stories. Finally she had crawled from her sleeping furs and sneaked to the boiling bag. If she had just a little to eat, she thought, that might help. But even in the darkness, Brown Water had seen her.

She had bounded out of bed, snatched up the ladle and cracked Yaa's knuckles with it. So Yaa lay, not only trying to sleep, but also trying to ignore the throb of her hand.

In just one moon, there had been many changes in their lodge. First Daes had been killed and Ghaden taken to live with Wolf-and-Raven. Then, just five days ago, Yaa's father had died. The ache of that death was still so fresh that it hurt worse than her hand.

The first night after his death, Yaa had dreamed of her father and of Daes. They had called her to join them. Since then, it had been difficult for Yaa to fall asleep, and when she finally did sleep, she would jerk awake in sudden fear, her heart beating so hard it felt as though it would break out through her chest.

During the day, Yaa dragged herself through her chores, earning blows and scoldings until her back ached and her ears were too tired to hear the words Brown Water yelled. But yesterday, Wolf-and-Raven had visited the lodge, had told Brown Water that Ghaden was ready to come back to them. After a night of songs and prayers, he would bring Ghaden to Brown Water's lodge.

Wolf-and-Raven's words lifted the gray of Yaa's world. Her hands and feet were suddenly able to do things in the old way, without stumbling or tangling.

She had helped her mother prepare Ghaden's bed. They had aired out his hare fur blankets and tucked good luck charms under the woven grass sleeping mats.

When they finished, Yaa's mother turned to her and said, "Now go get your own bedding and put it here beside Ghaden's. Brown Water and I have decided that you must be the one to take care of him. It will soon be spring, and we will be too busy."

She had smiled at Yaa then, and a great lump came into Yaa's throat. That night, Yaa was sure she would sleep, but though she willed herself into dreams, it seemed that her muscles danced under her skin. Now it was nearly morning, and Yaa was sure she had been awake all night.

She heard Brown Water clear her throat of the hearth fire's smoke, and she squinted to see through the dark of the lodge as the woman got up and stirred the coals. Yaa tightened her eyes against the firelight, and in that moment must have fallen asleep, because soon Brown Water was shaking her awake, calling her a seagull, a lazy bird that robs cooking hearths and meat racks.

Yaa's eyes popped open and she jumped up, pulled on her parka and ran outside to bring wood. She bumped each piece against the ground to shake out loose snow. Three days before, they had had a storm, but since then there had been only thick frosts that crackled on the caribouskin lodge covers and sparkled in the clear morning light.

Each day the sun came earlier. Yaa could tell the difference in the air, as though the trees were letting out the first smell of promised leaves from their bare and brittle branches.

She carried in six armloads of wood, then went out for another when Brown Water called out, "Enough!" and tilted her head toward the boiling bag so Yaa knew she was supposed to eat.

Yaa finished a bowl of meat, then settled down to weave a grass mat. Weaving was not her favorite thing. The dried grass always seemed to grow sticky under her fingers, and her eyes burned as she strained to see in the smoky lodge. But, she told herself, it was better than sewing.

Her favorite morning work was tending one of the boiling bags at the village hearths. She liked to hear the old women talk. They spoke with giggles of their husbands, so Yaa learned secrets about many hunters, men walking with chins held high, wearing parkas beaded with shells and adorned with feathers.

Old Blue-head Duck, honored for killing many caribou, liked to have his buttocks scratched before he went to sleep at night, and Dowitcher, whose nasty temper kept children away from him, was afraid of voles.

But this morning Yaa needed to stay in the lodge. If she was to care for Ghaden, she should be there when he came home.

Ghaden awoke to the sounds of Blue Flower laying out food. It smelled good. He was hungry. He rolled to his side and carefully pushed himself up.

The pain was there, catching at him like sharp-nailed fingers, but it was not as bad as it had been. He still hated to take long breaths. Each day the old woman Ligige' came, made him stand and fill his chest with air until he could do nothing but cough. Sometimes, when he heard her coming, he would pretend to be asleep. At first, that had worked. The old woman had gone away, promising to return the next day, but now, if he pretended, she merely shook him until he decided the shaking was worse than the long breaths.

It helped him, Happy Mouth said, and told him he must obey Ligige', and that he must eat, even if he was not hungry. Then he would get strong enough to return to their lodge. Then he could go home. Yes, he wanted to go home, more than anything, even more than having the pain go away.

"Ghaden, you are awake?" Blue Flower asked.

Ghaden smiled at her. She reminded him a little of his mother. "Hungry," he said.

"Hungry! Good!" She filled a bowl and handed it to him.

Ghaden crossed his legs and set the bowl in his lap. He fished his fingers into the broth and pulled out a piece of meat.

"Today?" he asked Blue Flower.

She raised her eyebrows. "Yes, today," she said.

His laughter rose like small round drops and popped from his mouth like the spit bubbles he and Yaa made with their lips. Today he could go back to Brown Water's lodge. Today he would see his mother.

Wolf-and-Raven did not come until the sun was high in the sky. By that time the waiting had made Yaa's skin feel as if it would crawl from her body. She jumped to her feet when she heard the scratch at the door, but Brown Water motioned for her to sit down. She sighed and drew the mat back onto her lap, wove another strand through the weft grass and used a notched bird bone to push it tightly into place.

Brown Water welcomed Wolf-and-Raven. To Yaa's disappointment, he did not have Ghaden with him, but after a few words of politeness, he ducked his head into the entrance tunnel and called to his wife. She came in carrying Ghaden.

Ghaden's face was a pale white circle swathed in furs. He seemed tinier than Yaa remembered him, though she had visited him often.

Brown Water gestured toward the boy's sleeping place, and Blue Flower carried him there, settled him into the blankets.

"Yaa," Brown Water said, and pointed with her chin toward the boy.

Yaa gratefully rolled up her mat and went to sit beside her brother. Blue Flower patted her on the head and left them, joining the adults at the hearth fire. Brown Water offered them food, and Happy Mouth filled bowls, then turned to Ghaden and asked if he was hungry.

He shook his head but struggled to sit up. Yaa scooted behind him to prop up his shoulders. "He says no," she told her mother, then leaned forward to catch the words Ghaden was mumbling.

"My mother," he said. "Where is my mother? Where is she?"

Yaa opened her mouth but did not know what to say. Had no one told him that Daes was dead? Had no one explained that she would not be here? Yaa looked at Wolf-and-Raven, at the important feathers he wore in his hair, at the amulets he had at his neck. His wife was dressed beautifully in a wolverine parka, the shoulders decorated with insets of white weasel fur. The woman was telling a joke. Brown Water laughed and so did Yaa's mother.

Yaa wanted to yell at them, to interrupt rudely and ask what they had told Ghaden. Perhaps they had said nothing. Perhaps they expected Yaa to tell him Daes was dead.

"I want my mother," Ghaden said again, and Yaa saw the shine of tears in his eyes.

She leaned forward, pressed her lips close to Ghaden's ear. "Your mother was hurt, like you were hurt, Little Brother," she said softly.

"But she was hurt too badly to get well. She had to go live with the spirits. She is there now."

Ghaden turned his head to look at her. "When will she come back?" he asked.

"She cannot come back for a long time," Yaa said, hoping her words were true, hoping that Daes would be content to leave them alone.

Ghaden's eyes grew large and round. He slipped his thumb into his mouth and sucked, something Yaa had not seen him do since he was a baby.

"Do not worry," Yaa said. "You will still live here with us."

Ghaden pulled his thumb from his mouth. It made a wet, popping noise. He pressed his lips together into a tight line, and for that moment, his small boy's face reminded Yaa of Daes. He looked over at the circle of people around the hearth fire. Several others had come to the lodge. Lazy Snow, who owned the lodge next to them, had brought a basket of dried blueberries. She had probably watched Wolf-and-Raven bring Ghaden home, Yaa guessed, and had sacrificed some of her prized berries to come over and see what was happening. Blue-head Duck, uncle to Brown Water, had also come, no doubt invited as an honored elder.

"Is Brown Water my mother now?" Ghaden asked in a small, quivering voice.

Brown Water sat straight and tall, her neck stretched out with her importance. What could be worse than having Brown Water as mother? Yaa thought.

"No," she said to Ghaden. "Brown Water is not your mother. I will be your mother."

Ghaden sighed, then relaxed against Yaa. He put his thumb back into his mouth, and Yaa leaned forward to rest her cheek on his head. Ghaden reached up and curled his fingers into her hair, then closed his eyes, his mouth working soundlessly around his thumb.

Chapter Ten

THE COUSIN RIVER VILLAGE

Chakliux studied the man sitting before him. Cloud Finder was large, but his body was soft and fat like that of an old woman who has many sons to feed her. His eyes, though, were bright and shrewd.

Cloud Finder was considered an elder, an honor bestowed more for his wisdom than his age. He was a good hunter, an honest man.

When traders came for dogs, they visited Cloud Finder first. His animals seldom fought, nor did they cringe or whine when men approached. Their muscles were firm and well-defined under their glossy fur. If Chakliux could bring dogs like those back to the Near River Village, then perhaps the elders would believe he worked to help their people.

"So during the days you have been with us, you have come to understand that the young men of our village grow weary of sitting," Cloud Finder said. "They think the best way to prove their worth is through war. You say that this is happening also among the Near River People? I am surprised. Their young men are bear hunters. You think they would find enough honor in hunting. If our men knew the trick of finding winter dens, they would be more content." He shrugged. "Spring is a bad time. Our young men—even my own four sons—have had enough of winter, enough of women's voices and children's songs. They grow hungry for fresh meat and honor."

"That is true," Chakliux said, "but perhaps the Near River men will no longer want to fight when I bring them good dogs."

"There is something more important here than dogs," said Cloud Finder. "Do the Near River elders want to fight or do they seek peace?"

"Like most of the elders in this village, they want peace," Chakliux said. "What good comes to an old man from fighting? Does a father want to lose his sons? You know He Talks sent me to the Near River Village to marry and in that way strengthen the bond between our peoples, but the woman did not want me. She was afraid our children would have feet like mine."

"What is so terrible about that?" Cloud Finder asked. "She did not want a man with the power of animal-gift?"

Chakliux lifted his hands. "Who can understand what a woman wants?" he said. "Dogs are dying in their village. Strong, healthy dogs. Some of the young men, trying to build anger against our people, have said I brought a curse to them. Perhaps the shaman's daughter also thinks I carry a curse. Their elders hope that if I bring back golden-eyed dogs, the people will understand I have not been sent to curse but to help."

Cloud Finder leaned forward, looked hard into Chakliux's eyes. "There is something more," he said.

Chakliux sat for a long time considering what to tell the man. Finally he said, "Less than a moon before I left to return here, two of the Near River People were killed. One was an elder, a respected hunter, the other a woman. Also, a young child was wounded. The elder was killed in his lodge, as he slept. The woman was outside, returning to her sister-wife's lodge. The child was her son. The killings were done with a knife."

"You think some of our young men did that?"

"I do not know. The Near River shaman says spirits killed them."

Cloud Finder blew out his breath in disgust. "What spirit uses a knife?" he asked.

"There was a trader in the village," Chakliux said. "Some think he did it."

"What do you think?"

"Why would he kill a village elder? The boy was the trader's son. Why would he try to kill his own son? The knife was still in the child's back when he was found. It was one of the knives the trader had brought to the village. Why would he leave his knife?"

"Is he stupid, this man?"

"Not in his trading."

"So you think perhaps one of our young men . . ."

"I am not sure. If a hunter from this village wanted to give the Near Rivers a reason for fighting, why kill a woman or child, why an old man?"

"Who needs protection more?" Cloud Finder asked. "When young men fight it is for their own honor and to protect those who cannot fight—the elders, the children, the women."

"That is true, but why leave a trader's knife? Why not let it be known that a Cousin River hunter did the killing?"

Cloud Finder nodded.

"Do you know of any hunters who were gone from this village for the time it would take to do such a thing?" Chakliux asked. "Probably six, eight days at least."

Cloud Finder frowned, looked up at the top of the lodge, pursed his lips. "My sons, Night Man and his brother Tikaani, were gone two days hunting," he said slowly. "They brought back a lynx, some hares, a fox." He was silent for a time. "There are no others that I know of. You have been staying in the hunters' lodge, have you not?"

"Yes."

"Young men often boast. You have heard nothing?"

"I have lain rolled in my robes, pretending to be asleep but listening long into the night. I have heard nothing."

"Then if something was done by one of our people, for some reason it was done in secret. There *is* one who might do such a thing, though not by herself. She would send another."

He raised his eyebrows at Chakliux, and Chakliux felt his belly twist. K'os. Who else but K'os, and if it was her, why tell the Near River People? It would give the young men reason to fight. Better only to wait and watch, ready for whatever she decided to do next.

"I understand," Chakliux said quietly.

"And you know that it is best to wait?"

"Yes."

Cloud Finder drew a long breath. "We must watch and listen, you and I," he said. "We will stop her." He stood and filled his bowl again to the top, lifted his chin toward Chakliux's bowl.

Chakliux shook his head.

Cloud Finder sat down. Through a mouthful of food he said, "Meanwhile, you need dogs. Why come to me?"

"You have the best dogs."

Cloud Finder laughed. "It is good to be known for something besides being fat," he said, though everyone knew he was proud of his size.

A man who was fat, even in spring, was a man who had chosen his wife wisely and who was skilled as a hunter. Either that or he was greedy, and no one who visited Cloud Finder's lodge had ever accused him of greed. Chakliux looked down at the large wooden bowl in his lap. He had been eating since he came, and the bowl was still half full.

"You offer a trade then?" Cloud Finder asked.

"I have goods of my own, and also things from the Near River People, furs and parkas, hare fur blankets, a sael of goose grease, fishskin baskets, fishnets, hooks, spearheads. I have a fire bow made by one of the elders. Many things."

"And for all this you want a dog?"

"A bitch that has recently whelped."

"And her pups?"

"Yes. You have more than one bitch. Several have just had litters."

"It is not easy for me to give up one of my dogs. They are like my children. I need to know they will be well cared for."

"You have known me since I was a boy, Cloud Finder. You know I will care for her."

Cloud Finder inclined his head. "I would not consider this if you were just a man seeking a good dog, but I do not want to see our people fight. We are cousins with those Near Rivers. We share the same grandfathers. What if some other enemy comes among us? Such a thing has happened before. It may happen again. There are strangers who live two, three handfuls of days from here. They use weapons we do not know how to make, and they do not respect sacred things. Their language is something no one understands. What if they attack our villages? What if they come to steal our daughters and wives? What would we do if we could not band together with the Near River People?" He sighed, then said, "Show me what you have brought. Perhaps I will trade."

"So," K'os said, her lips curling, "has he decided to give you a dog?"

Chakliux had avoided his mother since he had been in the village, but a hunter has to visit the village cooking hearths, otherwise how would he eat?

Now she stood, alone at the hearths, stirring one of the boiling bags as though she always took her turn cooking like other women in the village. She nodded toward his empty bowl. "Have you eaten yet?" she asked.

"This morning with Cloud Finder," Chakliux answered.

"Then why eat here?" she asked. "Besides, if you are hungry again, I have better food in my lodge."

Her food was good. The hunters often brought her the best meat for the favors she bestowed. She seldom shared any of it with other families, and she seldom used the village hearths except during celebrations when the men were nearby, and K'os did not have to worry about village women throwing ladles of hot food at the one who bedded their husbands and young sons.

"I cannot. I must return to the hunters' lodge. They wait for me."

"You are wrong. They have grown weary of your pleas for peace, your stories about the good and generous Near River People. They have not forgotten that the Near River People cursed our fishing. Have you told them that the Near River daughters do not want you?" She raised her eyebrows and laughed. "No, of course not. What honor would you have in this village if they knew what the Near River People know?"

Had he been younger, less experienced in dealing with his mother, anger would have brought careless words from his mouth. He would have told her that the young hunters did not care about the honor he received—or did not receive—at the Near River Village. They were more interested in learning the secrets of winter den hunting. But he kept his mouth closed, his thoughts hidden. The less she knew, the better for everyone.

Of course, she had many ways of discovering what she wanted to know. Under the joy of her hands, a young man would soon answer any questions she asked. As a child, Chakliux had listened from his sleeping robes and even then recognized her cunning.

An old woman made her way to the hearth. When she saw K'os, she wrapped her arms around herself, as though to hold the edges of her parka away from K'os's touch. The woman pushed back her parka hood and dumped a handful of dried berries into one of the boiling bags. Chakliux approached her, held out his bowl. She raised her eyebrows and glanced at K'os, a smile lifting one corner of her mouth. She filled Chakliux's bowl. He walked away without looking at his mother, but he felt her eyes burn against his back.

"I have decided," Cloud Finder said. He and Chakliux were sitting at the back of the hunters' lodge, an honored place given to them by the younger men.

Chakliux held his breath, then let it out in disappointment as Cloud Finder said, "There is not enough. I cannot give my dogs for what you offer."

Chakliux fought against the anger that pushed foolish words into his mouth. Cloud Finder had said he understood, had seemed to want peace between the villages as much as Chakliux did. Why then would the man ask for more? Chakliux had nothing else. In three days of bargaining, he had even borrowed pelts from his father to add to the trade goods.

"My dogs belong not only to me but to everyone in this village," Cloud Finder said. "How can I give them to another village without asking something for other hunters besides myself?"

Chakliux held out empty hands. "You know I have offered all I have, even my extra boots. There is nothing else. You know my wife and son are dead, so I cannot promise a child to be given in marriage."

"I ask nothing more from you," Cloud Finder said. "What I want is from the Near River People."

Chakliux held the man's eyes with his own. He did not see greed but wisdom, and so waited for Cloud Finder to speak.

"The Near River People need our strong, golden-eyed dogs, but they also have something we need." He paused and turned his head to look at the men around them.

Each was busy doing something—smoothing a spear shaft, hafting a blade, retouching a spear point. Though their eyes were not on Chakliux and Cloud Finder, Chakliux knew they listened to what was being said, and that they would take the words they heard back to fathers and uncles and the women they courted, so soon the whole village would know.

"What animal is more honored than the bear?" Cloud Finder asked. "What animal has more power? Yet in late winter and early spring when our people long for fat meat, we cannot hunt bears because we cannot find them.

"The dogs are yours," he said, "the bitch and her five pups, for the trade goods and one other thing. You must take me with you to the Near River Village. While I am there, I will teach the Near River People how to care for my dogs, and their hunters will teach me how to find bears. Then I will come back and tell these young men." He lifted his chin toward the hunters on the other side of the fire.

Chakliux felt hope glow in his heart. It was a good plan, something that might work. He wished Tsaani were alive to share his knowledge, but Sok was a gifted hunter, and he had sent trade goods. One of the pups would be his. Perhaps he would be willing to teach Cloud Finder what Tsaani had taught him.

Cloud Finder was wise. Why not, when buying peace for your village, also do something to help yourself? He would come back with knowledge every hunter wanted. With just a few bear kills, he could claim the honor of being chief hunter. There was now no true chief hunter in the village. Chakliux's father, Ground Beater, still held the respect of most men, but other hunters brought in more meat. It was time for one man to be seen as chief, one man to take the place of honor.

"Yes," Chakliux said, and felt the young hunters move close to him. Their excitement was like something alive within the lodge walls.

"You will take me back with you?"

"I leave tomorrow."

"That soon," Cloud Finder said, then added, "I will be ready."

Chakliux nodded. If they did not return now, there would be no denned bears to find. The warm weather would draw them outside. Besides, it was best to go before his mother found out, best to keep the knowledge from her as long as possible. She would not want Cloud Finder as chief hunter. He did not visit her, so how could she twist him into her plans?

Of course, Chakliux had seen most of these young hunters enter his mother's lodge at one time or another. Best to keep them here for the night until he and Cloud Finder were on the trail to the Near River Village.

When Cloud Finder left the lodge, Chakliux stood, spoke. "Any man who is willing to learn the sacred songs and who carries respect in his heart can hunt denned bears," he said. "Stay here this night. I will teach you songs given to me by the chief bear hunter of the Near River People. Even as an old man, his strength was legend. When Cloud Finder returns to this village, you will be ready to learn what he has to teach you, then you can hunt."

Several men moved nervously. Chakliux knew they were the ones who wanted to fight the Near River People. Now they were being told to honor them by learning their songs, but most spoke in excited voices. They asked questions, and Chakliux answered in such a way that even the men with downcast eyes began to listen. So when Chakliux again offered to teach songs, all the men stayed, singing with him until they knew the words that Tsaani had taught Chakliux, grandfather to grandson.

*   *   *

Early in the morning Chakliux went to Cloud Finder's lodge. He was met at the entrance tunnel by Cloud Finder's daughter, Star. Chakliux had heard stories of her strangeness, that at times she seemed like a child too young to leave her mother, and at other times like a woman, wise in all ways.

Looking into her large eyes, Chakliux felt himself drawn to her.

Star leaned forward, whispered to Chakliux, "Take care of my father. He thinks he is still young. Even now, my mother hides herself in our lodge, ashamed of her tears."

"Your father is a wise man," Chakliux answered, allowing his eyes to linger on the girl's face, on her smooth skin, the pink flush of her cheeks. "His wisdom will ensure his safety, and probably mine also, but I will do whatever I can to protect him."

"I have heard the Near River women wear shell-beaded leggings," Star said.

Chakliux, surprised by her boldness, thought for a moment, trying to remember what the women wore. "Yes," he said, "some do." He looked down at Cloud Finder's daughter, again felt himself caught by her eyes. "If I have any trade goods left after dealing with your father," he said, "I will try to get some leggings for you."

She smiled, showing a dimple at the corner of her mouth. Then her father called from within the lodge, and she ducked inside. Cloud Finder came out. In his fur parka, he was as large as a bear. How had such a man made himself a small, beautiful daughter? Chakliux wondered. Then he pulled his mind from the girl and watched Cloud Finder fasten the dog Snow Hawk to Sok's sled.

Chakliux was pleased when he found that Cloud Finder had decided to trade Snow Hawk. She was strong, with a wide chest and well-formed legs. Unlike other dogs, she would pull a sled, never fighting against the harness. She had also just given birth to a litter of healthy pups.

Cloud Finder handed them to Chakliux. They were in pouches of caribou skin hung from a sling.

"Put them inside," Cloud Finder told him, pointing to Chakliux's chest. He draped the sling around Chakliux's neck and slid the pups down under his parka. They were still small, each no larger than Chakliux's hand. He felt their warm tongues against his skin as he settled them into place.

Cloud Finder strapped on his snowshoes, hoops of willow bound into a circle with a webbing of rawhide. They were longer and wider than the snowshoes Chakliux wore. He gave a command, and Snow Hawk leaned her weight into Sok's sled.

"Four females, one male," Cloud Finder said, pursing his lips toward the bulge of pups under Chakliux's parka.

Chakliux raised his eyebrows to show he understood. Four females, five counting Snow Hawk, and a male. And Cloud Finder to teach the Near River People how to raise strong dogs. A better trade than he had dared hope for.

Cloud Finder clasped Snow Hawk's harness as she pulled the sled past the dogs still tied in the lee of his wife's lodge. Snow Hawk raised her nose and howled. Chakliux looked nervously back toward K'os's lodge. It was on the other side of the village, but she was a woman of sharp ears. He leaned toward Snow Hawk, cupped his hand over her muzzle. Her howling stopped, but she pranced as Cloud Finder untied one of his larger male dogs.

"Big Neck," he said to Chakliux.

Chakliux remembered the dog. He had been the runt of a litter so large, the mother had trouble feeding them all. The owner had decided to kill the pup and add his meat to the village boiling bags, but Cloud Finder had seen the dog for his true worth, traded some small trinket for him. Now any man in the village would be proud to own Big Neck.

Big Neck carried his curled tail high, ears forward, and his feet danced as he met Snow Hawk. The dogs touched noses, then, responding to Cloud Finder's command, led the way from the village.

"They are anxious to meet the Near River dogs," Cloud Finder said, and laughed.

Chakliux smiled but did not speak his gladness. What could be better? They had Snow Hawk and her five pups. Perhaps while Cloud Finder was visiting the Near River Village, Big Neck would father litters to Near River females. Then even the young hunters would have to admit the generosity of the Cousin River People.

They walked through that day, stopping only to break away balls of snow that formed between the pads of the dogs' feet and to allow Snow Hawk to nurse her pups.

That night they made a fire with wood Cloud Finder had loaded on the sled. They ate the hardened fat, berry cakes and dried meat Cloud Finder's wife had packed for them, then tipped the sled up on its side, a break against the wind, a shelter for the fire, and spoke of times they had shared in the village.

Finally Cloud Finder asked, "Tell me about these Near River People. I have been in their village often, have bedded some of their women, but I do not know them like you do."

"They are hardworking people," Chakliux answered. "Their ways are much like ours. They are gifted hunters, but their dogs are not as good as ours, and their women are not as beautiful."

Cloud Finder laughed, his voice loud in the cold air. "You told me the shaman's daughter did not want you, but have you spoken for some other woman among them?" he asked.

"No," Chakliux answered. He had taken the pups from beneath his parka. They lay now on a bed of spruce branches covered with a caribou skin, nursing from their mother. He leaned over and stroked Snow Hawk's flank. He thought of Blueberry, but said, "I have no wife among them."

Cloud Finder did not speak, and Chakliux understood the man waited for an explanation. Finally Chakliux said, "There is something I must tell you, something I did not know myself until I visited the Near River Village." He straightened and turned to face Cloud Finder. "There is a woman in the Near River Village who claims me as son. She says she threw me away, left me for the wind because of my foot."

"So," Cloud Finder said, "to the Near River People you are not animal-gift. Do they see you as cursed?"

"Some of them. Others do not. They remember that I swim. They see my feet as proof of otter blood."

For a long time, Cloud Finder watched the flames of their fire, then he said, "That is how I see you, as otter. A man who works for peace is a good man, no matter who his mother is."

And Chakliux knew he did not refer to his Near River mother, but to K'os.

They awoke to storm, the dogs curled tightly against the wind, tails tucked over noses. They had allowed the pups to sleep with their mother for the night, and Chakliux crawled on hands and knees from the shelter of fur robes and crusted snow to check them.

The wind flung snow and ice, sharp as stone. He spoke to the dogs, though the storm whipped away his words. He did not want to startle Snow Hawk, face her teeth as she leapt to protect her young. But she did not move. Carefully, he slipped his hand into the mound of snow that covered her, trying not to dislodge it, knowing it held in her warmth, but she raised her head at his touch. He slipped his caribou hide mitten from his hand and worked his fingers down to Snow Hawk's belly.

He found the first pup, mouth tight on one of its mother's teats. The pup's heartbeat was strong against Chakliux's fingertips. He moved his hand over each pup. They were warm, dry and alive. He went back to his own place, tucked himself close to the upturned sled.

He felt a tug at his arm and responded to Cloud Finder's question.

"Snow Hawk and the pups are fine. I did not check Big Neck."

"He has seen many storms," Cloud Finder said. "Do not worry about him." He handed Chakliux a stick of dried meat. Chakliux clamped the end in his teeth and cut off a bite-sized piece with his sleeve knife. The taste of wood smoke warmed him as though he held a small hearth fire in his mouth.

The storm left them the next night, and they started out under the clear shine of stars. Snow Hawk seemed anxious, the bitch pulling against the sled harness until Chakliux allowed her to begin.

As they walked, Chakliux heard a crackling sound that came first to his spirit then to his ears. He looked back over his shoulder, toward the high dark sky of the north, smiled when he saw the yaykaas—the flashing sky—bend and shimmer in greens and pinks.

"See," Cloud Finder said, and lifted one arm toward the lights that moved like dancers above the earth. "Our ancestors tell us we do well. They are the grandfathers of both villages and do not want to see their children kill one another."

"Yes," Chakliux said. He felt the squirm of the pups beneath his parka and sudden strength filled his body. Whatever the Near River People thought about him, when they saw the dogs they could not deny that he tried to bring them something good.

He looked ahead to Snow Hawk. No dog in the Near River Village could match her, not even Tsaani's good bear dogs. She seemed to pull the sled with little effort. Big Neck walked beside her, head high, eyes scanning as though he alone were responsible for their safety.

Suddenly Big Neck stopped, lifted his nose into the air. Cloud Finder slapped an arm against Chakliux's shoulder and pointed with a mittened hand toward the dog. Chakliux nodded as Big Neck pranced in a nervous circle, then darted back to look behind them. The dog raised his nose again, growled low in his throat.

"Wolves," Cloud Finder said. "They will be hungry after that storm."

He spoke sharply to Big Neck. The dog whined, then rejoined them, moving in close to Snow Hawk. Snow Hawk glanced at him but kept pulling, cocking her head back now and again to look at Chakliux's chest, the bulge that was her pups. Cloud Finder motioned her forward without speaking, and she continued, but she began a high-pitched whine Chakliux could hear over the sound of the sled runners.

He leaned down close to the dog and said, "Do not worry. They are safe." But she continued to whine, and increased her speed so Chakliux nearly had to run to keep up with her.

"Slow her down," Cloud Finder called. "She will make us sweat."

Yes, Chakliux thought, knowing the sweat would form a thin layer of ice against their skin, enough to freeze them before they got to the Near River Village. He caught the back edge of the sled and held it until, under the pressure of his hands, Snow Hawk slowed. He turned to look back at Cloud Finder. Cloud Finder nodded at him, then lifted his left hand, showing Chakliux he had taken his sleeve knife from its sheath.

Sok had given Chakliux a long-bladed obsidian knife the morning he left the Near River Village; not for trade, Sok had told him, but as protection. Chakliux drew it now from the scabbard tied on the outside of his right calf. The black blade drew a nod of admiration from Cloud Finder.

"From my brother," Chakliux said.

"You would consider a trade?" Cloud Finder asked.

"I cannot."

"So one good thing has come of your visit to the Near Rivers," Cloud Finder said. "Your brother."

"Yes."

"Perhaps his knife will bring us luck against the wolves."

Big Neck stopped, turned to face whatever followed them. Finally Cloud Finder also stopped, squinted down the trail.

Chakliux continued to walk, and when Cloud Finder caught up with him, he asked, "Did you see anything?"

"Nothing, but do not put away your knife. We should walk as far as we can. Perhaps we can reach the Near River Village without stopping."

"What about the dogs?"

"It will be easier for them than for us," said Cloud Finder, and tried to laugh, but his laughter was hollow under the dome of the night sky.

It is too far, Chakliux thought, already feeling the ache in his foot, already hearing Cloud Finder's ragged breathing. If he had two strong feet, if Cloud Finder was thin, agile, they might make it, but, no, not as they were. They would have to stop and face the wolves.

They walked through the night and on into the day, the sun glaring through the slits of their caribou antler snow goggles, and they continued to walk once the sun had set. Still they had not reached the Near River, so that Chakliux wondered if somehow, in the storm, they had begun to circle, losing themselves on the tundra. At least the dogs were no longer skittish. The wolves, Chakliux decided, must have grown weary of following them.

Finally they stopped. Even the dogs moved with stiff legs. Chakliux's eyes burned from the day of sun on snow, and in the dark all things seemed spotted with slits of light so he could not be sure of what he saw. His hands, now accustomed to Snow Hawk's harness, worked without the help of his eyes to unfasten the dog. He reached into his parka to give her the pups for feeding, but she leapt away as Cloud Finder threw out pieces of dog salmon for her and Big Neck.

Chakliux dug down to bare ground, then spread a layer of spruce branches and laid out wood for a fire. He took fireweed fluff and shreds of dried birchbark from a packet hung at his neck and set it around a piece of notched wood, then took out his fire bow. He twisted the string around the twirling stick, set the stick into the notched wood, then pressed his chin against the cup at the top of the stick. He used the bow to twist and untwist the string, twirling the stick until movement and pressure made heat strong enough to create fire. The flames caught the fireweed fluff, then spread to the bark and wood.

Cloud Finder squatted beside him on his haunches and fed the fire patiently until they had a blaze, then he set a tripod over it and hung a small boiling bag, a stew made by Cloud Finder's wife. During their journey it had frozen in the bag. Cloud Finder had almost left it, telling Chakliux they had enough dried meat and berry cakes to keep them. Now, after walking that long day and most of the night before, after waiting through two days of storm, Chakliux was glad for the chance to eat hot food. Both men scooped snow into their wooden bowls and set the bowls at the edge of the fire so the snow would melt into water.

Chakliux began to see better, and so felt himself relax, the tension in his shoulders and back subsiding to a pulsing ache. If they had been followed by wolves, he thought, they would attack now, in darkness, but the dogs showed no signs of nervousness, Snow Hawk nursing her pups, Big Neck asleep. Of course, the fire would help keep wolves away, but, he reminded himself, the smell of food would draw them. He had slipped his knife into its sheath when they stopped to make camp, but had thrust his spear point-up in the snow, within easy reach.

He poked at the snow in his bowl until it melted. He drank, then waited as Cloud Finder dipped his bowl into the boiling bag and filled it with stew. Chakliux filled his own bowl. They were still eating when Big Neck raised his head and growled.

The dog stood, his legs stiff, the fur on his back bristled. Chakliux grabbed his spear and jumped to his feet.

A shout came from the darkness, the voice of a man.

Cloud Finder threw back his head and laughed. "River Jumper, you always know when there is food!"

River Jumper came into the light of the fire, and Chakliux, too, grinned.

"You have been following us?" Chakliux asked.

"Ah, my wife, she threw me out again," he said, his face only a dark circle tucked back in the ruff of his parka. "I had to come this far to get fed!"

Cloud Finder dipped his bowl into the boiling bag and held it out to the man. "So that is what happened to our wolves," he said. "They were following us. They must have smelled you coming behind and left our trail. They are smart enough not to be caught between two groups of hunters."

River Jumper took the bowl from Cloud Finder. "I saw their tracks," he said. "There were five of them."

"It was good they did not turn and attack you," said Cloud Finder. "You should not have come alone. It is a dangerous trail for a man without friends."

River Jumper lifted his bowl of meat toward Chakliux. "This young one made it. I knew I could, too. I thought, though, that I would catch you before this. I want to help you make a good deal with the Near Rivers. They are a people of smooth words." He laughed. "But so am I."

Chakliux laid down his spear, picked up his bowl and stepped outside the circle of firelight. He drew his sleeve knife from its sheath and cut at the hardened snow. He knew River Jumper must be thirsty.

He heard Cloud Finder laugh, and River Jumper's loud voice, then a muffled sound, as though something fell into the snow. He turned, the bowl in one hand, his sleeve knife in the other.

At first he did not understand what he saw: River Jumper stood with a knife in his hand. Blood dripped from the blade. Chakliux dropped his bowl, crouched, looking for the wolves he thought had attacked. Then he saw Cloud Finder crumpled in a heap near the fire, and he realized there were no wolves. Only River Jumper.

Snow Hawk backed away, several pups trying to keep their hold on her teats. Chakliux nearly called to her, but then did not. Why draw River Jumper's attention?

Big Neck growled, and River Jumper turned to face him. The man shouted, and Big Neck attacked. River Jumper met him with Cloud Finder's spear, thrusting it into the dog's belly as he leapt. The dog yelped and fell. He cried out when he hit the ground, then was silent.

River Jumper pulled the spear free of Big Neck's body. Snow Hawk placed herself between the man and her pups, her ears flat against her head, her teeth bared.

"Do not worry, little mother," River Jumper said. "I will not hurt you." He bent slowly and picked up Chakliux's spear. Then he stood, lifted both weapons and called out.

"Your mother, K'os, sends her greetings."

Chapter
Eleven

"Why?" Chakliux shouted at River Jumper, and lifted one hand toward Cloud Finder. The man lay on the ground, his blood seeping into the snow.

"Look! What do I see?" River Jumper said, his answer coming in the familiar form of a riddle. "The winter grows old and in anger sends the wind."

"You are the wind?" Chakliux asked.

River Jumper laughed. "You honor me," he said, and shook his head. "You are a child, Chakliux. Do not try to understand."

Snow Hawk stood beside her pups, her eyes moving from Chakliux to the spears in River Jumper's hands. She crouched, and Chakliux saw the muscles in her flanks ripple. He knew Snow Hawk; he had watched her among the village dogs. She would fight to the death, but not for him. He had not yet earned such loyalty. She would fight for her pups. She would go for River Jumper's throat, even after seeing Cloud Finder and Big Neck killed.

Chakliux shifted the sleeve knife to his left hand and carefully drew the obsidian blade from his leg sheath. It was a fine knife, well-balanced, and he was good with knives, but who could say whether knives made in the Near River Village carried the same vision as those he had grown up with. Each weapon, like each man, was different. He set his eyes on the triangle beneath River Jumper's chin, the gap left by the ruff of his parka hood. That soft and vulnerable spot.

Snow Hawk growled, a low rumbling in her throat. River Jumper's eyes moved to the animal. In that brief moment, Chakliux pulled back his arm and threw.

He saw the surprise in River Jumper's face, then heard the hiss from the man's throat, saw the bubbling of blood. River Jumper's arms dropped, and he released the spears. Then, before Chakliux could stop her, Snow Hawk attacked the man, carrying him to the ground with her weight, sinking her teeth into his throat and ripping away flesh.

Chakliux called to her and she stopped, standing over River Jumper, her mouth dripping blood.

"Get away," he said, his voice loud but controlled. "Leave him."

She bared her teeth, guarding her kill.

Chakliux stepped carefully around her to the bed of spruce branches where her pups were huddled. One by one he picked them up and set them in the snow. The smallest, a black-and-white female, began to whimper.

Snow Hawk looked down at River Jumper's body. She lifted her head to growl at Chakliux, then went to her pups.

Chakliux stood still as Snow Hawk moved the pups back to the spruce bed, then he walked slowly past River Jumper's body to Cloud Finder.

He has to be dead, Chakliux told himself. No one can survive a spear in the chest. But to Chakliux's surprise, Cloud Finder's eyes fluttered open. Chakliux felt the beginning of hope. Perhaps the spear had been deflected by some weapon Cloud Finder had hidden under his parka. Then Cloud Finder tried to speak. Blood foamed from his mouth, and Chakliux's hope died. "Go," Cloud Finder said, choking on the word.

"No," said Chakliux. He knelt beside Cloud Finder and pulled up the man's parka, trying to find the wound, to stanch the welling blood.

"Fool!" Cloud Finder said. "River Jumper . . . would not come . . . alone. Others . . . out there . . ." His words were lost in a spasm of choking.

Chakliux lifted Cloud Finder's head to ease his breathing. He loosened the parka hood, pulled it away from the man's throat.

"Go!" Cloud Finder said again. "Do not stop until . . ." He took a long, shuddering breath. "Leave me," he whispered. "I am dead."

A high, thin keening rose into the air, and Chakliux realized it was Snow Hawk. She lay with her pups, but her eyes were on Cloud Finder.

"Bring my dog," Cloud Finder whispered, then reached out toward Big Neck.

Chakliux gathered the dog's body in his arms and laid him beside Cloud Finder. Cloud Finder curled his fingers into the thick fur, and looking up at Chakliux tried to smile. "Go," he said one last time.

Snow Hawk walked with her ears flat, neck fur bristled. He had left the sled—it would only slow them—and carried a small pack with few supplies.

Chakliux had taken Cloud Finder's sleeve knife from its sheath and placed it in the man's right hand, but when he was finally ready to leave, Cloud Finder was already dead.

Chakliux threw River Jumper's spear far into the dark of the night. He did not fit it into his spearthrower before he threw. Why risk that the spear would carry River Jumper's evil into Chakliux's own hunting supplies, to his thrower and blades and spears. But he did not want to leave the weapon for those who followed. He had traded away all but one of his own spears at the Cousin River Village, so decided to take Cloud Finder's spear with him.

He told himself the Near River could not be far. Chakliux wondered whether he should walk the river ice or follow the animal trails through the snow and brush of the banks. He was less likely to be seen in the brush, but the trees would slow him. He would not reach the village by morning, and in daylight his tracks would be easy to follow. If he walked the river, he might arrive at the village by morning, before they could catch him. Besides, there was a good chance the other men would stop for the night. It was a dangerous thing, walking in darkness.

Yes, Chakliux decided, they had probably stopped for the night, and sent River Jumper ahead to scout out Chakliux's camp. Perhaps by the time they decided to see why River Jumper had not returned, Chakliux would already be at the Near River Village.

Snow Hawk growled, but Chakliux told himself that dogs did not know everything. Perhaps she only growled at the wind.

He pulled his parka hood close around his eyes, still felt the aching cold of the night air against the bridge of his nose. "The winter grows old," he thought, remembering River Jumper's riddle. His mother had sent them. Perhaps she had even been the one who urged their old shaman, He Talks, to offer Chakliux as husband to Wolf-and-Raven's daughter. Even if Day Woman had not realized Chakliux was her son, it would take only a whisper to the right person for someone in the Near River Village to discover who he was—a curse given back to the Near River People. She might have been the one who had Tsaani killed.

But why? Perhaps she needed to know she could still control the young men, could make them fight or die at her whim.

Until Gguzaakk's death, he had been blind to the immensity of K'os's depravity. Gguzaakk had tried to tell him, but when did a man listen to what his wife said about his mother? Those were women things, a foolishness that men did not trouble themselves to understand. Even after Gguzaakk and their son had died, he did not want to believe. . . .

"My mother," Chakliux said aloud, so that Snow Hawk cocked her head and looked up at him. "My mother." He spat out the words, flinging them away.

"My mother is Day Woman," he said to the night. "My people are the Near River People. I am a hunter of the Near River Village. Not animal-gift, not Dzuuggi." He whispered it to the green light that spread undulating fingers into the north sky. Then he turned and said the same words south toward the Near River.

A hunter. What man needs to be more than that?

The night cold seeped into his joints, making his steps stiff and awkward. His knees groaned like trees in wind. He stopped to break the ice balls from between the pads of Snow Hawk's feet. She sniffed at the front of his parka.

"Not yet," he told the dog. "Not yet. Soon."

Then he saw the thin edge of darkness against the snow, the trees that marked the winding path of the river. The sight gave strength to his legs, and he began to walk more quickly. Snow Hawk seemed to sense his excitement and broke into a run, but he reached out, grasped her tail, slowed her to a walk. In cold like this, he could not risk running.

They worked their way through the brush until they came to a path made by animals, a gentle incline to the river. The river ice was solid beneath his feet and covered with a hard crust of wind-polished snow. Chakliux removed his snowshoes. The snow was hard enough to hold him without them. He strapped the shoes on his back and began to walk. The ache of his otter foot eased. It was good to be on the river. Even Snow Hawk moved with more assurance, as though she had followed the river before, as though she knew where it led.

Chakliux looked up. In summer, at this time of the night, the sky would be light, but now the sun still hid its face, ashamed, the elders said, at allowing the winter to stay with The People for so long. By the time he reached the village, the sun would be up, traveling its curve in the sky. He had a long walk yet, but was close enough to hope that if Cousin River men were following, they would turn back rather than risk facing Near River hunters.

He did not see the overflow until it was too late. He heard it first—the brittle song of the ice beneath his feet. The water must have oozed up through a crack during the day to flood the ice, then froze to slush. A man who walked through it would get wet, and unless he acted quickly, his feet would freeze.

Chakliux had known hunters who had done such a thing, remembered their suffering. Usually, even if toes and heels were cut away, the rot brought a slow and painful death. Those who survived, like old Net Maker, were crippled, a burden to The People when they moved to fish camp or followed the caribou.

But sometimes the ice gave warning, as it had for him, a voice that would save a hunter if he listened well enough, if he kept walking and did not stop. He quickened his pace, setting his feet carefully and pushing Snow Hawk ahead. It was a large flow. Many were only a few steps across, but this one spread the width of the river.

Then, ahead, he saw the clear dark of solid ice where wind had swept away the snow. Ice—or a crack where water shone through. Ice, he told himself. Ice, not water, then took two quick steps and jumped.

Ice, solid, hard. Ice under his otter foot. But his good foot, the foot he had pushed with as he jumped, broke through on that thrust and was wet, soaked and cold.

Snow Hawk was beside him, nosing his parka, a high, thin whine coming from her throat. He looked down at the dog, then knelt to break the snow from her feet. As he worked with her front feet, he held his mind blank, as if he could change what had happened by refusing to think about it. He set down one front paw, lifted the other. Both paws were dry.

If you do not stop, you will die, he thought, the words coming to him as though spoken by someone else. And it is not a good way to die.

"A man always has his knife," Chakliux answered. "I can live without a foot."

Besides, what choice did he have? If he stopped, made a fire, dried his foot and boot, the men from the Cousin River Village would catch him. What chance did he have against them? They would kill him, take Snow Hawk and the pups, and there would be no hope of peace. Many men would die, women and children also. What was his life compared to so many?

"We go, Snow Hawk," he told the dog as he set down her front paw and pulled up her left rear foot.

The dog whined again. Chakliux ran his fingers over the thick fur that padded the foot. He lifted the other back foot and then again, both of the front.

"You, too," he finally said, and gently squeezed each of her back paws. They were wet.

Chakliux walked until the slope of the bank grew shallow, then he led Snow Hawk up through the brush to a clear place, the snow scoured into a hard shining crust. He cut spruce boughs and willow, used his sleeve knife to break branches open to the dry heartwood. He started a fire and fed it carefully, then rummaged through his pack. He had a few hare pelts. He took off his boot and wrapped his foot with the pelts. He set the boot near the fire and watched the water steam from it.

Snow Hawk hunched herself into a ball and began to lick one of her back feet. Chakliux took a piece of caribou hide from his pack. He used it on her other foot, rubbing until the fur felt dry under his fingers. When both feet were dry, he pulled her pups from the sling and let her nurse them, then he put them under his parka again.

He turned his boot, moving it closer to the fire, rubbing it as he had rubbed Snow Hawk's feet, then he ate, sharing his dried meat with the dog. He ate quickly, then rubbed his boot one last time. It was not dry, but he did not want to wait longer. His foot at least was warm; perhaps walking would keep it from freezing before he arrived at the Near River Village.

He rewrapped the foot in a hare pelt and tied it snug at his ankle with a length of babiche. As he reached for his boot, Snow Hawk growled. He pulled the long knife from its sheath on his calf, moved his head slowly to look at her. Her ears were pricked forward.

"Men, not wolves?" Chakliux asked softly.

Snow Hawk lay her head again on her paws, her eyes open wide to stare out into the darkness. Chakliux stood and moved in a slow circle, looking away from the fire until his eyes adjusted to the night. He saw nothing.

Working quickly, he scored the hardened snow with his knife and dug into it with both mittened hands.

Snow Hawk lifted her head to watch as he mounded the snow into a heap and covered it with a hare fur blanket from his pack. Yes, he thought. It could be a man. If you believed it was. He fed more sticks into the fire, then picked up his and Cloud Finder's spears and backed away. He stepped carefully into the tracks he had made when he came from the river, until he reached a dense cover of brush. Snow Hawk stood as though to follow him, but he commanded her to stay. She lay down, nose pointing to the place he was hidden.

Chakliux wrapped his arms around his legs and did not let himself feel the cold seep up from the ground into the bottom of his wrapped foot. The hare fur was not enough to keep his foot from freezing, but for a while it would be all right. Especially if he stood now and again to shift his weight.

Like all young men, from the time he was a baby Chakliux had been set out naked for a few moments during freezing nights to harden his body. He knew how to fight the cold. He moved his fingers and toes, pulled his parka ruff close around his eyes, and let his mind drift to other things.

He had tucked his spearthrower up his left sleeve. It seemed warm against his skin, as though it were lending strength to his body. Chakliux had made the thrower himself—as most men did—to fit his own hand. He had carved a hollow in the underside so it lay comfortably against the pad of flesh at the base of his thumb. His first finger extended under the thrower and up into a hole; his thumb curled over one side of the thrower, his remaining three fingers over the other.

The spear lay in a groove at the top, the point aimed at the target. The weapon was held with the arm raised, hand extended back, opposite the direction the spear would be thrown. With the thrower, Chakliux could cast his spear farther and with more force.

The night passed slowly. Finally Chakliux turned to look toward the eastern sky. Was it his imagination or had the sky lightened? He stood, then saw the sudden snapping of Snow Hawk's head, heard the growl. Chakliux's fingers tightened on his spear, and he reached down to pull his obsidian knife from its sheath.

Their spears came quickly, two of them, slicing into the fur-wrapped snow at the side of the fire. Snow Hawk leapt to her feet as four men entered the narrow ring of firelight.

Night Man and Tikaani, Caribou and Stalker—Cloud Finder's sons. For a moment Chakliux nearly called out to them, but then he remembered that he had seen each of them at his mother's lodge. Were they acting on K'os's instructions? If so, they might think he had killed both River Jumper and their father.

The four men advanced slowly toward the fur-wrapped bundle. Chakliux wished he had taken time to make it more lifelike, a mitten or a bit of hair sticking out. Snow Hawk stood, still growling.

Night Man prodded the bundle with one toe, then groaned and pulled the blanket away from the heap of snow.

He lifted his voice and called out, "Chakliux, we came because that hunter you killed said you planned to kill our father. We mourn both men. We will kill you and anyone who claims you as friend!"

"Even this dog will die," the brother named Stalker said. He turned so his back was toward Chakliux, lifted his spear as though to thrust it into Snow Hawk's chest.

Snow Hawk growled and crouched, teeth bared.

"Cloud Finder, my friend," Chakliux whispered. "Forgive what I do."

He pulled out his spearthrower and fitted the notched end of his spear into the flat chip of ivory that held it in place. He raised it over his shoulder and threw. The spear landed with a quiet thud in the center of Stalker's back. The man sank to his knees with a groan. His brothers moved slowly, as if they could not believe what their eyes told them.

Chakliux fitted Cloud Finder's spear into his throwing board and threw again. His throw was high, taking Night Man in the right shoulder. Night Man cried out and spun, then fell writhing.

Snow Hawk began to bark, her yips high and frantic. "Shut your mouth, dog!" Night Man shouted, pain edging his voice. He pulled the spear from his shoulder, then fell back with the weapon still in his hands.

Chakliux knew as soon as he threw that he had aimed too high, but he had hoped the spear would wedge itself into the bone of Night Man's shoulder. It had not. Night Man had dislodged it too easily.

Night Man stood, using the shaft of Cloud Finder's spear to push himself to his feet. He coughed and gagged, retching into the snow. He spat, then tried to speak, but could not. For a moment Chakliux wanted to turn away, to run. They were boys, all of them. They had come, probably at his mother's urging, thinking to protect their father, to kill and find honor in killing. Until this night, Chakliux had never killed a man. It was not like taking an animal for meat. What animal taken did not give itself willingly? The People made songs and dances, praises and prayers. The animals' spirits understood and accepted such things as gifts, then they returned the next year to give themselves again, and to receive again.

In killing a man, what was gained? Were gifts given? Were children fed?

"Chakliux!" Tikaani called out. "You think we will allow you to live when you have killed our father?"

Chakliux did not move. He had thrown both spears and now had only knives to defend himself. What chance did he have? There were two of them. Three, if Night Man was not hurt too badly. Even Snow Hawk had moved to stand beside them, her teeth bared as she looked into the heavy brush of trees and shrubs where Chakliux hid. At least he had the darkness. If he stood still, did not move or call out, they would not know where he was until dawn.

Besides, they did not know all his spears were gone. They jumped at each gust of wind, each scratch of branches.

Night Man sat down beside the fire and pressed a handful of snow into the bloody rent in his parka.

"He can see you there, by the fire," Caribou said to his brother.

"He sees all of us," said Tikaani. He pulled his spear from the hare fur blanket. "He thinks we are fools," he said.

"We have been fools," said Caribou. He moved away from the fire so Chakliux could see only the white trim at the shoulders of his parka, two white lines moving in the darkness. "You spend a night in K'os's bed, then are ready to do whatever she says," Caribou continued, "to believe whatever she tells you. You think the Near River People sent Chakliux to curse us? If that is true then why did K'os raise him? She is the curse, not her son. You know what the women say. I have heard our mother whisper it—that K'os killed Chakliux's wife, that she did not want her cousin to have a child when she herself could not. Our father is dead, and our brother!"

"And was it a woman's knife that killed them?" Tikaani snarled. "It was Chakliux's own spear. Yet you blame K'os. Forget about her. Now is the time to kill this one who brings death to many. I think he has no more spears. Otherwise, he would have finished off Night Man. He is an easy target, sitting beside the fire."

Night Man began to whimper, and Tikaani turned on him, ripping back the man's parka hood to slap his face. Night Man drew his sleeve knife and held it point up until Tikaani turned away.

"Chakliux is probably already upriver toward his village," Caribou called to them from the darkness. "It is not far to the Near River People. While you two fight, he gets away."

"I think you do not want to kill him," Tikaani said, and also left the circle of light, walking into the darkness until Chakliux could not see where he had gone. "We must finish what we have started or all the men of the Near River Village will hunt for us. They will know who we are by our boot tracks alone."

Yes, Chakliux thought. The Near River women made boots with double soles, crimped at the front with seams sewn closer to the bottom of the boot. In soft snow, a man would know whether tracks had been left by Near River hunters or men from the Cousin River Village.

"They will know by our dead brother," Tikaani said.

"You think I will leave my brother?" Caribou asked from the darkness.

Chakliux shifted and moved his head, trying to see where the voice came from. The man seemed to be moving toward him. Chakliux stepped back carefully, slowly, so he would make no sound. If he could get to the river, sneak along the bank, perhaps he could put enough distance between himself and the men. They would not come much farther. The Near River Village was too close. There was even a chance that Snow Hawk would follow him to the village. He had her pups.

He reached into his parka, rubbed his hand over the pups' heads, then stroked his fingers on a tree trunk. He took several more steps, then stopped again, listened.

He heard the knife before he saw it, the hiss of the blade as it sliced toward him. He felt the scrape of the point as it cut into his chest, then heard the high thin cry of one of the pups. He pulled out the knife, then lunged forward with it in his left hand, his own knife in his right. Arms came at him from the darkness, and he felt the knife in his left hand bite into flesh. He heard a harsh intake of breath, then the arms were twisted away, and the knife as well. He slashed out with the blade in his right hand, but it was deflected by branches.

Chakliux stepped back and tripped. He fell into a tangle of willow and lost his knife, but he leapt up to meet his attacker. It was Caribou. He was a short, powerful man, stronger than Chakliux, and smarter than his brothers.

Caribou had a knife. Chakliux clasped his fingers around Caribou's wrist, but Caribou ripped at Chakliux's parka hood with his free hand until he could reach in, press a thumb against Chakliux's throat. Chakliux's arms begin to weaken as his breath was cut off, then he was borne in a rush to the ground, breaking off tree branches as he fell, snow closing over his head as the weight of Caribou's body pressed him down. Then he heard a snarl. Snow Hawk.

In falling, Chakliux's grip had tightened on Caribou's wrist. Now, as Caribou fought to turn toward the dog, to move his knife to slash at her, Chakliux dug his thumbnails into the man's wrist, pressing until Caribou finally dropped the knife.

Chakliux released the arm, raised his legs to push Caribou away, then raked his fingers through the snow until he found the knife.

Chakliux picked it up and, in one quick movement, thrust the blade into the soft skin under the man's jaw. A spurt of blood poured over his fingers, slicked his hands so that the knife slipped, fell into the parka hood. Then Snow Hawk was ripping at the man's throat, and Caribou's cries stopped.

Chakliux searched for his own knives, finally found the obsidian blade buried in the snow where Caribou first attacked him. He leaned against a tree, fighting to catch his breath, and peered out toward the fire. Only Stalker was still there, the man lying facedown in the snow. Chakliux's spear was gone.

Where were Tikaani and Night Man? he wondered. On the way back to their village or waiting for him in the darkness?

Chapter Twelve

THE NEAR RIVER VILLAGE

Ghaden reached out and patted the mound of sleeping robes beside him. He worked his fingers down through the blankets until he found Yaa's face. She was asleep. Otherwise she would have taken his hand, held it.

She was his mother now, a good mother. She told him stories and played games, and when his side began to ache, she rubbed his back. She never yelled at him like Brown Water did, but still, he missed his first mother, missed her so much that at times he could do nothing but cry.

Yaa did not know his other mother's songs and did not know the secret words she had taught him—First Men words that he was not supposed to say to other people.

Sometimes, too, Yaa did not seem big enough to be a mother. She could not bring him food whenever he wanted it. Mostly she had to sneak it from the boiling bag when Brown Water was not watching. And her lap was small so that when she held Ghaden, he always felt as if he was about to slip off. But he would rather have her as mother than Brown Water. She was even better than Happy Mouth. So he tried to hold in his tears and not think about his other mother. Mostly, he cried when Yaa was outside. Then he would remember what happened to his first mother and worry that someone might hurt Yaa, too. Who would be his mother if that happened?

He clasped one of Yaa's long braids, put his thumb into his mouth and rubbed the braid across his eyelids. It was soft and smelled of wood smoke. Ghaden felt the tears build in his throat until they almost choked him.

It was better here than in the shaman's lodge. He had Yaa, and the old grandmother Ligige' did not come as often. He knew that Ligige' was only trying to make him better, but her teas tasted bad, and when she had to put medicine on the knife wound in his back, it stung. She made him cough, and that hurt. If he cried, she called him a baby and told him he must be strong like a man. He knew she was right. He must be strong, but sometimes it was hard to pretend that something did not hurt or did not taste bad.

Once, he had asked her for some medicine to take away the inside pain. He was not sure what that pain was from. Perhaps the knife had cut something deep in his chest that did not show from the outside.

Ligige' had felt him all over, thumping his bones with hard, wrinkled fingers, and pressing her ear to him, front and back. Finally she said there was nothing wrong, nothing that needed her medicine. But even though the pain of the knife wound gradually went away, this inside pain stayed, hurting and hurting all the time.

After a while, Ghaden decided that Ligige' knew the pain was there, but that she did not have any medicine for it. He asked Wolf-and-Raven to make chants for him, but even that did not help. One day when Wolf-and-Raven's wife was playing the throwing bones game with him, the pain went away, just for a little while, and that made Ghaden hope that it would not be with him forever. Still, it hurt most of the time, especially at night or when he was alone.

He sighed and brushed the end of Yaa's braid against his nose. The pain eased just a little. Ghaden closed his eyes and tried to sleep, the braid clutched tightly in his hand.

The tug at her hair woke her. Yaa smiled. She lay still until she heard Ghaden's breathing soften into the rhythm of sleep, then she turned carefully, so she would not pull the braid from his hands.

Old Ligige' had invited Brown Water to come to her lodge in the morning. The boy was nearly well, Ligige' had said. She did not need to see him every day. She would teach Brown Water to give him his medicines.

To Yaa's surprise, after Ligige' left, Brown Water had asked her to come also. "You are the one who will care for the boy," she said. "You should hear all these instructions. I do not have time for such things."

Yaa had hugged her happiness to herself. If she smiled too much, Brown Water might change her mind. Besides, everyone in the lodge was still in mourning for Yaa's father. Yaa herself often found she needed to slip away to her animal den and cry, remembering her father's gentle ways, without others to see her tears.

Yaa pressed herself close to Ghaden. He was lying on his back, his face lit with the soft gold light of the hearth coals. His cheeks were becoming round and fat again, and his black lashes lay dark against his skin. Already, though he was still little more than a baby, the bone of his nose had a small hump in the center. Like the trader's nose, Yaa thought, remembering the man's face.

Then an idea came to her: the trader was probably Ghaden's father. He had brought Daes to the village. Yaa had been just a little girl when they came, but she remembered. That was why he came each year to see Daes and Ghaden, and probably why Daes sneaked out of the lodge to visit him. It was also why she put up with the blows Brown Water gave her for doing such a thing.

Though Wolf-and-Raven told everyone that some angered spirit had killed Daes and the old man Tsaani, some of the women still believed the trader did it. Yaa had heard them whisper about him around the village cooking hearths, but why would a man try to kill his own son? Why would he kill his son's mother? He always brought Daes and Ghaden presents. Sometimes he gave Yaa gifts as well, and told her to watch over Ghaden, to be a good sister to her little brother. If he was so concerned about his son, why would he hurt him or his mother?

She thought back to the night Daes was killed. Something had awakened her. A sound, she was sure. Perhaps it was Daes or Ghaden crying out, but she had been dreaming and had thought at the time the noise was part of her dream.

Her dreams had been about River Ice Dancer. He was teasing her, a throwing stick in his hand. A throwing stick. Yes. And it had suddenly turned into . . . what? A bola. He was swinging it. The stones made a wide circle, whirling up over his head, then arcing down toward the ground. Suddenly the stones were not stones but bits of antler, clacking together. Clacking in a rhythm like a person walking, the sound of a person with caribou hoof rattlers on the tops of his boots. Yes, ceremonial boots, worn in dances.

Many men had caribou rattlers on their dance boots, but this sound was a little different. It was the sound of rattlers, but something more . . . something more.

The effort to remember made Yaa's head throb.

Ghaden groaned and turned. Yaa pulled her hands from the warmth of her bedding furs and tugged the boy into the circle of her arms.

Was there a chance Ghaden had been awake when his mother was attacked? Yaa wondered. If not, surely the attack itself would have awakened him. Did he remember anything?

Even if he did, he probably would not have told Wolf-and-Raven or Ligige'. He had always been shy, but perhaps he would speak to Yaa, and then she might be able to figure out who had killed Daes.

The killer had to be someone strong. He had not only killed Daes but also Tsaani. Tsaani was an old man, but he was still a hunter. Surely he would have fought to save his own life.

Then Yaa thought of something that made her bones cold. What if the killer were afraid Ghaden would remember?

In Wolf-and-Raven's lodge, Ghaden had been safe. Who would try to kill in a shaman's lodge? But here, with only women and children, the killer would have no one to stop him. Yaa's heart beat hard under her ribs.

If I were old enough, she thought, I would marry a strong young man and bring him here to this lodge to protect us all. But no girl of seven summers was old enough to marry.

The best chance was for Yaa's mother or Brown Water to marry, but no one would want Brown Water. She was too old, and she was cross all the time. Someone might want Yaa's mother. At least as second wife, but she had to wait out mourning before a man could take her. How long was that? Yaa could not remember. One moon, maybe two.

Until then, their best protection was for Yaa to find out who had killed Daes and tell everyone. Tomorrow, when her mother and Brown Water were outside, she would talk to Ghaden. Perhaps he would tell her.

In the morning, Yaa did not want to leave Ghaden. Her fears of the night pressed heavily against her, and she imagined a man with a knife slashing his way into the lodge.

Yaa told herself that the killer would not do such a thing during the day when everyone could see him, but still she felt uneasy. She told her mother to watch Ghaden, to stay with him. She told her so many times that Brown Water finally gave her an openhanded cuff to the head and pulled her out of the lodge.

Tears stung her eyes, but Yaa blinked them back. Brown Water's cuff had not hurt that much, but the fear in Ghaden's eyes as he watched her leave seemed like a knife twisting in her heart. She followed Brown Water over the narrow village paths to Ligige''s lodge, then sat like a shadow at Brown Water's side.

Ligige' and Brown Water first spoke politely of unimportant things, then Ligige' served them bowls of broth from the small boiling bag that hung from her lodge poles. Finally when they had eaten, Ligige' began laying out herbs and bits of dried things, twigs and powders— alder bark shredded, boiled and cooled to lay over the wound site, yellow root for strength, the inner bark of willow for fever.

As she explained how to use each medicine, she often looked into Yaa's eyes, so Yaa knew the old woman understood she would be the one who gave the medicine, she would be the one responsible.

Finally the session ended and they walked back to Brown Water's lodge. Everything was just as they had left it. There were no slashes in the lodge walls, no blood or bodies lying outside.

See, you are foolish, Yaa told herself, and followed Brown Water into the entrance tunnel. But Brown Water stopped at the end of the tunnel, blocking Yaa inside. The woman made a strange choking noise in her throat, and Yaa felt her arms suddenly grow weak with fear.

"You should have told me you were coming," Brown Water said, then she asked, "Where is Happy Mouth?"

Yaa reached out to push against Brown Water, and the woman crawled aside, allowing Yaa into the lodge. Yaa's fear left with a suddenness that almost made her collapse to the floor. It was the elder Blue-head Duck. He was squatting on his haunches beside Ghaden. In his hands was a small brown-and-white puppy. Ghaden was smiling. He began to giggle as the puppy leaned forward to lick his nose.

"It is my puppy," Ghaden told Yaa, then looked seriously into Brown Water's face and said, "Mother, it is my dog. This grandfather says he will teach me to take care of it."

"Happy Mouth went to bring food from the hearth," Blue-head Duck said to Brown Water. "She will be back soon."

Brown Water nodded, threw back the hood of her parka, and gestured for Yaa to untie several water bladders. Yaa set the basket of Ligige''s medicines near her folded sleeping mats and hurried to do as Brown Water said.

What if Blue-head Duck had been the killer? she thought as she offered one of the bladders to him. With a puppy in his arms, who would have suspected him? He could have killed Ghaden and left before her mother returned.

Blue-head Duck took a long drink, then, lowering the bladder, looked at Brown Water. "This pup is from strong stock," he said. "He will be a good dog for hunting and for carrying. He should be kept inside."

Inside, Yaa thought in surprise. Who ever kept a dog inside? She looked at Brown Water, expecting her to explode in anger. Even an elder could not order a woman to keep a dog in her lodge.

But Brown Water did not grow angry. Instead she looked long and thoughtfully at the puppy. "It has a loud bark?" she asked.

"Yes."

"It will be a good dog for this lodge."

Then Yaa understood that she was not the only one who thought Ghaden was in danger.

Ghaden wadded the strip of hide into a ball and threw it. The puppy bounded after it, barking. Ghaden knew they were making too much noise. If Brown Water had been in the lodge, she would have scolded them, but he and Yaa and his new puppy were alone.

He was going to name the dog Biter, though he had told no one yet. When Biter grew up he would be a big dog with long, strong teeth, and everyone would be afraid of him. If Biter had been with them that night, he probably would have saved Ghaden's first mother.

The pup was light brown, with darker fur around his eyes. He had a little white spot, like a star, on his chin and a white chest and belly.

"What are you going to call him?" Yaa asked.

Ghaden looked into Yaa's round face and drew his lips back from his teeth. "Biter," he said, and growled.

"Biter!"

Ghaden growled again, looking at Yaa from the corners of his eyes, his lids half closed. "He is a fierce dog," Ghaden said.

"I had a pup once. I named him Tail-chaser," said Yaa. She bent her head to look into Ghaden's face. "Tail-chaser is a good name," she said.

Tail-chaser! Ghaden thought. Who would be afraid of a dog named Tail-chaser?

"His name is Biter."

Yaa lifted her arms and spread her hands. "He is your dog. You should name him what you want."

Ghaden crawled after Biter, grabbed away the strip of hide and threw it again. "Get it, Biter!"

The dog waved his plumed tail and ran after it. "What happened to Tail-chaser?" Ghaden asked.

"We ate him," Yaa answered. "It was the end of winter and our father could not hunt anymore." She rubbed her hands, thinking of the swollen joints that had changed her father from a hunter into an old man.

"Nobody will eat Biter," Ghaden said. "He will eat them first."

Yaa raised her eyebrows. "We need a protector dog in this lodge," she said. "Maybe Biter is a good name for him."

Yaa looked over at the puppy. He had the strip of hide in his mouth and was shaking his head. Now would be a good time, she thought. Her mother and Brown Water were at the cooking hearths, and Ghaden was talking more than he had since his mother had died.

"Now you are safe," Yaa began, and looked at Ghaden.

He raised his eyebrows in agreement. "Nobody will get me," he said, his voice firm.

"Ghaden," Yaa said, "no one knows who killed . . . who hurt you."

Ghaden crawled over to his puppy, put the dog on his lap and held the strip of hide up over its head. Biter lunged and tripped over Ghaden's legs, then bumped forward on his nose. He got up again, jumped toward the hide and caught it. Ghaden laughed.

"Do you know who hurt you?" Yaa asked.

It seemed as though Ghaden had not heard her question. He continued to play with the dog, dancing the hide strip around Biter's head.

"Ghaden, do you know?"

Yaa crawled over to her brother, clasped his arm and looked into his face. "Ghaden, I asked you if you knew who hurt you," she said, her voice stern.

Ghaden closed his eyes and shook his head until Yaa placed her hands on either side of his face to hold him still.

"Ghaden," she said softly, "if we know who hurt you, we can tell the elders. They will send him away, and he will never hurt you again."

Ghaden looked at her, his eyes round. He blinked back tears. "I saw . . . I saw . . ." he said, then patted his legs.

"You saw his legs?"

"Yes, saw them."

"I thought it was . . . I thought it was . . . Cen."

"The trader?"

Ghaden raised his eyebrows.

"But it was not?"

"No." He shook his head.

"Do you know who . . . ?"

Again he shook his head. "I saw the knife," he said. "Blood on it."

Ghaden stuck his thumb in his mouth and drew his legs up under him. He reached out toward one of Yaa's braids, then pulled his hand back. Biter jumped up to lick Ghaden's face. Ghaden pushed him away. The dog tilted his head, cocked his ears, then settled to sit quietly beside him.

Ghaden wrapped one arm around the pup, tucked his fingers into Biter's thick fur.

"Do you remember anything about him?" Yaa asked.

"Tall," Ghaden said around his thumb.

"Did you hear any noise? Did his boots have rattlers?"

Ghaden tried to think back to that night. The boots were different, but he could not remember how. It had been dark and he was sleepy. He had wanted to stay with Cen. There were things to play with in the trader's packs and always a lot to eat. But his mother said they must return to Brown Water's lodge.

By the time they got back, Ghaden was ready for his own bed, but for some reason his mother did not go inside. They waited in the cold until the chill of the air had seeped through his clothing.

He had looked back over his mother's shoulder as they crouched in the entrance tunnel, and saw someone. He thought it was Cen coming to get them, to take them back to his warm lodge. Ghaden slipped away from his mother, ran out to grab Cen's legs so he would not walk past them.

They were in the shadows. He might walk right by, and Ghaden was cold.

It was not Cen. Whoever it was carried a knife. Even in the dark, Ghaden could see blood on the blade. He still wasn't sure why he reached for it, but he remembered being frightened. He had run with the knife to his mother, and so had led the killer to her. . . .

Ghaden rolled to his side and curled himself into a ball. Biter licked his cheek, and Yaa asked more questions. Ghaden put one hand over his eyes so he did not have to look at her. She was like Wolf-and-Raven's wife, like old Ligige', like the man who had come into Wolf-and-Raven's lodge when Ghaden was there alone. They all asked too many questions.

Finally Yaa's questions turned into a lullaby, a song soft in her throat. "I will not talk about it anymore, Ghaden," she said. "Do not be afraid."

Biter lay down beside him, pressed his cold, wet nose to Ghaden's face. Ghaden patted his dog, and Yaa sang until he fell asleep.

Chapter
Thirteen

The morning was warm, the snow under Chakliux's feet softened by a south wind. Last year's grasses stood in dark clumps at the edges of the riverbank. Smoke lay in a thin layer over the Near River lodges. The dogs were barking—some for the joy of being fed; others, smelling the fish given to their neighbors, crying out for their share.

Snow Hawk perked her ears and stopped. She whined and looked up at Chakliux's parka where her pups were bound against his chest. One had died, killed by Caribou's knife. Chakliux had taken the pup from his parka, shown it to Snow Hawk, then made a small hole for it in the crusted river snow. Chakliux had allowed Snow Hawk to feed her other pups, then tucked them again in his parka, and continued the walk to the Near River Village. The dead man's boots on Chakliux's feet were dry, warm.

The children saw him first, boys feeding their fathers' dogs. They cried out at his approach, then stopped short when they saw who he was. So, Chakliux wondered, was he considered a curse or only a returning hunter?

"Whose dog?" one of the older boys called.

"She belongs to the elders," Chakliux answered.

The boy came closer, glancing back at his companions as if to see their reaction to his daring.

"Stay away from her. She is nervous. She does not know this village," Chakliux told the boy. "Her pups are here in my parka." He set his hand over his chest. "She will fight to protect them."

The boy nodded, then squinting at the dog shouted out, "She has golden eyes. Look at her! Golden eyes."

Chakliux reached into the pack on his back and pulled out a short length of braided bark rope. He fastened it around Snow Hawk's neck and led her through the village, around dogs that snapped at her from their tethers near the lodges.

He stopped first at Sok's wife's lodge, crept inside, taking the dog with him.

Red Leaf was sewing a pieced parka, something beautiful and most likely for Sok. She looked up as he entered, giving a little start of surprise when he brought the dog in with him. She lifted a hand toward the door, pointed rudely with one finger and said, "Get that dog out of my—" Then she stopped. "A golden-eye," she said. "You got one."

"Five, I have five," Chakliux answered, and reached into his parka, set the four pups, two dark-furred, the others mostly white, on the floor. "Three female, one male," Chakliux said, and lifted them to show Red Leaf the eyes. Snow Hawk nosed each of them, stopping to lick the darkened blood from the white-and-black fur of the smallest.

"It was hurt?" Red Leaf asked.

"No," Chakliux said, but told her nothing more. He did not want her to spread the story of his journey among the village women before Sok and the elders had a chance to hear it.

Red Leaf filled a bowl with warm broth and handed it to Chakliux. He left his parka on. Because of Snow Hawk's pup, the tip of Caribou's knife had left only a shallow wound in Chakliux's chest, but Red Leaf did not need to see it.

Chakliux tipped the bowl and sucked in a mouthful of warm liquid. It eased the ache in his belly and spread its heat out toward his arms and legs. He emptied the bowl then asked, "Where is Sok?"

"He and my sons have gone to feed his grand ... to feed your dogs."

Yes, his dogs. He had almost forgotten. During his journey, the world had become only himself, Snow Hawk and her pups. Here, he had dogs and a wife.

Red Leaf refilled his bowl. He drank several mouthfuls, then set the bowl on the floor for Snow Hawk. She was lying on her side, her pups crowded against her belly, nursing. Red Leaf squawked out a protest as the dog began to lap up the broth, but Chakliux said, "Snow Hawk has earned it."

"Why do you think they came after you?" Dog Trainer asked. His face was drawn, and the flickering hearth fire added to the lines that scored his cheeks and forehead.

Away from the fire, the lodge was so dark that Chakliux had to remind himself it was not yet night. His eyes were gritty, as though there were sand under the lids, and several times as he explained to the elders what had happened, he had to hold his mouth closed over a yawn.

Chakliux shook his head. "I do not know. Cloud Finder traded me the dogs. As an elder of the Cousin River Village he came with me, to speak to all of you, to tell you that the Cousin elders want peace, that only the young hunters, bored with the dark days of winter, speak of fighting."

"So then three were killed?" Dowitcher asked. He sat next to Dog Trainer in one of the places of honor at the back of the lodge. Sok was beside Chakliux, facing the half circle of village elders.

"Three, perhaps four. Another hunter was wounded," Chakliux said.

"But they killed this elder who traded you the dogs?"

"Yes," he answered. "One of the hunters killed him."

"Nothing has happened to us," Sok said. "None of our young men were killed. This elder was one of theirs. My brother"—he nodded his head at Chakliux—"he is also of their village. Perhaps this is not our problem, but one they must solve for themselves."

"But we do not know what the Cousin River hunters have told their people," Dog Trainer said. "Perhaps they will say that Chakliux stole the dogs, that there was no fair trade, and that he killed the elder and their hunters to get the dogs for us."

Chakliux felt the elders' eyes on him. What Dog Trainer said was true. Cloud Finder's sons probably believed he killed their father. Was it fair for this village to suffer because of something between people of the Cousin River Village?

"I will go back to them," Chakliux said. "I will tell them what happened."

"No," Sok began, but was interrupted by his stepfather.

"What about the dogs?" Fox Barking asked. "You traded away all our goods for those dogs. You cannot take them back."

"If he does not take them back," Dog Trainer said, "the Cousin River People will know they are here. They will think we killed to get their dogs."

"Wait," said Sees Light, grandfather to Blueberry. He pointed at Chakliux with his chin. "This man is now husband to my granddaughter. Do you think, if he returns to the Cousin River Village, they will allow him to live?" He paused, but the men were silent. "What if he had not returned here with the dogs? What could the Cousin River People say about that?"

"So where would he be?" Sok asked.

"Perhaps he went to the Walrus Hunters to trade this golden-eyed dog to them."

"What good will that do us?" Fox Barking said. "We sent Chakliux to the Cousin River Village in hopes that a golden-eyed dog would break the curse which has come to our own animals."

"She has four pups, does she not?" Sees Light asked. "How many of you have females with new litters?"

Several men muttered, nodding heads, raising eyebrows, Fox Barking among them.

"Perhaps some of the females will accept a new pup. These pups, if they live, still give us a chance to break the curse. If the Cousin River People send men to find Chakliux, we will hide the pups. That will not be difficult. They are small."

"And Chakliux?" Sok asked.

"He was a curse among us," Sees Light said. "We are glad he returned to his own village. We are glad he never came back."

THE COUSIN RIVER VILLAGE

"So you let him get away?" said K'os, her voice as smooth as ice. "He has the dog and the pups, and he is not injured?"

The man swallowed and said, "He killed my father."

"So the old man is dead, but my son, he is safe?"

"He will not be safe," Tikaani snarled.

"He killed River Jumper and Stalker and Caribou. Night Man is almost dead, and you expect me to believe you will kill Chakliux?"

K'os laughed, and knew Tikaani thought she laughed at him, but her laughter was for the ingenuity of her son. He was more resourceful than she had thought. It had turned out to be a fine game. Better than she had hoped. Who could believe the old fool Cloud Finder and her crippled son had any chance against River Jumper and four of the village's best young hunters? Of course, Chakliux did have the dogs.

"The female dog is not hurt?"

"I do not think so. I did not see the pups."

K'os shrugged. "Pups die easily," she said.

"It was the dog that killed my brother Caribou. She attacked him."

So perhaps it was not skill but luck that had saved Chakliux, K'os thought. Or power. The idea bothered her. He had been her joke, a terrible, terrible joke. . . .

She thought back to when she was young. She was beautiful now. Then she had been beyond words. Every man in the village had wanted her. The young hunters . . . ah, their bodies cried out for hers, but her father saw only the honor he would gain by giving her to an elder.

Name Giver's gifts had been wonderful, but he was like a dried-up old stick. K'os had wanted someone young.

She remembered the morning her father told her his decision. She had peeked out the doorflap, saw Ground Beater and River Jumper outside. They had set up a target of caribou hide, stretched taut around a frame of saplings, and were throwing blunt-tipped practice spears. Like boys, like little boys. She had watched from behind the doorflap, coughing once so they would know she was there. Then her father's hand had jerked her away.

"You think because you are beautiful that you can have every young man in the village," he had said to her. "You think because you found an animal-gift child you should have anything you want. You are no better than any other woman. You must have one husband; you must make sons to honor that husband. I have chosen Name Giver."

The words were like rocks falling into her stomach. She had pleaded with him, but he would not change his mind. K'os had curled herself into her sleeping robes and cried until her father left the lodge in disgust. Spitting out angry words, she had cursed Name Giver. Why would an old man want a young woman? There were widows in the village. What about Three Birds? She was not ugly. What about Morning Woman?

Later, K'os had walked to the Grandfather Lake, Chakliux strapped to her back. She did not want to see the other young women of the village, their smiles hidden behind raised hands, eyes snapping their delight when they heard K'os would be wife to Name Giver. At the lake, she cried out her anger to the Grandfather Rock, offered gifts, even promised to give Chakliux back to the Grandfather spirits if, when she returned to the village, old Name Giver was dead. The lake and rock did not hear her. Name Giver lived, and she became his wife, given by her father in exchange for the promise of dead caribou and dried fish.

Name Giver could do nothing in her bed. K'os told her mother and father, and asked them if she could throw him away, return to her mother's lodge, but they told her she could not. They said it was because of the honor she would lose, but K'os knew they did not care about her honor, only about Name Giver's gifts.

Worse, when Chakliux first tried to stand, K'os noticed the deformity of his foot. It was one more anger to add to those that plagued her life. She decided that Chakliux was not animal-gift but only a child someone had thrown away. By asking careful questions of men who came to trade from the Near River Village, she had found she was right.

One day when Name Giver was visiting another elder, Ground Beater had come to K'os's lodge, and she had talked him into her bed. Afterward, as she lay in Ground Beater's arms, rejoicing in the fullness that warmed her body, he told her he was to marry Three Birds. She had exploded in angry words, had driven him from her lodge.

That was when K'os began to visit Old Sister. Old Sister was a healer, wise in the knowledge of plant medicines. She taught K'os the plants and herbs that would ensure Name Giver's health. She taught those that should be avoided. Each day for nearly a year, K'os visited Old Sister. Each day, she learned until Old Sister had nothing more to teach her.

How sad when a strange sickness came to the village. K'os made many medicines, but for some reason, they did not help. She cut her hair in mourning when the disease took Old Sister. She comforted Ground Beater in his grief when it claimed Three Birds. She wore the rags and ashes of a widow when Name Giver himself succumbed.

Since then many things had changed. K'os turned her eyes to Tikaani. He was little more than a boy. His chest had not yet filled out, nor were his arms thick and strong, but his well-muscled legs foretold the man he would be, and she had still not tired of him in her bed.

"Go back to the hunter's lodge," she told him. "We will have our revenge, but it will not be something for you to do alone. Wait. I will tell you when the time is right. Then the Near River Village will be a ruin and the Near River People will be food for ravens and foxes."

K'os went to the uncles first, then to the cousins. She told them that Stalker and Caribou were too young to be dead because of the selfishness of her son and the greed of the Near River People. Night

Man lay in his mother's lodge, nearly dead, his shoulder festering. It was a miracle Tikaani had gotten him back to the village. River Jumper had been one of their best hunters. Now who would feed his children? Then there was Cloud Finder, a man of wisdom, an elder revered by many.

K'os hung her head in shame, knowing that her son had killed him. What could she say to Cloud Finder's young daughter, Star, who still lived in his wife's lodge?

It was her fault, K'os told them. She had brought Chakliux into this village, thinking he would bring honor and power to the people here.

She invited the men to come to her lodge, and by allowing each to think he would be there alone with her, she knew they would come.

She worked hard in preparation for their arrival, filling boiling bags with meat and water, carrying them to the village hearths to cook, guarding them so others would not take a share. She ignored the clacking tongues of the other women when she pushed their greedy ladles away from her meat.

When she saw Ground Squirrel's angry red cheeks and the pinched whiteness of Owl Catcher's face, she taunted them, saying, "Do not worry. Your husbands will be in your beds tonight. This food is for those families in mourning."

Then they left her alone, even helped her keep the children from the food.

When the meat was hot, bubbling in its own juice, rich with fat and flavored with dried berries, K'os carried the boiling bags to her lodge, hung them from her lodge poles and waited for the men to come.

THE NEAR RIVER VILLAGE

Chakliux sat down on the caribou hide floor of Red Leaf's lodge and rubbed his otter foot. It had ached since the fight with Tikaani and his brothers, but today the pain seemed less.

Red Leaf came into the lodge, her arms full of firewood. He stood, took the wood from her and piled it near the entrance tunnel as she removed her parka. She looked down at his foot.

"It still bothers you?" she asked.

"Yes."

"I have something." She held up a small packet. "Ligige' gave it to me. It is something the Sea Hunter woman told her about. It is called sixsiqax. Ligige' said fresh leaves are better, but she had only dried. I soaked them in hot water." She nodded toward the back of the lodge in the general direction of the village hearths. The women there always kept a caribou hide full of hot water, heated with rocks pulled from the edges of the cooking fires. "Sit down," she told Chakliux.

He sat and Red Leaf knelt beside him. She layered the wet, warm leaves over his foot. They seemed to draw the ache from his bones.

"Sixsiqax?" Chakliux said. The word was harsh in his throat, unfamiliar to his tongue. "A Sea Hunter name?" he asked.

Red Leaf shrugged, then asked, "Where is Sok?"

"With the dogs."

"What happened with the elders?"

Chakliux knew she would not ask Sok such a question, but she was more bold with him.

"They are pleased about the dogs."

"They should be."

Red Leaf waited, and Chakliux knew she wanted him to say more, but women did not need to know what happened in the elders' lodge.

"What do you think about our young men?" Red Leaf asked. "Some of them want to attack the Cousin River Village."

"They are foolish," Chakliux told her.

For a long time Red Leaf said nothing. Chakliux waited. She was a woman who spent much time at the cooking hearths hearing and telling. She would not be silent forever.

Finally she said, "There have been no deaths since you left our village, of dogs or people."

"So do the women think I killed my grandfather and the Sea Hunter woman?" Chakliux's throat felt tight as he asked the question.

"Most have decided the trader killed them," she said. "Most think he is dead. He was badly hurt when he left our village. Some of the young men thought you were the killer, but Blue-head Duck told them that if you were, you would not return to this village."

Chakliux took a long breath. "I am not the killer," he said.

"Now that you have brought the dogs, no one in the village thinks you are," Red Leaf said, but she looked away as she spoke the words.

Chakliux nodded. He knew that she did not tell him the whole truth. There were those still afraid of him.

"Some of the women say you will leave the village. Some say you will stay here and take Blueberry as wife. Others think you will throw her away."

"Some women talk too much," Chakliux replied.

Red Leaf picked up the parka she was making. She began to weave a sinew thread through holes she had punched with an awl. "If you do not take Blueberry, do you think Sok will?" she asked.

The question surprised Chakliux. It was something Red Leaf should not ask. "I do not know," he answered. "Ask your husband."

Red Leaf snorted. "Blueberry is better than Snow-in-her-hair," she said, then held up the parka so Chakliux could see the intricate sun design on the back. "But neither is good enough to make a parka like this."

THE COUSIN RIVER VILLAGE

K'os invited not only uncles and cousins who were already hunters, but also young cousins still considered boys. She needed the young ones, perhaps more than those who were experienced hunters. Each man seemed surprised as he entered her lodge—first to see her husband, Ground Beater, then to see others, among them their fathers, sons or brothers.

K'os laughed to herself as she watched each face, the change from eagerness to embarrassment, then the darkening of skin that told of anger. It would do her purpose well, that anger.

She acted the part of wife, serving each man a bowl of meat, the elders' flavored subtly with the root of the tall, purple-flowered plant she had found herself, something Old Sister had not even known. They would hardly notice its thin, sharp flavor, but it would make them calm, relaxed. They would sit quietly and do nothing as she worked on the young men, building their rage.

The hunters ate in silence, glancing at one another from the sides of their eyes. Stay angry, K'os told the young men silently. Stay angry. Slyly, she sought the gaze of each hunter, raised her brows, pursed her lips. Her husband was watching, she was sure. He knew far too much. How sad. It was not a good time to go through mourning, but some things could not be helped.

Finally she cleared her throat, looked at Ground Beater. At least he had agreed to this. She tightened her lips against a smile. He probably thought it was his own idea.

"I have asked each of you here," he said.

K'os saw the surprise in the men's eyes. She had said nothing to them about her husband's wanting them here, but what better way to feed the young men's anger?

"Each of you is in mourning. My wife and I want you to know we share your sorrow. We have gifts."

He waved his arm toward a pile of trade goods in the corner of the lodge, things he and K'os had gathered in the two days since Tikaani's return to the village. Most of the things K'os brought had been given to her by the men who visited her lodge. She kept the gifts in the back of their food cache, buried under bales of dried fish, frozen meat, and caribou intestines stuffed with fat and berries. She had little worry Ground Beater would find those treasures. What man ever dug past a good piece of meat?

K'os had told Ground Beater she traded meat for goods from her friends, from her aunt, from a cousin.

The men looked at the trade goods, and greed lighted their eyes.

"In this giveaway, we honor you," Ground Beater said. "We understand that our son is the cause of your mourning, and in that, we also mourn."

He was doing well, K'os thought, though his voice was thin, at times close to breaking as he praised each of the dead men, as he led a chant of healing for Night Man.

He had not been a bad choice for husband. In her young years, after Name Giver had died, when K'os still hoped for children and had not yet learned that a woman did not need a husband to feed her, she had wanted him. She would keep him, yet, for a little while. But he did not want to fight the Near River People, and because, for so many years, he had been the village's chief hunter, others would follow his decision, at least the older men. The young men would do as Tikaani said. After all, he was truly the chief hunter of the village. He brought in more meat than Ground Beater ever did, and Tikaani was always eager to spend time in her bed.

So perhaps she would give him what he wanted most, recognition as the village's only chief hunter. Then together they would continue their revenge against the Near River People—for what they had done to her.

Chapter Fourteen

THE NEAR RIVER VILLAGE

Chakliux stood beside the lodge fire and smoothed the goose grease over his skin. He dressed slowly: a new breechcloth Red Leaf had made him, his soft hare fur inner leggings, the caribou hide shirt rubbed clean with fine sand, then his inner boots of ground squirrel pelts, his outer leggings of caribou hide, and his ground squirrel parka, his sealskin boots.

He had gifts, things a woman would like: a wolf pelt, a needle case carved from ivory, a wooden comb, dried fish, dried berries, a jade woman's knife, and a fish lure carved from walrus ivory. Of course, these would not be enough for a bride price, but since Blueberry had been given to him by his grandfather, there was no need for gifts. He hoped she would like what he brought her. Perhaps it would ease this night they must spend together.

He had not had a woman since Gguzaakk had died—even before that. She had died shortly after their son was born, and what man takes a pregnant woman to his bed?

A man who cannot discipline himself to wait for a woman will not have the patience he needs to hunt well. What was hunting except watching and waiting? One move at the wrong time could mean the difference between a family that lived through a hard winter and one that did not.

Blueberry was a beautiful woman—much more beautiful than Gguzaakk, but Gguzaakk had been beautiful inside, beautiful and wise. Chakliux was not sure that Blueberry was either, though she had treated his grandfather well. At least according to what he had seen.

One night, he told himself. I must give her one night. That was enough to honor Tsaani. Finding her with Root Digger while she was still in mourning was just cause for Chakliux to throw her away, but out of respect for his grandfather, he would not mention that. Chakliux would break the marriage bond only because of the journey he must make to the Walrus Hunters. Who could say when he would return? Perhaps the Walrus Hunters would welcome him, and so he would stay and learn to hunt sea animals, to build an iqyax of his own. He might even decide to visit Sea Hunter villages.

A vague uneasiness came to him each time he thought of his journey. What did he know about the Walrus Hunters? Could he really learn to hunt sea animals? Could a grown man learn to do something that takes a lifetime to master?

Perhaps he could. If he was willing to be a boy again, if his pride did not stand in the way of his learning.

He placed the gifts into a fishskin basket. Tonight he would have his first lesson. Tonight he would begin learning how to live without pride.

"We will leave tomorrow," Sok told Sees Light. "I will go with my brother."

"How long will you be gone?" the man asked.

"Do not worry," Sok said. "Even now my brother arranges to have another man take your granddaughter as wife. She will not starve."

Sees Light nodded, then lifted his chin toward Sok. "And your wife?"

"She has brothers." For a moment Sok's voice grew hard. "She is a woman who can take care of herself. Besides, I will come back when my trading is done. Chakliux will return only if the Cousin River People do not seek him. Otherwise he will stay with the Walrus Hunters. Perhaps they will understand the honor he gives them as one who is both otter and man."

Sees Light looked away, and Sok sensed his embarrassment. Let him be embarrassed, Sok thought. He hoped Sees Light had reminded his granddaughter of the respect a wife owes her husband, especially someone like Chakliux.

Chakliux owned power. How else had he been able to come in, as youngest son, and receive all the things Sok wanted? Yet how could Sok complain? How could he hold any anger against Chakliux when he had earned Sok's respect in so many ways—by his hunting, his skill with weapons, even in the manner he treated Sok's sons? And Red Leaf, even she had softened in her feelings toward the man.

Chakliux once told Sok that his dream was to have an iqyax and learn to hunt sea animals. If he could do such a thing, perhaps he would stay with the Walrus Hunters. Or even go live with the Sea Hunters. Then one day he might come back to this village, teach Sok how to hunt sea animals. The thought lifted Sok's spirit, but he tried not to imagine what it would be like to return to this village alone, without Chakliux, the brother who claimed too much, the brother favored by the spirits since birth, the brother he had grown to love.

Blueberry stood up as Chakliux entered the lodge. She wore no ornaments, only a long caribou hide shirt and hare fur socks that reached her knees. Chakliux regretted that he had brought no necklaces, no feathers or weasel tails. He had been away from women too long. He had forgotten what they enjoyed.

He handed her the fishskin basket. "This is for you," he said.

She took the basket without speaking, lowering her head as she reached out for it, so Chakliux could see the long white part that divided her hair. She was a small woman, and narrow of hip, like Gguzaakk had been. His heart squeezed tight at the thought, then he reminded himself that this woman was only to be his wife for one night. He would never feel his soul torn apart in fear as she struggled through childbirth.

She set the basket on the floor and brought him a bowl of food. He sat down and ate, watching from the corner of his eyes as she examined the gifts he had brought her. She exclaimed over each one, her words soft but joyful, and he felt his heart fill also with her joy. Surely she had been given gifts before. Surely a woman as beautiful as Blueberry knew what it was to receive good things.

He handed her his empty bowl, and she flicked her eyes toward the boiling bag that hung from the lodge poles.

"It was very good," Chakliux said.

"The gifts, too, are wonderful," said Blueberry, her voice so soft that Chakliux had to lean forward to hear her.

"There is one more gift for you tonight."

She raised her eyebrows and looked down at his crotch.

"No," he said, and could not keep a smile from his face. He lifted his chin toward his bowl. "Fill my bowl again, and also another."

"I am not hungry," Blueberry said.

"It is not for you."

Someone scratched at the doorflap, and Chakliux called out, "Come."

Blueberry stared at the entrance tunnel with wide eyes, and when Root Digger came in, she dropped Chakliux's bowl and covered her face with both hands.

"Wife," Chakliux said to her, "our guest needs food."

Blueberry picked up Chakliux's bowl, filled it and handed it to him. She filled another bowl for Root Digger. Chakliux motioned for the man to sit beside him.

Root Digger was nervous. His long thin fingers shook as he took the bowl from Blueberry's hands.

Blueberry brought a water bladder, set it beside Chakliux, then went to her basket corner, tucking herself in among the reeds and grasses, the piles of fishskin baskets she stored there. She laid a sheaf of dried grasses across her lap and began to split a blade with her thumbnail.

Chakliux ate. He said nothing to Root Digger or to Blueberry, though he saw that, now and again, both looked at him from the sides of their eyes.

When Chakliux finished his food, he set his bowl on the floor. Blueberry jumped up to refill it, but he held up one hand so she settled herself again amidst her baskets.

Chakliux waited until Root Digger finished his food. The man ate more slowly than necessary, Chakliux thought, but then he reminded himself that Root Digger was a slow man, slow in feet and slow in thought. Why not also slow in eating?

"I have noticed," Chakliux began, turning to look straight into Root Digger's face, "that you live in your mother's lodge. Since I have been in this village only a few moons, I do not know everything about everyone, but I have heard that you do not have a wife."

"No, I do not," the man said, his words high and squeaky like a boy's.

"You need a wife," said Chakliux.

"Yes," Root Digger said, his face growing pale.

"There are many women in this village, young girls and widows who are not spoken for. There is Wolf-and-Raven's daughter, Snow-in-her-hair; there is Broken Grass, a widow still young enough to have children. There is Dog Trainer's granddaughter who just celebrated her woman's rites." He stopped, leaned down to run a finger over his bowl. He sucked the meat juice from his fingertip.

"Have you considered any of these women?" Chakliux asked.

"Only Broken Grass," Root Digger said.

Chakliux looked at Blueberry, saw the surprise in her face. Did she believe he thought only of her, this man? Her husband had been dead only a moon.

Root Digger followed Chakliux's eyes to Blueberry, then ducked his head, his face suddenly red.

"You know that I must claim Blueberry as wife," Chakliux said, looking again at Root Digger.

"I understand," said Root Digger.

Chakliux turned to Blueberry. "You understand this, wife?" he asked her.

"Yes."

"But there is something else I must tell you." He settled himself against the backrest that had once belonged to his grandfather. "I have just returned from the Cousin River Village, from my own people there. I traded in good faith for a golden-eyed dog and her pups. I brought the dogs here with hopes of breaking the curse that plagues the animals of this village. The young hunters in the Cousin River Village do not want to see good trading between us. They seek honor by becoming warriors. After I left their village, they attacked me."

Chakliux looked at Blueberry, saw that she listened with eyes round, mouth open. Root Digger also stared.

"Why?" he asked.

"Who knows? Honor is one thing to one man, another to someone else."

"I have seen the female you brought and her four pups," Root Digger said.

"There were five pups," said Chakliux. "They killed one, and a male dog I had brought to mate with our females. They also killed a Cousin River elder who came with me. Three of those hunters died. Three of five. Another was wounded. Then they returned to their own village, and I came here."

"They will come looking for you," Blueberry said, and she moved to their side of the fire, knelt down between them, as though she had forgotten her place as woman.

"They will come, and if we do not give you to them, they will attack," Root Digger said.

"That is what the elders believe," Chakliux answered. "What I and my brother believe, also. So tomorrow we plan to leave the village. We will go trade with the Walrus Hunters; perhaps we will travel even farther and trade with the Sea Hunters."

He glanced at Blueberry, saw the lines in her forehead, and knew what she was thinking.

"You will be gone a long time," she said quietly.

"I may not come back," Chakliux replied, and the words hung cold and empty in the lodge. "I may not be able to come back. The elders have agreed to say that I did not return here with the golden-eyed dogs. That way your people will hold no blame for the deaths of the Cousin River hunters. What fault is it of yours if one Cousin River man kills another Cousin River man? How can the young hunters use that to begin a war?"

"So you will take the dogs and leave?" Blueberry asked.

"Why take the dogs?" asked Root Digger. "You brought them for us."

Blueberry looked at the man, disgust in her face. "If their warriors come, they will recognize the female," she said.

"And the pups?" he asked.

"There are decisions yet to be made about the pups," Chakliux said. The elders had not yet chosen the men to whom the pups would go. One would belong to Dog Trainer, and perhaps one would be given to his stepfather, Fox Barking. But why say? The fewer men who knew about the pups being left in the village, the better.

"I have a bitch with a new litter," Root Digger said. "She could nurse another."

Chakliux bit at the inside of his cheek. "It is a decision the elders will make," he said. "Go speak to Dog Trainer. Perhaps they will decide it is not safe to leave any pups here."

"What man recognizes a pup once it is grown?" Root Digger asked.

"They have the eyes," Chakliux answered.

"There is a golden-eye born now and again among our litters."

Perhaps that was true, Chakliux thought. He had not lived long enough in the village to know. "My concern now is not dogs," he told Root Digger. "My concern is for my wife. I cannot take her with me. I do not know if I will return. Will you claim her as wife? That way she will have a hunter to care for her, and I will not worry whether she has the meat she needs for next winter."

Again Blueberry covered her face.

"I will take her if she will come to me," Root Digger said. His fingers tightened around the bowl he still held in his lap.

"Blueberry?"

"Yes, I will go to him," she said, her words muffled by her hands.

"I asked about you," Chakliux said to Root Digger. "I would not give Blueberry to you if you were not a good hunter and a good man."

Root Digger nodded, swallowed. He had a long neck, and his head stuck up out of his parka like the curled sprout of a new fern.

"Go then," Chakliux said. "Come to us in the morning when it is still dark. That is when Sok and I plan to leave." He turned and spoke to Blueberry, reached over to pull her hands away from her face. "You understand that I must throw you away. Otherwise, you will not be free to become Root Digger's wife."

"Yes."

"If we do this in the morning, early, no one will see except us. You will face no dishonor."

Chakliux took a long breath. He had nothing more to say. It was not an easy thing to give your wife to another man, even a wife you did not want.

Root Digger stood, dipped his head toward Chakliux, then looked into Blueberry's eyes. The woman lowered her head, glanced at Chakliux. Root Digger left, and the lodge was suddenly too large, too quiet.

Chakliux raised his bowl toward her, though his stomach was full. Eating was something to do, and, he reminded himself, there would be days during their journey when he would wish for the good food of Blueberry's lodge. Then he would remember this extra bowl of meat.

"Take one for yourself as well," he said.

She lay a hand against her belly, and he thought she would say she was not hungry, but she filled her bowl, then sat down on the opposite side of the hearth and began to eat. She kept the bowl tipped so it hid her face.

When she had finished eating, she lowered her bowl and looked at him. "Thank you," she said quietly.

Chakliux was not sure whether she thanked him for the food or for Root Digger. He wondered again whether Blueberry had broken mourning taboos with Root Digger or if she had welcomed him to her bed when Tsaani was still alive, but then he told himself it was not his problem. If taboos and promises had been broken, Blueberry's luck would leave her, and Root Digger's hunting success would falter. Now, since they would belong to each other, their curses would fall mostly upon themselves, as was best.

Then Chakliux pushed away all thoughts of Root Digger and led Blueberry to his bed. He removed his clothing except his breechcloth. Blueberry pulled her shirt off over her head. Her back was to the hearth coals, so in the shadows Chakliux could not see her clearly, only the mounds of her breasts, darker at the center, the shadow of the cleft between her legs.

She was thinner, finer boned than Gguzaakk. Looking at her, Chakliux first noticed only the differences between the two women, then it seemed as though he saw them side by side, and finally they began to flow into one another, like two streams joining—the dark, thin Blueberry, the fairer, wider Gguzaakk gradually mingling to become one. He pulled Blueberry close, stroked her back, her shoulders and arms.

Then Blueberry's hands were on him, light and gentle, the calluses of her palms small and rough against his skin. He had forgotten the joy of a woman's body, the heat. He was suddenly glad he had already promised her to Root Digger. He was not sure he could have after taking her as wife.

THE COUSIN RIVER VILLAGE

K'os carefully folded the powder into a bit of caribou hide. She had dyed the hide with five-leaves grass, and the red color would stand as a warning to her. She knotted it shut with many strands of sinew, then placed it at the bottom of her beaverskin medicine bag. Ground Beater had earned a reprieve. There would be another time for this, she thought, and patted the bag. For now, she would do as he suggested.

There was a risk. They were known in the Near River Village. Her husband had hunted with some of their men, and, of course, had traded with them. She also knew some of the Near River hunters. Knew them very well. But that was something they might wish to hide, especially when she was with her husband.

Ground Beater opened the doorflap at the entrance tunnel, called, "You are ready?"

She pulled up her parka hood, drew it tight around her face. It was early morning, a good time to leave, the ground hard and frozen. They could not wait for days, deciding what to do. Spring breakup was too close. Then no one would be able to cross the river until the flooding subsided. They would go now, confront their son in the Near River Village.

The dogs each carried a pack. There were three of them, a young female and two males, all with golden eyes. If the Near River People were eager for peace, perhaps they would be less so when they saw these dogs. When their young men realized that they could win dogs like these, they, too, might decide they wanted to fight.

Her husband bent over each animal, checked the straps that secured their packs. K'os backed away from him, leaned close to Tikaani and Snow Breaker, the two young hunters who would travel with them.

Her voice was quiet and low, softened by the fur ruff close around her face. "He thinks he will speak peace to these Near River People. I do not think there is a chance for peace. Guard him. When they see his dogs, I think they will try to kill him. They will say it is an accident, but . . ." She raised her hands, spread her mittened fingers.

Ground Beater looked back, waved them forward. Each of the men walked beside a dog. K'os followed. The village was quiet in early morning, smoke rising to spread a thin layer above the lodges, the stars still bright. Snow squeaked beneath K'os's sealskin boots. She carried her snowshoes and a small pack of supplies on her back. Women's knives rested in sheaths at her waist, and she had strapped a short-bladed knife to her left wrist. Under her parka, warm against her skin, was the medicine bag. She reached up to pat it and felt her heart thump as though in answer. She smiled, peering from the tunnel of her hood. It would be a long walk, but she looked forward to seeing her son again. She missed him.

Chapter
Fifteen

K'os removed her snow goggles. They were made from caribou antlers hollowed into small cups that fit over the circles of her eyes. Narrow eye slits and charcoal rubbed into the backs of the goggles helped cut the glare of sun on snow, but still her head ached and she saw spots. At least they had walked most of the day on river ice rather than pushing through the dense willow thickets or the melting tundra snow.

They had walked for three days, and now, as the river bent in a wide curve, Ground Beater turned back toward her and called out, "There, the Near River Village."

A path worn into the snow led up from the riverbank to a walkway of rocks that were easy to climb, so a person carrying something did not have to grab trees or scramble up on all fours. When they came to the top of the bank, K'os saw that the village was larger than she had remembered.

The lodges were set more closely together than in her own village. She wondered where they put the drying racks. There was no room for them between lodges. Perhaps at the edges of the village, she thought, where the sun would get at them better, but then so would the animals.

She leaned toward Tikaani and whispered, "The village is smaller than ours."

He nodded.

But the number of men in those lodges was the important thing, K'os reminded herself. How many men? How many capable of fighting?

They were met by a group of children, boys and girls bundled in parkas and leggings. Their cheeks were round, their eyes clear.

There is no shortage of food here, K'os thought. Children always showed it first—a village's weakness or its strength.

"We are visitors from the Cousin River Village," Ground Beater told them.

One of the older children came forward, a boy. He was stout and strong-looking, his chin set forward so his bottom teeth fit over the top. The other children kept their distance from him, leaving a small circle of cleared space.

K'os watched him. She might be able to use a boy like that someday.

He opened his mouth, but before he could speak K'os asked, "What is your name?"

Anger darkened his eyes. It was not a question a stranger—especially a woman—asked. A name was too sacred. When you knew someone's name, you had power over them.

"I am K'os," she said, giving her name, so he would feel the need to do the same. It was not an equal trade. There was little power the boy could use against her.

"We will take you to the elders," he said, turning his back on K'os and speaking instead to Ground Beater.

K'os smiled. He was not stupid, this one. A bully, yes, but not stupid. All the better. How many times had her plans been destroyed by stupidity? River Jumper, bah! He deserved what he got.

"Yes, tell them we come in honor to visit our brothers," Ground Beater said.

The children turned and ran toward the center of the village.

"Tell them we bring golden-eyed dogs," Tikaani called out to them.

"They are not blind," Ground Beater said. "They see what we bring."

K'os lifted her head, looked at the lodges around them. Soon not one will be left standing, she thought. Not one. A year from now, this will be a village of ground squirrels and ptarmigan. She held in her laughter. The Near River People deserved to be dead. They drew curses, then without thought spread those curses to others.

Soon the children returned. Two elders were with them. K'os studied the old men's faces but did not recognize them. Good, she thought, then lowered her head, stood behind her husband. Waiting as women must wait.

The elders' lodge was large. The lodge poles were crowded with the skins of sacred animals—white least weasels, flickers, marmot and beaver, and many wolverines. The men were seated in a circle around the hearth fire. K'os had been given a place behind her husband. Women scurried, bringing food from the outside cooking hearths. They ate well, then her husband presented the gifts he had brought: obsidian and jade blades for each man. They accepted the gifts with unsmiling faces, as was the custom in this village, but they could not hide the gleam of joy that came to their eyes. So the gifts—her husband's idea and one that she had not been sure about—had been a good decision.

The men spoke of many things, hunts and the spring melt, even of children and wives, which surprised K'os. Men in her village seldom spoke of their families. It was good that these Near Rivers valued their children so much, she told herself. They would be more willing to fight for them, but doubts crowded out other thoughts, doubts that she could not push away. Her last visit to the Near River Village had been when she was a girl. Her father had brought her. If she recalled correctly, the Near River People had been mourning a group of men drowned in the river. She did not know how such a thing had happened, most likely in spring breakup and flooding, but she did remember that the Near River Village had been far smaller then. Though she was only a child, she had been glad she lived in the Cousin River Village, and had asked her father not to promise her to a Near River man as wife.

She had realized that over the years the village would change, that it might grow strong. Now, as the men spoke, she contemplated how such a village could be taken by force. It would not be easy. Even the elders looked well-fed.

She was so immersed in her own thoughts that she almost missed her husband's question. "Have you seen our son?" he asked. "He brought several golden-eyed dogs from our village to all of you. He had hoped to bring more, and we were able to secure two males after he left. We have brought them to him."

K'os was almost hidden by her husband, and so, in the shadows at the back of the lodge, she was able to change her position to see each elder's face. They looked at one another, biting at lips, raising eyebrows until one finally said, "He did not come here. We have not seen him since he left our village to return to you nearly a moon ago."

Several elders shifted uncomfortably, but most nodded heads, raised chins in agreement.

It was not a woman's place to speak in a meeting of elders. It was unusual enough that they had allowed her to be here now, but she was a healer, and she knew several of these men—old Blue Jay and Camp Maker. She was sure they had not forgotten her. Besides, she was a woman afraid for her son. Who would blame her if she spoke?

She took a quick gasping breath, then put her hands over her face and moaned. "He is not here?" she asked. "He left our village six, seven days ago."

She blinked tears from her eyes and leaned forward so the hearth fire would show her face.

"There are other villages," one of the elders said, the man they called Dog Trainer. "Perhaps he went to the Four Rivers Village, hoping to find more dogs to trade before he came here."

K'os shook her head. "He knew we were trying to find dogs for him. He knew we might follow several days later."

She began to cry, hard shaking sobs, and Blue Jay asked, "You saw no sign of his camps on your journey here?"

"One," Ground Beater answered, and K'os looked up at him, set her teeth together. He spoke the truth. They had found one of his camps and two bodies—what was left of them—but she needed Ground Beater to be quiet, to let her speak. Of course, he did not know what she was doing. He thought they were only looking for their son, to warn him of the anger building against him in their village and to bring him dogs to trade so he could secure a place in this village or another.

K'os lowered her head, allowed her sobbing to subside.

Blue Jay stood, came to her. "She can go to my wife's lodge," he said, speaking softly to Ground Beater, then he bent to help K'os to her feet.

They were at the entrance tunnel when Dog Trainer said, "It is sad the young hunter has not returned to our village."

K'os turned and looked at the man, saw that his eyes were hard and fixed on Blue Jay's face. "Yes, it is sad," Blue Jay mumbled.

So, K'os thought, for now I will learn nothing, but there are others in this village besides elders, and women do not always do what a husband says.

Blue Jay's wife was called Song, simply that. A strange name, K'os thought, but soon she understood. The old woman did nothing without singing. Her voice, thin and raspy, grated against K'os's ears until her head ached.

Song crooned over her, clicking her sympathy, watching K'os with tiny black eyes, the lids so wrinkled that K'os wondered how the woman could open them to see.

"Your boy, he will be all right," the woman sang. "He is strong and healthy. His mother should not worry."

Yes, K'os thought, as the old woman sang the same words over and over again, Chakliux has been here. For some reason they do not want us to know. Perhaps Chakliux himself told them that hunters from the Cousin River Village sought an excuse to attack. If that was so, then she and Ground Beater were fortunate the elders had welcomed them. Of course, as Chakliux's parents they might be seen as friends rather than enemies.

Meanwhile, this was not a terrible place to be. The lodge was clean, well-cared-for. Fishskin and grass baskets were stacked in one area, bedding folded and piled in another. The caribou skins on the floor were well-scraped. She knew women in her own village who would make clothing out of such skins rather than use them on floors. But one look at the old woman's parka, hung on a peg near the entrance, made K'os understand. It was sea otter, she was sure, with a ruff of wolverine fur and cuffs banded with caribou hide, scraped and softened until it was almost white. The back of the parka came down in a wide pointed tail of some strange spotted skin, a stiff-haired pelt unlike any K'os had ever seen.

One side of the lodge was hung with weapons and men's clothing, sacred bundles of flicker feathers and a beaverskin pouch much like the one she carried under her parka, with the head as a flap that closed down over an opening cut in the throat.

There were several fire bows, one larger than any she had ever seen. How could a man build a fire using a bow that long? she wondered. The more she looked at it, the more puzzled she became. The wood part of it was very strong, reinforced, it appeared, by twisted sinew.

"Ah, you are hungry," the old woman said. She hummed something under her breath, then hobbled to the cooking bag that hung from the lodge poles. It was set over a hollowed stone.

K'os had seen such a stone before. It was made, she had been told, to hold a fire, something used by the people who were called Sea Hunters. It had seemed a foolish thing to her. How much heat could such a stone provide? And how did wood fit into it? Now she saw that the hollow was filled with oil. Bits of twisted moss floated in the oil. Song took fire from her hearth and lit the moss. It burned, but for some reason was not consumed by the flame. The stone was no wider across than the distance from her elbow to her wrist, and only small flames rose from the moss, but K'os could feel the stone's heat from where she sat on the other side of the lodge.

The old woman scooped out a bowl of food and brought it to her.

"That," K'os said, and lifted her chin toward the hollowed rock, "what is it?"

"Qignax," the old woman said. "The Sea Hunters use them to burn seal oil. It is cleaner than a hearth fire, and a good way to use old fat that is too rancid for cooking. My husband was a trader when he was young." She hummed again, something without words.

Yes, K'os thought. She remembered that he had bought her favors with a fine necklace of soapstone carved into intricately designed balls.

"He traded for that fire bow?" K'os asked, looking at the bow hanging among the weapons.

The old woman laughed. "It is not a fire bow," she said. "It is a strange kind of spearthrower. He got it from those people who live near the Far Mountains that edge the South Sea."

K'os had heard stories of such people. "They are not human, I have been told," she said.

The old woman lifted her shoulders in a shrug. "My husband says their language is different and their ways are different. They live in lodges of earth and dead trees. But they respect their ancestors and their children are healthy. He says it is good we do not live close to them. They are warriors, and their weapons would make it difficult for us to survive an attack."

"Weapons like that fire bow?" K'os asked. "What does it do?"

"I cannot touch it," the old woman said. "Even my husband seldom touches it. We do not take it with us to fish camp or when we follow caribou. We leave it here in the winter camp. It has great power, but he showed me how it works, and I will show you."

She brought a small fire bow, settled on her haunches beside K'os and tightened the string until it curved the bow's wooden back. She handed it to K'os, then crawled over to hunt through her stack of firewood until she found a stick. She notched the end of the stick with her woman's knife and set the notch into the string, pulled back and let the stick go. It flew across the lodge, stopping with a thud against the caribou hide wall.

"They do that with spears?" K'os asked.

"That is what my husband says. Small spears with feathers at the end like our men put on their bone-tipped throwing spears. The shafts are only this long," she said, and held her hands a shoulder width apart. "The spear points are small also, no longer than a finger, and made thin and light, of bone and slices of chert."

"So why would people use a weapon like this?" K'os asked.

"It is easy to carry. A man can take a handful, two handfuls, of little spears and shoot them quickly, and very far."

"Farther than a man throwing a spear with a spearthrower?"

"Yes," the old woman said, but she answered slowly, as though not quite sure she was right. "I am trying to think of what my husband told me," she said. She was quiet for a moment, then looked up at K'os with eyebrows raised. "A weak man is able to send his little spear nearly as far as a strong hunter can. That is the good thing. It helps a boy or an old man bring home meat for his family."

"That *is* good," K'os said, and raised the food bowl to her lips. The old woman's stew of meat and roots warmed K'os from her mouth to her belly. She settled her eyes on the bow, caressed it in her thoughts as it hung on the wall. She remembered all the young men she had welcomed into her bed during the past year—boys with thin arms, not yet able to match a grown man strength for strength. With these spear bows, would they be as formidable as older warriors? Was that possible?

K'os finished her meat, then reached inside her parka to the many necklaces she wore against her skin. The young men were always making them for her. Necklaces were not as good as some things. You could not eat them, and they would not keep you warm, but they had their uses.

"You have been kind to me," she said to Song. "Take this and remember my gratitude."

For a moment K'os saw a young woman shine through Song's faded eyes, then one clawed hand reached out for the necklace. K'os stood and draped it over Song's caribouskin shirt, then closed her ears to the old woman's pitiful song of praise.

"You would take a golden-eyed dog?" K'os asked.

"No," the old man said. "How can I trade it? It holds my luck. There is nothing you can give me for it, not even a golden-eyed dog. I still hunt, an old man like me. That spear bow keeps my spearthrower and spears strong. This year I have killed a bear. I also took many caribou. Look at my lodge. See the furs; see the baskets of dried meat. My cache is still nearly full. Soon I will have a giveaway. There is too much for my wife and me, so I will share what I have with others. We will feast and eat. I can do that before you leave. Your husband and the hunters from your village will see how much luck I have."

K'os narrowed her eyes, pulled her lips into a thin, tight line. Blue Jay was a fool. Why did he need luck? He was old.

"If I decided to give it away," he said, "I would give it to you. But a man cannot lose his luck. Especially an old man."

She heard the pleading in his voice and realized he was like all men, eager to please. She stood. "I understand," she said. "I will not ask such a thing of you, nor will my husband."

The old man smiled, relief in his eyes.

"You know I have been asked to visit my son's Near River mother," K'os said.

Blue Jay looked down at his hands. "I know you believe your son to be animal-gift," he said. "Some of us in this village also believe that. Do not let this woman take away your heart."

K'os smiled. "Chakliux is animal-gift, but if Day Woman thinks he is her lost son, then perhaps that belief brings her comfort. I will not take away her heart either."

"You are kind," Blue Jay said, then jerked his head toward Song's parka. "My wife will show you the way."

K'os nodded and followed Song from the lodge.

"He is a good man, worried for everyone," Song said.

"Yes," K'os answered. How sad, she thought, that his luck has run out.

After Song left them alone, K'os sensed Day Woman's nervousness. She could not raise her eyes, and her hands trembled when she gave K'os a dish of meat. K'os set the food on the floor beside her.

Day Woman's eyes grew large. "There is something else you would rather have?" she asked.

"I have had enough food," K'os said. She smiled at the stricken look on Day Woman's face, then asked, "You are Chakliux's true mother?"

She expected no answer from the woman. She had seen such wives before, knew many of them. They lived always trying to please others. She had heard a saying once: "Those who enjoy kicking dogs will find dogs to kick." Day Woman's husband was, no doubt, a dog kicker.

Day Woman's lodge alone was proof of that. Lodge poles were

crooked and small, the bedding furs were old and the smell of mildew was strong. The caribou skins on the floor were well-scraped, but many were falling apart.

"Yes, I am Chakliux's mother," Day Woman said.

K'os was surprised but pleased with the directness of Day Woman's answer. She always welcomed a challenge.

"No," K'os told her, "you are not his mother. He is animal-gift, given to me. His powers are for the people of my village."

Day Woman sat with mouth open, and K'os watched as the woman's eyes filled with tears.

"Crying will not change what is true."

"I do not cry for what you say," Day Woman answered, her voice louder than it had been, as though the tears had strengthened her throat. "I mourn the years I was not mother to him, and I thank you for being his mother when I could not."

K'os shrugged, then picked up her bowl of food, began to eat. Glancing up, she noticed that Day Woman, seeing her eat, seemed to relax. Hospitality was very important to these Near River People, K'os reminded herself. Even the Near River men who came to her village to trade, and then to her lodge for other reasons, always brought gifts and kind words, boring K'os with talk of things that did not matter. She had eyes; nothing stopped her from looking outside to see the sky, to know if it rained or did not, if it snowed or was clear. Why did they have to speak of such things as though she depended on their words for knowledge?

K'os lowered her bowl, looked into Day Woman's face. Yes, she could see some resemblance to Chakliux, the curve of the mouth, the way the right eye was a little larger than the left. "If you are his mother," she said slowly, "then you understand how I feel. More than two handfuls of days have passed since he left our village. He was coming here. We found the man he traveled with dead. There is no sign of my son, and your elders say he did not come to this village." She looked at Day Woman, then up at the top of the lodge. She held her eyes wide open, did not allow herself to blink until the smoke from the lodge hearth burned, then she raised one hand to wipe tears from her cheeks. "I cannot bear to think that he is . . ."

Day Woman leaned forward, shaking her head. "Do not cry, Sister. Do not cry." She crawled on hands and knees to K'os and wrapped her arms around K'os's shoulders.

K'os stiffened against the woman's touch but forced herself to be still. Day Woman smoothed K'os's hair as though she were a child.

"The elders are afraid of the young warriors in your village," Day

Woman said. "They are afraid the Cousin River hunters will think
Chakliux stole golden-eyed dogs for us." Again she stroked K'os's hair,
then rocked on her knees. "Hush, now. Chakliux is alive. Do not worry
over him. Even now he is on his way to the Walrus Hunters. Even
now he is safe, he and his brother, my son, Sok."

Chapter Sixteen

The screaming woke Yaa, and at first she thought it was Ghaden. When she realized he was asleep, she reached out for him. He was startled at her touch. Yaa gathered him into her arms, and he winced as she hugged him too tightly.

"What is it? What is the matter?" Brown Water called.

"Something outside," Happy Mouth said.

In the half-light of early morning, Yaa saw Brown Water roll from her sleeping mats, wrap herself in a hare fur blanket and duck out through the entrance tunnel.

"Yaa, Ghaden, you are awake?" Yaa's mother asked.

"Yes. We are awake," Yaa answered.

"Put on your boots but stay in your beds," said Happy Mouth.

Brown Water stuck her head back inside and said, "There is a fire. Song's lodge."

Yaa sucked in her breath. When a fire started, it spread rapidly, lodge top to lodge top, the greased caribou skins burning so quickly people were often trapped inside.

That was one of the reasons the women did most of their cooking outside, keeping only a small hearth fire in the lodge for warmth in winter and to drive away mosquitoes and gnats in summer. It was one of the first things Yaa had been taught, how to tend the fire, to keep it small.

Song's lodge, Brown Water had said. Fires often seemed to start in an old woman's lodge.

Yaa pulled Ghaden's parka on over his head, finished putting on his boots, then dragged him to the entrance tunnel. The puppy yawned, waddled to the tunnel and raised his leg, almost tipping himself over to urinate on the side of the lodge.

"Bad!" Yaa yelled at him, but had no time to do anything more. She took Brown Water's sewing basket and her mother's pouch of knives and skinning tools and set them beside Ghaden.

"Stay here until I come for you," she said to him. "Do not go back to your bed." Then pulling on her own parka and fetching their three largest wooden bowls, she went outside. Her mother and Brown Water were packing snow up against the lodge. Yaa gave them each a bowl, scooped her bowl full of wet, heavy snow and packed it against the caribouskin walls.

"My husband," K'os sobbed. "He tried to stop it. You have to get him out. You have to. Song is there and her husband. They are all inside." She made her voice rise into a scream, then she saw Tikaani and flung herself at him; she sank to her knees, clasping him around the legs. "Ground Beater, my husband, Ground Beater!" she cried.

Tikaani pulled her to her feet. "K'os, be still. They will get him out. I will get him out." He took a step away from her, toward the burning lodge, but she lunged for him, grabbed him so he had to stop. He called for someone to take her. An old man came, one of the Near River elders. He pulled away her hands, held them firmly.

The flames leapt from Song's lodge to the one beside it. The wind was not strong, so there was little chance the whole village would burn. Sad, K'os thought.

She smoothed back her hair. Her face and parka were full of soot, her hands also. She watched as Tikaani ducked in through the entrance tunnel. She held her breath, hoping he would not be hurt. She did not want to make the trip back to her village without him, and she did not want to remain in the Near River Village any longer than she must. It would be bad enough to be here through mourning, though perhaps they would not expect her to stay the whole moon, but only until her husband was wrapped and placed on a burial platform.

The people had the fire almost out in the next lodge. Only a portion of the caribouhide covering was burned away. Even the lodge poles seemed intact. Others in the village had begun mourning chants. K'os lifted her voice to join them.

Tikaani came out of Song's lodge pulling a body. It was Ground Beater. K'os took a long breath, let out a high screaming cry and broke away from the old man who held her. At that moment the lodge poles collapsed inward, carrying the flames with them. The fire roared, consuming the contents of the lodge.

K'os threw herself over her husband's body, ignoring the stench of burned flesh. She drew a woman's knife from her sleeve, slashed her forearm with the blade. The blood dripped dark red on Ground Beater's charred face.

For five days, K'os stayed with the Near River People, crying, mourning. She gave one of the golden-eyed dogs to Song's oldest son, another to the elders. She shook her head over the miracle that she was alive, nodded her gratitude to those who loaded a sled with gifts and food, and turned down offers from Near River hunters to accompany her to her village.

The Near River People promised they would honor Ground Beater, dissuading her with stories of wolves when she pleaded to take the body back with her.

On the sixth day, she rose early, finished packing, then excused herself to go to the women's place at the edge of the village.

Yaa lay just outside the animal den, a hindquarters of hot roasted hare in her hands. She had stolen it from one of the old women at the cooking hearths, half a hare, lean and tough from winter, but good. She had wrapped most of it in a piece of caribou hide to take back to Ghaden, to give him when they were alone, but she had been unable to wait to eat her own piece.

She lay on her belly, propped up with her elbows, peeking out from the low-lying branches of the black spruce that hid the den. It was good to be there. She had not had a chance to visit the place since Ghaden had returned to their lodge. He was worth it, though, and soon he would be strong enough to come with her. It was a fine hiding place.

She especially liked being in the den during early morning, when the women walked the path to the place where they relieved themselves. It was still very early, and only a few of the women—those whose turn it was to start the village cooking fires and the pregnant women whose big bellies forced them early from their beds—were on the path. Yaa sunk her teeth into the hare and pulled away a mouthful of meat.

When she saw the boots, she knew it was the Cousin River woman. They made their boots wrong, with seams too high on the foot. Yaa pulled herself forward with her elbows and peered out, watching her. Brown Water said the woman had slashed her arm in mourning, but her hair was still long, uncut. She was leaving today, River Ice Dancer had told her, then hit her several times in payment for his information.

Good, I have seen her, Yaa thought, and looked forward to telling her friends.

Yaa set her meat on the mat of dead spruce needles that littered the hardened snow and pulled herself closer to the path. Catching a spruce branch with one hand, she pulled it down to hide her face. Soon the woman was walking the path again. Yaa watched her feet, trying to see the details of the woman's boots so she could tell her mother. Her mother made the best boots in the village, warm and dry with the seams in the right places so they did not rub blisters into toes.

When the woman was well down the path, Yaa scooted out from under the tree, reaching back to grab her meat. She had lost food through carelessness before. Small animals came quickly. The path twisted behind a thick growth of willow, then dipped down toward the village, so by the time Yaa was standing, she had lost sight of the woman, but Yaa fixed her eyes where she would emerge from the bushes. Yaa waited a long time, then she saw something.

It was the woman, yes, and the two young hunters who had come with her. They had only one dog. One of the other two now belonged to Camp Maker. The other had been given to Song's oldest son.

So the woman would not return to the village. She must have come up in modesty to relieve herself. River Ice Dancer had said that it would take them three, maybe four days to return to the Cousin River Village. There would be enough times, on open land, that the poor woman would have to squat in front of those hunters, and they were not even her sons. Yaa hated it when they were following caribou and there was no place for privacy, though at least the girls went as a group together. The boys—ha!—they cared about nothing. Some of them stopped and went right on the trail. Of course it was easier for them.

Yaa took a bite of meat, watching as the young hunters greeted the woman. She gave something to one of the men. A fire bow, Yaa decided, then shook her head, no. It was too long for a fire bow. Ah, she knew what it was. That strange weapon from the Not-People. Something sacred that had belonged to old Blue Jay. He must have given it to her before the fire. She was lucky she was able to get it out. It might have burned.

Yaa watched the Cousin River People until they disappeared down the bank that led to the river, then she scooted back under the spruce tree. She had to eat quickly. She had been gone a long time, too long for only gathering firewood. She took another few bites, then tucked the rest of her meat inside her parka.

She came out from under the spruce tree and fitted her feet into the prints left by the Cousin River woman, walking the path toward the village. Yaa sighed. It was a sad thing for that woman. At least old Blue Jay had given her a gift, Yaa thought, but it was not much in exchange for a husband.

PART
TWO

Summer, 6460 b.c.

In anger I brought her into my lodge—into the warmth of my seal oil lamps, the safety of my thick ulax walls. I say this to make you understand that I did not want the path set before us. So do not tell me how an old woman gets her way by whining.

Our path was chosen by the chief hunter of our village and by the women of his ulax. They were given the same dream, each of them, those sister-wives, on the same night. Four women dreaming the same dream. Who can deny the sacredness of that?

Their dreams said that Aqamdax, daughter of Daes—one of those honored as a granddaughter of Shuganan—should come to me, sister of her father's grandmother, so that Aqamdax could learn to be the next storyteller.

For five tens of years, I have told the old and sacred tales of our people. How else would anyone know about the grandfather Shuganan and the warrior Samiq? From my mouth only came the stories of the otter-caller Chagak, of the trickster Raven and the carver Kiin, and of Kiin's grandson Ukamax, who gave the First Men their sacred dances. These stories have been passed down, storyteller to storyteller, from a time so distant that no one can count the years.

Those sister-wives, they said the spirits told them Aqamdax was the one. Hii! Their husband may believe them, but I do not.

He is a good man, and so he took the mother and child into his own ulax. Who else would take them with their husband-father dead, cursed by sea animals in his hunting? But did the woman show her gratitude? No.

Soon after her mourning had ended, she took a River People name—Daes—and ran off with a trader. They say she lives now with the River People. Fish-eaters who do not even know how to hunt sea animals!

Hii! What else should you expect from Water Slapper's daughter?

So listen to what I tell you, for I say the truth: those wives, the chief hunter's women, they had had enough of Aqamdax's quarrels, enough of her tricks. What better way to be rid of the girl than to give her to me? Have I not prayed for years that the next storyteller be revealed? Have I not set my eyes on each baby born and begged that it be the one? So how can I dispute the spirits' decision? After all, Aqamdax is a beautiful woman.

You would not know by seeing her that she is merely a seal bladder nayux, her skin given shape by the breath of her hate.

Chapter Seventeen

THE FIRST MEN VILLAGE

Bird Caller shuddered and released her. Aqamdax reached for him in the darkness, longing for the weight and warmth of his body, but he crept out of her sleeping place without a word. He was no different from the others. Once they were satisfied, they left.

What was he worried about, that the old woman would hear them? You had to shout to get anything into her ears.

There were other men. Aqamdax could fill her nights with them. She rolled herself into her bedding furs and wrapped her arms across her chest. Yes, she would do that. Some evening she would do that. She would get six men, perhaps seven, and all night she would have someone close to her, someone to hold her. Then the cold would leave her bones, and she would be warm like she had been when her father was alive, when the earth was as good and shining as her father's smile.

The young man walked through the ulax to the climbing log, but Qung pretended she did not see him. They thought she was stupid because she was old, but she saw who came to Aqamdax and how often.

It was almost night. Qung wondered if some other man would come or if Aqamdax would be content with only one. The girl was just like her mother. It would be a blessing to the whole village if some trader would come and take her away. Qung sighed and rolled up the grass mat she was weaving. It was a coarse mat, nothing like the ones she had made when she was young, but her finger joints were swollen and ached so much she could no longer weave split grass.

Until Aqamdax did something—took a husband or left the village—Qung had to teach her, and Aqamdax did not like to be taught. She was quick; it did not take her long to learn a new story. But she could not sit still. She paced as Qung taught her, so that Qung, in turning her head to keep track of the girl, often became dizzy.

Aqamdax practiced the stories; Qung had to admit that. She had even learned to throw her voice, making it seem to come from roof hole or sleeping place, oil lamp or rafter, and she was almost as good at it as Qung herself. But Aqamdax was prone to anger when there was no reason for anger, to throwing things and to pouting.

Aqamdax had lived with her for more than three moons now, and still Qung was not used to the girl's outbursts. During the first few days, Qung let herself feel hope each time a young hunter came to visit the girl. Aqamdax did have fifteen summers. Most women at that age were married, had children. Now Qung realized there was little hope Aqamdax would find a mate.

Why trust a woman who slept with any man who asked? Besides, what hunter would want a woman who, having had so many opportunities, had not yet become pregnant? And who would want a woman who was always angry, always fighting?

Qung sighed. She was old but still strong. She should live quite a few more winters, but what joy was a long life when you shared your ulax with someone like Aqamdax?

Qung pushed herself slowly to her feet, pinched out several wicks in the large oil lamp, leaving one burning. She waddled to her sleeping place, the lamplight throwing long shadows of her humped shoulders and thin arms on the wall before her. As she pulled back the grass sleeping place curtains, she heard a noise and turned. Someone was coming down the climbing log. Salmon. Why was he here? He had two wives.

Qung clicked her tongue in disgust and waited until Salmon saw her. She shook her head at him, and he looked down, avoiding her eyes. How did these men hope to have any luck hunting when they took so many women to satisfy their desires? Did sea animals respect such weakness? How did Salmon expect to keep his iqyax from becoming jealous when he came to it each morning with the smell of a woman on his hands? Someday it would flip him into the sea. Then who would hunt for his wives and their babies?

Qung settled herself into her sleeping place, taking care to wrap her feet in the thickest fur seal pelt. Old ways were being forgotten. Old taboos ignored. What good was it, being a storyteller, if the people would not listen and learn?

Qung turned herself so her back was to the grass curtain. Perhaps the people were tired of listening to an old voice telling them how things should be. Perhaps it was time to hear the stories told in new ways, by a strong, young voice. But what would happen to those sacred stories when they came from Aqamdax's mouth? Were they strong enough to keep themselves pure, or would Aqamdax's disrespect twist them like a woman twists a ptarmigan's neck?

Chapter Eighteen

"It is long-sun feast tonight," Qung said.

"I know," Aqamdax answered, and bit her tongue to stop the ridicule that came too easily into her mouth. Everyone knew it was long-sun feast.

"You have food prepared?" Qung asked.

Aqamdax raised her brows in surprise and spread her hands out over the dried fish and peeled iitikaalux stalks she had layered on grass mats.

Qung nodded as if she had just seen what Aqamdax had done. "Take some of our eggs," she said.

Again Aqamdax was surprised. The eggs, stored in seal oil and buried in sand, were Qung's favorite. She did not share them, and even Aqamdax had to sneak to get one from their store, though she had been the one who climbed the cliffs to gather them.

"Eggs?" she repeated, to be sure she had heard the old woman right.

"Eggs. I said eggs," Qung answered, her voice rising into annoyance. "Take eggs."

"Yes, Aunt."

"It is a celebration, you know."

Aqamdax smiled. "I know." Long-sun day always brought hope, and the First Men tried to show the sun that they appreciated its rising each morning. If they did not do such a thing, if praises were not made, who could say? Perhaps the sun would choose to stay wherever it went during the night and never return.

"The First Men will have a new storyteller."

Aqamdax opened her mouth but did not speak. A new storyteller. Qung must mean her, but did she know the stories well enough? What if the people would not listen when she talked? How could she hope to carry their respect as Qung did?

The men came willingly enough into her sleeping place, but she knew what was said behind her back. She understood the anger of wives and mothers. It was one thing for a man on a long journey to take his pleasure with a woman who was willing, but to have such a woman in their village, ready whenever a wife was not . . . If Aqamdax was wife, she might feel the same resentment.

Yet, she had never been claimed as wife, and each month her bleeding came. So how could she hope to be wife? Why give a bride price for a barren woman when she would welcome you into her bed anyway? Why have to worry about feeding her?

So, would the people listen to someone like her? How would they feel when their sacred stories came from her mouth?

"You are ready," Qung said. "I know. You are ready." She said the words with an assurance that settled the anxiety fluttering in Aqamdax's chest.

"I am ready," Aqamdax answered, and tried to make her voice sound as sure as Qung's. She smiled at Qung, at the face so lined with wrinkles you could hardly see the eyes. "Do you think our people are ready for me?"

She laughed when Qung did not answer her, then lifted her head. It would be no different than when she gathered clams with the women or joined the chief's wives to fish pogy. She was good at ignoring barbed words, sly smiles, narrowing eyes. If she told the stories well enough, perhaps they would forget who was telling and think only of what was being said.

The dancing did not end until the sun had sunk behind the northwest edge of the earth. Qung had kept the ulax dark, lighting only a few wicks in one oil lamp, and Aqamdax wondered if she had done that in hopes the people would forget who was speaking.

Aqamdax had left on her feathered sax, the long, calf-length coat that most First Men wore only outside the ulax. She wished she could wear a winter parka, the hood over her head to protect her from the people's thoughts. At least the sax hid her belly and breasts, caressed by too many men.

She had not participated in the dancing and had eaten very little during the feast. It seemed as though the people of her stories were alive in her mind, dancing, singing and shouting out their own celebration, whispering into her ears, pushing their songs into her mouth until she was so full of people inside she could not bear the company of those around her.

She had hidden outside in the shadowed lee of the ulax farthest from the celebration, crouching there to listen to the chattering in her head until she finally realized she was leaning against the death ulax.

Aqamdax had stood up to leave, but then decided she would stay. Here she would be left alone. No one would interrupt her as she retold the stories. Perhaps those bones inside the ulax would enjoy hearing the old stories once again.

She began with the Maker's stories, told how all things were created—sea and sky, earth and animals and man. Then she told of times long ago when sea otters and First Men were brothers. She told how a brother and sister, cursed by sleeping together, became the sun and moon. You could see them still, chasing one another across the sky. She told those stories and stories more recent, of hunters and warriors, of hard winters and good summers. Finally, when the sun had dipped into the earth, she returned to Qung's ulax.

Qung was waiting. The thin slits of her eyes sparked when Aqamdax climbed down into the ulax. Aqamdax wondered if the old woman would tell stories also, or if she wanted Aqamdax to do all the telling. Usually, when a village had more than one storyteller, they took turns, one telling, then the other, each spinning stories from what had already been told.

They sat in silence for a time, then Qung said, "I will tell the first story. When I have finished, it will be your turn. If anyone objects, do not stop. I will do whatever has to be done."

"Does anyone know I will be . . ."

"I have told the chief hunter. Perhaps he will tell his wives. Perhaps not, but what can they say? They are the ones who dreamed you here."

Aqamdax laughed. Yes, they had dreamed her here. What else could they have done with her? She needed to be a wife. If not that, then why not storyteller?

"Be still, Aqamdax," Qung said, and Aqamdax realized that she was pacing, moving in long, quick steps from one side of the ulax to the other. She made herself sit down, but her feet jerked and her knees twitched and the muscles of her legs danced under her skin.

"Here," Qung said, and slipped something into Aqamdax's hand. The girl opened her fingers. It was a whale's tooth, carved into the whorls of a shell. Smooth and cool, it lay as though it had been shaped to fit into a hand. Aqamdax's fingers followed the curves of the whorl, stroking. The nervousness seemed to slide out of her body as her fingers moved, slowly, slowly over the lines of the whale tooth shell.

"It is yours now," Qung said. "I do not need it."

Aqamdax was surprised. She had certainly given Qung no reason to offer gifts.

"Shuganan's?" Aqamdax asked. Her mother had had several of the man's ancient carvings, but she had taken them with her when she left the First Men.

"No, not Shuganan's," Qung answered. "One of his granddaughter's."

"Thank you," Aqamdax said, and realized that she had not thanked anyone for a long time—not since her mother had left.

"I do it as a favor for myself," Qung answered. She swept one arm toward Aqamdax's feet. "Now I do not have to put up with your wiggling." She cackled, an old woman's laugh, then stood and hobbled to the notched climbing log. She looked up expectantly.

Her hearing is not as bad as she pretends, Aqamdax thought, and reminded herself not to forget that. Then people were descending into the ulax, men followed by wives and children. Babies were slung on backs, toddlers on hips; young children climbed down cautiously; the older children jumped into the ulax from near the top of the log.

Qung sat down beside Aqamdax and bowed her head. Aqamdax, noticing, did the same. It was a wise thing to do, Aqamdax realized. The bowed head seemed to discourage anyone from starting a conversation, and it helped Aqamdax shift her thoughts back to the stories she would tell.

When Qung began the first story, Aqamdax raised her head, looked at the people. All of them had their eyes on Qung; each leaned forward as though ready to snatch up the words that came from Qung's mouth. Would they look at Aqamdax like that, or would they hiss their disgust?

She found each of the chief's wives. They sat behind the men but ahead of most other women. She found her cousin Kittiwake and Kittiwake's little son. Her mother's closest friend, Blue Fish, was there, and Blue Fish's aunt, her mind nearly gone, her mouth always dribbling saliva.

Aqamdax shifted her eyes to the men, saw the chief, and Salmon, then the one who had been her father's hunting partner, Afraid-of-his-hand, the man who could not save him from the sea.

Her toes began to wiggle, and she felt Qung squeeze her arm, pat the whale tooth shell Aqamdax still held in her hands.

Aqamdax rubbed her fingers over the shell, then took a long breath. Qung's story continued as though nothing had happened, and Aqamdax bowed her head, made herself sit still and listen until she was caught into the words, the ancient carver Shuganan alive again in the hills and beaches she saw in her mind.

When the story was done, Qung reached over, pressed Aqamdax's hand, smoothed gnarled fingers over the carving Aqamdax held.

"The woman Chagak was in the hills gathering berries when the warriors came," Aqamdax began. She stopped to take a breath, her heart hammering in fear. Would the people get up and leave? She heard several women hiss. Again Qung pressed Aqamdax's hand, and Aqamdax remembered what the old woman had told her. Keep speaking, do not stop. Continue the story.

Aqamdax opened her mouth, and the words came, halting at first, but then they flowed, beautiful words, honed through years of storytellers into something that carried the mind to far places and times long ago.

At first she spoke quietly, but as the story pulled the First Men's thoughts together, it also seemed to strengthen her. When Chagak spoke to the otter, Aqamdax used the knowledge Qung had given her to throw her voice up and out so it sounded as though the otter called from the top of the ulax, as though the animal were sitting there above them.

Several children looked up at the roof hole, and a number of women hummed their approval. The quiet praise glowed in Aqamdax's chest, filled her with joy. Her voice grew strong, and the story folded her into its magic like a sea otter folds itself into the kelp, safe. Safe.

Chapter Nineteen

THE WALRUS HUNTER VILLAGE

The storyteller spoke in a chant, using strands of knotted sinew stretched between quick fingers to illustrate his words, but the words were often spoken too quickly for Chakliux to understand, with allusions to other stories, to hunters and warriors that Chakliux did not know. When the people laughed, Chakliux could not join them, and when they nodded, adding comments of their own, agreeing or disagreeing with what the storyteller said, Chakliux felt like a child who understood only small pieces of the world around him.

He glanced across the circle of people that ringed the storyteller. They were outside, at the edge of the Walrus Hunters' summer village, the women and their children beside the men. He saw Sok with his arms shamelessly tucked under the parka of Little Ears, the woman hiding her giggles behind both hands.

Little Ears's father had already approached Sok, asking a bride price for the woman. Sok had made vague promises, offered possibilities, but Chakliux knew he wanted the woman only as long as they stayed with the Walrus Hunters. Sok had little enough chance to make

Snow-in-her-hair his bride as second wife. How could he win her if she were to be third wife? And who would take the brunt of the Walrus Hunters' anger when Sok left? Chakliux, of course. If Chakliux did not return to the Near River Village, then he would probably stay here, living with whatever mischief Sok left behind him.

Chakliux moved his eyes around the circle, away from his brother and Little Ears. There was Walrus Killer, the chief hunter, his two wives and their many children. Old Tusk, a hunter who was not old at all, sat next to them. He was helping Chakliux build his own iqyax. Together they had gathered driftwood for the frame. Old Tusk had been generous in trading Chakliux the ivory he needed to inlay at joints where wood rubbed wood. He had taught Chakliux how to mix red ocher into a paint which would protect the iqyax frame against rot and also show the sea animals that the iqyax was one of them, the wooden frame its bones, the lashings its tendons and sinews, the ocher its blood.

Old Tusk had offered to teach Chakliux how to paddle, had already taken Chakliux out in an old iqyak. Now Chakliux knew how to bend his body with the boat, to move his legs as though they were the iqyax's own muscles, his paddle as though it were flippers and tail. There was much Chakliux had yet to learn, even the simple knowledge of tides and rips, clouds and winds, but they had come to the place where Chakliux must learn to be the iqyax's true brother, and how could he be true brother unless he made the frame with his own hands, unless he built it to match the length and reach of his own legs and arms?

Now the frame was nearly done, but how could he complete an iqyax without a wife to sew the cover? Little Ears had offered, but Chakliux could not agree, knowing Sok's intentions.

Chakliux turned his mind back to the storyteller. He tried to follow the words, to focus his thoughts on the strands of sinew the man fashioned first into the head of a fox, next into a series of knots he called birds. Chakliux wondered if he could learn to do such a thing to strengthen his own stories, to help the Near River men decipher his riddles.

It was long-sun celebration, a time of feasting and giving thanks, but Chakliux felt uneasy being in this village on this day. What were his own people doing? Who was telling the stories now that they had no Dzuuggi? Were sacred ways being honored? Or were spirits angered because The People had forgotten what should be done?

And what about these Walrus Hunters? They did not do things in proper ways. Chakliux knew how to honor the sun; he knew the correct chants, the ancient stories, and yet here he was sitting like a child listening to the Walrus storyteller. Should he raise his voice, tell them what should be said? Yet how could he without enough Walrus words to speak clearly and in a manner the people would understand?

The Walrus Hunters seemed strong, healthy. Their food caches were full; their women were happy. Perhaps what they did was right for their beach, their village, but was it right for Chakliux and Sok? Should they have had their own celebration, remembering the way of The People, rather than relying on Walrus traditions?

There were too many problems for him in the Walrus Hunter Village, but would his life be better with Blueberry—or living with K'os?

Then Chakliux chided himself: So, like an old woman you whine out your discomfort? You mourn when your belly is full and your hands are busy, when good people are doing what they can to help you. Be still. I do not want to hear your complaints. You are not a child.

He listened again to the storyteller, watched the man's charmed fingers change his bird knots into the long-whiskered face of an otter. The storyteller held the otter up so all could see, then he turned to smile at Chakliux, the otter-man who had come to live among them.

THE FIRST MEN VILLAGE

Aqamdax flinched from Salmon's quivering fingers as he stroked her arm. At least his wives had left the ulax and did not see him. She wondered at herself. Why would something that had brought her pleasure yesterday now make her shudder? He was the same man. Of all the hunters, he was the only one who would stay in her sleeping place and hold her after he was satisfied.

Somehow the stories had filled her, made her feel as though she was complete, as though she did not need anyone to protect her against the night.

"No, Salmon," she said, but tried to keep the sharpness from her voice. Why offend the man? What if by tomorrow the stories were gone and again she was alone? She might need Salmon to hold her so she would not fly up into the dark skies and lose herself in the vast emptiness between earth and stars.

"I am tired," she said softly. "The people whose stories I told seemed to have taken a part of my spirit, so there is only enough left to guide me into dreams."

Salmon looked puzzled, but Aqamdax offered no other explanation. How could she? The stories not only filled her, but drew her soul into places she had never been before. It would seem like a betrayal to take a man who was not husband into her sleeping place. At least tonight it would seem so. Tomorrow, who could say?

Salmon left, as did other men who heard what she told him. After the storytelling many wanted to share her bed, some who had never come to her before, others who seldom came. Finally the last of the men was gone and there were only Qung and Aqamdax.

The old woman smiled. "You did well," she said.

Aqamdax, not used to compliments, lowered her head, unsure how to answer.

Qung lifted her hand toward the empty ulax. "No men tonight?" she asked.

"Not tonight."

Qung raised her eyebrows. Aqamdax shrugged, and Qung turned toward her sleeping place. She was muttering, but then spoke louder. "Perhaps those chief's wives did not lie," the old woman said. "Perhaps they did dream."

Aqamdax stood for a moment in the empty ulax, imagined that the people were still there. With her voice and her words, she had taken them from this ulax to places none of them had ever been. She had made them warriors and elders, children and traders. They had become Whale Hunters, and Walrus men, even faraway River People. She had done that.

She shook her head in disbelief. With only the words of her mouth, she had done that.

THE WALRUS HUNTER VILLAGE

The people of the Walrus Hunter Village told stories through the night, waiting until the sun showed its face in the morning. Then again they feasted, celebrating the light. Sok and Chakliux sat watching as the Walrus men helped themselves to the dried fish and walrus meat heaped on woven mats laid near the outdoor cooking hearths.

Sok and Chakliux did not eat until all the village elders and hunters were served, but when the boys began to bring their bowls, Chakliux and Sok went also. An old woman came to them with a bone dipping ladle and filled Sok's bowl. He grunted at her, then picked up several pieces of dried fish, laid them across the bowl, so the steam rising from the broth would soften the flesh.

Chakliux waited, assuming the woman would bring broth for him as well, but she pulled him with her toward a boiling bag as though he were a child. She was a tiny woman, her skin dark with age, but her eyes were bright, and she was as lean and straight as a young girl.

"Even before you came, I heard stories about you," she said, and Chakliux realized that she spoke the River language. Her words, though clipped too short by a tongue accustomed to speaking Walrus, were clear.

"You speak my language," Chakliux said.

"And what is so difficult about that?" she asked. "Even small children speak the River language, do they not?" She laughed, and Chakliux laughed with her.

"I am called Tutaqagiisix."

He tried to repeat the name, but the sounds wrapped themselves into a ball in his throat and came out wrong.

Again she laughed. "The children call me Tut. I am of the First Men, brought here to this village long ago as bride to a Walrus Hunter. I have kept my First Men name, though my husband was not happy I did so. It is a sign of my gift, given me as a child. I learn to speak languages easily. I hear the sounds and soon understand. *Tutaqagiisix* means 'hearing.'"

She dipped her ladle deep into a boiling bag, brought it out full of meat and small bones. "Seal flipper bones," she said, still speaking the River language. "They put themselves into my ladle to remind me what I must say to you." She pulled one of the bones from the ladle. She bit off one of the ends, softened by boiling, and sucked. Oil and broth dripped to her chin and she wiped the back of her hand over her mouth, then dumped the remaining meat and bones from her ladle into Chakliux's bowl.

"You also have a gift." She looked down at his caribouskin boots. "Dzuuggi, animal-gift."

Chakliux was surprised by her words. He and Sok had told few of his past. They were only hunters, trading, trying to earn a bride price for a wife, trying to find strong dogs for the River People.

As though she could hear his thoughts, the old woman said, "Remember my name. I hear much. You are otter, they say."

"Some say I am otter. Others say I am not."

"What do you say?"

Chakliux looked away from the woman. Where was Sok? Why was he alone with this old woman and her many questions?

She looked up at him like a child, waiting for his answer, but what could he say when he did not know himself what he was? Dzuuggi, yes, but otter? Animal-gift?

"I am Dzuuggi, trained as storyteller, and to know the many

traditions of our people, the memories of wars, hard winters and good hunts."

Tut again raised the bone to her mouth, sucked, then looked at him from the corners of her eyes. "And animal-gift?"

"If I am animal-gift, I am otter," Chakliux finally said. "More than that I do not know. The one who found me told me I was animal-gift. Sometimes I believe that is true. Other times I do not."

"Your words are honest, as the words of a Dzuuggi must be," the old woman said. "They say you have an otter foot. Show me."

Her request surprised him, but he did as she asked, showing first the three webbed toes of his right foot, then the bent and curved otter foot. She leaned over, poked at the foot, then said, "You are otter."

The words washed through Chakliux like warm rain, driving away doubt. Then he reminded himself that she was only an old woman. What did she know? But a small voice came to him, as though Gguzaakk spoke: Why doubt? Tutaqagiisix has also been given a gift. Who else is more apt to recognize the same in another?

"So then," Tut continued, "where do you build your iqyax?"

She handed Chakliux his bowl, and as though they were brother and sister, born to the same mother, sharing the same food, she reached in and pulled out another seal flipper bone.

"On the leeward side of the walrus rock," Chakliux told her, "beyond the high tide mark."

"Come to my tent tomorrow, early in the morning. You can carry the walrus hide. It is heavy for an old woman like me."

Then like brother to sister, Chakliux offered his bowl once more to her fingers.

Chapter Twenty

Chakliux angled his iqyax into the waves and turned his upper body to add thrust to his paddle, driving the bow forward, resisting the water spirits that wanted to tumble his iqyax back to shore.

His arms were strong, hardened during the four moons he had been with the Walrus Hunters, and now he had his own iqyax, Tut's fine stitches binding the walrus hide cover into one whole piece, like the skin of an animal.

She had also made a hatch skirt, and his chigdax, a watertight parka made of strips of sea lion gut with drawstrings at wrists and face. She had done all this and given it as gift, countering his protests with her own: Who did she have to sew for, now that she was a widow? What did he want her to do with her days? Sit with the old women and grumble?

The iqyax moved over waves like an otter. Sinew bindings at each joint allowed it to flex and bend as Chakliux paddled over each swell. He used his body and legs within the wooden framework as though the iqyax were skin and skeleton, and he its muscle.

Old Tusk had set out seal bladders, each blown full of air and tethered to the next, each weighted with a stone ballast on a long bull kelp line so it would not be lost in the waves. At each end of the tether line, Old Tusk had tied sealskin floats.

"You first!" Old Tusk called.

Chakliux pulled the rope that released his spearthrower from the deck of the iqyax. He fitted a harpoon into his thrower and raised his arm, pulled back, his hand tight on the thrower, fingers light against the harpoon shaft to hold it in place. The throw had to be accurate, had to hit the center of the target or the bladder would skitter away from the harpoon. He threw and his harpoon hit; the bladder popped. The tether line sagged under the weight of the ballast stone, no longer buoyed by air, and pulled the neighboring bladders closer together.

Old Tusk threw his harpoon. It, too, hit. Chakliux lifted his voice to praise, but Old Tusk called: "You are too noisy, brother. Remember, where there is one animal there may be many. Try again."

Chakliux coiled in his harpoon, fitted it into the spearthrower, and threw again. This time he missed, his throw only pushing the bladder sideways. Old Tusk threw again, hit again.

"See what happens when you are too noisy, brother," he called. "The animals leave you."

Chakliux took the scolding in good humor. Old Tusk was right. Hunting sea animals was very different from taking caribou or bears. He coiled in his harpoon and threw. He struck the bladder, and before retrieving the weapon, took another harpoon from the iqyax deck and threw it. Again he hit his target.

This time Old Tusk was the one to raise his voice in praise, and Chakliux could not keep the smile from his mouth. He began coiling in his harpoons. Besides the sealskins, there were two handfuls of bladders still floating. Chakliux and Old Tusk would aim only at the bladders so the whole line would not sink, costing them floats, kelp lines and rock weights. He tied one harpoon on his iqyax and fitted the other to his thrower. He raised his arm, then saw that Old Tusk had raised his thrower straight in the air.

Like all Walrus men, Old Tusk had painted his thrower black on the top, red on the bottom. When he held the red side up and turned it toward Chakliux, it meant his harpoon had hit its mark. This time, the black side was up, a sign he had sighted an animal. Had he seen a seal or otter, even with the noise of their practicing?

Old Tusk pointed with his thrower west, toward the horizon, and Chakliux saw them. Iqyan, three, perhaps four. He quickly tied harpoon and thrower to his iqyax and grabbed his paddle, ready to head back to the village, but Old Tusk called, "They are Walrus."

He began to paddle toward the iqyan. Chakliux followed. As they drew closer, he could see the yellow and red markings and realized the men were traders. He remembered the group that had left the Walrus Village not long after he and Sok had arrived. He had understood that they hoped to trade with Sea Hunters.

Chakliux thrust his paddle into the waves and pushed ahead to meet them, to see traders and iqyan that had been in the presence of sea otter men. Perhaps someday he would go himself to those far shores and learn what the Sea Hunters had to teach him.

Sok smiled. It was a forced smile, covering his anger. His trade offers were more than enough for the mask and shaman's pouch. Yehl was an old man who hid behind the power of his chants and medicines. His pleasures no longer came from the bodies of women or the accumulation of goods; now he found joy in withholding from others what he could not have himself.

The Walrus considered themselves a strong people, but how long would that strength last with a shaman like Yehl? Surely the spirits knew he was growing weak. Those evil ones out there would soon start playing their tricks. Would the sea animals continue to give themselves to the harpoons of men whose shaman had no power?

Sok had wasted four moons here in this village, surely long enough to know if the Cousin River People would seek revenge, but also long enough—more than long enough—for him to accumulate the trade goods he would need to change Wolf-and-Raven's mind about giving Snow-in-her-hair to him as wife.

But he had been too eager, and in foolishness had traded Snow Hawk during the first few days they had been in the village. Chakliux had told him to wait, but Sok, seeing the goods offered, had not. Since then, he and Chakliux had needed to trade away much of what he received for the dog in exchange for food, lodging and oil. How could he have known that the things he accepted in trade, though unusual to the River People, were of everyday use here in this village? How could he have known that in trading those things back to the Walrus, he would get so little in return?

Still, he had two walrus tusks and several obsidian spear points. Surely Wolf-and-Raven would find some value in those things, but probably not enough to pay a bride price for Snow-in-her-hair.

Yehl shifted on the fur mats where he sat, stood and reached for his caribouskin parka, another thing Sok had given to the man in trade. Sok stood, still unused to the rude ways of the Walrus. What man ever leaves a guest who is visiting? Chakliux's calm voice came to his ears: each village has its own way.

So then, Sok wondered, how should he respond? Finally he stood also, pulled the hood of his parka around his face, and when Yehl left the lodge, Sok followed him. His eyes had not yet adjusted to the sun when Chakliux came running to him, grabbed his arm as though they were both children, and chattered so quickly that Sok could not understand what he said.

Sok jerked his arm away. "What has happened?" he asked, his voice rough and low.

"The Walrus traders have returned."

Sok looked down at his brother. His eyes were bright, his face red and peeling from the long days he spent in the iqyax. Perhaps it was time for Sok to leave this village. It appeared that Chakliux would be happy to stay. He had even learned many of the Walrus words. Sok was able to communicate only with one of Yehl's sons, a man who spoke the River language, though in a poor and halting way, and to the old woman called Tut.

At least there was Little Ears. She knew only a few River words, but what need did he have to speak when he was with her?

"They have Sea Hunter things: otter skins, obsidian, grass baskets, shell beads, seal flipper boots . . ."

Chakliux's list continued until Sok's anger lifted enough for him to realize that his brother was suggesting they trade for these things themselves. Why not? Something brought from the far shores of the Sea Hunter People should be worth more to Wolf-and-Raven than mere Walrus goods. He clapped a hand on Chakliux's shoulder. His brother still wore the knee-length gut parka that hunters used to stay dry when they were in their iqyan.

"You were practicing today?" he asked Chakliux.

"Too bad the bladders were not seals," Chakliux answered.

Sok laughed. They pushed their way through the children and women to the group of Walrus men who surrounded the traders.

The traders were pulling packs from the bows and sterns of their iqyan. Several of the elders had already opened the packs, removing fist-sized nodules of obsidian, braided kelp ropes, packs of beads, whale teeth and fishhooks. Several children who had managed to creep through the crowd to the iqyan had opened a sea lion belly of dried fish. They ran, laughing, chunks of fish clasped in both hands, as one of the traders chased them away.

Chakliux noticed several whole seal skins turned inside out, stubs where the front flippers had been, the skins taut and bloated with the contents.

"Oil," Tut said, coming to stand beside him. "They do as we do, turning the skin whole, hair and all, and placing the fat strips inside to render on their own."

"I do not like the hair," said Chakliux.

Tut shrugged. "Good flavor," she said. "They render some also in pits or boiling bags, but that takes a long time. It is better to sew your husband's chigdax than wait on oil, eh?"

Sok gripped Chakliux's arm, pointed with his chin. One of the traders was holding a parka made of pieced bird skins. In the sunlight, the black feathers were as shiny as obsidian. It was trimmed with bands of hair embroidery and strips hung with iridescent shell beads.

"So what do you think?" he asked. "Would Wolf-and-Raven want such a thing?"

"What man would not?" Chakliux answered.

"Do not think you will get it," Tut said. "The Walrus are not ones to part with such trade goods easily."

The anger of his frustration with Yehl and the powerlessness he felt living with these Walrus Hunters honed Sok's words into sharpness, and he snapped, "What do you know, old woman?" He turned so she could see the sun Red Leaf had pieced on the back of his parka. "Not even for this?"

"I have heard men say good things about that parka. You should have brought more with you."

He had told himself the same thing many times, but who could believe that something a woman made would have more value to these Walrus Hunters than weapons or food?

He turned to Tut. "Tell those men not to trade away too many things. Tell them this River hunter has much to offer."

"I will tell them," Tut answered, "but do not expect them to give easily what has cost them many moons of hard travel."

He had taken the name Yehl, Raven, when he was young and strong, not yet as powerful in shaman ways as he would be, but, unlike many shamans, a gifted hunter, able to take both land and sea animals. Now his arms were the thin bony arms of an old man. His voice, once loud enough to carry chants over the whole village, was weak, and so were his eyes.

Someone scratched at the side of his tent, and Yehl pushed himself up.

"I am here," he called.

He recognized the large, square hand as it thrust in to push aside the walrus hide doorflap. Sun Beater. His mother claimed he was Yehl's son. Who could say for sure? The woman had never been one of his wives. She was not a woman to be trusted, and Yehl had never fully believed her claim.

Yehl treated the boy well, including him in hunting trips with his sisters' sons, sharing meat and oil with Sun Beater's mother each time she was between husbands, but the important things—chants and songs, weapons and amulets—those he saved for his wives' sons.

"Father," Sun Beater said even before Yehl had a chance to return to the soft furs where he had been sitting, "I have come to tell you my vision."

Yehl sighed. He was no fool. He knew that Sun Beater wanted to be the next shaman, and how could Yehl deny his claim? None of his true sons wanted to follow their father, nor did his sisters' sons. They were content being hunters. But Sun Beater was not a patient man. He wanted Yehl to teach him quickly, so he could claim powers he had not earned. He was too much like his mother. Wanting one thing, then wanting another, never satisfied for long with what he had.

"There is food in the boiling bag," Yehl said, and gestured toward the doorflap, the tripod just outside.

Sun Beater shook his head, squatted on his haunches. "I was sleeping but not sleeping, seeing but not seeing," he said, words that Yehl remembered saying to him long ago when he had explained one of his own dreams. "A woman came to me. Her voice was the voice of an otter, and when she spoke, it was like the wind sharing the secrets it has learned from the earth."

The young man's eyes glowed, and for once Yehl believed him. There *had* been a dream. Yehl knew when someone was lying. But a dream could mean many things—perhaps only that someone was afraid or wanted something. Perhaps only that the spirit was living its own life while the body rested.

"This woman," Yehl said, "who is she?"

Sun Beater shook his head. "That is why I came to you. Perhaps you know."

"You remember what she looked like?"

"Young, a round face like an otter. A large mouth, and she wore a parka of bird skins, much like the one the traders brought with them from the First Men Village."

"Did you dream this before you saw that parka or after?" Yehl asked.

"Before. Last night, before the traders returned."

Yehl raised his eyebrows. Then the dream was not because Sun Beater wanted the parka. Perhaps it came because he needed a woman. "Your wife, is she in moon blood time?"

Sun Beater frowned. "No."

"When was the last time you visited her sleeping place?"

"Last night," Sun Beater said.

Yehl closed his eyes, sat for a moment, then said to Sun Beater, "There might be something to this dream. Since she was wearing a birdskin parka, perhaps this woman is of the First Men. Perhaps we should go and speak to our traders, see if they found such a woman there. If she has some special power . . ." He glanced at Sun Beater and looked away. In his old age, sometimes he spoke too quickly, said too much. What if this woman did have spirit powers? Perhaps if he could get her as wife, her strength would compensate for his weakness. "You said she had a large mouth?" he asked.

"Too large. Her face was beautiful except for that mouth."

Yehl pulled on a parka and motioned Sun Beater to follow him from the tent.

"Perhaps I should eat," Sun Beater said, looking down into the food bag as they left.

"It will be here when we get back," Yehl said. "Those traders will soon remember their wives and close their doorflaps to all of us. Then even a shaman will not be welcome." He laughed, and Sun Beater joined his laughter.

Chakliux walked with Sok to the traders' tents. Tut had explained that the traders were brothers, four of them, and they shared the same lodge in the winter village. In this summer place near the North Sea, they placed their tents close to one another. They should go to the eldest brother's tent, Tut had told them. He was the one who did most of the trading. She told Sok to bring other trade goods, things the River People were known for—bark and fishskin baskets, caribou leggings embroidered with porcupine quills, and the warm hare fur blankets that their women made. But Sok had laughed at Tut's suggestions.

"She sees value in those things because she is a woman," he said to Chakliux. "What will a Walrus Hunter trader give for a basket that holds no more power than what some woman put into it?"

Instead he brought gaffs, traps and hooks for river fishing, snow goggles and snowshoes, chert knives with caribou bone handles and spearheads made with a bone base scored to hold thin stone blades, each no longer than a man's smallest finger, half as thick as the quill end of an eagle feather. He wore the parka, as Tut suggested he should, and he brought one hare fur robe.

"She knows nothing about trading," Sok said. "What woman does?"

"Most do not, at least among the River People," Chakliux said, "but perhaps here . . ."

"You have told me," Sok said. "Each village has its own ways."

Chakliux lowered his head and did not try to reason with his brother. Sometimes words only made things more difficult.

There were nearly as many people gathered around the traders' summer lodges as there had been when they beached their iqyan. As many women as men, Chakliux noticed, and the women often raised their voices, making offers for one trade good or another. Sok pushed his way through the crowd to where one of the traders stood. He was dealing with a man for a bone-tipped harpoon. Unlike Walrus Hunter harpoons, this one had a tip that carried most of its barbs on one side. The trader lifted the harpoon, unwrapped the sinew that covered the joint where the harpoon head met a bone foreshaft and showed the small beveled tongue of ivory that was inserted into a slot carved into the foreshaft.

"Like man into woman," the hunter joked.

"Yes," answered the trader, "and like man into woman, it works well. You will not miss seal or sea lion with this harpoon."

"Too small for walrus," the hunter said.

"They do not hunt walrus, those First Men."

"Then why do I need this small spear, good only for seals? Perhaps I am foolish to look at it."

"They also hunt whales," Chakliux said softly, speaking in Walrus words. He heard Tut hiss. Ah, he had probably broken some taboo.

The hunter spun, lifted his upper lip in derision at Chakliux, but the trader laughed, raised one hand as though in greeting.

"There, you see, friend," the trader told the hunter. "Even the River People know that First Men hunt whales."

"With that?" the hunter asked, and pointed at the harpoon.

The trader looked at Chakliux, raised his eyebrows.

"No," said Chakliux. "But I know stories that tell of Sea Hunters taking whales."

"So then," the trader said, "the same hands make both whale and seal harpoons. You do not see the power in that?"

Another hunter stepped forward. "If he does not, I do," he said.

The first hunter grabbed the harpoon and lifted a chin toward a summer tent pitched on the seaward side of the village. "I will give what you asked for. Two seal skins of oil. Two walrus harpoons. My daughter is in that tent. She will make you a willow root basket." He spun away from the trader, shot a look of disgust at Chakliux and left.

"So then, River man," the trader said to Chakliux, "you are next. What is it you want to trade for?"

Chakliux laid a hand on Sok's shoulder. "My brother is the one who has come to trade," he said.

Sok stepped forward, then leaned back to whisper to Chakliux, "Do not help me in the trading. Just tell me what they say. I do not need to follow the steps of that last hunter."

"My mouth is closed," Chakliux said, but he could not keep a smile from his lips.

Tut crowded close to Chakliux, and, as the trader began to speak, she translated the finer meanings of his words, those things Chakliux was not yet able to pick up.

"He asks what you want," Chakliux told Sok.

Sok pointed with his chin toward the birdskin parka. A hum of amazement came from the crowd of people, and the trader lifted his voice in a shout of laughter. He chattered out a series of words too quickly for Chakliux to follow.

"He says your brother must be a gifted hunter to have enough furs and meat to offer for the sax," Tut said.

"The what?"

"Sax, a First Men word. Sax. It means 'parka.' " Tut paused. "Almost, it means 'parka.' That garment you see lying there, that is a sax."

Sok turned back toward Chakliux. "Tell him that I will trade equal for equal. This fine parka I wear for that birdskin parka. Tell him this parka I have is caribou and wolf, fox and weasel, much more powerful than something made of bird skins. And warmer also."

"Offer less first," Tut told Sok.

"Old woman," Sok said, "leave the trading to the men."

Tut lifted her head and shrugged her shoulders. "Equal for equal," she said in the River language, then repeated the words in the Walrus tongue.

Sok turned, said the same words to the trader. Again the trader laughed.

"And what do you have that is equal?" he asked.

Chakliux translated his words, and Sok held out his arms, turned so the trader could see the sun design pieced on the back of his parka.

"It is worth something," the trader said. "But what woman does not know how to sew caribou parkas? Bird skins, though, that is something different. Are there any women here who can work bird skins?"

Sok turned to Chakliux, raised eyebrows to ask what was being said.

"Leave," Tut told Sok. "You have already lost. Leave. You have nothing he will take."

Sok spat on the ground. "Do not tell me what to do, woman," he said, then turned again to the trader, lifted the hare fur blanket he had draped over one arm.

The trader shook his head.

"What is the word for spear points?" Sok asked Chakliux without looking back. "For snow goggles, fish traps?"

Tut gave him the words, and Sok repeated them to the trader.

Again the trader shook his head.

"Your brother, he does not know how to trade," Tut whispered to Chakliux. "He has nothing else?"

"Nothing."

"I have grass baskets, leggings, a little oil."

"He does not need the sax, Tut. Do not give your things to satisfy his wants. He is not a child. Besides, he has already lost honor in this exchange in front of the whole village. He would not appreciate your help."

"So with a brother like Sok, how did you become so wise?" Tut asked.

Chakliux smiled at her. "In ways I would not wish on another," he said.

Sok turned away, pushed through the crowd. He had started down the path to the beach when Sun Beater came out of the trader's tent, called to him. Sok looked at Sun Beater with surprise in his eyes, then wended his way back through the crowd, whispering to Chakliux as he passed, "Wait for me."

"Be careful of that one," Tut told Sok. "He wants more than he should have."

"I am not a child, woman," Sok said, and pushed past her.

Tut watched him leave, then turned to look at Chakliux. She said nothing, but Chakliux saw that her eyes were dark with worry, and for a moment it was as though he were again with Gguzaakk, gaining wisdom through her wisdom.

Chapter
Twenty-one

THE FIRST MEN VILLAGE

Aqamdax cut the stalk of rye grass, holding the six leaf blades in her left hand as she cut with her right. The new grass grew from the pale remains of many previous summers' grass, as though each mound were a family, the parents and grandparents pushing the new green fronds up toward the sun. She laid the stalk in the growing bundle at her feet. Qung said the grass on this hill was best for baskets. Not as coarse as the rye near the beaches, it grew among the ferns and tried to mimic their lacy fronds, stretching tall and strong and graceful, until its outer blades were longer than a woman's arms.

The salmon were running in the river nearest their village, and all the women were busy cleaning and drying what the men brought in, but Qung was a woman of baskets, and insisted that, since she was too old to walk to this particularly good growth of grass, Aqamdax must go. She must go now, when the heads of grain had just begun to peak out of the stalks, before the early storms creased and twisted the grass, before snow and ice tore away the outer blades and made those pale center leaves brittle and sharp.

Aqamdax had argued with her. They would not be able to eat baskets when the hard moons of winter came. Better they had fish dried and stored than basket grass.

Others would bring food, Qung had told her. They always did, and Qung had been so sure in her pronouncement that Aqamdax had finally allowed herself to be persuaded. So here she was cutting grass a quarter day's walk from the village when she should be helping Qung with fish.

The sun had burned away the haze of morning and shone hot on her head. Now and again Aqamdax raised her eyes to the hills where ptarmigan grass and red-flowering fireweed grew; where coarse stalks of iitikaalux stood dark against the grasses, and yellow cup flowers, and orange paintbrushes bent in the wind. She knew what the village women would say. Not only was she a thief of husbands, she was also lazy, leaving an old woman alone to catch fish.

Hii! Let them whisper. She was pleasing Qung and that was the most important thing. Never had she known anyone to be so particular about basket grass, but then she had never seen anyone who made baskets like Qung's.

Qung slit the grass into fine strands as all women did, but instead of gathering the split grass into a coil and sewing with stitches tight enough to cover the coil as it wound its way up the basket, she tied several strands of grass together at their centers and fanned them out like a chuhnusix leaf. Then using two strands of grass as weavers, she twisted them in and out among the tied strands, making a circle that would be the bottom of the basket.

It was something that could not be done without the right grass, dried in the right way, Qung had told Aqamdax, then sent her to gather. In exchange she promised to tell Aqamdax two stories, old ones that most First Men had never heard. Aqamdax had not told Qung she would have gathered the grass for her anyway, without promise of stories.

Of course, the village women, especially the old ones, would talk, would use subtle words to shame her, but still, they came to hear her stories. Yes, they would listen and nod, hum their agreement, or sometimes interrupt to tell her another way they had heard the same story told. But that was good. How else did a person learn except by listening to others' ideas, then choosing what was best?

Usually in summer, there was little time for stories, save those a grandmother or aunt might tell in teaching, stories that were a part of every child's life. The story evenings, with most of the village people gathered in one ulax, were better saved for the long dark of winter.

This summer the salmon runs were small, not so that the people would starve—seals, sea lions and halibut were plentiful—but some worried about curses and spells, perhaps in punishment for old ways forsaken.

Now, to help the people remember those ways, He Sings had asked for story evenings. This night and the next and the next after that, Qung and Aqamdax would tell stories. They would talk until the elders could be sure all things were being done in honorable ways.

During the past few days, as Aqamdax worked gaffing salmon, cutting grass, sewing, weaving, she told stories to herself in silent words that colored her thoughts as brightly as the grasses and flowers colored the hills.

As she practiced the stories, she sometimes stopped to lift prayers, and each prayer was a request that the people would not realize that the greatest change in the village was the new storyteller, a woman who had once taken hunters to her bed without worry over hunting taboos or the hearts of their wives.

Chakliux switched his paddle, three strokes left, then again, three strokes right. The rhythm seemed as natural as breathing.

When Old Tusk first began to teach him, the iqyax was strange, like a man he did not know, someone to face with arms crossed, right hand drawing strength from the hard bone haft of a sleeve knife. Now the iqyax was as familiar to him as his own body. When he paddled he was truly otter, the sea as much his home as any grass-covered hill.

He looked back at his brother, Sok, and wondered if he regretted his agreement with Yehl, the Walrus shaman. The birdskin parka, a shaman's mask, a drum, a whistle, a medicine bag and the iqyax Sok was paddling were more than they ever could have gotten for a golden-eyed dog, but in exchange they had to bring back the First Men storyteller. How could they hope to convince a village to give up its storyteller just so she could be wife to an old Walrus Hunter shaman? Even if they persuaded her to come with them, who could say whether Wolf-and-Raven would agree to give his daughter as second wife for even all the powers of feather parka, mask and drum?

There were four iqyan on this journey: Chakliux's, Sok's and those belonging to two Walrus traders, Cormorant and Red Feather. Tut also accompanied them, the old woman requesting one last visit to her own village, to stay or perhaps not. She rode in Cormorant's iqyax, while Red Feather carried most of the trade goods, a bride price to offer the storyteller's father, brothers or uncles. Chakliux, Cormorant and Red Feather would each receive goods in exchange for accompanying Sok, but for Chakliux the greatest gift was the journey itself, the opportunity to visit a First Men village, to meet those hunters who were brothers to the sea otter.

Though Sok carried less than Chakliux did, though he was larger of arm and chest than the other men, he was always behind. Sometimes looking back, Chakliux could not even see him. Then he turned his iqyax, paddled until he knew his brother was not hurt or capsized. Sok had not learned to use his strength to aid his paddling. Instead, he fought the sea, using his paddle like a spear to be thrust and torn out, as though each wave were an enemy to be defeated. His face was raw and blistered from the salt—more than Chakliux's, more than Cormorant's or Red Feather's—as though the sea recognized his enmity.

After days of travel, they were near the First Men's village. They had already turned their iqyan into the broad inlet that led to the Traders' Beach. Now and again Cormorant would lift his paddle to point out a river or a stretch of sand where the First Men fished or hunted or set up summer camps. Soon they would be there, a place Chakliux had always hoped to see, had dreamed to visit, and Sok would begin trading for this storyteller.

A chill climbed Chakliux's spine even though the summer sun warmed the wind that swept into the inlet. Sok was not a trader. He did not understand the subtle use of words and eyes. Perhaps he would listen to Cormorant and Red Feather. Perhaps he would listen and learn how a man gets what he wants.

Qung had told Aqamdax to carry the grass carefully, holding it so it lay across her outstretched arms. Agamdax had not walked far on her return to the village when she wished she had cut less. Usually, walking back was easier, most of the way downhill, but by the time she saw the village, her arms and shoulders ached so badly she wanted to fling the grass into the wind, tell Qung she had been unable to find the place where it grew. But how could she do such a thing, when Qung had done so much for her?

Qung was old. Each day her arms hurt; each night the pains in her joints pulled her from her dreams. How could Aqamdax complain about a few more steps?

She began to recite one of the stories she would tell that evening, trying to find the words that sounded best, repeating phrases as she walked, listening to the sound of her voice. At the crest of the hill behind the village, she stopped, squatted for a moment on her haunches and rested her forearms on her knees. She closed her eyes, then opened them again, looked out over the bay. The hill was crowded with grasses, salmonberry bushes and heavy growths of stunted willow, but the hunters kept this place cleared so boys could watch the bay for signs of salmon, seals and sea lions.

Today, the bay was full of men in iqyan, some fishing, others practicing with darts and harpoons. Several women fished from the beach with handlines, but most were gathered at the river end of the bay, taking red salmon.

Aqamdax noticed several traders' iqyan drawn up on the beach. That was not unusual. There was still at least a moon, probably more, before storms would hinder travel. When some of the ache in her shoulders had subsided, she stood and continued toward the village.

Walrus Hunters often came to the village to trade. Since she was a child, Aqamdax had learned many of their words, as did all the First Men children. Sometimes Walrus Hunters took First Men wives, but usually when they did, the men lived in the First Men Village. Aqamdax wished her mother had gone with a Walrus trader. She probably would have returned by now, at least to visit.

Aqamdax carried the grass to the top of Qung's ulax and laid it there. She saw Qung was not inside, so she hurried toward the beach. She would go to the salmon stream, do what she could to help Qung. In words loud enough for other women to hear, she would tell her that she had cut a large bundle of grass. Then they would know it was not laziness that had kept Aqamdax from the salmon.

She walked to the beach, stopped when she saw a group of men gathered around the traders' iqyan. Each time traders came, she hoped they might be River men, but this late in the summer, she knew there was little chance, and so she felt no true disappointment to see the marks of Walrus traders on the iqyan bows. She turned her steps toward the salmon river. She would help Qung until it was time to tell stories, then they would help each other as they tried to guide the people back to old and sacred ways.

Sok knew she was Daes's daughter. She looked so much like her that she had to be. But she was stronger than Daes. In her voice, even in the bones of her face, she was stronger. At first, she had spoken slowly, her words spaced with pauses. There were times when she spoke so softly that Sok could hardly hear what she was saying, but as the story grew, the woman also seemed to grow, until she sat so tall among them that he had to look up to see her face.

Now she spoke in a new voice, something that came from the top of the lodge. At first, Sok thought that there was someone outside who called down to them from the smoke hole. Then he realized that Daes's daughter made both voices.

Ah, this woman would take Wolf-and-Raven's heart even more than a birdskin parka or a shaman mask. Who would not want her as wife? Then Snow-in-her-hair would belong to him, if he could get Daes's daughter away from her First Men husband. Her place as village storyteller gave her so much honor that no husband would willingly throw her away. Perhaps if her husband was a weak man, someone who did not understand the true value of things, he might consider some kind of trade, especially when Sok showed him the goods he had brought.

Sok was anxious for the stories to end, but they continued, Daes's daughter alternating with a woman so old her face was as brown as a river otter's. Tut sat between Sok and Chakliux, translating as the storytellers spoke, but the hard paddling of the day, the beach meeting with the hunters and chief of the First Men, the time spent making a crude shelter with caribou skins and their upturned iqyan, made Sok long for sleep. Sometime during the old woman's last few stories, he closed his eyes and allowed Tut's whispers to pull him into dreams.

He woke when those around him began to stand, and at first did not know where he was. Then he saw Tut. Chakliux was speaking to Cormorant, and Red Feather had joined a group of First Men, but Sok sought out Daes's daughter. He watched for her husband, but no one seemed to claim her, though several hunters hovered over her, greed on their faces. Finally, when all the women and children had left the lodge, two men approached her. She spoke to them, her face shadowed in the lamplight. Tut also watched, and Sok asked her, "Which man is her husband?"

He waited while Tut, speaking in the throat-rich First Men tongue, asked a hunter.

"He tells us she has no husband," Tut told Sok.

Sok did not hide his surprise. Daes's daughter was not ugly. Her face was round, with a small chin and large eyes, a well-shaped nose, and when she smiled, which was seldom, you could see she had good teeth.

"She is a widow?" he asked, and when Tut repeated the question to the First Men hunter, the hunter laughed.

"She is a woman who has a different man in her bed each night," Tut said to Sok, translating the hunter's words. "He says that if you want her, you can probably have her, but for all the men she has known, she is barren."

Sok nodded but tried to keep his interest hidden. The First Men hunter spoke again, and Sok impatiently waited for Tut to tell him what was said.

"She is called Aqamdax. Her father is dead. She lives with Qung, the old storyteller."

The First Men hunter jutted out his chin toward the old one. The woman's back was so humped, she had to tilt her head to look at anyone who stood in front of her. She had told many stories, and though Sok did not understand her words, he had heard the strength in her voice and sensed the honor of her place among these people.

The First Men hunter spoke again. This time he spoke in Walrus, his words broken and slow, though strangely easier for Sok to understand than when Cormorant or Red Feather spoke. "Qung much power. Food cache." He laughed and drew a large circle with his arms. "Much full."

He reverted to his own language and spoke long with Tut. Sok turned to Cormorant and Chakliux, the two speaking in the Walrus tongue. Chakliux spoke nearly as well as any Walrus Hunter, and Sok felt a quick barb of irritation.

Finally Tut pulled at Sok's arm. "Listen," she said, "this hunter says the young storyteller is called Aqamdax. Some years ago her mother left with a trader said to be of the River People. Do you know him?"

Sok shrugged. "There are many traders," he said. "What is his name?"

Tut turned to the First Men hunter, asked Sok's question.

The hunter spread his arms wide, shrugged, then went to talk to Aqamdax, but Sok stayed hidden in the shadows of the lodge. Tomorrow, he thought, when her stories have left her and she is only a woman, then I will speak to her.

Chapter
Twenty-two

"I need to know the First Men word for *grandmother*," Sok said to Tut.

Tut smiled at him. "You plan to do some trading?" she asked.

"What does it matter to you, old woman?"

"Perhaps it matters in many ways," she told him. She had begun to wear her hair like the First Men women, hanging loose or pulled back into a thick roll at the base of her neck. She was a proud woman—something Sok had realized the first time he met her—and she held her head high. For some reason, she looked almost young now. Chakliux said she had found all three of her brothers still living and many nephews and nieces. "I do not want you to cheat my family."

"I will cheat no one."

For a moment she tilted her head, studied him. Finally she said, "I believe you. Say *kukax*. That is *grandmother*, but be careful how you use it. Some women do not want to be grandmother to a River man." She walked away, looking back over her shoulder to smile at him, and Sok knew that she was almost laughing.

* * *

They were the only traders visiting the First Men, though Tut told Chakliux that often whole villages of traders stayed in tents near the beach.

"It is a sheltered bay," she had said. "A good stopping place between First Men villages on beaches to the west and the Walrus villages to the east."

"I have heard it said that First Men live on islands all the way to the edge of the earth," Chakliux had said.

Tut had shrugged. "Who can say? We know of villages a moon's travel to the west. Storytellers say we once came from an island far out in the sea and that our hunters killed whales. If it is true, then somehow we have lost those powers."

Cormorant and Red Feather laid out trade goods on mats near their upturned iqyan. They muttered that they had had no chance to replenish their stores since their last visit to the First Men. They had stopped at one village between the Walrus summer beach camp and this village, but the people had little there, only fish, grass mats. Chakliux had managed to trade for several rolls of dried sea lion throat, not enough for a chigdax, but a start. That was the best trade any of them made, and Sok had traded for nothing, holding all he had as bride price for the storyteller.

Chakliux squatted on his haunches and looked out at the water. The wind was small, and the bay was nearly flat. Two young men had come to the beach early, had pulled their iqyan from the racks and taken them out into the water. Fog lay over the inlet, pushed long fingers up the beach and into the low valleys between hill ridges. Chakliux watched the men until they were swallowed up in the gray. He wished he could take his own iqyax and paddle out with them, but he did not want to do something that would break taboos or show disrespect.

When they returned he would go to them, ask if he could look inside their iqyan, to see the size of ribs they used and how they attached the hatch coaming to the frame. Cormorant had told him they used sea lion skins instead of split walrus for their iqyan coverings. He wished he could speak the First Men language. He had so many questions to ask, but perhaps by the time they returned he could find Tut to translate as he spoke.

They had been here only one night, and already she seemed to belong again in the village. Her oldest brother gave her a place in his lodge. No, not lodge, *ulax*. That was what the First Men called their lodges. He would not be surprised if she decided to stay with the First

Men, but he would miss her. She was outspoken like a child, and like a child seemed to delight in all things.

As though his thoughts had brought her, Chakliux saw Tut walk out of the fog, and with her an old woman, bent and stooped. Tut waved him to come, and he broke into a run, slowed by the sand under his feet.

"You remember Qung?" Tut asked when he approached them. "She wants to see your otter foot."

A sudden tangle of beach peas wound around his ankles and he stumbled, but righted himself before he fell. He brushed sand from the palms of his hands and tried to stand with dignity, but Tut burst out laughing, and then so did he.

"Yes, I remember Qung," he said. "The storyteller."

Tut said something to the woman in the First Men tongue and Qung answered, her words carrying a sharpness that made Chakliux wonder if Qung were angry.

"She scolds me for my rudeness," Tut said. "She tells me the Walrus Hunters have made me forget the polite ways of the First Men. So now then, I will be polite. What do you think of the fog? It is like this always here. I had almost forgotten. What do you think of the village? It is large and the people are strong, eh? Did you enjoy the stories last night?"

She did not pause long enough for Chakliux to answer, and finally said, "Now we are done with politeness. Show her your foot."

Smiling at Tut's strange ways, Chakliux pulled off his boot and unwrapped the hare fur pelts he used to cushion his foot. Qung bent so close to the ground that Chakliux was afraid she would tumble over. She spoke, her voice rising as though she asked a question.

"She wants to touch it," Tut said to him.

"Tell her she may."

Qung's hand was cold against his skin. Again she spoke; again Tut translated. "She wants to know if you say chants, if you are trained in prayers and songs."

"Tell her I am Dzuuggi. You know what Dzuuggi is?"

"Yes. A storyteller, as Qung is. Are you also shaman?"

"I claim no spirit powers. My strength comes from the stories I have learned and from my people's riddles."

Tut spoke to Qung and again Qung asked questions, her hands still on Chakliux's foot. Finally, she straightened as much as she was able, groaning with the effort, and Tut said, "She wants a riddle. Not something about the River People, but something a First Men woman might be able to figure out."

Chakliux thought for a moment, trying to remember some of the information Tut had given him about the First Men and their beaches, something simple that might be made into a riddle. Finally he said, "Look! What do I see? A fool follows its path."

Tut told Qung, and the old woman raised her head, lifted her brows and smiled.

"Does she want the answer?"

"Let her think about the riddle for a time," Tut said. "The First Men are a quiet people. They use up most of their words in their thoughts. She will ask if she wants to know."

Qung pointed with her lips toward his foot, and Tut said, "She is grateful you let her see the foot."

Then Qung turned and walked back into the fog.

"They ask about you," Qung said as she worked her way slowly down the climbing log into the ulax.

Aqamdax looked up from the seal skin she was piercing with a birdbone awl. "Who?"

"Those Walrus traders."

"They are the same ones that were here about a moon ago?"

"Two are."

They had probably been told that she took many men into her bed. Aqamdax wondered what baubles they would offer her, then shook her head to rid it of such thoughts. There were still times when she could not sleep, but they had become fewer, and now that the village was about to have three story nights, she did not want the interference of men to pull the new stories she had learned from her mind.

"I do not want them to come here," Aqamdax said.

"Even the two that are from the River People?"

Qung's words jerked Aqamdax's head as though it were an air-filled seal bladder tied on a string. "Two are River People? Do they understand our language? Did you speak to them? Do they know anything about my mother?"

"You ask too many questions," Qung said, and stepped down from the last notch of the climbing log. She settled herself on a pillow of fox fur stuffed with goose feathers and said, "The big one and the small one, they are brothers. They are River. The small one has some special gift. His foot is like an otter foot with toes webbed, and he is a storyteller among his people. He Sings says the man is almost as good in an iqyax as a First Men hunter. The tall one I do not know much about. Some of the women say he wants a wife. Basket Keeper said he asked about you."

"No one has asked about my mother?"

"Who would ask about your mother except you?"

"They understand the First Men language then?"

"No. I spoke to the otter one. The woman who came with them, Tutaqagiisix, she is one of us, married to a Walrus Hunter before you were born. Her brother is Small Lake. She has come back to stay with him. She translated the man's words for me, and mine for him. He gave me a riddle. Do you want to hear it?"

Aqamdax folded away her seal skin and slipped the awl and finger protector into her ivory needle case. "Are the River men on the beach?" she asked.

"You do not want to hear the riddle?"

"The riddle?"

"The otter-foot man told me a riddle. It is a puzzle of words."

"Yes, but not now. Save it for me."

Aqamdax put on her sax and started up the climbing log.

"You should take something to trade. Traders give nothing away, not even information." But it seemed that Aqamdax's ears were closed to anything but her own thoughts.

Chapter Twenty-three

"Two," the Walrus trader said. "That is all. Look, the otter skin is old."
He held it to his nose, sniffed. "I can trade it to the Caribou People.
They will not know the difference, but Walrus Hunters, other First
Men, and even the River People will know. How could I give you
more when I will get so little for it myself?"

White Hair lowered her head. Aqamdax had watched traders deal
with old women before. Village hunters made sure they did not starve,
but because their husbands were unable to hunt, the best animal hides
no longer came to them. The women gradually traded off their best
pelts—even those they had kept for themselves. If they had done a
good job scraping and softening, and stored the pelt carefully, an old
one was nearly as valuable as one that was new, but why tell the man
that? If he was any trader at all, he would know.

And, of course, he had not lied. Walrus Hunters and First Men
would know the pelt was old, but they would also know its value.

"How much do you eat, grandmother?" the trader asked.

The old woman rubbed her hands over the surface of the dark
dense fur but did not answer.

"Not much," the trader said. "Two seal bellies of oil will last you a long time. Longer than it would have when you were young."

"I have a husband," White Hair said.

"Here then." The trader pulled a thin ivory nose pin from one of his trade packs. "Take this, too. He will be happy."

The woman reached for the nose pin, but Aqamdax clasped it first. The trader looked up into her face.

"Yes," she said. "My uncle will like this." She took the pin and dropped it into the old woman's hands. "What did he offer you for that pelt, Aunt?" she asked.

"Two bellies," White Hair said.

Aqamdax snorted. "You can get four, five caribou skins for this, can you not?" she asked the trader.

"It is old," he replied, but stepped away from her, from the truth of her words.

Aqamdax picked up the fur. She held it to her nose, then turned toward the women closest to her. "Do you smell any rot?"

Several women stepped forward, fingered the pelt, sniffed it.

"No rot," Calls Loud said. She was a bold woman, usually the first to cry out nasty names when Aqamdax passed her ulax, but now she smiled, a sly gladness in her eyes, a quick lift of her chin to show Aqamdax her approval.

Aqamdax pushed the fur into the trader's face, held it against his nose. "Do you smell any rot?" she asked.

The trader pushed the fur away. "Take it. I do not want it," he said.

"I would think this is one of the finest furs I have ever seen," Aqamdax said. "I would think just to see this fur would be worth something." She looked over her shoulder at Calls Loud, at Grass Eyes and Spotted Leaf. They murmured their agreement.

She stepped closer to the trader, again raised the fur to his face. "Two bellies of oil, just to see it, I would think," she said.

Again the women murmured their agreement, several of them calling out, "Two bellies, yes. Two bellies." Others came and added their voices to Aqamdax's.

The trader opened his mouth to speak but then looked at the women.

"There are many of us," Aqamdax told him. "And we have all brought things to trade. I am sure if you treat our elders well, we will continue to welcome you to our village."

"Two bellies?" the trader asked.

Aqamdax nodded.

"He says two, Aunt. And also the nose pin?"

"What is happening here?"

Aqamdax recognized Day Breaker's voice.

The other women parted to allow him through to the trader, but Aqamdax stood her ground.

"This man is a good trader," she told Day Breaker. "He has offered our aunt two bellies of oil and a nose pin just for the chance to see this otter pelt."

Day Breaker looked at the trader, then at Aqamdax.

"That is true?" he asked.

"Yes," the trader said. His voice was weak. He cleared his throat. "Yes," he said again. "Two bellies. The nose pin is a gift."

Day Breaker nodded, but he fastened his eyes on Aqamdax, raised one eyebrow at her, a look that pulled at her heart, a look he now usually saved for his wife. "I will send other people your way, trader," he said, then picked up the pelt and two seal bellies of oil and escorted White Hair back to the village.

Chakliux and Tut sat together in the lee of the iqyax racks, watching and listening as the storyteller Aqamdax dealt with Cormorant, first helping one of the old women, then trading for two birchbark saels, two caribou skins, necklaces and a few dyed porcupine quills.

Several times Chakliux had to hold his laughter in his mouth as Tut translated the storyteller's words. She was a woman who knew how to get her way.

When she was done trading, Qung, the other storyteller, came. Cormorant and Red Feather gave her good deals. A caribou hide and some dried fish for a small seal skin and coil of sinew. A necklace thrown in as a gift, which Red Feather himself fastened around her neck.

After the old woman left, Chakliux let his thoughts dwell on Aqamdax. Her storytelling was a gift. He wondered if she knew how good she was. Sok had boasted to Chakliux that if Yehl did not take her, he would keep her himself. Why not? He could probably get trade goods from those who came to listen to her. Trades for the words that came from a woman's mouth. What could be easier than that?

The Walrus traders had set out their goods earlier than Sok thought they would. When he woke, it was to the sound of men and women dickering, voices rising and falling, making offers, rejecting and accepting. He had hurriedly put out his goods, the few things he owned himself, things he had not set away as bride price for Aqamdax—things that would not mean much to River People but perhaps would have some value to Sea Hunters.

The first to look through his trade goods were several young girls, each full of giggling and with nothing to trade, but soon one of their mothers walked over. She called to others, and finally the crowd around him was nearly as large as the one around the Walrus traders.

The old storyteller came and, with her, Aqamdax. Sok tried to keep his eyes from Aqamdax but found himself watching the graceful movements of her hands as she picked up a hare fur blanket. She bent down to whisper into the old woman's ear, and they both studied the weave of the blanket.

She was a good woman to look at. No wonder the men came eagerly to her bed. He wondered if they gave her trade goods in exchange for their pleasure. In some villages, women got many things that way—furs and necklaces, oil and meat. According to the Walrus Hunters, the practice was not common among the First Men. The men did not share their women except with hunting partners or a brother who had no wife, and not even a husband could make his wife go to a man she did not want. But Aqamdax was no one's wife. She had no brother, no father, no uncle to speak for her. And worse, she was barren.

So what would happen if Sok asked her to come with him and be wife to the Walrus shaman? What woman, even a storyteller, even one who readily shared her bed, could survive without being a wife? It would not be long before she was old. Then what? Who would want her? Besides, what would he lose by asking?

From the corners of his eyes, Sok watched her. She stroked the weasel furs and looked through a birchbark sael full of quills. She picked up a fishskin basket, then joined several women in derisive laughter. Sok ignored their ridicule.

He had used rocks to make a platform and set the trade goods on the rocks. Though the rocks were uneven, it was better than having things flat on the ground. Men and women were careful, but children, in the excitement of trading, often started to run and play. Cormorant had told him he had lost more than one fishskin basket to a child's feet.

Aqamdax finally came to him. She offered a shell necklace for a handful of carved soapstone beads. It was a good trade for him. The Caribou People would give much for a shell bead necklace. "How many?" he asked her, speaking the words in Walrus.

She held up five fingers twice. "Take more," he said. He smiled as she lifted her eyebrows in surprise. She picked up three more beads and he nodded at her, then accepted the necklace.

Tut pushed through the crowd, squeezed around the trade goods and back to where Sok stood. "Do you need help in knowing what they say?" she asked.

"Yes, yes," Sok said, then looked back at Aqamdax.

She had already turned her back and was standing on tiptoe to look over people's heads toward the other traders. He could not be rude, reach out and clasp her arm, so he spoke, leaning forward across his trade goods.

"Your stories," he said, raising his voice over the babble of women. "They are very good."

Tut also leaned forward, spoke the words in the First Men tongue.

Aqamdax turned and looked at Tut, then at Sok. Her smile made her beautiful, smoothed the creases between her brows, and pushed her eyes into shining crescent moons. He had thought Daes was beautiful. This woman was better. Yes, the Walrus shaman would be pleased, especially if no one told him she was barren.

"I did not leave a gift last night. Could I come by later, when the trading has ended, and bring something?"

As Tut spoke, Sok saw surprise in Aqamdax's face. She opened her mouth, then hesitated.

"Is there something you or your husband would like, something you see here?" He extended one arm out over his trade goods.

"My husband?" she asked. "Ah," she said, "he has always wanted a good fishskin basket." She laughed and several women beside her also laughed.

As Tut translated, a wedge of anger forced its way into Sok's chest, but he said, "I will save him one," and took the largest basket, crouched on his heels and filled it with skins, furs and necklaces. Then standing, he said, "I will bring it to him tonight. You live in the storyteller's ulax?"

"Yes," Aqamdax answered, looking first at Tut, then at Sok. She said something else, and Tut translated, explaining that Aqamdax had no husband, but Sok looked out over her head at the hunters who waited. Cormorant had told him they would not come until the women left, that then Sok should bring out his weapons and chert. He pretended not to hear what Tut was saying, and instead rearranged the chert and the seal skin floats he had brought from the Walrus Hunter Village.

*   *   *

Aqamdax hugged the beads to her chest and backed out through the women, allowing others to take her place. She got more than she had hoped for, beautiful beads from the River trader, necklaces and birchbark containers from the Walrus men, and the River trader was going to bring a gift, though part of that gift was a fishskin basket— something she deserved, she told herself, for making a joke at the man's expense. Most men would have lashed out with angry words or retreated into a seething silence.

She was already walking back to the village when she remembered that Qung was still trading. Aqamdax should have waited for her, should be there to carry whatever the old woman got. The traders had been generous with the old ones since Aqamdax had stood up to the one they called Cormorant. She pursed her lips to hide her smile. It was good to do something that helped someone.

She quickened her steps toward the ulax. She would carry her own trade goods home, then return to help Qung. She cut up over the small sand hill that separated the village from the beach. Four women walked ahead of her—Basket Keeper and her older sister, an aunt and the woman called Mouth. Mouth was not a good one to have as enemy. Her words were as sharp as winter-dried beach grass.

Aqamdax slowed her pace so she would not have to walk with them. The wind had grown since early morning, pushing a line of thick gray clouds in from the horizon. It molded her birdskin sax around her legs, and, as she walked down the back of the sand hill, it also brought the women's words to her ears.

Basket Keeper was whining, as she usually did, about too much to do. Aqamdax shook her head. Compared to most wives, she did little. She had given her husband only one child, and all the women in the village knew that her sister-wife did most of the sewing and cooking.

Basket Keeper's sister laughed. "You are lazy," she said. "You should live with my husband, then you would know what work is."

"Or live through a year when the salmon are plentiful," her aunt added. "There are so few this year, I have filled only two drying racks."

Mouth snorted. "What do you expect? We have a curse. We are lucky to have any salmon at all."

"There are good years and years not so good," the aunt said.

"I do not argue with that," said Mouth, "but no one, not even the oldest among us, remembers a year with so few fish. There is always a reason for such things."

Basket Keeper hummed an agreement. "The Two-beach People

have a strong shaman. . . ." She waved a hand west toward their village. "Perhaps he can tell us why this has happened."

"Hii! I do not need a shaman for something as simple as that," Mouth said. "Only one thing has changed in this village since last summer. One woman who is honored and should not be. One woman . . ."

"I have been a good wife," Basket Keeper said. "Ask my husband. All things I do to honor—"

Mouth's snort cut off her words. "Little fool," she said, bending to look into Basket Keeper's face, "do you always think everything is about you? Who lives now with Qung? Who has been honored with knowledge not even our elders know?"

Mouth's words cut like knives into the happiness of Aqamdax's trading. The carved beads were suddenly sharp in her hands, the new necklaces rough against her skin.

"Ah," Basket Keeper said.

"Ah," said her sister.

Angry words pushed into Aqamdax's mouth, slid over her tongue as thick as oil. Almost, she shouted out to the women; almost, she told them what she thought. But what good would anger do? Perhaps only prove Mouth's accusation. What was more rude than to listen to others' conversations? What was more rude than interrupting?

Instead, she quickened her steps, strode up to them and passed, calling out a greeting. She turned, walking backward, her arms full of trade goods, a smile on her face. "It is a beautiful day, is it not?" she said.

They blinked at her cheerfulness, and finally Basket Keeper stammered out, "The sun, the sun is good."

"The wind carries rain," said Mouth.

Aqamdax shrugged. "We have had rain before," she answered. "Truly we are a village blessed by good fortune." Then she turned toward Qung's ulax and walked on, closing her ears to whatever they said as they walked behind her.

"I told you he is coming," Aqamdax said, and set out more fish, another pile of sea urchins. "He is coming to see my husband. He would not listen to me when I told him I was not married."

Qung watched, wondered at Aqamdax's nervousness. Many men had come to this ulax. Aqamdax had never set out food before, or worried because she had no husband. Why worry now? He would eat, he would go to her bed, he would leave, and in the morning Qung would see what Aqamdax had earned by opening her legs to another man.

"Aunt," Aqamdax said, "I . . . it . . . now I am storyteller . . ." She tipped her head back on her shoulders and let out a long sigh. Her hair hung in a glossy flow to her hips, and, for a moment, Qung envied the girl's beauty. "I do not want him in my bed," she finally said. "The stories are enough. I do not need the men now. The stories changed things for me. I cannot explain it, but . . ."

"What makes you think he wants to come into your bed?"

"Every man wants to come into my bed. You know that."

"There are men who do not come to you. You said he is bringing a gift to your husband. He will not expect anything from you if he plans to see your husband."

"You think none of the men have told him about me?"

"You think men talk about women? There are too many other things to fill their mouths. Fishing and hunting and weapons. I was married for many years. I never heard my husband speak about me or our children. Men are not like women. They do not have much interest in people."

"Bedding a woman is different," Aqamdax told her. "For a man, it is not about people."

Qung lifted her hands. "Who can say? I have never understood men, and I do not think they understand women." She pointed up at the roof hole with her chin. "He is here," she said.

Aqamdax straightened her sax, arranged the necklaces she wore, and held her breath as the man climbed down into the ulax. She recognized the feet on the climbing log and exhaled with sudden impatience.

"So now your wife is pregnant, you come to me again?" she asked.

Day Breaker set his feet on the ulax floor and turned slowly to face her. "I have no interest in your sleeping place," he said to her. As though realizing for the first time that Qung stood watching him, he nodded at the old woman, muttered a greeting, called her grandmother in honor of her age. "My wife heard one of the traders say he was coming to visit you."

"Your wife hears many things," Aqamdax answered.

Day Breaker's face darkened, and Aqamdax enjoyed his anger. He had told her she would be his wife. She had believed him, though the chief's wives laughed when she told them. Now she understood their laughter. How could Day Breaker marry a woman without a father, a woman without uncles or brothers or a grandfather?

"Is it the trader called Sok?"

"Yes," Aqamdax told him. "The tall one."

"I saw him try to cheat an old woman."

"That was one of the Walrus traders," Aqamdax said. "Sok did not cheat anyone."

"He gave me a whole caribou skin and dried fish for a small seal skin and a coil of twisted sinew," Qung said. "He did not cheat me."

"I have come to tell you to be careful," said Day Breaker. "My uncle told me no one should ever trust a trader."

"Your uncle does not trust anyone because he is dishonest himself," Qung said. "Aqamdax has learned many things in her life. She has had men make promises to her before this." She stepped close to Day Breaker. "She knows how to be careful," she said, and stared at him until he turned and started up the climbing log.

"Do not think you are the only one with wisdom," Qung called after him, then she looked at Aqamdax and giggled like a girl.

They met on old Qung's ulax roof, so it was difficult to pretend they did not see each other, but neither man spoke. A sudden thrust of anger burned in Sok's chest—was this one of the men who visited Aqamdax's bed? But then he chided himself. Why should he care? The woman did not belong to him.

The Sea Hunter man jumped from the ulax roof, and Sok watched as he walked to another, larger ulax. Sok tightened his grip on the salmonskin basket he carried, then paused at the roof hole. He did not know the First Men's customs about visiting. Did a man call out? Did he use a stick to rap the wood that framed the square roof hole? Tut had said she would meet him here. Should he wait for her?

Finally he called down from the roof hole, then climbed into the ulax. It was a small ulax, less than half the size of many in the village. Of course, most ulas housed several families. This one, as far as he had been able to learn, belonged to the old woman Qung, and only she and Aqamdax lived here. Tut had told him that it was unusual among the First Men for a woman to own a ulax. Most belonged to men.

It seemed the most difficult thing about being a trader, besides the traveling, was learning the customs of each village. It was easy to offend without realizing. Cormorant had told him to speak softly and seldom, especially when he was invited to some villager's lodge.

The two women stood at the bottom of the climbing log, and Qung made some nonsense of words that Sok guessed was a greeting. He reached into the basket, pulled out two birdbone necklaces and handed one to each women, then turned and looked around as though he were searching for Aqamdax's husband.

"I have brought these things to honor your husband," he said in the River language. "He is not here?" When they did not answer, he spoke in Walrus, one word, "Husband?"

"No husband," Qung said, also speaking in Walrus.

Someone called from the roof hole, and in relief Sok recognized Tut's voice.

She came down the climbing log, spoke for a moment to Qung, then said to Sok, "They understand that I am here to translate. What do you want to tell them?"

"Tell them I now know Aqamdax has no husband. Tell them I want them to have these things themselves."

Tut explained in long words, then Qung smiled and took the basket from Sok and set it on the floor. She squatted beside it and pulled out his gifts, exclaiming over each thing as though she were a child.

Sok watched her, then felt a hand on his parka sleeve. "Would you like something to eat?" Aqamdax asked, pantomiming a bowl cupped in one hand, her other hand scooping toward her mouth with two fingers.

"Yes. I am hungry." He pointed with his lips at Qung and the basket. "You do not want to see what I brought?"

Tut repeated the question, and with laughter lifting the corners of her mouth, translated Aqamdax's reply. "She says that Qung is not greedy. She will give Aqamdax a fair share."

Aqamdax filled a bowl from a boiling bag that hung over an oil lamp and handed it to Sok. He squatted on his haunches and ate. Most women would have found something to do—sewing, or weaving grass—but Aqamdax squatted beside him and watched him. It made him uncomfortable. He kept his eyes straight ahead, and when he finished the bowl, he handed it to her.

There was no politeness in the woman. She did not offer him more to eat or wait for him to speak first, but turned and said something to Tut.

Again Tut laughed. "She says that she is not a fool. She sees by your gifts that you knew she did not have a husband. So she asks, since you did not come to see her husband, why are you here?"

He matched her rudeness with his own and answered, "I am still hungry."

Tut told Aqamdax, and Sok waited for a scowl or angry words, but she did not seem insulted. She simply stood and filled his bowl, then handed it back to him. Again she watched him eat; again he ignored her.

Finally, as he finished the food, she spoke. Tut left Qung's side, not bothering to stand, waddling like a puffin, her legs bent beneath her.

"Aqamdax says her mother lives with the River People," Tut told Sok.

Before Sok could say anything, the old woman Qung called out in a strong voice.

"Qung says that you did not answer Aqamdax's question," Tut said. "She wants to know why are you here. Why do you bring these gifts?"

"I enjoyed your stories," Sok answered.

"So that is worth a belly of oil, perhaps a seal skin," Qung continued, pausing now and again so Tut could translate. "You give too much. It is not expected in this village. We will take one thing, and you can have the rest to trade."

A rude people, these First Men, Sok thought, then wondered if it was more rude to say what you thought or to hide true intent under a cloak of words or a basket of gifts.

"I have come to ask Aqamdax to return with me to the Walrus Village and become a wife," he said.

Tut translated, and both Qung and Aqamdax stood with mouths open. Sok waited for one of them to speak, but they said nothing.

Finally he said, "I know it is not an easy decision. I will leave you now and come back tomorrow."

Without waiting for Tut to translate, Sok stood, thanked them for the food and left the ulax.

"What did he say?" Aqamdax asked.

"He will come tomorrow for your decision," Tut told her.

Aqamdax looked at Qung with worried eyes.

"You would give up being storyteller to become a trader's wife?" Qung asked her.

Aqamdax could not answer.

Chapter
Twenty-four

Aqamdax waded into the bay, first up to her knees and then beyond. The water rose to cover the sparse dark hair that protected her woman's cleft, then past her belly and up to her small round breasts. For a moment a wave caught her up off her feet and a swell of fear made her draw in her breath, but then the water set her down again. She had never been in so deep and, like most First Men, could not swim. Usually, each morning, she went to the river, to the shallow pool it had carved out where it emptied itself into the bay. There she and the other women would stand, knee-deep, facing the new sun, splashing their bodies with water to cleanse and strengthen themselves.

Today she went to the bay, like hunters did, to the challenge of deeper water and the harsh, bone-aching cold. She had chosen the bay water to harden herself so she would be ready for what she must do next, not only to harden her flesh, but also her soul. Otherwise, how could she hope to survive? Surely her spirit would abandon her and come back to this place she loved, to the rocks and grasses and beaches that were her home.

*   *   *

"So you asked her?"

Sok nodded.

Chakliux watched as Sok cracked the knuckles of his left hand, then his right. "And?"

"And she will give me an answer today."

"You think she will come with us?"

"There is a chance. They say she is barren. Though her storytelling powers are great, she is unable to give a husband a child."

"Perhaps she is content being only storyteller."

"What woman does not want to be a wife? Even a storyteller cannot expect the village hunters to provide as much food as a husband and sons."

"Perhaps that is true," Chakliux answered, "but sometimes a gift is in itself enough, worth more than meat or oil."

"I have told her I would give many gifts," Sok answered.

Chakliux looked away, did not try to explain to his brother what he had meant.

They were sitting at the iqyax racks, their backs to the wind, hoods up to protect their ears from the cold.

"Do not hope too much, brother," Chakliux said.

The wind cut suddenly around the racks, sending a spray of sand into their faces. Chakliux closed his eyes and tightened his hood. Tut had told him that the wind was stronger here than where the Walrus Hunters lived, and traders claimed it was stronger still farther to the west. Chakliux blinked the sand out of his eyes, then noticed that something moved out on the water.

An otter, he thought, and pushed back his hood to see better. The dark otter head rose from the water, lifted and became not otter but woman, hair as black and shining as obsidian, molded like a garment over the woman's shoulders and breasts.

He heard Sok gasp beside him, then felt his brother's hand hard on his arm. "Turn your head, brother," Sok said.

And Chakliux knew his words were not because the woman was naked. The First Men took less care about hiding their bodies from one another than the River People did. It was because the woman was completing some sacred washing, a tradition among the First Men, as Tut had once explained.

Still, the woman's grace held him, and suddenly he knew she was the storyteller Aqamdax. She lifted her hands toward the sky, then lowered herself again into the water, where again she seemed to become otter. Sok was right; this was something sacred.

He turned his head, closed his eyes.

Qung did not look up when Aqamdax entered the ulax. The old woman was weaving one of her grass baskets. It was small, no larger than her fist, not much use for gathering or storage, a basket for the eyes, as Qung would call it.

"Sit here," she said without looking up from her work.

Aqamdax sat down beside her.

"Watch," Qung said.

Aqamdax focused her eyes on Qung's deft fingers. The body of the basket rested in her left hand, and she held thin strands of split grass in place between her left forefinger and middle finger as her right hand twisted weft strands over warp. Usually after Qung told her to watch, both women sat in silence, but this time Qung began to speak, her fingers working in rhythm to her words.

"Making a basket is little different from weaving a story," she began. "The strands of grass are like words. Each has its own place; each has strength to add to the whole. I choose the grass carefully— strong inner blades, dried slowly—just as I choose my words." She dipped her fingers into a small wooden bowl of water. "I keep it wet, so it will remember how it grew strong under the rain, and thus remain strong as I weave, just as stories remain strong, and grow stronger with each remembering."

Again she was silent, and Aqamdax bent her head to watch Qung's fingers. She wove a long time, then she stopped, inverted her basket over a carved wood form, the same size and shape as the basket itself. She sorted through the split strands of grass at her side, selected two, crossed them at their centers, looped them over each other, twining them together. Now they were weft strands, weavers. She added a warp strand between them, twined the weavers over it, continued to add warp grass. She looked up at Aqamdax.

"You have decided to go with the traders, have you not?"

Aqamdax twisted her fingers together in her lap. "My mother lives among the River People. Perhaps I will find her." She did not mention what Mouth and the other women had said.

Qung pulled herself into a ball, tucking her arms around her up-raised knees, lowering her head so Aqamdax could not see her face. Finally she spoke, her words almost a whisper. "If you marry a trader, perhaps you will come back."

"Perhaps each year," Aqamdax said.

Qung lifted her head. "You will not forget the stories?"

"I will never forget the stories."

Again silence. Qung fingered the basket she had just begun, then suddenly thrust it at Aqamdax. "You have much to learn. Watch me, and follow my hands." She took up her own basket and began to weave. Aqamdax, her fingers sticky with nervousness, watched, tried to imitate. It was difficult. The grass was so thin, the circle of warp and weft so frail under her hands. She wove, and Qung set her own basket down to watch, shook her head, ripped out Aqamdax's work, told her to start again.

All afternoon, they wove, and still Aqamdax had no more done than when she had begun. Finally, Qung checked her work and nodded her head, allowed Aqamdax to continue, then showed her how to add more warp strands. Aqamdax wove, though her neck and shoulders ached, her eyes burned.

"Enough," Qung finally said. "Put it away. Your River man will come soon."

Aqamdax set aside the small circle of weaving she had completed. She combed out her hair, oiled her skin until it shone, changed her woven grass aprons for those she saved for celebrations, woven in bright colored bands and hanging to her knees, one from the front of her belt, the other from the back.

When she came out into the ulax, Qung looked at her, squinted her eyes and said, "They named you well. Aqamdax—cloudberry. The cloudberry holds its single berry on a stem high above the plant. That way, it sees all things, but it is also the first to die in the frosts of winter. Just like the cloudberry, you lift your head too high, always trying to see too much of the world around you. You should be more cautious like the crowberry, nestled safe in its heather branches."

Aqamdax had hoped for Qung's compliments, or even some suggestion about dealing with the River trader. After hearing Qung's words, she nearly fell back into the practiced retorts she had used with He Sings's wives, but she closed her lips tightly over the harsh words and instead replied, "But, Aunt, what tastes sweeter than the cloudberry after the first frost?"

Qung did not answer.

He came with the old woman Tut, not a woman Qung was anxious to have in her ulax. After all, she had chosen to leave the First Men for a Walrus Hunter, not even a good hunter, Qung had heard, but who can be sure that whispers tucked behind hands are ever true? She looked good. Old, but who did not grow old? Only those who died young.

She was a woman of voices, that Tutaqagiisix, with some magic in her tongue that allowed her to speak the languages of traders after only a few days of listening to them. Qung had always envied the trick. Once, as a young girl, she had even tried to trade some treasured bauble for the knowledge of how Tut did it. But Tut claimed not to know—as if such a claim could be true—and so in that way Qung also learned of the woman's greed.

It was good that she had gone to the Walrus. When a person allows greed in one part of life, it soon spreads. No one needs a woman who takes more than her share in oil or food, in good luck or in bad.

Besides, if Tut had stayed, Qung might not have been chosen as storyteller. Then how would she have lived after her husband died? She owed much to Tut's decision to leave this village, Qung reminded herself, and for that reason, she gave the woman a seat of honor near the oil lamp, beside the River trader who had come to take Aqamdax away from her.

Sok had asked Tut the ways of politeness followed by the First Men. Silence, Tut had told him. Quietness. At first Sok had smiled, sure she was making a joke. What man goes to a lodge and keeps his words in his mouth? Why else did people come together but to eat and talk? But Tut had repeated her claim, then said, "How better to show your respect for another person's thoughts than by silence? Is it polite to cover those thoughts with your own ideas? What is polite about that?"

It was a strange way of thinking, but Sok could understand how a people might come to believe such a thing. There were times when he needed to leave his own lodge, if only to get away from Red Leaf's many words, her need to fill all the space around him with her songs and chatter and constant touching.

So now as he took the place indicated by Qung, he followed Tut's lead, waiting for her eyes to tell him when he should speak. At first the silence made him uncomfortable. It was louder in his ears than if someone had been screaming. Then he began to look around the ulax, at the stone lamps that burned oil, sending up a nearly smokeless flame so the air of the ulax was much clearer than that of River lodges. He studied the woven grass mats that hung from wooden frames around the large central room. Behind those mats Tut had told him, were separate places for sleeping. The ceiling was thatched with grass and grass mats held in place by strips of driftwood and willow branches. The floor was padded with grass. Where sleeping curtains did not block his view, Sok could see that a trench, a handlength in depth, had been dug into the floor near the earthen walls, and he wondered if there were times during the year, perhaps in spring, when snow melted, that the walls seeped water.

Now, in summer, the ulax seemed dry and warm, sturdy enough to stand against the high winds that often swept the beach.

Finally Qung spoke, uttering a few words. Tut replied but did not bother to translate. Tut had told him they would speak of the weather, of small happenings in the village, much as the River People did when anyone came to visit. Then they would eat, and when that was finished, Tut would broach the subject of a bride price.

Aqamdax sat quietly in a place that seemed filled with piles of dried grasses. Whatever her hands were making was so small, Sok could not really see it. Perhaps she was beginning one of the grass baskets the women of the village worked on, but this one seemed very small. Of course, he supposed that all baskets began small, not that he ever paid much attention to women and their basket making.

Aqamdax was a tall woman, taller than Red Leaf, but smaller boned, narrower, though most of the First Men seemed to be of stocky build. She wore her hair long and loose, tucked back over her ears. Her face was round, her eyes long.

Qung and Tut talked together for a long time. Finally Qung said something to Aqamdax. She raised her head, and Sok felt the heat of her eyes on his face. His body tightened with desire, but he reminded himself she was to be Yehl's wife.

Aqamdax got up, filled a bowl with dark, sweet sea lion meat. She offered him the bowl, then also a seal bladder of water. Qung gave Tut food, then both First Men women filled bowls for themselves, sat and ate. In some villages, Tut had told him, the men ate first, the women later, but here the women often ate with their men and it was not taken as something impolite. Such a thing would not be done among the River People, especially during the starving moons of late winter when people's lives depended on the strength of their hunters.

When they had all finished eating, Tut spoke to Qung, then said to Sok, "Now you must ask."

For an instant he did not see the women sitting beside him, but instead the small face, the large eyes of Snow-in-her-hair. The words he had rehearsed came to him and he spoke of Yehl, the Walrus shaman, the strength of the man, the wisdom. He talked about the gifts that Aqamdax and Qung would receive, the honored place Aqamdax would have in the Walrus Hunter Village as storyteller, and as he spoke, Tut translated his words for Qung and Aqamdax.

* * *

Chakliux walked the edge of the beach. This night Sok would know whether or not the storyteller would come with them. Chakliux shook his head. Why should she? She had every reason to stay here, with her people, her family. Sok was foolish to think he could get her, but why complain about Sok's foolishness? It had given Chakliux an opportunity to come to this First Men village, to study their iqyan, to watch their paddling and to think of ways he could make his own iqyax stronger and improve his skills. Two men had even taken him with them to hunt sea otters. They had lent him otter darts to use in his spearthrower, had let him make the first throw when they found a group of otters. They had come back with two, and generously given Chakliux the otter teeth.

They were a good people, these First Men, full of jokes and laughter, with rich, strong voices they lifted in song when they were in their iqyan. Chakliux had been told they were not quite human, but now that he had come to know them better, he thought those who said so were wrong. Perhaps other First Men, far to the west in the islands at the edge of the world, were not quite human, but these First Men were as human as he was. He looked down at his otter foot, then laughed at himself. How many thought he was not quite human? Even Blueberry. Even the children in the village where he grew up.

The sky was darkening for the short summer night. Chakliux turned and walked back toward the tent shelter he and Sok shared with the Walrus traders. He could see the light of their fire near the entrance. He wondered if Sok had come back from the storytellers' ulax. Whatever had happened, they would soon leave this village and return to the Walrus Hunters.

He sighed. How strange. Though he did not know their language, had no wife or family here, he wanted to stay.

Aqamdax drew her brows together and frowned. She said something to Qung, and Qung spoke to Tut.

Sok leaned toward Tut. "Is she angry?" he asked.

Tut held one hand up toward him. Sok clenched his fists. For all that Tut was telling him, he might as well not even be here. Again he gestured toward the pile of trade goods he had brought as bride price. He had things he could yet offer, gifts he had held back in case Qung and Aqamdax needed more persuasion.

He started to stand. "I have more. In my tent," he said.

Tut, still speaking to Qung, glanced at him. "Sit down and be still," she said, as though he were a child.

He had to bite his cheeks to keep his mouth closed over his anger.

There was a problem, but how could he help if Tut did not tell him what it was? Did she think she knew more than he did? He was a man, used to dealing in trades, used to fighting with words. What did she know? She was only an old woman.

He wished he had brought Chakliux with him. His brother had been quick in learning Walrus, and though he could not carry on a long conversation, he knew enough to make his needs known. Perhaps in the few days they had been here, he had also picked up a few First Men words, at least enough to guess at what was happening. But Sok had been afraid that if Chakliux came he would expect some portion of the Walrus shaman's payment, then perhaps there would not be enough for Sok to give Wolf-and-Raven for Snow-in-her-hair.

"Aqamdax's mother left this village with a River People trader. Aqamdax asks if you could help find the woman. Her name is Daes."

"I could try."

Tut spoke to Qung for a long time, but Qung said little, holding her lips tight as though to keep in her words.

Finally Tut sighed and said to Sok, "I can do no better."

"I told you I have more goods."

Tut shook her head. "Qung says that what you have offered is enough. She tells you to keep the rest so you can take good care of your wife."

"You told her about Red Leaf?" Sok asked.

Tut's slow smile moved only one side of her mouth. "Aqamdax will come with you," she told Sok, "but not as Yehl's wife. She will come only as *your* wife."

Sok could not keep the surprise from showing in his face. He looked at Aqamdax, and she stood. The lamplight shone from her oiled skin, casting a red glow against the dark tips of her breasts, the smooth fall of her hair. Her eyes were shadowed, dark hollows in the smooth circle of her face.

She reached out to him. Slowly he lifted his hand, felt her long thin fingers against his palm.

"There is no ceremony?" Sok asked Tut.

She shook her head. "Only to go with her," she said. She stared into his eyes, and he saw the questions there, but Sok looked at Aqamdax and pushed those questions from his mind. There would be other days to think about Yehl, other days to decide what to do.

He followed Aqamdax into her sleeping place.

Chapter Twenty-five

Aqamdax could not look at Qung as she led the River trader into her sleeping place. Qung would probably think that she agreed to be wife only to get this man into her blankets. What else could she think, considering the way Aqamdax had lived her life before she was storyteller?

But this was not the same. Now she could be a wife in an honorable way. It was also her chance to find her mother, and because her intent was honest perhaps she would someday bear children.

Qung would have to choose another to be the next storyteller. Surely that one would be more respectable than Aqamdax, and if the salmon had been offended by her, now they would see that the First Men were again doing things in honored ways.

The River trader was named Sok. Tut told her that the name meant "raven's call." It was a good name for him, a powerful name. He was a strong man, the muscles of his arms and chest thick and heavy. He had the large beaked nose she had seen before on other traders, full lips and deep-set eyes, thick dark hair that he bound into two short, stiff braids. He sometimes put bone ornaments in his earlobes, but unlike the First Men he did not wear a nose pin.

"Sok," she said softly, and reached to touch his face. Her eyes had not yet adjusted to the darkness of the sleeping place, but she felt him smile.

"I am called Aqamdax," she said. She laid a hand on her chest and again said, "Aqamdax."

She waited for him to repeat it, but he did not, and for some reason she was disappointed. You are foolish, she told herself. You are wife now, act like one. The thought sent a shiver of joy through her, and she leaned forward, slipped her hands under his parka. It was a well-sewn parka, as fine as any she had seen, and she wondered if he had another wife. Second wife would be better than none, she told herself. Of course, since he was a trader, perhaps he had bought it from some village where the women prided themselves on their sewing skills.

She ran her hands up his sides and then around his chest. His skin was hot. Suddenly he crossed his arms, gripped the bottom of his parka and pulled it off over his head. He sat for a moment without moving, then he lay back on the fox fur blankets and pulled Aqamdax with him, pressed his face into her neck and flicked his tongue to her skin. Aqamdax closed her eyes, lost herself in the pleasure of his touch. She moved her hands to his thighs, heard the soft intake of his breath, and then his hands were on her, moving too quickly, with too much urgency.

Again Aqamdax did not allow herself to feel disappointment. Most men had little patience for the gentle, slow touching she enjoyed. He wanted her now, and he was her husband. She lifted herself up, straddled him. His hands clamped over her hips, pushed her down. She began to move, hoping to please him, hoping to bring him joy.

Qung tried to listen to Tut rather than the noise Aqamdax and the trader were making behind the sleeping curtains. What was more honorable than the union of husband and wife? she asked herself as Tut's chatter clouded the ulax. What was better for Aqamdax than to have a husband of her own? He might even help her find her mother. Not, of course, that Daes deserved to have such a daughter, no, but every child needs a mother, and though Aqamdax was grown, what woman was not at times a child?

Yes, it was best. And it would be good to have the ulax to herself again, to know that what she put in the food cache would still be there the next time she looked for it. How good not to dread the clicking tongues of the women. Who could criticize Aqamdax for becoming wife, and who could criticize the fine bride price Sok had given for her? It was more even than Day Breaker gave for Smiles Much. Yes, it was good, very good.

Now if Tut would only leave and allow her time alone for foolish tears.

The next morning, Chakliux walked into the bay until the water reached his thighs. He had been in cold water before. The Cousin River was never warm, and he often swam into the depths. He reminded himself that the difference he felt was that of a river otter first swimming the sea, and then he plunged quickly, crouched then ducked his head under, pulling himself into the cold with strong strokes of his arms, until he skimmed the bottom, feeling the lift of waves as they passed over him, the pull of a current that ran parallel to the shore. He swam until his lungs ached for air, then cut up toward the light.

His head broke the water some distance from where he had started, closer to the shore, where two First Men hunters waded in knee-deep water. One spoke to Chakliux, but Chakliux could not understand him. He set his feet on the bottom and stood.

"No understand," he said in Walrus.

"You speak Walrus," the other hunter said. They looked to be brothers, but Chakliux was not sure. Many of the First Men seemed to look alike.

"A little," Chakliux said.

"You are the one they call otter," the hunter told him.

Chakliux was surprised. He did not know what the Walrus or the First Men called him.

"People do not swim. You must be otter."

"Anyone can swim."

The men laughed and began to wade toward shore. Chakliux followed. When he reached his clothing, he rubbed feeling back into his arms and legs with one of his hare fur boot liners, then saw that the First Men only sluiced the water from their bodies with the sides of their hands, so Chakliux did the same.

He pulled on his leggings. The leather stuck to his wet skin. He put on his liners, boots and parka. Someone called him. It was Sok. Tut was with him; no, not Tut. Tut did not wear First Men clothing. It was Aqamdax, the storyteller.

When Chakliux drew close, Sok placed an arm around the woman's shoulders. Chakliux looked hard into his brother's face. Sok had been away all night, and now he was acting as though the storyteller was his woman. In many villages, the people would be offended to have a man so careless in his touching.

"She is mine," Sok said, and smiled.

"She has agreed to come with us to the Walrus Hunters?"

Sok laughed. "She is my wife."

When Cormorant and Red Feather, the Walrus traders, saw the woman, they crowed out their delight.

"So now," Chakliux said to Sok as the traders celebrated and Aqamdax looked on, smiling, laughing, "when do Cormorant and Red Feather find out that she is your wife? Now or tonight when you take her into your sleeping robes? Have you prepared yourself for their knives?"

"I have done my part," Sok said. "I have taken the woman in trade, and she has promised to come with us to the Walrus Hunter Village. Do you think that was easy? You are the one who must tell the Walrus traders. After all, how can I speak to them? I do not know their language."

Anger tightened Chakliux's chest. Sok's foolishness could cost them their lives.

"Then, brother," Chakliux said, "perhaps I will tell them what they want to hear. That you secured the woman for their shaman. Then it will be your choice whether or not to bed her, your throat that is slit if you do."

"You cannot tell them that. Tut will hear the truth and let them know."

Chakliux shrugged. "Still, better your life than mine."

Sok clamped his hands on Chakliux's shoulders. "I asked her to be the shaman's wife, and she refused. She would only agree to come as my wife."

"At least that gives us a starting point," Chakliux told him. "I will find Tut. It is best if we ask her advice, and better to rely on her words than mine in explaining all this. Try to keep your hands away from Aqamdax until I return."

As he left, he thought he felt the eyes of the storyteller on his back, but perhaps it was only Gguzaakk waiting to see what would happen.

He found Tut in the chief hunter's ulax, her voice rising above the chatter of the wives. He called down from the roof hole, asking for her. Tut invited him to come inside, and so he entered, surprised at the size of the ulax as he climbed down the notched log. It was clean, well-kept, the floor covered with long sheaths of dried grass, the lamp wicks burning with little smoke. Braided leaves and roots, sometimes whole plants, hung from the high ceiling rafters.

They knew how to build lodges, those First Men.

He waited beside the ladder, trying to catch Tut's eye, but she would not look at him. She knows I want her to come with me, Chakliux thought, but she does not want to leave the women. Why should she?

He thought of how often he remembered his own village, his own people. He missed the wisdom of the elders, their stories of hunts and hard winters. Tut must have missed the people of this village in the same way.

Finally, the oldest woman said something to Tut, lifted her chin toward a curtained area of the ulax wall. Tut shook her head, then stood and walked over to the climbing log.

"Grass Eyes wants to know if you are hungry."

"I need you to come with me," he said.

"Now?"

"Yes. I am sorry, but my brother has done something that could bring us trouble."

"He has taken the storyteller as wife."

"You have heard?"

"I was there when he asked her."

"Do others in the village know?"

"Do you think something like that could remain a secret through a whole night?"

"These women, what do they think?"

"They are glad," Tut said. "They say she will be a good wife. They want to know if you will take her back with you to the River People or if your brother will live here with us."

"He plans to take her back."

Tut shrugged. "Then what is the problem?"

Chakliux lowered his voice. "Tut, you know the Walrus traders came to get her as wife for their shaman."

"And Sok has not yet told them he himself is the husband?"

"No."

Tut threw back her head and laughed. "And I am supposed to worry about this?"

"Tut, please come."

"You speak the language. You tell them."

"You would risk something like this to my poor knowledge of their language?"

Tut gave him a sour look, then sighed and turned, spoke in quick words to the First Men women, then gestured for him to climb the log. He waited at the top of the ulax, and finally she came. He helped her down the side, then she pulled away from him, walked in hard steps, stomping her feet against the earth like an angry child. Finally she said, "And what do you want me to tell them?"

"Tell them the truth," Chakliux answered. "Say that she would not come with us except as Sok's wife and that it will be up to the Walrus shaman to win her with gifts and promises when we get to their village."

She nodded and said nothing more until they arrived at the traders' tent.

Chakliux heard Aqamdax's voice even as they neared the tent, and, though she spoke in the First Men's language, he could tell by the cadence of her words that she was telling a story. Her voice rose to meet them as they entered the tent, though the storyteller herself did not move from the center of the shelter. The Walrus traders were sitting, listening, as was Sok, his face creased with a smile. When he saw Chakliux, he said, "She tells us a story. You see the powers she has. Listen."

She spoke in many voices, and her face glowed with her words; her body moved with the rhythm of her speech. To his surprise, Chakliux felt his loins tighten with desire, and finally he closed his eyes so he could not see her. It was a foolish thing to want a brother's wife.

Then in the darkness, he heard Tut tell the Walrus traders of Sok's marriage. To Chakliux's surprise, they seemed to think Sok had acted wisely. Whether they expected Sok to give her to Yehl once they returned to the Walrus Hunter village, Chakliux was not sure. And what of Sok? Would he be willing to give her to another once she had been his?

For two nights, Sok and Aqamdax stayed in Qung's ulax, slept in Aqamdax's sleeping place. During those nights, Aqamdax woke often, sometimes to respond to her River husband's lovemaking, but most often because something in her dreams reminded her that she was wife. She would wake and listen to Sok's breathing, to the sound of him as he slept. The word *ayagax*—"wife"—would come to her, and it seemed that Sok's breath became the rhythm of that word: *ayagax, ayagax.*

Then her heart would fill as though it were a nayux, buoying up her spirit, lifting her from the darkness of the years since her father's death.

On the third day, Tut drew her aside, sat with her in the lee of

Qung's ulax and together they scraped sea lion hides. They worked in silence, enjoying the heat of summer sun, the sound of wind in the grass of the ulax roof, the noise of children playing. Aqamdax's scraper spoke in the silence between them, loud enough so that she was sure Tut also heard and understood her joy: *ayagax, ayagax.*

Finally Tut said, "You know that they plan to leave tomorrow?"

The question seemed to catch in the notched edge of Aqamdax's scraper, so that her hands had to stop. "Tomorrow?"

"They return to the Walrus, then your husband and his brother will go on to the River People."

Aqamdax thought of her mother, drew out the faded remembrance of her face, then Aqamdax's hands were free to move again. She pressed her weight against the scraper, peeled a thin strand of membrane from the hide and watched it float away, caught on the wind.

"Then perhaps I will find my mother," Aqamdax said, speaking with strength so Tut would not think she regretted her decision to marry.

For a long time Tut said nothing, and Aqamdax let her eyes wander from what her hands were doing to rest on the small familiar things she could see from this side of Qung's ulax. The high growth of salmonberries near Fish Caller's ulax; the black lava rocks He Sings kept as remembrance of grandfathers and great-grandfathers; the long fringe of Qung's basket grass strung point down on the drying racks.

She spoke to her eyes, told them to see and remember, told her ears not to forget the sound of the sea at this beach. Then she told herself, You are wife! with words fierce enough to tear away the sadness. Someday, you will come back. You will bring your babies to listen to Qung's stories.

Qung is old, came the thought, unbidden, but Aqamdax pushed it away. Qung was strong in spite of her age. She would live to see Aqamdax's children. It would not be easy to tell the old woman goodbye, but Aqamdax must remember what had been given to her. A strong husband, a new home and the chance to see her mother again.

"If you have questions, you should ask now," Tut said. "There will be no one you can ask once you leave here. No one in the Walrus Hunter Village speaks much of the First Men language. It has always been the First Men who spoke both tongues. Though any trader will know some. So ask, and I will do what I can to answer."

Aqamdax set down her scraper and looked at the woman. Tut was old, but she held herself straight, and her hands showed no signs of the bone sickness that knots joints and twists the body. Aqamdax had thought the woman would return to the Walrus Hunter Village with them, and the knowledge that she would not filled Aqamdax's stomach with sudden unease.

"You will not return to the Walrus?" she asked.

"My Walrus husband is dead. My daughter married a First Men hunter and lives in a village a day or two west of here. It is better for me to be here, with my brothers, with my First Men family."

"I will be alone then," Aqamdax said, her voice soft, as though she spoke to herself.

"You will like the Walrus Hunter Village," Tut told her. "The people there are good people. They will be a new family to you."

"I will probably not be there long," Aqamdax said. "My husband will soon return to his River village."

"You know the Walrus shaman has asked to have you as wife?" Tut said.

"Yes," Aqamdax said, "but now Sok is my husband. I will not stay with the Walrus."

"I will tell him that for you. I will be sure he understands."

Aqamdax picked up her scraper, then set it down again. "I will not go with him if he plans to give me to the Walrus shaman." Her words were strong, but she felt a sickness inside, as though something were eating her heart. Had Sok taken her only so she would go with him, then when she was away from her own people, no longer storyteller of her village, would he give her away? She remembered his hands on her body, the strength of his arms around her. No, he would not trade her. Already, they had formed the strong bond that comes to husband and wife. She did not need to worry.

"Is there anything else I can ask him?"

"Do you know if he has other wives?"

Tut thought for a moment. "He has two sons," she finally said. "He speaks often of them. They are still boys, but old enough to hunt."

"Then I am second wife."

"Probably."

"Will you ask him what the River People expect of a second wife? I do not want to offend."

"I will ask for you. And I will ask what other things you should know about River customs."

Aqamdax nodded but said nothing. They worked in silence, the two together. Aqamdax tried to think of other things to ask Tut, but her thoughts were like the bits of flesh she scraped from the sea lion hide, carried quickly away on the wind.

Chapter
Twenty-six

THE NEAR RIVER VILLAGE

Ghaden heard the clatter of the killer's boots, the clicking of caribou hoof rattlers like the ones dancers wore during celebrations. He opened his mouth to scream out a warning, but he had no words, nothing but a quiet moan that sounded more like wind than his own voice. Suddenly a dog barked, chased the one with the knife, and instead of the clicking noise, Ghaden heard Brown Water's voice, loud and angry.

"Yaa, put that dog outside."

Ghaden took a long breath. He had been dreaming. He was safe in Brown Water's lodge. Yaa untangled herself from her hare fur blankets. Ghaden felt her warmth leave his side, heard her angry whispers scolding Biter as she untied the doorflap and let him out. A few moments later, he heard the dog come back. Yaa snuggled beside him in the sleeping mats, bringing with her a waft of cool air and the fresh smell of outside, the whine of mosquitoes.

Biter flopped down at Ghaden's feet, and Ghaden sat up, patted Biter's head, felt the dog's tongue hot and wet on his hand. For a long time, Ghaden sat in the darkness and stroked his dog's head. When he finally lay back down, he fell asleep easily, and that night, the dream did not return.

Ghaden shook the string of bone beads, then slapped the floor of the lodge with a stick until Biter barked. Ghaden barked with him, making his face as fierce as he could, trying to show Biter that he must be ready to fight.

Again Ghaden shook the beads, then he threw them down, growled at them, hit them with his stick. Biter jumped at the beads, took them in his mouth, flung them back over his head and barked.

It sounded like a fierce bark, but Biter did not look fierce. He looked like a dog who was playing a game. He looked like a dog who was almost smiling, if dogs could smile. Would barking be enough to scare the killer if he came again, rattling his bones?

He and Biter were making so much noise that he did not hear Brown Water come into the lodge, did not know she was behind him until she grabbed his shoulder. He was so caught up in his game that at first he thought she was the killer. He screamed and whirled, the stick in his hand, ready to strike. At the same time, Biter jumped toward Brown Water, teeth bared. Suddenly Yaa was there, her hands at Biter's neck, caught deep into Biter's fur, holding him away from Brown Water.

When Ghaden realized Brown Water was the one who had him, he dropped his stick and crouched down, raising his arms over his head.

"What were you doing?" she asked. She lifted her hand, but did not hit him.

"Teaching Biter," Ghaden said in a small voice, and tried to hold in a sob that threatened to break through his words.

"You were making so much noise that Lazy Snow came over to see what was wrong. Her nose is long enough. We do not need it sticking into our lodge." She lowered her hand. "Play quiet games."

She looked at Yaa. "Where were you?"

"You told me to get wood."

"Well, where is it?"

"Outside."

"Bring it in," she told Yaa. "When you are done, take the boy and do something with him. I think he is strong enough to be outside more. Take the dog, too."

Yaa left, and Ghaden braced himself for Brown Water's quick hand, but she only pointed toward the rolled sleeping mats with her chin and said, "Go sit down until Yaa is finished."

Ghaden walked over to his sleeping robe and sat down. It was rolled so tightly that it looked like a plump, furry log. Biter sat beside him, and Ghaden began to stroke the dog's ears. He almost put his thumb into his mouth, but he stopped himself. Why give Brown Water something else to yell about?

Yaa was slow about bringing in the wood. She knew Brown Water would soon go to the cooking hearths, then she and Ghaden would have the lodge to themselves. But Brown Water, also, seemed in no hurry. Yaa had brought in almost all the wood by the time the woman left. Yaa picked up one more armload and watched until Brown Water disappeared down toward the cooking hearths, then she went inside.

Ghaden was sitting with one arm draped over Biter. The dog was nearly full-sized now, though still with the lankiness of a puppy. She noticed that as soon as Brown Water left the lodge, Ghaden had stuck his thumb in his mouth.

"So, Ghaden, Brown Water says you can go outside. It has been a long time since you played with your friends. Do you want to try to find Little Fish and Spear?"

"No."

"Why not?"

Ghaden lay his head against Biter. "Can Biter come?"

"If he stays away from other dogs."

"He will."

"Why were you and Biter making so much noise?"

Ghaden pulled his thumb out of his mouth and smiled at her. "I was teaching Biter to be fierce."

"With this?"

Yaa picked up the string of beads from the floor. She shook them and Biter growled.

Ghaden laughed and threw his arms around his dog. "Old bone man won't get us!" he said.

"Who is old bone man?"

Ghaden stuck his thumb back into his mouth. "Secret," he said, the word slurring past his thumb. "Can't tell you."

Ghaden felt small when he was outside. Smaller than when he was in the lodge. And the village seemed strange—too quiet. Most of the people were at fish camp, but Brown Water had decided not to go this year. She said the walk was too far for him. He was not strong enough yet, and mostly she made him stay inside. It had not been a good summer.

Even Yaa treated him like a baby. When they did go out, she coated his face with goose grease to keep the bugs away and made him wear his caribouskin boots, though he wanted to go barefoot like she did.

Ghaden followed her to the edge of the village, to a clearing near the steep bank that dropped off into the river. The older boys were playing a game, kicking a caribou bladder to one another, trying to keep it from touching the ground. Ghaden watched, eyes sparkling. Both he and Yaa had to keep a grip on Biter so he did not join the game.

Several of the smaller boys came to Ghaden, tried to get him to play with them, but Yaa would not let him go. Ghaden turned away, and Feet First, a boy of about five summers, began calling him names.

"My dog will bite you!" Ghaden screamed out.

Biter bared his teeth, but Yaa clamped a hand over his muzzle, then pulled him and Ghaden with her to the cooking hearths, where Yaa's mother gave both of them a bit of meat.

"You want to go back to the lodge?" Yaa asked Ghaden.

"No."

"You want to watch the boys?"

"No."

She knelt down in front of Ghaden. Sometimes, when she wanted an answer from him, she had better luck when she looked into his eyes. "Tell me what you want to do."

He turned his face away.

"All right. We'll go back to the lodge. You can stay there with Biter. I have friends I can be with. You can stay by yourself."

He grabbed her hand. "No, Yaa. Stay with me."

"I know what we can do," Yaa said, thinking the words out loud. "There's a place I want to take you."

"Can Biter come?"

"If he is good."

"He is always good."

"Ghaden," she said slowly, "this is a secret place. You cannot tell anyone."

He looked into her eyes. "I won't tell."

With most of the children at fish camp, it was a good time to show Ghaden her den. She did not want someone like River Ice Dancer to find her hiding place. He might ruin it. Besides, the best part of having the den was that no one else knew about it.

She took Ghaden's hand and led him out of the village toward the women's place, then off on the little hidden path to the den. She held a finger to her lips, knelt down in front of the black spruce, and crawled in under the bottom branches. Ghaden and Biter followed her. She picked up the stick and poked it into the den, then crept inside. She loved the darkness, the sweet earth smell. She reached back, pulled Ghaden in, then laughed as Biter followed on his belly.

"Are we foxes?" Ghaden asked.

The idea brought a smile to her face, and Yaa laughed. "Yes," she said, "foxes. I am the mother. You are the father and Biter is the baby."

"He's the dog," Ghaden said solemnly.

"Foxes don't have dogs," Yaa told him.

"We do."

"All right, Biter's the dog. Do you like it in here?" she asked, then lifted her hand to the top of the den. "Look, I bet you can almost stand up straight."

He stood but had to bend his head to the side.

"Almost," Yaa said.

"I like it," Ghaden whispered. "What do you do in here?"

"Sometimes I bring food."

"I'm hungry, Yaa."

Yaa rolled her eyes, though she knew it was probably too dark for him to see. "You just ate."

Ghaden didn't answer.

"Sometimes I like to sit and think about things," she told him.

"What do you think about?"

"Ummm, sometimes you. What happened to you."

She felt Ghaden suddenly stiffen. "It's all right in here," she told him. "The best thing about this secret place is that we are safe here. No one knows about it except us. If someone ever tries to get you, you can come here and be safe. Whatever words you say here, no one can hear you. It's a good place to tell secrets."

Ghaden was quiet for a long time. Finally he said, "I have secrets."

"You do?"

"You won't tell?"

"No." She held her breath, hoping he would talk to her about the night Daes was killed.

"I took food last night from the cooking bag."

Yaa was disappointed, but she reminded herself that big secrets were not easily told. It was best to start with small ones. She giggled. "I did, too," she said.

Ghaden laughed out loud.

"Be quiet," Yaa whispered, but was careful to keep the laughter bubbling through her words so Ghaden would know she was not mad.

"You have any more secrets?" Yaa asked.

Ghaden was suddenly very still, and Yaa hoped he would decide to tell her something. Each day when she hauled wood, stirred cooking bags, wove mats, each night when she lay trying to sleep, she thought about the killer, wondered if whoever it was would try to hurt Ghaden again. She thought about Daes and who in the village might have hated her enough to kill her.

So far, she had come up with nothing. The village women had not been friendly to Daes, except perhaps for Yaa's mother, but only Brown Water was openly mean, and Brown Water had been in the lodge all night; at least she had been there when Yaa fell asleep, and was still there when Yaa awoke in the morning. Besides, why would Brown Water want to kill Daes? Without Daes each woman in the lodge had more work to do.

When Ghaden finally spoke, it was with a voice so small Yaa almost did not hear his words. "I have secrets," he said again. "Biter and me have secrets."

"So are you going to tell me those secrets?" Yaa asked.

"Not today," he said.

"I won't tell anyone. I promise."

"Not today. Someday. Not today."

"Can you tell me who the old bone man is?"

"No."

"You don't know who he is?"

"No, I don't," Ghaden said, then whispered, "He has a bloody knife."

Chapter
Twenty-seven

THE BERING SEA

During the first days of their journey, Aqamdax wondered whether she would have agreed to come had she known the cold and fear and hunger she would face. Her chigdax kept her dry, but even with a warm sax underneath, the cold that rose from the sea found its way into her bones until even her teeth ached.

Before they left the First Men Village, He Sings showed Sok how to enlarge his iqyax hatch so both he and Aqamdax could sit inside, back to back. At least Sok's body blocked some of the wind, and his back, pressed against her own, gave warmth.

The waves were worse than the cold. They thrust from the sea, huge under the iqyax, sometimes so large that Aqamdax could not see the other men, and it seemed that she and Sok lived alone in a world of water, without the hope of land. She did not allow herself to consider the thinness of the iqyax walls, and she blocked out stories she knew of sea animals rising from the depths to bite holes in iqyan.

On the second day, she found that the men did not eat before they left the beaches in the morning. Perhaps they would take a mouthful of dried fish, and always they drank water, but that was all until they beached their iqyan each night. Aqamdax did the same, though by the end of each day her belly ached with hunger.

The Walrus traders chanted as they paddled, and sometimes Sok's brother sang River People songs, yet the words, sounding strange and without sense, brought her only despair. How would she live with a people she could not understand?

Her skin peeled and cracked, leaving her face and hands sore and red. Sok gave her goose grease to use as salve, but the salt water ate through grease and skin until she had bleeding sores on her lips, in the corners of her eyes and at the edges of her nostrils.

As the days passed and her terror lessened, she found herself mourning for her village, her own people, and for the sound of words she could understand. Then one morning as she woke to the shaking dread that preceded each day, a voice came to her as though Qung were speaking.

It was a scolding voice, grandmother to child. "You are storyteller, yet you waste your days in regret. The songs of your husband's brother come to you as he paddles his iqyax, yet you do not hear them. Now is the time to learn words. How will you be storyteller among the River People if you do not speak their language? Do you expect them to learn yours?"

Then, after Aqamdax packed away their caribouskin tent, and bundled her feet into the warm hare fur socks that her husband had given her the second day of their trip, as she pulled on her chigdax, she grabbed a piece of dried fish and held it up. She told Sok the First Men word for fish, lifting her voice so that he would understand she was asking the River word, but he only shook his head at her. She picked up several things—her seal flipper boot, a knife, and finally a rock—but he only looked at her in puzzled silence. Finally he lashed out, pointed at the work she had left to do, and flicked his hands at the water so she understood that they needed to go soon or they would have to wait on this rocky beach until the tide rose again.

She packed Sok's iqyax, trying to hide her discouragement. What husband wants a wife whose mouth is filled with sighs, whose lips never smile? Then Chakliux came to her, walking carefully on his otter foot. He picked up a fist-sized stone, white with speckles, like a puffin's egg.

"Ts'es," he said, then repeated the word.

Aqamdax did her best to twist her tongue around the strange sounds, and he smiled and nodded at her. "Ts'es," she said, then, pointing with her chin at rocks under their feet, said, "Ts'es, ts'es, ts'es."

He laughed, and for some reason his laughter lifted some of her sadness. During that day of paddling, she repeated the word to herself, "Ts'es," until at the end of the day, when the dim glow of sun under clouds told her they would soon beach their iqyan for the night, she realized that, of all the words she could have chosen, ts'es was one she needed least. As they turned their iqyan toward the shore, she found herself laughing at her foolishness, and so decided what things she would ask to know this night: dried fish, caribouskin tent, water, husband, eyes, nose, mouth. Each day she would learn more until she could understand as a River wife should understand, and speak as a storyteller should speak.

They came to the Walrus Hunter Village in the middle of a day. Sok first noticed the change in the color of the sea, then strands of ribbon kelp that lifted brown blades to catch at paddles so the whisper of his chigdax as he moved no longer kept the beat of the traders' chants. He raised his voice and called to Aqamdax, naming her as wife, a River word she now understood. He used his paddle to point out the kelp, giving her the Walrus name for it, since his own people had none. He tried to remember the few River words she knew, finally said, "Walrus Village, out there. Soon."

He was not sure she understood, but when he paddled, quickening his pace as best he could in the kelp, she leaned against his back as though she, too, were pressing onward, toward land, toward the Walrus Hunter Village.

In summer, though some Walrus Hunters went to fish camps on nearby rivers and small inland lakes, most stayed in tents near the sea. It was a good time to hunt sea lions and seals, and hunters could also go together to hunt the few walrus that came to these waters.

Sok wondered what the Walrus shaman would think of Aqamdax. The journey, though not long, had been hard for her. The skin on her face was no longer smooth but full of sores, and she had lost some of the plump fullness of her breasts and belly. Now when he held her in the night, he felt the bones of her ribs rather than sleek, smooth skin. The first days in the iqyax, he had regretted bringing her, but then she began to learn River words, and she seemed to be happier in all things. As they traveled, she repeated the words she had learned, sometimes tangling them together in a way that made Sok smile.

He did not look forward to the rest of this day when she would learn that he had given her to the Walrus shaman. He would miss her.

She was good in his bed, much better than Red Leaf, but with the shaman's mask, the amulets and feather sax he would get for her, there was little doubt Wolf-and-Raven would give him Snow-in-her-hair. What would be better than to finally have that one who had lived in his heart since she was a child?

The Walrus Hunter Village was as Aqamdax had imagined. Like all children in her village, she had listened to the traders' stories, had eventually learned enough Walrus words so as an adult she could make trades or even flatter a Walrus man who chose to come to her bed.

When she and Sok beached the iqyax, women and children, as well as hunters, came to help them. Children gathered close to look at Aqamdax, and the women watched her from the sides of their eyes, speaking to one another with hands over lips in words she could not hear.

Finally Sok came to her, untied the hood string of her chigdax and helped her slip the garment over her head, then, clasping her long hair in both hands, he pulled it from her sax and smoothed it down over her back. Aqamdax felt joy in the gentleness of his touch, in the pride with which he turned her to face the people.

"Aqamdax," he said, giving her name the lilt of the River People language.

She looked at him, her tall, strong husband, and whispered the River word for wife, then also spoke that word in the Walrus tongue. Suddenly the days in the iqyax were worth the joy that filled her.

Then Sok called out, "Where is Yehl?" And though his next words were a broken mix of River and Walrus, Aqamdax understood, and in her horror, could not move, could not speak.

"Tell Yehl I bring Aqamdax. Tell him I have his wife."

Chakliux turned away and fixed his eyes on the horizon. He could not bear to see the look in Aqamdax's eyes as she realized what was happening. When Sok told Chakliux that he would give her to Yehl with all the people watching, Chakliux had told him there were better ways, had said that he should speak to Aqamdax privately. But Sok answered, "What woman wants to be dishonored before a whole village? If I announce my intent so everyone hears, she will have no choice but to act as though she came knowing she would be the shaman's wife."

And Chakliux found he could not disagree. As wife to the shaman, she would have a place of honor in the village. Living here, she would be closer to her own people, perhaps able to do as Tut did when she grew old—return to the First Men Village. She would also have opportunities to visit with First Men traders, those few who came each year to the Walrus Hunter People, and in that way hear her own language spoken.

In the next few days, after Sok had done his final trading, he and Chakliux would leave for the Near River Village, and, if Chakliux was welcome there, they would not return to the Walrus Hunters. If they found the Cousin River People were still seeking revenge, Chakliux would return here. Either way, Aqamdax would not have to see Sok again. She would not have his face to feed her anger or his voice to bring back memories of times shared as husband and wife.

Chakliux walked up the beach toward the iqyax racks. He needed to oil his iqyax and to repair some of the seams. Sok planned to walk back to the Near River Village, but Chakliux would go by water. Sok had laughed at him, asked him how the iqyax would help him in hunting bear or caribou, but Chakliux had reminded Sok that the few First Men traders who did come to River People Villages came upriver in their iqyan, traveling much more quickly than if they had walked.

Besides, his iqyax was more than wood and walrus hide. It was the way he became true otter. In his iqyax, he was whole and strong. How could he explain such a thing to Sok? How could Sok understand that Chakliux's iqyax was like another brother?

A sudden shout of laughter made Chakliux turn, retrace his steps. He pushed his way through a crowd of Walrus Hunter People. A fight, Chakliux thought. Someone has started a fight. Probably two young men, then he realized it was not young men who fought but Aqamdax.

He forced his way to the center of the group and saw that she had somehow pushed Sok to the ground and was astride his shoulders, one hand twisted into his hair, the other with the curved blade of a woman's knife at his throat. One of the Walrus traders had grabbed her around the waist, and he held a blade to her neck. He was shouting a First Men word at her, a word Chakliux did not know, and Aqamdax was shouting back, handfuls of words, full of anger. He saw the despair in her eyes and knew that she did not care if the trader cut her throat.

Sok roared and, with one strong heave, threw both the Walrus trader and Aqamdax backward to the ground. Chakliux placed himself between the woman and his brother. He stepped on her hand, pinned it to the ground as one of the Walrus men pried the knife from her fingers and another checked the sleeves of her sax for other weapons.

It took several men to lead her away; one finally brought a rope to bind her hands and hobble her feet.

During the days in the iqyan, Chakliux had begun to realize how strong and determined Aqamdax was, but still, he had not thought she would react in anger, but more likely do as K'os would have— stand proudly, as though she had always known what would happen at the Walrus Village. His Near River mother, Day Woman, might have lifted her voice in mourning, but how many women would have tried to kill their betrayer?

Sok had one hand pressed against his neck, stanching the flow of blood from a shallow cut.

"How bad?" Chakliux asked.

"Nothing," Sok said, but his words were a growl. He curled his lips to show his teeth. "What man would want a woman like that? She is worse than a dog, that one."

Almost Chakliux answered yes, but then he knew his agreement would not be the truth, so he kept his words behind his teeth and did not tell his brother that he thought Aqamdax was not dog but warrior.

They threw her into an empty Walrus tent. She shouted out in the Walrus words she knew, filled in with First Men language: "You think you can keep me here? I can tear through these hide walls with my teeth. You think you can keep me in such a place? Your stink drives me from this village. I cannot stand the sight of you. You are like dead fish, white and rotting on the beach. You are dog vomit. Your wives are the feces of seals."

Her hands were bound, but they had tied them in front of her, so she was able to loosen the knots with her teeth and pull free. She unwound the rope from her ankles and began to rip the furs from the raised bed platforms. She trampled fishskin baskets, unplugged a sea lion belly of oil and poured the oil over the bedding furs. Her insults became screams, then tears, and finally sobbing cries that seemed to tear her heart and rip the breath from her lungs.

Why had she trusted him? Had she learned nothing from Day Breaker? What man had ever been honest with her? What man had ever done what he promised?

For a long time she gave in to her tears, but finally her anger subsided to a slow rhythm, like the throbbing of a wound, and she found herself thinking of the Walrus shaman.

She had seen him at the edge of the crowd, seen his horror as she attacked Sok. He had been wearing many amulets and charms, skins and furs of animals she did not know. Had he thought that would impress her?

He was an old man, but that would not matter, especially if in his knowledge as shaman he could give her a child. Then she realized that it was not the thought of him as husband that fed her anger, but of Sok's betrayal.

Of course, the first time Sok had come to her, he had asked her to go with him to the Walrus Hunter Village to be the shaman's wife. In her foolishness, she had believed she had the power to change his mind.

She had bought enough from traders to know they did not cheat themselves, and the shaman had probably given Sok much to bring her here. She had only added to the trade goods by giving Sok nights of pleasure in his sleeping robes.

She thought of Sok's brother, Chakliux. He was not as large or strong as Sok, but he had a strength of spirit that she liked. Had he known Sok's plan? How could he not? What had the shaman offered them so they would betray her in such a way?

She looked at the mess she had made, then wiped her eyes dry with the edges of her hands, sniffed up the tears that were running down her nose. She had acted like a child. How could she be so foolish? First Men traders came to this village each summer. She could get back to her own people. Surely Qung would welcome her.

Meanwhile, if she did not want to spend her life alone in a Walrus tent, she needed to act like a good wife.

Perhaps before she left this village the shaman would put a child in her belly. Perhaps she could learn to speak the Walrus language well enough to understand some of their stories.

She began to pick up the bedding furs, wiping the oil from those she had doused, then rubbing the excess into her hair and on her legs and arms.

When they returned for her, they would find the tent in good order and Aqamdax ready to go to the shaman as wife, but if Sok ever came to this village again, she would find some way to have her revenge. She would find some way to make him regret what he had done to her.

Chapter
Twenty-eight

THE FIRST MEN VILLAGE

Cen pulled his iqyax above the reach of the waves, then began to unload his packs. He liked this village. The people were strong, healthy; they laughed often and traded well. With his left wrist still weak, it had taken him almost a moon of paddling to get from the nearest Walrus Hunter settlement to the Traders' Beach, but if all went as he planned, his efforts would be worth it.

The First Men had chosen their village site wisely, so they could hunt both sea and land animals, and fish the inlet as well as the rivers that fed it. But each winter the ice brought new shoals and new rocks. A man had to be careful, always watching as he paddled.

If one of the village hunters saw a trader coming, he would act as guide, but this time no one was on the beach. Cen had paddled in alone. High tide helped him avoid any damage from rocks or sandbars and allowed him an easy landing. He heard voices, looked up to see several elders coming to greet him. Cen met them with palms up and the assurance he had come in friendship. Their language did not sit easily on his tongue, but he knew that a day in their village would bring most of it back to him. His years visiting Daes had given him more than the warmth of a woman in his bed.

"You have come to trade?" one of the elders asked.

Cen answered the man politely, listing some of his trade goods—walrus hides, wolf fur parkas, split willow baskets and large wooden halibut hooks. He did not have as much as he usually did—nothing left from the River People but a few knives.

He had thought his luck was gone, was sure the cache he kept near one of the two Walrus villages where he usually traded would have been found by men or animals, but it had been untouched. The wolf fur parkas, caribou skins, a sael of fat, seal skins of oil, and of most importance, his iqyax, had been waiting for him.

He set out for the First Men Village, not only to trade but to find Daes's family. She had told him her father was dead, that she had no brothers, but surely she had cousins, and of course a daughter, who by now would have a husband. When Cen explained what had happened to Daes, surely they would come with him to seek revenge. They would help him win back his son, Ghaden.

He straightened, easing the pain of newly healed injuries, rubbed a finger across his nose. It was crooked now, wide and flat. A scar gathered his mouth toward one corner, but in this village it was good he did not look the same. There must be First Men hunters who were not happy that he had taken Daes, those men who had wanted her themselves. If they recognized Cen, they might act in anger before he had a chance to explain why he had come.

Cen had been especially careful when he was with Daes, aware of the mourning taboos that kept her from men. Perhaps that was why she had seemed so desirable—because of the taboos. There were other First Men women he could have chosen, but his eyes had filled themselves with Daes.

It had been a mistake, after bedding her, to return on his way back from his trading farther to the west. But how could he forget her? She still haunted his dreams. He should have stayed with her at the River village. What did it matter to him what village he lived in? His mother had been of the Caribou People, his father of the Walrus, and he had spent summers in River villages as his parents traveled between their peoples. He had grown up speaking all three languages, and easily picked up the First Men language.

He should have lived with Daes, claimed her child, the boy whose face was so much like his Walrus grandfather's, whose voice held the clear, singing timbre of the Caribou People. But Cen had known that each time Daes looked at him she wished he was her First Men husband. Besides, what trader needs the encumbrance of a wife and baby? He had found her a River elder who was still a strong hunter, who would be a good father to the child and a good husband to Daes.

Though he had left her behind, during the next winter Cen's thoughts had stayed with Daes. No matter how many Tundra women warmed his bed, the smooth brown skin under his hands had always belonged to Daes. So he returned each year to visit her, and finally she had agreed to go with him. Then he dared to believe that she no longer wished he was that dead husband, that she had learned to care for him because of his own strengths.

All things had seemed so good. His throat ached to think of it. But he would have his revenge, and those River People—the few he allowed to live—would never forget him.

THE WALRUS VILLAGE

Aqamdax expected them to come in the night, so she waited, keeping herself awake with songs and stories, but finally she fell asleep where she sat, leaning against the bedding platform. She awoke in early morning with a stiff neck and cramped legs. The entrance was still braced shut, and Aqamdax, feeling the need to relieve herself, searched the lodge for some kind of urine trough or night waste basket. Finally she squatted over a fishskin container, hoping it would hold her water and that she was not breaking any Walrus taboos.

The oil in the stone lamp was low, and several wicks had gone out. There was a small amount of oil left in the seal belly, and she poured a portion of it into the basin. The fire blazed with greater strength, but still she was cold. She sorted through baskets and hides, searched the walls for a food cache, but found nothing. She seemed to remember from stories that the Walrus stored their food in outside caches, but she was not sure. She had eaten the day before. She would not starve, and there were full water bladders hanging from the lodge poles.

Ah, Tut, she thought, why did I not ask more questions about these people? Surely in refusing their shaman she had insulted the whole village. She would wait one more day, then during the brief darkness of night, would cut her way out using the small skinning knife she kept in the belt under her sax. They had not found that one, and though the blade was short, it was sharp. If she was careful and worked slowly, it might be strong enough to cut through the split walrus hide.

Then what? Without food, without her woman's knife, what could she do? She would have to find Sok and his brother, beg them to take her with them, or go to the shaman, make her apologies and ask to be given to some Walrus Hunter as wife. She sat on the edge of the bedding platform, stroked the smooth feathers of her sax.

No, she would not return to Sok. Why trust the man? It was better to stay here in this village, closer to her own people. She would offer herself to the shaman. If he no longer wanted her, she would ask to be wife to a hunter, second wife if necessary.

Hii, she had been stupid! But now she would be wise, and if she could keep her anger from directing her hands into more foolishness, she would find her way back to her people.

Chakliux walked through the village to the iqyax racks. During the days it took them to paddle to this village, he had spent much time considering the First Men iqyan and whether he might change his own to be more like theirs—narrower for speed and with a keelson made of three pieces of wood rather than one to allow the iqyax more strength, more flex in the waves.

Perhaps rather than change the iqyax he had, he should make another. Why ruin something that already worked and worked well? Then he could compare the two, how each rode the waves, how each responded to his paddle in currents and tides, in rips and breakers.

He passed the small tent where they had put Aqamdax. He felt sorry for the woman. She had seemed to care much about Sok, to try in many ways to be a good wife.

He remembered with a flood of warmth how it had been to have Gguzaakk as wife, and remembered the horror of her death. Their son had died the next day, and in his grief, Chakliux had not wanted to live. But what Dzuuggi could choose the luxury of death?

He continued to work for peace, though he knew K'os worked against him. It was not until his grief brought him to visit Gguzaakk's burial platform that he knew the extent of K'os's hatred. As he approached the sacred place, he saw K'os there, and he waited, thinking she also had come to grieve. She stooped to lay something on the ground. When he drew near, he saw it was a spray of purple flowers, and knew, as every child knows, the deadly poison of the plant and its hooded blooms.

"My son also?" he had asked her.

"Children die easily," she had said, and lifted a hand to cover her nose and mouth.

He should have killed her then, but he was unable to move, as though his body, too, had been gripped by that poison that stills the muscles, stops the heart. He went to the elders, the hunters, even his father, but no one believed him. To make his revenge would mean his own death, the whole village against him. Then what chance would he have to work for peace?

Sometimes it was almost too difficult for any man to be Dzuuggi. The moons with the Walrus and First Men, a time when he was only hunter, had been good.

He envied Sok. What man could want more than a woman who honored him? Red Leaf and Aqamdax, two good women. It was sad Sok could not keep Aqamdax. Yet every man must value his life, and if Sok had not given her to the Walrus shaman, the shaman might have killed him or cursed him with illness.

Of course, when Aqamdax refused to come with them except as Sok's wife, he could have left her with her own people. But if they had not brought her back, would the Walrus shaman have allowed Chakliux to stay in the village if he could not return to the Near River People? So, then, though Sok had earned trade goods, he had also helped Chakliux.

As Chakliux passed Aqamdax's tent, he heard the soft sounds of a song, something she had sung when they were in the iqyan. He felt his heart twist as though touched by her sorrow, but told himself that soon she would feel happiness in being wife to the village shaman, joy in finding new stories here in this village.

It was not until he came to the beach that he heard the first wails of women mourning.

THE FIRST MEN VILLAGE

"I know you," the old woman said. She leaned forward, and because of the large hump that deformed her back, Cen thought she might topple face first to lie at his feet, but she twisted her head so she was looking up, eyes squinted into slits. His heart gave a lurch, then he chided himself. Was he afraid of an old woman?

"I have been here before," he said boldly. "Do you see anything you want?" He swept his hand out over the trade goods he had displayed beside his iqyax.

For a moment she looked down, and he thought he had distracted her, but again she turned her head to study him, again she said, "I know you. You were here . . ." She paused. "Four summers ago. No, five."

"Grandmother, I have been to many villages in five summers. I cannot say for sure that I was here. Perhaps. I did make a trip out this way about that time, though I have not been back until now."

She seemed not to hear him, and instead began to murmur to herself. She fingered his trade goods and finally left. Then the younger women were looking, all speaking at the same time, several of them snapping their dark eyes at him, in insult, he knew, but also to see if he noticed their impertinence. These First Men women were not ones to throw themselves into a man's bed, but usually, in most First Men villages, there were one or two who might show favor to a trader. He counted on finding such a one at this village as well. In the privacy of her dark sleeping place, he would ask about Aqamdax, would say that some other trader claimed she was good in a man's bed. The young woman, in her eagerness to show Cen she could please better than Aqamdax, would probably answer all of Cen's questions—and his needs.

Through the day, Cen traded, building his supplies with First Men trade goods that would bring much to him among the Caribou and Tundra People, but no woman gave sly hints that she would welcome him.

Later, when hunters were trading, Cen ventured to ask if any woman in the village gave hospitality.

One hunter smiled at him, showing a broken front tooth and high pink gums. "You are too late," he said. "There was one, but a River trader came and took her as wife."

Cen shook his head. River trader? They seldom came this far. Though their log rafts allowed them to travel the quieter rivers, they were not able to handle the harsh winds and high waves of the North Sea. Of course, a man could travel overland, but why waste so many moons in order to visit a few First Men villages? In the same amount of time he could trade in many Caribou and River settlements, even perhaps cross the great rivers to the land of the North Tundra People, those hunters who had no true villages but lived in thin tents, following the wind.

But Cen reminded himself that the First Men considered any trader who was not Walrus or First Men to be River. Did they not also call him a River trader?

"So there is no one?" Cen asked.

The First Men hunter shrugged, held out his hands, then picked up several bone-tipped bird darts, set them down again. Perhaps, Cen thought, it would be best to come out and ask, though often when someone was named, people acted with suspicion and refused to say anything. He could not truly remember what she looked like, though she had often been in his thoughts on this journey. He had watched all the young village women, seeking one who might look like Daes, but none had. Of course, daughters did not always look like mothers. Perhaps she had grown to look like that father who had drowned, or like one of her grandmothers.

He leaned toward the hunter who had again gone back to the bird darts. "Two for a handful of bola stones," Cen told the man.

The hunter looked at him with surprise in his eyes.

"But do not tell other hunters until I have left. I cannot do that for everyone. I would have nothing to trade at other villages."

The man held a hand up, palm out. "Save them for me. I will be back."

"Choose the ones you want," Cen told him.

The hunter chose his darts, each fletched with silver-white shear-water feathers. Cen tucked them under his upturned iqyax, then waited, offering other hunters other deals, bickering and challenging, always trying to make them feel they had bested him, that their trading talents were greater than his.

Finally the hunter returned, a double handful of sharp andesite bola stones bound in a square of seal skin. Cen studied them, turning several in his hand. Without speaking, he took the darts from the iqyax and handed them to the man. Then he leaned forward and, speaking in a low voice, asked, "There is a woman I have been told about. They call her Aqamdax."

The hunter began to laugh. "You have been told," he said. "Yes, I am sure you have been told." He laughed again. "There is not a man in this village who does not miss that one."

"She is no longer here?" Cen asked.

"She is the one who left with the River trader. He claimed to want her for her stories, but no one in this village believed that."

"So she had no First Men husband?"

"No."

"And no brothers or uncles?"

"No one. The chief hunter took her into his ulax for a time, but finally she stayed with old Qung." He lifted his head toward a group of women who had settled themselves on a grassy knoll above the beach. "The old one there at the center of the group."

She was the humpback who had claimed to know him. She sat on her haunches, her head bent so far forward it appeared to rest on her upraised knees. Though he could not hear what she said, Cen could tell she was speaking.

"She is our village storyteller. Aqamdax went to her to learn. The women were not happy about that, but she did well. Her stories were good to hear."

The man continued to speak, telling Cen about Aqamdax's talents, in storytelling and in bed, but soon Cen no longer heard. Why listen? Aqamdax could not help him. He had wasted his time coming to this village, and now he had to return, risking his life again in the North Sea. Worse than that, he had to make a new plan, a way to get revenge on the River People—and to take Ghaden, for what father would allow his son to be raised by an enemy?

THE WALRUS VILLAGE

The hunter's spear was tipped with a bone and clamshell point stained the color of old blood. He held it just below Aqamdax's jaw, the point pressing into her skin.

Several Walrus Hunters had brought her from the summer tent. They walked her out of the village and told her in a mixture of Walrus and First Men to stand at the edge of the beach, then all but one left. That one now stood between her and the village, as though she were a danger to those who lived there, as though she must be held at bay with threats and weapons.

Women gathered behind the hunter and shouted out their anger, but Aqamdax could also hear high thin wails coming from the village. Were they mourning cries?

Had someone died? Were the Walrus a people who killed to show their sorrow? She knew of wives who died grieving the loss of a husband or a child, of elders who, on losing a son, went to their sleeping places and waited for death. But why kill? For revenge, yes, but in sorrow?

Her heart beat so rapidly it made her hands and arms shake. She took a long breath, tried to see beyond the hunter to find Chakliux or even Sok, but she saw only the Walrus women, crowded together in a close circle.

She thought back to her own father's death, remembered how another person's smile would make her lash out in anger. How could anyone smile when her father was dead? Did they not feel the sorrow that had burned her heart until it was nothing more than a hard, dark cinder?

So if these Walrus were mourning, perhaps they would lose some of their anger when she shared their pain.

Then, in spite of the spear at her throat, in spite of the old women who leaned in to spit at her, Aqamdax lifted her voice into the ululation that was the First Men's mourning song.

By the time she saw Chakliux, the spear had been withdrawn and the women had joined her mourning cries.

Aqamdax sat between them without speaking, without looking at either of them. Chakliux could feel her anger, and Sok's. Old Tusk was chosen to watch them. He had taken them to an open stretch of beach a short distance from the Walrus Hunter Village. He had threatened to tie their wrists and ankles, but had left the leather thongs lying at his feet. Though he did not bind them, he thrust his spear toward them in quick jabs if they tried to speak.

Old Tusk did not look at Chakliux, but now and again made quiet comments about wind and tides, as if they were hunters sitting together to watch the sea.

For a time Chakliux listened to him, but finally he asked, "Who died?"

Old Tusk raised his spear, hissed, but said, "Who do you think? That one she was to marry."

"The shaman?" Sok asked.

Old Tusk lowered the point of his spear so it was only a handsbreadth from Sok's throat. "You are not allowed to talk," Old Tusk said. His eyes shifted to Chakliux. "They think the woman killed him."

"How could she do such a thing? She was in a lodge all night," Chakliux said.

Old Tusk lowered his spear. "Some say she is a shaman. Others think she holds evil spirits."

"The shaman was old. He just died," Sok said.

Old Tusk shrugged his shoulders. "Some say that is true."

"So the elders will decide whether or not she killed him?" Chakliux asked.

"They will decide."

"Then what will happen?"

"They might let you leave. They might kill you. Perhaps they will kill only the woman."

"There is nothing you can do?"

"How can I let you go if you killed our shaman?"

"We killed no one!" Sok said, his words almost a shout.

Old Tusk lowered his spear once more to Sok's neck. "Be quiet. You cannot talk," Old Tusk told him. And again he was guard, not friend, watching them carefully, shifting his spear to point at one, then another, and lifting his eyes on occasion toward the edge of the village where the elders had gathered to make their decision.

*   *   *

Aqamdax was thirsty; the wind had dried her throat, even her eyes. It would be good to have some water before she died.

That morning, before they had come for her, she had been hungry, but now she did not think she could eat.

She should not have lifted her voice in mourning. She should have been glad to let the Walrus man kill her. There were worse ways to die than by the quick thrust of a spear.

How foolish she had been to leave her village. Even the years she had spent in He Sings's ulax had been better than her life since she had left.

Who was a better teacher than Qung? Who had more patience? If the Walrus killed Aqamdax, all that learning would be lost. Qung was old. Would she live long enough to train another storyteller? Perhaps thinking Aqamdax had a long life yet to live, Qung would be in no hurry to teach someone else. Perhaps she would wait too long, and many of their people's stories would be lost.

Aqamdax looked up at the Walrus man who guarded them. He was a young man, his face made dark with a line of tattoos across his nose and cheeks. He had pushed back the hood of his parka, and Aqamdax could see that his hair was greased and pulled into a tight braid on either side of his head.

She began to speak, knowing her words might bring the spear, but perhaps they would also float to her village, so Qung would understand she must teach another to be storyteller.

"I am here, Qung," Aqamdax said, speaking in the First Men tongue. "It might soon be said that the Walrus killed me. It might soon be told in ulas that I am dead."

The Walrus Hunter growled out in anger, but Aqamdax spoke more loudly, and when she had finished her message to Qung, she began to tell stories. If she must die, then why not die as storyteller?

From the edge of her eye, she saw the Walrus Hunter move his spear close to her face, but she did not stop speaking. Her words were in her own voice, then in the voice of sea otters and of the wind, in the voice of children and hunters. She closed her eyes so she would not see the spear, closed her eyes so she would not stop speaking when the clamshell cut into her throat, so her words would flow even as her blood spilled.

PART
THREE

I listen to Sok, this man I must again call husband. His face is layered with a thick coat of grease. He hates the gnats, he says, though there are not that many of them. A person can scoop a hand before the eyes and clear a path for seeing. Who needs more than that?

Gnats stick to his face like knots of black hair, and I hate to hear him call me to his bed.

I try to see him as he was in my village, his hair smooth and shining, his arms sleek with muscle, legs as thick and strong as the driftwood climbing log that leads from Qung's ulax.

On the journey to the Walrus village, we slept under his iqyax, its curved back like the shell of a clam, shiny and wet from the tide flats.

But now I see myself as clam, dug up and waiting. His hands seek their way through the feathers and skins of my sax, under careful seams and small stitches to my bare legs. He enters me, devours me, then he sleeps, head resting on my head, his grease-killed gnats pressed into my hair.

Chapter
Twenty-nine

THE NEAR RIVER VILLAGE

Chakliux had taken his iqyax up the Near River, waited two handfuls of days for Sok and Aqamdax, who had walked with the dogs from the Walrus Hunter Village. They had camped with him last night. This morning, after Chakliux had hidden the iqyax high in the sheltering branches of a black spruce and covered it with bark, they started out together to the Near River Village. They had less than a day's walk, most of it along a trail the Near River People had made through the brush that grew beside the river.

Sok told him that Aqamdax had been no trouble, that though at first she was afraid of the dogs, she soon learned to secure their packs and to tie them so they wouldn't gnaw away their ropes, how much to feed them so they wouldn't be lazy the next day. Already, she knew the River words all dogs understood. But though Sok spoke of his wife with praise, Chakliux did not have to look hard to see the anger in Aqamdax's eyes, the disdain. When she accepted something from Sok's hands, or followed him meekly to his sleeping blankets, he saw that she mocked him with curled lips and slitted eyes.

What else should Sok expect? Chakliux asked himself. Aqamdax had been tricked into becoming wife, had been given to a people who almost killed her, and even then, Sok had done nothing to save her.

Though her mockery displeased Chakliux, he, too, found reason to praise her. How many women—how many hunters—would have thought to join the mourners' song when their lives were threatened? When she was accused of causing the death of that old one they called shaman, she had not denied it, but used her storytelling voices to show the people her powers.

How could the Walrus Hunters risk killing her when she might be able to seek revenge? Without their shaman to guide them, how could they protect themselves?

Chakliux had seen the dead man. He had been curled like a child, hands clutched over his chest. There was no mark of fire or knife, no fear caught in the open eyes. He had been an old man. Old men die. Why think Aqamdax did it? He had said as much to Sok when Sok did not want to take Aqamdax with them, had reminded Sok that if the woman truly did have powers, most likely she would have killed them rather than the shaman. So to save her life, and perhaps theirs as well, they agreed to leave, agreed to take back all their trade goods, even Snow Hawk and Gray, the dogs they had brought from the Near River Village.

Old Tusk told Chakliux that they would place the shaman's body in the lodge where Aqamdax had stayed, then would burn the place over him when the days of mourning had ended. If a woman could kill a shaman, what hope did anyone have of standing against her powers? Had she not walked across the floor of that lodge, her power seeping out at each step? Better to send that power away in smoke so it would settle far from the Walrus Hunters, who always tried to live lives of respect.

Yaa was the first in the village to see them. She was checking her mother's trapline, the one she set for hares near the riverbank. Ghaden trailed behind her, Biter at his side. The boy was as quiet as a shadow, crowding close each time she stopped and staying three steps back when she walked. She had just found the second hare, the animal strangled in the trap's clever sinew loop, when she heard the sound of brush snapping. Her first thought was of bears, so she pulled Ghaden close to her, crouched down, gripped the scruff of Biter's neck and clamped his muzzle closed with one hand.

Then the leaves parted and she recognized Sok. The Cousin River man, Chakliux, walked with him, and behind them was a woman, tall and dark-skinned, who wore a strange feathered garment. Almost, Yaa called out to them; almost, she spoke a welcome, but then did not. She did not know the woman. With her dark-feathered parka, she might be some relative of Raven. Why draw the attention of one so powerful as that? Yaa let them pass.

Once they were gone, Yaa wanted to run and tell everyone in the village what she had seen, but she knew Brown Water would scold her for leaving without checking and resetting the traps. Even her mother would be angry with her. There were only three more. She looked back to be sure Ghaden was following her. He walked with one hand entwined in Biter's fur, the other rubbing his eyes. She stopped, knelt down in front of him.

"Ghaden, are you hurt?"

He looked down, shook his head.

"What's wrong?"

"Nothing," he murmured. He took a long shuddering breath.

She knew him well enough to guess that more questions would do no good. What boy ever admitted he was crying? She reached for his hands, turned them over, pushed his hair off his forehead, then ran her fingers down his leggings to his feet. No blood. Probably a bruised foot from a stick or rock hidden in the riverbank sod. She slowed her pace but went on to the next trap. At the last trap, they would rest, but even a little boy had to learn to finish his work. If hunters stayed home each time they got hurt, who would feed the people?

Aqamdax was glad when the path led out into an open space of grasses. The trees were taller here than where her people lived. Though their branches were high over her head, it seemed as though they pressed against her shoulders with whatever thoughts and powers trees had. Some were so large that they blocked out the sky. When she looked up at them, she felt as though they pulled her spirit out through her eyes and into the hidden places of their dark boughs.

The open grasses were better. Though there was little wind and a river instead of a sea, it seemed more like her home. How could a person know what was happening in the world if the sky was covered by trees? How could anyone know of storms coming or rain? Snow or sun?

The men had stopped, and Aqamdax, seeing them, stopped also. She lay a hand on each of the dogs' backs to be sure they did not run on ahead. They had learned to obey her, these dogs, but sometimes they seemed to turn wild, even snarling at Sok's commands. She could not blame them. There were times when she, too, wanted to run, to leave the packs she was carrying, to forget the many River taboos Chakliux had taught her.

First Men taboos made sense, but the taboos she must follow now that she had a River husband—ways of cutting meat, words that must be said when she took water or something from the earth—were foolish. Would not her own words be better? Now that she was River wife, now that she was here in the place where River People lived, did that mean the First Men taboos, First Men wisdom, should no longer be followed? Finally, she had decided to follow both ways. She spoke First Men chants and River chants, followed First Men taboos and River taboos, but their weight was like the heaviness of the tree branches, and she found herself watching the birds, following their flight, and wishing she, too, could soar above trees and earth, taking nothing with her but a cloak of feathers and the wind.

"Aqamdax! Come." It was Sok. He gestured for her to join them, and so she walked to his side. He held out one arm, fingers splayed, and she saw that he was pointing toward a village, the ulas crowded close in a valley that was shaped like a bowl.

Aqamdax could not hide her curiosity. Who could believe how many different ways people made ulas?

"Listen, you can hear the dogs," Sok said.

Aqamdax nodded. Looking back at Snow Hawk and Gray, she saw their ears were pricked forward, bodies stiff.

"This is your village?" Aqamdax asked, then realized she had spoken in the First Men tongue. She searched for River words, lifted her chin toward the village, then pressed fingertips against Sok's arm and asked, "Your?"

"Yes," he answered.

Chakliux stepped forward, told her the River word for "village," and corrected her pronunciation when she repeated it.

They started again, Sok walking so quickly that Aqamdax saw Chakliux had difficulty keeping up. Finally Chakliux dropped back to walk beside her, and she slowed her pace. What did it matter if Sok arrived first? She had many days to live here in this village, time to learn their language and then to find her mother, a long time to devise a way to return to her own people. She thought of Tut, who had grown into an old woman before she got back to the First Men, and wondered if she, too, would be old before she found her way home.

They went first to the elders' lodge. They set their heavy packs at the entrance, left the dogs and Aqamdax outside.

Dog Trainer greeted them, and when Chakliux's eyes adjusted to the smoky light of the hearth fire, he saw that Wolf-and-Raven, Blue-head Duck, Fox Barking, Sleeps Long and Camp Maker sat at the back of the lodge. Fox Barking rose and made much of seeing his wife's sons again, but after his greetings, Chakliux heard the man's greed as he asked subtle questions about dogs and trade goods.

Finally Sok interrupted him. "Yes, we have trade goods," he said, "but most important, we must know if my brother is welcome in this village."

"You are both welcome," Blue-head Duck said. "In this lodge and in this village. Sit down and I will tell you what has happened."

They sat, and soon Blue-head Duck's wife came carrying a boiling bag of thick, hot stew. They ate before they spoke, the hot food filling Chakliux with contentment, and he hoped that Blue-head Duck was not being only polite when he said they were welcome in the village.

Finally, when he had emptied his bowl, Blue-head Duck said, "After you left, a woman and her husband and two young hunters came from the Cousin River Village." He looked at Chakliux. "She claimed to be your mother, and the man said he was your father. They brought golden-eyed dogs to help you in your trading. We told them that you had never arrived here, that you must have gone on to trade with the Walrus, or perhaps to other River villages."

"They did not seek revenge?" Sok asked.

"They only seemed concerned for Chakliux's safety," Blue-head Duck said.

"My mother," said Chakliux. "K'os?"

"Yes," said Blue-head Duck. "It was not easy to pretend you had never come to the village. She was afraid for you, that you might be dead. It was a hard time for her. She found much sorrow here during her stay."

Fox Barking leaned forward, used his bowl to point at Chakliux. "Now you have only one man to call father," he said. "Be grateful your mother Day Woman has a husband."

At first Chakliux was puzzled by Fox Barking's words, but as understanding came, his breath seemed to leave him, and he could not speak.

"You are telling us that Chakliux's father is dead?" Sok asked.

Blue-head Duck looked at Fox Barking. "There are better ways to tell such a thing," he said, then reached out to clasp Chakliux's arm. "I am sorry. In the few times I traded with him, I found your father to be an honorable man."

Chakliux's voice returned, and he asked softly, "How did he die?"

"A fire," said Blue-head Duck. "Your mother and father were staying in an elder's lodge, with his wife, that one who was always singing. The lodge burned in the night. Your father and the two old ones, they died. Your mother spent mourning days here, then went back to her own village."

"She was not hurt?" Chakliux asked.

"No, she alone survived."

Chakliux kept his face still, did not show his anger or his grief. Of course his mother had survived. Of course. And the two elders who died—he remembered the woman, Song. And her husband was... Blue Jay. Yes. There were many reasons for his father Ground Beater to die, many ways he might have displeased K'os. But why kill the two old ones? Perhaps only to cover her part in Ground Beater's death. Perhaps only that.

"Brother," Sok said, "I share your sorrow."

Chakliux looked into Sok's eyes, and grief tightened his throat so he could only nod acknowledgment of his brother's words.

"Blue-head Duck," Sok said, "there were no others who came from the Cousin River Village? No one seeking revenge? No one who asked about Chakliux and where he had gone?"

"No one."

"Who were the two young hunters that came with Chakliux's mother and father?"

"Tikaani and Snow Breaker," Blue-head Duck said. He looked at Sok. "You know them?"

"No," said Sok.

"I know them," Chakliux said softly.

Yes, he thought, and if they were the two who came with his mother, they came seeking revenge. Perhaps, though, they believed what the elders told them, that Chakliux had not returned to the village. But there are many people in a village, old ones, wives, children. Someone might have told them that he had stopped, then gone to the Walrus. Either way, the elders did not seem to think the Cousin River People planned any revenge.

It was best, then, to stay for a while, Chakliux decided, at least until he saw what happened with Aqamdax. Besides, someone had to keep watch. Who could say what plans K'os had made? There should be someone in the village with eyes open.

"You are welcome to stay here with us. We need a good storyteller in this village," Blue-head Duck told Chakliux.

The others murmured their agreement, and Camp Maker said,

"You should know that your mother left your father's bones in our burial place."

The man's words gave comfort. His father's bones—another tie to hold him to this village. "I will stay," Chakliux said.

Yaa pulled Ghaden into the lodge's entrance tunnel. She was close to losing her temper with him. He had kept up with her as long as they followed the trapline, but on the way back to the village, he kept lagging behind until finally she had to carry him. He was in his fourth summer—too big to expect her to carry him, too old to act like a baby. She stuck her head out of the entrance tunnel. Brown Water was sitting inside the lodge, poking holes in a caribou skin with a birdbone awl.

Yaa turned and pulled Ghaden's thumb from his mouth, then crawled into the lodge. Ghaden followed her, sliding across the floor on his knees, then flinging himself into the rolls of bed mats. He curled up with his back toward Brown Water, and Biter flopped down beside him.

Yaa held out the two hares, but Brown Water ignored her to say, "Hunters do not curse their throwing sticks with wet thumbs."

Ghaden lay still, and Brown Water sighed, then turned her eyes to Yaa. She looked at the hares, then said, "Did you reset the traps?"

The question was an insult. Of course she had reset the traps. Even Ghaden knew better than to leave trap strings loose. "Yes," she said.

"Gut the hares and skin them," Brown Water told her. "Then take them to the hearths. Sok and his brother are back, and they have brought a Sea Hunter woman. Wolf-and-Raven has decided to show her that we are a strong village. She was a storyteller among her own people, Sok says."

Yaa widened her eyes and looked over at Ghaden. They loved storytelling evenings, but Ghaden lay still, as if he were asleep.

"She is Chakliux's wife?" Yaa asked.

"Someone said she is Sok's wife."

"But Sok already has a wife, and Chakliux has none."

Brown Water shrugged her shoulders, then said, "You talk too much. Do your work. If every woman in this village was like you, we would never have anything to eat."

Chakliux waited outside Red Leaf's lodge with Aqamdax. His nephews had run out to welcome him, the youngest with a wild fling of arms and happy chatter. The older boy had greeted Chakliux with a shy smile and then questions, many questions—about the First Men, how they hunted, about their iqyan, their weapons. All the while, Aqamdax waited, crouched on her haunches beside the dogs, her eyes straight ahead. She said nothing, though soon a crowd of villagers, mostly women, had gathered, pointing at her with pursed lips and chins outthrust, speaking about her as though she were not there to hear their words.

Of course, Chakliux thought, she would understand little, which was good since they were not always kind, though all spoke in awe of her feather sax.

When Sok finally came outside, several women rudely asked questions, but he did not answer. He leaned over to clasp Aqamdax's arm, then to gesture for Chakliux to follow them inside.

Chakliux did not know what to expect from Red Leaf. Some first wives were angry when a second wife came into their lodge, but others, especially those who welcomed sisters or cousins as second wife, were glad—one more person to help with sewing and cooking, with preparing hides and maintaining traplines. But how would any River woman react when she found the second wife was a First Men woman, one who could scarcely speak the River language? One who was as beautiful as Aqamdax?

He glanced quickly at Red Leaf, saw her swollen eyes, her tears.

"You will always be my wife," Sok told her, but Red Leaf looked away.

"Even if she gives you many sons?" she finally asked in a small voice.

"What son could be better than Carries Much?" Sok answered. "What child could bring me more joy than Cries-loud?"

Sok tried to laugh, but the sound was strange, as though the laughter were not his own.

Red Leaf pursed her lips, then drew close to watch as Sok brought out several finely woven grass baskets and a split walrus hide needle case, as large as Sok's hand and filled with strips of seal skin pierced by many needles of all sizes and shapes.

"I have also brought walrus meat for our sons," he said, "and a bladder of whale oil. What will bring them more power than the oil and meat of animals as strong as whales and walrus?

"This woman," Sok said, and pointed at Aqamdax with his chin, "she is nothing in a man's bed. She is good, though, to weave baskets and mats. She can do the things you do not want to do. She can take care of our dogs and gather wood. She can clean fish and keep the snow banked around our lodge in winter. I thought that of all the gifts I brought you, she would please you most."

Red Leaf tipped her head and studied Aqamdax. Aqamdax met the woman's stare.

"Here," Sok said, and pulled a sea otter skin from one of his packs. "This, too, I brought you."

Red Leaf took the pelt, smoothed her hand over the thick, soft fur, turned it to the skin side and sniffed.

"It is beautiful," she said. She looked again at Aqamdax. "She does not understand our language?"

"Only a few words," Sok replied.

"I do not have time to worry about her," Red Leaf said. "I cannot teach her to speak the true language and sew also."

"I did not bring her to make you more work," Sok told his wife. Looking over his shoulder at his brother, he said, "Chakliux will teach her. Whatever you want her to do, tell Chakliux."

"Stay here, then!" Yaa shouted, and she left Ghaden alone in the lodge. "I'm going to the cooking hearths." She carried the hares, gutted and skinned, in one hand, holding them out at arm's length, away from her parka.

It was not easy to be a mother, especially now that Ghaden's wound was healed. The stronger he got, the more often he disobeyed her. Well, she was not going to miss the feast. Besides, she wanted to tell her friends that she had seen the First Men woman before anyone else had.

She wished now she had left the trapline and rushed back to tell everyone Sok and Chakliux were coming. Now her friends might say she only made up the story, though they knew she was not one to tell lies.

Her thoughts were so full of what she would say to her friends that she did not see River Ice Dancer until he was beside her.

"Sok and the Cousin River brother are back," he said. "I saw them when they were coming into the village."

"I already saw them," Yaa said, then wished she had said nothing. "You liar."

River Ice Dancer curled his lips, and suddenly Yaa remembered the joy of punching him, the blood that had flowed from his nose. He was big, and older than she was, but he was not as brave as he pretended to be.

This time she did not answer him, but only shrugged. When he saw that she was not going to ask any questions, he tossed his head back and broke into a run, leaving her behind. Yaa let out a sigh and slowed her pace so she would not catch up to him. When she passed

Red Leaf's lodge, she walked even more slowly, hoping to see the First Men woman, or Sok or Chakliux, but even the dogs near the lodge were quiet, save one that Yaa recognized as a golden-eyed dog from the Cousin River People. She was surprised to see that dog back in the village. One of her friends had told her that the elders did not want it here, though why that was so, Yaa's friend was not sure.

Next she came to Spotted Flower's lodge. Spotted Flower's mother was outside and called to Yaa, told her that Spotted Flower was already at the cooking hearths. Yaa hurried then, and when she came to the hearths, she scanned the group of children, took the hares to the cooking bag farthest from where River Ice Dancer stood. A group of younger boys had already gathered around him, and River Ice Dancer was telling them about the Sea Hunter woman.

The grandmother Helps-herself took the hares from her hand. Since they were so large, Yaa thought she might skewer them on cooking sticks, but Helps-herself laid the hares on a slab of wood and began to cut them into pieces with her woman's knife.

As though she knew Yaa's thoughts, she looked up and said, "These are too fine to allow their fat to drip away into the fire."

Of course everyone knew that fat dripped into the fire was not wasted. The grass and berries and trees used it to grow. The spirits smelled it in the smoke and refrained from whatever evil mischief they had decided upon. But the people must have fat, too, and Yaa was proud that her hares would bring joy to bellies, strength to arms and legs. She sucked the raw hare juice from her hand and fingers, then she saw Spotted Flower sitting with a group of their friends. They had chosen a place where the wind brought smoke from the cooking fires to keep away the mosquitoes and gnats.

Yaa joined the group, listening for a while before she spoke, laughing when Best Fist told about the fight she had had with her brother, and then standing to see the new comb Breaks-wood-fast had at the top of her head, a gift from the young hunter who had been promised to her as husband as soon as she came into her moon times.

Breaks-wood-fast was two years older than Yaa, but it seemed strange to think of her as someone's wife. Yet, in some ways she was further from being a woman than Yaa was, as were all these friends. None of them was mother like Yaa was mother. Green Stripe had her new brother strapped to her back in a cradleboard, but caring for a brother or sister, cousin or nephew was not like being mother. Sometimes when she was with her friends, Yaa felt like an old woman sitting with children; their eyes were not yet open to the hard things in life.

Finally the discussion turned to Sok and Chakliux. Several girls giggled their gladness that the new woman was wife to Sok, not Chakliux. Ah, Chakliux, they said, who could not find joy in being wife to that one, though Blueberry had been fool enough to choose Root Digger, and Snow-in-her-hair . . . They clapped their hands over their mouths and laughed. Some of the older girls remembered when Snow-in-her-hair played with them, before moon blood separated her from games and children. Fool! Now she had no husband at all, and what man would want her when she had no respect for someone with the powers of an otter foot?

"They say this First Men woman is ugly," Green Stripe whispered.

The girls leaned their heads together and Breaks-wood-fast said, "My father told me not to look at her, that her ugliness could come into my face and Muskrat Singer would not want me."

Yaa shook her head. Breaks-wood-fast always tried to twist the conversation so she might mention Muskrat Singer. He was her father's sister's son, and she had been promised to him since she was a baby. Yaa's aunts had no sons, and Spotted Flower's aunt was old; her sons all had wives. The same with the other girls. Their aunts were dead, or without sons or with sons too young or too old. Breaks-wood-fast had no real reason to consider herself better than they were because she was promised. It was not as if some hunter had asked for her because she was beautiful or gifted with sewing.

"You're wrong," Yaa said.

The girls looked at her in surprise. Even Best Fist's little three-year-old sister, Net, who was bent over a handful of colorful pebbles, looked up. Net stuck one of the pebbles into her mouth, and Best Fist, without moving her eyes from Yaa's face, hooked a finger into Net's mouth and popped the pebble out.

"How do you know?" Spotted Flower asked.

"I saw her."

The questions came too fast for Yaa to answer until one of the oldest girls, Blue Necklace—whose complaints of sore breasts let them all know she would soon leave their children's circle for a place among the women—told them to be quiet, then ordered Yaa to explain.

Yaa felt her chest expand in excitement. It was not often she earned the attention of Blue Necklace. Yaa spoke quickly, telling how she and Ghaden were checking the trapline. She said that the woman was not ugly, but that her clothes were different, like the ones worn by Ghaden's dead mother. She did not say Daes's name, would not take the risk of doing such a thing, but even so, the girls turned their heads away from her at the mention of that dead woman.

After Yaa had told her story, they asked questions until Yaa could tell them nothing more. Then their interest turned to other things, and soon Breaks-wood-fast was boasting again about Muskrat Singer.

For a while Yaa sat with them, but finally she began to feel uneasy, suddenly remembering that she had left Ghaden alone in the lodge. Who could say what a child might do to himself, alone, without anyone to watch him? What had she been thinking, to leave him? She had agreed to be his mother; that was not something that you forgot when you were tired of the extra work.

She stood up and, pointing with her chin toward Best Fist's little sister, said, "I have to go take care of Ghaden. I'll be back."

But most of the girls were talking to each other about something else, and Blue Necklace had already left the circle, walking with swaying hips to stand at the edge of the boys' group, leaning close to one of the young hunters to whisper something in his ear.

That one would soon be married, Yaa thought. But as the older girls left to become wives, babies grew up enough to fill their places, and that was good—the way things were supposed to be.

Soon Ghaden would sit with the boys. It seemed such a long time since last winter, when he had been stabbed. With Biter living in their lodge, Yaa had begun to feel safe. But perhaps, if the killer was someone in the village, that one was waiting for them to forget, waiting for Yaa to grow so busy with her own life that she no longer worried about Ghaden.

When Yaa got to the lodge, she crawled inside, calling for Ghaden. Biter made a quick bound, licking her face before she could stand and push him away. Ghaden sat up, rubbing his eyes. Yaa took a long breath and smiled at herself for her foolish worries.

"I came to take you to the cooking hearths to get food," she said.

"I'm not hungry."

"Ghaden, you are always hungry!"

"No."

"Ghaden, you have to come." He started to cry, but Yaa grabbed his parka and pulled it on over his head, then rubbed his checks with grease to protect him against the bugs. At first he struggled against her, but finally let himself go limp so that Yaa felt as though she were dressing a baby.

"Can we take Biter?"

"You know Biter will steal food if we take him."

Ghaden popped his thumb into his mouth. Ordinarily, Yaa would have pulled it out, but this time she left it. She got their eating bowls, then fastened a braided rope around Biter's neck and tied him outside.

Ghaden hugged Biter and followed Yaa. He walked slowly, but without crying or complaining.

As they came to the hearths, River Ice Dancer and three other boys shoved past them. River Ice Dancer stopped and pushed his face close to Yaa's.

"You liar," he said. "I know what you told Blue Necklace and the girls."

Yaa grabbed Ghaden's hand and hurried past, but River Ice Dancer grabbed Ghaden's parka hood, then crouched down and said, "Your sister's a liar. You know that?"

Ghaden stuck his thumb in his mouth, and River Ice Dancer laughed. He pulled Ghaden's hand up and opened his own mouth wide, lowered it over the thumb. "I should bite that right off for you. Otherwise you might stay a baby all your life."

"My dog would kill you," Ghaden said.

Two of the other boys laughed. "That's the way, you tell him!" the one named First Tree said to Ghaden.

River Ice Dancer stood up and grabbed First Tree. Yaa pulled Ghaden away. River Ice Dancer called something after her, but she did not hear what he said. She saw her mother stirring the contents of a cooking bag and went over to stand beside her. For all his boasting, River Ice Dancer was not one to cause trouble where adults might see him.

The other men had eaten by the time Sok and Chakliux, Red Leaf and the First Men woman came to the hearths. When Ghaden saw them, he began to wail until Happy Mouth finally told Yaa to take him home.

When they got to the lodge, Yaa added wood to the fire and pulled off Ghaden's parka, wiped the bits of food from his mouth and wrapped him into his sleeping robes. Biter lay down beside him, chewing a piece of dried meat Yaa had stolen for him from a food basket.

She stroked Ghaden's hair and sang until his crying was only an occasional sob, then she leaned over him and whispered, "You need to tell me why you are crying, Ghaden. Are you afraid of Sok? Are you afraid of Chakliux?"

Ghaden would not answer her. He closed his eyes and rolled closer to Biter, lifted his head to bury his face in the soft fur of the dog's neck.

Chapter Thirty

It was more difficult than the pain he had faced the last time he was in the Near River Village, worse than discovering that Aqamdax had left the First Men Village. Cen's hands tightened on the paddle, and the muscles in his legs spasmed as if they could take him from his iqyax through the dark water of the river to the lodge where Ghaden slept.

He had purposely spent days idle—his tent pitched beside a slow-moving stream—waiting for this night of new moon, dark and still. Now he paddled past the village, hugging the far bank of the river, and though in the darkness he could see nothing, his eyes kept turning toward those lodges, and his thoughts were of his son.

Two times, he almost crossed that river, almost decided to go into the village, but as he moved his paddle to the left side of his iqyax, as he leaned into a turn, he remembered the villagers' accusations, their anger, and reminded himself that he would never win his son back if he died. And though, as a spirit, he might have some chance of revenge, it was better to stay alive and seek revenge as warrior, and have the joy of teaching his son to hunt and trade.

The people of the Cousin River Village would welcome him. They always had. Since it was late summer, they might yet be in their fish camps near the river.

Though they shared grandfathers with the Near River People, anger often seemed to fuel skirmishes between the two villages. He might find Cousin River men who would help him get his son and earn his revenge. He had last visited that village two, three summers ago. The woman K'os had welcomed him into her lodge. She was a healer, and her husband was chief hunter, though he was growing old, losing the respect of the young men.

If K'os was still there, he would visit her first. She was always greedy for trade goods, and he had many fine things from the First Men that she would like.

He heard several village dogs begin to bark. They might have heard his paddling, but the river was so wide he did not think so. Most likely they saw a porcupine or an owl, but he paddled more quickly in case some hunter was aroused by the noise.

He paddled hard until he was well past the village. He would not stop until morning, and then only for a short rest, a bit of dried fish. He did not want a Near River hunter to see him and decide again to take revenge for Tsaani and Daes.

Dogs. They were fighting, biting Aqamdax's arms, flinging heavy bodies against her legs to bring her down into their teeth and jaws.

She woke with a jerk, breathing heavily until the dream left her. She lay still and finally realized that Sok's arm lay across her belly. She wished he would not sleep with her until she had her own lodge. She could not bear the sorrow in Red Leaf's eyes each time Sok touched her.

She had tried to tell Red Leaf that she had no true feelings for him, that she would do nothing to win his favor, but Red Leaf had begun to scream out Sok's virtues, listing, as far as Aqamdax could understand, his skills and strengths until her shouts filled up the lodge and pushed Aqamdax outside. A group of women had gathered there, hands over mouths, but she was used to being scorned by women, and so held her head high, walked to the village hearths, stirred boiling bags as though nothing had happened.

Across the lodge, Red Leaf sighed and murmured in her sleep. Sok groaned and lifted his arm from Aqamdax's belly. She pushed herself away from him, turning her back. She had not slept well since she had been in this village. She woke during the middle of each night and lay with worries weaving themselves into her thoughts until it was time for her to stoke the morning fire and bring in wood.

She had lost count of the days she had been here. More than ten, she was sure, but not yet from full moon to full moon.

Each day, Chakliux taught her more of the language. He seemed to know which words she should learn first, but she still had to think of each phrase in her own language before she could remember the River People word. It made her thoughts slow and her speech cumbersome. Red Leaf was no help, and seemed to rejoice in confusing Aqamdax's attempts to learn. Sok was impatient, but his two young sons had begun to treat her like a friend, laughing at her mistakes but also helping her correct them. She had already begun each of them a caribou gut raincoat, though Sok had expressed his doubt about such a coat's worth to a River boy and Red Leaf had reacted in anger.

She had also woven Red Leaf a gathering basket, but Red Leaf had tossed it away, crushed it disdainfully under her heel.

Aqamdax told herself things would get better. Soon she would be able to speak the River People's language well enough to tell stories, and Sok had already given her the caribou hides she needed to make a lodge, though she was not at all sure how to do such a thing. She hoped there were women in the village who would teach her.

They seemed to treat her well when she took her turn at the cooking hearths. One woman—her name was Happy Mouth—even sought her out, chattered away in bright words that Aqamdax only vaguely understood. Still, Happy Mouth's acceptance gave her hope that other women, too, would someday count her as friend.

Aqamdax turned her head so she could see the smoke hole. It was very dark, a night of new moon, but soon the sky would lighten and then she could get up. Remember, she told herself, you will not be here forever. Someday, one of the First Men will come to trade.

Then she would go back with him, to her own people, to her own village, and again be storyteller.

Dogs barking woke him. Ghaden reached out for Yaa, stroked the soft mat of her dark hair and stuck his thumb in his mouth. He felt Biter move beside him, heard the low rumble of a growl in Biter's throat. He laid his hand on the dog's back, but Biter rose stiff-legged and moved toward the door. Ghaden waited, his breath in his throat.

It might be her. He knew that she would come for him. Biter could protect him from people, but what about ghosts? What did ghosts do? Did they turn people into ghosts? If he were a ghost, would he still live in this lodge with Yaa and Brown Water and Happy Mouth?

Could he play like other boys or would he have to float around like smoke? Worse, would the ghost kill Biter?

He heard the dog growl again, so he shook Yaa's arm until she woke up.

"What?" she asked, her voice full of sleep. She was cross with him, he could tell, though in the dark he could not see her face.

"Something's outside," Ghaden whispered.

"Just dogs barking. Go to sleep."

She flopped back down into her sleeping robes, but Ghaden leaned over her and said, "It might be the ghost."

Yaa sat up. "What ghost?"

"The one who came with the hunters. The one who lives with the otter man."

"The First Men woman?"

"She's a ghost."

"Ghaden! She's a woman. She's just like us. Well, almost like us."

Ghaden felt tears closing up his throat. Yaa didn't like him to cry, so he shut his eyes tight and tried to hold the tears inside.

"Ghaden," Yaa said softly, "why do you think she's a ghost?"

"She's my other mother," Ghaden said, but when he spoke the words, a sob came with them. He clamped his mouth shut in the bitterness of knowing that Yaa could tell he was crying.

"Sh-h-h," she said. She sat up and pulled him into her lap. Biter came to them, stuck his nose into Ghaden's face and licked away the tears. "Don't worry, Ghaden," Yaa told him. "She's not a ghost, but even if she is, you're safe with us."

In the morning Yaa left Ghaden in the lodge and went to the cooking hearths. She walked past the place where Sok's Sea Hunter wife was to put her new lodge, hoping to see the woman working there. Several elders were digging a circle into the earth with broad slate blades. Usually the women did that, but many were still with their families at summer fish camps, though they would return to this winter village before they left for fall caribou hunts.

Yaa could barely remember the last time she had been on a caribou hunt. That was when her father was still strong enough to hunt, but then he became old, and now with no man in the lodge, they had to depend on Brown Water's married son to provide caribou meat, though she and her mother and Brown Water had been able to do their share in catching and drying salmon for winter food.

She walked slowly past the lodge site, finding reason to stop and tighten the rawhide that laced her boots from insteps to ankles. She did the left boot, then the right, but still the Sea Hunter woman did not come. She stood and watched the elders until Blue-head Duck stopped digging and scolded her, telling her she was lazy. Then she hurried to the hearths, chose a cooking bag and emptied Brown Water's meager contribution of dried salmon and a handful of fresh blueberries. She fed one of the fires, then used a willow loop to pull a cooking stone from the coals. She carried it to the cooking bag, dropped the stone and watched it sizzle its heat into the meat and broth.

She was disappointed that the Sea Hunter woman had not been working at her lodge. She must mostly stay inside, Yaa thought, for she seldom saw her. Well, as second wife, the Sea Hunter woman would have to do what Red Leaf told her, just like her own mother did what Brown Water said.

Yaa stirred the cooking bag again and looked up at the sky. Brown Water had told her to stay here until the sun was two hands past the tops of the northeast trees. She held a hand up to the edge of the trees. One and a half. She fed two of the fires, adding the wood where it would least disturb the coals. She didn't mind hauling wood and feeding fires or stirring the food, but she didn't like to carry hot rocks and drop them into the cooking bags. Even the most carefully chosen rocks—smooth and round—sometimes cracked into pieces when you added them to the meat. There was always the chance a sliver of stone would fly up and cut hands or face. Best Fist had a scar above her left eyebrow where a rock had cut her last year. Then, of course, someone had to try to find all the pieces of rock and get them out of the food. Yaa had had to do that more often than she liked to remember. Still, as careful as she was, Dog Trainer had once chipped a tooth on a piece she did not get out.

Yaa moved to the next cooking bag. For the moment, she was alone at the hearths, although since the fires were burning so well, she knew other women had recently been there and would probably return soon. She stirred the meat, felt the heat rise, but knew it needed another stone. She was lifting the stone with the willow loop tongs when she saw the Sea Hunter woman walking toward her. As much as she wanted to look at her, Yaa made herself keep her eyes on the rock until she got it to the cooking bag. She dropped it in, then looked up and greeted the woman.

The Sea Hunter woman smiled at Yaa and held up a caribou cooking skin, pointed at the cooking bags with her chin, then at the skin so Yaa knew she wanted some meat to take back to Red Leaf's lodge.

"Red Leaf tell . . . come . . . take."

It seemed as though the woman's broken speech stole Yaa's words, and she could only nod. The woman brought the skin and Yaa filled it.

The Sea Hunter woman thanked her, and Yaa inclined her head, then went back to stirring. The woman had turned away before Yaa thought to call after her: "I am Yaa. My mother is Happy Mouth. My brother is Ghaden."

The woman turned. "No speak," she said.

Yaa laid a hand on her chest. "Yaa," she said.

"Aqamdax."

Yaa lifted her chin toward the woman. "Aqamdax?" she asked.

"Yes."

The woman walked away. Aqamdax, Yaa thought. It was a word she did not know. A Sea Hunter word, no doubt, and hard to say, the last part more like a choke deep in the throat than a sound. No wonder the people did not say her name.

Daes had had a River name. Perhaps this woman, too, after living in the village for a time, would take a name everyone could say. Then, thinking of Daes, Yaa realized how much this new woman looked like her. Of course, it was the same among many people. The hunters of the Cousin River Village, when they came here to trade, all seemed to look much alike.

Daes had kept her hair long, seldom binding it back from her face. She cut it in a fringe across her forehead, as did this new First Men woman. Suddenly, Yaa stopped stirring. No wonder Ghaden did not want to go outside. Aqamdax *did* look like Daes. Ghaden probably thought she was his mother's ghost.

THE COUSIN RIVER FISH CAMP

K'os rolled her sleeping mats into a tight bundle and secured them with a braid of babiche. She hated the long three-day walk to their winter village. They would stay there only a moon, then leave on a caribou hunt, and what was worse than that? Piling rocks and rebuilding brush driving fences to direct the caribou to the hunters. Then butchering and hauling, most of which the women did.

For the past few years she had chosen to remain in the winter village, had found a young woman willing to go with her husband, do his work in hopes of becoming a second wife. She certainly did not mind having another woman warm Ground Beater's bed during the caribou hunt, but second wife? No. Why chance that Ground Beater would be influenced by another woman's needs, by her wants, or by her father's ideas? K'os always saw they were paid well in meat, and even a few necklaces, but also always found reason for them to return to their mothers' lodges.

This year, though, she had no husband, and that meant she had to go on the hunt again. She would do her share—build fences and butcher and skin—but all the while she would be watching.

This year the young hunters had chosen to break with tradition, and she was afraid that without her there, they might allow the elders to convince them to return to their spears and spearthrowers without the chance of proving that their bows and small-bladed arrows would work as well, perhaps even better.

She added her rolled sleeping robes to the pile of her belongings. Her two dogs would take the caribou hide tent, her bedding and her cooking utensils. She would carry her medicine bag, the plants she had gathered and dried, as well as the few weapons she owned.

She shaded her eyes from the sun and looked across the camp. There were few families left, so it was easy to see that Tikaani's tent was still up. His sister was slow. K'os took two dried fish from a sael and gave one to each of her dogs. Most of the elders thought dogs worked better on an empty stomach, but she had always fed dogs well and never had trouble with them.

Dogs and men were much alike: mean when their bellies were empty. She laughed and sat down on her bedding roll. She pulled out a fish for herself and began to eat, her back to the summer camp so she could look down the path that led from the river.

She thought at first she was seeing a vision—the body of a bear with the head and beak of a giant eagle. By the time several of the elders found courage to go forward and meet the strange beast, she realized it was only a man carrying a large pack and a skin-covered boat. A Sea Hunter trader this far from the sea?

She had never been one to rush forward, to greet traders or hunters until she decided what kind of men they were. Once such foolishness had cost her much. She would not repeat her mistake. She crouched between her dogs, an arm around each animal's neck, and spoke in a stern voice until their barking had faded to thin, high whines.

When the man finally drew close enough for her to see his face, she remembered him, recalled inviting him into her bed. He had been in too much of a hurry for her taste, but had been generous in his trading. His face had changed—more than what would be expected only from the passing of years. His nose had been broken and a scar drew his mouth into a pucker, but still his eyes and the bones of his cheeks were the same.

The shaman He Talks puffed himself up to hold his shoulders straight, his sagging belly in. He approached the man, soon was arguing with him, telling him that he had never been to their village. K'os drew her mouth into a smirk. What did He Talks know?

K'os rose, walked slowly toward the trader. He had set down his boat, and she could see that he wore a peaked hat. It seemed to be made of wood, thin and bent into the shape of a woman's breast, but large enough to fit over a hunter's head. It was waterproofed with strips of gut. She could understand the reason for such a thing, especially on the sea. It would shade the eyes and even protect against rain. It might be something a hunter would wear, or a shaman. Either way, it must hold power. She wanted it, and by the time the trader left them, she would have it.

"He has been here before," K'os said to He Talks.

He Talks turned to her, and K'os saw that his eyes were dark in anger. He did not like her. She was a woman, and younger than he was, but her power was greater. He was afraid of her. He had been the first to throw accusations against her in Gguzaakk's death, the first to withdraw them after three nights of stomach pains and loose, bloody stools. He had not even had the decency to thank her for the medicine she had given him, a medicine that took away the pain almost as quickly as it had come.

"He has been here before," she repeated. "He was a guest in my fish camp lodge, a friend of my dead husband." That reference to Ground Beater should be enough to convince those few who still doubted. Who would risk mentioning someone dead unless that mention carried great importance?

She stepped forward and looked into the trader's face, so close that the beak of the hat extended forward over her head. Yes, he was the same one. She was not wrong. Ah, but what was his name? Something about the earth. Yes, tundra—Cen.

"What happened to your face, Cen?" she asked, and smiled at her boldness.

Her question surprised him. She was not a young woman, but a man would have difficulty knowing such a thing. Her face was beautiful, but who could have accumulated the cold knowledge in those eyes without living a long time?

He almost answered her with a joke, but for some reason the words that came out of his mouth were harsh, angry. Words that told the truth.

"The Near River People killed my wife and nearly killed me," he said. "They still have my son—unless they have killed him also."

More people had gathered now, the hunters crowded so close that they pressed against him on all sides. They spoke to one another quietly, their voices like a low rumble in the throat of a dog. He pulled up his sleeve so they could see his misshapen wrist.

The growl rolled into a deep roar of anger, but the woman who stood before him lifted her voice to call out, "We have a common enemy. They steal our fish and curse our hunting. They have turned my own son against us."

Cen saw several elders step back, pull at young men in the crowd, but the hunters pushed them away.

"Do you seek revenge?" she asked, hissing the words into his face.

"Yes," he told her. "And I want my son."

She turned with arms spread, and in that way widened the circle of people. "You see," she said, "we are not the only ones the Near River People have cursed." She looked over her shoulder at Cen. "Those with the same enemies should lend their strength to one another. Our winter village is three days' walk. Will you come with us?"

He looked at her. The question was more than something asked in hope of trading.

"There is a traders' lodge where I might stay? I no longer have my own lodge poles."

"There is a lodge where you can stay," she said. Then she clasped his left hand, pushed up his sleeve, her hand hovering for a moment over the haft of the blade he had sheathed there. She ran strong fingers over the wrist, palpitating the swelling that extended up his arm.

He noticed that her hands were the hands of an old woman, with pocked skin and large purple veins. He wondered how far that oldness extended—to her breasts, her belly? Or was her body young like her face?

"I have something that will take the pain from your wrist," she said.

"I can bear the pain, but I need to regain my strength."

"I may be able to help with that," she said, then shrugged. "And I may not, but pain weakens the will."

"I will go with you," Cen replied.

The woman left then, and again the hunters crowded close, asking questions about the First Men hat he wore and about the seal flipper boots on his feet.

He had been wise to come to these people. If nothing else, he would make good trades. He lifted his eyes to where the woman had been sitting. But he might gain more than that. Perhaps much more than that.

Chapter
Thirty-one

THE NEAR RIVER VILLAGE

Green Stripe giggled, and Best Fist said, "Dats'eni."

"Dats'eni," Aqamdax said, correcting herself.

"You are getting better," said Best Fist.

Aqamdax smiled at her and said, "Because you help me." Best Fist, a girl who had not been blessed with comely face or quickness of hands, straightened her back and lifted her eyebrows at Aqamdax, and Aqamdax continued her story. It was about a duck and a raven, one of the few the River children had told her. She had made it her own by adding voices and giving the duck a good amount of wisdom as weapon against the raven's cunning.

When she finished the story, one of the children sang out a request for another. "The last one," Aqamdax told them, though she truly enjoyed telling stories, and the telling did not slow her fingers as she sewed a caribouskin parka for Red Leaf's youngest son.

More than two tens of children had gathered to listen to her stories that day. Even a few of the oldest boys stood at the edge of the group, each with a practice spear or bola in his hands, as though he had stopped for only a moment.

First the children had merely watched her when she sat outside her new lodge to sew or scrape hides. She had tried to speak to them, but found they slipped away if she looked at them. So one day she did not lift her eyes from her sewing, but began to sing songs using the few words of the River language that she knew. One day she began to tell stories, simple things about animals or plants, speaking as though she talked to herself.

Finally the children grew bold enough to sit near her, and then to tell her stories as well, and to correct her words, to answer her questions about the way things were done in the village.

She found they were remarkable teachers, and so during the two moons she had lived in the village, she had already learned much of the language. It was good, too, to have the children as friends. Now that she had her own lodge, she was often alone, though Sok came some nights to share her bed, and each day Red Leaf brought her more work to do.

Usually Chakliux came each morning, at first to share new River words and perhaps a bowl of food, but now they were friends. She told him about her people, and she, too, was a teacher, sharing First Men words as Chakliux shared his language with her.

For the past four days, Chakliux had been away hunting bear, and soon, after a short time home, he would leave for the caribou hunt. She would not go on that hunt, Red Leaf had told her, though Red Leaf, Sok and their sons would go. Someone had to stay with the dogs left behind. Someone had to watch the lodges. It did not matter to Aqamdax. Having never been on a caribou hunt, she would be like a child, always in the way.

She was glad Red Leaf was going, but she would miss Chakliux. Even now, with him away on the bear hunt, she felt a small ache under her ribs each time she thought of him. He had taught her not only River People words, but also some of the riddles spoken in the Cousin River Village, the village where Chakliux, though he was brother to Sok, had been raised.

Aqamdax ended her story and stood up, bringing groans and sighs from the children. "Come tomorrow. There will be more stories then," she said.

"A riddle before we go," pleaded Yaa, a girl whose little brother sat with his face hidden against her chest each time they came.

"Look," Aqamdax said, beginning as Chakliux had taught her, "I see something."

"A bird," one of the boys called out before she could finish.

"A cloud," said Best Fist.

"A dead animal, stinking," said River Ice Dancer, a boy Aqamdax had learned to ignore.

"It brings a feast," said someone behind her.

Aqamdax turned at the voice, a sudden gladness in her heart. "An easy riddle," she said, then asked, "You bring meat?"

"If the riddle is so easy, why do you ask?" said Chakliux.

He looked thinner than he had when he left, and his parka needed to be brushed, one of the sleeves was torn at the seam, but his eyes were bright and he was smiling.

"Hunters are back?" several of the children asked, then bounded off to tell the news.

"It is good my lodge is here at the edge of the village," Aqamdax said. "I am first to learn good things."

"You speak well, Aqamdax," Chakliux told her. "Even in these few days I have been gone, you have learned more, though you still speak your words like First Men do."

"I *am* First Men," she said softly. "I will always be First Men. I will not change. I will learn, but I will not change. You, Otter Foot, should understand that as well as anyone."

He smiled at her, and she looked into his eyes, found she had to look away. It was not good to have her heart quicken for Chakliux when she did not feel that way about Sok.

She turned as though to enter her lodge, but looked back over her shoulder to ask if Chakliux was hungry.

"We have spent the last day eating, honoring the animals we have taken, and tonight, I am sure, the women will prepare another feast, though only with the meat the women can touch."

Aqamdax shook her head. There were strange taboos among these people. Some were what anyone would expect—the burial of bones, the honoring of animals. Others, such as the eating and preparation of bear meat, the use of certain birds and animals, seemed strange and senseless. But who was she to comment? She was a woman of the First Men, and Sea Hunters seldom took a bear.

"They will cook the meat at the hearths?" she asked.

"Yes."

"Are there taboos I should know?"

"Do you have a new ladle or stirring stick?"

"I can get a stirring stick," she said.

"Good. Bring that. I told you women should not say the name of the animal?"

"Yes."

"Remember that, and also, do not eat until Red Leaf has eaten."

Aqamdax raised her eyebrows. "It is taboo?"

"It is a custom of politeness."

Aqamdax felt the first stirrings of anger, like the anger she had often known when she lived with He Sings's wives and their foolish rules.

"Perhaps I will not go. I have good food here." She nodded toward the food cache near her lodge. It was a high platform that held a small square of logs where she kept meat and dried fish, berries saved in oil, and the few bellies of seal fat she had brought all the way from her village. "I have walrus meat, too," she said, though Chakliux himself had been the one to give it to her.

Chakliux looked away, and she thought she saw disappointment in his eyes. No, she told herself, do not believe he cares for you. You have a husband. He has given you your own lodge. Perhaps someday you will have the good luck to bear children.

But as Chakliux walked away, he said softly, "Two of the animals are mine."

"Perhaps I will have the honor of preparing their meat for you," Aqamdax called after him.

THE COUSIN RIVER VILLAGE

Cen held his breath, pulled back the bowstring and loosed the arrow. It flew toward the tree, hit hard against the grass-stuffed goose skin the hunters had hung from a low branch.

Tikaani let out a shout of approval. "Soon you will be as good as any of us," he said, but Cen knew the words were an exaggeration.

Though his first shots were usually accurate, the longer he practiced in any one day, the worse he became. Finally, his left wrist would throb so hard from the strain of holding the bow, his eyes could no longer guide the arrow to its target.

He shot again, but the arrow flew wide to the left, his wrist buckling as soon as he released the string. "Enough," he said, and did not miss the sly smile that twisted the side of Tikaani's face.

Why fault the man? They shared an uneasy peace, the two of them, united by their need for revenge, he for Daes, and Tikaani for two brothers who were dead and another who might as well be, one of his arms crippled, his body weakened by whatever spirit had come in through the wound to fester in sores and lumps.

They also both shared K'os's bed. No one man could keep K'os as his own, but Cen was not sure Tikaani understood that.

Cen did not hold the same feelings for K'os that he had for Daes, but with his wrist aching, his thoughts had already strayed to K'os's fingers kneading away his pain, layering hot wet strips of ground squirrel hide tightly over his hand and wrist, the smell of partner grass pungent in the lodge.

"You are ready to go with me," Tikaani said.

"You are going somewhere?"

"K'os has not told you?" he asked.

She had, but Cen was wise enough to feign surprise. "Told me what?"

"That the hunters are almost ready, that they want us to go first, to scout out the best place to stand for attack. Perhaps we will be able to bring back your son."

"When do we leave?"

"Tomorrow, early, before the sun rises," Tikaani said.

"We will take dogs?"

"No dogs. Only hunting weapons, and if our elders ask, we tell them that we go to see if our bows will be honored by bears."

"You think we will not break our luck by claiming something that is not true, something that might make bears think we do not respect them?"

"You believe we cannot find your son and also hunt?"

Cen thought for a moment, then said, "And perhaps trade as well."

"Trade?"

"Life for life."

"Life for life," said Tikaani.

THE NEAR RIVER VILLAGE

"I will stir for you," Yaa said, raising her voice above the chatter of the women at the cooking hearths. The sun had set and most of the people had eaten. Soon the dancing and stories would begin.

Aqamdax handed Yaa the stirring stick. "It is a new one?" Yaa asked.

"Yes."

"You have the same custom in your village?"

"We do not take many—" She stopped, clapping a hand over her mouth before she said the word for bear.

"What do you eat?"

"Mostly fish and seal meat. Sea lion."

"Caribou?"

"Some."

"You can sit there." Yaa lifted her chin toward a pile of hare fur blankets.

"Your brother?"

"He is asleep. You cannot see him?"

In the darkness, lit only by the yellow flames of the dying hearth fires, Aqamdax had missed the shadow of the boy's head against the fur.

"He does not like me. What if he wakes up?"

"He likes you, but he is afraid. He thinks you are a ghost."

"A ghost? Why?"

"His mother died." Yaa had lowered her voice to a whisper and Aqamdax had to lean forward to hear her. "He was hurt."

When Aqamdax first came to the village, Chakliux had told her the story of a woman killed and a son injured, but that was before Aqamdax knew much of the River language, and she had not understood all of his words, had never been sure which boy he meant.

"So he is the one," Aqamdax said. "But your mother . . ."

"Was his mother's sister-wife."

"Ah."

"I am Ghaden's mother now," Yaa said, and her smile was that of a woman much older, a woman who speaks with pride of her son. "He thinks you are ghost because you look a little like his mother."

"I will sit beside him, but if he wakes, come over. I do not want him to be afraid."

Aqamdax handed Yaa the stirring stick, then crouched down with a sigh, sitting as the First Men sat, feet flat against the ground, arms clasped around raised knees. The River People wasted many furs in their preference to sit with legs crossed, padding the ground when it was wet or cold with woven hare fur blankets and mats of caribou hide. Any pelt grew weak when it became wet. Who did not know that?

She closed her eyes for a moment, wishing someone would leave so she also could go without fear of breaking taboos or showing rudeness. For all his desire to have her come to this feast, Chakliux had not spoken to her, even though he came to her cooking bag each time he wanted his bowl filled.

She looked down at the boy lying beside her. Her heart made a small jump in her chest. Each time she saw him, she felt as though she were seeing a child of her own village. He looked as if he belonged to the First Men. He had a wide face, and his nose, though humped, was small, unlike the larger noses of these River People. She remembered, though, that he had River People eyes, tilted at the corners and narrower than the eyes of her people. He was lighter of skin also. Still, looking at him, she could imagine she was home, perhaps in an ulax, celebrating with a feast and stories. She could almost hear her people's drums, beating hard then soft, the rhythm of a heart.

Aqamdax closed her eyes. Dreams called her, and almost, she let herself follow them, but then came a scream, a hunter's voice. Aqamdax's eyes flew open, and she jumped to her feet only to hear the laughter of the women sitting around her. One, still laughing, leaned close to draw Aqamdax back down, to whisper that the men would now tell stories of their hunts.

Aqamdax smiled, realizing that their laughter was not done out of spite, then settled herself again beside Ghaden, the boy still asleep, and opened her eyes wide to wake herself up. Two elders came into the center of the hearth circle, the place left bare but lit by remnants of the cooking fires.

Their stories were easy for her to follow because the words were accompanied by actions, so that everyone could see the way the hunter stalked the bear; everyone could watch as he told of placing a spear in his thrower and making the kill.

Aqamdax watched carefully, trying to remember the words they used to begin and end their stories, such things having importance as tradition in a village, and perhaps also some connection to good luck and proper respect. She tried to remember their hand movements, small things she might adapt for her own storytelling, ways of placing pictures in the listeners' minds. For what is storytelling if not ideas brought full and whole to the inner eyes of those who listen?

After the elders, two men came out, one wearing a mask that hung to his knees; its mouth was agape and studded with bear teeth. The other man was dressed as a hunter and carried weapons. Their story was told without words, only actions set to the rhythm of drums. When they had finished, Sok came out. At first he was alone, wearing no mask, carrying no weapons, the beautiful patterns of his parka and boots catching the light, bringing honor to Red Leaf's handiwork, so that there was a murmur among the women.

Aqamdax turned her eyes to where her sister-wife sat and saw that Red Leaf's head was held high, her face set and proud. In that moment, though Red Leaf had been a difficult woman to call sister, Aqamdax felt a thrill of pride, as though she herself were being honored. The women raised a high ululation, one rise, then a fall, and Aqamdax joined them, purposely turning her head toward Red Leaf so everyone knew she praised her sister-wife.

Red Leaf saw Aqamdax, eyes meeting eyes, and in that quick moment, Aqamdax read the woman's surprise, then her understanding.

Sok began to dance, setting his own rhythm with the clatter of the hoof rattlers sewn at the tops of his boots. His body moved in strong, sharp swings. Aqamdax knew each step must carry some meaning, though here among the River People that would be different from what she had learned among the First Men. As he danced, she noticed that he often looked in one direction, often turned his eyes in one way. At first she thought he was watching Red Leaf, but then she realized that he looked beyond her to the place where the younger women of the village sat, and finally, by watching carefully, she saw that his eyes were on a woman named Snow-in-her-hair. Aqamdax had met her sometimes at the cooking hearths, though Snow-in-her-hair ignored her when they were the only ones at the hearths and cut her eyes rudely away if other women were near.

Aqamdax looked quickly at Red Leaf, but the woman did not seem to notice, her eyes totally on her husband, her lips moving as though she counted his steps in an effort to help him keep the rhythm. Aqamdax felt an uneasiness, a sudden weight of apprehension, then scolded herself for her foolishness. What man did not want to impress young women, especially someone as pretty as Snow-in-her-hair? But Sok had two wives. He was not a chief hunter to take three or four like He Sings, and among the River People, most men had one wife.

Finally, another masked hunter entered the dance circle. This one also wore a bear mask, though it covered only his face and was painted with bright colors. The dancer was barefoot, so it was not difficult to tell he was Chakliux. He moved gracefully, as if he had the normal feet of a man, and Aqamdax's thoughts were so filled with his dancing that at first she did not hear the thin keening that rose from beside her. When the keening turned into a wail, she realized it was the child Ghaden. He was staring at the dancers, mouth open, eyes wide.

Aqamdax scooped him into her arms, and he looked up at her, then began to scream, "The ghost! The ghost! She is here! Yaa, don't let her get me!"

Yaa took the sobbing child from Aqamdax, soothed him with quiet humming. Yaa's mother and Brown Water came, moved the two children away from the dance circle and toward the comfort of Brown Water's lodge.

Aqamdax watched them until they disappeared into the darkness, then she squatted on her haunches, gathered the boy's blankets so she could return them when the dance was finished. For a time, the women around her whispered among themselves, but Aqamdax turned her thoughts back to Sok and Chakliux. Almost, she missed that one word, the name, spoken quietly, then hushed with a hiss of fear, covered with a charm of words and a flurry of hands to prevent a curse.

Suddenly many things became clear. Suddenly she did not feel like a daughter betrayed but like one who was loved. Then she watched her husband not in pride but in anger, saw his brother not with fondness but in loathing, and only because she did not want to disgrace Red Leaf did she stay until their dance was finished. Then she stood, and before the women could nod their heads in acknowledgment of her place as second wife, as sister-in-law, before Sok or Chakliux could look toward her expecting praise, she left, and carrying the bundle of Ghaden's blankets, she walked to Brown Water's lodge.

She heard Yaa's singing through the walls of the lodge and scratched against the caribou hide covering until Brown Water called for her to come in. She crawled through the entrance tunnel.

Yaa's eyes widened when she saw her, and she pulled her brother close, turning his head against her breast.

Choosing her words slowly, carefully, Aqamdax said to Brown Water, "I am not of your people. I do not know all taboos, but I must ask something."

"Come with me then," Brown Water said, and Aqamdax followed her from the lodge.

Aqamdax knew Brown Water must be a strong woman. She had kept her place of respect even after the death of her husband and now lived alone, as widow, she and her sister-wife and the two children. Strange, the ways of these River People. Among the First Men, once the mourning was complete, each woman would have gone to another hunter, at worst to a brother, to his ulax. How did they live, these women, without a hunter in their lodge?

Brown Water walked a short way from the lodge, then turned and said to Aqamdax, "What is it you want to know?"

"This sister-wife of yours, Ghaden's mother," Aqamdax said, "how did she die?"

Brown Water wrapped her arms around herself. "It is not a good thing to talk about," she said.

"It breaks taboos?"

The woman would not look at Aqamdax, and instead moved her eyes to the lodge, then to the ground and up to the sky. "No one knows," she finally said.

"She was of the First Men—the Sea Hunters," said Aqamdax.

"Yes. You knew her?"

Aqamdax sighed. "I knew her. Someone told me there was a knife."

Brown Water nodded. "There was a knife," she said. "But Wolf-and-Raven says a spirit killed her."

"With a knife?"

"Who knows what a spirit might do? Who knows what spirits she might have offended? She should not have been here." Brown Water fastened her eyes on Aqamdax, but Aqamdax did not look away. Brown Water raised one hand, rudely pointed with one thick finger at Aqamdax's chest. "You should not be here. It is one thing for your people to come to trade, but when hunters take wives, too many things can happen."

"This woman had enemies?"

"I did not like her," Brown Water said. "I did not want her in my lodge. If she had an enemy, I was that one, but I would not dishonor my husband. I did not kill her. She was killed by a spirit. It was what she deserved."

Aqamdax looked at the woman for a long time, clasped her amulet, then fingered the whorls of the whale tooth shell she wore at her waist. She believed Brown Water, but there was some evil here she did not understand.

"You think the boy, Ghaden, is safe?"

"As safe as Wolf-and-Raven can make him. As safe as I can make him. Why?"

"Tell him I am not the ghost of his mother," Aqamdax said softly. "Tell him I look like that dead one because she was also my mother."

Chapter
Thirty-two

Cen slipped the parka hood back from his face. The fur blended with the grays and yellows of the autumn grasses, but he was too hot. Tikaani had insisted they wear hare fur parkas, but except at night, when the warmth was welcome, they made Cen sweat. Better to have worn ground squirrel, he thought, warm but not hot, and lightweight. But perhaps Tikaani's suggestion was a good one, he told himself. Each morning small puddles of water had thin crusts of ice at the corners. There might be a day when he was glad for the warmth of hare fur.

They had come without dogs, and through some magic that still made Cen cringe when he saw his face reflected in calm water, K'os had made a salve to darken and wrinkle the men's faces. With her clever needle, she had sewn white tufts of caribou hair into their braids so they looked like old men, not hunters, not warriors. She had shown them how to wad grass in the bottoms of their boots, so they walked like old men, though they had not used the grass until they were within a half day of the Near River Village. She had also given them something to drink that scalded their throats and left them hoarse and soft-voiced.

She had turned them old and assured them she had the power to make them young again. Cen did not doubt that she had the power. Whether she would choose to make them young again, that was his concern. And what price would she ask in exchange?

Now they hid in the dark woods at the edge of the village under branches of black spruce. With leaves stuck into their clothing, they lay at the rim of the earthen bowl which cradled the Near River Village. They watched as women and children passed, and they counted warriors as K'os had told them to do. During the night they had scaled each food cache to see how much fish the people had for winter, but they took nothing, did nothing to let anyone know they watched.

During the next two days, Aqamdax did not speak to Sok, avoided Chakliux. In that time, she won Ghaden as brother, gave careful explanation to Brown Water, Happy Mouth and Yaa, and tried to keep from accusing her husband of deception. After all, perhaps she had not told him her mother's name, though she thought she had.

In the five years since Daes had left the First Men Village, Aqamdax had held much anger against her mother. The woman had left her, forced her to live with those who did not want her. Now, at least, Aqamdax understood what had happened.

The First Men mourned their dead four tens of days, and after that a widow was expected to stay away from other men, to show her respect to her husband, for four moons. The traders had come about two moons after Aqamdax's father's death, and her mother, like Aqamdax, had not been able to bear the emptiness of nights alone. She had given herself to a trader, become pregnant, then left with him to protect the village against the curse of broken taboos. To protect Aqamdax.

"She spoke of you often," Happy Mouth said. "She wanted to go back to you and her people."

Aqamdax glanced at Brown Water, saw the surprise in the woman's face, though she tried to cover it with narrowed eyes and nodding head. Yes, Aqamdax thought, she, too, would confide in Happy Mouth, but never in Brown Water. Who could trust the woman's thin, harsh mouth, her angry words?

The day that Aqamdax told Ghaden she was his sister, he only looked at her from the safety of Yaa's lap, but gradually he began to watch her without fear. This morning, three days later, when she came into the lodge, he ran to her, showed her a ball Yaa had made him of rawhide strips wound together to the size of his fist.

"Biter, get!" he cried, and threw the ball, sending the dog in a scramble to the pile of baskets where the ball landed.

"Better to play outside," Yaa warned, and flashed her eyes to where Brown Water usually sat.

Aqamdax praised both dog and ball, then took Ghaden and Biter to the edge of the village, where they played together until Yaa came and got Ghaden to help her carry wood. Then Aqamdax went to Red Leaf's lodge. She had practiced her words and built her courage to the point of speaking to Sok, and she planned to do so before another day passed. She found Sok still wrapped in his sleeping blankets, the lodge empty except for him.

"Red Leaf is at the cooking hearths," he told her, mumbling the words with closed eyes.

"I came to see you and your brother," she said.

"Three, four days we will leave for the caribou hunt. You cannot let me sleep knowing I will get little rest during this next moon?"

As though he had said nothing to her, Aqamdax asked, "Why did you let me think I would find my mother if I came with you?"

Slowly, Sok opened his eyes.

"You and Chakliux knew my mother was dead."

He sat up. "Who told you she was dead?" he asked.

"My brother, Ghaden."

He grunted, stood, kicked his sleeping furs over toward the neat rolls piled at the back of the lodge.

"I cannot talk to you now," he said.

"Where is Chakliux?"

"He did not know," Sok said. "At least I never spoke to him about your mother. Did you?"

"No."

"Then keep your anger for me, not him."

For some reason, his words calmed her. "Why didn't you tell me?"

"Would you have come with me if you knew your mother was dead?"

"Perhaps not. But if I knew I had a brother . . ."

Sok shrugged. "Sometimes brothers are good things; sometimes they are not. How could I know how you would feel about him? He is only a child."

"Surely you knew I would discover my mother was dead once I got here."

"I did not intend to bring you here. I brought you to the Walrus shaman."

"I did not kill him," Aqamdax said.

"Do you think I would take you as one of my wives if I believed you did?"

"So then, what did that shaman offer to make you travel to my village? Why did he want me?"

"Do not pretend you are ignorant of your powers. What better wife for a shaman than a storyteller?"

"Perhaps," she said softly.

Again Sok shrugged. "He wanted you, and he offered me something useful."

"What?"

"Many things. Many trade goods."

"And for that you would chance the seas, a man who had little experience in an iqyax?"

"I do well enough in an iqyax."

She snorted. "For one who hunts caribou."

"You do not want to be my wife?" he asked.

She took a long breath. "No."

"What if another man offered for you?"

"Who?"

"Someone honored in this village. Someone whose powers are as great, perhaps greater than yours."

She held her breath. Almost, she spoke his brother's name. Almost, she said her hope out loud, but too many times she had seen hopes vanish. It was always easier to lose a dream when no one else knew.

"Who?" she asked again.

"The shaman, Wolf-and-Raven."

Suddenly she understood. Snow-in-her-hair. Why else would Sok risk his life for trade goods? He needed a bride price.

"So now, with the Walrus shaman dead, I am to be bride price for Snow-in-her-hair."

"You do not want to be a shaman's wife?"

"I am not one to want power or to think power over spirits is a desirable thing. It is too often misused."

"Wolf-and-Raven is not like that. He is a respectable man."

"Strong? A good hunter?"

"Good enough."

"If he is a man of so much power, why would he be interested in my poor storytelling? I am not one of your people. Why would a shaman want a wife who is not quite human?"

Sok began to pace in quick hard steps from one side of the lodge to the other so that Aqamdax wondered whether he had yet spoken to Wolf-and-Raven, if he had made any offer to the man.

"Among my people," Aqamdax said, "a woman chooses the man she will have as husband. A father or uncle might promise her, but if she does not want to go, no one forces her. And a woman whose husband is not good to her or to her children, she can leave him and choose another."

"I would expect such a thing among people who are not quite human," Sok told her, and stopped pacing long enough to look into her face. "You are not among your people. You are here. You are my wife. You will do as I say."

"If you must give me to another, give me to your brother." She spoke the words quickly, before she lost the courage to say them.

"Chakliux?"

"Yes."

Sok threw back his head and laughed. "He does not want you. Besides, he has nothing to give as bride price."

"He has dogs and his iqyax."

"You are fool enough to think he will give those things for you!"

The words stung, and Aqamdax cursed herself for her foolishness. Once a person knows what you care about, he also knows how to hurt you.

"You are like your mother, without respect, without honor. She dishonored her husband and went to the trader Cen. What did he give in return? A knife, death. If you are not careful, you will earn the same."

"A trader killed her?" Aqamdax asked.

"Some say he did."

"Brown Water says spirits killed her."

"I do not know who killed her. Whoever it was also killed my grandfather. If I knew who it was, they would be dead by now." He pawed through a pile of clothing and pulled out a pair of caribou hide leggings. "What you must know," he said, glancing up at Aqamdax, "is that if you have no husband, there is no one in this village who will protect you. What if I throw you away? What will you do?"

Aqamdax realized he was right. She must make her own protection by finding a good husband, having sons, and strengthening the tie between herself and Ghaden, but all those things would take many years. Now she had no one, and nothing to barter except her willingness to help Sok get what he wanted.

"What do you want me to do?" she asked softly.

"I want the people to hear your stories, to see your powers."

"You will arrange a storytelling, then?"

"Chakliux and I will ask for such an evening, a way to show respect and gain honor before we leave to hunt caribou."

"And I will also tell stories?"

"Yes."

"Once Wolf-and-Raven hears my stories, you think he will want me?"

"He will see your powers, then I will speak to him of a bride price for Snow-in-her-hair."

"And if I do this?"

"You will have a new husband."

"I want more than a new husband."

"What else do you want?"

"I want to keep my lodge."

"No. I have promised it to Snow-in-her-hair."

"Let her build another."

"What choice do you have?"

"The choice of telling stories or saying nothing."

"The choice of dying or living."

"I want my lodge."

"Perhaps Wolf-and-Raven will want you to stay in Blue Flower's lodge."

"He has only one wife?"

"Yes."

"You think he will risk displeasing her?"

"I think she will understand the powers he might gain by taking you as second wife. I think she will be pleased to have another woman do some of the work."

"What if I tell Wolf-and-Raven that I will not be wife without my own lodge?"

Sok tilted his head and looked up at the smoke hole. "You have not been an easy woman to have as wife," he said.

Almost, Aqamdax smiled.

"If Snow-in-her-hair wants your lodge," he said, "you must leave it, but I will give you enough caribou hides to make another."

"And you and Chakliux will help cut the lodge poles?"

"We will help."

Aqamdax laughed. "You promise your brother's help without asking him?"

"I gave three, four moons of my life to see him safe among the Walrus Hunters until we knew the Cousin River People would not try to kill him. He can give me a few days."

"I will tell stories," Aqamdax said. "I will show these people the powers of a First Men woman. Let them think about that and be glad they do not call the First Men enemy."

The third day of watching, Cen saw him. Ghaden, taller and thinner than he remembered, but Ghaden. The sight of the boy was like a fist to Cen's belly, knocking away his breath so that at first he could say nothing to Tikaani, only watch, eyes caressing. He had never totally believed that the boy was alive, and now told himself that the knife might have left Ghaden with some deformity. But as Cen watched, he saw that the boy did not limp, and though it was difficult to tell from this distance, his face did not seem to be scarred. He had a dog and was throwing a ball in high arcing curves, laughing when the dog caught the ball, scolding if the animal did not drop it at his command.

Cen opened his mouth to tell Tikaani, but tears filled his throat. He had to swallow, and when he finally did speak it was with the quiver of an old man. K'os's throat-scalding tea, he told himself, and would not admit to the tears that burned his eyes.

"My son," he said, and extended one arm to point.

"You said he was injured," Tikaani said. He watched the boy for a while. "He seems strong."

"Watch. He throws the ball with his left hand," Cen said. "He carries his right shoulder higher, sometimes presses his right arm to his side."

"He did not always favor his left hand?"

Cen shook his head.

"A warrior should hunt with his right hand. It is the way things should be done."

Ghaden picked up the ball, threw it with his right hand. The throw was not as hard, and the ball did not curve as high, but it was a good throw. "He needs a man to teach him," Cen said. "That is all. Do you know the woman who is with him? It is not one of his mother's sister-wives."

Tikaani was still but finally said, "I was in the village with K'os at the end of last winter, but I do not recognize her."

"Perhaps one of the men brought her from another River Village."

"She wears a strange parka."

The words brought the truth in suddenness to Cen's mind, but he did not say anything to Tikaani until he watched her for a time, saw, with heart beating hard in sorrow, how much she looked like Daes, even in the way she walked, the way she pushed her hair from her eyes. Then he whispered, "It is a First Men sax, made of bird skins. I know her, though she has changed in four years. She is Aqamdax, Ghaden's sister."

"A First Men woman? Your . . . the dead one's . . ."

"Daughter."

"Not your daughter?"

"No."

"How did she get here?"

"I do not know. Perhaps looking for her mother. I was told she took a River trader as husband."

"At least she is someone to take care of your son."

"How can I let him grow up with the people who killed his mother?"

Tikaani looked at him, smiled slowly. "We must leave soon, tomorrow, the next day. You want to take him back with us?"

Cen pulled the knife from his arm sheath, thrust it into the soft sod where they lay. "Yes," he said. "I want him. I would kill every man in this village to get him."

Chapter Thirty-three

"He wants a storytelling tonight?"

Aqamdax nodded. "Should I provide food? I do not have much in my cache. Do the people eat seal oil?"

"No food," Red Leaf said. "Let them eat at the cooking hearths. It is not a recognized celebration, only a time for people to gather before the families leave to hunt caribou. Besides, on a caribou hunt usually the women go, too. How can we get ready to go if we have to give a feast? We will have the feast later—when we bring back the meat."

Aqamdax carefully watched Red Leaf as she spoke. She wished she knew the woman better. It was difficult coming to a new village. She had not realized how much knowledge a person gathered during childhood years. In her own village, she had been able to tell by the tone of a voice or the expression on a face each woman's true thoughts. Here among the River People, it was difficult to know. Only a few days before, she had realized that they expressed agreement not with words but with raised eyebrows.

Now, as she listened to Red Leaf, Aqamdax reminded herself that the woman did not like her, would probably dislike any sister-wife.

So then, did she speak the truth about the food, or did she hope to shame Aqamdax by telling her to do something that was not according to village traditions?

To be safe, when Red Leaf left Aqamdax would find Chakliux and ask him.

Since she had discovered that her mother was dead, it seemed as though her mind was not clear. She had made her own mourning, singing the First Men death songs alone in her lodge, and Happy Mouth told her that she and Brown Water had made chants and songs during the four days after Daes's death. Still, it seemed as though Aqamdax's thoughts were as frayed as old sinew threads.

Even if she had known Red Leaf better, it was not a good time for Aqamdax to trust her own insight. Yes, she should ask Chakliux.

"I do not want to embarrass our husband," Aqamdax said, knowing that Red Leaf did all she could to honor Sok. "I still stumble in my words. I have much to learn."

"I will try to help you," Red Leaf said, and again, though the woman looked into Aqamdax's eyes as she spoke, Aqamdax was not sure she could trust her. "If you do not know a word, I will try to say it for you."

"Thank you," Aqamdax answered, but wondered if Red Leaf would risk making a fool of Sok in order to humiliate Aqamdax. Probably not. She seemed to value order and did not often laugh or pull jokes. Her eyes always followed Sok when he was near, and she mentioned him often in her conversations with other women.

Red Leaf's hands were always busy, and now, even though she had come to Aqamdax's lodge only to bring a few hare furs for Aqamdax to scrape, she had also brought her sewing. She was making a pair of dance boots for Sok, though the ones he had were new and beautiful. She rolled the caribouskin uppers and slipped her needle into a bit of hide and tucked it into her needle case. She held the walrus hide case so Aqamdax could see it, and Aqamdax, knowing the woman's pride in it, commented, admiring the sewn pattern of lines and circles.

"I go now," she told Aqamdax. "I will see you tonight. I will help if I can." She stopped at the entrance tunnel. "You should have water. How many bladders do you own?"

"Four."

Red Leaf cocked her head to one side, pursed her lips. "I will bring three. That should be enough."

She left and Aqamdax sat considering their conversation. It did not seem that Red Leaf wanted Aqamdax to fail in the storytelling. Perhaps she had grown accustomed to the idea that she would have to share Sok, if not with Aqamdax, then with some other woman. Better he have me, Aqamdax thought. As a First Men woman, I will never have the status that one who was born here would have.

She lifted two bladders from the lodge poles. She would take them to the river, fill them with fresh water. She should also gather firewood, have a good heap of it near the door, ready to bring inside if rain threatened, ready to light if insects or cold disturbed their storytelling.

She walked through the village, wondered if Ghaden and his sister Yaa were near. If so, they would see her and come. Yesterday Ghaden had sat on her lap when she told him stories. She loved the weight of him against her chest, the smell of his soft hair, the sound of his laughter when she told a joke. She was also beginning to see Yaa as sister. The girl was an unusual child—an adult in a child's body—always busy, always serious. If Aqamdax could choose a younger sister, Yaa would be the one.

There were others at the river, some fishing with thin handlines of twisted sinew. Aqamdax still used her kelp line, though some of the women laughed at her. Let them laugh; kelp was strong. She would not have to worry about a broken line if she caught a large fish.

Aqamdax walked to the place where the women filled their water bladders. The bank sloped gently to the river and a curve of sand made a beach large enough to launch boats, a good place to sit and repair nets or wade out in shallow water.

When she heard Chakliux's voice, she turned and smiled at him. He squatted on his haunches as though he were First Men and offered her a strip of dried fish. She finished filling her bladders, then came to him, took the fish and offered him a bladder of water. He drank, squeezing a bit of water out onto the fish to soften the meat.

She squatted beside him and ate without speaking. When he had finished his meat, he took another drink, then handed her the bladder. She drank, replaced the ivory stopper and set the bladder at her feet.

"You are telling stories tonight," Chakliux said.

"Yes, but it is too soon," she replied.

"You tell stories each day to the children."

Aqamdax laughed. "They tell me as many stories as I tell them. They teach me."

"They have taught you well."

"There is much I do not know," she said. Often she chose the wrong word. Often she had to repeat herself.

"You will have to speak slowly. Some of the old ones who do not hear well, they will get caught by the sound of your First Men voice and in that way lose the River words."

"I will speak slowly," Aqamdax said. She was disappointed. She had hoped he would take her side and try to convince Sok to wait. "You are storyteller, as I am. I do not have to explain the magic of words to you," she said. "But how can I be sure my First Men stories will come out strong and whole when I must use River words to tell them?"

For a long time, Chakliux watched the river. Finally he drew a long string of sinew from a pouch at his waist. He twisted it in his fingers until Aqamdax could see the form of an otter outlined in knots and turns.

"Walrus Hunters use strings to help them tell their stories," Chakliux told her. "I have heard that Tundra women draw their stories in the snow using knives of wood and ivory." He reached over and took her left hand in his, looped the sinew string around her wrist and tied it.

Aqamdax's breath caught in her throat, and for a moment she forgot everything but the warmth of his touch.

"When your words seem thin, remember this sinew bracelet." He circled her wrist with his fingers. "Remember that it is stronger than it looks. Remember that I am here with you."

He dropped her hand and stood.

"I still have many questions," Aqamdax told him. "Do you have time to help me?" She knew she sounded like a child, pestering, but she wanted to keep him beside her, if only for a moment longer.

He looked up at the sun. "Yes. I have weapons to prepare, but I have time."

"Bring your weapons to my lodge," Aqamdax told him. "You can work there."

Aqamdax knew he would tell her of some taboo. He seldom entered her lodge. When he did, he usually brought one of his nephews with him.

"Bring Carries Much or Cries-loud if you want," she told him, hurrying to get her words in before he could speak.

"I will come," he said, and then he was gone, striding away toward the village.

"A man like you should have more than one wife," Sok said, gesturing with the half-empty bowl he held in his right hand. "The old shaman at the Walrus village had three wives."

"My woman would not be happy," Wolf-and-Raven said.

Sok lifted the bowl to his mouth, sucked in some broth. Wolf-and-Raven was not a man who easily made up his mind. Even in repeating chants and prayers, it was better if someone told him what was needed.

Sok, like most hunters in the village, often tired of old Ligige"'s loud voice—the woman should have been a man, she was so fond of making decisions—but now he wished his aunt were here. If he had thought she might agree with him, he would have brought her, but who could say what she might decide? He had avoided her since his grandfather's death. She could talk about little else. She seemed to live that day over and over, as though by her thoughts alone she could change what had happened. If thoughts could change what had happened in the past, there would be much in Sok's life that would be different. Yes, many, many things.

"Your daughter needs a good husband, someone who might someday be chief hunter of this village," said Sok.

Wolf-and-Raven slurped noisily from his bowl, then looked at Sok over the rim. "My wife also tells me that."

"I will be a good husband to her."

"She would be second wife."

"I would honor her as though she were first wife."

"We had this same conversation before your grandfather's death. I told you then I would give Snow-in-her-hair only as first wife."

"You know that since she would not take Chakliux, the hunters fear her. They think she might bring them bad luck."

Wolf-and-Raven raised his eyebrows. "And you are not afraid of her, even though she refused your brother?"

"Why should I fear someone who refused my brother? You think he would curse me? We are hunting partners. He lives in my wife's lodge."

"That is true," Wolf-and-Raven said. "That is true."

"You know I have much I will give for her, more than just the First Men woman, as much as any daughter could bring."

"Why do you think I would want the Sea Hunter woman?"

"You must hear her as she tells stories. She has powers you cannot believe. When words come from her mouth, they carry you to other places, other times. She is gifted, that one."

For a long time Wolf-and-Raven sat without speaking. For a long time Sok waited. He had nearly decided to stand, to leave and tell Aqamdax they would not have the storytelling, but then Wolf-and-Raven spoke, slowly, quietly.

"Say nothing to your wife Red Leaf. I do not want my wife to know yet."

The words put hope in Sok's heart, and he leaned forward, gripping the food bowl so tightly the wood groaned within his hands.

"You say this Sea Hunter woman will tell stories tonight?" Wolf-and-Raven asked.

"Yes."

"I will be there. I will listen. If she pleases me, we will make a trade. Tomorrow, you will give her to me as second wife, but my daughter stays with me during the caribou hunt. You can claim her when the hunt is over."

No fool, this one, Sok thought. He would have two wives and a daughter to help him butcher his meat and prepare his hides. He would get little help from the First Men woman, but at least she would learn and be ready for the next year. Perhaps Blue Flower would be more willing to teach her than Red Leaf was.

"It is good," Sok replied. He left the lodge quickly, before Wolf-and-Raven could change his mind.

Aqamdax scattered fresh grass and dried fireweed flowers over the floor. The River People covered their floors with caribou hides, but she used grass as she had been taught. What smelled better than grass and dried flowers? She had brought woven mats with her and hung them against the walls. The pattern of the weaving drew the eye away from the ashes of the hearth fire to the beauty of the lodge walls. The first time Red Leaf had seen Aqamdax's lodge, she had covered her mouth with one hand, hiding surprise or laughter, Aqamdax did not know, but who could expect these River women to understand something that was beautiful when they made their baskets from fish skin?

There was a scratching at her door, and she bent to call through the entrance tunnel, welcoming the one outside, hoping it was Chakliux.

When she lived with the First Men in the chief hunter's ulax, she had always been glad when men came to see her, glad to know she would not face the darkness of the night alone. With Chakliux, she felt a different kind of gladness. She wanted to look into his eyes when she told him a riddle. She wanted to hear his voice, deep and full from his chest, when he spoke to her. Even with Day Breaker, she had never felt that way.

She was not sure why Chakliux pleased her. He was not a large man, though his arms were strong. Perhaps it was the power of his otter foot. Perhaps it was the quickness of his mind. Often before she slept her thoughts turned to him, and just as often she told herself she should not think so much about her husband's brother. But even in her dreams he came to her, and who could control dreams?

She smiled, but her smile changed to a mouth open in surprise when the one who entered her lodge was not Chakliux but one of the old women of the village, one of Chakliux's aunts, though Aqamdax could not remember her name.

"W-welcome, Aunt," she stammered.

The woman cocked her head at her as though considering the relationship Aqamdax so easily claimed. "Aunt to your husband, that is true," she finally said.

There was a sharpness in her voice that drew Aqamdax's anger, and the words came too quickly to Aqamdax's tongue. "You are not sure you want to be aunt to someone who is not quite human. According to my people's stories, we are brothers to the sea otter. Considering your nephew Chakliux, perhaps we are more closely related than you think."

The old woman narrowed her eyes and opened her mouth, and at that moment Chakliux came into the lodge. Hii! Aqamdax thought, a good way to begin my first storytelling, insulting one of the elders, aunt to my husband. Why do I always speak before I think?

Then, to Aqamdax's surprise, the old woman began to laugh. It was a deep, rolling laugh, something that might come from a young woman's mouth, and Chakliux, watching, also began to laugh, until even Aqamdax found her lips curling into a smile.

The old woman sat down near the center of the lodge, near the fire, and Chakliux sat down beside her, his legs crossed. Aqamdax brought them bowls of fish soup and a bladder of water.

The aunt wiped her eyes on her sleeve and accepted the soup from Aqamdax's hands.

"Red Leaf told you that you need not prepare food for the listeners?" Chakliux asked.

"Yes," Aqamdax answered, grateful to find out that the woman had told her the truth. "But it is not yet time for stories, and you are family." She looked into the old woman's eyes, saw the slight raising of her eyebrows. A good sign.

"This wife of Sok's," the old woman said, turning to speak to Chakliux as if Aqamdax had left the lodge, "she has the wrong husband."

Aqamdax's hands were suddenly still. Did she know about Sok's plans to trade her to Wolf-and-Raven?

Chakliux opened his mouth, then closed it again as though he could not decide what to say. Finally he looked at Aqamdax, holding her eyes as he spoke. "My brother has told me of his plans to trade her. Perhaps to Wolf-and-Raven."

"Wolf-and-Raven could do worse," the old woman said, "but you are the one who should have her."

"Yes, I am," Chakliux said, and did not move his eyes from Aqamdax's face.

Sok wore his finest parka. Red Leaf had made it of wolf and marten, the lighter, longer-furred wolf skins worked diagonally and alternating with the smooth, dark brown marten pelts. At the center of the back, she had made the sun pattern from pieces of a yellow-white hide Sok had bought in trade. It was so thick and stiff, Red Leaf's hands had cracked and bled in the sewing. She had decorated the parka sleeves with scraped caribou intestine, some frozen and dried into a pure whiteness, alternating with strips she had dyed red, and others dyed black. The front of the parka was hung with fish teeth, drilled and sewn to dangle in two long rows from his shoulders to his waist, and behind each fish tooth she had hung a dark, iridescent cormorant throat feather.

It was a parka that pulled the eyes, so when Sok entered the lodge everyone looked at him, watched him. He took the honored place at the back of the lodge, his words loud and joking. Aqamdax stood near the entrance, two bladders of water hanging from each of her wrists. She had decided to dress as she did when telling stories among her own people, her woven aprons tied at her waist, and, because the lodge was not warm—at least not as warm as Aqamdax was used to— she also wore her black cormorant feather sax. She had worn it with the feathers turned in toward her body during the long journey over the North Sea, so some of the feathers were broken, and she had had to resew several seams, but it still looked beautiful, as fine as anything she had seen a River woman wear. Sok lifted his chin toward her, then gestured that she should take her place as storyteller. She had arranged a pad of sea otter skins at one side of the fire, so now she sat there, hardly aware that Red Leaf came to her, took the water bladders and hung them from her own wrists.

Suddenly Aqamdax could not remember any River words, could only recall the language of her own people. Her eyes widened in fear, and she glanced at Chakliux, who smiled at her. Yes, she should be his wife, Aqamdax thought. Then she would not be trying to tell stories before she was ready, trying to earn her way into the lodge of a man she did not want.

They were waiting, the men and women and children who had crowded into her small lodge; others peered in from the entrance tunnel. Perhaps if she began in the First Men tongue, she could more easily change to River words, but who could say? The River People might be insulted.

Finally Chakliux stood, his eyes firmly on Sok, as though telling him to be still, to wait. "I begin the stories in the tradition I learned as a child," he said, and with his words, spoken so clearly in the River tongue, the language again came into Aqamdax's mind. "First a riddle."

There was a murmur from the people, of anticipation or of discontent, Aqamdax was not quite sure, but she could only feel gratitude.

"Look, I see something," Chakliux said.

"What?" asked one of the children, a small boy of about three summers.

His question brought a rill of laughter from the people, and Chakliux laughed, too.

"They grow together in sacredness to help the people," he said.

There were many guesses: trees and animals, fish and birds, until finally the old woman, the aunt, lifted her head and said, "What is more sacred to our people among growing things than the plants that give us berries? They live close to the earth, pull strength from the soil and give it to us through their fruit."

"Ligige', you are wise," Wolf-and-Raven said, then asked, "Who can tell Chakliux the answer to his riddle?"

Ligige', Aqamdax thought. She had to remember the woman's name. Aqamdax could go to her with questions, and perhaps someday . . . but no. She could not let herself wish to become Chakliux's wife. Not when she was promised to Wolf-and-Raven. Not when she still belonged to Sok.

"Crowberries and cloudberries grow together," said Carries Much, one of Sok's sons.

Aqamdax saw Sok lift his eyebrows and glance at Chakliux. Chakliux nodded his head at his nephew, and Sok crowed out his pleasure at his son's answer.

"You are wise," Chakliux said.

The people murmured their agreement, and Aqamdax realized her fear was gone. The storytelling would still be difficult, and she would make no claim to the place of storyteller. In this village, that place belonged to Chakliux. She was content to tell stories to the children, but tonight she would help Sok catch the wife he wanted. Perhaps in return, someday, he would help her find a way to become Chakliux's wife.

Aqamdax settled herself on the otter fur pads, crouching on her haunches as her people did. "Among my people, I am a storyteller, trained by a storyteller," she began, and she did not stumble over her words.

"Each of you knows the River stories better than I do, so I will not try to tell them to you. It is better that you tell them to me." They nodded their heads, eyebrows raised. A good beginning. "So tonight my husband offers his hospitality in hopes that you might like to hear new stories from the people you call Sea Hunters. They have long been your trading partners, and sometimes we trade wives as well."

She smiled and there was a wave of laughter.

"So first I tell you of the sea otters, our brothers, and how they came to be." She spoke of that brother and sister, found to be lovers, and so dishonored among their people; how, still needing to belong to one another, they had jumped into the sea and were made the first otters. When she finished that story, she told another, of the great carver Shuganan, then she began the story of Chagak. Although the River words did not flow as easily from her mouth as her own language, she knew the people had begun to live her stories, to become the ones she spoke about. Sometimes she had to pause and search for a word, but if she could not remember what she needed to know, she would look at Chakliux. Each time, he formed his lips so she could see the word before he spoke, and it seemed as though she used her breath to give life to what he said.

When she came to the otter part of the story, she changed her voice as she had done among her own people, so that it seemed as though the otter rather than Aqamdax spoke.

She tightened her throat, brought the voice from the darkness that was now closing around the smoke hole. The first sound after the otter voice was the delighted crowing of the children. She had used her voices with them before, and they had learned to expect them. But with a rumbling like the grinding of the earth when it moves beneath a village, the hunters began to murmur, and she heard the women's higher voices, calling out in small whimpers as if they, themselves, were suddenly children.

Then Wolf-and-Raven was on his feet, screaming at her, pointing with his walking stick, singing out words that seemed to be curses. She looked at Chakliux, but he had his back to her, his hands already clamped on Wolf-and-Raven's arms. Then Sok was beside her, shouting to the people as they shoved their way from the lodge.

"There is nothing to fear here. She does not call spirits. It is her own voice. She makes these voices herself. She is a storyteller, that is all. Why are you afraid?"

But they did not stop, and finally only Sok and Chakliux, Ligige' and Wolf-and-Raven were left with Aqamdax in the lodge.

"You expect to trade someone who has no respect for a shaman's powers? You think I will take her in exchange for my daughter?" Wolf-and-Raven shouted at Sok. "The spirit voices are something only a shaman has the right to use."

Sok stood with his mouth open. Aqamdax waited for him to speak, to explain to Wolf-and-Raven, and when he did not Aqamdax said, "I hold no disrespect. I am a storyteller. I made the voices myself. I can do it now if you want. Many voices. That is how the First Men tell stories."

"I will hear no more of your stories," he said, and left the lodge. Sok followed him.

Chapter
Thirty-four

"Blue Necklace thinks she is a witch," Yaa said, "but I don't. She doesn't call spirits. She just tells stories."

Yaa brushed her hair from her eyes. She had snagged it in a root at the top of the den and pulled a hank loose from her braids. In the dim light, she could not see Ghaden's face clearly, but she could hear him as he ate.

"She's my sister," he said, his words slurring over the fish in his mouth.

"Yes, and she's a storyteller."

"You're my sister."

"We're both your sisters," Yaa told him patiently. It was a litany they seemed to have to go through each day, the assurance that Aqamdax was his sister.

"You're her sister, too?" he asked.

Yaa frowned. He'd never asked that question before. "No, well, maybe, since her mother and my mother were sister-wives." Relationships between people were complicated. Sometimes cousins were also husband and wife. Then were their children sisters and brothers to each other or were they cousins? Best Fist said both, but sometimes Best Fist had strange ideas. There were many rules about the ones you could marry and those you were related to. Yaa was just learning them herself. They were too complicated for Ghaden to understand.

Since Yaa had been bringing Ghaden to the den, she had swept the floor and removed all the debris. She had even thought about leaving a blanket, but knew some animal would smell it and either take it or rip it up, maybe even decide to move in, although she had been urinating in the far corner to leave her scent, marking the place as her own.

"Wolf-and-Raven was mad at her, right, Yaa?"

"He was just cross. You know sometimes he gets cross. Like Brown Water."

"Umph," Ghaden said, and Yaa was not sure if it was a sound of agreement or disagreement.

She took a bite of her fish and chewed it slowly, trying to make it last a long time. It was a trick she had learned one spring when she was Ghaden's age. If she ate slowly, her mouth remembered the taste, then when food was scarce, she could close her eyes and pretend she was eating.

Now even Brown Water's caches were full, packed with dried fish and fish roe, with small birds left whole and dried berries stored in oil. They had layered fish heads in pits and left them to ferment, and soon, if the hunters had good fortune, there would be caribou meat, smoked and dried.

"He's mad at big man," Ghaden said, interrupting Yaa's thoughts.

"Who's mad?"

"Wolf-and-Raven."

"Oh." She wished she had had the sense to take Ghaden home after the first few stories. Before Aqamdax had done the voices. It seemed as if he could not think about anything but what had happened. "I told you he was just cross," she said.

"At big man, too?"

"Who's big . . . oh, Sok."

"Umph," Ghaden said again. "Wolf-and-Raven was cross with Sok."

"Sometimes that happens, but usually they're friends."

"Will my sister have to go back to her other village?"

Yaa tipped her head and looked up toward the darkest part of the den. She hadn't thought of that before, that perhaps someone would make Aqamdax return to the Sea Hunters. She hoped not. It was good to have a grown-up person who was like a sister, not a mother. It was good to have another lodge to go to when Brown Water was angry.

"She has a husband, so she can stay here," Yaa told Ghaden, but she wondered what Aqamdax would do if Sok threw her away. She hoped when she was old enough to be a wife that she found a husband from her own village. It was easier that way. One thing was sure. She would never agree to go as far away as the Sea Hunter Village.

"What about the girl?" Tikaani asked.

"Leave her."

"She'll go back and tell her mother, then they'll have hunters follow us."

Cen snorted, but he knew Tikaani was right. They needed to get the boy alone, but his sister seldom left him.

"We could kill her," Tikaani suggested.

It was not a wise thing to kill a child. What parent would not want revenge?

"We'll take her, too," Cen finally said. "Someone will buy her, if not in your village then in another. She is not old enough to be a wife, but she looks strong. Someone will want her for a slave, a girl they will be able to trade for a bride price in a few summers."

"Do you think the boy will remember you?"

"I think so, but not like this." He gestured toward his face, lined and dirty, the tufts of white caribou hair in his braids. "But I have things a boy would like. A small spear, fishhooks and a handline."

"If we do not take him soon, we must leave. I thought we would have him three, four days ago."

"Sometimes he is alone when the girl is at the hearths."

"The dog."

Cen pulled a haunch of a fresh-killed hare from a pouch he wore slung at his waist.

"So then, we wait," Tikaani said. "K'os can wait as well. We will have a good report for her when we return."

Cen thought about K'os. She was not one who appreciated waiting, but he didn't care what she thought. He wanted Ghaden.

Chakliux sat on a rock at the edge of the forest. He had found this place when he first came to the Near River Village, when Sok had been more like enemy than brother and Red Leaf had complained loudly of the extra work he caused her. It had been a long time since he had come to the rock. He was welcome now with Sok and Red Leaf, true uncle to Carries Much and Cries-loud. Red Leaf had no brothers to help her sons with weapons and hunting, to teach them the ways a man must know, so he tried to teach them, both the ways of the Near River and the Cousin River hunters.

When Sok gave Aqamdax her own lodge, she began to sew for Chakliux, all her clothing sewn with fine stitches in double seams according to the tradition of the First Men. She had already made him a new chigdax and was working on a birdskin parka, not as warm as parkas made of caribou or wolf, but good in summer, and good to shed the rain.

Sometimes, it almost seemed that they were married, and once when Sok suggested that he share Aqamdax's bed—something allowed a brother who had no wife—Chakliux almost agreed. But he was not sure what Aqamdax might want, so he did not go to her.

Now he still did not know what was best. Perhaps before asking her to be his wife, he should offer to take her back to her own village. A journey to the First Men Village would be dangerous at this time of year, but he could tell her that he would take her back next summer. Perhaps she would be willing to be wife for the winter—but then how could he bear to let her go?

He was working on soapstone bola weights, carving each one into the beaked head of a raven. The bola would be a gift to place with his father's bones, a sign of the mourning Chakliux made for him in his heart. Chakliux was not a good carver, but the work relaxed him, the soapstone soft under the chert blade of his sleeve knife. In spite of the frost that hardened the ground each night, the morning sun was warm, and the trees that circled three sides of the rock shielded him from the wind.

Chakliux heard a noise and looked up, saw Sleeps Long, hunting partner to his mother's husband, Fox Barking. The man had wrinkled his face with a frown, though usually his lips were slack, as though it was too much effort to close his mouth.

Chakliux nodded at the man, and Sleeps Long said, "Your father has asked that I speak to you."

"What does Fox Barking want?" Chakliux asked, trying to keep his voice from showing that he would never consider Fox Barking father, never be able to give the man that honor.

"Two more dogs have died."

"His dogs?"

"No, they belong to Blue-head Duck. One was a bitch with a belly full of pups."

Chakliux shook his head. With the golden-eyed dogs now in the village, he had hoped all talk of dogs being cursed was past.

"How did they die?"

"No one knows."

"They were not sick?"

"No."

"What does Fox Barking expect me to do? I have no more golden-eyed dogs to give."

"He wants you to know that some of the hunters think the curse has returned. He wants you to know they think you have brought bad luck again to our village."

"Tell him that dogs die. Remind him that they died before I came here and will die after I leave. I brought strong dogs from the Cousin River Village, and strong dogs from the Walrus Hunters. That is all I can do. Except for my grandfather's dogs, I have not even kept a dog for myself. Until Black Nose has another litter, I cannot offer Blue-head Duck a dog to replace the ones he lost. Tell Fox Barking that if he wants something done now, he should give Blue-head Duck one of his own dogs."

Sleeps Long muttered under his breath, but Chakliux did not want to know what the man said, so did not ask him to repeat it. Chakliux returned to his carving, and finally Sleeps Long walked away.

No, he could do nothing about the dogs, but there was something he could do. He would go to Sok now, tell him he wanted Aqamdax. Perhaps Sok would be angry, but why should he care? He had said last night that he did not want Aqamdax as wife. Would he expect the woman to spend the winter in the Near River Village without a husband?

Aqamdax had stayed inside her lodge all morning. She was sure Sok would come to her and throw her away. She had hoped he would come early, before most of the women were awake. She did not know the customs among the River People. If he threw her away, did that mean she had to leave the lodge? Or even the village? Would there be some family willing to take her in until she found a way back to the First Men?

She wished Chakliux would come to her. His advice was always good, always wise, and her best chance was if he would take her as wife. But if he wanted her, wouldn't he have come before now? Perhaps he had changed his mind. Perhaps he, too, wanted her to leave the village.

She picked up a basket she had begun weaving several days before. She had tried to weave it as Qung did, twining split strands of grass into delicate stitches. She had nearly completed the circle of the bottom, but today her fingers shook, and she could do nothing. She set down the work and paced the lodge, side to side. She heard a sound in the entrance tunnel and waited, her heart squeezing out tight, hard beats under her ribs. She recognized the top of Sok's head and moved away from him as he stood.

He looked long at her. His eyes were cold.

"I am sorry . . ." she began, but he interrupted.

"Be quiet," he said. "I do not want to hear your voice again."

She closed her mouth, clasped her hands together, forced herself to keep her fingers still.

Sok was wearing the same ceremonial parka he had worn the night before, but his boots and leggings were the ones he wore each day, without caribou hoof danglers or dyed hair embroidery.

"You are no longer my wife," he said, and the words were like a slap against Aqamdax's face. "I throw you away. You have not been my wife long enough to keep this lodge. Unless you find a husband who can pay me for the caribou hides, you must leave it as well."

Again, she opened her mouth to speak, but he pointed at her, thrusting one finger close to her face. "Do not speak to me," he said, then ducked back out through the entrance tunnel.

She stood still for a long time, his words pressing against her until she felt she could not breathe. Then she slipped on her leggings and boots, the parka she had made in the manner of the River People.

A dog, she thought. I must have a dog. She might be able to walk to her people's village if she could find a dog for protection and to help carry supplies. She had things to trade, a chigdax—but no, what if she found a trader willing to take her by boat? She would need a chigdax.

She had baskets. They would bring something. She had little food to spare. Perhaps some of her seal oil.

She would go to the old woman Ligige' first. Perhaps she knew someone willing to trade a dog. Perhaps she would know if Chakliux was also angry with her.

No, first she should go to Ghaden and Yaa, tell them good-bye. Perhaps when he was grown Ghaden would choose to be a trader like his father. Someday he would come to Aqamdax's village, and she would get to see him again. But the knowledge that that would probably never happen was a hard lump in her throat, and she felt tears prick at the backs of her eyelids.

She reminded herself that she might have never come here, might never have known she had a brother. Just knowing, having met him, was worth much, even if she had to leave.

She packed what was hers, rolled mats and sleeping robes, then paused and looked around her lodge. She smiled, one quick smile, remembering that she had wanted her own lodge when she had lived with the First Men. Now that she had one, she was leaving it. She reached up, took a half-filled water bladder from the lodge poles and slung it over one shoulder, picked up a pack she had prepared as trade goods and left the lodge.

Sok came into Red Leaf's lodge bringing a rush of chilled air, pungent with the smell of smoke and old leaves. He looked at Chakliux. "She is yours," he said, "but she is not welcome in this lodge." He lifted his chin toward Chakliux. "You are welcome," he said.

"I will give Red Leaf caribou hides, half my share from our hunt for the hides in Aqamdax's lodge."

Sok shrugged, looked away. Chakliux reached for his parka, but Red Leaf stopped him. "Wait," she said. "You cannot go yet."

Sok narrowed his eyes at his wife, spat out a few words in anger, then left the lodge.

Red Leaf smiled. "You cannot go to a bride without preparing yourself. I have oil. I have dried fireweed to sweeten your hair. Do you have a gift you can take her?"

Chakliux felt his face grow hot. He had spent the night thinking of a gift, but that was not something he wanted to tell Red Leaf. He had finally decided on the shell-and-jasper necklace he wore for ceremonies.

"I have a necklace," he said.

"Good. Here." She handed him a sael of goose grease, rendered to a light yellow. He took a small amount, smoothed it carefully into his hair, then relaxed as Red Leaf combed it in with her fingers.

Wife. The last time he had prepared himself to take a wife, the woman was Blueberry and he had felt only sorrow. Now he thought of Aqamdax and knew joy, as bubbling and full as the day he had taken Gguzaakk.

Ah, my Gguzaakk, be glad for me, he thought. Find a good hunter for yourself in that spirit world and someday we will all be together, you and I and our little son, your spirit hunter and my Aqamdax, and perhaps other sons and daughters.

"I do not want people to see you here," Brown Water told her. "You are not welcome in my lodge. Do not come in. Leave us."

The woman's eyes were hard and dark as stone, but Aqamdax did not turn away. "I need to see my brother," she said.

"He is not your brother."

"Daes is my mother. Ghaden is my brother."

Brown Water gasped as Aqamdax spoke Daes's name aloud, and Aqamdax saw the fear in her eyes.

"You think I am not human to speak a dead one's name? You are wrong. But I do not fear my own mother, and what more can I lose, now that I have lost everything? I want to see my brother."

"He is gone. I do not know where. He is with Yaa."

Aqamdax did not know if Brown Water was telling her the truth. Perhaps it would be best to pretend to believe her. She would find Ligige', then return and ask again if she could speak to Ghaden.

"I will be back," Aqamdax told Brown Water, and smiled at the woman as though they were friends exchanging greetings. She walked to Ligige''s lodge with her head high. Surely by now some of the women knew Sok had thrown her away, but was that worse than the ridicule she had known in her own village?

Ligige' had left a stick propped against the lodge entrance. Aqamdax picked it up and scratched at the worn caribou hides.

"I am here!" Ligige' called, the raspy voice of an old woman, but louder than Aqamdax had expected.

She ducked through the entrance. Rich smells of meat cooking filled the air. Ligige' was stirring something in a cooking skin hung on a tripod. "I am too old to always go to the village hearths," she said to Aqamdax. "Are you hungry?"

Aqamdax almost refused the food, her stomach too small and twisted with worry, but she was not sure of the politeness of refusing here among the River People.

"Yes," she said. "It smells good."

Ligige' pointed with an out-thrust chin toward a clutter of wooden bowls hanging in a net on the other side of the lodge. Aqamdax reached in and took one for herself. "For you also?" she asked.

"Yes," Ligige' said, then filled both bowls and handed one to Aqamdax.

She sat down on a mat not far from the hearth and began to eat. Aqamdax squatted on her haunches beside her. Ligige' stopped eating long enough to lift the bowl toward Aqamdax's legs and ask, "You do not get tired sitting like that?"

"It is the way I always sit," she said. "Why get a feather sax wet by sitting on it?"

"Sometimes I think the Sea Hunters are more human than we are," Ligige' said.

Aqamdax raised her eyebrows in surprise at the remark, then remembered that, to the River People, raised eyebrows meant agreement, so she ducked her head quickly, hoping Ligige' had not seen.

"I think we are all human," Aqamdax said softly. "Just different, that is all."

"Perhaps," said Ligige' through a mouthful of meat.

When Aqamdax emptied her bowl, Ligige' offered more, but Aqamdax told her she was full. The old woman looked wistfully at the cooking bag, then took a little more.

"Eating seems to be the only pleasure left me," she said.

Aqamdax smiled. "Chakliux tells me you enjoy a good riddle."

"Ah, that, too," said Ligige', and slapped a hand against her knee. "That, too. It has been a fine thing to have Chakliux in our village. He and his riddles are good company."

"I have found that also," Aqamdax told her.

"Some of the women have been talking," Ligige' said. "I see you have a pack. Are you leaving us?"

"I have no choice. My husband has thrown me away."

"And there are no other men for you in this village?" Ligige' asked.

"None that will take me."

"I think you are wrong."

"Who wants me after seeing Wolf-and-Raven's anger?"

"Do not be afraid that Wolf-and-Raven will curse you. He is not one to do such a thing."

"He thinks I do not respect his shaman powers."

"In his heart he knows you did not mean to show disrespect, but sometimes it takes Wolf-and-Raven a little while to be honest with himself. He is my cousin, and I have known him since the day he was born. I had thirteen summers then, and spent much time the next few years carrying him around, cleaning him, changing the moss that padded his carrying board. It is difficult to take a man too seriously if you remember wiping his bottom when he was a child." She tipped her chin at Aqamdax. "You have known him only as shaman. I see him also as crying baby and little boy. I understand him better, and of course he remembers me as a girl and so understands me better, too."

Ligige' leaned toward Aqamdax and took her bowl, set it inside her own.

"I miss my brother Tsaani," she said.

Aqamdax did not remember anyone in the village named Tsaani. "He lives in another village?" she asked.

"No, he lived here. He died before you came. Do not worry that I speak his name. You are safe here with me."

"I do not worry," Aqamdax said, then asked, "He has been dead a long time?"

"Not long. As long as your mother. That is all."

"You know she was my mother?"

"Speak her name if you wish, unless it is taboo to you. I am old. I do not fear her. I knew she was your mother when I first saw you. You look like her. Others said it was only because you are Sea Hunter, but I knew. Some people are foolish, thinking Sea Hunters should all look alike. Here is something you should know." She leaned toward Aqamdax and lowered her voice to a hoarse whisper. "My brother and your mother died by the same knife."

"He is Chakliux's grandfather?"

"Yes."

"He is the one who died the same night my mother died?"

"Yes. Both. The same night. Chakliux told you?"

"Brown Water."

"Ah. I am surprised Sok did not tell you."

"I have found there is much Sok did not tell me."

"He is not a man good with words, but he is a fine hunter."

For a moment, Aqamdax felt the burn of anger, but then she turned her thoughts from Sok to the night her mother had died. If Daes was killed because she was First Men, then why was Tsaani killed? If the trader had some reason to kill Daes—the trader who was father to Ghaden—why would he also kill Tsaani? Why would he try to kill his own son, then leave a knife that most people knew was his? Traders were not fools. Fools did not survive long traveling village to village, dealing with many people.

"Were they together that night, your brother and my mother?" she finally asked Ligige'.

"No. My brother was in his wife's lodge. Your mother and brother were found outside Brown Water's lodge."

"Chakliux has told me some things," Aqamdax said. "That he found my brother and that the knife was still in his back."

"Yes. I helped Wolf-and-Raven care for the boy."

"Then I owe you much," Aqamdax said.

"What does anyone owe when an old woman cares for one who will someday hunt?"

"Who was your brother's wife?"

"Blueberry."

"The one who is now wife to Root Digger?"

"Yes."

"She is young."

"She was a good wife to my brother. He had sent her to her parents that night because Wolf-and-Raven came to speak to him."

"About what?"

Ligige' frowned, and Aqamdax held up one hand. "I am sorry. I did not mean to be rude."

Ligige' shrugged. "Customs are different, village to village, and people to people," she said.

"It would be rude in my village also," Aqamdax told her.

The old woman smiled. "I understand that you want to know what happened. I cannot tell you much, only that Blueberry said she was at her mother's lodge, and even her youngest brother, yet only four summers, will tell you the same. She did not know what Wolf-and-Raven wanted to speak about—you see, I asked also—so I went to Wolf-and-Raven and asked him."

"He told you?"

"He grumbled about it, but yes, he told me. He said he wanted to tell Tsaani that Sok could not have Snow-in-her-hair, that his daughter would not be second wife to any hunter."

"For a long time, Sok has been trying to get Snow-in-her-hair."

"Yes, for a long time. You know that was the reason for last night's storytelling?"

"I know."

"Wolf-and-Raven is not a terrible man, but he guards his shaman powers. If he were stronger, more sure of himself, I do not think he would have been so angry. He worries that there are others more deserving of such power than he is."

"I understand," Aqamdax said.

"You are a child. How do you understand?"

"I was storyteller in our village, but before that . . ." She paused, considered her words carefully. "Before that I was not a woman a man would want as wife."

"But Sok wanted you."

"No. The Walrus shaman wanted me. Sok gave me to him to get trade goods for Snow-in-her-hair's bride price."

"Why are you here then?"

"The Walrus shaman died before I could become his wife."

Ligige''s eyes grew round, and Aqamdax suddenly wished she had not told the woman. "I did not kill him," Aqamdax said. "I had nothing to do with his death."

"You wanted to stay with the Walrus then?"

"At that time, I wanted to be wife to Sok. Then I found he had taken me only to trade to the Walrus shaman."

"But you came here with him."

"The Walrus would not let me stay with them, and after I was here . . ."

"You stayed because of Chakliux," Ligige' finally said.

"No . . ." Aqamdax began, then suddenly knew that Ligige''s words were true. She had stayed because of Chakliux. "Yes," she said.

"Do not leave before you speak to him."

"I have other things I must do first. Do you know anyone who has a dog to trade?"

Ligige' shook her head. "Go to the hearths, ask the women there."

"I must also find my brother, Ghaden, and his sister, Yaa. They were not at Brown Water's lodge."

"Children play," Ligige' said. "There is a fine fox den on the path to the women's place just outside the village. You remember the old spruce, the tallest one, at the bend in the path?"

Aqamdax nodded.

"Under that tree. Look there if you cannot find them in the village."

"Thank you. It would be good to call you aunt."

"Then do so." The old woman pushed herself to her feet. "Do not leave without speaking to Chakliux."

Aqamdax smiled, looked into the old woman's eyes. "I will speak to Chakliux," she promised.

Chapter
Thirty-five

"My father will never let me go to you now," Snow-in-her-hair said.

Sok reached out to lay a hand on her shoulder, but she jerked away and turned her back. Her hair hung thick and loose, almost to her waist. She had taken off her parka in the warmth of Red Leaf's lodge and wore only a caribou hide shirt with long slits under the arms. When she moved, he could see the shadowed skin at the sides of her breasts.

"I have enough in bride price to buy three wives," Sok said, raising his eyes to the lodge roof so he would not lose himself in his desire for her.

"There is still a way," Snow-in-her-hair said, and she spoke so quietly that Sok had to lean close to hear her words.

She looked into his eyes, and he felt his belly quiver as though he were hunting, spear and thrower poised in his hand, the animal watching.

"If you threw away Red Leaf ..."

He turned from her. "I cannot," he said. "How can I bear to see my sons go to another man?"

She pressed herself against his back, wrapped her arms around his waist and leaned into him so he could feel the mounds of her breasts, the hard rise of bone that guarded the soft folds of her vulva. "I can give you sons," she whispered. "Many sons. So many sons we will have to build two lodges." She laughed, a deep joyous sound that he loved. "So many sons that you will have to marry another wife just to help take care of them."

He could not move—the joy and horror of what she wanted him to do was like the noose of a trap around his neck. Then he heard her gasp, and she released him. He looked up to see Red Leaf.

Red Leaf was a tall woman, nearly as tall as Sok, and at that moment she seemed larger, taller. He thought she would scream out her anger, but instead she lifted her head, held her chin high.

"Two strong sons are better than promises of sons," she said, directing her words to Snow-in-her-hair. She looked at Sok and said, "You do not have to throw me away. I know how you can get Wolf-and-Raven to let you have this girl you want. Something easy. Something a woman can do. Something I could do. And if I did, you would not even have to give him much for a bride price." She cocked her head, looked at Snow-in-her-hair from the corners of her eyes. "But," she said, "the furs you do not give to Wolf-and-Raven, those furs are mine."

"They are yours," Sok agreed.

"Yaa?" Aqamdax crouched in front of the spruce tree and called into the branches. Surely this was the spruce Ligige' meant. It was the only large tree where the path turned.

"Ghaden? It is your sister Aqamdax."

She heard a rustling in the branches and stepped back. She did not know much about the animals that lived close to the Near River Village and was not sure what to do if one confronted her.

Then Ghaden peeked out, a small white face, round with a smile.

"Ghaden!" The call was a whisper, but Aqamdax recognized Yaa's voice. Suddenly Ghaden was jerked from her view, his face disappearing under the spruce branches. Aqamdax crawled after him.

"It is too late. I know you are here, Yaa. Ligige' told me."

"Ligige'!"

Yaa crawled out, her face flushed with annoyance. "Ligige' said we would be here?"

"She did."

"How did she know? No one knows about this place but me and Ghaden." She thrust her lower lip into a pout. "And now you."

"Old ones know many things, but I do not think you have to worry. She will not tell, and I will not tell. It will still be your secret place. I will not come here again."

Yaa sighed. "I guess you could if we invited you. But not very often."

Aqamdax smiled and slowly shook her head. "No, Yaa, I will not come again," she said. "Walk with me. I need to talk to you and Ghaden."

Chakliux went first to Aqamdax's lodge. Most of her things were packed. Even the mats she had hung from the walls were rolled together next to a seal belly of oil. Had she decided to leave the village? Hadn't Sok told her that Chakliux wanted her as wife? Surely she knew he would come for her.

She must be with Ghaden or Ligige'. Of course. But though Chakliux knew she was probably still in the village, he was suddenly afraid. She was First Men and had no husband's protection. Who could say what the spirits might do to her?

He went to Brown Water's lodge, found the woman outside scraping a fox skin she had laid over a log. Her scraper was a caribou foreleg bone, and when he spoke to her, she lifted it as though it were a weapon, grasping it like a man holds a spear.

"Do not mention her name," Brown Water said when he asked about Aqamdax. "She is like her mother, always finding some way to show disrespect, some way to make problems. I was not surprised the spirits killed her mother, and I will not be surprised to see the same thing happen to Aqamdax."

Chakliux faced the woman as a warrior, crossing his arms to lay one hand on the knife scabbard at his waist. "You have seen her," he said, and drew a reluctant nod from Brown Water. "Where did she go?"

"She wanted to see Ghaden. That's all I know."

"Where is he?"

"Gone with her, I hope," Brown Water said. She pointed the scraper at the center of Chakliux's chest. "She is right to leave this village. That is one thing I will say. She should not be here. She is not one of us."

Chakliux finally turned away, but he could still hear Brown Water's voice, scolding and whining.

He went to Ligige''s lodge and found her inside, sitting doing nothing. He expected her to make some excuse for her idle hands, but she said only, "I am an old woman," as though that were reason enough for everything done or not done.

He did not have polite words ready in his mouth, and so fumbled for a moment, trying to remember whether or not the sun was shining, how cold it was outside.

Finally Ligige' said, "You are looking for Aqamdax?"

He closed his mouth, swallowed. "Yes," he said.

"I knew you would be. She is with Ghaden."

"Where is Ghaden?"

"Ah, that is something I cannot tell you. It is a secret place only he and his sisters can know."

"Ligige', she is leaving. I have to find her."

"I cannot tell you the place, but perhaps you will be able to find it yourself," she said, and gestured for him to bend closer.

"You are ready?"

Cen nodded.

"And the woman?"

"Do not kill her," Cen told him.

"So you want someone alive who is not even human."

Cen turned and looked into Tikaani's face. Did the man truly believe a person who was not River was not human?

"She is my son's sister. Do not kill her."

"But the little girl. You do not care about her?"

"I will not kill her. You do what you want."

Tikaani started down into the Near River People's valley, his steps careful, toe settled in first, then heel. Suddenly he was running, swiftly, quietly. Cen struggled to keep up with him, to place his feet in the same places Tikaani had stepped.

They came upon the three so quickly that only the youngest girl had time to cry out. Cen grabbed Ghaden, one arm across the boy's belly, one hand over his mouth. He picked him up and ran back the way they had come.

He did not realize until they had ducked back into the shelter of the trees that the young girl had followed him. He felt the sting of a stick across his legs, then across the back of his neck. He stopped, and she jumped on him, kicking and hitting as Ghaden, still in Cen's arms, opened his mouth wide, caught an edge of Cen's hand and bit.

Cen jerked his hand from Ghaden's mouth and slapped the girl. The force of the blow landed on her temple. For a moment she looked at him, eyes dark, then she crumbled into a heap and lay still.

"My sister! My mother!" Ghaden cried.

"She is all right. She is asleep, that is all. Just asleep. Look at me, Ghaden. Remember? I am Cen the trader. I am your father. I have come to take you away from this village. Someone here killed your mother. They might kill you, too. I am going to take you to a safe place. I want you to come with me."

Ghaden looked down at his sister, then slowly up at Cen. "She is asleep?" he asked.

"Yes."

"I need Biter."

"Who is Biter?"

"My dog. He is at Brown Water's lodge. I need him."

"We will have to get him later," Cen said.

Ghaden's face crinkled so that Cen thought the boy might cry, but he stuck his thumb into his mouth and closed his eyes.

Cen shifted him into one arm and started deeper into the trees. They could not risk walking the river paths by day, but had marked a trail through the woods, bending stems of grass, chipping out small chunks of bark, signs that would not be noticed unless someone was watching for them.

The weight of the boy in his arms brought a sudden joy, and Cen did not allow himself to think of the girl he had left lying on the ground. Finally Tikaani caught up to him, the First Men woman slung over one shoulder, her pack over the other.

They walked a long time without stopping, but eventually Tikaani groaned, crouched and let the woman fall forward to the ground.

Cen set Ghaden down, straightened his arm to relieve the cramps in his muscles. Ghaden knelt beside Aqamdax, laid his face against hers and clasped a handful of her hair. Cen shook his head. She looked so much like Daes. Somehow she had discovered where he had taken her mother, had come to this village. He wondered if he could persuade her to go with him. She could take care of Ghaden, help carry his packs. He had once thought a wife would be a hindrance, but since Daes had died, he had thought of little else but having a wife. He knelt beside her, placed a hand against her neck, felt her pulse strong under his fingers.

"What did you do to her?" he asked Tikaani.

"Better to ask what *she* did to me." Dried blood marked four cuts that ran from his forehead to his chin. He held out one hand and Cen saw a line of tooth marks. "I hit her." He leaned forward and pointed to a bruise that darkened Aqamdax's jaw. "There." He raised his hand to his mouth. He sucked, spat out a mouthful of blood, then said, "Tie her now."

"She will remember me," Cen said. "She will not fight." But he raised her sax and took the woman's knife from the packet she had tied at her waist, then patted her sleeves to see if she had knives sheathed there.

"You watch her. I'm going to eat, then sleep. It will be easier if we do not take her."

"And do what instead?"

"Kill her, or tie her and leave her here."

"She will not live long if we tie her."

"She does not deserve to live long."

"So you would not fight if someone took you and your brother? It is right if you seek revenge, but not if she does?"

Tikaani muttered something under his breath, then stalked to a mossy rise under a tree and sat down. He opened the pack the First Men woman had been carrying and found a sael of dried fish. He threw a piece to Cen. "A heavy pack for a woman to carry," he said through a mouthful of fish. "Lots of food in here."

"She was leaving," Ghaden said, his voice small. "She was going home. She said I could come see her when I was a trader."

"Come here, Ghaden," Cen said.

The boy stayed beside the woman for a moment, but when Cen held out his arms, he came. Cen pulled him into his lap and gave him part of his fish.

"When can we go get Biter?" Ghaden asked.

"His dog," Cen explained to Tikaani.

The man smirked, then bent his head over Aqamdax's pack, pulled out more supplies.

"Not today," Cen said.

"I told Yaa we should bring him, but she said he was too noisy. Someone would hear him. Is Yaa awake yet?"

"The little girl, her name is Yaa?" Cen asked.

"Yes."

"She is awake now."

"Brown Water will be mad."

"Why?"

"Because I am not home. I have work to do."

"Let her be mad. You are with me, and I am not mad."

"She might not feed Biter."

"Yaa will feed Biter."

"Yaa will?"

"Yaa will."

Ghaden put his thumb into his mouth and leaned back against Cen. "Make Aqamdax wake up," he said.

"I think it is better if she sleeps."

Grasses were trampled. There was blood. The broken strand of a necklace. Chakliux picked it up and recognized it as Aqamdax's. His heart began to hammer, thick, hard beats that echoed in his throat. What had happened here? Had she and Sok had a fight? Would his brother hurt her, perhaps kill her? He was a man to act in anger, without thought to consequences. Chakliux picked up the remaining beads and began to search the area, walking the path almost up to the women's place, and then down into the village. There were footprints, some large enough to belong to a man, but it was a path worn hard by women, and it was impossible to see any clear track.

He went to Red Leaf's lodge, found Sok there, staring into the flames of the hearth fire.

"Where is Aqamdax?" Chakliux demanded.

"How should I know? I threw her away."

"You did nothing to her?"

"What?"

"Where was she the last time you saw her?"

"In her lodge. I told you I threw her away. She is probably there now."

"After that, where did you go?"

"Chakliux, what has happened?"

"Where were you?"

"I went to find Snow-in-her-hair. I was with her and with Red Leaf all day. Ask them."

Chakliux left the lodge. How could he know if his brother was telling the truth? How could he trust anyone in this Near River Village? Perhaps his own people were right. Would good people allow men like Fox Barking and Sleeps Long to remain in their village? But then he thought of Blue-head Duck and Tsaani. Of Camp Maker and Dog Trainer. All good men. Even Wolf-and-Raven was a good man, though weak.

Among the Cousin River People were there not good and bad as well? Why judge a whole village by one or two?

He would go back to the path where he had found the necklace. He ducked into Aqamdax's lodge as he passed. It was still empty. Though he did not want to, he went back through the village, stopped at Brown Water's lodge, scratched at the entrance tunnel.

"Yaa?" a thin voice called out.

Brown Water shouted, "Where have you been, you and Ghaden? It is nearly dark."

Her head popped out of the entrance tunnel. She scowled when she saw him. "You have not found the woman?" she asked.

"No."

"You'd better find her. She's taken Ghaden and Yaa with her."

"She would not take your children."

"You know her so well? She is evil, that one. If those children are not back soon, I will send hunters after her. I will send my son and he will kill her."

She pulled herself back into the lodge, but as Chakliux turned away, a dog yelped, then scooted out through the entrance tunnel, tail tucked between his legs. The dog cowered when he saw Chakliux, but Chakliux knelt down, extended a hand for the dog to smell. He had seen the animal before, always at Ghaden's side. It had long gangly legs, and the chest was still narrow, but it had already grown to a good size. What had the boy named him? A strange name for a dog.

Biter. That was it. He had heard people say that when the dog hunted, he brought his kill back to the boy. Whoever heard of a dog doing such a thing?

"Biter," Chakliux called softly. "Biter. Will you help me find Ghaden?"

Chakliux had to coax the dog away from Brown Water's lodge, but finally he followed. "Good boy. We will find Ghaden and Yaa and Aqamdax," he told the dog, a promise he made to Biter and to himself.

Chapter Thirty-six

At first Ghaden did not believe the man who carried him was Cen, the trader. Cen, the one who always had good things to give him, who always had good food. How could Cen be so old? Cen was a trader, not an elder. How could he get white hair? How could his face be so full of wrinkles and spots?

But when they rested, the old man opened a pack, pulled out some of the same things Ghaden had played with the last time he was in Cen's lodge, in the trader's tent with his first mother. He looked carefully into the old man's face. The nose was not Cen's nose. And there was a scar, pink and shining. Cen had not had a scar. But the eyes, they looked like Cen's eyes, and the hair . . .

Ghaden reached up, touched a tuft of white hair. The old man laughed, then tugged at the white hair, pulled it right out of his head and handed it to Ghaden. Ghaden did not want to touch it. It had some kind of magic in it, he was sure. Otherwise it would not have come out of the old one's head so easily, but the man had given it to him. Like a gift. You did not throw away gifts or act like you didn't want them. He held the hair but did not close his fingers over it.

The old man laughed, reached out to rub the hair between his thumb and fingers. "Look," he said. "It is caribou hair. See?"

Ghaden leaned down, looked closely, rubbed the hair as the old man had. It *was* caribou. He had heard stories of men who became animals, and animals who became men. "You are caribou?" he asked softly.

The old man laughed. "No," he said. "I told you I am Cen, your father, Cen."

His father? No, his father was dead. He had died while Ghaden stayed in the shaman's lodge, while he was getting over the knife wound.

"My father died," Ghaden said.

"One of your fathers," the man told him. "I am your other father. Your first father. When your mother decided to stay with the River People, you got another father."

Ghaden tilted his head, stared at the man. He did look a little like Cen. Just a little, and his voice was Cen's voice. When Ghaden closed his eyes and listened, it was like Cen talking. He had Cen's trader packs. Even the boots he wore looked like Cen's boots, though maybe not exactly.

"Why do you have caribou hair?" Ghaden finally asked.

"To make me look old."

"Why?"

"So I could sneak close to the village and take you to live with me."

"Why?"

"Because I am your father."

"Brown Water will be mad."

"Do not worry about Brown Water. I will protect you from her. How could I let you grow up with Brown Water when I want to teach you to be a trader like me, and to hunt and to paddle a trader's boat?"

Ghaden stuck his thumb in his mouth, spoke around it. "I want Biter. I want my Yaa."

"I will get you a dog. A better dog than Biter, bigger and better."

Ghaden shook his head slowly. "No," he said, then got up and went to where they had laid Aqamdax. He sat down beside her, his back turned so he could not see the old man who said he was Cen. Ghaden wound his hand into Aqamdax's hair. He would wait for her to wake up, then they would leave these old men and go back to their own village. The next time Yaa said they couldn't take Biter with them to the den, he wouldn't go either.

"Leave the woman." A man's voice. He spoke the River language.

Aqamdax lay with eyes closed. She knew Ghaden was beside her, could feel his small hands stroking her head, clutching her hair. He shuddered now and again, as though he were trying to hold in tears.

"I will not leave her," another man said. Though his words were River, his voice held the accent of a trader, a man who spoke many languages, each leaving some bit of itself, like a stone holds the colors of the seeds and dried berries ground on it. "She was my wife's daughter. I will not leave her."

Aqamdax's eyes almost flew open at his words. His wife's daughter? Her first thoughts were of her own father, drowned in the North Sea. Had she left the earth and gone to live in the spirit world? Then she realized her foolishness. This man was a trader. Probably the one who had brought her mother to the River Village. Perhaps Ghaden's father.

Slowly, she opened her eyes to narrow slits, tried to see through the fringe of her eyelashes. Yes, there were two men. They were squatting on their haunches near their packs. Her pack, too, was there. Though it was difficult to see the men clearly, they seemed to have the white hair of elders, but held their bodies erect like young hunters. Who were they? Why had they attacked her and Ghaden and Yaa?

Yaa! Where was she? Had they killed her?

"How will you bring her? She is too heavy to carry. She will only slow us down. They will find the other one and come after us. A good tracker will soon see the signs we left to guide us back through the trees."

If I lie still, Aqamdax thought, they will leave me. Then I can go for help. But they will take Ghaden, and what if our hunters cannot find them?

She turned her head, opened her eyes and smiled at Ghaden. He smiled at her, a wide smile.

She raised her head, clenched her teeth against the pain and sat up. The whole side of her face ached.

"I will go with you," she said. The words were slurred, and she raised her hand to her mouth. Her lips were swollen, crusted with blood.

Both men looked startled. One stood, came toward her. Even in the shadows of the forest, she could see that the white in his hair had been sewn in, like embroidery, that it was . . . caribou hair. His face was wrinkled and dark, scarred as well, but his eyes were the eyes of a young man, his teeth white, his lips not yet thinned with age.

"I am Cen," he said, speaking in the First Men language. "I have no knife." He held his hands out, fingers open, in the greeting Aqamdax had seen so often. The words, in her own language, were like a gift, but she warned herself that just because a man spoke her language did not mean he was a friend.

"I will go with you and my brother," she said, and reached to pull Ghaden into her lap.

"You can walk?" the other man asked. "We cannot carry you. As soon as it is dark, we will leave."

"Where are you going?"

The man squinted his eyes into slits, and Aqamdax wished she had not asked.

"A long way," he finally said, then spoke to the one called Cen. "You know the choice you have. If you take her, you are responsible for her."

"I want them both," the man said, then went to his pack, untied a water bladder and pulled out dried fish. He thrust them at Aqamdax. "Eat and be sure your brother eats. We will not stop until morning."

The thought of food nauseated her, but she forced herself to take a bite, then gave the fish to Ghaden. "Eat," she told him, and prayed he did not refuse.

"I want Yaa. I want Biter," he said in a small voice.

"Ghaden, you have to eat." He stared into her eyes, watched as she took another bite, then he, too, ate.

How could the dog disappear? It had been with him, only a little ahead of him, then the path turned and Biter was gone.

How does any animal disappear? he asked himself. Ground squirrels, foxes, even ptarmigan in snow? They have holes, safe places, hidden dens.

Unlike most of the black spruce that grew at the edge of the village, the branches of those at the sides of the path grew to the ground. He lowered himself to hands and knees, pushing aside grass and branches, peering into the dark recesses under the boughs. The tree at the corner, where the path turned toward the women's place, was the largest. Its branches were a jagged circle that extended out almost the length of a man's body from the trunk. He lifted up the largest branch. There was another, smaller, growing under it. He lifted this branch, then caught his breath as something shot from under the tree.

Chakliux reached for his sleeve knife, whipped the blade from the sheath before he saw that the animal was a dog. He dropped the knife before Biter, in his eagerness, could impale himself on the point.

"Where were you?" Chakliux asked, then lifted the branch again, held it up as the dog wiggled back under the tree and into a dark hole that seemed to dip down beneath the roots.

Chakliux followed the dog, pushing himself into the hole. His shoulders stuck, the earth like hands, holding him. He kicked hard with his strong right leg, once, twice, then found himself in a den, his hair caught painfully in a tangle of tree roots. Gradually his eyes adjusted until he could see Biter and something huddled beside him.

It moved, and he heard a small voice, Yaa's voice: "Biter, now everyone knows where our secret place is. You bad dog."

Chakliux carried her as he had once carried Ghaden, but this time, Biter was at his heels, snapping at anyone who came too close. By the time they were at Brown Water's lodge, a troop of children were behind him, the older boys asking questions, one of the girls crying. He called at the lodge entrance, then went inside. When she saw him, Happy Mouth cried out, began a high screaming lament that Brown Water stopped with a quick hand over the woman's mouth.

"Do not invite death," Brown Water said, and tucked her fingertips against the girl's neck. "She is alive."

Happy Mouth rolled out sleeping furs, and Chakliux laid the girl down. He held Biter away from her face as Brown Water and Happy Mouth checked her arms and legs, lifted her parka and palpitated her belly and chest, then finally ran quick hands over her head.

"Here," Brown Water said, her fingers probing over Yaa's left ear.

Happy Mouth pressed her own fingers in the same place, and Chakliux saw Yaa wince. "It hurts?" Happy Mouth asked the girl.

"Yes," Yaa said in a tiny voice.

Chakliux, kneeling behind the women, felt a hand on his shoulder. He looked up to see Ligige'.

"Best Fist came and got me," she whispered to him. "Where did you find Yaa?"

"Out by the women's path there is a large spruce. Under it—"

"I know the place," Ligige' said. "Do you know what happened to her?"

"No."

Yaa lifted her head, struggled to see past her mother and Brown Water, her eyes seeking out Chakliux. "Ghaden?" she asked.

"He was not there."

She fell back against the bedding furs, closed her eyes. "I should have . . . he wanted to bring Biter. They took him."

"Who took him?" Chakliux asked.

"And Aqamdax," she said.

"That woman," said Brown Water. "That woman took him. I knew she would. We should send hunters after them. She can't be too far, a woman with a child."

"No," Yaa said, but Brown Water had lifted her voice, was telling Chakliux to speak to the elders, was asking Ligige' to find young hunters.

"No!" Yaa said again, and then she suddenly sat up, cupped her hands over her mouth and began to retch.

Happy Mouth grabbed a bark sael and held it under her daughter's chin, but Brown Water turned to Chakliux. "You know that Sea Hunter woman as well as anyone. What do you think?"

"I don't know," he said quietly.

"Her husband threw her away this morning," Ligige' said. "She came to me after. She had a pack of trade goods, and she was looking for Ghaden and Yaa."

"You told her where they were?" Brown Water screeched. She flung one arm back to Yaa's bed. "Look what she did to our little daughter."

"She might have decided to leave the village," Ligige' said, ignoring Brown Water. "She might want to return to her own people, but I do not think she would hurt anyone, especially a child."

Brown Water pressed one finger into Chakliux's chest. "You and your brother, this is your fault. Go find her and bring back Ghaden."

Chakliux looked past Brown Water to Ligige'. "She did not say where she was going?"

"No."

"I will find her," Chakliux said. "Take care of the little daughter." He pulled a sinew string of smooth shell beads from his neck. It was one of the gifts he had planned to give Aqamdax. He handed it to Happy Mouth. "For Yaa," he said, "when she is feeling better." Then he left the lodge.

"I found it. It is mine," River Ice Dancer said.

"We all found it. We were all together. It has to belong to all of us," said Black Moon.

The four boys stood around the iqyax. It had been nestled inside a bark cache set high in a tree.

"It might be my uncle's," Carries Much told the others, but they hooted out their derision.

Carries Much shrugged his shoulders.

"Did your uncle say he had an iqyax?"

"He never talked about it," Carries Much said. "But he knows how to make them. So does my father."

"Do you see their mark on it?" Black Moon asked.

Carries Much ran his hand over the smooth walrus hide cover. "Maybe that," he said, and lifted his chin toward a series of white circles near the pointed bow.

"Maybe that," River Ice Dancer said, his voice pitched higher to imitate Carries Much.

River Ice Dancer was the oldest of the boys, several years older than Carries Much, and larger than all of them. "It's mine," he told them again. "I'm going to keep it." Suddenly he lunged out and grabbed the front of Carries Much's parka, twisted his hand into the fur until Carries Much began to choke. "And if anybody tells his uncle or any uncle, he can count himself happy to be dead." He released Carries Much so suddenly that the boy nearly fell to the ground.

The other boys laughed nervously, then Black Moon leaned down and offered Carries Much his hand.

"I think I'll put it in a different place," River Ice Dancer said. "If we find a tree with some good-sized branches, that should be rack enough for it. Just to keep it off the ground."

He set his right shoulder under one side and lifted. "Here, help me. Black Moon, you get on the other side. Stone Thrower, you take the back. Carries Much, go home to your mother. You might need to suck on her teats."

She wouldn't leave without talking to him, Chakliux told himself. Their friendship had been too deep . . . but perhaps only to him. He was brother to her husband. Why should she think Chakliux would want her once Sok in anger threw her away?

Perhaps she only pretended friendship. As storyteller, he had something to offer her. He had told her tales from Caribou traders, even shared stories the North Tundra men said were from people who lived so close to the rising sun that they lit their cooking hearths from its flame.

But whatever had been between them, whether it was true or not true, if Aqamdax had decided to return to her own people and take her brother with her, how would she go? She would have to follow the river to the sea, then walk the shore. She could take birds with nets and fish with a handline, but her brother would slow her down. He was too old to carry far and too young to walk any great distance. Surely she knew it was too close to winter to make such a journey. Surely she knew someone would come after her, if only to get the boy back.

Then a thought came that pulled his breath from his chest, as though someone had sunk a fist into his belly. She might have taken his iqyax.

With the iqyax her brother would be no hindrance, and she could paddle wide around the Walrus Hunter Village, where the people might still want to kill her. So then, he asked himself, do you sit here and wonder, or do you go and see if your iqyax is still there?

He stopped at Red Leaf's lodge, took spear and throwing board, another knife and a bladder of oil. It was foolish to think Aqamdax would have taken the iqyax, he told himself, but he should go and oil the cover, remove it and store it in a dry place for the winter. By the time he reached the storage cache, it was nearly dark.

He climbed up into the tree, then called out his anguish, a warrior's cry.

Chapter
Thirty-seven

They did not believe her. Not Brown Water. Not the elders. Not even her mother. At first, it did not matter. Yaa's head had hurt so badly that she could not think around the pain, but now that she felt better, now that her eyes could focus again, her anger grew each time she tried to talk to them. Finally she decided that she could not remain in Brown Water's lodge, doing nothing. It was bad enough that Chakliux stayed in Aqamdax's lodge, did not look for them. He would not even eat, some of the women said.

There were many angry people in the village: elders mad that Aqamdax had stolen Ghaden; Chakliux mad that she took his iqyax; Brown Water mad that Yaa was hurt. Everyone was mad that Wolf-and-Raven did not have the power to stop Aqamdax, and Wolf-and-Raven was mad about everything.

Now, according to what Best Fist told her this morning, Wolf-and-Raven had new reason to be angry. Women were saying that his daughter Snow-in-her-hair was sleeping with many men in the village, trying to catch a baby in her belly so one of them would decide she was worth claiming.

Yaa's mother and Brown Water spent much time at the village hearths, talking and talking. Other families were leaving for the caribou hunts. Brown Water said that soon Sok and Chakliux would go, that River Ice Dancer and his family had already left. Perhaps this was a good time for her to go also, Yaa thought. With everyone thinking about other things, it would take them longer to notice that she was gone. She would need food and extra boots, water and a woman's knife. Maybe she could sneak one of her father's throwing spears, one of the few that had not been left with his body on the death scaffold. She would say she was going to visit Best Fist, to spend the day teaching her how to make coiled grass baskets. Then she and Biter would leave.

It would be difficult to follow those two men after so many days, but Biter had a good nose.

Besides, she knew where those men were from. The last thing she had seen before the darkness came and pulled her away was the old man's boot, with seams made in the foolish way of the Cousin River People.

Chakliux's body ached, his tongue was swollen. Sweat had plastered his hair to his neck and shoulders. It was his third day of fasting, his third day of praying, and for most of that time he had also lived without water. He left his prayers only to dream, and now his dreams were visions of war, the Cousin and the Near River Peoples destroying each other.

Chakliux, too, fought, moving in his dreams to attack first one group, then the other, but no matter which village he fought against, the person always at the other side of his knife, at the tip of his spear, was Aqamdax, her hair loose and flying and Ghaden slung on her hip. Each time he pinned her to the ground, spear poised over her heart, he stopped, suddenly unable to move. In this dream, they fought from iqyan, and as he lifted his spear to thrust it into her heart, she threw her spear first, not into his flesh but into the taut cover of his iqyax, piercing the deck and hull, so that Chakliux felt the cold water flood his craft and pull him down into the sea.

He cried out, and suddenly he was in Aqamdax's lodge, the place he had chosen to use during his fast, away from the shouts and conversations of Carries Much and Cries-loud, from the fussing and worry of Red Leaf, from Sok's sly plans to take Snow-in-her-hair as second wife.

The lodge walls were close, pungent with the smell of hearth fire smoke. His body was heavy, his arms and legs slow and burdensome, as though he had forgotten how to use them. He stood, and his head spun. He pulled a bladder from a lodge pole. The water was tepid, dusky with the flavor of its storage container, but as he swallowed it, his thoughts cleared. He saw two faces, not those he might expect—Aqamdax or K'os, even his own Gguzaakk—but instead the girl Yaa and his young nephew Carries Much. He shook his head, took another drink, but the faces stayed, Yaa and Carries Much.

He used the remaining water in the bladder to clean the soot from his face, then he pulled on his parka and left Aqamdax's lodge.

Yaa told her story slowly, this time with hope, her hands rubbing Biter's ears as she spoke. Chakliux sat and listened, and seemed to ignore Brown Water's sighs and protests, her rudeness once she realized that he intended to listen to Yaa.

Yaa lifted her voice to speak over Brown Water's sudden decision to sing, over the woman's clatter of wooden dishes, over a loud conversation she had with herself about the foolishness of young girls. Yaa told her story as best she remembered it from the time she and Ghaden first heard Aqamdax outside their den to the last blow to her head. She did not tell Chakliux she thought the men were Cousin River men. Why insult him? After all, was he not also from the Cousin River Village? But she did tell him that she thought they were old, and that the short one went for Aqamdax, that he had much white hair, that the other man wore a necklace of sea lion teeth.

She held her breath when she had finished speaking, hoping that he believed her, that he would go after Ghaden and Aqamdax. But he said nothing, merely nodded as she spoke, and then, when she was done, he thanked her and left the lodge.

She was disappointed, but even from the first he had seemed a little strange, his eyes focused above her head, his face drawn and pale, his hair dull and in strings, as though he had not combed oil through it in many days.

After he left, Brown Water scolded her and ordered her to go out and get firewood. It was the first time Brown Water had told her to do anything since she was hurt, but she was glad to get outside, to feel the wind on her face. Even the rough pieces of wood felt good under her fingers. When her mother saw her working, she came, concern in her eyes, but Yaa told her she felt strong. Then she asked if she could go to Best Fist's lodge tomorrow and spend the day.

Happy Mouth, looking at the heavy load of wood in her daughter's arms, at the whiteness of her daughter's face, told Yaa it would be a good thing for her to spend a day in Best Fist's lodge.

He slept a night and a day and another night, rousing himself only to take water. His sleeping seemed not so much a time to rest but to consider what Yaa had told him and to think back over all the conversations he and Aqamdax had shared.

He awoke hungry, and with the certainty that he knew what had happened. Yaa had said one of the attackers wore a necklace of sea lion teeth. Who else but Walrus Hunters and First Men wore sea lion teeth? Of those two peoples, who would seek revenge against Aqamdax? How like the Walrus Hunters to send elders to avenge the death of a shaman. If they were lost, the people would not suffer from their deaths as much as they would from the deaths of young hunters.

Chakliux sat up, peeled back his sleeping robes, then saw that he was not alone in Aqamdax's lodge, that Carries Much was also there with him.

The words came to Chakliux's mouth before he thought about them: "There is something you have to tell me," he said.

"Yes," Carries Much answered, and did not seem surprised that Chakliux knew.

When Carries Much began to speak, his voice was so soft Chakliux could barely hear him, but the more he spoke, the more he seemed to gather courage, and when he had finished, his voice was as strong as a man's.

Then Chakliux spoke to him as though he were an adult, in the same manner that he might speak to Sok. "I have to make a journey, and I need my iqyax."

Chakliux's heart twisted at the thought that Aqamdax might already be dead, but the pain was not as great as it had been when he believed she had gone of her own choice, stealing what was his, something she knew he valued more than any other possession.

Chakliux stood and gestured for Carries Much to do the same. "So you will show me where River Ice Dancer put my iqyax?" he asked.

Carries Much nodded.

"Good. Then you will also help me take the food and supplies I need. Afterward, you will tell your father that I have gone to the Walrus Hunter Village. You will tell him that Walrus elders came and took Aqamdax, and since Ghaden was with her, they took him as well. Tell him I will try bring them both back. And from now on you will not do what River Ice Dancer tells you to do."

"No, I will not."

Chakliux laid a hand on his nephew's shoulder. "Good," he said. "It is a lesson every man has to learn. There are many River Ice Dancers in the world. At least one for each of us, it seems." He looked into his nephew's eyes until the boy finally smiled.

PART
FOUR

WINTER, 6459 B.C.

Sometimes I dream I am back again with my own people, in our village by the inlet. I hear the gulls and kittiwakes. I see the grasses bend with the wind. When I awake, I lie very still, and though my bed is hard, and I sleep in the cold of the entry tunnel, I can almost believe that I am home, that soon I will hear Qung's quiet wisdom or the scolding voices of He Sings's wives.

When I first came to this village, my dreams were always bad, but then Biter led Yaa to us. By the time she reached us, she could walk only by clinging to his fur, but somehow she survived the journey. She and Ghaden were adopted by a young woman. They call her Star and say her mother has lived on the edge of madness since Star's father died. He was killed, K'os tells me, by her son Chakliux, but I have come to know K'os, slave to master. It is a peculiar kind of knowing, and makes me cautious in what I believe. I do not think Chakliux would have killed the man without good reason.

On cold nights, Yaa sends Biter to sleep with me. His body warms mine, and I am sure his thick fur catches evil dreams, for I have yet to have one when he sleeps beside me.

K'os gives me much work to do, and worst of all, lends me to hunters and traders to warm their beds. At one time, I would have thought nothing of doing such a thing, but it is different to come to men as a slave. For all that is bad, there is also some good. K'os recognizes my worth as story-teller. I have had many times during this long winter to practice my skills, and no shaman in this village cries out to protest when I speak in other voices.

Qung taught me well. There is no way I can repay her, or even tell her of my gratitude. But I owe her for more than stories. During the years Qung lived alone in our village, using her stories as a hunter uses his harpoon, to bring in meat, she learned to live as a hunter lives, earning good fortune with respect, with quietness and with skill.

Now I practice what she taught me: I do not speak of my discontent, I watch, I survive.

Chapter Thirty-eight

THE COUSIN RIVER VILLAGE

Aqamdax lifted her head and looked at K'os.

"Go get wood," K'os told her. "Not from the piles at the edge of the lodge, but from the woods." She smiled. "Put it in the entrance tunnel so it will dry."

Aqamdax kept her face still, her mouth straight. She had discovered that K'os did most things to show her own power, to rejoice in what she could make Aqamdax do, and Aqamdax had scars to remind her of the times she had tried to defy the woman.

The wind found their smoke hole and hurled soot back at them, stirred the ashes in the hearth. A drift of ice crystals slanted in from the entrance tunnel. K'os had allowed her to keep only one of her sleeping furs, a woven hare fur blanket, too old to remember the warmth of the animals it had come from. Cen had one of her blankets, made of sea otter fur, thick and heavy. He used it in his own bed, but on the coldest nights, he would give it back to Aqamdax. She was careful to hide it under her hare fur blanket so K'os did not see.

Aqamdax pulled the hood of her parka tightly around her face and slipped into the boots Cen had given her, good warm boots of caribou and seal skin. K'os had already paid Cen back for giving Aqamdax those boots—a meal that left Cen writhing in agony, clutching his belly for two days. Aqamdax had eaten nothing from K'os's hands for a long time after Cen's illness. A slave that ill might be killed. Who had time to care for her?

Aqamdax put on her snowshoes and went out through the entrance tunnel, working her way through the drift that blocked off the door, opening the frozen caribouskin doorflap carefully so it would not crack in the cold. She had made herself mittens from the fur of the ground squirrels she had killed last fall when she was gathering firewood outside the village. She had hidden to eat their meat, had eaten it raw so K'os would not know she had extra food. Their skins made warm mittens with small pouches for her thumbs and high cuffs that nearly reached her elbows.

The wind was so strong and the snow so thick that Aqamdax could not see the next lodge. It would be difficult enough to bring in wood from the piles she had stored around the lodge, let alone to find her way into the forest.

K'os's request had not surprised her, though. Cen had left several days before on a winter trading trip to the Black River Village, and since he'd left, Tikaani had not come to K'os's lodge as he usually did when Cen was away. K'os had finally visited Tikaani in the hunters' lodge, the only woman in the village ever to do such a thing, Aqamdax heard the women at the cooking hearths say.

That day, K'os had returned to her own lodge so full of anger that Aqamdax had quickly made an excuse to leave, telling K'os that one of the elders had requested she bring him some of K'os's willow bark tea.

K'os had thrown a packet of bark at Aqamdax, and Aqamdax had grabbed her parka and boots, scooted into the entrance tunnel to put them on. She had taken the willow bark to old Twisted Stalk's lodge, had told the woman K'os had sent her and that the tea would help soothe the ache of her husband's hips and knees.

In return, Twisted Stalk gave her a bowl of meat and broth, more food than Aqamdax usually had in a day, and when she had eaten, Twisted Stalk gave her a poorly made floor mat to take back to K'os.

Aqamdax had walked the village, hoping to see Ghaden or Yaa before she returned to K'os's lodge, but though other children were sliding down a snow-covered hill on caribou hides, Ghaden and Yaa were not among them. Aqamdax had watched the children for a while, thinking how smart the Cousin River mothers were to allow their children to do such hard work for them—wearing the hair from the hides by their sliding.

She had finally returned to K'os, to the woman's anger, her sharp words and slapping fingers. K'os cut Twisted Stalk's woven mat into strips, then told Aqamdax to feed it to the fire, but Aqamdax saved part of it and hid it in the entrance tunnel, later used it to pad her own bed.

Today, there would be no children outside. Even the dogs were curled close to the lodges, tails covering noses, snow mounding over them. She walked lodge to lodge, remembered the stories some of the women had told her about people lost in snowstorms, some not found until spring. Who in this village would even notice she was gone if such a thing happened to her?

Star did not allow Ghaden and Yaa to be with Aqamdax, shielded their eyes with her hand if they walked past her or met her at the village hearths. They were not even allowed to come when K'os planned a storytelling. Star claimed it was because Aqamdax was slave, but Aqamdax thought it more likely that the woman feared she would steal the children, take them back to the Near River Village.

But why should she return to the Near River Village? No one there wanted her. Not Sok, or Red Leaf; perhaps Chakliux, but if he had cared for her, why hadn't he come after her?

Aqamdax turned and walked backward into the wind. She ran into the next lodge, tripping over a pile of wood and driving snow up under the back of her parka. It was too cold to do such a foolish thing, she told herself as she got up and brushed out the snow before it could melt. She fought her way through the village and to the tree that stood just beyond the last lodge. She stopped there in hopes that she might find a limb broken off by the wind, but there was nothing, and branches that had once been within her reach had been taken by other hands for other hearth fires.

The path that had been easy to find in the morning was now buried, but even in the snow and wind, Aqamdax thought she could see the dark edge of the forest. She walked toward it, pulling her hood so tightly around her face that only her eyes showed. Her toes were like pieces of wood and her fingers ached with the cold.

As she entered the forest, the wind pulled a strange song from the trees, and Aqamdax wrapped her arms around herself. The First Men were not a people of forests. Who could tell what spirits hid in those gnarled branches? Who could say what amulets and songs would appease them?

Aqamdax opened her mouth and chanted her thanks, a praise song for the trees, something she made up as she sang. Then she heard a cracking above her head, a sound that vibrated through the earth. She pressed herself against a tree trunk, looked up through the branches. The top of the tree tipped and fell, breaking away lower branches, moving slowly as though in a dream, and flinging snow into Aqam-dax's face when it hit the ground.

Biter scratched at the side of the lodge, and Yaa made a face at the dog. He had not been out all day, so she was sure he had to go, but the storm was fierce, and for some reason the wind seemed to scare Ghaden. Star ignored the dog, as she always did, as she had since she and Ghaden had screamed at each other over the dog's right to stay in the lodge rather than be tied outside like other dogs. Often Yaa felt as if she were mother to both Ghaden and Star, though Star had the face and body of an adult.

There were good days when Star took care of Ghaden, fed him, made clothes for him. She taught Yaa to sew caribou hair into patterns of leaves and flowers on her clothing. Then she would suddenly become as whiny and fretful as a child, arguing over small things and pinching when she couldn't get her way.

Star's mother, Long Eyes, was worse than Star. She sat all day, rocking side to side and singing a song with words Yaa could not understand. Long Eyes left the lodge only twice a day to visit the women's place, and once a month to spend four or five days in the moon blood lodge. Those were the best times, if Star was also good. The worst times were like now, when both women were in the lodge and Star was behaving like a child, screaming out her demands, sometimes even trying to curl herself into her mother's lap. It was a curse, Trail Climber had told her. Something that happened to the mother when her husband was killed by K'os's son. That son was gone, had left the village in shame, and everyone was forbidden even to say his name, but the hunters in the village were preparing to seek revenge, were going to attack the village where this son now lived.

They even had new weapons, Trail Climber had told her, but had whispered that Yaa could tell no one, not even Ghaden. She had promised, then had asked Trail Climber if Star had also changed into this strange woman-child at the death of her father. Trail Climber told her that Star had always been that way, spoiled and expecting more than others had, but that she became worse after her father died.

During bad times, Yaa reminded herself of the three handfuls of days it had taken her and Biter to find the Cousin River Village. She remembered the howling of wolves, the bear tracks. She had not known the night sky was so wide, the stars' light so feeble against the darkness. When they ran out of food, she had eaten berries that made her so sick she could walk only a short way before resting, and when Biter had caught a ptarmigan, she did not even have the strength to make a fire. She and Biter had eaten it raw, slept, then started out again. They came to the Cousin River Village that evening, Yaa so weak that she had to lean on Biter just to walk.

When Yaa remembered that, she was grateful for Star and Long Eyes, for the warm lodge they shared with her and with Ghaden, especially on storm days like this one.

"Star," Yaa said, seeing that Biter's scratching was becoming more frantic, "I have to let Biter out."

Star looked at Yaa with empty eyes, but Ghaden gripped Biter's fur.

"He cannot go into the bowl like you," Yaa told him. "If he goes inside maybe Star will get angry and tie him outside."

She did not want to remind him that the Cousin River People often ate dogs, more than the Near River People did, especially dogs that did not have golden eyes. She saw the knowledge in Ghaden's face. He released his hold, and Yaa whispered, "Go to Star. Climb into her lap. You might distract her enough for me to let Biter out."

"He will come back?" Ghaden asked, looking up at the crust of snow that had formed over the smoke hole.

Yaa, too, looked up, told herself she would have to clear the snow away now, and also during the night, if the storm did not stop.

"Biter's too smart to stay out in this storm," Yaa told Ghaden, then waited as he climbed into Star's lap and used his fingers like a comb to stroke Star's hair. Yaa crept to the entrance tunnel, opened the flap for the dog, crawled after him to the outside doorflap, broke the snow away from the edges and let him out. She waited for a moment, then called him. She peeked outside, could see that he stood with his nose pointed up, as though to smell the wind, then he turned and followed her back inside.

"Stay away from the tunnel. Don't go out," Star said when Yaa returned. Ghaden was sitting in front of her and had her hair combed down over her face. Yaa found a shell comb from one of Star's baskets and crouched beside him. She motioned with her head toward Biter, and Ghaden crawled over to the dog, wiped the snow from the dog's fur.

Yaa pulled the comb through Star's long, thick hair. "I'm right here," she told Star. "Don't worry. We won't go outside."

*   *   *

The men sat together in the hunters' lodge. Those with wives grumbled of too much time spent listening to children whine and women complain.

Tikaani looked at his brother, Night Man. He seemed to be a little stronger, able to stand now and hobble across the lodge if he braced himself with a walking stick. Though his legs were not injured, the wound in his shoulder had not yet healed, and it had spread its poison through his body, leaving painful lumps at his groin, the backs of his knees and under both arms.

It was a poison that even K'os was not able to stop, and she blamed its power on the Near River People, told the men that they must destroy that village or the poison would spread from Night Man to every Cousin River hunter. In the autumn, with food and wood plentiful, it was something to think about, killing those Near Rivers. The warriors honed their skills with spears and spearthrowers, with knives, and also with the new sacred weapon K'os had won for them through her cunning.

But now there was more to think about than revenge. Now, the village food caches were nearly empty. With the poor salmon runs, they did not have enough food to get them through until spring, even though their caribou hunting had brought them more meat than usual. The hunters' lodge was also nearly out of firewood, though he knew K'os had a large supply brought to her by the hardworking First Men woman he and Cen had captured from the Near River Village. She would not be slave for long, that one. Already the children looked forward to hearing her stories, and elders also made one excuse or another to listen.

Storytelling was a good diversion for children, but young hunters lost patience listening to old men. What good were their stories? Could they fill bellies or warm lodges?

Black Caribou was speaking, his tale long and rambling, but finally he finished, and before another old man could begin, Tikaani interrupted with a riddle.

Black Caribou narrowed his eyes, but Tikaani ignored him.

"Look! What do I see?" Tikaani said. He glanced at the old men who looked at him in surprise. Did they think it strange that a young warrior would speak? Hard times called for new ways. "Look! What do I see?" Tikaani said again. "There are no tracks under it."

The old men did not look at him. Some moved their jaws as though they had to chew on his words, to tear them into pieces to understand the hidden meaning.

Finally Night Man spoke, drawing the old men's eyes. "An empty food cache," he said.

"An empty food cache," Tikaani repeated, proud of his brother's quick mind.

"I have food enough," said Black Caribou.

"For you or for the whole village?" Tikaani asked. "Because if you have only food for yourself, then that is not enough."

"For myself and my wife," Black Caribou answered in a smaller, less boastful voice.

"It is because of the fish," another of the elders said.

"The Near Rivers, their curse," said one of the young men. "Chakliux, that one."

Some agreed; others lifted voices to disagree, and though Tikaani might have welcomed the debate at another time, today there were more important things to talk about.

"How will we gain revenge if we die before summer?" he asked.

The men were silent.

Finally Black Caribou said, "Tikaani is right."

"So then you will go out in this storm and hunt?" Night Man asked, and lifted his hand toward the top of the lodge, where the wind cried out against the warmth of their fire. "Even our wood supply is running low."

"The women are lazy."

Night Man shrugged. "They worry about their own lodges first. What else do you expect? They think about their children."

"Who do they think feeds their children?"

"I will go out to hunt," Tikaani said. "Once this storm ends."

"You expect to find anything other than hares?"

"I have no problem eating hares." He looked at Black Caribou's soot-stained face, at the other hunters in the lodge. They were thin, but not yet starving, at the stage of hunger that brings irritation, not lethargy. Still it was a difficult time to get men to hunt. The women's traps had taken all the small game close to the village, and the caribou had traveled south to their sheltered winter feeding grounds. What hunter wanted to spend days in the snow only to bring back women's meat—hares, ptarmigan?

"So who will come with me?" Tikaani asked.

He waited but no one spoke.

Finally Night Man said, "I will go."

Tikaani nearly refused the offer, but then saw the pride in his brother's eyes. "Good," he said. "Night Man and I will go." He waited again, sure that Night Man's offer would shame other hunters into joining them, but the men kept their heads lowered, eyes averted.

"There is nothing to hunt," someone said. The words were whispered so Tikaani could not tell who spoke. What good was a man's pride if it kept him from taking hares in a time of little food? And who could say? Even a man out looking for hares sometimes found a caribou.

"When the wind dies, when the snow stops, Night Man and I will go," Tikaani said. "It is good for our women that there are two hunters in this village."

The wood was heavy, and her hands were numb, so sometimes Aqamdax did not realize she had lost her grip on the branches until they fell at her feet. She dragged the tree top, and cradled the smaller broken branches in her left arm. At the edge of the woods, she stopped, looked out into the white of the storm. Without the trees to catch a portion of the wind and snow, she could see nothing but the next step. Even the prints of her snowshoes had been filled, as though she had never come to the woods, as though she had stayed warm and safe in K'os's lodge.

The lodges of the Cousin River Village were spaced farther apart than those of the Near River People, and she was afraid she might have the poor fortune of walking between them, walking through the village and beyond. She wished she had counted her steps from the last lodge to the edge of the woods.

Ten tens, she thought. Surely no more than that. She tightened her grip on the branches, ducked her head against the wind and began counting. After each ten steps, she stopped, but every time saw only a curtain of white. The wind seemed to suck the air from her lungs, but she went on until she had counted ten steps ten times. There was nothing. Only white, snow, wind.

"You are not far enough," she said, speaking the words aloud, thinking the sound of her voice would give her courage, but the wind took the words before they could come to her ears.

She did not realize she had sunk to her knees until she leaned forward and felt the snow against her face. She closed her eyes. Perhaps if she rested, only for a short time . . .

No. Had she forgotten the many River stories of people lost in storms who had slept themselves into death? She lifted one leg, planted her foot on the ground, dropped the wood to push herself up, hand on knee, then picked up the wood and continued to walk.

She concentrated on her feet, moved one then the other. Surely she was past the village by now. There were ways to build caves in the snow, to make a shelter. Chakliux had told her a story about a snow cave. . . .

Her mind worked so slowly that her thoughts seemed as thin and foolish as dreams. They dig, they stop and dig and . . . But they have dogs in the stories. Don't they have dogs? To help dig? No, perhaps not. Wolves? Bears? Fool, who would share a den with a bear?

Suddenly the wind and snow were dark, as solid as the earth. She hit hard against that blackness, then slid down, forcing splinters from the branches through her mitten and into the palm of her hand. Then she was in the snow, buried by it, the softness folding over her head like water, cutting away the wind but also taking her breath. She drew in a mouthful, felt it burn her lungs. She battled to her feet and realized that she had run into a lodge.

She began to laugh, high foolish laughter. Then there were people around her. She looked into the faces of Cousin Village hunters. Tikaani and Black Caribou, Runner and Speaks First. She had found the hunters' lodge.

"You are not hurt?" Tikaani asked, bending over her.

Then Aqamdax's thoughts were clear, as though she had not made the hard journey for wood, as though it was a day without winds or snow or deep, harsh cold.

She tilted her head toward the tree top she had dragged from the forest. "I thought of you," she said to the men. "I know you must spend much time hunting. I thought I should bring you wood."

Chapter
Thirty-nine

"You know Star does not take care of Night Man, and my mother . . ." Tikaani lifted his hands. Why say anything more? His mother had lost too much, too quickly.

"Aqamdax is a slave. She has no lodge, nothing. Where will they live?" Black Caribou asked.

"With my mother and Star."

"Who will hunt for them? Night Man barely has the strength to walk across the village. Is it not enough that you must bring meat for your mother and Star and those children Star decided she must have?"

"I feed Aqamdax already," Tikaani said, and after a moment Black Caribou nodded, though he said nothing about K'os and the fact that Tikaani also supplied much of the meat that went to that woman's lodge.

"Then if you think you can get her, do what is best. She is a hard worker. I still do not know how she managed to bring that wood to the hunters' lodge. Do you know that she came back later to cut and stack it?"

"Night Man told me."

Black Caribou narrowed his eyes as though he had just thought of something. "Does Night Man want a wife?" he asked.

"What man does not want a wife?" Tikaani replied. He did not mention the argument he and Night Man had had about K'os's slave woman. When Night Man was strong enough to hunt again, then he could throw her away and take another woman, or if she had pleased him, keep her and take a second wife. Night Man had finally agreed, but was still worried that a Sea Hunter woman would change his luck.

A foolish thing to worry about! It would be a good thing if she did. Their family had had nothing but bad luck since Chakliux had convinced Cloud Finder to give the Near Rivers some of his golden-eyed dogs.

Tikaani and Black Caribou left the hunters' lodge, walked together to Black Caribou's lodge.

The storm had lasted for three days, but now the sky was the clear high blue that sometimes comes in mid-winter, a cold day when breathing curls the inside of the nose and makes the lungs ache.

"You will go to K'os now?" Black Caribou asked as he ducked into the entrance tunnel.

"Yes."

Black Caribou shook his head, chuckled deep in his throat

Tikaani said nothing, but he understood what the man meant. Asking K'os would be the most difficult part. More difficult because he had not visited her for many days. He was too busy, had too many people to hunt for, too many worries. Besides, he had filled her cache that fall, even before he filled his share of the hunters' cache, before he gave meat to his mother and sister. Why should K'os complain when he had given her so much? But he wondered what it would cost him to win his brother a wife.

K'os threw the scrap of caribou hide at Aqamdax and screamed out her frustration. Her hands ached so badly she could not even grip the needle. Worse, her fingers had begun to turn in on themselves, and now she could not straighten them. They looked like claws, hooked and deformed. She had tried all the medicines she knew, but winter limited her. There were roots and leaves that were best used fresh, and she would not be able to find those until spring.

K'os had thought it would be a good winter. With her husband, Ground Beater, dead, she thought other hunters would be more likely to visit her, but those hunters had not come, not even Tikaani, though he had brought meat. The few men who did visit usually asked for Aqamdax. And if they pretended to want K'os, their eyes still strayed to the Sea Hunter woman. Were they fools? Aqamdax had no power to give them. She was only Sea Hunter, only a slave.

Someone scratched outside the lodge. K'os heard a hunter's voice. Tikaani. She hid her hands under a hare fur robe, then invited him inside.

He stood before her, and she lowered her eyelids, met his eyes, then looked away quickly, an insult most women learned when they were still young. What else should he expect? He had not come to visit her for a moon of days or longer. She lifted her chin and looked at him, but did not get up to give him food or water, did not offer a place by the hearth fire.

She knew Aqamdax was watching her, saw the indecision in the woman's eyes. Should she be the one to offer food? Should she fetch water?

"I have come to speak to you about something important, K'os," Tikaani finally said.

K'os held a smile in her cheek, hid it well behind her teeth. She had forced him to speak first, to break silence rudely and thus give her the advantage of his disrespect.

She sat quietly for a time, enjoyed the discomfort she saw in Tikaani's eyes, the confusion she felt coming from her slave as Aqamdax waited for K'os's orders. Finally K'os nodded her head toward the caribou boiling bag where a thick soup of meat, broth and dried berries simmered.

K'os and Tikaani ate in silence, Aqamdax standing behind them. K'os knew the woman would jump at the snap of her fingers, bring water or more food, even hurry outside to fetch firewood. K'os had learned how to control her. Anger and blows did not work with this one, and it had taken a few days of frustration for K'os to finally understand what would, but since then, all things had been easy. Very easy.

"So what is it you want to tell me?" K'os finally said, making sure she asked the question just as Tikaani had lifted the bowl to his lips and filled his mouth.

Again, she held a smile behind her teeth as she watched Tikaani struggle to swallow quickly, then nearly choke on his meat.

"I have come to find my brother Night Man a wife."

"You think I will marry a cripple, someone who cannot hunt, who cannot even fish in the summer with the old men?"

As soon as the words were out of her mouth, K'os realized that Tikaani had not meant her but the slave Aqamdax. In horror she saw the corners of his mouth curl, saw his shoulders shake with silent laughter. When was the last time anyone had laughed at her? Not since she was a girl. Was Tikaani such a fool that he did not know her power? Had he forgotten the sacred weapon she had stolen from old Blue Jay? Had he forgotten the price she had been willing to pay for that?

"You have taught me too well, K'os," Tikaani said to her. "There is not a man in this village who would dare ask you to be wife." His words were as smooth as oil.

K'os narrowed her eyes, trying to see through those words, to discern other meanings under what he said.

"Not even you?" she asked him.

"What do I have to offer? I have a sister and mother, two children and a brother to hunt for. Perhaps I will also have to provide for my brother's wife. How can I ask for a woman like you when I have so little to give?"

K'os pressed her lips together. It would be good to believe him. Perhaps she did believe him, but it would be best if he did not know it.

She crossed her arms over her chest, hid her hands under her sleeves and laughed. Then, still smiling, she said, "The woman has already gathered enough wood for me to last the winter, and I am tired of feeding her. What do you offer me in exchange?"

"What do you want?"

"What I truly want cannot happen until spring. I assume your brother wants the woman before that."

"Yes."

"Ah, then," she said, and looked at Aqamdax, did not miss the shine that had come into the woman's eyes, "there are several things. Have her make me three more baskets. You have seen her grass baskets?"

"I have seen them."

"Three of those—large ones. I want wolf pelts. Two. Well-scraped. And you will fill my cache this spring, when the caribou pass through again."

Tikaani nodded, looked at Aqamdax. "You will make the baskets?" he asked.

"Yes, I will make them."

"Soon," K'os said.

"Soon," Aqamdax repeated.

"I will fill the cache this spring. I have one of the wolf skins. A black one. I will get another."

"Black is good," K'os said.

"If I bring it to you now, may I take her?"

K'os turned and looked at Aqamdax, let her eyes linger long on the woman's face. She was a good slave, a hard worker, but K'os did not like her. She did what she was told, took the men K'os sent her into her bed, had even braved a storm to bring back wood.

She was a beautiful woman, too, although her beauty was almost too strange to appreciate. When the eyes grew accustomed, then it was apparent.

But her spirit was not the spirit of a slave. That was the worst thing, and nothing K'os had done to her had yet changed that. Perhaps it would be best to let her have a sickly husband. Allow her to discover how difficult it was to care for someone who could never hunt or protect her, who could not give status by his deeds.

Of course, there was one thing yet K'os could do, only a small thing really, not close to the threats she had made against those River children, Yaa and Ghaden.

"Well then, if she will go, you can have her." K'os stood up and turned to face Aqamdax. "You have seen Night Man," K'os said to her.

"Yes," Aqamdax said softly, but the flashing in her eyes belied the quietness of her answer.

"He has not recovered from an injury to his shoulder—something my own son did to him, something that lies like stone against my heart. Perhaps by offering you I will repay in part what my son has done. But like all women, you have a choice. Stay here with me if you wish or go if you wish. Either way, I am happy."

Aqamdax waited before giving her answer. She had lived with K'os long enough to know that the woman did not offer good things without reason, and most often that reason was to rejoice in the disappointment when that gift was taken away. Be wife? Yes, to get out of this lodge, she would be wife to any man, old or young, sick or healthy. From what Tikaani had said, by becoming Night Man's wife she would live in the same lodge as Ghaden and Yaa. Surely, K'os could see the wanting in her eyes, the hope there. And what gave K'os more pleasure than destroying hope?

Finally she said, "I will be wife to Night Man," and the image of the man's thin, white face came to her mind.

For some reason, at the same time, she also saw Chakliux's face, but she forced that image away. If the man had cared about her, he would have come for her—long before this.

"When do you want me?"

"Take her now," K'os said, cutting off whatever answer Tikaani would have given. "Do you think I want to feed her longer than I must?"

"I can take you now," Tikaani said, but Aqamdax could see by the look on his face that he had not intended for her to come with him at that time, and she wondered if he had spoken yet to Night Man. "Come to the hunters' lodge when you are ready, but do not go inside. Call and I will come out to you."

Tikaani had already ducked his head into the tunnel when K'os cleared her throat and said, "There is one more thing I would ask." She paused and smiled at Aqamdax. "There is a dog that comes some nights to my lodge. I believe he even sleeps in my entrance tunnel. I do not want him there. Bring him to me for my cooking bag. I will add his meat to my caribou stew."

Aqamdax opened her mouth but could find no words. What good would words do anyway? she asked herself. What K'os said was true. The dog slept in the entrance tunnel—something dogs were not supposed to do.

"Do you know who owns him?" Tikaani asked.

"He came with that girl from the Near Rivers."

"Ah, Ghaden's dog," Tikaani said. "He will not want the dog to be killed. It has been trained to protect him. You are sure it is that one? He is a dog who obeys commands. It seems that if Ghaden wanted him to stay home, he . . ." Tikaani's words trailed into silence, and he looked at Aqamdax. "So this dog protects others besides Ghaden," he said.

Aqamdax tried to think of some way to save Biter. Perhaps the only thing she could do was refuse to go as bride. No, K'os would use Aqamdax's refusal against her, just as she was now using her acceptance. Either way, something would happen to the dog or—perhaps worse—to Ghaden or Yaa.

"Bring me the dog and the first of the wolf pelts, and she is yours . . . or your brother's," K'os said.

"I will be back tonight with both," Tikaani told her, but Aqamdax stepped forward, held a hand out toward the man, careful not to touch him.

"Not tonight," she said quietly. "When you came to this lodge, I was just about to tell K'os that I must go to the moon blood lodge."

K'os hissed. "You might have cursed him had he brought a weapon. How could you be so careless?"

"Among my people, we do not separate ourselves except in first bleeding."

"Leave us then," K'os said, flicking her fingers toward Aqamdax.

Aqamdax slipped on her parka and picked up the grass basket she had been working on. The days in the women's lodge would give her uninterrupted time to finish it.

Tikaani followed her from K'os's lodge, called to her. He came closer than she thought he would, close enough so she could hear his quiet words.

"You do not bleed," he said.

She shook her head. "But this will give me five days. Perhaps I can think of some way to save Biter."

He shrugged his shoulders. "What is a dog? I will give the boy another—a golden-eye."

"Please let me try."

Again Tikaani shrugged. "Do what you want. I will tell my brother you will come to him in five days. It is custom among our people for a bride to make something for her husband. Perhaps boots."

"I have nothing to make them with."

"I will bring something."

She watched him walk away from her, then went to the moon blood lodge. It was a good place, a quiet place, and though the women there seldom spoke to her, she did not care. It gave her opportunity to be away from K'os.

She would weave and decide how she might save Biter. She would also make boots for Night Man. She had made several pairs in the manner of the River People. These for Night Man she would also decorate, and in that way show him she was glad to be his wife. Her designs would have to follow those of her own people. A woman did not take another woman's design. Patterns were passed as gift from mother or grandmother, and so she owned no River People designs, but perhaps Night Man would find there was strength in the designs of the First Men, power that would recall the strength of sea mammals, swimming through long days toward the warmth of summer.

THE FIRST MEN VILLAGE

Chakliux closed his eyes and listened as the old woman began her story. In all the months he had been at the First Men's village, it was the only time Qung had allowed him to come into her ulax.

It had been a long journey to the First Men Village. After hearing Yaa's story, he was sure the Walrus Hunters had taken Aqamdax, and so had first stopped at the Walrus Hunter Village. He had little hope that he could arrive in time to stop them if they planned revenge, but if he could not save Aqamdax, perhaps he could find Ghaden. Besides, how could he wait and do nothing?

The Walrus had not welcomed him, but neither did they seem to blame him for what had happened with Aqamdax. He had spent three days with them, asking hunters, women, even children about Aqamdax and Ghaden. They all claimed to know nothing, but late one night Sun Beater, a son of the dead shaman, came to him, spoke to him about the First Men hunters who had passed their village only a few days before Chakliux had arrived.

They had not stopped to trade, Sun Beater claimed, an unusual thing for First Men, and so he had taken out his iqyax, had followed them. He said he did not get close, but thought he saw a woman in one of the iqyan, perhaps a woman in each. He had not been sure.

Almost, then, Chakliux had returned to his own village. If Aqamdax's own people had come to get her, what chance was there that she would want him? But since he had come such a distance toward the First Men Village, why not go on? Why not see if she was willing to be his wife? If she would not return to the Near River Village with him, perhaps the First Men would allow him to live in their village. They had welcomed him as trader, why not husband?

If he did not find Aqamdax, or if she refused him, he could at least stay with them for the winter, trading caribou hides from summer kills for meat and a place in a First Men ulax. He had battled autumn storms, spent days hunkered under the iqyax, trying to escape rain and wind, but finally he had come to the wide inlet that led to the First Men Village. They had welcomed him as trader, surprised to have him come so near winter. His queries about Aqamdax had brought the storyteller Qung and several other women to him the first day.

Qung had asked about Aqamdax, soon managed to find out that Sok had thrown her away as wife and that Chakliux was seeking her. The other women had begun a mourning song, but Qung had quieted them with dark looks and angry words. Also that first day, Tut had greeted Chakliux as friend and invited him to live with her family.

For most of the winter, Qung had avoided him and had, through Tut, told Chakliux he was not welcome in her ulax, not even during storytelling evenings.

This evening the village was celebrating a feast of ancient hunters and warriors, of people long dead. To Chakliux's surprise, Qung had asked him to come. As storyteller, Chakliux had accepted the invitation, though Tut had warned that Qung might plan some way to embarrass him.

"I have been embarrassed before, Aunt," Chakliux had told her, speaking in the First Men tongue, earning a smile from Tut.

"You know you cannot sit with the men. You are not a Sea Hunter."

"So then, Aunt, will you be embarrassed if I sit with you?"

"I will not be embarrassed," Tut had said, and now they sat together in the women's row in Qung's ulax.

Qung's climbing log had been strung with lines of seal bladders, blown full of air and tied to cover each step. He had known what to expect when he saw a crowd of children gathered on the roof, hiding their giggles behind their hands. Aqamdax had told him about this trick, and that the best thing was to laugh also, enjoy the joke, even if it made you fall.

He looked down into the ulax, feigned surprise and broke into a garbled combination of First Men and River languages. Finally he asked the children what he should do.

They told him he must climb down. He planted his feet firmly, popping two bladders before deciding he could make a good act of slipping off the log to the floor. The children's voices floated down to him as he lay looking up, unhurt and able, after catching his breath, to join them in laughter. He glanced at Qung, whose face was impassive, almost stern, but then she lifted her chin slightly at him, acknowledging his performance.

When the storytelling began, Qung's voice, as strong as if she were a young woman, filled the ulax, and now, many stories later, she still spoke, giving herself a rest only now and again to allow the chief hunter to tell of hunts, those recent and some remembered from the past.

She had said nothing derogatory about Chakliux, nothing in anger about the River People, though one story mentioned a River People child raised by the First Men who taught them to hunt land animals, a skill they had forgotten when they lived on islands far to the west.

Suddenly, Qung looked at him, and even in the dimly lit ulax, he could see the fire in her eyes. "There is another storyteller here," she said, "though he calls himself a trader. Storytellers always recognize one another. We are a people of too many words. We make our living by theft, taking ideas from everyone around us, pulling stories from other people's lives. You admit to such thievery, River Man?" she asked.

"No," Chakliux answered. "I am storyteller, as you have said, but not a thief. Rather I am trader, exchanging story for story, and I am weaver, twining bits and scraps of words into whole baskets able to hold ideas and the remembrance of lives lived long ago."

Qung's eyes, so tiny in a face full of wrinkles, winked at him, and he thought she might smile. She did not, but he heard the beginning of laughter deep in her throat when she said, "Do you have one of these stories you might give in trade?"

Aqamdax had told him many First Men stories, stories that Qung, for all her talking, had not yet told. He could tell River People stories or legends he had learned from Caribou and Walrus and North Tundra People, but there was another tale he decided to tell them—a story they needed to know if Aqamdax ever returned to them, if she brought her small brother Ghaden with her.

"Look! What do I see?" he said, then explained that elders in his village used riddles to teach their children and to say things that could not be politely said in other ways. "From afar, it looks black. When it is close, you can see through it."

He did not expect an answer, but Qung said, "A feather. A cormorant feather." Then, plucking at the front of her sax, she lifted a feather and held it close to her face, reminding those who might question that the eye can see through a feather, just as it can see through its own lashes.

Chakliux nodded his approval of her answer, then said, "So it is when we look at the way others live their lives. We see more clearly when we look more closely." Then he began the story of Daes, as Aqamdax had told him.

When he finished his story, there was a murmur of approval, and later, long into the night, when the stories were finished and the people were leaving the ulax, Qung caught his hand before he left, pulled him to the back of the ulax and asked, "Do you know who killed the woman?"

"I do not," Chakliux said.

"Those River People, they will not kill Aqamdax?"

"She is no longer with them."

"Tut says you do not know where she is. Why do you search for her?"

"I want her to be my wife."

"So in spring you will leave here and continue to search?"

"Yes, I will return to the River People and try to find her."

"She might be dead."

"She might be."

Qung sighed, turned away from him, mumbling. "I told her not to go."

Chakliux was halfway up the climbing log when Qung called to him. "If you find her, come back here. We need good storytellers in this village."

"I will come, Aunt," Chakliux told her. "I have much to learn."

Chapter Forty

THE COUSIN RIVER VILLAGE

Aqamdax hoped she might have an opportunity to slip out of the moon blood lodge at night, in darkness make her way to Star's lodge, to whisper her plan to Yaa. Each night the women took turns getting firewood, tending the hearth. The second night was Aqamdax's turn. Who would notice if she was gone longer than it takes to get an armful of wood?

Then Third Daughter had come, she and her baby. It was unusual for a nursing mother to have bleeding times. Usually a baby kept the blood from flowing so the next child waiting would know it could not come until the older one was weaned. But though Third Daughter's baby was still small, her milk had almost dried up and her bleeding had started again. Some taboo broken, the other women in the lodge told her.

Third Daughter rocked her baby, giving him her breast to try to stop his wailing, but still he cried, all day and most of the night. How could Aqamdax slip away when Third Daughter's baby kept them all awake?

Aqamdax spent her time weaving a basket, but her thoughts were always on Biter, her chest full with the ache of Ghaden's sorrow.

She reminded herself that the dog was fortunate to be alive. It was a hard winter, and soon they would begin killing dogs for food. Would they choose to kill one of their own before Biter? If she could just get away from the lodge, for only a little while, if she could have a moment to speak to Yaa . . .

The doorflap was pulled aside; a gust of cold air swirled into the lodge. Third Daughter's baby stopped crying, held his breath against the cold, and in the sudden silence Aqamdax looked up, saw Star with Yaa behind her, the two letting in the winter air until Star stepped inside and allowed the doorflap, weighted with stones, to fall down into place.

Star went to the back of the lodge, and Yaa followed her, carrying food and sewing supplies. Aqamdax returned to her weaving, kept her head bent over her basket, but from the corners of her eyes she watched until Star had settled herself, had flicked her fingers for Yaa to leave. Then, Aqamdax stood and said, "I will bring in wood."

She did not bother to put on her outer parka. She was afraid Yaa would slip away before she had a chance to catch her. But she found Yaa waiting for her, the girl crouched down with her back to the wind. "You and Ghaden are all right?" Aqamdax asked.

"It is a good time for us, when Star is in the women's lodge," Yaa told her.

"It is not too difficult to take care of Star's mother?"

"She mostly sits. Sometimes she sews. Sometimes she holds Ghaden. She eats when I give her food and goes with me when I lead her to the women's place. Star is not so easy."

"Yaa, I have something important to tell you," Aqamdax said. "Tikaani has asked K'os to let me be Night Man's wife."

Yaa's eyes grew large. She clapped her mittened hands and said, "You would live with us?"

"Yes."

Yaa opened her mouth as though to scream out her joy, but Aqamdax hushed her. "There is a problem. K'os has asked a bride price. She wants Biter."

"She would take Biter? She has dogs."

Aqamdax pressed her lips together, bit at the insides of her cheeks. "She wants Biter dead. She has asked that they bring him to her for food."

"Biter? No! Ghaden couldn't stand it."

"Listen, Yaa, even if I turn down Tikaani's offer . . ."

"You can do that?"

"Be quiet and listen. I have to go back in soon. They will take Biter for food anyway, not yet but soon. The caches are getting low and winter has been hard. We have to show them that he is a dog worth keeping.

"I have a plan that might work, but there is something you must do. It will be easier now that Star is here." She nodded toward the women's lodge. "Tomorrow, I will leave the women's lodge. The next day Tikaani wants my answer. That morning I want you to feed Biter and feed him well, then take him out to K'os's trapline and leave him there. Afterward, go back and dress Ghaden warmly and make him play outside. Keep him outside until Biter comes back. You can do that?"

"Yes."

Star's voice, raised in complaint, came to them through the lodge walls. "I have to go inside," Aqamdax said. "Do not forget. Two days from now. In the morning."

"I will do it."

Aqamdax scooped up an armload of wood, then crawled back into the lodge. She set the wood near the door, then listened to Star's complaints about the snow she had brought in, the cold, and the laziness of those people who called themselves Sea Hunters.

When Aqamdax left the moon blood lodge and returned to K'os, the woman barely spoke to her. Aqamdax brought in wood, melted snow for water, fed K'os's dogs, then she offered to check the traplines.

"You only want to steal my food for your husband," K'os said.

Aqamdax lowered her head, pulled on her boots. The woman was right. She did plan to steal food, but only one hare. Her stomach twisted as she suddenly pictured each snare gaping and empty.

"I will bring back what I find," Aqamdax said, then pulled on her parka. She took a pair of snowshoes from the lodge entrance and carried them as she walked through the village to Star's lodge. Yaa was outside.

"Do I bring Biter now?" Yaa whispered as Aqamdax walked by.

"Not until I am out of the village," Aqamdax said, stooping to put on the snowshoes. "Take him to K'os's traps and stay with him until he is following my trail, then go back and get Ghaden ready."

She straightened and went on.

The first snare was empty, the string still tied into its loop with fine strands of grass. The next snare held a hare, stiff and frozen. Aqamdax sighed her relief, loosed it from the snare, brushed off the snow, and slipped it under her parka to thaw. The rest of the trapline was empty.

Aqamdax started back toward the village, and at the halfway point, stopped to wait for Biter. Yaa should have released him by now.

Aqamdax waited until the cold began to seep into her feet, then finally she walked to the next snare, and the next. Still Biter did not come. Could Yaa have forgotten? No, Yaa was as reliable as any grown woman. Most likely, Biter had been distracted by some animal.

She decided to see if she could find Biter's tracks. If he had followed some animal into the woods, she might yet find him. At the edge of the woods, she found his trail, then noticed that there was another line of tracks a short distance to her left. They were Biter's. He had turned and doubled back.

Fool! Aqamdax said to herself. Do you think your plan would have worked anyway? Someone would have realized the hare was killed by a snare rather than a dog, even if you thawed it enough to make it look like a fresh kill.

She had taught Biter when he was half-grown to hunt small animals and bring them back to her or Ghaden, but in this village, he was almost always tied. He had not hunted for a long time. Even if she had been able to get him to take the hare back to Ghaden, some old woman would probably claim Biter had robbed her snares.

She pulled the hare from her parka and tied it on the stringer she had fastened to a belt at her waist, then continued to the village. She rounded the curved path that led to Star's lodge, then stopped. A small group of women were gathered outside the lodge. Then she saw Biter. The dog sat on his haunches, his head lifted, tongue out. A large hare, its neck discolored with blood, was lying on the ground beside him, left at the entrance of the lodge, just as a hunter leaves his kill for his wife.

Several of the older women turned, saw Aqamdax and looked away, but she could hear what they said to one another, so was able to understand that Biter had brought the hare to Ghaden, the boy sitting outside the lodge, digging in the snow, playing as children play.

Finally one of the younger women turned to Aqamdax, asked her, "This dog, did it come from the Near River Village?"

"Yes. One of the elders gave him to Ghaden."

Then many women were asking questions: How old was Biter? Who had taught him to hunt? Did the animal ever eat his kill and refuse to give it to the boy?

Aqamdax answered the questions as best she could, hiding a smile in her cheek when she realized that some of the older women were speaking to her for the first time, women who usually would not consider talking to a slave, let alone a slave owned by K'os.

Finally, as the group got larger, several men joined them, and they, too, began to ask questions. Aqamdax heard Tikaani's voice, the man working his way to the center of the crowd until he stood before the dog. His words were for Biter, a quick praise, something one hunter might say to another. He leaned forward, reached for the hare.

Biter bared his teeth, growled and set one paw over the animal, then he picked it up in his mouth, dragged it to Ghaden's lap and dropped it.

Tikaani tilted his head back and laughed.

"Who taught the dog to hunt like this?" he asked, and Yaa, standing beside Ghaden, one hand lying on her brother's shoulder, lifted her small chin toward Aqamdax and, speaking in a clear voice, said, "Our sister, Aqamdax."

The next night Aqamdax was no longer slave but wife. Ignoring K'os's angry eyes, she moved her few belongings into Star's lodge, then helped Night Man move his things from the hunters' lodge. Even Star's mother, Long Eyes, seemed to come out of the strange dreaming world she lived in and prepared food, though she called Ghaden by one of her dead son's names. She seemed not to see Aqamdax, even walked into her several times, then pulled back, startled but staring through her, as though Aqamdax were as clear as water.

That night, after Tikaani had left the lodge and Ghaden and Yaa were asleep—Biter, in his new status as hunter, was now allowed to sleep in Ghaden's bed—Aqamdax rolled out her mats beside those of her husband.

Though she had lived with the River People for nearly a year, she had never grown accustomed to the way they slept, all in one place, with no curtains to close off sleeping areas, to separate husbands and wives from other members of the family. She noticed that in politeness Star and Long Eyes had turned their backs on them, unlike K'os, who seemed to derive some strange pleasure from watching when Aqamdax had been forced to please a man. But why judge the Cousin People by K'os?

Aqamdax sat down beside Night Man. He was lying against a backrest of woven willow, his bad shoulder cushioned with a pad of soft wolf fur. He was thin and pale, a tall man with a large beaked nose that grew straight out from the bridge and bent halfway down so it reminded Aqamdax of an elbow. His eyes were the lighter brown of the River People, the same color as Chakliux's eyes, and they were

set deeply into their sockets. His mouth was full and wide and sometimes quirked up into a short quiet laugh, and she had noticed that
when the pain from his shoulder was most severe, he pressed his lips
together, drawing them tight across his teeth.

Unlike the First Men, the River People made a ceremony of marriage, more than just a father or uncle pushing the hunter and woman
together in laughter into a sleeping place. They had been given a blessing of words, then afterward a feast celebration. Since Night Man
could not bear the jostling of a crowd, he and Aqamdax had stayed in
the lodge, waited for village people to come to them.

Aqamdax had no new clothes for the celebration, though Star gave
her a slim belt of caribou hide embroidered with red-dyed caribou hair
and small disk beads made of shell. Aqamdax had allowed her hair to
hang loose, had worn her hoodless inner parka, ground squirrel fur
facing out, and tied the belt at her waist. Star's mother had stayed in
the lodge with them, humming some strange song that sounded like
wind moaning.

Night Man, like most hunters, spoke only when necessary. When
they were first in the lodge, alone except for Long Eyes, Aqamdax had
leaned close to her new husband, whispered, "Thank you for making
me your wife." But even then he only grunted, nodded, averted his
eyes.

For a brief moment she thought of Chakliux, a man with whom
she had discussed many things, had argued and joked and made riddles. She fingered the twisted string of sinew she still wore on her
wrist. K'os had not deemed it worth taking, unlike Aqamdax's necklaces. Aqamdax's sudden longing for Chakliux, his gentle wit, his stories, was as sharp as a knife, but she reminded herself of her life with
K'os, the nights she was forced to take men into her bed, the cold days
she was sent on foolish errands. Then she could see Night Man only
with gratitude, could only be glad she was no longer slave.

Yaa turned on her bed and squeezed her eyes shut. She did not
want Aqamdax or Night Man to think she was watching them, though
she was curious about what they would do on this first night together.
She had seen her father in bed with her mother when she was very
small, had watched them moving together and sometimes heard them
make happy moans in their throats. She wondered if it would be the
same with Aqamdax and Night Man.

Night Man did not look strong like most hunters. He walked
slowly and used a walking stick like her father had. Night Man was
young, but he did not seem young. He had been hurt somehow, one

of the Cousin River girls had told her, though mostly the girls would not play with her, seldom spoke to her. That was all right. She had enough to do, trying to please Star and take care of Ghaden, and, until today, worry about Aqamdax. It would be better now, though she felt sorry that Aqamdax had to be wife to a man who was probably too sick to hunt, a man who smelled strange, almost like rotten meat.

She could hear the two whispering together, then Aqamdax was on her knees in front of Night Man and the two of them pulled off his shirt. Yaa forgot to keep her eyes closed, opened them wide when Night Man cried out as the shirt slipped over his shoulder. A wave of the rotten meat smell wafted across the lodge, then Aqamdax was helping Night Man settle himself against the backrest.

Yaa suddenly remembered she was supposed to be asleep. She closed her eyes and listened as hard as she could, even slowing her breath so it would not cover the sounds of their voices.

She heard a rustle next to her bed, then realized Aqamdax was beside her.

"I know you are pretending, sister," Aqamdax said, but her voice was gentle. "Open your eyes and help me."

Slowly Yaa opened her eyes.

"Where does Star keep the medicines?" Aqamdax asked. "Where does she keep scraped hides?"

Yaa scrambled out of her bedding furs and brought Aqamdax an armful of hides, some with fur, some without. Aqamdax chose a few smaller ones, well-scraped on both sides.

Yaa stood and watched as Aqamdax moved cooking stones into the hearth coals and stoked the fire. "My husband is sick, and I do not want to wait until morning to help him," she told Yaa, then poured water into an empty cooking bag, ready to add the stones when they were hot.

"Will he die?" Yaa asked.

"No, he will not die," Aqamdax told her. "I will not let him."

K'os had not gone to the feast. Why celebrate? What respect would come from allowing a woman, not even human, to be wife? Besides, who could say where Aqamdax's loyalty would lie? She had lived with the Near Rivers. If she heard K'os's plans, would she somehow contrive to warn them? There was little danger that she could do so now, when both villages were in winter camps, but what if the young hunters decided, after this hard winter, that they were not strong enough to fight in the spring? Then they would have to wait through the summer—what good would it do to attack when so many families were scattered to various fish camps? But during summer, there were times when Near River and Cousin River People were less than half a day's walk apart. What would keep Aqamdax from slipping away to warn them?

Of course, K'os might be able to convince the hunters to attack before the village families went to their fish camps. If she could not do that, she would have to kill the Sea Hunter woman. That would be difficult, especially now that Aqamdax lived in a lodge with many other people. If food was poisoned, too many would die; others in the village might be suspicious. She had to be more careful now. She had used poison too freely when she was young. But she had found that sometimes there were better ways to achieve revenge than by killing, and often there were better ways to kill than by doing it herself.

Aqamdax used hot poultices to draw out the poison in Night Man's shoulder. The wound had rotted deep into the muscle of his arm. There were painful lumps in his neck and down his side, even at the joint between his left leg and groin. She was able to draw some of the poison out, and by morning he said the pain was less. Even his eyes were clearer.

"You are a healer," he had whispered during the night, but she had told him she was only a wife.

Near morning, Night Man slept, and Aqamdax also allowed herself a few moments of sleep, listening, even through her dreams, to the sound of his breathing.

She awoke with Star standing over them, her nose wrinkled at the wooden bowl of clotted blood and pus.

Star poked Aqamdax with one toe and asked, "What did you do to him?"

"I cleaned his wound," Aqamdax answered, and sat up. She had slept in her ground squirrel parka, without bedding furs, content to be inside a warm lodge.

"I do not want Ghaden to see this mess," Star said.

Aqamdax nodded. Star was right. It would not be a good thing. She put on her outer parka and carried the bowl and the worst of the hide rags to the refuse pile just beyond the women's place.

When she returned to the lodge, Night Man was awake. His eyes brightened when he saw her, and he held out his good hand. "Wife," he said, and the word was warm in Aqamdax's heart. "I am hungry."

"You know where our cache is?" Star asked her.

"Yes."

"Good. Get what you need for him and yourself. Most of what we had in the lodge was eaten last night."

The cache was close to K'os's, a square of logs held high on log legs. It was a strange way to keep food, Aqamdax thought, but then the River People did most things in strange ways. Their boats were rafts of trees tied together. They were so heavy, it took several men to carry one around rapids and shallow water.

Each cache had a ladder—two long poles tied together with cross-bars made of stout branches. They were easy to climb, even with an armload, and could easily be taken down so animals did not get into the cache. She climbed up, untied the door string and opened the cache. It was still at least half full. Even K'os's did not have that much meat, and K'os made sure any man who slept with her or Aqamdax paid in caribou or fish.

Aqamdax pulled out a caribouskin storage container, opened it and removed a frozen chunk of meat. Near the door were baled stacks of dried and frozen fish. She took several fish to give to Biter.

She stopped at the top of the cache and looked carefully around, checking for clouds of frozen breath that might mean wolves or a loose dog had followed and were waiting for her to come down with meat, but there was nothing except the drift of smoke from the roof holes of each lodge and the gray twilight of morning. She fastened the door and climbed down.

Walking back to the lodge, she met other women. She lowered her head, prepared to hear their abusive words, as she had every morning, tongues clicking against the roofs of their mouths as they spoke about the strangeness of those who were not River People. But this morning the women greeted her as they greeted one another. One even stopped to ask how Night Man was feeling. Then Aqamdax saw K'os, the woman walking toward her, eyes straight ahead, as though no one was worthy of her gaze.

One of the children had told Aqamdax that K'os was old, and she must be, to be Chakliux's mother, but her face did not look old. Only her hands, gnarled and dark, told of her age. Aqamdax held her head high, meeting the woman as wife to widow. She expected that K'os would pass her as she had other women, without speaking, without even a flash of the eyes to show recognition, but she stopped, extended a mittened hand and said, "Tikaani tells me your husband is in much pain."

"The wound has never healed," Aqamdax said, hoping her words were not an insult to the one recognized as healer. When K'os said nothing, Aqamdax, too eager to fill the quietness between them, asked,

"Does this village have a shaman who knows the chants and prayers that might drive away evil spirits?"

K'os's eyes darkened. "He died last fall," she said. "Right after we returned from our summer fish camp. He was old, but he did not know much. I have plants that will help Night Man. I gave some to his mother before winter started. If I had known he was not getting better, I would have brought more."

Surely the woman understood that giving things to Night Man's mother was worse than giving them to a child, Aqamdax thought. Besides, she did not trust K'os. She might decide to give poison rather than medicine.

"I will bring you some."

Aqamdax nodded her thanks, then continued toward Star's lodge. She would accept K'os's medicine but not give it to Night Man. Perhaps her own poultices would be enough to help him grow strong again. Aqamdax entered the lodge, saw that her husband was sitting up, his lips tightened in concentration as he and Ghaden worked together to string rawhide into the web of a snowshoe.

It is good to be wife, Aqamdax thought. Had she ever wanted anything more than that?

Chapter
Forty-one

THE NEAR RIVER VILLAGE

Sok lifted the dog's body, stood without speaking as Sleeps Long spat full into his face.

"That is what I think of your brother's dogs. That is what I think of you. If your brother ever returns to this village, tell him he owes me two handfuls of caribou skins, enough to pay for three good dogs."

Sok held in his anger. "You think I have not also lost dogs?"

"I know you have. Yours were among the first to die. But now your brother's foolishness—trying to bind us in friendship with the Cousin River People—has not only killed your dogs but also most of the dogs in the village. I have nothing more to say to you, Sok."

Sok stood holding the dog, unsure what to do. He had lost count of the dogs that had died in the past year—four handfuls? Five? He should go to Wolf-and-Raven. A shaman would know some way to lift a curse from the village, but Wolf-and-Raven was still angry with Sok for taking Snow-in-her-hair to be his second wife.

His anger was foolish. Snow-in-her-hair was happy. Sok had not forced her into his bed. She had come willingly, and he had taken her as wife when she became pregnant. He had paid the same bride price he would have had she come to him as first wife. Now she lived in Aqamdax's lodge, and Sok spent most nights there even though he could not enjoy her during her pregnancy.

The village rumors—that Snow-in-her-hair had slept with many hunters so she could get pregnant and be taken as wife—were not true. She slept only with Sok. The rumors were part of Red Leaf's plan to force Wolf-and-Raven to allow his daughter's marriage. How else would he give her to Sok unless he believed that, in her disgrace, she would never find a husband?

Wolf-and-Raven should be grateful. Did the old shaman think he was powerful enough to make his daughter a husband from stones, from twigs or mud? The many days he spent speaking to spirits seemed to cloud his mind so no one could truly understand him.

Why should Sok take the dead dog to Wolf-and-Raven? He would only berate Sok, call down curses on Chakliux.

Better to go to Blue-head Duck. Sok started toward Blue-head Duck's lodge, carrying the dog, keeping his eyes straight ahead and away from those along the path who stopped to stare. He did not scratch at the door-flap. How could he with his arms full? Blue-head Duck's old wife gasped as he came inside, as he lay the dead dog down.

Blue-head Duck was sitting near the hearth fire, a bowl of food raised to his mouth. He lowered the bowl, but his mouth stayed open.

He did not speak, so finally Sok said, "First they blamed my brother. Now they blame me. They say I do not have the gifts my grandfather had, that all our dogs will die, then worse will happen. Perhaps our children—"

"Shut your mouth!" Blue-head Duck cried out. "Do not open the spirits' ears with such words."

"Those words have already been spoken," Sok replied. "Whispered from lodge to lodge by old women who have nothing better to do."

"Whose dog is it?"

"Sleeps Long brought it to me."

"He has always prided himself on his dogs. What does he say you should do?"

"He has no advice. He only blames, as does everyone in the village."

"Did he say you should come here?"

"No."

"Then why did you? I know little about dogs. I have only the one I need to help my wife carry our supplies when we move to fish camp in the spring. I no longer hunt bear or follow the caribou. I am an old man. Why do I need dogs?"

Sok chose his words carefully. "You are the eldest of the hunters in our village. You know the prayers and chants to appease the spirits nearly as well as Wolf-and-Raven. I ask you to join your prayers and chants with mine and Wolf-and-Raven's to protect our dogs. If some disrespect has angered the spirits, perhaps that will help. The rest of us, we are like children. We do not know what to do."

As Sok spoke, Blue-head Duck straightened, then finally stood up and faced Sok, locked eyes with Sok.

"Leave the dog. I will pray until I decide what must be done."

At dusk, Ligige' left her lodge. Her arms ached and her finger joints also. She could sew only a little while, and then had to stop. She did little but sleep and eat. What good was that to the village, a woman who took a share of food but gave nothing in return?

She had decided to go to the cooking hearths, take a turn stirring so some of the younger women could get back to their lodges, and also so she could scrape away the layer of soft warm fat that coated the tops of the bags where the liquid had boiled down. She would rub it into her hands to soothe the joints, and it would be good to lick off later.

She nearly ran into Vole, Blue-head Duck's wife, who was pulling a dead dog from their lodge.

"Your dog?" Ligige' asked, and wondered why Vole had not butchered it for its meat.

"No," the woman told her, her voice muffled by the front of her parka as she bent nearly double, pulling the dog outside.

Ligige' saw Blue-head Duck's dog leap to its feet from where it was tied at the back of the lodge. It ran to the end of its rope and lunged toward the dead dog, its voice raised in a howling bark.

"Sok brought it."

"Another dog dead?"

"Yes. My husband said I was to give it to you. He has taken any curse from it, and says you can have it."

"Whose dog is it?"

"Sleeps Long gave it to Sok."

"He does not want it?"

"He told my husband to give it to someone who needs the meat."

Ligige' bent to help Vole pull the dog's body to her lodge. Ligige' thanked her, told her to give her thanks also to Blue-head Duck and to Sleeps Long, but after Vole left, Ligige' only sat and stared at the carcass. If the meat was free of curses, why did Blue-head Duck or Sleeps Long not want it? If it was so safe to eat, why would someone like Vole, whose love of dog meat was well known, give it so willingly?

All day until late into the night, Ligige' sat beside the dead dog; all day, she thought about the dogs that had died. They had not started dying until Chakliux came to the village. The people had blamed him, but now he was gone.

He had traveled to the Walrus Hunters, Happy Mouth said, to find Ghaden and Yaa, but who could believe that? Why would he go after children who were not his, not even a sister or brother, not even a cousin? Happy Mouth only hoped he went, and her hope had made her believe something that was not true. Besides, who could doubt that Aqamdax had taken Ghaden? Of course there was little chance she would survive a journey all the way back to her own people.

Red Leaf had claimed that she took Chakliux's iqyax. Who even knew Chakliux had an iqyax? It was hidden in the forest, Sok had said, but why did he hide it? It would be safer in the village.

After a few days, Red Leaf had changed her story. Walrus Hunters had taken Aqamdax, the woman said, in revenge for something she had done. If that was true, what chance did Aqamdax have of survival? If that was true, why would they have also taken Ghaden, and what had happened to Yaa?

Brown Water said Yaa had not been right in her head since Chakliux had found her, and no one knew how she had gotten hurt. Most of the women thought she had been hit by a falling branch and that after Chakliux had left the village, she had probably just wandered away on her own. Someday a hunter would find her bones.

Once Chakliux was gone, the elders claimed there was no more reason to worry about dogs. They were safe. But even without Chakliux in the village dogs were dying again. Now the people blamed Sok. They said he was not as powerful as his grandfather, that he did not know how to protect the dogs. She had heard some of the men speak out against the Cousin River dog, Snow Hawk, and the four pups Chakliux had brought from that village. Some said those dogs should be killed, but they were healthy dogs, and their owners wanted to keep them. Two had already delivered litters of strong pups, and some of those, Ligige' had heard, were also golden-eyed.

Besides, did those elders forget that the first dogs had died when Tsaani was still alive? Perhaps she should remind Blue-head Duck. He seemed to be the elder with the loudest mouth, and usually the wisest of those men whose age had earned them the respect of the village.

Strange that all the animals had died in cold weather. Strange, too, that most had seemed healthy. The ones that died were often the favorites of their owners. If there was some curse, even if it was something the spirits sent as punishment for disrespect, it would seem that the old and weak would still be the first to die.

Ligige''s thoughts began to circle, twining themselves into confusion. Her eyes burned from spending the whole day in the smoke of her lodge.

"Well, old woman," she said out loud. "You need to do something with this dog." She seemed to recall that the other dogs that died had not been eaten. Some were burned, and the pups were buried. Perhaps Blue-head Duck was afraid that the waste of meat had angered the spirits. Perhaps that was why he gave her the dog.

If she ate it and the spirits were pleased, then perhaps the deaths would stop. If she ate it and the spirits were angry, then she would be the one to suffer—she, and not some hunter or a young woman who might yet have children. The thought made her angry, then she reminded herself that this was a way to help everyone. Why complain?

She found a knife with a sharp, newly retouched stone blade. She was not strong enough to lift the carcass, to hang it from a tree limb; besides, it was too cold and dark for her to work outside. She pulled out old mats to set under the dog, then rolled it to its back and made her first cut, throat to anus. She would eat the liver and kidneys, pancreas and heart, but would set aside the intestines and belly to clean outside. Otherwise the stink would never leave her lodge.

Ignoring the pain in her joints, she worked to free the organs, then carried the belly and intestines into the entrance tunnel. They would stay cold there until she was ready to work on them. She gave the bundle one last heave to clear the inner doorflap, but lost her balance and fell forward.

She landed face down on the viscera, and cried out in disgust as the thick smell of fecal matter filled the entrance tunnel.

"Fool, fool, fool," she screeched at herself. "You should have waited until morning. There are plenty of young girls who would have helped you."

She pushed herself up, winced. She had fallen on something sharp, pierced her left hand. She crawled back inside her lodge, pulled down a bladder of water and washed away the dung. Her hand was bleeding, a puncture wound. She found a clean knife, made the cut larger. She had lived long enough to have seen such wounds fester, especially when they did not bleed enough. She washed the hand again, then sucked at the wound, drawing out more blood. She heated water, made a salve from fat and dried violet leaves, then bound it to her hand with a thick pad of caribou hide.

She pulled the dog's remains into the entrance tunnel and left them there. Enough, she told herself. Time for an old woman to sleep. She would decide what to do with the dog in the morning.

THE COUSIN RIVER VILLAGE

Two tens of days had passed since Night Man had taken Aqamdax as wife. During that time, she had gone to his bed only once, three days after their marriage ceremony. During those first three days, Night Man had grown stronger, and Aqamdax had waited for him to ask her to his bed, but when night came, he said nothing, so she went to the women's side of the lodge and rolled out her sleeping furs beside Star and Long Eyes.

The third day she had come in from gathering wood. She had brushed the snow from her parka and hung it from a lodge pole. She was cold, and she held her hands to the fire. Ghaden and Yaa were outside playing, and Star, too, was away; only Long Eyes sat, singing her strange song, staring at the lodge walls.

Night Man called Aqamdax, and she left the warmth of the hearth fire with regret.

"You want food or water?" she asked.

"No food, no water," he said softly, then held out his good hand. She knelt beside him, and he stroked her cheek.

"Are you cold?" he asked softly, then said, "It is warm here, in this bed." He lifted the furs that lay over him and held her eyes with his own. She slipped in beside him, felt herself relax as the warmth of his body enveloped her. She lay still, waiting, not sure if he wanted her body or only the comfort of having her beside him.

He turned so he could look at her, and she saw the pain his effort cost him, so she raised herself on one elbow, pressed him back against the bedding furs, and began to stroke his good arm, then his uninjured shoulder, gradually moving her hands down his body. She drew back the blankets, saw that he was ready for her, even before she touched him. She slipped off her shirt and leggings, and he raised his hand to her breasts, trailed his fingers down over her belly.

Their touching became a rhythm, and soon she moved over him, murmuring her delight, praying that somehow the joy of this union would drive away the evil of his sickness.

For two days, she thought it had. For two days, he seemed to grow even stronger, sitting up for most of each day, and once, with Tikaani's help, walking to the hunters' lodge.

Aqamdax waited in eagerness for Night Man to invite her back to his bed. She even sat down in his furs, began the first tentative strokes of lovemaking, but he only smiled, made no move to encourage her, and so to hide her embarrassment at his quiet rejection, she had moved behind him, kneaded the muscles of his back and neck, then returned to the women's side of the lodge.

Six days after their marriage ceremony, she had awakened to find Night Man frantic with strange dreams. His skin burned to the touch and his lips were cracked, scored with dried blood. Star, also awakened by Night Man's cries, piled furs and stored food, much of what was left after the marriage feast, and over Aqamdax's protests, took it to K'os's lodge.

K'os came that night. She brought one of her medicine bags—a river otter skin, the bones of the skull still in the head, the empty eyes refilled with glittering black stones, the belly bulging with packets of roots and dried plants.

"You have been giving him the medicine I sent?" she asked Aqamdax.

Before Aqamdax could answer, Star said, "I have. She was throwing it out. I saw her take it to the midden pile, so I followed and brought the packet back. I made my brother hot teas whenever Aqamdax was outside."

K'os looked at Aqamdax through half-closed eyes, curled her lips into a smirk. "You do not trust me?" she said. "You know I am a healer. I would not hurt anyone."

"You have forgotten that I lived with you, K'os," Aqamdax replied. "You will not touch my husband."

"Star?" K'os said, holding her hands out, palms up.

"Do not leave. I will get Tikaani."

Star went to the hunters' lodge, and while she was gone, Aqamdax stood over Night Man, guarding him. When Tikaani came, he asked K'os to give Night Man medicine. Aqamdax argued, then pleaded, and all the while K'os worked, boiling powders into teas, mixing roots with fat, pulling away the heat of Night Man's skin with her raven feather fan, directing it to the hearth fire smoke so it rose out of the lodge.

The next day, Night Man seemed stronger, and his fever abated, but he no longer spoke, seldom opened his eyes. Sometimes, seeing him lie so still, Aqamdax bent close until she could feel his breath against her cheek and reassure herself that he was still alive.

THE NEAR RIVER VILLAGE

Ligige' awoke from dreams of dead dogs. With glazed eyes and swollen tongues they performed one of The People's dances to appease those spirits that steal souls. They did not wear the large wooden masks of death dancers. Instead their dog faces were bare to those who watched, both the living and the dead, and their feet sank into the earth with each step, as they reached down to pull power from the ground.

Ligige' awoke breathless, and the parody of that dream-dance pulled away the sight of her lodge, its caribouskin walls strong and real.

She shuddered and pushed herself from her bed, hissing when she leaned against the palm of her left hand. She peeled away the strips of caribou skin she had used to cover her wound. A dark scab had already begun to pull the raw edges together, and no red lines told of poison trying to find its way to her heart.

She had to get the dead dog out of her lodge. She had been foolish to allow it to stay for the night. Who could say what spirits it had drawn, lying there in her entrance tunnel? She took a long breath, pushed her fingers into her stomach to see if there were any lumps or pains that had not been there the day before.

She felt nothing, only the ache of hips and hands, knees and neck, pain that comes to everyone with age, pain she had learned to live with long ago. She felt her anger rise at Blue-head Duck. What foolishness to give her the dog.

She pulled on leggings and boots, parka and mittens, then went out into the entrance. She dragged the carcass outside. Let Sleeps Long carry it away. He was strong. She was just an old woman. She returned for the innards.

They were bulky, and when she got outside, she slipped in the snow. She fell heavily on her knees, then pitched forward to her hands. She had closed her eyes when she fell, now opened them and saw that a long strip of what looked like ivory protruded from the dog's belly.

Ligige' pulled and it came out easily. It was nearly the length of her forearm, as thin as a fingernail and sharpened on both ends. One end curved up, as though it had been tightly coiled. She crawled back into the lodge, found a long-bladed knife, then came outside, squatted down and cut into the belly.

She found three strips like the first, one still partially coiled in a ball of hardened fat. She took off her mittens, pushed her hands into the belly contents, and pulled out four balls, each no larger around than a child's fist. She set them in the snow, then called to the first woman who passed by.

"Go get Blue-head Duck. Tell him Ligige' needs him. Tell him he must come now!"

The dog was not killed by spirits or disease. Did spirits wrap something as wicked as these ivory strips in fat and set them where dogs would swallow them? Did disease do such a thing?

Then Blue-head Duck was there, sputtering his outrage at being called from a warm lodge early in the morning.

"Shut your mouth and look at this," Ligige' told him.

Still muttering, he squatted beside her.

"Look. This is what killed the dog." She held up one of the balls of fat, and he took it from her, turned it in his hands.

"This? Is it poison?"

"Break it open."

He took off a mitten and stuck his thumbnail into the fat. He jumped as the coiled ivory suddenly straightened, flinging bits of fat and the sour contents of the dog's stomach into their faces.

"Have you ever seen anything like it?" Ligige' asked him.

"I have heard of it. North Tundra hunters use them to kill wolves. Wolves eat like dogs. They swallow without chewing. The heat of their bellies melts the fat and releases the strip of ivory. They bleed to death, if they are lucky. Sometimes the wound festers. . . ."

Ligige' nodded. "So there is no evil spirit killing these dogs," she said.

Blue-head Duck studied the ivory, plucked at the sharpened point with his thumbnail. "Do I tell the elders?" he finally asked.

"If you tell the elders, then soon whoever did this will know that you know."

Blue-head Duck nodded. "Perhaps I will wait, though it might cost our village more dogs. Will you keep the ivory for me, and these?" He pointed to the balls of fat that were still intact.

"I will keep them."

"Someplace cold."

"I am not a fool."

"No," he said. He smiled at her. "You are not a fool." He stood and poked at the dog with his foot. "I will get my daughter's husband to take this outside the village . . . unless you want the meat."

"No," Ligige' said. "I do not want the meat. Tell your daughter she can have it. She is carrying a child. I have only myself to feed."

When Blue-head Duck left, she placed the ivory strips and balls of fat in an old fishskin basket. She set the basket just inside her entrance tunnel, packed snow around it, then went into her lodge.

Ligige' was hungry, and her bladder was uncomfortably full, but she sat for a long time beside the hearth fire, staring into the flames.

Chapter
Forty-two

THE NORTH SEA

He had left before they said he should. The ice in the bay had gone out, driven into the North Sea by high storm winds, but when the hunters took their iqyan beyond the inlet, they said the ice still floated in chunks the size of an ulax roof. They told Chakliux there was a slush between the floes that a man could guide an iqyax through, but wind at the wrong time, in the wrong direction, might drive the floes together, crush an iqyax as if it were no more than a sea urchin shell.

They told him one moon, maybe a little more, then he should go, but Chakliux followed them into the ice, learned how to maneuver his iqyax around the floes.

He wanted to check the beaches and to stop again at the Walrus Hunter Village, to see if Aqamdax had come to them during the winter. Each night, his sleep was disturbed by dreams of her bones lying without honor somewhere between the Near River Village and this village that was her home. How could he wait?

From full moon to new moon—three handfuls of days—he had paddled without problems, a strong south wind driving the ice from the shore. Each night he had found a good beach, had slept under his iqyax, in the lee of its tight skin. But then the wind changed, packing the ice back into the beaches, and freezing the floes into a hard solid sheet, forcing Chakliux to paddle far beyond the shores.

Day turned to night and back to day again. His body ached in weariness, but he was afraid that if he slept the iqyax would turn sideways to the waves and flip him upside down in the sea. Under the guidance of Day Breaker, he had learned to right himself if he flipped, but he was still uneasy in the skill. Better to stay awake. To watch.

The First Men had taught him how to carve a bailing tube, so much easier to handle than the wooden bowl he had once used. The tube was longer than his arm, wrist to elbow, narrow at both ends, flaring out wider in the center. He could lower it into the iqyax, place his mouth over one end and suck, drawing the tube full of water. He had learned to lift the tube by clamping his teeth around it and picking up his head, then blowing the water out. The last few days in the iqyax, water had seeped in almost constantly, and he had been very glad for the bailing tube, and always afraid that a shard of ice would pierce the softening sides of his iqyax.

At the end of the next day the winds calmed, and he found a lead as wide as his iqyax was long. It stretched toward land as far as he could see, and the ice on either side of the open water was thin enough to break with his paddle. He had heard First Men stories of hunters caught in leads, their iqyan crushed when the winds shifted, but he pushed those thoughts to the back of his mind and started paddling, working as fast as he could to reach land before the calm ended. The lead soon narrowed in thickening ice, so that Chakliux had to use his hand ax to chop space enough for himself to turn around. He paddled back out to sea and in the calm waters paddled east, telling himself he did not need sleep.

Finally, he could no longer lift his arms, and he knew there was no choice but to tie his paddle to the deck of the iqyax and follow the dreams that called him.

THE COUSIN RIVER VILLAGE

K'os hid herself well so they did not know she watched. Why remind them that she held the power of life and death over every man and woman, every child? Why chance that her power would overshadow their own and consume their ability with this new weapon she had given them?

Already, few of them spoke of where their bows came from. Surely not from her. Had they not made them with their own hands? Carved the wood themselves, strengthened it with strips of caribou hide? Had they not twisted the sinew strings, made the small notched spears that those bows threw so far and so quickly?

Let them pretend. She knew who had brought the bow to their village. Surely that was enough. At least for now. At least until they had accomplished what she wanted.

She watched as the men practiced. Arrow after arrow pierced the center of the padded caribou hide they used as target. She watched and held in her joy. They were ready, and soon she would give them more than caribou hide to shoot at.

Tikaani lowered his bow and nodded his head at Three Furs. The new arrowheads were what they had needed. He felt his chest swell in pride, as though the idea had been his rather than his brother Night Man's.

Their first points had been of stone. Less than half the size of those they made for throwing spears, they had still weighed down the arrows so they curved too quickly in their flight and fell short of most targets.

Night Man had spent many days during the winter knapping various stones into arrowheads. None were light enough. Finally, he made several of bone. They were light but fragile.

It was not worth worrying about, Tikaani had told him. They could use stone heads for close targets, bone for those farther away and for smaller game, like geese. But Night Man had continued to work, and Tikaani did not discourage him, hoping that the man forgot his pain as he spent the dark winter lost in thoughts of stone and sharpness, bone and blood.

Now Tikaani studied the arrowhead his brother had made and tried not to remember that, during the past moon, Night Man had seemed to lose what little strength he had left. Aqamdax cared for her husband now as though he were a baby: cleaning him, turning him, forcing water down his throat. Almost every day, K'os brought medicine. Sometimes it seemed to help; other times it did not.

The thought of K'os made Tikaani uneasy. He needed to visit her more often. Since Ground Beater's death, he no longer found the joy he once had in her bed. Perhaps because he was now recognized as chief hunter, he did not have to prove himself worthy of the honor by claiming the old chief hunter's wife. Then, too, there were many mothers anxious for him to know their daughters. This summer he must take a wife. Why take K'os? He must choose a young woman who would bear him strong sons. He could still spend any night he chose in K'os's lodge. Perhaps even this night. . . .

He again studied the arrowhead in his hand. Night Man had carved a piece of caribou antler into a shaft as long and nearly as big around as his smallest finger. He tapered it to a point at one end and thinned it at the other so he could bind it to the arrow shaft. He had cut two vertical slits about half the length of the antler beginning at the point, one on either side of the shaft, then fitted a thin sharp edge of slate into each slit.

The arrowhead was light and strong, easier to make than knapped chert or obsidian heads.

Tikaani watched as Three Furs shot several arrows at their target. The man's aim was true, and the new arrowheads easily penetrated the caribou hide. Tikaani sighed. Three Furs was a good hunter, but Night Man should be the one here with Tikaani, trying out the new points. Night Man was the kind of hunter any village needed. Strong and loyal, with a good mind. He deserved better than what he had—a living death and a Sea Hunter wife.

Little more than a year ago they had so much. Their father, Cloud Finder, was strong and alive, honored in the village. His sister Star had two young men who wanted her as wife. His mother had been full of laughter. His brothers Caribou and Stalker were both promising young hunters. Now only he himself was left whole and unchanged.

No, not unchanged.

Someday, he would find Chakliux. He would take great pleasure in being the one who killed him. In dishonor Chakliux would die, and he and Star and K'os, they would dance on his bones.

THE NORTH SEA

Chakliux awoke with the burn of salt water in his nose. He inhaled before he could stop himself, choked and panicked. When he realized he was upside down, he began to tear at the drip skirt that held him to the iqyax, then gathered his wits enough to pull the string that freed his paddle. He was still choking, his lungs starved for air, but he swung the paddle down and back, turning his body to gain momentum. The iqyax shuddered but remained inverted.

Again, he struggled with his drip skirt, but then he asked himself how long he would live outside his iqyax in the cold of the North Sea—even if he was able to swim free. Better to die now, better to take in that next mouthful of water.

His chest heaved, and darkness edged his vision. Then he saw Aqamdax, not her bones but her face. She opened her mouth to speak, and her voice came to him as clearly as if she were with him, in the water, in the cold.

"Look, I see something." She held up one hand, and he saw the knotted sinew on her wrist, the shape of an otter head in a design of knots.

Like an otter, he twisted his body, thrust back, then forward, with his paddle. He felt the iqyax turn, rise beneath him, respond to his movement, lift him from the sea. He drew in a long breath, partially air, partially the water that streamed from his head and face. He gagged and choked. Vomited water. Choked again. Inhaled. Filled his lungs. Filled his lungs. Was alive.

THE COUSIN RIVER VILLAGE

K'os called and the boy came to her. He was young, eight summers, perhaps nine. A fine, strong boy and Fire Eater's only son—in a lodge of girls, the only son. She dangled the charm before him.

"It is something I made for you," she said.

He narrowed his eyes. A smart one, this boy, and that was why she had chosen him. A promise, he was, for the whole village. A boy like this might well be chief hunter someday. He had already been taken on a bear hunt, a rare honor for one so young. His first kill had not been a yellowlegs—that small, weak bird that was first-kill feast for so many boys. A lynx had been stalking him and his youngest sister, and the boy had killed it, earning himself a new name.

"Lynx Killer," she said to him, speaking in a voice that would flatter—the voice she used when she spoke to men. "Lynx Killer, I have had a vision. You are to be the next chief hunter, after your cousin Tikaani. The spirits told me to make you this charm."

He tilted his head, reached for the caribouskin pouch that dangled by its drawstring from her fingers.

She pulled the pouch away before he could touch it, then she smiled and allowed a rift of laughter to lighten her words. "It must be earned," she told him.

"How?"

His voice was hard, held no respect, and a spark of anger burned in her chest. Too bad the child would not live long enough to know her true powers, though perhaps as he died he would begin to understand. Surely, as his spirit rose from his body, he would know who killed him. She smiled a sweet smile, tender, as a mother smiles at her son.

"You know the stand of black spruce that hunters call seven sisters?"

She saw his surprise.

"You wonder that I know such a thing, knowledge that is for men only," she said. "I am the healer in this village. There are certain things a healer must know to hold the power needed to make medicines. Do not worry. This is not taboo for me. I am different. Ask your cousin Tikaani. He will tell you."

The boy nodded slowly, but his eyes never left her face. "I know the seven sisters," he said.

"Go there. You are to tell no one where you are going or why. Go there, if you are brave enough. Then sit down and close your eyes. Wait, and the spirits will tell you what to do. Take water with you, but no food. Take your knife and your spears. Once you leave the village, if you see someone and they ask you where you are going, only raise your spears and say, 'I hunt.' "

"My father will not let me go there alone."

"You are not alone. No man is alone when he goes on such a quest. Besides, your father already knows that you go. He has already given you his blessing. Go now, do not wait. Get your weapons and go."

She watched as the boy ran back through the village toward his mother's lodge. The woman was at the cooking hearths. K'os had seen her there only moments before, and he would have no trouble with his father. She walked back through the village, past Lynx Killer's mother, her dark head bent toward the woman next to her, the two covering their mouths and whispering together as K'os dipped a bowl of meat from one of the boiling bags.

When K'os came to her own lodge, she lowered the hood of her parka before crawling into the entry tunnel, then she stood, smiled at Fire Eater. The man was lying naked in her bedding furs. She set aside the bowl of meat she had brought from the hearths, laughed and said, "Perhaps you will want to eat later."

He joined her laughter.

She pulled off her parka, boots and leggings, knelt over him, lifted his hands to her breasts, then straddled his torso. "I saw your son," she said. "He told me he is going hunting."

A shadow passed over Fire Eater's eyes, but she raised up and slid herself down over him. "I told him not to go far," she said.

*   *   *

Ghaden arranged the pebbles between the two lines he had scratched out in the snow. Lynx Killer ran past him.

"Lynx Killer!" Ghaden called out, but the boy did not stop, did not even look at him.

Ghaden felt his disappointment well up into tears. Lynx Killer was the one boy in the village who almost always talked to him, even though Lynx Killer was nearly old enough to be a hunter. Ghaden lowered his head over his pebbles. He rubbed his fists across his eyes. What would Lynx Killer think if he saw Ghaden cry over such a silly thing? He blinked back his tears and swallowed them. They were salt in his mouth; they burned his throat.

He returned to his game. Each pebble was a caribou. They were crossing a river and would soon head into the hunters' trap. He was not sure how hunters caught caribou, but the Cousin River boys talked about caribou hunts all the time. Aqamdax said if Night Man got stronger, they would go on a caribou hunt themselves, but Ghaden didn't think Night Man was getting stronger.

"Ghaden!"

Ghaden looked up. It was Lynx Killer. The boy held several throwing spears in his left hand and had a hunting knife in a sheath on his right leg, bird darts and a dartthrower in his right hand.

"I am going to hunt. That's why I couldn't stop and play. Sorry." His words were quick, spoken as though he was out of breath. Ghaden raised up on his knees and watched Lynx Killer run through the village until the lodges hid him from Ghaden's eyes.

It was a good place, this Cousin River Village, Ghaden thought. Especially since Aqamdax came to live with them. Old bone man couldn't get them here. He didn't even know where they were.

Ghaden looked down at his caribou game and drew in his breath. A bird dart lay across the pebbles. Lynx Killer must have dropped it. If Ghaden hurried, he could catch him before he left the village.

He jumped up, then looked back at the lodge. He should tell Yaa, but she was at the cooking hearths, so was Star. The old grandmother, Long Eyes, was inside, and Aqamdax and Night Man, but he didn't want to disturb Night Man. He would run fast and be back to the lodge before they knew he had left. Ghaden untied Biter's rope, and the dog followed him.

THE NORTH SEA

Though his chigdax had shed most of the water, Chakliux was cold, his hands stiff, his fingers·numb. He untied a bag of dried fish from the deck of the iqyax and ate. The food strengthened him, and he looked out again over the ice, east then south. He blinked twice before he allowed himself to believe what he was seeing. Though ice still blocked his way, the shore was close. Surely, if he was patient, he would find an open lead that would allow him to beach his iqyax.

Winter had scoured the inlets and beaches into new shapes, but he thought he recognized a few hills that were just south of the Walrus Hunter Village. Soon he would be back at the Near River Village.

THE COUSIN RIVER VILLAGE
"Biter! You stupid dog turd."

Ghaden had run through the village, Biter at his heels, but as they passed the last lodge, ignoring the jeering daughters who belonged to the woman Grebe, a hare had cut across the path. Biter jumped after it, disappearing into the brush before Ghaden could even react.

He followed the dog a short distance, called him, but Biter didn't return. Finally Ghaden returned to the path, to the laughter of Grebe's daughters. He held up Lynx Killer's hunting dart and asked if they had seen him. The youngest girl said that he had walked north from the village and disappeared into the spruce forest just before Ghaden and Biter came. She was giggling, even as she told him.

Ghaden ran down the path, into the dark of the spruce. He and Aqamdax had walked through a lot of woods on the journey from the Near River Village, but that had been mostly leafless willow and birch, the low brush that grew close to the river.

This was different. The trees were so big they blocked out the light. The ground was spongy with melting snow, and he could feel the crunch of the spruce needles under his feet. How far should he go? He looked back often. Finally the path's opening was only a tiny brightness in the dark of the trees.

He listened, hoping to hear Lynx Killer walking, but the only sound was that of the wind pushing through the spruce boughs, the tree voices talking softly, like old women sewing around a winter hearth fire.

He'd better go back. He'd never find Lynx Killer, and besides, Biter might catch that hare and take it to the lodge. He liked to be there when Biter did something like that. After all, Biter was his dog, and when he brought back meat, Star was always a little nicer, not so apt to do the small mean things that plagued his days—pinching, a foot thrust out to trip, angry words about things Ghaden did not understand, and worst of all, the quick sharp slaps with a willow stick across his cheeks and hands, something that she also did to Yaa, though Yaa was better at holding in her tears than he was.

Those things did not happen when Aqamdax was in the lodge, but she could not always be there, and, of course, there were those days when she had to be in the women's lodge, five long days of Star's willow stick and of different women coming to help care for Night Man. Sometimes even the tall, strange K'os came. When Ghaden saw her, he always tried to hide.

He knew she was good, though she did not look like a good person. She brought Night Man medicine. She had medicine for Star, too. After Star took K'os's medicine, she was quiet, often smiled, though she would forget to give Ghaden food when she was like that, and afterward she slept for a long time.

He turned back down the path, walked a short way and stopped. If Grebe's daughters were still outside, they would know he had not gone very far. Maybe he should sit down and wait. Maybe Lynx Killer would come back this way, or maybe Biter would sniff out Ghaden's trail if he was still and allowed his smell to stay in one place for a while.

Ghaden crouched on his haunches. He thought about being old enough to hunt like Lynx Killer, to have his own spears and bird darts and a hunting knife. His right leg began to ache. He and Biter had been wrestling the day before, and Biter had jumped on him, left two dark bruises on his thigh. Ghaden stood, stretched the leg, then saw a tree with a wide low branch. He climbed to the branch, settled himself back against the trunk. He closed his eyes. It was still too cold for mosquitoes or flies, and the ground was not yet soupy with melt water. It was a good time of year.

During the past moon, they had all been a little hungry, but no one was starving, and maybe Biter would catch that hare. Then they would have fresh meat in the stew . . . and soon they would go on the spring caribou hunt. That would be good. Then they would eat until their bellies almost burst. That's what Lynx Killer had told him. They would eat and eat and not be hungry for a long, long time. . . .

Chapter
Forty-three

The snap of a twig woke him. Ghaden rubbed his eyes and shook his head. Where was he? For a moment he was afraid, then he remembered he had followed Lynx Killer into the woods. The bird dart was lying across his stomach. He clasped it and looked toward the spot of light that marked the path to the village. It was getting dark. Yaa would be worried. He climbed out of the tree, pushed his way through its lower branches, then heard another snap.

He heard the sound again, then a quick, muffled cry. Was it Lynx Killer? He looked at the bird dart in his hand. It was the only weapon he had. How foolish to come into the woods with nothing but a bird dart. What if some animal were stalking him? What good was a bird dart? He slid back into the spruce branches, hoping their strong tree smell would help mask his scent.

He heard the crunch of footsteps and held his breath. Ghaden strained to see through the branches, but they were so thick he could make out only a bit of dark fur. Then he saw it, not animal, but human. Lynx Killer, he thought—no—a woman.

The parka had strips of white at the shoulders and red fox tails hanging across the back. It was the healer, K'os. She carried a gathering basket slung on one arm. He sighed his relief, slid from his refuge in the tree. He opened his mouth to call out to her, but in his hurry to get from tree to path, he dropped Lynx Killer's bird dart. In the darkness under the low hanging spruce branches, it was difficult to see. He moved his hands quickly over the ground, but it took him a long time to find the dart. He pushed his way out of the branches and saw that K'os was nearly out of the woods.

At least he had the bird dart. Besides, he didn't need an old woman to walk him back to the village. He was almost old enough to be a hunter.

Mourning cries pierced the still dark sky. Star was the first out of her lodge; Yaa and Aqamdax followed. Even Long Eyes went out, lifted her voice. Ghaden rubbed the sleep from his eyes and glanced over at Night Man. He must have died. Ghaden felt a lump of sadness for Aqamdax and a thrill of dread for the women who would come to their lodge. They would push him into a small corner, scold Biter, tell harsh stories of death.

Biter poked at Ghaden with his nose, tried to roust him out of the sleeping robes. The day before, Biter had returned before Ghaden, a hare in his mouth. He had carried it from lodge to lodge looking for Ghaden. Ghaden had missed the praise the village women heaped on the dog, but at least he had been able to enjoy the fresh meat in their stew, the good rich broth that made last year's fish seem almost palatable. But now Night Man . . .

Ghaden looked over at Night Man's bed, squinted so Night Man's spirit could not look fully into his eyes. Then Night Man moaned, moved and moaned again. Ghaden jumped from his bed. Wearing only his breechclout, he ran outside, caught Yaa's hand.

"He is alive, Yaa. Come back inside. He isn't dead. I saw him move."

"Who?" Yaa asked, looking down at him, her mouth screwed into a frown.

"Night Man."

"Night Man isn't dead."

"I know. I saw him move. He . . . isn't dead?"

"No."

"Who's dead?" He saw the tears in Yaa's eyes. Suddenly he was very afraid. "Who's dead, Yaa!"

She leaned down to whisper the name into Ghaden's ear so the dead one's spirit would not hear, would not think they spoke in disrespect. "Lynx Killer," she said.

Ghaden smiled. It was a joke. She was teasing. Sometimes Yaa teased him, told him something that wasn't true. Sometimes she did that. "No," Ghaden said.

She nodded her head, and he saw the tears floating in her eyes.

"No," Ghaden said again. "I have his bird dart. I have to give it to him."

Aqamdax put her arms around him. "I am so sorry, Little Brother," she whispered. Then Ghaden knew it was true.

"He went hunting yesterday. I saw him," Ghaden said. "I saw him go. He dropped a bird dart. I went after him, to give it to him, but I couldn't find him." A chill coursed down his back. He had followed Lynx Killer. Did an animal get him?

"Was it a bear?" Ghaden asked.

Aqamdax pressed herself closer. "They say it was a spear, a Near River spear."

Then again the fear came, swallowed Ghaden like a wolf swallows meat. They were Near River, he and Yaa. Would the elders think they did it?

"Who found him?" Star called to one of the men passing their lodge.

"K'os," the hunter answered, then quickened his pace toward the hunters' lodge. "She was out this morning gathering plants," he called back over his shoulder. "She found him in the spruce woods, not far from the village. The spear was in his heart."

K'os, Ghaden thought. She had been gathering plants yesterday—in the spruce woods. She was lucky the Near River People did not kill her, too.

Tikaani came to K'os that night. She did not welcome him to her bed. Why welcome a man who had ignored her for most of the winter? Why pretend she was not angry?

He came into her lodge. He was larger, stronger than she remembered, and suddenly, though only for a moment, she felt the years bend her spine, the weight of them heavy on her shoulders. But she raised her head, straightened and stood tall, felt her own power move toward him, mold him back into the young man she remembered, brash and sometimes foolish.

"I am sorry about your little cousin," K'os said.

He narrowed his eyes as if trying to see past her words. She turned her back on him and sat down, picked up a parka she had been sewing and held it so he could see the fine lines of dyed caribou hair that made a multicolored design at the shoulders, wrists and on the top of the hood. Once, not that long ago, she would have made the parka for him. This one was for Sky Watcher, a man younger than Tikaani but with the promise of being a great hunter, a skilled warrior. She saw Tikaani's eyes on the parka and knew he could not miss the sacred symbols she had embroidered: the dark sharp wing that was raven, the circles that were sun, the lines that stood for animals taken. What man would not want to own such a thing, to have the power it would give the wearer?

"It is for Sky Watcher," she said, and sucked in her cheeks to keep from smiling when she saw the frown on Tikaani's face.

Tikaani crouched on his haunches across the hearth fire from her. "They will fight," he said, his words loud and harsh. "They have decided the bows give advantage."

She tried to keep her face set, to show no sign of gladness, but she could not. She smiled. "When?" she asked.

"Now, before the river melts, before they go to hunt caribou. Before our own hunts."

"They have a plan?" K'os asked. Too often the men of this village did things without thinking, without deciding how they should act. Too often each went with his own ideas, believed that everyone thought as he did. Too often they kept their words to themselves until it was too late for anything but to survive. She had said as much to Tikaani over the years. Since he was little more than a boy, she had told him that hunts and battles were better when plans were made, when ideas were shared in wisdom and without rivalry for power or honor.

"We have a plan," he said. "You taught me well."

She did not try to hide her smile this time, but held up the parka on her lap. "It could be for you. I can make another for Sky Watcher." She lifted the caribou hide shirt she wore and opened her legs.

He shook his head. "The only gift I want is for my brother," he said, and looked hard into her eyes. She felt his anger, his hatred. "My hope is for my brother, that someday he will be strong again."

He left the lodge. K'os ground her teeth. Yes, she had taught him well. Too well. How could she control him if she could not get him back into her bed?

She sat still for a long time, until the hearth fire nearly died and the chill of the night crept into her lodge. Then suddenly she threw back her head and laughed, stoked the fire and pulled out her medicine bag. Tikaani thought he was a man, but he was still a child. Only a boy playing with a new toy. How foolish of her not to realize it.

Chapter
Forty-four

THE NEAR RIVER VILLAGE

The young children came first, screaming, afraid. Something terrible was coming, those little ones said, and they cried for their mothers. It was a giant, huge, with a head so large he banged it against trees when he turned, they said. They pointed back toward the forest, to the path that followed the river.

Sok ignored the small children, instead waited for the older boys, his son Carries Much among them.

They, too, were breathless, but told the men that it was no more than a hunter carrying something over his head.

"An iqyax," Carries Much said. "Like my uncle's."

It might be a trader, Sok thought, but most likely it was Chakliux, returned at last from searching for that useless one, Aqamdax. Evidently, he returned alone.

Chakliux was foolish to bring the iqyax to the village. Who could say how the elders would react? Would they say it broke the River People's taboos? What if the young boys did not show respect? What if the women thought they could touch the iqyax, use it as they used their own rafts? Better first to prepare the people with stories, then later this summer show them the iqyax, teach the men how to build them, and remind the women and children that such boats must be treated with respect.

Sok saw the man walking from the woods, noticed the limp, and knew that it was his brother. He hurried to meet him, lifted the iqyax from his shoulders. The iqyax cover was badly worn, so Sok knew Chakliux had spent long days on the North Sea. He saw the shreds that had once been Chakliux's boots, now stained dark with blood, and knew his brother had walked far. Sok carried the iqyax to one of the drying racks that had survived the winter, leaned it belly side down, told the women and children not to touch it, then stood there to keep small hands away.

Chakliux came to him, unstrapped his carrying pack and lowered it to the ground. Sok, seeing his brother's eyes, did not ask about Aqamdax.

They sat together in Red Leaf's lodge. Even Snow-in-her-hair had come, her belly bulging with Sok's child. Chakliux wanted to ask when they expected the baby's birth, but it was not something one hunter asked another. If Aqamdax were here, he could ask her, but he did not want to ask Red Leaf. Though she was smiling and cordial with Chakliux, gentle with her sons and Sok, her shoulders stiffened, her mouth puckered when she had to speak to Snow-in-her-hair.

"The Sea Hunter woman never returned to this village," Sok said. "Everyone says she is dead."

Chakliux could find no words to answer his brother. Sok was probably right, and if she was not dead, then she had left by her own choice, not taken by Walrus Hunters in revenge or by some First Men hunter who wanted her as wife.

Let her go, he told himself. There are other women. You thought you would never find anyone to compare to Gguzaakk, and yet Aqamdax made a place for herself in your heart.

He had told himself the same thing with each step he had taken walking the river ice to his brother's village. Chakliux had pulled remembrances of her from his mind, scattered them behind him, left them on tree branches, on the winter-flattened grasses.

That night, as he lay in Red Leaf's lodge, on the soft furs and clean sleeping mats, Chakliux did not let himself think of Aqamdax, did not carry the image of her face into his dreams, but when he had almost let sleep swallow him, he heard Red Leaf's voice as she lay with Sok in her sleeping furs.

"So then, perhaps Happy Mouth's young daughter spoke right before she disappeared. Perhaps two old Cousin River men took Aq- amdax and the boy as well."

The next morning, after he had eaten, Chakliux went to Ligige'`s lodge. She beckoned him inside, welcomed him as though he were a child.

"Do you stand there, your mouth empty of good words, when you have been gone so long? Do you stand there without a greeting for an old woman whose prayers followed you?"

He sat down on a pad of fur she arranged for him, and waited in silence as she filled bowls, as she offered water and fish broth. He took the broth, sipped, then said, "Aunt, I have missed your wisdom," a politeness he had learned when he lived with the First Men.

Almost, she smiled at him. He saw her cheeks quiver, and knew she was pleased.

"So you have returned to us with oil on your tongue," she said. "Your words shine like a new wife's hair."

He laughed, and she joined his laughter, then asked: "You went to the First Men? You found the Sea Hunter woman?"

Chakliux shook his head. "I did not find her, but, yes, I went to her people. It was a good winter. I learned much. They are wise. Es- pecially their women."

"And will you tell our hunters that the men were the wise ones?"

"I could," he answered, "and it would not be a lie, nor have I lied to you."

"So why do you come to my lodge? Surely Red Leaf has better food and a warmer fire."

"I have a question about Happy Mouth's daughter," Chakliux told her.

"No one has found her," Ligige' said.

"They think she is dead?"

"Wolf-and-Raven does, and the elders."

"And you?"

Ligige' raised her eyebrows, then took a long draft from the bowl of broth she held in her hands. She lowered the bowl and said, "You have heard the girl's story about the two old men?"

"Yes. Do you think she told the truth?"

"I think she told what she believed to be the truth. You spoke to her before you left last fall. What did she tell you about the ones who attacked her?"

"That they were old and that one wore a sea lion tooth necklace."

"Nothing about the Cousin River Village?"

"Nothing."

"Happy Mouth says she claimed they were from the Cousin River Village."

"Did she have a reason for thinking such a thing?"

Ligige' gestured toward her feet. "Their boots."

She took another drink from her bowl, and when she was finished, Chakliux asked, "Did anyone look for her?"

"A few hunters. They found wolf tracks, scraps of bone, and decided she was dead."

"I believed the ones the girl spoke about were Walrus," Chakliux told her. He laid one hand against his chest. "Because of the necklace. When I did not find them at the Walrus Hunter Village, I went on in my iqyax to the Sea Hunters, hoping the woman's own people had taken her. When I returned here, Red Leaf said the girl was gone, that she had disappeared like the Sea Hunter woman and her brother."

"So now what will you do?"

"Go to my own village. If I find any of them, I will bring them back here."

"You will risk meeting those hunters who tried to kill you?"

"I will go quietly. I will watch without being seen."

Ligige' swept one hand across her face, as though fanning away smoke, then said, "There is something else I want to talk to you about, something I need to show you."

She crawled into the entrance tunnel and brought back a fishskin basket. She reached into it and brought out a frozen ball of fat, dropped it into his hand.

THE COUSIN RIVER VILLAGE

It was the second day of new moon. Aqamdax went outside and searched the sky, rejoiced in the strengthening sun. She placed one hand over her belly, felt the warmth of her body even through the fur of her parka.

The sound of drums and singing came from the hunters' lodge. She had heard whispers among the women at the cooking hearths. The spear in Lynx Killer's chest had carried the marks of the Near River People—a black band crested with a white circle—and now that the days of mourning were over, there would be revenge. Someone would die for the boy who was killed.

She could not let herself think about who that might be. Possibly a boy who had joined the story circle in her Near River lodge. A young man who would never be hunter, would never know the joy of sleeping with his wife, of watching his children grow strong. But who was she to protest? Some foolish hunter, probably a young man not yet wise enough to see beyond the moment he was living, had taken the life of a Cousin River boy, a young man with much promise. What else could the hunters do but repay?

She went back into the lodge. Night Man moved restlessly on his bed. That morning, with much loud singing and chants, K'os had brought a new medicine for him, had even called Night Man's brother Tikaani from the hunters' lodge to watch her performance. Aqamdax had crouched quietly in the corner beside her husband's mother, had clasped the woman's cold, still hands and waited until K'os left the lodge.

She had expected Tikaani to follow K'os, as most men in the village did, but he had not. Instead, he had stayed and waited with Aqamdax, had watched as she straightened her husband's bed, as she fed him gruel, as she combed his hair and wiped his face. Then Tikaani, too, had left, and Aqamdax had been able to coax Long Eyes to her feet, to support her as she walked with small shuffling steps to the women's place to relieve herself and then back again to the lodge. Aqamdax gave her food, and though she had to remind the woman now and again to eat, Long Eyes finished everything and held her bowl out for another portion.

During all that time, Aqamdax had held her thoughts away from her hopes, but now, she again allowed herself to reflect on the heaviness that rested just below her belly, and she knew she carried Night Man's child.

She crouched beside her husband, again whispered his name. He opened his eyes, but they were opaque, as though he saw nothing, as though his body lived but without his spirit. She struggled with his backrest until he seemed to be comfortable, then she placed a hand at his groin to feel the pad of moss she used to catch his urine. It was dry. She stood and pulled a caribou belly of water from the lodge poles, knelt beside him and held it while he drank. Finally he turned his head away. Aqamdax pushed the ivory stopper back into the neck of the container and rehung it, and sat down again beside her husband.

Usually she stayed beside him, sewing or weaving, sitting close enough so she could press one leg against his thigh. She often spoke to him, in spite of Star's mocking glances, but now she only sat, watching his eyes, hoping for some sign that he knew she was there. She clasped his hand and thought she felt him tighten his fingers. She leaned close to him, then whispered into his ear.

"Husband," she said, "my husband, I carry your child in my womb." She took his left hand with both of hers and laid it over her belly. "A child," she whispered again.

Did she see the smallest flicker of understanding in his eyes? Perhaps the child, as it grew larger, stronger, would have the power to pull his father's spirit back from wherever it had gone and return it to Night Man's body.

THE NEAR RIVER VILLAGE

"You have seen such a thing before?" Ligige' asked, and put the fat ball back into the basket.

For a moment Chakliux sat still. There was something buried deep in his memories. A story he had heard. . . .

"The North Tundra People use them to kill wolves," he finally said.

"They are poison, then," said Ligige', but something in her words told Chakliux she knew they were not.

Chakliux pulled his sleeve knife from the sheath at his wrist and sliced open the ball, holding one hand out in caution as Ligige' bent too close. "Shield your eyes," he told her, and turned his own head away.

He need not have worried. The coil of sharpened ivory stretched out slowly in his hand. "It pierces the wolf's belly after the heat of his body melts the fat. Usually they die, though a North Tundra hunter told me he found a wolf with one in his belly and that it had remained coiled."

"How could that happen?"

Chakliux shrugged. "I do not know, but he carried it as something sacred in his amulet pouch, and the other hunters claimed he always had good luck in hunting wolves."

Ligige' snorted. "North Tundra People will tell you anything. They are not quite human, you know."

"Ligige'," Chakliux said softly, "they are much like us."

She frowned, and Chakliux asked, "Where did you get this?"

"I found it in a dog's belly."

"Do Near River hunters use these to kill wolves?" Chakliux asked as he handed her the strip of ivory.

"No."

"Ligige', how long have dogs been dying in this village? Healthy dogs, not pups or old ones."

"Since you came," she answered.

"None died before I came?"

"Perhaps a few old dogs. Always a few pups. Nothing that people would notice."

"This past winter, how many died?"

"Four handfuls, probably more. Grown dogs. Not old, not sick."

"Puppies?"

"Yes, some. Most of them belonged to elders."

"Were they sick or deformed?"

"Two were born without the lower jaw. That has happened before. It is Camp Maker's dark-colored bitch. Sometimes her pups are like that."

"But the others? Were they sick?"

"I do not know. You should talk to Dog Trainer. He knows these things."

Chakliux sighed. He needed to leave, to begin his journey to the Cousin River Village, but this, too, was important. If Aqamdax and Ghaden had been taken to the Cousin River Village, then they had been there all winter. What would one more day matter?

"I will talk to Dog Trainer," Chakliux said. "How many of these were in the dog's belly?"

"A handful or more. Four still coiled."

"You kept them?"

"Yes."

"Do you have enough fat to make them into balls again?"

She shrugged her shoulders. "An old woman's cache does not have much fat at the end of a long winter."

"I will bring you fat."

"That would be good," she said, and licked her lips.

"Does anyone else know how the dog died?"

"Only Blue-head Duck."

"For now do not tell anyone else."

"No one will know," she said.

He left Ligige' and went to the elders' lodge. He scratched at the lodge entrance and called out, then waited for someone to beckon him.

A voice came, Blue-head Duck's, then also Dog Trainer's. They were the only ones inside, and both were grumbling because the women had not refilled their food bag. They looked at Chakliux warily. He was too young to come to the lodge only to talk or tell stories, at least without invitation. Why else did young men come but to request favors?

"I need to talk to you about dogs," Chakliux said, and earned looks of disgust.

Chakliux reminded himself that he should have spoken of other things. What man is so impolite as to forget the praise and honor due an elder? "Both of you are gifted with wisdom," he said, hoping the praise would make them overlook his rudeness. "In this village and even in the village where I was raised, the people know your names. I count it an honor to ask advice from men who are wiser than I."

Both elders straightened their shoulders, so Chakliux knew that he had finally said the right thing. Questions pressed into his mouth so he could hardly pull in breath, but he waited until Blue-head Duck said, "If you need advice about dogs, you must speak to Dog Trainer. He knows far more than I do, but I will help you if I can."

Dog Trainer inclined his head, and Chakliux asked, "Did you lose any dogs this winter?"

"None," Dog Trainer said.

"And you?" Chakliux asked Blue-head Duck.

"Three healthy dogs and four pups."

"They were not sick?"

"Only just before they died. They howled, chewed at their bellies, choked up blood. Several days later they died."

"The pups also?"

"No, I found them dead in the morning. All four dead."

"There are many ways a pup can die," Dog Trainer said.

"And there were other grown dogs in the village that died after choking up blood?" Chakliux asked.

"Yes," said Dog Trainer. "More than two handfuls, and others last winter. You know that most of your brother's dogs died last year. Did he tell you that only one of your grandfather's dogs is still alive?"

"No," Chakliux replied, and felt a sudden regret that he had not stayed in the village, caring for the dogs his grandfather had entrusted to him. "Which one is alive?" he asked.

"The female."

"Black Nose," he said, and nodded. Of the three, she was the strongest. He would watch her more carefully. Perhaps, if he offered Ligige' meat or oil, she would allow the dog to stay in her entrance tunnel.

"Did any die in the summer?" Chakliux asked.

"We did not lose any, except a pup now and again or an old dog."

"But those dogs that died in the way you told me," Chakliux said, "that happened only in winter?"

"Yes."

Blue-head Duck looked at him. "Some hunters believe you cursed our dogs. But this last winter, you were gone, and still dogs died. Perhaps it is not you."

"Perhaps it is not," Chakliux said softly.

THE COUSIN RIVER VILLAGE

Cen saw the thin layer of smoke in the sky and knew he was close to the village. He had had a good winter of trading. Though he had begun with little, he had managed to accumulate much. He anticipated the look in K'os's eyes when she saw the white bear skin he had managed to get from an old man in a village on the Great River.

His pack was heavy, but he quickened his steps and soon was greeted by the calls of children at the edge of the village. They remembered his name, and it felt good to have a place that he could regard as his home. At the back of the group he saw Ghaden. He set down his pack, then opened his arms and called the boy's name.

At first Ghaden seemed confused, but the other children pushed him forward until Cen could grab him and hoist him to eye level. Cen laughed and set him down, saw a slow smile tug at the boy's mouth.

"You have grown!" Cen's voice came out loud and rough, as it always did when he spoke his first words after long days on the trail. "Here," he said, and reached into his pack to pull out a handful of wooden whistles carved from willow twigs. He put one into his mouth and blew, laughed at the squeals from the children.

"I do not have enough for all of you," he told them, "but if you show them to your uncles they can carve enough for everyone."

He handed one to Ghaden and then threw the others into the group of children, chortled as they dropped to hands and knees, scrambling after them. Soon the children were running home with their treasures.

"Go show your sister," he said to Ghaden, and sent the boy off with a pat on his shoulder.

Ghaden had grown. He had the sturdy build of the First Men, already broad of shoulder. The elders might have given him to Star, but they would not stop Cen from taking the boy when he was old enough to travel as a trader.

Besides, having Ghaden in Star's lodge was not all bad. It gave him time to be alone with K'os.

He strode through the village to K'os's lodge, set his pack down outside and untied the bear skin. It was heavy and stiff, but he had managed to roll and bind it to the left side of his pack. He pulled the pack into the entrance tunnel, took the bear skin and crawled into the lodge.

In the dim light, he heard the groaning before he saw them. The boy, Sky Watcher, was on top, his body bare and slicked with sweat. K'os, also writhing and naked, was under him.

She was a woman who had many men, he knew that. Had he not also enjoyed other women during his trading journey? He should not expect anything different from her, but still the sight of them was like a knife thrust into his belly. This was not Daes with some poor old hunter, a man kind enough to raise Ghaden as his own, a man who could not compare to Cen. Sky Watcher was young, already a good hunter.

K'os smiled, heaved the boy off her belly, and came to Cen, hands open.

Almost, he reached for her, but then, as though some other man dictated his actions, he turned and left the lodge, dragging his pack, the bear skin still in his arms.

THE NEAR RIVER VILLAGE
"You will tell the others, then?" Chakliux asked Blue-head Duck.

"Tonight, outside the elders' lodge," Blue-head Duck said. "I will tell them."

Chakliux nodded, then after a time of polite conversation, he left the elders' lodge and went to the cache he shared with Sok. He took out a pack of hardened caribou fat. It was precious, especially at this time of year, and it did not really belong to him, but he had given Sok several seal bellies filled with seal oil. Surely they were worth more than a pack of caribou fat. He took the fat to Ligige''s lodge, scratched and listened for her call.

She sounded distracted, irritated at the interruption, but he went inside anyway. When she saw it was him, she smiled.

"I thought you were Leaf Weaver. That old woman comes every day to help herself to my food and fill my ears with her foolish words."

Chakliux set the pack on the floor beside her, and Ligige' grinned at him, showing teeth worn almost to her wide pink gums.

"Good," she said. "I had only enough fat to make two balls. It is not easy, you know. It took me a long time on the first one. It is not truly cold enough to freeze the balls hard, so the fat would not hold the ivory in a coil."

"How did you do it?" Chakliux asked.

She handed him a ball of fat, and he saw that it was circled in several places by thin strands of sinew thread.

"Tonight when it is cold, they will freeze, then you can take the sinew off."

She suddenly narrowed her eyes and looked at him. "You will not let any of our dogs eat these," she said.

"I will not give them to anyone's dogs," he promised.

"If you put them out for wolves, some dog might get them."

"I will not even give these to wolves." He crouched down on his haunches and looked into her face. "You knew what it meant when you found the first ivory strip in that dog's belly."

"I knew," she said softly.

"It is not a curse," Chakliux said. "It is not a sickness."

"Someone is killing our dogs," said Ligige'.

"Do you know who it is?" Chakliux asked.

She again looked up at him, and he was surprised to see tears shimmering in her eyes.

"I know," she said softly.

THE COUSIN RIVER VILLAGE

Aqamdax had stayed with Night Man through days when he lay so still she thought he might have died, and days when his arms and legs thrashed in the agony he suffered in whatever world he now lived. So she did not look up from her weaving when his arm moved, when his body shifted on his sleeping mats. She did not look at him until a soft groan came from his throat, and within that groan the sound of her name.

Then with a cry she dropped her weaving, called to Star and Long Eyes, Ghaden and Yaa. She brought a water bladder so Night Man could drink, pulled it away after he gulped down several large mouthfuls.

"Let him drink," Star said.

"It will make him sick," said Aqamdax, remembering hunters who had returned from long sea journeys, their fresh water gone. They drank slowly, a few sips at first and later a few more sips. If they did not, their stomachs seemed to harden and convulse in spasms, making them retch.

Star opened her mouth to argue, but Aqamdax looked away. She did not want to fight just when Night Man's spirit had finally returned to them. Instead, she went to the cooking bag that hung near the hearth fire and dipped out a bowl of broth from the top of the bag. She brought it to her husband and knelt beside him, fed him slowly. Star flung herself away from them and pulled Ghaden and Yaa with her, settled Yaa at her knees and began to comb the girl's hair with Aqamdax's shell comb, something Aqamdax treasured because she had brought it from her own village.

Aqamdax ignored her, murmuring soft words to Night Man. Finally he raised one hand to signal he had eaten enough. Again, she offered him water and he drank, this time slowly. Then he asked, "How long did I sleep?"

"Two moons, almost three," Star called out, and Aqamdax noticed that even Long Eyes had turned so she could see her son, her face shining from within as though she understood some of what was happening.

Night Man slumped back on his bedding mats.

"Do not worry, husband," Aqamdax said, whispering her words to keep them private from Star. "It was a good time of the year to sleep."

He looked at her with raised eyebrows, then made an effort to laugh, but the laughter ended in a cough that racked his body. He closed his eyes, and Aqamdax wanted to call out to him, fear rising in her chest that he would escape back into that world where he had been lost for so long.

But as though he heard her thoughts, he said, "My wife, do not worry. I only sleep."

Aqamdax leaned close and pressed her cheek to his forehead. His skin was dry but cool, and even his breath did not seem to carry the sour odor it once had.

Suddenly he opened his eyes wide, moved his head to look at her. "I had a dream . . ." he said, but his words were interrupted by a scratching at the entrance tunnel. Cen.

Aqamdax felt the breath leave her chest. He and Tikaani had been the ones to bring her here. Tikaani, in his concern about Night Man, had long ago won Aqamdax's friendship, but she felt nothing except anger and hatred for Cen. He might have fathered Ghaden, a fine young brother, but he had taken too much from her in exchange.

When Star saw him, she jumped to her feet, clapped her hands and danced like a child. Cen dropped a heavy white pelt on the floor of the lodge. "This is for me?" Star squealed, and pounced on the rolled hide.

Cen looked at her for a moment, opened his mouth, then closed it again. "No," he finally said. "It is my bed."

His words did not seem to bother Star. Instead she called Yaa to her side and together they untied the braided babiche that held the hide and unrolled it. Star stretched out over the fur, and looked up at Cen, licking her upper lip.

Aqamdax looked away in disgust, bent down over Night Man. "Cen?" he asked, his words a raspy whisper.

"He has returned," she said.

Night Man nodded and again closed his eyes.

"You had a dream?" Aqamdax asked, hoping he would stay awake a little longer, but he only sighed and slipped away into sleep.

Cen stayed in their lodge that night, and though Star openly offered herself to him, he placed his bedding close to Night Man and told Star he was too tired from long days of walking to do more than sleep. She pouted for a short time, but then, as though Cen's presence had reminded her that she was a woman, she began to act the part of sister and mother, seeing that Night Man was comfortable, that Yaa and Ghaden had food.

Aqamdax lay awake long after others were asleep. Through that night the drums in the hunters' lodge continued to beat. She had not asked Cen if he had joined the men there before coming to Star's lodge. He was not truly one of the Cousin River People, and so might not be welcome when the men planned revenge raids.

Finally, she, too, slept, only to awaken suddenly in the early dawn. Her first thought was of Night Man. Had something happened to him, some sudden passing of his spirit? She moved her hands to his face and he mumbled something, brushed at her hand sleepily, bringing a smile to her face. Then she realized that silence had awakened her.

"The drums have stopped," Star whispered from across the lodge.

"Even warriors must sleep," Aqamdax murmured, and turned on her side, pulled her woven hare fur blanket up over her shoulder.

She did not notice that Tikaani had come into the lodge until he was beside her, bending over Night Man, laying his hand on Night Man's forehead.

Aqamdax raised up on one elbow. "He came back to us last night. Now he sleeps."

"I am awake," Night Man said, and Aqamdax covered her mouth in surprise.

As though he did not realize that he was crowding himself into Aqamdax's bed, Tikaani slid closer to his brother, squatting cross-legged and bending his head over Night Man's face.

"You are awake?" Tikaani asked.

"How could I sleep with all your talking?" his brother answered.

Tikaani laughed, glanced at Aqamdax, joy dancing in his eyes. "It is the right thing, then, what we do," he said. "I told the elders it was. I told them the deaths, the salmon, all things were because we did not appease our dead with revenge. Look, now as soon as our plans are made, you are back with us."

"Probably not strong enough to fight," Night Man said, trying to smile.

"I will fight for both of us."

"What is the hunters' plan?"

"We have a new weapon. Do you remember it?"

"The bow."

"Yes. Instead of a few men trying to kill one or two of their hunters for what was done to us, this time we all go, hunters and elders, even the older boys." Tikaani drew his hands together in a circle. "Remember how their village is set in a hollow, like a bowl, with trees around it?"

"I remember."

"With bows, we can sit in the trees and shoot down into the village, taking men from a distance so they will not even know who has attacked."

Night Man raised his good hand, and Tikaani clasped it in his own, then he was gone, slipping out into the dawn, leaving his brother to sleep and Aqamdax to stare into the dim morning light with horror, the faces of the Near River People clear in her mind. Women and children, elders and hunters. Chakliux.

THE NEAR RIVER VILLAGE

"I only tell you this," Wolf-and-Raven said to Sok. "My daughter wants to be your first wife."

Sok had been up all night waiting through Snow-in-her-hair's labor, the woman's screams. He had been afraid she was dying. What woman screamed unless spirits were pulling her away from her husband and new child?

His thoughts had returned to that first night they had shared together, the joy of having her in his bed. She had been shy, averting her head when he first stroked her breasts, gasping in surprise when he slid his fingers to the damp warmth of her woman's cleft.

He had held those memories as though they could keep Snow-in-her-hair with him even through childbirth. He had fought down his fears with prayers and chants.

When his wife's aunt came to him just before dawn, his fear was so great he thought he could not bear to hear what she had to tell him, but she said the birth had been an easy one. That their son was strong and Snow-in-her-hair was as well as any woman could expect to be after giving birth and yelling so loudly that she kept the whole village awake all night.

Now her father was in his daughter's lodge insisting that Sok throw away his good first wife, a woman who had given him two strong sons, boys who already showed promise as hunters—a woman who had not screamed once in delivering those two boys.

They were alone, Sok and Wolf-and-Raven. Sok had stayed in his wife's lodge for the night, a custom in their village, a way to lend Snow-in-her-hair strength during her labor. He did not look forward to facing the other men in the village, or the women, their sly looks of disdain, the laughter they would pretend to hide behind their hands. Better to stay inside for a while, he had thought, but then Wolf-and-Raven had come.

"She is second wife. She will stay second wife," Sok said, his voice a warrior's voice.

Then Wolf-and-Raven stood, and as though he had come for no other reason, he said, "Your brother has asked for a meeting of all people in the village this evening."

"Chakliux has?"

"He has." Wolf-and-Raven jutted his chin toward Sok. "Few hunters will come. What has Chakliux to tell us that carries any importance?"

"I will be there," Sok said.

Wolf-and-Raven left the lodge, and Sok lay back on the hare fur blanket that Snow-in-her-hair had made him. It was thin and poorly made. Red Leaf's blankets were woven so tightly that even the smallest shaft of light could not pass through them.

He heard a scratching at the side of the lodge. "Come!" he called, his voice gruff. It was probably Wolf-and-Raven with another piece of foolishness.

Red Leaf came in carrying a boiling pot. "My husband," she said in a quiet voice, "I am glad to hear of your new son." She left the lodge without looking at him.

Chapter
Forty-five

Chakliux could feel the men's hostility. Who was he to call the whole village together, ask them to listen for an evening? There were many things to do this time of year—nets to mend, knives to knap, blades to retouch. They did not have time for the foolishness of a Cousin River man.

But they came. Grumbling, frowning, they came. Even the children seemed to feel the irritation of their parents; squabbles broke out among them and had to be quelled by adults; babies cried. Chakliux closed his eyes and reached for the peace he always felt when he was in his iqyax, when the only sounds were those of water and birds and wind.

Ligige' had prepared the balls of fat, coiled bone or ivory in each, two handfuls in all. She had wrapped them in thin pieces of dried and softened gut, then placed them in a fishskin basket. He was careful to keep the basket beside him but not too close. He did not want the heat of his body to soften the fat and release the coils.

They gathered outside the elders' lodge. The young men had made a large hearth fire, and the elders sat in the circle closest to the flames.

The hunters were next, in order of their age, then the grandmothers, women with babies, and last, unmarried women and the children. The women had brought food, but the elders had turned it down, as did most of the hunters. The children begged for the leftovers, and a few grandmothers complied, adding to the confusion as scuffles broke out among the children who had food and those who did not.

Chakliux, sitting with the hunters, waited until Wolf-and-Raven stood, until with a loud voice he told the children to stop fighting. When most of the noise had died away, he looked at Chakliux and said, "Tell us now what you have to say."

Chakliux walked to the center of the circle, stood with his back to the elders' lodge, his face toward the people. The spring evening was still light, the sky a deep blue, shadows long. Firelight touched the people's faces, and he searched for Ligige', Fox Barking, Sleeps Long, Blue-head Duck, Dog Trainer, Root Digger, Sok.

"I have asked you to come so we could talk about your dogs," Chakliux began.

A low murmur came from the hunters, and Chakliux heard Ligige' say: "Be still. Listen."

The murmuring stopped, and Chakliux continued. "You know that another dog has died. It died of the same sickness that has killed many of our dogs. It is a sickness that none of us could understand until Ligige' discovered what was wrong."

Many turned to look at Ligige'. She held her chin high, kept her eyes on Chakliux.

"Ligige' has asked that I tell you."

There was sudden quiet. Even the children's voices were still. Chakliux reached for the basket at his side. He lifted one of the fat balls.

"Root Digger!" he called out. The man looked up at him, and Chakliux threw the ball. Root Digger caught it, held it up so others could see.

"Sok!" Sok also caught one of the fat balls, raised it to his mouth as if to bite into it.

Ligige' called out, "No. Do not eat it. Wait."

"It is poison?" Sok asked.

"No," Chakliux said. "It is not poison."

He threw fat balls to Fox Barking and Sleeps Long, to Dog Trainer, even to the boy River Ice Dancer. They sank fingers into the balls, sniffed them.

Finally there were only two left, yet Chakliux had not found the reaction he had hoped for. He looked at Ligige'. She met his eyes with a clear, steady gaze and lifted her hands, cupped them together. He threw one of the balls, and she caught it easily, then, leaning on the shoulder of the woman next to her, she pushed herself up, and standing, she tossed the ball to Wolf-and-Raven.

He bobbled it, dropped it to the ground and allowed it to lie there.

"Pick it up, Little Cousin," Ligige' said to him, and the people smiled, holding in laughter at the diminutive she used to address him.

He picked it up, held it so others could see, then again set it on the ground.

"It does not kill unless it is inside, Little Cousin," Ligige' told him, and Chakliux heard the terrible sadness in her voice.

There was a sudden yelp from Root Digger. The heat from his hand had melted one side of the fat ball, had allowed one end of the coil to pierce his thumb.

"What is it?" he cried out, and dropped the ball to the ground while sucking at the puncture wound.

"Blue-head Duck took pity on an old woman," Ligige' said. "He gave me a dead dog. When I butchered the animal, I found this." She held up an ivory strip. "It was in the belly of the dog. There were many of them, more than a handful."

Chakliux noticed that the others had set their fat balls on the ground as Wolf-and-Raven had. He handed the fishskin basket to one of the women. "Pick them up and bring them back to me," he told her. "We do not want our dogs or our children to get them." He turned to Wolf-and-Raven. "You would not hold the fat ball. Why?"

"I do not trust a man from the Cousin River Village," Wolf-and-Raven said. "That is why."

Chakliux turned to the elders. "I accuse no one," he said. "Decide for yourselves who killed the dogs. You saw what the coil of bone did to Root Digger's hand. Think what they do inside a dog's belly."

There was a rise of sound—a growl of anger, men's and women's voices together.

"Why?" one of the hunters asked. "Why kill our dogs? We need them for hunting and for food. Why would anyone do this?"

A woman at the back of the circle stood up. Chakliux did not realize it was Wolf-and-Raven's wife until she spoke.

"For power," Blue Flower said. "Only for power. To be able to accuse others of causing such a curse, and then to say he himself was able to stop it."

"I throw you away," Wolf-and-Raven screeched, jumping to his feet and thrusting his walking stick toward his wife.

"No," she said to him. "I throw you away. Get your things out of my lodge. I do not want to see you again."

Then everyone was speaking, shouting, arguing. Most raised angry words at Wolf-and-Raven. Some shouted at Chakliux, others at Ligige'. Wolf-and-Raven had worn his shaman's headpiece, heavy with beads and raven beaks. He took it off and held it toward anyone who drew near, sweeping a path through the people as he stomped away. Some of the men shouted out their disagreement with Chakliux. Others came, clapped hands on his back, thanked him, peered into the fishskin basket at the fat balls, then, shaking their heads, walked away.

Soon everyone was gone except Chakliux and Ligige'. She was huddled on the ground, her blanket pulled up over her head. Chakliux knelt beside her. "Aunt," he whispered softly. "Would you like to stay in Red Leaf's lodge tonight?"

"I do not think Sok would want me there," she said, her voice trembling. "I have destroyed his wife's father."

"Wolf-and-Raven destroyed himself," Chakliux said, and helped her to her feet.

"I think I will go to my own lodge," Ligige' told him. "I think this village has heard enough of my voice."

"Then could I stay with you?" Chakliux asked her.

"Yes, come and stay." She blinked away tears and put a sly smile on her face. "The old women say you have more seal oil. They say it is very good on dried fish."

Chakliux also smiled. "Yes, Aunt, it is very good, as you shall see."

THE COUSIN RIVER VILLAGE

Cen did not want to go with them. He had not yet mastered their bow weapons. Besides, he was trader. What trader wanted to encourage fighting? But the Near River People were the ones who had killed Daes. They were the ones who had almost killed him. Even yet his ribs ached on cold days, and his left wrist would never be as strong as it once was.

He had considered Aqamdax's words. She had gone lodge to lodge, pleading with hunters, telling them the Near Rivers were a good people, urging them to take only one life for the boy who had been killed. But even Ghaden had gritted his teeth, raised a fist and screamed out his anger against the Near Rivers for killing a boy who had been a friend.

They took no dogs with them. Only packs with food and supplies. Only weapons. Bows and throwing spears, arrows and knives.

Cen had a bow, but still his left wrist buckled when he pulled back the string. Better for him to use a spear. At least his right wrist was strong, his throw far and accurate.

It usually took three days to make the journey to the Near Rivers' winter village from the winter camp of the Cousin River People, and that was with dogs carrying packs. But anger seemed to lend strength to the men's legs, and at the end of the first day they found themselves already at the Near River. They slept through a night of wind and snow, the last bite of winter as it was defeated by the new strong sun.

The second morning, they began early, and by midday they moved from the river ice into the forest, then made a camp near the village. Now all they could do was wait for morning and hope some hunter would come from the village to be their first kill.

The day had faded to dusk when that one came—a man alone, not even a dog at his side. He carried a large pack, as though he were a trader. He carried a spear as walking stick.

Cen was sitting on a fallen tree, had brushed the snow from the trunk and cushioned the wet bark with a pad of caribou hide. His thoughts were not on the battle, the attack that Tikaani and others had decided would begin in early morning. His thoughts were instead on K'os. She was a woman, like Daes, who seemed to push wisdom out of his head, who made him act without thinking, without considering consequences. Now that he was away from her, when her face did not cloud his thinking, it was a good time to decide what to do.

Even if she became his wife, she would probably still invite many men to her bed. He had heard the stories about her two husbands. Both had died in terrible ways, the first man consumed by some sickness that seemed to eat away his belly until all he could do was vomit blood. The other was killed in a fire that K'os herself escaped. Surely some spirit of bad luck followed K'os and would soon attack anyone she took as husband. Some of the hunters said K'os was old, too old to give children. That was difficult to believe. Her face said she was young, but she seemed to be barren.

Cen was grateful for Ghaden, but he wanted more sons, even a daughter. What was better for an old man than a daughter to take care of him in his last days?

He could marry Star, but he did not want a wife who whined and threw tantrums like a child. There was also Aqamdax. She looked much like Daes and was a hard worker. The First Men claimed she was a storyteller. She was wife to Night Man, but who could expect him to live long? The night Cen had stayed in Star's lodge, he had had to turn away when Aqamdax changed the poultice on Night Man's shoulder, the flesh was so rotten.

When Night Man died, what would Aqamdax do? Perhaps Tikaani would take her, but he was chief hunter now. It would not be wise for the chief hunter to take a woman from another village for first wife. Who would want the trouble that could cause?

Cen was drawn from his thoughts by a soft hiss that passed hunter to hunter among the Cousin River men. He crouched beside the log, reached for his spear, tucked it close to his shoulder, point out.

Suddenly arrows were flying, some ricocheting off trees, others flying true, their voices higher, thinner than the voices of spear and spearthrower.

Cen heard screams, then the cries of the Cousin River men calling out as though they had made a successful hunt. He stood, still clutching his spear, then went to see what had been killed. An animal, he thought, perhaps a bear just coming from its winter den. What better sign of favor?

No, it was a man. A heavy pack, bristling with arrows, was on his back, and his legs and arms leaked blood into the snow. Then Cen saw the medicine bundle, the skin of a river otter, and another of a wolverine. A flicker wing hung from the pack, and a beaded head covering.

"Wolf-and-Raven," he said.

Some of the men near him gasped; others, the younger men, drew brows together as though they were puzzled.

"A shaman," Tikaani said.

Some looked at Cen for confirmation. "Yes, a shaman," he answered.

"Cut his joints, quickly," one of the young men said.

Tikaani looked at the man, really yet a boy, and handed him his knife. Clasping his amulet, Tikaani walked away, a thin chant rising from his throat. The others did the same, leaving the boy there alone. Finally, the boy dropped the knife, backed away, lifted his hands in signs of protection, held his amulet high over his head.

Later, as the others slept, Cen crept away through the forest. He walked the river ice all night and all the next day, then continued north toward the Great River and east toward the villages of the Caribou People.

THE NEAR RIVER VILLAGE
Chakliux thought the sound was part of his dream, but then he heard a voice, and pulled himself from sleep. He sat up and remembered he had decided to spend the night in Ligige''s lodge.

The hearth coals were only bits of glowing red, but he could see well enough to tell that Ligige', too, was sitting up.

"It is Wolf-and-Raven," she said. "I know his voice. "

"He left the village," Chakliux reminded her. Blue Flower had come and told them herself.

"It is Wolf-and-Raven," Ligige' insisted.

Chakliux wrapped a hare fur blanket around himself and crept out through the entrance tunnel. There was no moon, and clouds had covered the stars. In the darkness he could see nothing.

"Who is here?" he called, keeping his voice low. Why wake others for something that was probably only an old woman's dream?

There was nothing, no sound. Not even the barking of dogs, the cry of a baby. He turned to go back inside, then heard the moan. He stood and listened, again heard a moan, then walked in careful steps toward the sound. In the darkness, he tripped, catching his leg on something, then realized it was a man lying in the snow. Chakliuk called Ligige', told her to bring coals for light. She came out, already bundled in her parka, carrying a bowl with coals burning inside.

She knelt beside Chakliux, set the bowl in a patch of snow to keep the coals from burning through, then with words edged by tears said, "Wolf-and-Raven. I told you. Someone has killed him."

"Help me," Chakliux said. He gathered the man into his arms, and together they carried him into the lodge.

"What are these?" Ligige' asked, shaking her head, scattering her tears. She pointed at feathered shafts of wood, one in Wolf-and-Raven's shoulder, two in his left arm, another in his leg, one in his belly.

"Not a weapon the River People use," Chakliux said. He leaned close, saw a familiar band of red, black and white on one of the shafts.

Then he heard the rattle of breath, another moan. Ligige' whimpered and moved to cradle Wolf-and-Raven's head in her arms. He opened his eyes but did not seem to see her.

"How did this happen?" Chakliux asked, speaking slowly, his words loud so Wolf-and-Raven's spirit would hear him before it floated up and left his body.

Wolf-and-Raven opened his mouth, said what Chakliux already knew. "The Cousin . . . They are coming. . . ."

"You took this from the shaman's leg?" Sok asked, turning the arrow in his hands.

Chakliux nodded. They were in the elders' lodge with most of the Near River hunters.

"It looks like one of the spears the old trader once kept in his lodge," Sok said. "He told us the large fire bow somehow threw them." He glanced at Chakliux. "That trader died in the same fire which killed your father."

"The trader never used the weapon," said one of the elders. "He kept it for good luck."

"My father stayed there, in that lodge?" Chakliux asked.

Blue-head Duck nodded. "And the woman."

"K'os?"

"Yes."

"Then we know how they got the weapon," Sok said.

"And why the old ones died," Chakliux added.

"This woman would do such a thing?" Dog Trainer asked.

"She would," said Fox Barking.

Chakliux looked at his stepfather in surprise.

"Long ago I knew her," Fox Barking said.

Chakliux, remembering the many men who came to his mother's lodge, did not doubt that Fox Barking spoke the truth.

"So our shaman said the Cousin River hunters are coming?" Blue-head Duck asked.

"Let them come," said one of the younger men. "I am tired of their foolishness." He nodded toward the arrow in Sok's hand. "Our spears are stronger than that. We will kill them all, then go to their village and get their women, take the food in their caches."

One of the elders stood, First River, a man not as old as Blue-head Duck but weaker, one who had nearly died during the winter. He used a walking stick to give his legs strength, and he looked straight ahead, most of his vision robbed by the white cauls that covered his eyes.

"Once I was a trader," he said, and his words were so weak that Chakliux could barely hear him.

Some of the younger hunters did not even seem to be aware he was speaking and continued their conversation among themselves until Blue-head Duck raised his walking stick and rapped one of them on the shoulder.

"Once I was a trader," First River said again, then stopped and coughed with the effort of forcing out his words. "I was partner with that one who died in the fire. We were hunting partners and trading partners. My first wife was his wife's sister." He stopped, leaned forward on his walking stick. One of the young men rose and went over to First River, wrapped an arm around the old one's shoulders and helped him stand, took long breaths as though he could, through his own breathing, lend strength.

"We went far once. Beyond the south mountains. Two years we were gone. Our wives thought we were dead. The dead one's wife, she even took another husband." He pushed out a laugh and shot a sharp glance at Blue-head Duck as he said, "She left him when her husband returned.

"We saw people who used these small spears. Their spearthrowers look like fire bows, only longer. Some of you saw such a thing hanging on the wall of that dead one's lodge. They are small, those spears, but they go through an animal's hide almost as well as a large spear, and a hunter can shoot quickly, more quickly than a man can throw a spear, and yet not grow as tired. The small spears also go farther. So a hunter does not have to be as close to the animals he is trying to kill."

The old one stopped, and for a long time no one else spoke. Finally Chakliux said, "First River, if you were going to attack this village using those weapons, how would you do it?"

The other men seemed surprised by Chakliux's question, but First River answered quickly, as though he had already thought about such a thing. "From the ridge," he said. "You know we put our lodges in this place because it is near the river, and the earth, being shaped like a bowl, shields us from the winds. Yet enemies can surround us on all sides, sit in the trees and shoot down, knowing our spears cannot reach them."

"No," some of the younger hunters called out. "These small spears cannot fly that far."

"Yes," First River said, "I have seen them. They can. And who among us is strong enough to send his spear that distance? Perhaps only Sok."

Sok nodded, but said, "And only a few times. Then my strength would be gone."

"Those small spears, even if they hit a man, will not kill him," said the boy River Ice Dancer.

It was a foolish thing to say, and most of the men did not even bother to answer, leaving River Ice Dancer to puff out his chest, thinking he had said something important, but old First River said, "They killed the shaman."

"Can they penetrate the walls of our lodges?" Sok asked.

"Perhaps not," Blue-head Duck said, "since our lodges are made with two layers. Maybe we should just stay inside, wait for them to come close, then we will kill them."

"But how long until they think of fire?" First River asked. He was leaning heavily now on the young man beside him. "Those faraway hunters tied oil-soaked moss to the ends of their spears, lit them and shot them into lodges. The people who survived the spears died in the flames."

"What should we do?" Sok asked.

"Let us go now," said Chakliux. "We can climb to the ridges, meet them there with our spears."

"First River," said Blue-head Duck, "in a close space, which is the better weapon, our spears or theirs?"

"Ours," First River said.

Some of the younger men began boasting, but Blue-head Duck shouted them down. "Remember our shaman. Remember that, even in his disgrace, he defied death to warn us. Go now, get your weapons and leave the village in quietness. Wait in the willow at the edge of the ridge, and when the Cousin River hunters come, they will find we are stronger than they think."

Some of the Cousin River men did not want to fight. They saw that the shaman was gone, leaving only his pack to mark the place where he had died. They were afraid his spirit had taken his body and would fight with the Near Rivers against them.

"Wolves took him," Man Laughing said, and Tikaani raised his voice in agreement, but he did not let himself wonder how wolves took the man without disturbing the pack.

He was afraid their luck had begun to leave them, so he urged the men to hurry to the ridge that encircled the village, go while it was still dark, before they could lose all their good luck. When the first Near River hunters left their lodges in the morning, the quick silence of the Cousin River warriors' arrows would await them.

Each Cousin River warrior had thrown gaming sticks to determine his place to fight. The largest stick had four sides, one marked to show north, the others for south, east and west.

On Tikaani's throw, the stick had fallen to north, the river side of the village. A good place to be, Tikaani had thought, closest to escape if their luck was not as strong as they hoped. The second stick had eight sides, and his had fallen on the side for one of the center positions. Who could know if that was good or bad? The third stick was flat, with only two sides, one for standing, the other for climbing into a tree. Each hunter who had thrown for the north side had also thrown to stand.

The elder Take More told the men of the north side to throw again, but again, the stick told each of them to stand. Then Take More said the spirits were speaking to them, that all those on the river side should stand, though on the other sides hunters should both stand and climb trees.

Perhaps that was best, Tikaani thought, but he had never been sure of Take More's wisdom. He would stand at first, but later, if the battle was not going well, he would climb a tree. Better to see, better to shoot his arrows far.

He crept to his place, pulled an arrow from his quiver, and waited. It was too dark to see into the village except for the glow of those lodges where hearth fires burned, and in this time just before sunrise, even that light was dim. Suddenly one of the lodges glowed brightly, then another and another. Did the Near River women rise so early?

A movement drew his eye, and he heard a hiss of indrawn breath, as though all the men on the ridge were one, watching together, breathing together. People were moving between the lodges. Tikaani could see their heads like shadows.

"They have spears," someone to his left whispered.

Tikaani squinted and moved his head, giving his eyes greater vision in the darkness. Then came the command, whether from one of the men near him or from within he did not know.

"Shoot!"

He drew back his bow and released his arrow.

Chapter Forty-six

Chakliux crept low between the lodges. Some of the men had watched Wolf-and-Raven leave the village. They said he went east into the forest, so they, too, went east, hoping to place themselves between the Cousin River men and their families.

Chakliux wished for more time. Even a few days would have made a difference. First River could have given them a better idea of what they were facing in the fire bow weapon. How far could something like that send its arrows? Could they penetrate lodge walls? With a few days' warning, they could have moved the women and children from the village or ambushed the Cousin River men in the forest.

The top of the lodge to Chakliux's right suddenly glowed bright. Then another farther ahead. The women were awake. Who could blame them? Their men had returned only long enough to grab weapons and protection charms. Chakliux did not want to fight. The fear in his chest was so large it seemed to hamper the beating of his heart, but he was glad he was not a woman, waiting.

The sound came from above him, a hiss that made him duck. Then a thump, a cry, and he saw Least Weasel, one of the youngest hunters, pinned to the lodge just ahead, an arrow through the soft flesh of his side, the arrowhead embedded in the caribou hide lodge covering. Chakliux ran to him. Least Weasel struggled against the arrow, sobbing out his anger.

"Be quiet, be still," Chakliux told him.

He used his sleeve knife to cut through the shaft just above the arrowhead, then he pulled the shaft from the wound. Least Weasel slumped at his feet, and Chakliux lifted him up. They moved just as another arrow pierced the lodge where they had been standing. Chakliux did not stop to wonder whose lodge it was. He only dragged Least Weasel through the entrance, called to the women inside to help, then he left.

What magic gave the Cousin River hunters the power to see in darkness? he wondered, then ducked again as another arrow thudded into the ground in front of him. He pulled the arrow free and thrust it into his spear sheath. Perhaps the magic was in the arrow itself. Perhaps if it was beside his spears, they, too, would see in darkness. He raised his head. Root Digger was ahead of him, his body dark against a lodge. Then before Chakliux could react, a Cousin River arrow caught Root Digger in the throat. In horror, Chakliux rushed to his side; in horror he watched the death throes rack Root Digger's body. When Root Digger lay still, Chakliux stood, but he dropped quickly as an arrow sliced into the lodge just above his head.

Then he understood. There was no magic, only the silhouettes of the Near River men against the lodges. As the women stirred the hearth fires, the light allowed the Cousin River hunters to see the men that moved from the village.

"Stay low," he called. "They can see us against the lodges."

More men cried out, echoing his call, then Chakliux heard others, men at the edge of the village: "They are on the ridge above us."

Chakliux lay flat against the ground. If the Cousin River men were on all sides of the village, there were few places to hide from their arrows. The ridge was like the lip of a bowl, with only the rock steps that led to the river breaking the edge. If some of the men could get to that break before the sun rose, they might work their way behind the Cousin River men, could attack them from the back.

Chakliux looked to his left, waited until he saw movement, then crept over to catch the leg of Blue-head Duck, the old man crawling on his belly. He turned with his knife raised.

"I am Chakliux."

"You were almost dead," the old man said.

"Come with me toward the river," Chakliux told him. "Stay low."

"Our stupid women," Blue-head Duck whispered. He raised his hand, beat against the side of the nearest lodge and called out, "Douse your hearth fire. The Cousin River men can see us. You give their eyes light to find us."

Chakliux heard the muffled sound of voices from inside the lodge, then suddenly the light was gone. He crept ahead to the next lodge, poked his head into the entrance tunnel and told them the same thing. All along the edge of the village, as they moved toward the river path, they warned the women, and when they found a hunter, told him to follow. As they gathered more men, they split into threes and fours, moving separately, afraid a large group would catch the Cousin River hunters' eyes, even in the darkness.

Chakliux, Blue-head Duck and Carries Much were the first hunters to reach the path. The shadows were deep, and for a moment Chakliux considered standing and throwing a spear at the Cousin River hunters who stood closest to them on the ridge. But he could not see well enough to be sure of his target. Besides, if one fell, the hunters closest to him might send their arrows into the cleft the path made through the ridge.

Chakliux clasped Blue-head Duck's wrist, whispered, "Do not throw your weapon. They will know we are here," then said the same to Carries Much. He felt the boy let out his breath, realized he had a spear in his thrower, ready.

"Go to the river," Chakliux told them, "then where the bank is low, creep up into the forest. Take a place behind the Cousin River men, pick your target, but do not throw your spear until you hear me call out." He squeezed Carries Much's shoulder, felt the boy tremble. "Go now. Go quietly."

Blue-head Duck and Carries Much left him, and Chakliux waited for the next group. They came, led by Sok. Chakliux could think of no words to express his joy that his brother was still alive, so only told them what he had said to the others, sent them also to the river, and waited again.

Five groups of men came, three or four hunters in each group. Finally, Chakliux also went to the river, followed it to the low bank and climbed up to disappear into the spruce forest. He found the Near River men just inside the forest, waiting, each a few running steps behind the trees that hid the Cousin River hunters.

Many Cousin River hunters were standing at the rocky lip of the ledge. Some were laughing, calling out insults, as they sent their arrows into the village. They were men Chakliux had grown up with, and he could not let himself think of the years they had lived together, could not let himself imagine the destruction that would come to both villages no matter who won the battle. He stepped forward, called out, threw his spear. It hit solidly between a Cousin River hunter's shoulder blades. The man slumped, and the hunter next to him turned to look. His exclamation of surprise became a froth of blood when he, too, was hit.

Then the Near River men were crying out their victory. Several hunters stood on the ridge to crow their delight, and arrows took them, but the others—most of the Near River hunters—crept back into the forest, hid, waited for light, waited for the Cousin River men to come to them.

They did not come. At dawn they swarmed down from the trees and into the village, where they began fighting lodge to lodge. Chakliux led the Near River men into the village, and they fought, knife to knife, hunter to hunter. Chakliux's strong arms allowed him to kill two men, but then his legs grew weary and his muscles were torn with cramps. He crept into a lodge, fended off the knife in the hands of one of the Near River women. She wept her regret, then gave him water, offered food. He took the water, but did not think he could eat anything. His belly was twisted too tightly in anger, in fear.

When he went outside again, he crept up behind a Cousin River hunter who was fighting with Fox Barking. Chakliux killed the Cousin River man with his long-bladed knife, then in the same way killed a hunter who was fighting with Sok.

Chakliux fought one man then another until he lost track of the sun and no longer felt his pain. Finally there were no more to fight, and he heard the cries of victory, the ululations of the women, then affirmations that the Cousin River hunters had fled.

As the women found husbands and sons dead, mourning songs drowned out cries of celebration, but Chakliux's weariness was so great that at first they did not pierce his heart. He stared up at the sky, saw that the sun was still high. How could so much have happened in such a short time? Surely they had fought for years. Surely it had taken them longer than one morning to destroy themselves.

K'os counted out the days on her fingers. Three to walk to the Near River Village, though the men, being hunters and not slowed by women and children, should make it more quickly than that. Another day to prepare weapons and complete plans. One day to fight. Perhaps two? She counted two. Another day to celebrate and take the spoils, divide the women and children. Then what, four days to return home?

With women and children hindering them, with their wounded, yes, probably four. That made one more than two handfuls. She should not be worried yet. It had been only one handful and three more.

She squatted beside her fire and stirred the coals. The village seemed too empty without the men, and for some reason, K'os could not stay warm. It was as though the wind, knowing the women and old ones were alone, blew harder. She dug through the bundle of furs she stored for making boots, leggings and parkas, found a large wolf pelt, turned it fur side in, and wrapped it around her shoulders.

She had intended to sew a parka while the men were gone. She would make it beautiful to celebrate their successful battle. She would wear it to honor her revenge against Fox Barking and Sleeps Long. They deserved to die, as did their wives and children. And what about that woman who had left Chakliux on the Grandfather Rock and tricked K'os into raising a cursed child? She, too, should die.

But though K'os had planned to sew, her fingers were too full of nervousness. They dropped awls and needles, tangled sinew thread. She had cut out the pieces of the parka, had even dyed the caribou hair she would use to embroider a pattern on shoulders, cuffs and chest, but that was all she had done.

She heard a shout just outside her lodge, raised her head. It was a woman's voice. Some child had probably managed to hurt himself. Or a woman had foolishly dumped hot broth on herself. K'os dropped the wolf pelt from her shoulders and went to get her medicine bag. She had goose grass for burns, though the dried stems were not as good as juice taken fresh from the crushed plant. She had yellow violet leaves mixed into a goose grease salve for scrapes, cuts and bruises, and she knew how to make birchbark casts for broken bones.

More shouting, a scream. K'os sighed, then smiled. She got a good price for her work—usually some charm highly valued by the one who was sick or hurt. Later, K'os would wear it often, or better yet, destroy it and leave the remains in plain sight at the refuse pile at the edge of the village.

She took out several strings of beads, fastened them around her neck, then picked up her medicine bag. Why make them come and get her? Why not go now? People who lived in the same village should help one another.

"Listen," Night Man said. He propped himself higher against his backrest, flinched at the jostling to his shoulder.

He had good ears, far better than Aqamdax's. She crawled into the lodge entrance, heard the thin sound of voices, women crying.

"Stay here," she told Ghaden, who had followed her, then she went outside.

She could see nothing, but again she heard the voices. They seemed to come from the south side of the village. She went back into the lodge.

"Something has happened," she told Night Man.

She pulled on leggings and boots and her outside parka. Ghaden began to struggle with his parka, but Night Man shook his head at the boy. "Stay," he said. "If you go, Biter will go, and he could cause problems if someone has been injured."

"Do you think the men have returned?" Yaa asked.

"If they had, Star would be here to tell us," Aqamdax said, but did not miss the look of dread that passed over Night Man's face. If the men had returned, it was not good. There were no celebration cries.

"I will be back," Aqamdax said, and hurried outside. She ran through the village, joined other women who also ran, and, when she saw the group of men, she, too, lifted her voice in mourning.

Only six hunters had returned: Fisher, Runner, Sky Watcher, Take More, Man Laughing and Tikaani. Each of them showed some sign of injury. Tikaani lay on a travois; he was so pale Aqamdax thought he was dead. Star and K'os were huddled beside him. K'os looked back over her shoulder and saw Aqamdax.

"This man, we must get him to my lodge," K'os said. She raised her voice and spoke to the women. "Take the others, each to a lodge. Check their feet and hands for frostbite, give them water and food, wash any wounds and let them sleep. I will come later and bring medicines." She turned and looked at the men standing beside Tikaani's travois. "Do any of you have strength enough to get him to my lodge?"

"I do," Sky Watcher said. Then Take More, an elder, slumped to his knees.

"Bring him as well," K'os said, lifting her chin toward the old man.

Aqamdax leaned down beside Star, helped her get Take More to his feet. On the way to K'os's lodge, Aqamdax saw one of Yaa's friends and asked her to tell those in Star's lodge that the men had returned. "Tell them I am in K'os's lodge with Tikaani and that I will come home when I can."

The girl ran off, and Aqamdax wished she could have been the one to go. How would Night Man react, hearing that his brother was wounded? She needed to be with her husband but did not want to leave Tikaani alone with K'os.

Aqamdax helped Star settle Take More on pelts K'os had laid out on the floor, then the two of them removed his outer parka, his boots and leggings. The man had several gashes on his arms, another across his forehead, but none seemed infected. He opened his eyes, looked at both of them, croaked out a request for water. Aqamdax got a water bladder and held it so only a trickle went into Take More's mouth.

He roared out a protest, and Aqamdax told Star, "This one is just tired."

"I cannot see right," he whispered. "I see two of all things."

Though K'os was working over Tikaani, she asked, "Did someone hit you in the face or head?"

"The back of the head," Take More said. "For a whole day I did not know anything. They had me on a travois with Tikaani."

K'os lifted her chin toward Aqamdax. "Put your hands on the back of his head. Touch with your fingertips."

Aqamdax did what K'os told her.

"Do you feel a lump or a sunken area?"

"A lump," Aqamdax said, and made a circle with her thumb and forefinger to show K'os how large it was.

"You will see better tomorrow, at least by the next day," K'os told Take More. "Stay with me tonight. I have a tea Aqamdax will make for you." She thrust her hand into the medicine bag and drew out a packet, tossed it to Aqamdax.

"Only a pinch. Heat it to boiling, then let it cool. Make him drink it all." She laid out several packets of powdered woundwort leaves and told Aqamdax and Star to skim fat from her boiling bag and mix it with the powder, smooth the fat over Take More's cuts.

She turned back to Tikaani and worked over him for a time, probing with her fingers, cleaning wounds. Finally she looked up. A smile on her face gave Aqamdax hope, but K'os said, "He is dead. A belly wound, not an easy way to die, at least the first few days." K'os looked at Sky Watcher. "You should have left him, saved your strength," she said.

"He was my mother's cousin," the young man answered. "He fought well. I could not leave him."

"Are any more of our hunters coming back?" K'os asked him.

"No. We are the only ones left."

At his words, Star raised her voice in a hard wail of mourning.

K'os whirled toward the woman. "Shut your mouth!" she shouted, then she lowered her voice and asked the young man, "And how many Near Rivers died?"

"Many," he said.

K'os tipped back her head and sang out a chant, strange words mixed with laughter.

"Did you know any of them?" she asked. "A man named Fox Barking, another named Sleeps Long, did they die?"

"I do not know," he answered.

Take More said, "I fought Fox Barking. He is still alive, but cut here." He drew a finger down his forehead and over one eye to his jaw. "Sleeps Long is dead. I killed him."

"Hah!" K'os screamed out. "I celebrate your bravery." She reached into her medicine packet. "Put this into the tea you are making," she told Aqamdax. "It will taste better and will relieve some of Take More's pain."

She went over to Take More, began to check his wounds, finally nodded as if satisfied. "There is nothing serious here," she said, then pressed her hand to the back of his head. "Even this. I have seen worse."

"My son Chakliux. Did you see him?" she asked Sky Watcher.

"He is alive," he said. "I saw him as we were leaving. I thought he would kill us, but he held back the hunters, though some were angry. I could hear their shouts. Still, they did as he said."

K'os sucked in her cheeks, said nothing for a long time, and when she spoke again, Aqamdax saw blood froth at the corners of her mouth.

"You are so proud to drag that one home," she said, and lifted a foot to prod Tikaani's body. "Are you proud enough to carry him to her lodge?" She nodded toward Star. "Let his mother and sister prepare him for burial. I do not have time. My work is with the living. Besides, if any of our men deserved death, he did. He was the one who planned the attack against the Near Rivers."

"I know who planned the attack," Sky Watcher said, then he lifted his head and spit full into K'os's face.

She screamed curses, but the man ignored her. He hoisted Tikaani's body to one shoulder and followed Star and Aqamdax from the lodge.

THE NEAR RIVER VILLAGE

Blue-head Duck was dying. The wounds on his body were shallow, not enough to kill, but at some time during the battle, someone had cursed the man's heart, and he had fallen as though hit by an arrow, clutching his chest in pain, though there was no blood.

"You must lead this village now," he said to Chakliux. "There is no one else. Tsaani is dead. Wolf-and-Raven is dead." He spoke the names as though he, too, were dead and did not have to worry what their spirits might do to him. "Sok does not have the wisdom."

Blue-head Duck paused, took a long breath, lay his hand over the center of his chest, winced, and Chakliux wished he could share the man's pain.

"We do not want Fox Barking. A man who is too lazy to provide for his wives should not lead a village. We do not want Dog Trainer."

A moon before, Chakliux would have smiled at Blue-head Duck's words. Everyone knew of the rivalry between Blue-head Duck and Dog Trainer. Dog Trainer would have been a good leader, wise and strong enough to stand for what he believed to be right. But Dog Trainer was dead. Chakliux looked away so Blue-head Duck would not see the knowledge of that death in his eyes. He would know soon enough. Let them compete with one another in the spirit world.

"I have asked the people to meet tonight. I will be there. They will listen to me."

Chakliux nodded and did not express his doubt. Why would they listen to a man who was dying? Most of the men acknowledged Chakliux's part in saving the village from complete destruction, but many hunters and most of the elders had died. When the Cousin River men had seen they were losing, they set lodges on fire, killing two old women and several others: Blue Flower and No Teeth; New Grass and her baby; the sister-wives Brown Water and Happy Mouth. Half of the young hunters had died in the battle—and most of the boys, including Sok's son Carries Much.

Chakliux could not allow himself to remember his nephew's face. When he did, his sorrow was like a wound in his heart, and he could do nothing but cry out his anguish.

They had enough hunters to keep their village strong, to supply food for the winter, to fish, but only a handful of the Cousin River men had survived, and of those, Tikaani and Take More had been dragged away on a travois. Chakliux had persuaded the Near River men to let them go. Perhaps that was foolish, but how would their women survive if there were no men to hunt?

Chakliux left Blue-head Duck's lodge and walked into the woods, past a group of young men practicing with bows and arrows captured in the battle. He found a rock at the base of a large spruce, sat down on it, drew his feet up, away from the cold of the still-frozen ground.

He called to his mind all the faces of the Cousin River men he had known. Although they were the ones who had started the battle, he mourned as much for them as he did for the Near River People. It was probably also a Cousin River hunter who had killed Tsaani and Daes. Why did people do such stupid things?

He leaned his head back against the tree trunk, thought through all the stories he had been told, Cousin and Near River, North Tundra and Caribou, the First Men stories he had heard from Aqamdax and Qung. He heard them again as though he were a child, learning all things for the first time. He listened, and the words were like a poultice for the wounds of his body, and those larger, deeper wounds that pierced his soul.

Sok took his place among the hunters. With so many killed in battle, the circle of men was small, but its smallness made him feel larger, more important. They would choose a leader tonight. Who else could it be but him? Blue-head Duck was dying—Chakliux himself had told Red Leaf. Sleeps Long and Dog Trainer were dead. Chakliux would not be chosen. How could a man with only one good leg lead his people? How could a person who had been raised in the Cousin River Village carry the respect of the Near River hunters? No one wanted Fox Barking. Who could trust the man? The oldest person in the village was probably Ligige', and she was a woman. Who would listen to her?

Sok had worn his finest parka, had brought both his wives, as well as Cries-loud and the infant son born to Snow-in-her-hair. Red Leaf's face was dark with charcoal, her hair chopped short in mourning. He, too, carried the pain of his son's death, but the boy had died bravely, and what father could not find solace in that? He would name Snow-in-her-hair's child Carries Much, and in that way call the boy back to live with them. Perhaps Red Leaf would find comfort in that, though the two women were often sharp with one another, using words like men used weapons.

Four hunters brought Blue-head Duck from his lodge on a blanket of caribou skins, each man holding a corner. His old wife scurried beside him, poking at his hair and clothing, fussing until Sok had to look away, lest he speak out against her foolishness.

They set him down on a pad of soft furs next to the fire. The three remaining elders clustered close to him, but Sok stayed with the younger hunters, waited until Blue-head Duck's wife left his side and found her place among the women. Then he went to Snow-in-her-hair, lifted his son from her arms and took him along with Cries-loud to Blue-head Duck. He knelt beside the man and spoke.

"I bring my sons to honor the elders of this village," Sok said. "I bring them so they understand the sacredness and respect these men give to the Near River People."

He waited, hoping Blue-head Duck would open his eyes, would say something, but the old man lay as if he were already dead, though Sok could see the labored rise and fall of his chest. Finally, Sok began a chant, something soft, a hunting song he had learned from his grandfather. He took the baby and Cries-loud back to their mothers, reclaimed his place among the hunters. He calmed his anger with the hope that even without Blue-head Duck's acknowledgment, his action would be enough to win the people's favor, to make them realize who should be their chief hunter.

He waited then, uncomfortable in the silence, wondering who would speak first. Of the elders still living, Blue-head Duck was too close to the spirit world to know what was happening in the village. Fox Barking held no one's respect. Sun Caller was a man of stuttering tongue and few words, and Giving Meat had long ago retreated into a world where no one could reach him. He sat with spittle hanging from his mouth, his leggings dark with fresh urine.

Then Blue-head Duck raised one hand, made a whispered request, and Sun Caller moved behind him, propped him up until he was almost sitting.

"I am dying," he said, the words so sudden that all whispers, all movement stopped, and it seemed as if even the wind held its breath. "For more than a year we have lived without our chief hunter. Some say his life was taken by spirits; others claim it was by those enemies we just defeated. We have now lost our shaman. Our healer is an old woman."

Blue-head Duck moved his head slowly to look at Ligige'. Her eyes stared back at him from a face blackened in mourning. "Some have called me leader," Blue-head Duck said. "Among the elders, I often spoke first." He coughed, took several deep breaths, and when he spoke again, his voice was louder, stronger. "You must choose a new leader. I do not say to choose a shaman, that is something the people cannot do, but choose someone to lead the elders, someone as chief hunter, perhaps one man, perhaps two." He paused, "My choice would be . . ."

Sok held his breath, waited impatiently for Blue-head Duck's eyes to come to him, but they did not. They stopped, and Sok leaned forward, saw the old man was staring at Chakliux.

"Chakliux," Blue-head Duck said. "Both for leader of the elders and chief hunter."

Sok opened his mouth to make a protest, but his words choked him, and before he could say anything, Blue-head Duck gasped, clutched at his chest, twisting his body as if to flee the pain. He cried out, then was still, both mouth and eyes open.

Women and men gathered around him, and finally old Ligige' raised her voice to tell everyone that he was dead.

No one started a mourning song, and Sok wondered if sorrow had piled too high on the people, so that they had no songs left.

Then suddenly Fox Barking was speaking, standing among the elders. "This man was a good man, wise, strong; we will miss him," Fox Barking said. "I was glad to call him friend, but now that there are only three of us counted as elders, I must speak. How can we allow a man who is young, one who—although he is my son—was raised among those we call enemy? He fought for us, and I hold pride in my heart at his strength, but I say that we who are elders will lead ourselves. You young men, go out, hunt and protect our women, give them sons and daughters, teach your nephews to hunt. When the years have taught you wisdom, join us as elders, but not until then.

"Chakliux," he said, and smiled at him, "I mean you no dishonor. You are storyteller. Find praise in that, but let the elders lead themselves."

Sok looked at Sun Caller and at Giving Meat, knew in his heart that all things would be decided by Fox Barking.

"So then," Fox Barking said, "I lift my voice to honor our storyteller." He began a chant of praise, and others did the same, though Sok sat still and silent, as did Chakliux, both with eyes on Blue-head Duck, a good man lying dead without the honor of mourning chants.

As the praise song died away, one woman began a mourning song, but again Fox Barking spoke. This time his voice was loud, and all warmth had left it. "With such honor given my son Chakliux, I cannot ask that he also be called chief hunter. There are others who bring in more meat. Now, after this battle with our enemies, we must have a chief hunter whose good luck will spread to all the men of the village."

Several hunters called out Sok's name, and again he felt hope grow in his heart. Fox Barking was right. Chakliux was raised as Dzuuggi by the Cousin River People, and he should be storyteller. But with his weak leg, surely not chief hunter.

Fox Barking raised his hands, looked at Sok, smiled. "Again, I am honored to hear one of my sons named. Who is a better hunter than Sok? Even his grandfather knew he was gifted with spear and spear-thrower, but he carries a curse. He is my son, and so I did not want to tell you this, but I must. Already too many have died."

Sok stared at his stepfather. What did he mean? What curse? He looked around the circle, seeking out Chakliux. His brother often understood things Sok did not, but he saw the same confusion on Chakliux's face. Then he saw Red Leaf stretch her hands out toward Fox Barking, as if she could stop his words before they came from his mouth.

"Look! What do I see?" Fox Barking said. "The snow is red, as is the floor of a lodge." He spoke to Chakliux. "I have come to appreciate your riddles," he told him, then he turned to Sok. "Look! What do I see?" he said again. "She fears she must build a lodge in the midden piles and no longer see the sun."

Sok looked at Chakliux, saw understanding, then sorrow, dawn in his brother's eyes.

Chapter
Forty-seven

Fox Barking narrowed his eyes. The wound that slashed his face from brow to jaw was as dark as blood. "You do not understand?" he said to Sok. "Ask your brother. With his mind and your feet, the two of you make one good warrior." Then, spreading his arms to the circle of people, Fox Barking said, "We should wait before we decide who is chief hunter. After the caribou hunts, then we will know and make a wise decision. Until then, the elders will decide when we hunt and where we go. The three of us," he said, nodding toward Sun Caller and Giving Meat.

There was a low hum of disapproval from the people, and finally one of the young men spoke out. "Sok is our best hunter, and Chakliux knows about sea hunting," he said. "Sok has many strong dogs, and Chakliux brought us the golden-eyed pups. I think you are wrong about this curse."

"I know things you do not," Fox Barking said. "Remember Chakliux has only one dog now, and most of Sok's dogs have died." He waited, but no one spoke. "Do not misunderstand. Perhaps Chakliux or Sok will lead us. All I say is we should wait. After we have hunted through the spring and summer, when winter is near, then we will decide who is our chief hunter. Who can say what will happen by then? Many things might change."

He raised his eyebrows at Chakliux, but Chakliux pretended he did not see. Perhaps Fox Barking's riddle was not true. He often lied, especially for his own gain.

"What is most important now," Fox Barking continued, "is this dead one, long honored as an elder. We must mourn him as we have all the men and women who died in this battle."

A few of the women lifted voices to begin mourning, but the men lifted knives and throwing spears.

Fox Barking gestured for the men to lower their weapons. "When our mourning is finished," he called out, "then we will speak of revenge. Six of their hunters left this village alive. Some of our men said we should not follow them. I say we are foolish to let them live. No, they cannot attack our village as they once did, but what will stop them from stalking our hunters and killing them one by one? What will stop them from attacking our women and children when they go to set traplines?"

Hunters raised their voices, and several men jumped to their feet, began a chant of victory. Chakliux also stood, made his way to Sok's side and pulled his brother from the circle.

"What do the riddles mean?" Sok asked, his breath coming in quick gasps as though he had been running. "Do you understand what he just did to us? Together we might have been the leaders of our village, I as chief hunter and you leading the elders."

"He wants the power for himself," Chakliux said.

"You think because I do not understand his riddles that I do not know he wants all power for himself?"

Chakliux heard the fear under his brother's words. "Sok," he said quietly, "there are more important things to talk about now. Is Red Leaf's lodge empty?"

"Yes."

"Let us go there."

Ligige' watched as Sok and Chakliux left the fire circle. She listened as Fox Barking continued to speak, and her mind worked at the riddles he had told, turning them and shaking them like a woman cleaning floor mats. Riddles were a foolish thing, she thought. Why did the Cousin River People enjoy them so much?

Her irritation continued to rise as Fox Barking spoke. Did the people believe him? His words were like nets ready to catch them all.

Though now he praised Blue-head Duck, had they forgotten how often Fox Barking made jokes about the man, told lies about his children, even his dogs? Did they think he was trustworthy just because he could shed a few tears?

Fox Barking told several old women and two of Blue-head Duck's nephews to take the man's body to his wife's lodge, then when those few were gone, he spoke again about revenge, promising the young men they could take Cousin River women as wives, telling the women their men would bring them back food and furs from the Cousin River storage caches. Finally, Ligige' could not bear to listen any longer.

She pushed herself up with her walking stick, called out to anyone who would listen, "He is a fool; he is a liar. If you follow him, you are no better than he is."

She turned to leave the circle, ignoring those who called to her. As she walked away, her anger seemed to clear her mind, and suddenly she knew what Fox Barking meant with his riddles.

The knowledge was like a fist to her stomach, and she had to stop, gasp for breath. Almost, she turned her steps toward Red Leaf's lodge, but then decided she must spend time thinking before she spoke to Sok.

Her thoughts had been as thin as smoke, drifting in circles, since the battle. Who could believe that a village could lose so much in one day? Who could believe so many people could die? And who could believe her sorrow had not killed her?

Sok stirred the hearth coals then they pulled back their parka hoods, held open hands toward the fire. Finally Chakliux said, "I do not think many people understood the riddles."

"Perhaps I understood the first," Sok said. "Red on the snow and on a lodge floor, that means blood. He was talking about the two deaths, our grandfather's and that of the Sea Hunter woman."

Chakliux nodded.

"But I do not understand the second riddle."

Chakliux closed his eyes, tightened his hands into fists. He did not want to say this to Sok. If it was not true, then why repeat it? But if it was true and Fox Barking knew, they must be prepared; they must think before taking action.

"What do we put in midden piles?" he asked softly.

Sok pulled his parka off over his head, laid it on the floor, then snorted. "Things thrown away, things not wanted."

"Who lives in lodges?" Chakliux asked.

"We do," Sok said, an edge of irritation hardening his voice. "All of us."

"People," Chakliux said. "Not animals, not rocks, not plants, people."

"Yes," Sok said.

"Who owns our lodges?"

"The women."

"The second riddle was 'She fears she must build a lodge in the midden piles and no longer see the sun.' "

"A woman thrown away," Sok said. "He is talking about a woman thrown away by her husband." He frowned. "The only women thrown away in this past year were Blueberry and the Sea Hunter woman."

Chakliux shook his head. "Fox Barking spoke about a woman who was afraid she might be thrown away."

"Then it could be any woman."

"Remember, she is afraid that she will no longer see the sun." He pointed at the sun motif on Sok's parka, and saw understanding, then horror, fill Sok's face.

"Red Leaf?" he said softly. "Not Red Leaf. She cared too much for our grandfather. She would not . . ." Suddenly, he jumped to his feet. "Fox Barking!" he shouted. "He tries to destroy us. He wants the others to drive us from the village!"

He tore open the doorflap, then stopped, backed into the lodge, his mouth hanging open. Red Leaf entered, her eyes on his face.

"You understand the riddle?" she asked.

"He lies. It is not true," Sok said.

Then Fox Barking was also in the lodge, his mouth stretched wide in a smile.

"Tell him," Fox Barking said to Red Leaf.

Her voice was soft, like a whisper. "I killed your grandfather," she said, "and the Sea Hunter woman."

"She would have killed me, if she could have," Fox Barking said, "but she thought I would keep her secret. She thought I would rather preserve my son's honor. Most times I would, but there are other times . . ." He looked at Sok and laughed.

"Why?" Sok asked softly.

Red Leaf held her hands out to him, palms up. "So you would get his dogs. So you would have his songs. So you could be chief hunter."

Sok buried his face in his hands. His shoulders shook, but Chakliux heard no sound. Finally Sok looked at his wife. "A man does not want to be chief hunter in that way," he told her, and he spoke softly, as if he were talking to a child.

"I was afraid you would throw me away so you could take Snow-in-her-hair as first wife. I knew you wanted her even before I became your wife. I thought I could make you forget her, then I thought that she could be second wife, but Wolf-and-Raven would not give her to you. I thought he might let her come to you if you were chief hunter. Then you would not throw me away. I did not mean to kill the Sea Hunter woman. But she saw me, she and her boy. I thought the boy might tell others, but I dressed as a man, and he must not have known who I was. But Fox Barking saw me. . . ."

"I had just left your grandfather's lodge," Fox Barking said. "I saw her from the shadows, but she did not see me. I did not know anyone had died until the next day. Then I remembered who I had seen. I went to Red Leaf and told her I would say nothing, that I did not want my son to be hurt by something his wife did. But sometimes a man can no longer live with lies."

Sok turned his back on Fox Barking and said to Red Leaf, "We had two strong sons. I would not have thrown you away, but now . . ." His words faded, and he clenched the knife he wore in a scabbard at his waist. "Do you know how many times I have vowed to kill the one who killed my grandfather?"

"I will leave the village," Red Leaf said. "I will find some other place to raise your son."

Sok clenched his teeth. "If I let you leave, you will not take Cries-loud. He will stay with me. Snow-in-her-hair will be his mother."

"I do not speak of Cries-loud," Red Leaf said. She placed a hand over her belly. "I speak of this son that I carry under my heart."

Fox Barking laughed. "So what choice do you have?" he asked. "Keep her. She is a strong woman. Who else can make parkas like Red Leaf? But I must tell you that she is not welcome in this village. You can stay, but she cannot." He laughed again. "Nor can her son. Either son."

Sok whirled, scooped up his parka and threw it on the fire. The fur caught, filling the lodge with smoke. "Get out!" he bellowed at Fox Barking. "This woman and I and our sons will leave the village tomorrow morning. Until then, I do not want to see you." He pushed Fox Barking toward the entrance tunnel.

Chakliux pulled the charred remains of the parka from the hearth fire with a stirring stick and heaved it outside after Fox Barking.

Sok sank to his haunches, sat with his head in his hands. Chakliux sat beside him.

"I will go with you," he told his brother. "I still hope to find Aq-amdax."

"Aqamdax is dead," Sok said. "I have seen her death in my dreams."

"I have not," Chakliux said quietly.

"So where will we go?"

"To the Cousin River Village."

"They are our enemies."

"They were my people. I cannot let Fox Barking plan a revenge raid without warning them."

"Why should they believe you? Why should they listen? They know you fought against them."

"I will go quietly, in the night, to my mother."

"You think she will not kill you?"

"She may try to kill me, but she will listen first."

"What good will it do them, to know our hunters come? They have only a handful of warriors left." He looked hard into Chakliux's eyes. "Do not expect me to fight against my own people. I will not. Against Fox Barking I would seek revenge, not against any other."

"So then you understand how I feel about my people. I have few I owe revenge: Night Man and Tikaani, though both may now be dead. I did not see Night Man in the battle or among the survivors, and Tikaani was taken away on the travois. That leaves only my mother."

"And in this village, Red Leaf," Sok said, staring at the woman until she huddled against the wall of the lodge, covered her face with her hands.

For a long time, neither man spoke, but finally Sok broke the silence. "I will take Red Leaf and Cries-loud and leave in the morning. I will travel near the Cousin River Village. If you choose to come with me, then come. I will wait for you while you visit the Cousin River People. If you do not return, I will go on, try to find a River village that will welcome a hunter and his wife. Or perhaps I will build a lodge near the Grandfather Lake and stay there." He looked into Chakliux's eyes. "It has been a good thing to have a brother."

They rolled out sleeping mats, but Chakliux could not sleep. They had already packed many of their belongings and would empty out their storage caches in the morning. Though Wolf-and-Raven had killed most of Sok's dogs, he still had Snow Hawk and two others. Chakliux had Black Nose. With the dogs and the four of them—Chakliux, Sok, Red Leaf and Cries-loud—they could take much with them, even Red Leaf's caribouskin lodge cover.

Cries-loud had come to them as they were packing, but Sok had refused to answer the boy's many questions. Finally Red Leaf drew him aside, spoke to him for a long time. Then the boy, too, helped them, his face somber, his eyes red and swollen, though Chakliux saw no tears on his face.

Halfway through the night, Chakliux heard someone outside the lodge. He sat up, reached for his knife. If others had solved Fox Barking's riddles, they might come for revenge, but then he heard the scratching on the lodge wall. What enemy scratched before entering? He crept through the entrance tunnel. Snow-in-her-hair stood outside, her son bound to her back.

"I need to talk to my husband."

Chakliux beckoned her into the lodge and saw that Red Leaf and Sok were awake. Sok sat down beside the hearth.

Chakliux wrapped himself up in his sleeping robes, lay down and turned his back.

"Fox Barking came to me," Snow-in-her-hair said. "What he told me, is it true?"

"Yes," Red Leaf said quietly, and came to stand beside Sok.

"Why did you do such a thing?"

"To keep my husband," Red Leaf said.

"Almost, I can understand," said Snow-in-her-hair, then she asked, "If I come with you, will I and my child be safe?"

"You will be safe," Sok said, his words loud after the quietness of the women's voices.

"No," Snow-in-her-hair said, "I am asking Red Leaf."

"You will be safe, and any of your children."

"When do you leave?"

"In the morning," Sok said, "after we have taken the lodge cover down."

"Can you help me with my lodge cover also?" she asked.

"I will help you," Sok said, and Chakliux heard the gladness in his voice.

She left, and then their mother Day Woman came. Her tears and sobbing woke even Cries-loud. She would come with them, she said, and no argument from Sok or Chakliux could convince her otherwise. She had already brought her pack. Fox Barking was angry, she said, but he did not stop her. What good was she, a woman without sons in the village, a woman too old to bear more sons? Fox Barking would probably throw her away at the beginning of the next winter. He was better off with a younger wife.

What could Chakliux and Sok do except agree to take her?

In the morning, when they rolled up their sleeping robes, when Red Leaf and Day Woman went to empty the food cache, as Criesloud and Chakliux began to take the lodge cover from the poles, then Ligige' came to them. She was leading Wolf-and-Raven's dog, her belongings strapped to the dog's back. She sat on her haunches and watched them work, called out advice now and again.

By noon, they were ready to leave the village. Ignoring the curses shouted against them, and acknowledging the cries that were blessings, they started out: two hunters, two wives, a boy, a baby, five dogs and two old women.

Chapter
Forty-eight

For the third time since the men had returned, K'os's dreams took her back to the day at the Grandfather Rock. For the third night, she was not K'os, healer, feared by all, but K'os, daughter of Mink, a girl without power. She awoke with a start. Her bedding was wrapped around her, pinning her arms as Gull Wing had pinned her arms, and her hair had come loose from its braid and lay across her face, smothering her as her parka had smothered her.

Then she heard the man's voice. Because she was still in her dream, she thought it was Gull Wing. She opened her mouth to scream, but in taking a breath, drew her own hair down her throat. Hands were on her face, but they were gentle, pulling away the hair, loosening the blankets. Then her mind cleared and her eyes, and she knew it was Chakliux.

She pushed away his hands, then stood, shook off her bedding furs, catching one to wrap around her waist. She stirred the hearth coals, moved a tripod that held a caribou skin of stew closer to the coals, then squatted on her haunches and looked at him.

He was larger than she remembered, and his face had changed.

Boy to man? No, that had happened long before. Storyteller to warrior. Perhaps that.

"So you are alive," she said to him.

The words were harsh, rough with the phlegm of sleep.

His silence reminded her of Ground Beater, and she wondered if the spirit of her dead husband had come to Chakliux, had strengthened him with a need for revenge.

"Our warriors say the Near River men fought bravely," K'os said. "They also tell me you led them."

"We fought to protect the women and children, the old ones," Chakliux said.

K'os rose and took two wooden bowls, filled them with meat from the cooking bag. "You will eat?" she asked, holding both bowls out to him.

He took one, wrapped his hands around it and waited until K'os took the first bite, then he ate.

"You are afraid I would poison you?" she asked, mocking him.

"You have taught me to be careful," he answered.

"And because I eat, you think you are safe? What if I, too, have decided to die? What if I decided to sacrifice myself in order to kill the one who has killed so many of my people?"

Chakliux smiled. "You do not care about your people. Why should you die for them?"

"Why not? I will die someday anyway. I am an old woman."

Chakliux studied her. "Yes," he finally said, "you are an old woman."

His words enraged her, but she held her anger in check. "Wisdom comes with age. Strength, power, respect."

"For some."

Her throat burned with unspoken curses, and she gripped her bowl tightly to keep her fingers from flying to his face.

"So you have come to laugh at our defeat, to take your pick of women? Only five have husbands, six if you count Aqamdax, though Night Man will die soon." K'os heard his gasp as she mentioned Aqamdax's name. "You did not know the woman was here?" she asked. She laughed. "She was given to me by Tikaani and Cen. She was my slave until Tikaani decided his brother needed a wife. I used her well." Again she laughed, and felt the laughter bring back a portion of her power. "So she has found a place in your heart. I thought you had no room for anyone but a dead woman and her dead son."

Chakliux gave no answer, so K'os continued. "Yes, Cen and Tikaani captured her and the boy, her brother. He is here also. Star took him as son, but do not worry about avenging their capture. Tikaani is dead, and since Cen did not return from the battle, I assume he is also." She slitted her eyes and watched Chakliux. He lifted his bowl to his mouth, ate until the bowl was empty.

"I asked why you are here," K'os said, and did not refill his bowl, did not offer water.

He stood, took a water bladder from the lodge poles and drank, wiped a hand across his mouth, then held the bladder out to her. She shook her head.

"I am here to tell you that the Near River men plan an attack in revenge."

"How many?"

"I do not know."

"Do they know you have come to warn us?"

"I do not think so."

"Why did you come? Why not stay with them and fight?"

She saw him hesitate, and remembered his doing the same as a small boy when there was something he did not want to tell her. He might be a man, a warrior, even Dzuuggi, but still, he was a child, and she knew that child well.

"They do not want you with them. Why?"

Chakliux squatted again beside the fire. "I did not lead by choice or decision—theirs or mine. I led because I was the first to understand the plan your men used in fighting us."

"And you devised a way to meet their attack."

He rested his wrists over his knees. "The elders say you were the one who gave the bow weapons to the Cousin River men. They say you took a bow from one of our elders."

K'os raised her eyebrows. "A fine old man," she said. "Perhaps you remember him from his visits to my lodge. He was a trader and sometimes enjoyed our hospitality. Sad how he died." When Chakliux said nothing, she finished the meat in her bowl, then rose and got herself more but did not offer any to him. "So why warn us?" she asked as she sat down again. "Surely you must consider us your enemy."

"Truly, I have only one enemy," he said.

"You think so?" she asked.

"I think so."

"You are wrong. Star hates you for killing her brothers. Aqamdax hates you because you left her here and did not try to find her. Those five warriors who survived, they hate you also."

"I warn you because of the women and children. I warn you so you can leave the village before the Near River men come."

"That is what you think we would do? Run away? Hide? You think we are so frightened of the Near Rivers that we would leave our wounded, our old ones?"

"I think," Chakliux said slowly, "that you have three, four days to decide what to do. Three, four days to carry your children and wounded and old ones to a safer place."

"And you will fight with them?" K'os asked.

"I will not," he said. "I fight to save lives, not take them."

He pulled his parka hood up around his face and turned toward the entrance tunnel.

"Chakliux," K'os called. "The man Fox Barking and the one they call Sleeps Long, did they die in the battle?"

"Sleeps Long is dead."

"And Fox Barking?" she asked.

"He now leads the Near River People."

He left the lodge, and it was not until K'os raised her food bowl to her mouth that she realized she had sunk her teeth through her bottom lip.

Chakliux crept through the dark shadows of the village to Star's lodge. He expected to hear the howling of Cloud Finder's dogs, but though they raised their heads as he passed, only one barked—two short yips. They remembered him. Knew him as part of the village.

He came to the lodge, crouched beside the entrance tunnel. He did not want to go inside, to risk waking Star or her mother or Aqamdax's husband, Night Man. But how could he leave the village without seeing Aqamdax?

He was still for a long time, until the cold numbed his feet and crept up into his ankles. Finally, he pulled the doorflap aside. It was a square of caribou hide, sewn double and weighted at the bottom with rocks to hold it in place against the wind. No one spoke, no dog barked, so he crept inside, settled the doorflap behind him and again waited, listened.

Finally he pulled aside the inner doorflap. He heard a low growl. Star, too, kept a dog inside her lodge? Then he realized it was Biter. The knowledge brought a smile, and he held his hand out from the tunnel, whispered the dog's name, removed a stick of dried meat from his sleeve and offered it. Biter came slowly. In the light of the hearth coals, Chakliux could see that his fur was bristled. He sniffed at the meat, took it carefully from Chakliux's fingers, then slowly wagged his tail. Chakliux stroked the dog's wide chest, again whispered his name. Biter took the meat back to a mat on the women's side of the lodge.

Still partially hidden in the tunnel, Chakliux could make out Ghaden, lying with mouth open. The boy moved, flung an arm over the dog, muttered in his sleep, then was still. Someone was lying beside him. Aqamdax? Star? Chakliux raised himself higher on his knees. No, a girl. She turned, and he saw her face. Yaa. Why not? If Biter had made it here, why not Yaa? Her mother had said she and the dog disappeared only a few days after Chakliux had left the village. Perhaps Cen and Tikaani had taken her, too. Or perhaps she had followed them. He tried to imagine himself as a child doing such a thing, but could not.

He moved so he could see the other side of the lodge. Two women—Star and one with gray hair. Her mother. He pushed himself farther into the lodge, saw Night Man, asleep, then raised his eyes to the face of the one who sat beside Night Man.

Aqamdax. She smiled, a sad smile, motioned for him to go back into the entrance tunnel. He waited, and then she was there beside him, a hare fur blanket wrapped around her shoulders and up over her head. In the darkness, he reached out to her face. Her cheeks were wet. She lay her head on his shoulder and they sat without speaking for a long time.

"I prayed you would come for me," she finally whispered.

"Come with me now," he said, tucking his hand into the warmth between her hair and the blanket.

"I cannot leave my husband," she told him. "I cannot leave Ghaden or Yaa."

"Bring them. All of them."

"Night Man is too ill. I cannot move him."

"Aqamdax," he said, "the Near River men are coming to attack the village. You have three, four days, that is all. Is Night Man strong enough to walk into the woods? If you bring him that far, I can take him on a travois, get him away from the village before the attack."

"Let me think," she said, and again leaned her head on his shoulder.

He placed his arm around her, drew her close. She was wife to another, but to find her, after searching so long—he could not believe it was true.

"Tomorrow, when the sun is highest in the sky," Aqamdax said, "wait for us in the woods. Do you know the black rock that is next to the path?"

"I know it."

"We will try to be there. Should I tell the others, our few men, that the Near River warriors come?"

"I have told K'os," Chakliux said.

"You cannot stay here. The men, they will kill you."

"Do not worry. I am with my brother."

"Sok is here?"

"He waits for me, but he does not know you are here."

He felt her mouth move in a smile under his fingertips.

"He will not be happy you have found me," she said.

"Yes, he will," Chakliux told her. "He knows how long I searched for you."

"Why did you wait until now to come?"

"First I went to your village," he told her.

He heard her gasp. "To my people?" she asked.

"To your people, and the Walrus."

"You saw Qung and He Sings; you saw Tut?"

"All of them. I lived with Tut and her brothers."

"Qung is well?"

"She is well." He leaned his cheek against the top of her head, held her. She raised a hand to his face, and he clasped her wrist, felt the string of sinew she wore as a bracelet. He fingered the knots, recognized the shape of the otter.

"I kept it," she said, then wiggled away from him, fumbling with something tied at her waist. In the darkness of the entrance tunnel, he could not see what it was, but she placed it in his hands, and it was cool and smooth under his fingers.

"It is a whale tooth carved into a shell," she whispered. "Something the storytellers of my village wear. Qung gave it to me. It will remind you of the bond we share as storytellers just as the sinew at my wrist reminds me that we both came from the otter."

A soft moan echoed from within the lodge.

Aqamdax pressed close to Chakliux, whispered, "My husband." And suddenly she was gone, as quickly as she had come.

Aqamdax finally slept just as dawn lighted the sky. Then she was pulled from dreams by a loud voice, Fisher calling, scratching at the lodge until Biter's barking woke everyone.

Fisher came inside without Star's invitation, took a place beside Night Man, who had also been awakened by the man's rudeness.

"K'os sent me," he said to Star. "She says that everyone in the village will soon be here."

Star gasped.

"You do not have to feed them. It is only so we can meet and discuss plans. Last night Chakliux came to the village, told K'os the Near Rivers will soon attack. She wants us to plan how best to fight them. She decided we should meet in this lodge, especially since Night Man cannot be moved." He nodded toward Night Man. "She wants your wisdom," he said.

Night Man's eyes cleared, and he straightened himself on his mats.

Aqamdax got up from her bed, pulled on leggings and a caribou hide shirt, then rolled her bedding and got food. Star spent a long time dressing, combing her hair. She did everything in front of Fisher, watching him with slow-blinking eyes.

Aqamdax asked Yaa to help her take Long Eyes to the women's place. Yaa opened her mouth, and Aqamdax knew she was going to ask why Long Eyes had to go outside. At night and in the morning, she usually urinated in a wooden trough. But Aqamdax frowned at the girl and shook her head, then bundled Long Eyes into leggings, boots and parka, and the three went outside.

When they got to the women's place, Aqamdax helped Long Eyes with leggings and parka, held her as she crouched and made water. Then as the old woman adjusted her clothing, Aqamdax drew Yaa aside and told her of Chakliux's plan.

"Go and tell him I cannot get away, that K'os probably guessed what we would do and called a meeting in our lodge." She cupped the girl's chin in her hands. "Take Ghaden and Biter and go with him. Do not stay in the village."

"It is only Chakliux? He is alone?" Yaa asked.

"He and Sok," Aqamdax told her.

Yaa shook her head and looked away. "We cannot go with him," she said. "Ghaden cannot go. I cannot."

"Yaa, that is foolish. The Near River men—"

"Aqamdax, when we were in the Near River Village, you told me to keep talking to Ghaden, to try to help him remember who killed . . . his . . . your mother."

Aqamdax's breath stopped. "Yes," she said softly.

"At the dancing, when the men here were preparing to fight our village, do you remember the boots they wore, the fancy ones with rattlers?"

Aqamdax nodded.

"The noise of the boots helped Ghaden remember. The killer's boots had rattlers, and on the sides the fur was cut to look like the sun."

"Sok," Aqamdax said softly.

"We will stay with you," Yaa said, her words loud. "We will fight with you against the Near Rivers. If they try to kill Night Man, we will kill them."

They helped Long Eyes back to the lodge, then cleared away bedding and mats, making as much space as possible for the village people. Aqamdax tried not to think of Chakliux waiting for her, or what he would do when she did not come.

That morning, K'os sent boys out to watch, to wait on all sides of the village, the youngest to the north where the Near Rivers were least likely to come, the oldest to the south, hidden in the brush of the Cousin River.

When the meeting started, and K'os told the people that Chakliux had come and brought a warning, they scoffed, but then several of the old women, those who had often spat at K'os, took her side.

How foolish to think they would not come, one old woman said. She remembered other battles. When a village is left with only children and women, why not come, raid caches, take slaves?

The men spoke as though they wanted to fight, but in their eyes K'os could see they did not. She let them talk for a long time, but she asked questions now and again to remind them what the battle had been like. Finally she offered her own plan.

"Let the women meet them," she said, and ignored the horrified gasp that came from the old ones, from women with children at their breasts. "Not all of us, just a few. I will go. I will act surprised that they are coming to attack. I will say we were traveling to the Near River Village to surrender. We will be loaded down with stores from our caches. We will promise to go with them, and we will say that we do not want to fight."

"You think that will keep them from attacking those who are left here?" said Sky Watcher.

"No, of course not," K'os replied. She nodded her head at Fisher and asked, "If a group of women came to you, offering to surrender, what would you do?"

He thought for a moment, then said, "I would leave one or two elders with them and take the rest of the men to fight as we had planned."

"Would any of you do differently?" K'os asked.

They murmured their agreement.

"But what if the other women, the boys and old ones in the village—anyone able to leave their lodge—went to the forest, hid until the men attacked, then came from the woods in a surprise attack? Then we who met the hunters also returned to fight with the spears and knives we had hidden in our packs."

"Women do not know how to use spears and knives," Take More said.

"We have a day or two to learn something," said Star, her eyes shining. She bared her teeth. "I would like to kill one of them."

Twisted Stalk tottered to her feet. "The Near Rivers killed my grandson and two of my sons," she said. "I do not care if we win. I only want to take as many as we can."

She began to sing, a battle chant, a warrior's song. For a time, her voice rose alone, then one of the men joined her, and several boys. Then everyone sang, hitting the ground with feet and fists to beckon the force of the earth to help them with their revenge.

K'os sat silent, head bowed, deciding which women, which boys, she would take with her to meet the Near River hunters.

Chapter
Forty-nine

There were twelve of them, not counting the babies. They used walking sticks as though prepared for a far journey. They and their dogs carried heavy packs. K'os had chosen carefully, taking women who were docile but strong, with some beauty to face or body. Three were young mothers, all widows, all with babies; two had children old enough to walk. She had included three unmarried girls, all past their first bleeding. One of their mothers, Keep Fish, had insisted on accompanying her daughter Sun Girl, though K'os did not want her. Keep Fish was a woman of strong will. K'os had also taken two boys, nearly grown, in case they needed protection, but both took orders easily.

The three boys who watched the forest trail had come to the hunters the night before and told of sighting fires, hearing war songs from a group of men camped half a day's walk to the south. The next morning K'os started out with her group.

When they broke from the far edge of the woods, one of the boys ran ahead. When he came back, his mouth was drawn tight against his teeth, and K'os sensed his fear.

"They are close," he said to her.

"Good," K'os replied, and ignored the look of surprise on the boy's face. "The Near Rivers do not yet know it, but the next battle has begun."

Chakliux watched from the forest. This day also Aqamdax had not come. When he saw K'os and those with her, he followed them. Walking silently behind, hidden in the brushy places of alder and birch, he watched them and wondered where they were going. When they disappeared in the convolutions of the land, he made his way to the river, walked through the brush there until he came to the group again. They were slow, with mothers and children, and though the river was still frozen, the earth in midday was soft, the mud sucking at their feet.

He saw the boy run to them, heard his message and K'os's reply.

So the village had a battle plan, some way to fight. He wanted to stay hidden, to see what happened, but instead, he crept down to the river, walked carefully over stones and ice, trying not to leave tracks, and made his way back to the forest. If there was going to be a battle, he should be with Aqamdax, to offer her whatever protection he could.

They were led by Fox Barking, as Chakliux had told her. Hatred boiled in her heart. It would be difficult to surrender to him, but, K'os reminded herself, it would be only the first of many difficult things. She would have to spend time as slave, but she knew how to please men. Soon she would be wife, perhaps even to Fox Barking. Yes, most likely to him.

Suddenly she was glad he was still alive. She would enjoy being his wife, and he would be grateful that she was a healer.

They met on open ground. K'os stepped to the front of her group, called out, "I am K'os, woman of the Cousin River Village, a healer among the River People. I and these few, we travel to our brothers in the Near River Village. We hope to find a place for ourselves among the people there."

Fox Barking stood with his mouth open as though he would speak, but he said nothing. Finally a smaller man beside him, another elder, spoke, his words coming out in short bursts of sound, as though he were not used to speaking his thoughts in front of others. "How m-many are . . . in the village?" he asked.

"Few," she answered. "Six hunters, one nearly dead, two of the others wounded. Six handfuls of young women." She shrugged. "Another four handfuls of old women. Children and babies. Several boys."

Finally Fox Barking found his voice. "Those others, they are in the village?"

"Some are," K'os answered. "They will fight you, but we have had enough of war. We have no argument with the people of the Near River Village. Why should we? We share the same grandfathers. Allow us to go on to the Near River Village. We will wait there for you."

Fox Barking raised his voice into laughter, and the men behind him also laughed. There were about six handfuls, K'os decided, which meant that the Cousin River men had killed more than she thought, or that some of the Near River men had chosen not to come.

"So I allow you to go on your own," Fox Barking said. "What if you decide to walk to the Black River Village? What if you decide you will join the battle and attack us from the rear?" The boy nearest K'os looked up at her, but she ignored him.

"We will not," K'os said.

"You think I do not remember you, K'os?" Fox Barking asked. "You think the years have changed you that much?"

"We have both changed," K'os answered. "Things done are often regretted. I have had my revenge. I seek peace."

"I have not had *my* revenge," Fox Barking said. "You will stay here. You and your group. Set up shelters and wait until we return. There are those among us who will be glad to have slaves." He lifted his chin toward the elder beside him, then at two young men, not much more than boys. They both groaned when he chose them.

"If you complain, you will get nothing," Fox Barking said, "but if you keep these people here until we return, you can have your pick among them as slaves and split their goods and dogs between the two of you and Sun Caller." He looked back at K'os, then said, "All save the healer K'os. She and her belongings are mine."

K'os clamped her teeth together to keep from smiling.

When Fox Barking and his men left, K'os and her group set up their shelters. They made lean-tos of bark and caribou hides, placing two so they faced one another, a shared fire in the gap between. K'os set up a lean-to for herself, and as she worked, the young boys came to her, each of them, and asked when they would kill the men who watched them, when they would set out to attack Fox Barking and his warriors.

"Tonight, when it is dark," she told them. She promised to put a powder into the men's meat that would make them sleep.

When she had finished building her lean-to, she sat near the fire she shared with Keep Fish and her daughter, skewered strips of dried caribou meat on a sharpened stick and held the meat over the flames to soften. When the meat was ready, she took some to one of the young Near River men, invited him to share the food with her.

Soon they were wrapped together in her sleeping robes, and K'os whispered into his ears, told him that the boys planned to kill them that night. She told him that there was supposed to be something in the stew to make them sleep, then the boys would attack, slice open their throats.

The hunter looked at her with anger in his eyes, then he laughed. "They are boys," he said. "They can do nothing against us."

"Then eat only the meat I give you," she told him.

"Why should I trust you?" he asked.

"You think I want to be slave to Fox Barking? By helping you, perhaps I will show my worth. Perhaps you will decide you need another wife."

He smiled at that, puffed out his chest, took her quickly, with strong thrusts and loud groans. Afterwards she lay under him, his body limp and heavy on her chest. She poked him until he stirred, then whispered: "You would sleep after what I told you?"

He left her bed, and she pulled leggings and boots back on, twisted her parka down over her hips and went to find the Near River elder Sun Caller.

Aqamdax gasped when Chakliux crawled into the lodge, but as her husband reached for his throwing spear, she grabbed his wrist, stopped him.

"Wait," Aqamdax said.

"He killed my brothers!" Night Man's words seemed to suck away his breath, and he had to lie back for a moment, but he held his face in a grimace, his eyes open and staring.

"I am here to help, not to kill," Chakliux said. "The Near River People are less than a day's walk away. Since you did not come to the forest, I have returned to fight with you."

Night Man looked at Aqamdax, questions in his eyes.

"You know Chakliux visited this village three nights ago," she told him. "You heard K'os. He also came to this lodge, offered to help us escape so we would not be here during the attack."

"You would not go," Night Man said softly.

"I would not leave you," she told him, and did not look at Chakliux. It had been easier to say those words to him in the night, when she could not see his eyes.

"You should have sent the children," Night Man told her. "They are Near River."

"They would not go," Aqamdax said.

"They know me," said Chakliux. "Ghaden, why wouldn't you

come? My brother and I have a camp three days east. You would be safe there."

Ghaden hid his face in the dense fur of Biter's back.

"He wouldn't go because of Sok," Yaa said. "We have a chance here, even in a battle. Sometimes they do not kill children. We are also Near River. If they see us, they will leave us alone. With Sok, we are not safe."

The long days of waiting, the worry and frustration of wondering why Aqamdax did not come, brought out Chakliux's anger. He looked at Aqamdax. "What foolishness is this?"

She spoke slowly, with eyes lowered, as though it were difficult for her to say the words. "On the night before the Cousin River men left to attack the Near River Village, they made chants and prayers and dances of war. We heard the noise of their voices, the clatter of caribou hoof rattlers on their feet.

"Ghaden had been asleep, but he awoke and told Yaa about the boots the one who killed his mother—my mother—wore. They had caribou rattlers and were decorated with pictures of the sun on the sides." She spread her hands like rays of light. "Only Sok wears boots like that."

"It was not Sok," Chakliux said quietly. He turned to Ghaden. "You are not the only one who saw the killer. Fox Barking also saw. He was visiting my grandfather that night, and hid himself in the darkness between lodges. He saw the killer leave my grandfather's lodge."

"And he did nothing to help?" Aqamdax asked.

"He is a selfish man," Chakliux said. "These many moons since, he has had many favors given to him because of what he knew, and finally, when it was to his benefit to tell the killer's name, he did, but only to Sok and to me, because we were chosen to lead the Near River People, Sok as chief hunter and I as chief of the elders. Fox Barking wanted all power for himself."

"If Sok is not the killer, then who is?"

"Red Leaf."

Aqamdax sat without moving, the words like the thrust of a knife to her chest.

"She took her husband's boots and parka to disguise herself," Chakliux said. "She used one of his knives."

"Why?" Aqamdax asked.

"Red Leaf thought Sok would throw her away so he could take Snow-in-her-hair as wife. She thought if he could get his grandfather's dogs and weapons, he would become the chief hunter and hold enough honor in the village that Snow-in-her-hair's father would allow her to come to Sok as second wife."

"And my mother . . ."

"Just happened to see her."

"So Fox Barking drove you and Sok from the village."

"Yes. Our mother also chose to come with us, and Ligige', Snow-in-her-hair and her baby, Cries-loud and—"

"Snow-in-her-hair is Sok's wife?"

"Yes. She was pregnant with his child, so her father let her become second wife."

"And you have Sok's sons?"

"Only Cries-loud."

Aqamdax sighed, pressed her lips together. "The other . . . is dead?"

Chakliux nodded. "We also have Red Leaf."

Aqamdax pulled in her breath. "No one killed her?"

"She carries Sok's child in her belly. Still, Ghaden has no reason to worry. She has nothing more to hide."

"And when the baby is born?" Aqamdax asked.

"Then Sok and I will decide what we must do to avenge our grandfather."

That night Aqamdax and Chakliux took turns sitting at the door. Star had taken her mother with the others to wait outside the village, then they would use bows and spears against the Near River hunters in ambush while the few who remained in the lodges fought from within.

It was not until dawn that Aqamdax noticed the first sign of movement. Her heart quickened, and she squinted, trying to see in the gray light. Their best chance for survival was for the Near River hunters to recognize her, to realize she also had Ghaden and Yaa, so she stood outside the lodge, waiting for the first men to come.

Chakliux had asked her to awaken him as soon as she saw anything. With the two of them, they had a better chance the Near Rivers would leave their lodge alone, but still she knew that in the frenzy of fighting the Near River men might not care.

She had raised chants and prayers when she awoke; in the tradition of the First Men, she had thanked the Maker for her life and welcomed the sun. She had stilled her heart with quiet songs each time the fear of death washed over her.

Now, for a moment, the horror of what she was seeing held her captive, and she could not move. The Near River men came from all sides of the village, each with spear and spearthrower in his hands. The head of each spear glowed with fire.

Aqamdax's scream woke Chakliux, and he jumped to his feet, grabbed his spear. Night Man was sitting up in his bed, knives in both hands.

Aqamdax ran into the lodge, grabbing not for weapons but for water bladders.

"Fire!" she screamed. "They shoot fire at the lodges!"

"Stay inside!" Chakliux called to her, then grabbed one of the scraped caribou hides that lined the floor, took it with him, waited in the tunnel until one of the fire spears hit the top of the lodge. Then he jumped out, flipped the caribou hide over the fire, smothering it before the flames could spread.

Already other lodges were burning. People fought the fires with water and hides, but soon the flames spread through the whole village. Near River spears took a few of the boys and men, but most of the Near River hunters stood by the food caches, stomping out flames that caught in nearby brush, preventing the fires from consuming the caches.

When the flames roared at their worst, Chakliux knew he could no longer keep Star's lodge from catching. "Bring what you can carry," he called to Aqamdax. "Get the children outside. I will help your husband."

The smoke had seeped into the lodge so that Chakliux almost had to feel his way to Night Man's bed. His eyes burned, and the heat from the fire seared his throat and lungs as he fought to draw in breath. He grabbed the corners of Night Man's sleeping mats and pulled him outside. The smoke was not as dense lower to the ground, so he bent almost double, gulping in the cooler air.

He could not see Aqamdax and the children, and though he called out for them, the voice of the fire, as loud as wind or sea, smothered his words. When they reached the edge of the village, he told Night Man he would go back for Yaa and Ghaden, for Aqamdax, but then, as though he had been given a gift, they were beside them, their hands also on Night Man's mat, and the four of them pulled Night Man to safety.

They did not fight. Why die for no reason? Two Cousin River boys and a woman who had tried to attack were killed. Fisher also was dead, and Runner had a spear in his back. He would not live, the old women said. That gave the village only three hunters and Night Man.

The Near Rivers left that day, taking whatever they could carry from the caches and most of the young women, all the dogs except Biter. They left the elders, the wounded, to live in the charred remains of the village with not even enough food to last through the next few days.

And what about K'os and those she had taken with her? Why had she not returned? the few who remained in the village asked themselves. Had the Near Rivers killed her? More likely, she and the boys had been unable to overpower their guards. Well, less mouths to share what food they had. Besides, the old women said, they did not need a healer. They would be dead before the next winter. Most of them would be dead before summer arrived.

When the Near River men returned to where they had left K'os, they came with shouts, as though she should rejoice with them in their victory. Instead, she lifted her chin and looked away, answered them in anger.

When the Cousin River women who had come from the village asked why K'os did not return to join the attack, she pointed at the bodies of the two boys and Sun Girl's mother, the three who had volunteered to slit the Near River guards' throats. So the Cousin River People came to the Near River Village in mourning, soot still black on their faces, their arms and clothing cut to show their grief.

K'os's greatest sorrow was over the number of Cousin River women who had chosen to go to the Near River Village. She had thought more would be killed in the battle, especially after she convinced the men to let the women use weapons.

Who could believe the Near River hunters would use fire against the Cousin River Village? Who could believe Fox Barking would think of an idea like that?

Now with so many women from the Cousin River Village, there was less chance she would become wife, more chance she would stay slave. But she walked into the Near River Village with her head held high and did not let herself remember the last time she had been there, with Ground Beater, Tikaani and Snow Breaker, now all dead.

It did not matter what had happened to them, she told herself. She was alive. There were Near River men, wounded in battle, who could use her help. She had brought her medicines, and soon it would be summer, a time to gather new plants. If there were not enough wounded men for her to heal, she was sure there were those who would become sick. She patted her medicine bags. She was also sure she could heal them.

Chapter Fifty

Of those who remained in the Cousin River Village, five were hunters, including Chakliux and Night Man. There were six boys seven summers and older, one handful of younger women, three handfuls of old women. Five handfuls of children and babies. Twisted Stalk had hidden two tiny female pups under her parka, and a young mother who had recently lost her baby said she would nurse them. So with Biter, they had three dogs.

Aqamdax sighed and continued to sort through the contents of K'os's burned lodge. Knife blades, scrapers, cooking stones, an assortment of beads had all survived the flames. She also found a bundle of fox furs, charred only at two edges, a few tattered pieces of woven sleeping mats and a water bladder.

Three old women were fighting over the contents of the lodge next to K'os's. Aqamdax, her despair spilling into words, raised her voice and interrupted their squabbling.

"Aunts," she said, "everything must belong to all of us. If we fight among ourselves, what hope do we have?"

The three women were suddenly silent, then all of them turned on her, shouting insults and taunts. Aqamdax closed her eyes against tears, then opened them to see Chakliux beside her.

He led her out of the smoking ruins, down the path and into the cool quietness of the forest. "These are not your people, Aqamdax," he said. "Why do you stay? Come with me; bring Yaa and Ghaden. We will find Sok, spend the summer fishing and hunting together. Our lodges will be warm next winter, and we will have enough food. During those long moons when we wait for spring, I will build an iqyax frame. Then next summer, when we have enough fish put away to keep us through a long journey, you and I can return to your people."

"Chakliux, I cannot leave Ghaden," she told him. "Yaa may want to return to her mother, but. . . ."

"Yaa's mother was killed in the fighting," Chakliux said softly. He caught Aqamdax's mittened hands in his own. "I will build two iqyan. We will wait until Ghaden is old enough to paddle one, then we will go, but until then, bring your brother and Yaa, and come with me."

Aqamdax pulled her hands away. "I cannot leave my husband."

"There are many women in this village who need husbands. Let him be husband to one of them."

"Chakliux," Aqamdax said and began to cry. She laid one hand across her belly. "I cannot leave Night Man. I carry his child."

They made one lodge, using lodge poles and caribou hides that had survived the fires. The women with babies, the children, were crowded inside. The others, mothers with older children, the hunters, and the old women made lean-tos. They set them in a ragged circle, their open sides toward the lodge, as though to draw warmth from those within.

They lifted their voices in mourning songs, and the words rose into the night sky, riding the smoke that spiraled up from the hearth fires.

Chakliux approached the lean-to where Night Man lay. His sister Star sat on one side of his bedding mats, Aqamdax on the other. Yaa and Ghaden were huddled together at the back of the shelter, and Star's mother sat twisting her hands, staring off into the distance as though she waited for those dead ones who would never return.

Night Man purposely averted his face, but Chakliux went to him, lay two large hares on the ground beside the fire.

"We do not need your meat," said Night Man.

Star looked anxiously at her brother, began to gnaw her bottom lip. "We need the meat," she said. "We need the pelts."

Night Man raised his voice. "This lodge has a hunter."

"I have come to ask for a wife," Chakliux said. "There is no shame in taking meat from a man who will be husband to your sister."

Though Aqamdax understood that Chakliux was doing this for her, the words were knives to her chest. Chakliux had grown up with Star. Surely he knew she would not be a good wife.

It would not be an easy thing to have him live in the same lodge, to see him share Star's bed during the night, but he was a hunter. He would bring meat. She lifted her head to look at Night Man and could see that he was torn by Chakliux's offer. Chakliux had been enemy. How could Night Man welcome him as brother? But if he did not, was he throwing away the lives of his wife and their child, his sister and his mother?

"You would take this man as husband?" he asked Star.

Star stood and walked slowly to Chakliux's side. "You think you can live again as Cousin?" she asked.

"I can live as Cousin," he said.

"Then I will be your wife," she told him. "Do you have bride price gifts?"

"Only the promise of my hunting."

Star pursed her mouth into a pout, but Night Man said, "That is bride price enough." He lifted his good hand as though to encompass the ruins of the village beyond the circle of lean-tos. "What more can we ask?"

"There is one thing I must do first," Chakliux said. "My brother Sok, his wives and children, our mother and an aunt have made a camp three days from here. They wait for me. I must tell them I will stay in this village."

"I have heard of the hunter Sok," Night Man said. "Tell him he is welcome here."

"I will tell him."

"When will you leave?"

"If you allow me a place beside your fire tonight," Chakliux said, "I will leave in the morning, and return as soon as I can."

"You have a place beside my fire," said Night Man.

Chakliux picked up the two hares, handed them to Star. "Not a bride price," he said. "Someday I will give something better."

She took the hares, sat down, laid them across her lap and stroked their fur. Biter pulled away from Ghaden, his eyes on the hares, but Yaa caught him around the neck and held him back.

"Wife," Night Man said to Aqamdax, "skin them. We need meat tonight."

Aqamdax took the hares from Star, and Star wailed like a child.

Her mother looked at her, startled, then raised her voice to sing a mourning song. Star glanced at Chakliux, then changed her cries from petulance to mourning.

A handful of days passed, then two handfuls, and still Chakliux did not return. Star shouted out her anger at the old women in the camp, at the children, and twice Aqamdax had to stop her as she stood, knife in hand, ready to shred the sides of their lean-to.

He would not be back, Aqamdax told herself. Surely, when he had time to think, time to realize how difficult it would be to have Star as wife, he would stay with Sok, and Aqamdax would not see him again.

The people had made another lodge, this one smaller, the covering pieced from caribou hides charred and weakened by the fires, but now the old women and some of the older children had a place. Ghaden and Yaa spent the nights in that lodge, though Ghaden was not allowed to take Biter with him.

The first few days after Chakliux left, Star had joined Yaa and Aqamdax to set out traplines. Now she did nothing except lash out in anger or crouch inside the lean-to, refusing to eat, refusing to speak.

Each morning Night Man worked to sit longer, and finally he was able to push himself up, first to his knees, and then to his feet, though he stood only a short time. His right arm still hung useless, and Aqamdax made a sling to bind it against his body.

Several of the old women salvaged bits and pieces from half-burned baskets and wove fish traps. The three men strong enough to hunt prepared spears and weapons for caribou. The boys made bolas to bring down birds that would soon come from the south.

The twelfth day after Chakliux had left them, Aqamdax took Biter with her to check traps. She hoped the dog might catch a hare or ptarmigan. She stopped by a tangle of highbush cranberry and picked a few wizened berries, offered several to Biter. "Next year will be better," she told him. Biter, his fur ragged, his body gaunt, whined as though he understood her words. Suddenly, he jumped away from her, began to run. She followed him for a few steps, then saw that he chased a hare. She returned to her trapline. Each loop was empty.

Such things always happened at this time of year, she reminded herself. Winter traps had already caught most of the small animals that lived near the village. She would have to move the trapline farther away.

When Biter returned, he carried the front half of a hare in his mouth. She praised him, surprised that he would bring anything at all when they shared so little with him.

It was a sign, that hare, Aqamdax thought, a reminder of all good things. She was alive and deep inside her belly she carried a child—a son who would be a strong hunter, or a daughter who would sew and weave and someday give Aqamdax grandchildren.

She smiled, raised her eyes to the blue sky. The wind was a spring wind, and it swept through the forest with a warmth that lifted the last of the winter's cold from the brown and gray earth. Aqamdax began a soft song of praise, a thanksgiving for her life, for the life of Night Man's child, for Ghaden and for Yaa. For her husband and his family.

Suddenly, Biter's ears pricked forward. He whined, laid the hare carcass on the ground, set one of his front feet on it, then barked.

Aqamdax slipped her knife from its scabbard and crouched beside the dog, clasped a hand over his muzzle to quiet him. She waited, then heard someone call her name. "You will let me have this?" she asked Biter and reached for the hare.

He lifted his foot, and she took it slowly, slipped it into the carrying bag slung from her shoulder. Biter gave her one backward glance and began to run. She followed him, then saw them, all of them—Chakliux and Sok, Red Leaf and Snow-in-her-hair, Cries-loud and Day Woman, last, her voice rising above all the others, old Ligige'.

"We have come with my brother," Sok called out. "We hear there is a village near that needs hunters."

Aqamdax allowed her eyes to meet Chakliux's, a long look of joy and welcome. She called Biter to her, then waited as the others passed, greeted them as they greeted her, though Red Leaf said nothing, only walked by, her hands cradled over her belly.

Aqamdax joined Ligige', last in line. "I am glad you chose to come, Aunt," she told her, "but even with Sok and Chakliux, we have only five strong men to hunt for us."

"Ah, child," Ligige' told her, "Perhaps we have only five hunters, but how many villages have two storytellers? You and Chakliux will help us forget our bellies. Your stories will give us strength for what we must endure, and remind us that life is sacred and the earth is good."

Author's Notes

Perhaps the greatest gift that any novel can bestow is when, under the guise of entertainment, it allows the reader to defy the boundaries of time and space and live the lives of its characters. This transliteration of the reader's inner vision offers an incredible possibility: a mind open to new understanding.

When we step away from ourselves and see through the eyes of another, we are blessed not only with a vision different than our own but also with a more accurate portrait of ourselves, of our political and social environs, and the preconceptions that color our thinking.

While I make no claim that *Song of the River* will be able to do that for its readers, during the research and writing of this novel I found that I developed a better understanding of the human weaknesses which precipitate war, the prejudices we use for justification and the devastation that can be brought about by hatred.

Even when war is reduced to the fundamental level of intervillage conflict, traditions of prejudice and mythologies of superiority are used to justify elitist and even vastly deviant behavior. In both primitive and complex societies, material comfort has a tendency to camouflage the most destructive of social ills, not those that deny us wealth and leisure but those which strike at the most basic and vital level of our existence: our souls, our consciences—the very things which make us human.

Although there is general consensus that the ancestors of the present-day Aleut people lived on the Aleutian Archipelago thousands of years ago, archaeologists, anthropologists and ethnologists disagree as to the identity of the descendants of the Denali Complex people, those users of microblades who also lived in Alaska thousands of years ago.

Though novelists are allowed freedoms not given to scientific researchers, please be assured that my speculation has been tempered by research into many North American and Asian aboriginal cultures, both prehistoric and historic, including Aleut, Diuktai, Nenana, Denali, Denbigh, Yup'ik, Athabascan, Cree, Eyak, Tlingit, Tsimshian, Haida, Kwakiutl, Nootka, Koryak, Even, Chukchi, Itelmen, and Yakut.

I have long believed that one of the best ways to learn about a people is through their language. In *Song of the River*, I include a number of Native words, most from the Aleut and Ahtna Athabaskan languages, with spellings as standardized in the *Aleut Dictionary, Unangam Tunudgusii*, compiled by Knut Bergsland, and the *Ahtna Athabaskan Dictionary*, compiled and edited by James Kari. Both dictionaries are published by the Alaska Native Language Center, University of Alaska Fairbanks.

Those readers familiar with my first three novels—*Mother Earth Father Sky, My Sister the Moon* and *Brother Wind*—and the Aleut words used in those texts will notice minor changes in spelling. When I wrote *Mother Earth Father Sky* and its sequels, Bergsland's fine dictionary (published in 1994) was not available to me, and so I used a variety of sources for Aleut words. Because I believe Bergsland's dictionary is and will continue to be lauded as the definitive lexicon of the Aleut language, I use his spellings in *Song of the River*.

My decision to use an Athabascan language for the River People was not merely by whim, but because Athabascan peoples of Alaska evolved a riparian culture and also hunt caribou, bear and various smaller animals and birds.

The Athabascan language family is comprised of some thirty-five languages spoken in Alaska, Canada and the southwestern and western United States. At the time of the publication of this novel, fewer than one hundred people, most over the age of fifty, speak Ahtna Athabascan, though there are more than one thousand people living who are of Ahtna descent.

Through *Song of the River* and my other novels, I hope to engender an awareness of the treasure inherent in North American Native languages, and to that end, I ask that the reader accept the Native words in this novel, not with irritation or in resignation, but with contemplative wonder and joy.

The riddles in this novel are based on the riddles of one of the northernmost Athabascan peoples, the Koyukon. Each riddle, however, is an original, none copied from any known Koyukon riddle, in recognition and respect of ownership rights.

(For those readers who are admirers of the oddities and possibilities of language: in Chakliux's riddle as presented in chapter eight ["Look! What do I see? It runs far, singing, and Sok's is the first to fill its mouth with meat." Answer: Sok's spear], the Ahtna word for a bone-tipped, birch-shafted caribou or bear spear is *c'izaeggi*, from the root *zaek*, much similar to *zaek'*, which means "voice" or "spit," and also to the word *zaa*, which means "mouth." In addition to posing a riddle, Chakliux is also making a pun, thus giving an added dimension to the unraveling.)

Two last comments: many Athabascan hunters will not use dogs to take bears. They consider such hunting an insult to the bear. Second, please do not confuse the disdain some of my characters carry for fishskin baskets to be a reflection of my own preferences. These references are meant only to illustrate the small prejudices that color our lives. Fishskin baskets, examples of which may be seen in many of Alaska's fine museums, are incredible examples of the beauty, variety and ingenuity of items produced by Native peoples.

GLOSSARY OF NATIVE AMERICAN WORDS

AQAMDAX (Aleut) Cloudberry, *Rubus chamaemorus*. (See Pharmacognosia.)

AYAGAX (Aleut) Wife.

BABICHE (English—probably anglicized from the Cree word *assababish*, a diminutive of *assabab*, "thread") Lacing made from rawhide.

BITAALA' (Ahtna Athabascan) A foot-long organ located between the stomach and liver in the black bear. Among the Ahtna, it is considered taboo for anyone except the elders to eat the bitaala'.

CEN (Ahtna Athabascan) Tundra.

CET'AENI (Ahtna Athabascan) Creatures of ancient Ahtna legend. They are tailed and live in trees and caves.

CHAGAK (Aleut) Obsidian, red cedar.

CHAKLIUX (Ahtna Athabascan, as recorded by Pinart in 1872) Sea otter.

CHIGDAX (Aleut) A waterproof, watertight parka made of sea lion or bear intestines, esophagus of seal or sea lion, or the tongue of a whale. The hood had a drawstring, and the sleeves were tied at the wrist for sea travel. These knee-length garments were often decorated with feathers and bits of colored esophagus.

CHUHNUSIX (Aleut) Wild geranium, *Geranium erianthum*. (See Pharmacognosia.)

CILT'OGHO (Ahtna Athabascan) A container hollowed out of birch and used to carry water.

DAES (Ahtna Athabascan) Shallow, a shallow portion of a lake or stream.

DATS'ENI (Ahtna Athabascan) Waterfowl.

DZUUGGI (Ahtna Athabascan) A favored child who receives special training, especially in oral traditions, from infancy.

GGUZAAKK (Koyukon Athabascan) A thrush, *Hylocichla minima, H. ustulata* and *H. guttata.* These birds sing an intricately beautiful song that the Koyukon people traditionally believe to indicate the presence of an unknown person or spirit.

GHADEN (Ahtna Athabascan) Another person.

HII (Aleut) An exclamation of surprise or disgust.

IITIKAALUX (Atkan Aleut) Cow parsnip, wild celery, *Heracleum lanatum.* (See Pharmacognosia.)

IQYAX(s.) (Aleut) A skin-covered, wooden-framed boat. A kayak.

K'OS (Ahtna Athabascan) Cloud.

KUKAX (Aleut) Grandmother.

LIGIGE' (Ahtna Athabascan) The soapberry or dog berry, *Shepherdia canadensis.* (See Pharmacognosia.)

NAYUX (Aleut) A float made of a seal skin or seal bladder filled with air.

QIGNAX (Aleut) Fire or light resulting from a fire.

QUNG (Aleut) Hump, humpback.

SAEL (Ahtna Athabascan) A container made of bark.

SAX (Aleut) A long, hoodless parka made of feathered bird skins.

SIXSIQAX (Aleut) Wormwood, *Artemisia unalaskensis.* (See Pharmacognosia.)

SHUGANAN (Ancient word of uncertain origin) Exact meaning unsure, relating to an ancient people.

SOK (Ahtna Athabascan) Raven call.

TIKAANI (Ahtna Athabascan) Wolf.

TIKIYAASDE (Ahtna Athabascan) Menstruation hut.

TSAANI (Ahtna Athabascan) Grizzly bear, *Ursus arctos.*

TS'ES (Ahtna Athabascan) Rock, stone.

TUTAQAGIISIX (Aleut) Hearing.

ULAX(s.) ULAS(pl.) (Aleut) A semisubterranean dwelling raftered with driftwood and covered with thatching and sod.

YAA (Ahtna Athabascan) Sky.

YAYKAAS (Ahtna Athabaskan) Literally, "flashing sky." The aurora borealis.

YEHL (Tlingit) Raven.

The words in this glossary are defined and listed according to their use in *Song of the River*. Readers interested in pronunciation guides may write to the author at: P.O. Box 6, Pickford, MI 49774.

Pharmacognosia

Plants listed in this pharmacognosia are *not* recommended for use, but are cited only as a supplement to the novel. Many poisonous plants resemble helpful plants, and even some of the most benign can be harmful if used in excess. The wisest way to harvest wild vegetation for use as medicine, food or dyes is in the company of an expert. Plants are listed in alphabetical order according to the names used in *Song of the River*.

ALDER , *Alnus crispa*: A small tree with grayish bark. Medium green leaves have toothed edges, rounded bases and pointed tops. Flower clusters resemble miniature pinecones. The cambium or inner layer of bark is dried (fresh bark will irritate the stomach) and used to make tea said to reduce high fever. It is also used as an astringent and a gargle for sore throats. The bark is used to make brown dye.

BEDSTRAW: See **Goose Grass**, below.

BLUEBERRY (bog blueberry), *Vaccinium uliginosum*: A low-branching, extremely hardy shrub. Leaves are medium green with rounded tips. Small, round blue-black berries ripen in August. Berries are choice for food, fresh or dried, and are high in iron.

CARIBOU LEAVES (wormwood, silverleaf), *Artemisia tilesii*: This perennial plant attains a height of two to three feet on a single stem. The hairy, lobed leaves are silver underneath and a darker green on top. A spike of small clustered flowers grows at the top of the stem in late summer. Fresh leaves are used to make a tea that is said to purify the blood and stop internal bleeding, and to wash cuts and sore eyes. The leaves are heated and layered over arthritic joints to ease pain. Caution: caribou leaves may be toxic in large doses.

CHUHNUSIX (wild geranium, cranebill), *Geranium erianthum*: A perennial with dark green palmated leaves and purplish flowers. It grows to a little over two feet in height. Dried leaves are steeped for tea that is used as a gargle for sore throats and a wash to dry seeping wounds.

CLOUDBERRY (salmonberry), *Rubus chamaemorus*: Not to be confused with the larger shrublike salmonberry, *Rubus spectabilis*, this small plant grows to about six inches in height and bears a single white flower and a salmon-colored berry shaped like a raspberry. The green leaves are serrated and have five main lobes. The berries are edible but not as flavorful as raspberries, and are high in vitamin C. The juice from the berries is said to be a remedy for hives.

FIVE-LEAVES GRASS (cinquefoil), *Potentilla tormentilla*; (marsh fivefinger), *Potentilla palustris*: These potentillas have five-fingered palmate leaves, and root at the joints. Plants of the *Potentilla* genus have yellow flowers—except *palustris*, which has purple blooms. They branch out from the root with flowers at the end of eighteen- to twenty-inch stems. *Palustris* leaves are used for tea (nonmedicinal). *Tormentilla* root is boiled and applied as a poultice to skin eruptions and shingles. It is said to be useful as a tonic for the lungs, for fevers and as a gargle for gum and mouth sores.

GOOSE GRASS (northern bedstraw), *Galium boreale*: The narrow leaves grow in groups of four under the fragrant white flower sprays. Young plants warmed (not boiled) in hot water and placed on external wounds are said to help clot the blood. The dried plant, made into a salve with softened fat, was used to treat external skin irritations. Teas (steeped, not boiled) made of young leaves, seeds or roots may be diuretic. Roots produce a purplish dye.

IITIKAALUX (cow parsnip, wild celery), *Heracleum lanatum*: A thick-stemmed, hearty plant that grows to nine feet in height. The coarse, dark leaves have three main lobes with serrated edges. It is also known by the Russian name *poochki* or *putchki*. Stems and leaf stalks taste like a spicy celery but must be peeled before eating because the outer layer is a skin irritant. White flowers grow in inverted bowl-shaped clusters at the tops of the plants. Roots are also edible, and leaves were dried to flavor soups and stews. The root was chewed raw to ease sore throats and was heated and a section pushed into a painful tooth to deaden root pain. Caution: gloves should be worn when harvesting. Iitikaalux is similar in appearance to poisonous water hemlock.

LIGIGE' (soapberry or dog berry), *Shepherdia canadensis*: A shrub that grows to six feet in height with smooth, round-tipped, dark green leaves. The orange-colored berries ripen in July and are edible but bitter. They foam like soap when beaten.

PARTNER GRASS (pineapple weed), *Matricaria matricarioides*: Finely feathered leaves grow on stems up to twelve inches in height. The rayless yellow flower heads emit a pineapple smell when crushed. Plants are used for teas and are said to soothe stomach upsets. Caution: some people experience skin irritation from handling these plants. Large doses may cause nausea and vomiting.

PURPLE FLOWER (purple boneset), *Eupatorium purpureum*: A tall (five to six feet) perennial, its clustered purple flower heads appear in September. Coarse leaves grow in groups of three or five. The root, crushed in a water solution, is said to be a diuretic and tonic as well as a relaxant.

RYE GRASS (basket grass, beach grass), *Elymus arenarius mollis:* A tall, coarse-bladed grass that is dried and split, then used by Aleut weavers to make finely woven baskets and mats.

SIXSIQAX (wormwood), *Artemisia unalaskensis:* Some Aleut people used the leaves of this plant as a hot poultice. See **Caribou Leaves**, above.

SOUR DOCK (sorrel, curly dock), *Rumex crispus;* (arctic dock) *Rumex arcticus:* Leaves are shaped like spearheads, wavy at the edges, and fan out from the base of the plant. A central stalk grows to three or four feet in height and bears clusters of edible reddish seeds. Steamed leaves are said to remove warts. The root of these plants is crushed and used as a poultice for skin eruptions. Fresh leaves are abundant in vitamins C and A, but contain oxalic acid, so consumption should be moderate.

WILLOW, *Salix:* A narrow-leafed shrub or small tree with smooth gray, yellowish and/or brownish bark. There are presently more than thirty species of willow in Alaska. The leaves are a very good source of vitamin C, though in some varieties they taste quite bitter. The leaves and inner bark contain salicin, which acts like aspirin to deaden pain. Bark can be chipped and boiled to render a pain-relieving tea. Leaves can also be boiled for tea. Leaves are chewed and placed over insect bites to relieve itching. Roots and branches are used to make baskets and woven fish weirs.

WOUNDWORT (goldenrod), *Solidago multiradiata, Solidago lepida:* Serrated leaves grow in an alternating pattern up stalks that can attain three feet in height. Golden clusters of flowers top the stem in August and September. Powdered or fresh leaves and flowers were used as dressings for wounds. Tea made from flowers is said to be helpful for internal bleeding or diarrhea. Flowers are used to make a yellow dye.

YELLOW ROOT (gold thread), *Coptis trifolia:* A creeping fibrous perennial root, the leaves grow in threes on foot-high stalks separate from flower stalks. Tea made from boiling the root is said to be an invigorating tonic and also a gargle for sore throats and mouth lesions.

YELLOW VIOLET, *Violaceae:* Small yellow five-petaled flowers are borne on stems that grow to approximately ten inches. Flowers carry irregular dark lines at the center of each petal. Serrated leaves are heart-shaped. Both leaves and flowers are edible. Leaves are a good source of vitamin C. Leaves were mixed with fat and used as a salve on skin contusions. Caution: leaves and flowers tend to have a laxative effect.

ACKNOWLEDGMENTS

None of my novels could have been written without the patience, encouragement and wise advice of my husband, Neil Harrison. He is my best friend, business partner, confidant and travel companion. I also owe a great debt of gratitude to our children, Krystal and Neil; our parents, Pat and Bob McHaney and Shirley and Clifford Harrison; and to our brothers and sisters. A loving family is a gift I can never repay.

To my agent, Rhoda Weyr, whom I am privileged to count as friend as well as adviser, forever my thanks. She saw possibility where others did not, and in addition to her astute business skills, continues to enrich my life as encourager, advocate and sounding board. My most sincere gratitude to Ellen Edwards, an editor blessed with skill, vision and patience. I count myself fortunate to have had her help because my work requires an inordinate amount of all three. My heartfelt appreciation also to her staff, and to Ann McKay Thoroman and her staff.

To those friends and family members who have had the patience to read *Song of the River* in its various forms, many, many thanks: my husband, Neil; Pat and Bob McHaney; friend and gifted writer Linda Hudson; and my sister, Patricia Walker.

With each of my novels, and with each of the journeys Neil and I make to Alaska, we find we are more indebted to those who share their knowledge, expertise and advice. There are never enough words to express our gratitude and the awe we feel when people open their homes and their hearts to us.

For those families who have offered the hospitality of their homes during our Alaska travels, many thanks: Dort and Ragan Callaway and Mike and Rayna Livingston of Anchorage; Karen and Rudy Brandt; Kaydee Caraway and her family: Candie, Joe and Hollie of Anchorage and Beluga; Mark Shellinger, Superintendent of the Pribilof Islands School District (who made our visit to the Pribilofs possible, gave us a place in his home, and escorted us on incredible walking tours of the island); B.G. and Lois Olson of St. Paul Island; Bonnie, Chris and Samantha Mierzejek of St. George Island (who gave us a place in their home and treated us like family); Mike and Sally Swetzof and their daughters Crystal and Mary of Atka; Bill Walz, Superintendent of the Aleutian Region School District and his wife Lani and son Wilson of Unalaska (who engineered our trip to Unalaska and Atka and allowed us to stay in their home, including us in Unalaska's wonderful Aleut Week); head of the Akutan Traditional Council, Jacob Stepetin, and his wife, Annette, and Pat Darling (who arranged our visit to Akutan).

Our sincere appreciation also to the teachers, staff and students of the St. George and the St. Paul schools who quickly found a place in our hearts, and to those in the communities of St. Paul and St. George who welcomed us with receptions, warm food and warm hearts; the dancers at St. George and St. Paul; and the members of the St. George and the Atka Russian Orthodox churches who allowed this Methodist to join them in their services and helped me discover that worship transcends the boundaries of language; to Chris Lokanin for taking me to an old barabara site on Atka and for carving me an Aleut nose pin; and Tamara Guil, my Atka guide via a four-wheeler; Katia Guil, Ethan Pettigrew and the Atka Dancers (How can words express my gratitude that you would don your beautiful regalia and dance for Neil and me?); the staff and teachers at Unalaska School who welcomed me into their classrooms and sent us home with jams and jellies, salmon and many wonderful memories; the staff and teachers at Atka School and the people of Atka for their hospitality; and to the people of Akutan for the reception of food and fellowship; and to the late Nick Sias and his *Blue Goose*. In our hearts, they will both forever fly the Aleutian skies.

Any historical novel requires long hours of research. I owe an incredible debt to many people who shared experiences, knowledge and resource materials. Errors contained in *Song of the River* are solely my own and not the fault of those cited in these acknowledgments.

A special thanks to Andrew Gronholdt and his instruction during the Aleut Ceremonial Hat Class arranged by Jerah Chadwick and conducted through the University of Alaska Fairbanks extension services at Unalaska. Neil was privileged to learn this ancient art from Andrew and also to enjoy Andrew's wit and his store of wisdom. For Ray Hudson, whose books have inspired, informed and entertained, my gratitude for the privilege of an early reading of *The Bays of Beaver Inlet* (Epicenter Press). For readers who hanker for a taste of what modern life is like on the Aleutian Islands, Ray's book is a must read. You will learn much, but beyond the learning, you will find that it speaks to your heart.

My sincere appreciation to Dr. William Laughlin and his daughter

Sarah, for their continued support and for answering questions on their archaeological work on the Aleutian Islands; Dr. Mark Mc-Donald, for information on geology and ocean habitats; Forbes Mc-Donald, for information on bear hunting; Don Alan Hall, Center for the Study of the First Americans, Oregon State University, editor of the very fine magazine *Mammoth Trumpet*; Dr. Douglas Veltrie, for taking time to show us many Native artifacts in storage at the University of Alaska Anchorage and to answer my many questions; Dr. Rick Knecht, for slide presentations during Unalaska Aleut Week on his various dig sites in the islands; Clint Groover, doctor of veterinary medicine, and his wife and assistant, Barbara, for answering my questions about dogs; Crystal Swetzof and Clara Snigaroff, for information about the Aleut language, Atkan dialect; Mike Swetzof, for historical perspectives on the Aleut people and for demonstrating an authentic Aleut throwing board and harpoon; Katia Guil, for dance and Koryak legends; Ethan Petticrew, for Aleut dance and legends; Bonnie Mierzejek, for hours of answering my questions, for sharing childhood Aleut stories and for allowing me to sit in on her Aleut language classes at the St. George School; Edna at St. Paul, for allowing me to sit in on her Aleut language classes; Jacob Stepetin, for showing us the artifacts at the Akutan Library Museum and answering questions about fishing; Denise Wartes, University of Alaska Fairbanks, for her patient replies to my questions about her work in interior Alaska; Okalena Patricia Lekanoff-Gregory, for sharing Aleut stories and for her basket-weaving presentation during Aleut Week; Candie Caraway, for information on bears; Kaydee Caraway, for information on wolves; June McGlashan, for poetry that is the fragile and robust echo of the Aleut soul; and Phia Xiong, for answering my questions about the Hmong culture.

My gratitude also to those who shared resource material:
Ernest Stepetin; Richard Herring; Phyllis Hunter; Mick and Kathleen Herring; Jerah Chadwick; Kristi and Mike Lucia; Bill White; Don Darling; Margaret Lekanoff; James and Esther Waybrant; Ann Chandonnet; Dort and Ragan Callaway; Mike and Rayna Livingston.

My sincere appreciation to my husband, Neil, for his computer work digitizing the map for this book.

And to Dora: your words to me as I left St. Paul will forever be in my heart.